RUIN

JOHN GWYNNE studied and lectured at Brighton University.
He's been in a rock 'n' roll band, playing the double bass, and has
travelled the USA and lived in Canada for a time. He is married
with four children and lives in Eastbourne, running a small family
business rejuvenating vintage furniture. His first novel, *Malice*, won
the David Gemmell Morningstar award for best debut fantasy.
Ruin is his third novel, following *Malice* and *Valour*.

www.john-gwynnc.com

By John Gwynne

The Faithful and the Fallen series

MALICE

VALOUR

RUIN

JOHN GWYNNE

Book Three of
The Faithful and the Fallen

PAN BOOKS

First published 2015 by Tor

This edition published in paperback 2016 by Pan Books
an imprint of Pan Macmillan
20 New Wharf Road, London N1 9RR
Associated companies throughout the world
www.panmacmillan.com

ISBN 978-1-4472-5964-0

1 3 5 7 9 8 6 4 2

A CIP catalogue record for this book is available from the British Library.

Typeset by Ellipsis Digital Limited, Glasgow
Printed and bound by CPI Group (UK) Ltd, Croydon, CR0 4YY

Visit **www.panmacmillan.com** to read more about all our books
and to buy them. You will also find features, author interviews and
news of any author events, and you can sign up for e-newsletters
so that you're always first to hear about our new releases.

For William, my memory and my joy.

And for Caroline, the air that I breathe.

Acknowledgements

I can't believe we are three books into The Faithful and the Fallen. I'm still not used to seeing them on shelves in bookshops, with paper and cover art and everything, and here we are now with the third! As with *Malice* and *Valour*, writing *Ruin* has been a rollercoaster of an experience, with a small warband of helping hands throughout.

First of all I must thank my wife, Caroline, and my children, Harriett, James, Ed and Will for their unceasing and passionate support of all things Banished Lands, and also for allowing me to retreat into my very own fantasy world for a large chunk of last year. I did emerge from my ivory tower (messy desk!) for brief periods of weapons sparring (read: helping with homework), in which I tended to come off worse. This book wouldn't have been written without their support.

Thanks must also go to my agent, John Jarrold, without whom The Faithful and the Fallen would never have seen the light of day. He is a man of immeasurable class and a fantastic agent. There is no one I'd rather have in my corner.

Also my wonderful editor at Tor UK, Julie Crisp, one of the few people I've met more bloodthirsty than myself. Her talent and polishing skills are a constant source of amazement to me, without which The Faithful and the Fallen would have been a much duller affair. Of course, along with Julie I must thank Bella Pagan, Louise Buckley, Sam Eades, Rob Cox, James Long and all at Team Tor, a host of people that make this writing malarkey look easy – which I can assure you it is not!

Thanks must go to my copy-editor Jessica Cuthbert-Smith, a lady with a most remarkable eye for the minutest of details.

And thanks of course to Will Hinton, my editor across the pond, as well as the whole team at Orbit US.

Acknowledgements

I'd also like to thank those who have taken the time to read *Ruin* and provide feedback. It is not a small book; indeed, I suspect it's large enough to bludgeon a fully grown giant to death. Firstly Edward and William Gwynne – to say they have read *Ruin* is really an understatement. They've buried themselves within its pages, frequently reminding (catching me out!) on details I've neglected or overlooked (forgotten!). I must also confess to the dubious fact that *Ruin* reduced Edward to tears – something I am coming to realize equates (hopefully) with a good bit in the book.

Others who have read and commented on *Ruin*: my wife, Caroline; Mark Roberson; David Emrys – whose knowledge on the details of close-quarter combat has been both extremely helpful and mildly disturbing. I do not want to know how he's come by his expert knowledge! And of course, Sadak Miah, my oldest friend; one of two geeks who formed their very own Tolkien Club at school, with a quiz for any who wished to join! Reading seven chapters of *Ruin* really isn't good enough, you know!

I'd also like to thank my good friend Robert Sharpe, his brother John Sharpe and their friend Ciarán Mac Murchaidh for help and translatory (that's a word, now) skills in the use of Gaelic within this book.

And finally, a huge thank you to all of you who have bought the books and taken The Faithful and the Fallen to heart. Truth and Courage!

Cast of Characters

Brenin – murdered King of Ardan, father of Edana.

Brina – healer of Dun Carreg, owner of a cantankerous crow, Craf.
Escaped with Edana from the sack of Dun Carreg. After reaching
Domhain, along with a few companions, she accompanies Corban to
Murias in search of Corban's sister, Cywen.

Corban – warrior of Dun Carreg, son of Thannon and Gwenith, brother
of Cywen. Escaped with Edana from the sack of Dun Carreg and
fled to Domhain. Travelled to Murias, a giant fortress of the Benothi
clan, in search of his sister, Cywen. Some claim that he is the Bright
Star of prophecy.

Cywen – from Dun Carreg, daughter of Thannon and Gwenith, sister of
Corban. Taken as both prisoner and bait by Calidus and Nathair.
Rescued by Corban and his companions during the Battle of Murias.

Dath – fisherman of Dun Carreg, friend of Corban. Escaped with Edana
from the sack of Dun Carreg. Accompanied Corban in the pursuit of
Cywen to the fortress of Murias.

Edana – fugitive Queen of Ardan, daughter of Brenin. At present on a
ship sailing away from Domhain, accompanied by a handful of
faithful shieldmen and Roisin.

Evnis – counsellor and murderer of King Brenin and father of Vonn.
In league with Queen Rhin of Cambren. Now regent of Ardan,
ruling as Queen Rhin's right hand.

Farrell – warrior, son of Anwarth and friend of Corban. Escaped with
Edana from the sack of Dun Carreg. Accompanied Corban north in
search of Cywen.

Gar – stablemaster, secret guardian of Corban. A Jehar warrior and son of Tukul, lord of the Jehar. Escaped with Corban and Edana from the sack of Dun Carreg. Accompanied Corban north in search of Cywen.

Glyn – shieldman of Evnis.

Meg – orphaned child from a village on the outskirts of Dun Crin's marshes.

Pendathran – battlechief of King Brenin, injured during the fall of Dun Carreg. Held prisoner and tortured by Evnis. Escaped with the help of Cywen.

Rafe – young warrior belonging to Evnis' hold. Childhood rival of Corban. Trained as a huntsman, and present during the escape of Edana from Domhain.

Vonn – warrior, son of Evnis. Escaped with Edana from the sack of Dun Carreg and remained with her during the fall and flight from Domhain.

CAMBREN

Braith – warrior and huntsman. One-time leader of the Darkwood outlaws, now huntsman of Queen Rhin.

Geraint – warrior, battlechief of Queen Rhin.

Morcant – warrior, once first-sword of Queen Rhin, defeated and replaced by Conall. Now one of Rhin's battlechiefs, loaned to Evnis to assist in the suppression of resistance against Rhin in Ardan.

Rhin – once-Queen of Cambren, now Queen of the West, having conquered Narvon, Ardan and Domhain. Ally of Nathair. Servant of Asroth, Demon-Lord of the Fallen.

CARNUTAN

Belo – Baron of Tarba, a fortress in Carnutan. Uncle of Gundul. Hostile and suspicious of outside involvement in Carnutan.

Gundul – King of Carnutan and ally of Nathair's. Son of Mandros, who was thought to have murdered King Aquilus of Tenebral and was in turn slain by Veradis.

DOMHAIN

Baird – one-eyed warrior of the Degad, Rath's giantkillers. Now guide and protector of Edana.

Brogan – warrior of Domhain. Shieldman of Lorcan and Roisin, one of the survivors who fled with them and Edana.

Cian – warrior of Domhain, shieldman to Roisin and one of those who escaped the fall of Dun Taras and fled by ship with Edana.

Conall – warrior, bastard son of King Eremon. Brother of Halion and half-brother of Coralen. Sided with Evnis in the sack of Dun Carreg. Now the lord of Domhain, ruling in Queen Rhin's name.

Coralen – warrior, companion of Rath. Bastard daughter of King Eremon, half-sister of Halion and Conall. Accompanied Corban north.

Halion – warrior, first-sword of Edana of Ardan. Bastard son of King Eremon, brother of Conall and half-brother of Coralen. Captured by Conall as he fought rearguard to enable Edana's escape.

Lorcan – young fugitive King of Domhain, son of Eremon and Roisin. Escaped from Domhain by ship with Edana.

Roisin – Queen of Domhain, widowed wife of Eremon, mother of Lorcan. Fled by ship with Edana.

Helveth

Lothar – once battlechief of Helveth, now its king. Murderer of previous king of Helveth, Braster. Ally to Nathair and Calidus.

Isiltir

Dag – huntsman in the service of King Jael of Isiltir.

Fram – warrior of Isiltir. First-sword to King Jael.

Gramm – horse-trader and timber merchant, lord of a hold in the north of Isiltir. Father of Orgull and Wulf. Allied to Meical.

Haelan – fugitive child-King of Isiltir, fleeing Jael. In hiding at Gramm's hold, in the far north of Isiltir.

Hild – woman of Gramm's hold. Wife of Wulf, son of Gramm. Mother of Swain and Sif.

Jael – self-proclaimed King of Isiltir. Allied to Nathair of Tenebral.

Kalf – man of Gramm's hold. Overseer of Gramm's river trade and boatwright.

Maquin – warrior of Isiltir and the elite Gadrai. Taken captive during the fall of Dun Kellen by Lykos of the Vin Thalun. Enslaved and thrown into the fighting-pits, where he fought his way almost to freedom. Escaped Lykos during rioting at Jerolin, capital of Tenebral, on Lykos' wedding day. Now a fugitive on the run with Fidele of Tenebral, once-regent of Tenebral and recently wedded to Lykos.

Sif – child of Gramm's hold. Daughter of Wulf and Hild, sister of Swain.

Swain – child of Gramm's hold. Son of Wulf and Hild, brother of Sif.

Tahir – warrior of Isiltir and the elite Gadrai. Protector to Haelan, child-King of Isiltir.

Trigg – orphaned child raised at Gramm's hold. She is a half-breed, part giant.

Ulfilas – warrior, shieldman of Jael. Captain of Jael's honour guard.

Wulf – warrior, son of Gramm and brother of Orgull. Wed to Hild. Father of Sif and Swain.

Yalric – warrior of Gramm's Hold.

NARVON

Camlin – outlaw of the Darkwood. Now companion to Edana. Fled with her from Domhain, fought in the rearguard to protect Edana as she boarded a ship and fought Braith before escaping on the ship.

Drust – warrior, shieldman of Owain. Escaped the defeat of Owain and his warband, aided by Cywen.

Gorsedd – villager who joins Corban's warband.

Owain – King of Narvon. Conqueror of Ardan, with the aid of Nathair, King of Tenebral. Executed after his warband was defeated on Queen Rhin's order.

Teca – woman from a northern village of Narvon, joins Corban's warband as she flees Nathair and the Kadoshim.

Uthan – Prince of Narvon, Owain's son. Murdered by Evnis on Rhin's orders.

TARBESH

Akar – captain of the Jehar holy warrior order travelling with Veradis.

Enkara – warrior of the Jehar holy order. One of the Hundred travelling with Tukul.

Hamil – captain of the ten Jehar left by Tukul to guard Drassil and Skald's spear.

Javed – slave and pit-fighter of the Vin Thalun.

Kulla – warrior of the Jehar, part of Akar's company that joins Corban.

Sumur – lord of the Jehar holy warrior order.

Tukul – warrior of the Jehar holy order, leader of the Hundred.

TENEBRAL

Alben – swordsmaster and healer of Ripa.

Atilius – warrior of Tenebral. Fought with Peritus against the Vin Thalun during the uprising. Captured, enslaved and put to work on a Vin Thalun oar-bench.

Caesus – warrior of the eagle-guard, captain of the shield wall.

Ektor – son of Lamar of Ripa and brother of Krelis and Veradis. A scholar where his brothers are warriors.

Fidele – widow of Aquilus, mother of Nathair. For a time Queen Regent of Tenebral. Lykos uses dark magic to bewitch and control Fidele, eventually marrying her. Riots break out in their wedding celebrations, during which the spell controlling her is broken. She stabs Lykos and with Maquin's help flees in the confusion.

Krelis – warrior, son of Lamar of Ripa and brother of Ektor and Veradis.

Lamar – Baron of Ripa, father of Krelis, Ektor and Veradis.

Marcellin – Baron of Ultas.

Nathair – King of Tenebral, son of Aquilus and Fidele. In league with Queen Rhin of Cambren. Believes that he is the Bright Star, the one prophesied to be the chosen champion of Elyon. Recently completed his quest to claim the starstone cauldron, one of the Seven Treasures of ancient myth.

Pax – son of Atilius. A young warrior captured during the uprising in Tenebral. Made a slave and set to work on a Vin Thalun galley, alongside his father.

Peritus – once battlechief of Tenebral. Now leader of the resistance against Lykos and his Vin Thalun.

Valent – a warrior of Ripa.

Veradis – first-sword and friend to King Nathair. Son of Lamar of Ripa and brother of Ektor and Krelis. He commands a warband of Tenebral, instrumental in the defeats of Owain of Narvon and Eremon of Domhain.

Cast of Characters

THE THREE ISLANDS

Alazon – chief shipwright of the Vin Thalun.

Demos – Vin Thalun ship-lord. Friend of Lykos.

Jayr – Vin Thalun healer.

Kolai – shieldman of Lykos.

Lykos – Lord of the Vin Thalun, the pirate nation that inhabits the Three Islands of Panos, Pelset and Nerin. Sworn to Asroth, ally and co-conspirator of Calidus. Appointed regent of Tenebral by Nathair. Has used sorcery to control and marry Fidele, mother of Nathair.

Nella – one-time lover of Lykos. Mother of his child.

Senios - Vin Thalun pirate. Captive of Maquin and Fidele for a time.

THE GIANT CLANS

The Benothi

Balur One-Eye – Benothi giant. Joined forces with Corban and his company during the Battle of Murias. He took the starstone axe from Alcyon.

Eisa – Benothi giantess, companion of Uthas.

Ethlinn – Benothi giantess, daughter of Balur One-Eye, also called the Dreamer.

Laith – female giantling, one of the survivors of the Battle of Murias who joins Corban and his companions.

Nemain – Queen of the Benothi giants. Betrayed and slain by Uthas.

Salach – Benothi giant, shieldman of Uthas.

Uthas – giant of the Benothi clan, secret ally and conspirator with Queen Rhin of Cambren. Slayer of Queen Nemain and now self-proclaimed Lord of the Benothi. Dreams of reuniting the giant clans and being their lord.

The Jotun

Ildaer – warlord of the Jotun.

Ilska – giantess. Battle-maiden and bear-rider.

The Kurgan

Alcyon – servant and guardian of Calidus.
Raina – giantess. Mother of Tain.
Tain – giantling. Son of Raina.

The Ben-Elim

Meical – high captain of the Ben-Elim. Chosen as the one to leave the Otherworld, to be clothed in flesh and sent to the Banished Lands to prepare for the coming war.

The Kadoshim

Asroth – Demon-Lord of the Fallen.
Belial – a captain of Asroth, one of the Kadoshim spirits that travels through the cauldron and possesses the body of Sumur, lord of the Jehar warriors.
Bune – a Kadoshim spirit that possesses the body of a Jehar warrior during the Battle of Murias.
Calidus – High captain of the Kadoshim, second only to Asroth. Chosen as the Kadoshim to be clothed in flesh and prepare the way for Asroth in the Banished Lands. Adversary and arch-rival of Meical, high captain of the Ben-Elim.
Danjal – a Kadoshim spirit that possesses the body of a Jehar warrior during the Battle of Murias.
Legion – many Kadoshim spirits that swarmed into the body of a Jehar warrior as the gateway through the cauldron was closing during the Battle of Murias.

THE
BANISHED
LANDS

THE BONE FELLS

OTUNHEIM

Kavala mountains

ARCONA

Drassil

ORN FOREST

Haldis

rihan

Halstat

Bairg mountains

HELVETH

Taur

Ultas

Jerolin

Agullas Mountains

ENEBRAL

Balara

Tethys Sea

Ripa

TARBESH

PELSET

Telassar

NERIN

'Havoc and spoil and ruin are my gain.'

John Milton, *Paradise Lost*

CHAPTER ONE

ULFILAS

The Year 1143 of the Age of Exiles, Eagle Moon

Ulfilas touched his heels to his horse's side, urging her up the incline before him, a slope of grey rock and gravel littered with the remains of long-dead trees. Beside him King Jael kept pace, his face set in rigid lines. A dozen paces ahead of them rode Jael's huntsman, Dag.

Jael should not be here, Ulfilas thought, a knot of worry shifting in his gut. *The King of Isiltir, wandering in the northern wilderness on a fool's errand.* It was not that Ulfilas felt any great sense of loyalty to Jael; he didn't even like the man. It was more that after all they had been through, to die now on a journey like this, which he considered a waste of time, would feel foolish.

Ulfilas was aware that times were changing, there was war on the horizon, and the power in Isiltir needed consolidating. He had been Jael's shieldman since he'd sat his Long Night, and despite his dis-like of Jael's character and practices, Ulfilas was also a pragmatic man. *I'm a warrior. Got to fight for someone.* Recent events had proven his choice well made. King Romar was dead. Kastell, Jael's cousin, was dead. Gerda, estranged wife of Romar, was dead. Her young son, Haelan, technically speaking still heir to the throne of Isiltir, was missing. Running. He knew that Jael felt little to no loyalty towards the men who followed him, that the new self-proclaimed King of Isiltir was scheming, vain and power hungry and would do whatever it took to keep his newly won crown. But he was a man on the rise. And so Ulfilas had stuck with him, when a voice in his mind had been telling him to walk away and find another, more worthy, lord to serve.

A conscience? he wondered. *Hah, a conscience doesn't put food on my plate or keep my head from a spike.*

'How much longer?' Jael called ahead.

'Not much longer, my lord,' the huntsman Dag called back. 'We'll be with them before sunset.'

Close to the top of the incline Ulfilas reined in his horse and looked back.

A column of warriors wound up the slope behind him, surrounding a wain pulled by two hulking auroch. Beyond them the land stretched grey and desolate, further south the fringes of Forn Forest were a green blur. A river in the distance sparkled under the dipping sun, marking the border of this northern wasteland with the realm beyond.

Isiltir. Home. Ulfilas looked away, back up the slope towards his King, and spurred his horse after him.

They travelled ever northwards as the sun sank lower, shadows stretching about them, their path winding through empty plains and steep-sided ravines. Once they crossed a stone bridge that spanned a deep abyss; Ulfilas looked down into the darkness. His stomach shifted as his horse stumbled on loose stone, the thought of falling into the unknown making him snatch at his reins. He let out a long breath when they reached the far side, the sharp rush of fear receding as quickly as it had appeared.

They rode into a series of barren foothills, eventually cresting another slope to find Dag silently waiting for them. Ulfilas and his King drew level with the huntsman and pulled their mounts to a standstill at the sight before them.

A flat plain unfolded into the distance, the tips of mountains jagged on the horizon. Just below the travellers lay their destination: a great crater, as if Elyon the Maker had punched a fist into the fabric of the earth, barren of life and no breeze or sound of wildlife to disturb it.

'The starstone crater,' Jael whispered.

Ulfilas had thought it more tale than truth, the rumoured site of the starstone that had fallen from the sky.

How many thousands of years ago was it supposed to have crashed to the earth? And from it the Seven Treasures were said to have been forged, over which past wars had changed the face of the Banished Lands, not least of all here, where the stories told how Elyon's Scourging had broken the land, scorching it black.

Ulfilas stared up at the sky, slate-grey and swollen with clouds, and imagined for a moment that they were filled with the white-feathered Ben-Elim and Asroth's demon horde. He could almost hear their battle-cries echoing about him, hear the clash of weapons, the death-screams.

Elyon and Asroth, Maker and Destroyer, their angels and demons fighting for supremacy over these Banished Lands. I thought it all a faery tale. And now I am told it is happening again.

Riding through these lands now Ulfilas found himself believing what, only a year ago, he had thought to be bedtime stories for bairns. He thought of the time he had spent at Haldis, the burial ground of the Hunen giants hidden deep in Forn Forest. He had witnessed a king betrayed and slain over a black axe said to be one of the Seven Treasures carved from the starstone; he had seen white wyrms, and earth magic where solid ground turned into a swamp, suffocating the life from his sword-brothers. He was a man of action – of deeds. Monsters made real were not something he'd found easy to accept. Fear churned in his gut at just the memory of it.

Fear keeps you sharp.

Further down the slope and built on the lip of the crater was the carcass of an ancient fortress, walls and towers broken and crumbling. Figures moved amongst the ruins, mere pinpricks in the distance.

'The Jotun,' said Jael.

The giants of the north. Rumoured to be strongest and fiercest of the surviving giant clans. Not for the first time Ulfilas questioned the wisdom of this journey.

'No sudden movements,' Dag said, 'and keep your wits about you.'

Some of the Jotun's number filtered out of the ruins, gathering on the road that cut through the derelict walls, their spear-tips and mail catching the sinking sun. A handful were mounted on shaggy, lumbering creatures.

'Are they riding bears?' Ulfilas asked.

'We've all heard the tales of the Jotun in the north,' Jael said. 'It would appear some of those tales, at least, are true.'

They stopped at the first remains of a wall, the column of riders behind them rippling to a halt. Warriors spread from the path, curling about Jael like a protective hand. Ten score of Jael's best shieldmen. Ulfilas could feel the tension amongst them, saw the way hands gripped spear shafts and sword hilts.

Giants appeared from the ruins, moving with surprising grace despite their bulk. Some sat on the path ahead of them upon the backs of dark-furred and yellow-clawed bears. Ulfilas knew Jael was right to be wary, they'd seen first-hand at the Battle of Haldis how deadly an attacking force of giants could be. If it hadn't been for the men of Tenebral forming their wall of shields and stopping the Hunen giants' attack that had been tearing the warbands of Isiltir and Helveth apart, then Ulfilas knew none of them would be here today.

Too late to learn the shield wall now, but I swear, if I make it home . . .

One of the bear-riders moved ahead of the others, a tremor passing through the ground with the bear's every footfall. It halted before Jael, looming over him.

The giant slid from a tall-backed saddle and strode forward, blond hair and moustache bound in thick braids. A cloak of dark fur wrapped his wide frame, the glint of iron beneath it. In his hand he held a thick-shafted spear, a war-hammer was left strapped to his saddle. His bear watched them with small, intelligent eyes. It curled a lip, showing a line of sharp teeth.

'Welcome to the Desolation, Jael, King of Isiltir,' the giant said. His voice sounded like gravel sliding over stone.

'Greetings, Ildaer, warlord of the Jotun,' Jael replied. He beckoned behind him, his warriors parted to allow the wain forward. One of the shaggy auroch that pulled it snorted and dug at the ground with a hoof.

It doesn't like the smell of bear any more than I do.

Jael pulled back a cloth that covered the wain's contents. 'It is as my envoys promised you. A tribute. Weapons of your ancestors, hoarded at Dun Kellen,' he said, reaching in and with difficulty pulling out a huge battle-axe. 'My gift to you.'

Ildaer gestured and another giant moved to the wain, a broadsword slung across his back. He stood as tall as Jael did upon his horse. The giant took the axe, turning it in his hands, then peered into the wain. He could not hide the look of joy that swept his face.

'They are the weapons of our kin,' he said with a nod to Ildaer.

'I return them to you, as a token of my goodwill, and part payment of a task that I need your aid in.'

The giant gripped the aurochs' harness and led them forward, Ildaer peering in as the wain passed him. Giants pressed close about it.

'And what is to stop me from killing you and your men, and giving your carcasses to my bears?'

'I am of more value to you alive. You are a man of intellect, I have been told. Not a savage.'

Ildaer looked at Jael, his eyes narrowing beneath his jutting brow. He glanced back over his shoulder at the wain full of weapons.

'And besides, who is to say that we would not kill you and all of your warband?' Jael said.

The giants behind Ildaer all glowered at Jael.

A bear growled.

Ulfilas felt the familiar spike of fear – the precursor to sudden violence. His fingers twitched upon his sword hilt.

'Hah,' Ildaer laughed. 'I think I like you, southlander.'

Ulfilas felt the moment pass, the tension ebbing. *Southlander? Isiltir is not one of the southlands. But then, we are in the northlands now. They call anything south of here the southlands.*

Ildaer looked back at the wain again. 'That is of great worth to my people,' he admitted.

'It is nothing compared to what I am prepared to give, if you can help me.' Jael told him.

'What is it that you want?'

'I want you to find a runaway boy for me.'

CHAPTER TWO

CORBAN

Corban woke with his heart pounding. The remnants of a dream, dispersed with wakefulness, just a hint of black eyes and immeasurable hatred remaining for a moment. Then that too was gone.

It was cold darkness all around.

He heard Storm growl and he sat up, one hand feeling for his sword hilt. *Something's wrong.*

He felt Storm's bulk beside him, reached out and felt her hackles standing rigid.

'What is it, girl?' he whispered.

The camp was silent. To his left the fire-pit glimmered, but he avoided looking at it, knowing it would destroy any night vision he possessed. He made out the dense shadow of a guard standing on the incline of the dell they were camped within. The moon emerged, revealing another figure close by, tall and dark-haired. *Meical.* He was standing perfectly still, his attention fixed on the dell's rim. Behind Corban a horse whinnied.

There was a flapping up above and then a croaking bird's screech. '*WAKE, WARE THE ENEMY, WAKE. WAKE. WAKE.*'

Craf or Fech. Corban leaped to his feet, all around him other shapes doing the same, the rasp of swords pulled from scabbards. Shapes appeared at the dell's edge, figures outlined for a moment in the moon's glow before they swarmed down the incline. There was a crunch, a collision, a scream.

'Kadoshim,' Meical shouted, then all was chaos. Bodies were swirling, solid shadows blurred with starlight, then an explosion of sparks burst from the fire as it blazed brightly, scattering light. Corban caught a glimpse of Brina calling out incantations beside the fire, making it burn higher and directing tongues of it towards their enemy.

The new light revealed a dozen attackers amongst them, dressed like the Jehar but moving differently, with none of their fluid grace, as if their bodies held too much power to contain within the confines of flesh and bone. They carved their way through the camp, sending those that attacked them hurtling away. Corban remembered how the Kadoshim had fought in Murias, just after they'd been raised from the cauldron, tearing limbs from bodies with a savage, inhuman ferocity. A wave of fear suddenly swept him, pinning his feet to the ground. He heard a strange language screamed in defiance and looked to see Balur One-Eye the giant, his kin gathered behind him, hurling defiance at the Kadoshim, who paused for a moment, then surged towards Balur.

They have come for the axe.

As he watched them charge together, Corban remembered his mam, their attack on *her*, how he had tried to stop the blood flowing as he'd held her, how the light had dimmed from her eyes. Hatred for these creatures swept him, burning away the fear that had frozen him moments before, and then he was moving forwards, running faster with each step, Storm at his side.

They saw him before he reached them, or perhaps it was Storm that marked him out. Either way, the Kadoshim obviously recognized him, and who he was supposed to be: the Seren Disglair – Bright Star and Elyon's avatar made flesh. Some of them broke from the main bulk that was now locked in combat with Balur and his giant kin. Tukul and his Jehar swirled around their edges, slicing, cutting.

Storm lengthened her stride and forged ahead of him. Corban glimpsed the muscles in her legs bunching as she gathered to leap, then she was airborne, colliding with one of the Kadoshim in a mass of fur and flesh, her jaws tearing at its throat.

Instinct took Corban as he reached them; gripping his sword two-handed he raised it high, slashing diagonally, shifting his weight to sweep around his target. He felt his sword bite through leather and mail, shattering bone and carving through flesh. It should have been a killing blow. The Kadoshim staggered, one hand gripping Corban's blade. It stared at him, black eyes boring into him, then it grinned, blood as dark as ink welling from its mouth. These were no longer the human Jehar whose bodies they'd possessed upon emerging from the cauldron, but something far stronger.

Corban yanked his sword away, saw severed fingers fall as the Kadoshim tried to keep its grip. Its other hand shot out, grabbing Corban around the throat, lifting him from the ground. Impossibly strong fingers began to squeeze. He kicked his legs, tried to bring his sword round, but could put no strength in his blows. Stars appeared at the edges of his vision, a darkness drawing in. The pounding of his heart grew in volume, drowning all else out. Panic swept him and he found new strength, bringing the wolven hilt of his sword down on the Kadoshim's head. He felt the skull crack, but still it gripped him.

It regarded Corban calmly, head cocked to one side.

'So you are Meical's puppet,' it growled, startling Corban. Its voice was unsteady, a basal rumble that seemed too deep for the throat it issued from.

Corban tried to raise his sword, but it was suddenly so heavy. Too heavy. It slipped from his fingers. The strength was fading from his limbs, leaking from him, a great lethargy seeping through him.

So much for everyone's hopes of me being the Bright Star. Is this what dying feels like? At least I'll get to see Mam again.

There was an impact, a crunch that he felt shudder through his body and he saw sharp teeth sink into the Kadoshim's neck and shoulder.

Storm, he realized, distantly.

The Kadoshim was spun around as Storm tried to drag it off Corban, but it would not release its grip on Corban's throat. Then there was another impact – this one accompanied by what sounded like wet wood being split as an axe-blade hacked through the Kadoshim's wrist, severing it completely.

Corban crashed to the ground, his weak legs folding beneath him. He looked up to see Tukul wrestling with the Kadoshim, Storm tearing at the creature's leg. Then someone else was there, sword a blur, and the Kadoshim's head was spiralling through the air.

Its body sank to the ground, feet drumming on the turf as a

black vapour in the shape of great wings poured from it, eyes like glowing coals regarding them with insatiable malice for a moment before a breeze tugged it apart. A wail of anguish lingered in the air.

Gar stood over Corban, reaching to pull him upright.

'You have to take their heads,' Gar said.

'I remember now,' Corban croaked.

'Remember earlier next time.'

Corban nodded, massaging his throat. He touched his warrior torc, felt a bend in the metal.

This must have stopped it from crushing my throat.

The battle was all but done. The grey of first dawn had crept over them as they fought, and by it Corban saw a handful of giants pinning the last Kadoshim to the ground, Balur standing over the creature. His axe swung and then the mist-figure was forming in the air, screeching its rage as it departed the world of flesh.

There was the silent, relief-filled moment that comes at the end of battle. Corban paused, just glad to still be alive, the fear and tension of combat draining from him. He could see it in those around him, the shift and relaxing of muscle in bodies, a change on their faces, a gratitude shared. Then they were moving again.

As dawn rose they gathered their dead, laying them out along the stream bank next to the cairn they'd finished building just yesterday. Corban stood and stared at the pile of rocks they'd dragged from the stream.

My mam is in there, beneath those rocks.

A tear rolled down Corban's cheek as grief and exhaustion welled in his belly, swelling into his chest, taking his breath away. He heard a whine: Storm, pressing her muzzle into his hand. It was crusted with dried blood.

A cold breeze made his skin tingle as he stood before his mam's cairn. *How can she be gone?* He felt her absence like a physical thing, as if a limb had been severed. The events of yesterday seemed like a dream. *A nightmare.* His mam's death, so many others, men and giants and great wyrms. And he had seen the cauldron: one of the Seven Treasures, remnant from an age of faery tales. He had seen a bubbling wave of demon-spirits from the Otherworld pouring from it, Asroth's Kadoshim, filling the bodies of transfixed Jehar warriors like empty vessels. He knew the group who had attacked them had only been a small part of those remaining a dozen leagues to the north; Nathair and his demon-warriors camped within the walls of Murias.

What are we going to do?

He watched as the rest of his followers started to break camp. He searched for Meical but could not see him. Brina stood close to the fire-pit, Craf and Fech fluttering about her. He glimpsed Coralen moving quietly to the camp's fringe, checking on the pad-docked horses. Her wolven claws were slung across her shoulders. Corban remembered their words before the battle at Murias, when they had heard of Domhain's fall, of her father King Eremon's death. She'd fled into the trees and he'd followed her, wanted to comfort her but not known how. They'd shared a handful of words and for a moment he'd seen through the cold hard walls she'd set about her. He wished he could go back to that moment and say more to her. He saw her head turn, her gaze touching him for a moment, then turning sharply away. Beyond her, a huddle of figures stood – the giants who had fled Murias, clustered together like an outcrop of rock. Closer by, the Jehar were gathering beside the stream, making ready to begin their sword dance. He felt the pull of habit drawing him to join them. Without thinking he approached them, seeking comfort in the act of something familiar amidst the whirl of fear, death and grief that threatened to consume him.

They were gathered about their leader, Tukul, Gar beside him; a few score stood further behind the old warrior – the ones who had saved Corban in Rhin's fortress. Others were grouped before Tukul, at least twice their number. As Corban approached Tukul raised his voice, saying something in a language Corban did not recognize. The mass of Jehar before him dropped to their knees and bowed their heads. There was one who did not – Corban recognized him as one of the Jehar who had been with Nathair before realizing they had been betrayed. It seemed he was angry about something. Gar stepped forward. From years of knowing him Corban could tell he was furious, a straightness in his back, a tension in the set of his shoulders.

For a moment the two men stood staring at one another, a sense of imminent violence emanating from both of them, then Tukul snapped an order and they stepped apart, the other man stalking away.

Gar saw Corban and walked towards him. His eyes looked raw, red-rimmed. Corban remembered him weeping before his mam's cairn. The first time he'd seen him display such emotion.

He has always seemed so strong, so in control. Something about seeing Gar weep had made him seem more human, somehow. Corban felt a sudden surge of emotion for the man, his teacher and protector. His friend.

'What's happening?' Corban asked him.

'The Jehar that followed Sumur and Nathair,' Gar said with a nod towards the Jehar, who had risen and all started forming the lines for the sword dance practice. 'They have recognized my father as their captain.'

'Good. And him?' Corban said, looking at the one who had spoken with Tukul.

'Akar. He was Sumur's captain. He is ashamed that they followed the Black Sun, that they were fooled by Nathair. That he was fooled. And he is proud. It is making him say foolish things.' Gar shrugged, the emotion of a few moments ago gone or well hidden.

'He looked like he wanted to fight you.'

'It may come to that.' Gar looked at the warrior, mingling now in the line of the sword dance. 'And we have a history.'

Corban waited but Gar said nothing more.

'Where's Meical?' Corban asked.

'Scouting. He set off soon after the attack – took a giant and a few of my sword-brothers and left.'

'Shouldn't we go and find him?'

'I think Meical can look after himself. He'll be back soon. Best use our time.' Gar ushered him forward amongst the ranks of Jehar warriors. Corban drew his sword and slipped into the first position of the dance, his mind sinking into the rhythm of it, muscle memory automatically taking over from conscious thought. Time passed, merging into a fusion of contraction and extension, of focus and sweat, of pumping blood and his beating heart and the weight of his sword. Then he was finished, Tukul stepping from the line and ordering the Jehar to break camp.

Corban stood there a moment, savouring the ache in his wrists and shoulders, clinging to the familiarity. He looked around and saw his friends were nearby, watching him – Farrell and Coralen, standing with Dath. A figure walked towards him – Cywen, their mam's knife-belt strapped diagonally across her torso.

'Happy nameday, Ban,' Cywen said.

'What?'

'It's your nameday. Seventeen summers.'

Is it? He shook his head. *It's been over a year since we fled Dun Carreg, since I last saw Cywen. A year of running and fighting, of blood and fear. But at least I have spent it amongst my kin and friends. What has she been through? A year by herself, surviving who knows what. And only to come back and be reunited with us and help bury our mam.* He took a long look at her – thinner, grime on her cheeks highlighted by tear tracks. The bones in her face were starkly defined, and her eyes were haunted. They hadn't spoken much last night before sleeping. There'd been too much happen to all of them that day for them to relive anything else. Instead they'd sat by the fire for hours, just comfortable in each other's company, Dath teasing Cywen and trying to make her smile, Farrell quietly watching and Coralen pacing as if she couldn't quite settle.

Before he could respond to Cywen's greeting there was a drum of hooves as a handful of riders crested the dell. Meical led, with the hulking forms of giants following behind. Corban could barely believe that what had once been mankind's fiercest enemy was now their ally. Meical rode into the camp, dismounted smoothly and strode to Corban. Balur and another giant, a female, accompanied him, with Tukul following behind.

'Only one of the Kadoshim survived last night's attack. We tracked him halfway back to Murias before we gave up the chase. The land between us and the fortress is clear, for now,' Meical said. 'My guess is that the Kadoshim will stay within the fortress walls a while and become accustomed to their new bodies.'

'Fech is watching them for us,' the female giant said. 'We will not have another surprise like the one last night.'

'Good,' Corban nodded, then looked at Meical. 'What next?'

'That is what we have come to ask you,' Tukul said, staring at Corban.

'Me?'

'Of course you. You are the Seren Disglair. We follow you.'

Corban felt a shift around him and looked about to see the whole camp still and silent, all watching him.

He gulped.

CHAPTER THREE

UTHAS

Uthas of the Benothi stared down at the dead. He was standing just within the great doors of Murias, the sun warming his back. The bodies of his kin were laid out before him, scores of them, the might of the Benothi laid to waste. Here and there survivors of his clan moved, a handful remaining of those who had joined him – little more than two score – pulling fallen Benothi from the mass of the dead. The whole chamber was clogged with corpses, giants, men, horses, the stench of blood and excrement underlying all else.

Other figures lurked in the shadows, the Kadoshim. They moved awkwardly, not yet fully accustomed to their new bodies of flesh and bone. Uthas suppressed a shudder and looked away; the sight was unsettling now the chaos and rush of battle had passed.

Most of his surviving kin were gathered around a large ink pot, dipping bone needles as they inscribed the tale of thorns on their bodies. All had killed during yesterday's battle; all would have fresh thorns to tattoo into their flesh. He saw Salach, his shieldman, bent close over Eisa as he tattooed her shoulder. Uthas' eyes strayed back to the corpses lined at his feet, searching the faces of the dead. One that he had hoped he would find was not there. *Balur. I should have known he would not have the good grace to die.* He felt a flutter of fear at the knowledge that the old warrior was still alive, knew what Balur would wish to do to him. *He will carry this blood-feud until the end of days. He needs to die.* His gaze came to rest upon the corpse of Nemain, once his queen, now so much food for carrion.

What have I done? Fear and doubt gnawed at him. He cursed the events that had led to this. Cursed Fech, the damn bird that had warned Nemain of his betrayal. He put a hand to his face, felt the claw marks that Fech's talons had raked into his forehead and cheeks.

Things could have been different if I'd had time to reason with Nemain . . . He gritted his teeth. *No. It is done, no going back. I must salvage from this what I can, protect and rebuild my clan. I am King of the Benothi now.*

Voices drew his attention and he looked up to see Nathair's adviser, Calidus, emerge from a hall, the giant Alcyon looming behind him. After the battle they had set a makeshift camp in the chamber of the cauldron, deep in the belly of the mountain, but Uthas could not stand it in there; the stench of so many dead wyrms was making him retch. Besides, it was foolish to leave the great gates unguarded, the only entrance and exit to the fortress of Murias. Their enemies had seemingly fled, but who knew what they were capable of? Meical and his followers had already stormed their way into Murias once and shattered the ceremony, preventing many of the Kadoshim from passing through the cauldron into the world of flesh.

Calidus saw him and strode over.

'How many of the Benothi live?' Calidus asked. A cut across his forehead was scabbing, the skin puckering as he spoke. After the battle he had appeared weary to Uthas, face drawn, his silver hair dull. For the first time he had looked frail, like an old man. Now that was gone. He stood straight, his body alive with new energy, his yellow eyes appearing feral, radiating power.

'Forty-five, fifty maybe of those who stood with me. Others still live who fought against us, or at least, their bodies have not been found. Balur is one of them.'

'Balur has the starstone axe. He took it from Alcyon.' Calidus flickered a withering stare at the giant beside him who stood with head downcast, his face stained with a purple bruise. Uthas noticed Alcyon had a war-hammer slung across his back, replacing the black axe that had been there. *Taken from a fallen Benothi, no doubt.* That stirred anger in his belly and he scowled at Alcyon, a member of a rival giant clan, the Kurgan.

No, he told himself, *if my dream is to become reality I cannot think like that. We were one clan once, before the Sundering. It can be so again.*

Looking at Alcyon, though, he realized just how deep the old grudges ran.

'You have something to say?' Alcyon growled at him, standing straighter, returning his dark look.

Control your temper, build bridges, he told himself.

'I see you carry a Benothi weapon. There is much honour in that.'

'Honour, in the Benothi?' Alcyon sniffed.

'Aye,' Uthas growled, anger rising. 'As there is in all of the clans. Even the Kurgan.'

Alcyon looked slowly around, his gaze lingering on the fallen Benothi. 'I see little evidence of Benothi honour here.'

'I did what had to be done,' Uthas snarled. 'For our future. Yours, mine, all of the clans'. If Nemain had continued to do nothing all of the clans would have faded, become a tale to frighten wayward children.'

'And instead we will slaughter ourselves to extinction.'

You fool, you do not see the long path, only the next step. His temper was fraying.

'You would be better served by concentrating on the task set for you.' Uthas shrugged, feeling the spite rise in him like bile after too much wine. 'But you were unable to do that, as you could not even hold onto the starstone axe.'

'Do not judge me, you that have betrayed your kin, your queen.' Alcyon looked about the room, eyes resting on Nemain's broken body. 'And I lost the axe to Balur One-Eye. I feel no shame in that, when I can smell the fear in you at the mere mention of his name.'

Uthas felt the words like a blow across his face. 'We have both served the same master here,' he said.

'Aye, but you out of *choice*,' Alcyon glowered.

'Enough,' Calidus snapped. He glared at Alcyon until the giant looked away from Uthas. 'Balur is a problem. I hoped that he would have been slain in the battle.'

As did I. 'He will do all in his power to see me dead.' Uthas felt a stab of shame at the tremor in his voice. He gripped his spear tighter, his shame shifting to anger. 'He could be dead, slain by those that left in the night.'

There had been a disagreement after the battle; one of the

Kadoshim had argued with Calidus. It had been unsettling, hearing a voice so alien issuing from the Jehar's mouth – rasping and sibilant.

'You have failed Asroth,' the Kadoshim had accused Calidus, arms jerking. 'We must regain the axe now, before it is too late, and reopen the pathway.'

Calidus had taken a long shuddering breath, mastering himself. 'It is too great a risk, Danjal,' Calidus had said. 'Battles are still being fought. We must secure the fortress, make sure the cauldron is safe. Would you have us abandon it?'

'Our great master must be allowed to cross over. For that we need the starstone axe.'

'Seven Treasures are needed to open the way for Asroth, not just the axe. It will happen, but we must wait. I seized an opportunity, and over a thousand of our brothers are now clothed in flesh. Be content with that. Asroth waits to enter this world wrapped in his own form, not filling someone else's, as you have done. And, besides, to pursue Meical now would be foolish; it would put the cauldron at risk, and many of you will lose your new skins.'

'Your body of flesh and bone has made you craven,' the Kadoshim had snarled. 'Asroth will reward me when he knows it was I who secured the axe and made his passage possible.'

Calidus took a step back from the Kadoshim and unsheathed his sword, the rasp of it drawing all eyes. 'Craven? I have just fought Meical, high captain of the Ben-Elim, and seen him flee. I have fought countless battles to reach this place and made a bridge between the Otherworld and the world of flesh, to bring your worthless spirit here. You will not call me craven. Or would you challenge me, reckless Danjal?'

Muscles clenched and unclenched in the Kadoshim, a spasming ripple. Eventually he lowered his eyes.

'I seek our master's glory,' he growled.

'As do I,' Calidus said. 'Go after Meical and you will be rejoining our master in the Otherworld before you know it.' Calidus had turned his back and walked away. The once-Jehar looked about, called for help and then ran from the chamber, a dozen or so Kadoshim surging after him.

'If you find them, try and kill Meical's puppet, his Bright Star;

you may actually achieve something useful with your death that way,' Calidus called out after them.

Uthas had felt a glimmer of hope. To retrieve the starstone axe they would need to slay Balur.

He wished it was so, but as yet there had been no sign of the Kadoshim that had left during the night.

'Your comrades that went after the axe, they may have killed Balur, retaken the axe.'

'Maybe.' Calidus shrugged. 'But I doubt it. More likely is that the Kadoshim that went after the axe are slain, their spirits returned to the Otherworld. Meical may be foolish in some things, but he would have set a guard, and he knows how to fight.'

Uthas could not hide his disappointment as his hope flickered and died.

'It is of no matter. Danjal has always been a fool; we are better off without his rebellious nature. Do not fear Balur. I will protect you. Your future is with me, now. Your loyalty to Asroth will not be forgotten. I have the cauldron because of you, and I am grateful.' The old man paused a moment; Uthas took strength from his words.

'How many are with Balur?' Calidus asked him.

'A score that cannot be accounted for, his dreaming bitch of a daughter Ethlinn amongst them. And none of our young have been found – they were hidden in a higher chamber. Around the same number again.' He shook his head, a wave of regret sweeping him. 'The Benothi are close to extinction, our numbers . . .'

'Too late for remorse. You've made your choice. And a wise one – you have chosen the victorious side. The Kadoshim walk this world, and this is only the beginning.' Calidus grinned a smile that didn't reach his cold eyes

He is right. And added to that, what other road is there for me to follow? The Benothi's fate is entwined with the Kadoshim now.

Uthas took a shuddering breath. 'And what now?' he asked Calidus. 'You have the cauldron. What would you do with it?'

'Make it safe.'

'It is safe enough here.'

'Clearly not. We took it. No, it must be taken to Tenebral. There it will be at the centre of a web that has taken me many years to build. I will have Lykos and his Vin Thalun, and Nathair's eagle-guard to protect it, along with your Benothi and my Kadoshim.'

Uthas frowned. 'A long journey. Much could happen.'

'Aye, but it will have an honour guard this world has never seen before. You Benothi and over a thousand Kadoshim.'

'And once it is in Tenebral?'

'One thing at a time. First, to journey there with the cauldron. I would have you and your Benothi build a wain for the cauldron to travel upon, sturdy and strong.'

'We shall do it. To Tenebral, you say. For that you will need Nathair.'

Calidus looked thoughtful and frowned. 'Yes. The time has come for me to speak with our disillusioned King.'

Calidus had tasked Uthas with keeping a watch over Nathair. During the battle he had sat on the dais steps before the cauldron, the truth of his actions unfolding before him, settling upon him like a shroud. After having believed himself to be the Seren Disglair for so long, witnessing the events he'd set in action had only left him questioning his true position. After the battle he had attempted to confront Calidus, who had just ignored him. It seemed that was the last straw for Nathair. He had flown into a rage and attacked Calidus, spraying spittle as he spat curses, denounced him as a traitor, but Uthas had grabbed Nathair, held him, and Calidus had struck him unconscious. He had then cut a lock of hair from Nathair's head.

'Where is Nathair?' Calidus asked him.

'Out there,' Uthas waved at the gates.

'Accompany me. I need Nathair's cooperation. Some persuasion will be necessary, and your example may be helpful.'

'And if he does not agree?'

'There is always this,' Calidus said. He opened his cloak to show a crude clay figure, strands of dark hair embedded within it.

Does he have strands of my hair bound within an effigy of clay? Uthas felt a shiver of fear at that thought.

'But I'd rather it didn't come to that,' Calidus said, dropping his cloak.

'Compassion?'

'Don't be an idiot,' Calidus said with a sneer. 'It would be one more thing that I have to maintain – it is hard work, conquering a world.'

As they strode towards the gate one of the Kadoshim called Calidus' name. Uthas recognized its body as Sumur, the leader of the Jehar who had followed Nathair. 'This body,' the Kadoshim said, its voice a serpentine growl. 'It is weakening, not responding as it did.'

'Men of flesh must eat, to restore their energy,' Calidus said. 'Ideally every day.'

'Eat?'

'You must consume sustenance: fruit, meat, many things.' Calidus waved a hand.

As Uthas watched, ripples of movement ran across once-Sumur's face. The black eyes bulged, lips pulling back in a rictus of pain as a scream burst from its lips. For a moment the flesh of the face writhed, fingers trying to gouge their way out. With a twist of the neck and a groan the features became smooth again, calm, expressionless.

'This human objects to my presence,' the serpentine voice said. Something passing for a smile twisted its face, a tongue licking its lips. 'It gives good sport.'

Uthas was horrified. He had assumed the souls of the hosts had been displaced, were not still residing trapped within their own bodies, struggling to evict those who possessed them. He shuddered – such a thing would be a living death.

'He was a master swordsman, all of your new hosts were,' Calidus said, raising his voice to all the Kadoshim in the great hall. 'Examine their souls, pick them apart, absorb their skills. Learn the ways of your new bodies. And eat.'

Sibilant laughter echoed about the chamber as Calidus walked away. Uthas saw one Kadoshim drop to the ground, burying its face in the belly of a dead horse, the wet sound of flesh tearing.

'They are like children,' Calidus sighed. 'I have much to teach them in little time, which is why I need Nathair to cooperate.'

They found the King of Tenebral a short way along the road that approached Murias, the tattered bodies of Jehar warriors and their horses scattered around him, shredded to a bloody mess by the raven storm that Queen Nemain had set upon them. He was stood with his great draig, holding its reins loosely in one hand while it feasted on the corpse of a horse. It pulled its snout from a smashed ribcage to regard them with small black eyes, gore dripping from its jaws. As they drew nearer to Nathair, Uthas glimpsed amongst the fern and gorse one of his kin whom he had set to watch the King of Tenebral.

Nathair heard their approach and looked up. He whispered something to the draig, which went back to devouring the horse's innards. Nathair turned his back to them, looking out over the bleak landscape of moorland, gentle hills undulating into the horizon.

'He is out there,' Nathair said quietly.

'Who do you speak of?' Calidus asked.

'The Bright Star. For so long I have believed that title was mine.' He turned, calm now, Uthas saw, his rage from the cauldron's chamber gone, spent. His eyes were dark-rimmed and red. A bruise mottled his jaw.

'You have deceived me, all this time.' Nathair looked first at Calidus, then past him, to Alcyon. The giant dropped his head, not meeting Nathair's gaze.

'You would not have understood,' Calidus said.

Nathair raised his eyebrows at that. 'Something we agree on. My first-sword Veradis will have your heads for this. Thankfully he is not here to witness how far we have fallen.'

'Time will be the judge,' Calidus said with a shrug. 'But there is still a future for you. For us.'

'What, this is not to be my execution, then?' Nathair's eyes flickered to Alcyon and Uthas behind Calidus, and then further off, to the Benothi guards lurking in shadows.

'No. I came to talk.'

'It seems to me the time for that has passed. But go on . . .'

'You see things as you have been taught. Good, evil; right, wrong. But things are not always as they seem—'

'No, they are not. You are living proof of that. Claiming to be one of the Ben Elim, yet you are the opposite: Kadoshim, a fallen angel, servant of Asroth.'

'You speak of things about which you have no understanding,' Calidus snapped. 'Kadoshim, Ben-Elim, they are just names given by those too ignorant to comprehend. Remember, history is written by the victors. It is not an unassailable truth, but a twisted, moulded thing, corrupted by the victor's perspective. Elyon is not good; Asroth is not evil. That is a child's view. The world is not scribed in black and white, but in shades of grey.'

'So you would have me believe that Asroth is good? That Elyon is the deceiver?'

'No, something in the middle of that, perhaps, with both parties capable of both good and evil. Like you. More human, if you like. Would that be so hard to imagine?'

Uthas saw something flicker across Nathair's face. *Doubt?*

'Your histories tell that Asroth would destroy this world of flesh,' Calidus continued. 'They claim that was Asroth's purpose in the War of Treasures. Ask yourself: if that were true, then why is he so desperate to come here, to become flesh?'

'I would not dare to guess after having been proved so monumentally naive,' Nathair said with a sour twist of his lips. Something of his earlier rage returned, a vein pulsing in his temple.

'Don't be so dramatic,' Calidus scolded, 'like a sulking child. I have come to you to speak hard truths and would hear you speak in return as the man you can be, the leader of men, the king. Not as a petulant child.' He took a moment, waiting, letting the weight of his words subdue Nathair's anger. 'Now think on this. Asroth would come here not to destroy, but to rule. He would fashion an empire, just as you have imagined. A new order, one defined by peace, once the dissenters were dealt with. No different from your plans. And you could still be a part of it. Our numbers are too few; we will need someone to rule the Banished Lands. Someone who could unite the realms. I believe that someone is you.'

'And you think I would believe anything that crosses your lips, now. After this?' Nathair gestured at the towering bulk of Murias.

'Yes. I would. Put your anger, your pride and shame aside and think. War has raged in the Otherworld for aeons. It has been bloody and violent and heartbreaking. I have seen my brothers cut down, broken, destroyed. And I have returned the violence upon the Ben-Elim a hundredfold. I did what I had to do. Withholding some of the truth from you was necessary. Difficult decisions must be made in war, for the greater good. You know this.' Calidus paused, holding Nathair with his gaze.

'There are some lines that cannot be crossed, regardless of the greater good,' Nathair spat.

'You forget, Nathair. I know you. I know what you have done. What lines you have already crossed in the name of the greater good.'

Nathair raised a hand and took a step back, as if warding a blow. His draig stopped crunching bones to cast its baleful glare upon Calidus.

'I do not say it as a criticism, but as a compliment. Once you are committed to a cause you will do whatever is necessary to see it through. Whatever it takes, regardless of the cost. A rare ability in this world of frailty and weakness. And one that we need. I respect that. So I ask you, Nathair: join us. Commit to our cause and you will gain all you desire, see your dreams come to fruition, your ambition rewarded. And if you think on it, it is not so different from all that you were striving for before the scales fell from your eyes.'

Alcyon shifted from behind Calidus. 'Someone comes,' he said, pulling his newly acquired war-hammer from his back.

'Where?' Calidus asked, hand on sword hilt, eyes narrowed.

Alcyon pointed south-east, into the moorland. A dark speck solidified, moving at considerable speed.

'It is one of my brothers,' Calidus said. 'One of those that left with Danjal.'

They stood in silence as the figure approached. It covered the ground quickly, running with a loping gait. As it drew near, Uthas saw it was weaving.

And something is wrong with its arm.

It must have seen them standing on the road, for it veered towards them, collapsing before Calidus. Its hand was severed just above the wrist, blood still trickling from the wound. It was pale as milk, veins black within its skin. Nathair's draig gave a low rumbling growl.

'I am weak,' the Kadoshim rasped. 'This body is failing.'

'I warned you,' Calidus said. 'These bodies are still mortal. Soon it will die from loss of blood.'

'Help me,' the Kadoshim whispered.

'Swear to obey me in all things,' Calidus said, voice cold as winter-forged iron.

'I swear it. Please . . .'

'Bind his arm,' Calidus snapped at Alcyon, kneeling to put an arm about the injured Kadoshim. 'You must look after your new body, Bune. Like a weapon, it must be cared for. You have lost much blood, but if we treat your wound and feed you, all will be well.'

'My thanks,' the creature croaked. 'I would not return to the Otherworld so soon.'

'Then no more of this foolish charging off to fight unwinnable battles. Danjal? The others?'

'All gone, back to the Otherworld. There were too many against us, and these bodies . . .' Bune held up his uninjured arm. 'It is taking me some time to adjust to it.'

'It will. Come, back to our kin where we can tend you better.' Calidus glanced at Alcyon, who finished binding the wrist and then lifted Bune in his arms. Calidus led them back towards the gates of Murias, Nathair and his draig following slowly behind. Birds circled lazily above, the remnants of Nemain's ravens lured by the stench of carrion. Uthas glared at them with something akin to hatred, thinking of Fech. As they stepped within the shadow of the fortress, Uthas saw a raven perched on a ledge in the cliff face. It stared back at him. For a moment he was convinced it was Fech and he raised a hand involuntarily to his scarred face.

Surely not. Fech is not brave or stupid enough to return here.

Calidus looked back to Nathair.

'Think on my words, King of Tenebral. I would have you fight beside me in the coming war. No more deceptions.'

Nathair paused before the gates and put a hand upon his draig's neck. Together the King and beast watched Calidus and his companions enter Murias.

'Watch him closely,' Calidus whispered to Uthas. 'If he tries to leave, stop him. Whatever it takes.'

CHAPTER FOUR

MAQUIN

Maquin ran through the undergrowth, trees thick about him. With one hand he pushed aside branches, with the other he held onto Fidele, the Queen Regent of Tenebral, recently married to Lykos, Lord of the Vin Thalun. *Until she tried to murder him. I'm guessing that's the end of their happy nuptials.*

She stumbled and he snatched a glance back at her, saw she was breathing heavily, her bridal gown snagged and torn, stained with blood. *She needs to rest.* The sounds of combat drifted behind him, faint and distant, but still too close for his liking.

It will not be long before Lykos and his Vin Thalun have put down the rioters. Then he'll be looking for his absent bride. Still, if we run much more she'll be finished anyway. With a frown he slowed, heard the sound of a stream and changed direction.

Maquin caught his breath as he splashed his face and naked chest with the icy cold water, washing away the blood and grime of the fighting-pit. A hundred different cuts began to sting as the adrenalin of his escape faded, his skin goose-fleshing. He shivered. *Should have grabbed a cloak as we fled.* He was still dressed for the heat of the pit: boots and breeches, a curved knife in his belt, nothing on his torso except blood and dirt and scars.

I'm free. He sucked in a deep breath, savouring the earthy scents of the forest, reminding him of Forn. Of another life. He closed his eyes as memories flickered through his mind. The Gadrai; his sword-brothers; of Kastell, slain by that traitorous bastard Jael; of Tahir and Orgull, the only other survivors of the betrayal in Haldis. It felt so long ago. *The time-before.* He looked at his hands, blood still ground into the swirls of his skin, stuck beneath his fingernails. *Orgull's blood.*

His friend's face filled his mind as it had been when he had cradled him – beaten, bloody, dying. A swell of emotion bubbled up, tears blurring his eyes. He remembered Orgull's last words to him: a request to find a man named Meical and pass on a message. *That I stayed true to the end,* Orgull had said.

So much death, and yet still I live. More. I am a free man. All right, a refugee, with enemies behind me, and I'm a thousand leagues from home. But I'm free. Free to hunt down Jael and put him in the ground. Even now the thought of Jael burned away all else. He could see his face, lips twisted in a mocking sneer as Maquin had been chained and led to the Vin Thalun ships. Hatred flared incandescent, a pure flame in his gut. He felt himself snarling. A tearing sound drew his attention. Fidele was standing in the stream close by. She was ripping away the lower part of her dress.

'Easier to run,' she told him. 'Here.' She bunched the fabric and dipped it in the stream, then began washing the filth from his back. She gasped and paused a moment as the myriad scars were revealed, telling the tale of the whip as a slave, countless other cuts and reminders from his time in the fighting-pit. She'd seen him earn some of those scars, watched him fight, kill others. Shame filled him at the things he'd done and he bowed his head.

'Where are you from?' she asked quietly.

He blinked; for a moment he had to think about that. 'Isiltir,' he said, pronouncing it slowly, like a forgotten friend.

'What is your name? Who are you?'

In the pit I was called Old Wolf, the only name I've gone by for a good long while. I am a trained killer. Have become that which I hate.

'My name is Maquin,' he said with a twist of his lips, a step towards reclaiming himself. 'I was shieldman to Kastell, nephew of King Romar.'

'Oh,' Fidele breathed. 'You are a long way from home. How did you end up . . . ?'

'In the fighting-pits?' He paused, the silence stretching, thinking back to before his enslavement, to the life he had led, the friends he had known, pulling at memories buried deep within, of the events that had preceded his life as a slave. 'Jael has usurped King Romar's throne – murdered the King, crushed the resistance in Isiltir. I fought him as part of that resistance, but Lykos and his Vin Thalun came, allied to Jael . . .' He shrugged, his voice was a croak, unused to conversations of more than a few words.

Her hands touched his shoulder, hovering, tracing a swirling design, sending an involuntary shiver through him.

'Lykos gave me that one,' he said. 'Branded me as his slave, his property.'

'Do you think he's dead?'

Maquin remembered the last time he'd seen the man, fallen to one knee in the arena, a knife hilt protruding from beneath his ribs, blood pulsing. Combat had swept Maquin away, and when he had looked back Lykos was gone.

'Doubt it. He's a tough one.'

'I want him dead,' Fidele hissed, a flash of rage contorting her face.

He looked at her a long moment, taken aback by the vehemence in her. He had always thought of her as unapproachably beautiful, calm, serene. 'Bit strange to marry him, then.'

She stepped away, eyes downcast. 'I was under a foul magic – he had an effigy, a small clay doll, with a lock of my hair cast within it. You crushed it when you fought him. That set me free.'

Fidele shuddered, her eyes closed. Then she straightened and looked him in the eye.

'I have not thanked you, for protecting me in the riot, for getting me away to safety.'

Maquin looked about. 'This is not exactly what I would call safe.'

'It is safer, by far, than the arena.'

'True enough.'

All had been chaos back in the arena before Jerolin, and Maquin had taken advantage of it, using the mayhem and confusion to rush Fidele out of the arena. The closest cover had been woodland to the south; Maquin led Fidele in a mad dash across open meadow towards the trees, all the while his heart thudding in his head as he waited for the expected cries of pursuit. None had come as they reached the treeline and so they continued to run deeper into the woodland, Maquin's only thought to put distance between him and the Vin Thalun. Something had sparked the riot. Maquin's duel with Orgull had played a part in it, but Maquin had also seen warriors amongst the crowd, urging them on. They had been wearing the white eagle crest of Tenebral. There was some kind of resistance forming against the Vin Thalun, that was clear. But how strong was it? Had they managed to crush the Vin Thalun? To drive them from Jerolin and Tenebral? Maquin doubted it – the Vin Thalun had numbered in their thousands; it would take a lot of manpower to finish them. 'And what would you do now, my lady?' Maquin asked her.

She frowned and sat upon a rock. 'I don't know is the short answer. I would find out if the Vin Thalun have been defeated –' she paused, a tremor touching her lips – 'but I am scared to go back. The thought of being caught is more than I can bear.'

Maquin nodded. *I can understand that.* For himself, he wanted to leave. To point himself north-west instead of south and aim straight for Jael. *What about her, though?* He could not just abandon her in the woods.

'Will you help me?' she asked. 'I have seen that you are no friend to Lykos or the Vin Thalun. We have a common enemy.'

'I've had enough of fighting other people's battles,' he said. 'I've got my own to fight. I need to go home. I have something to do,' he muttered quietly, almost to himself. He looked at her face and saw a determination of purpose there, battling with the fear of her circumstances. 'But I will see you safe first, my lady. If I can.'

She breathed a relieved sigh. 'My thanks. I will do all in my power to repay you, and to speed you on your way.'

'First, we must survive the night and the cold.'

'Wait here,' Maquin whispered to Fidele.

They were crouched behind a ridge, looking out upon a wide stretch of land covered in tree stumps. On the far side was a row of timber cabins, piles of felled trunks surrounding them. It was dusk; the forest was grey and silent.

'Do not come after me for anything. Nothing, you understand?'

She nodded and he slipped away, staying low to the ground, keeping to the outskirts of the manmade clearing, stalking within the shadows amongst the trees. Eventually he was behind the row of cabins. Gripping his knife he slipped to the front and entered. Grey light filtered through gaps in the shutters and he paused to let his eyes adjust to the gloom.

Cots lined the walls, covered by rough woollen blankets, boots, breeches, and cloaks. A long table ran down the centre of the room, cups and plates scattered upon it. Axes and great two-man saws were all about, and there were racks of water skins, gloves, other work tools. *Men live here. Woodcutters. Question is, where are they now?*

It came to him quickly – *Jerolin and the arena. It's a big day – celebrations and games to mark Lykos being wed to Fidele.*

He quickly grabbed cloaks from pegs, woollen shirts, breeches, some cheese and mutton, water skins and a roll of twine, stuffing them all into an empty bag he'd found.

There was a groan; a blanket shifted on a cot in the corner of the room. A figure sat up – a man, rubbing his eyes.

In heartbeats Maquin had crossed the room and had his knife held to the stranger's throat, his eyes drawn to the man's beard, the iron rings binding it.

He is Vin Thalun. A rage bubbled up, threatening to consume him.

'Please, no—' the man gasped.

Can't kill him here – too much blood. His friends will be onto us as soon as they return.

'Up,' Maquin ordered.

Slowly the man stood, eyes flickering to the sheathed sword hanging over the cot.

'Don't,' Maquin grunted, kicking the back of the man's leg, sending him tumbling away from the cot. He slung the sword and belt over one shoulder.

'Why are you here? Not at the arena?' Maquin asked as the Vin Thalun climbed to his feet.

He glowered at Maquin. 'Someone has to stand guard; Lykos' orders. I pulled the short straw.'

'Outside,' Maquin ordered and followed his prisoner out of the door, directing him behind the cabin, into the trees. It was twilight; the world was slipping into degrees of shadow. Maquin dropped his bundle of provisions. 'On your knees, hands behind your head,' he grunted.

The Vin Thalun lunged forwards, turning as he moved, reaching for Maquin's knife arm.

Maquin was too quick for him, sidestepping, slashing at the warrior's hand, his blade coming away red. He barrelled forwards, the Vin Thalun somehow managing to grip his wrist. Maquin headbutted him, blood spurting from the Vin Thalun's nose. He staggered and dropped to the ground.

Time for you to die.

The Vin Thalun must have read the thought in Maquin's eyes, and he began to plead.

Undergrowth rustled and Fidele stepped out from amongst the trees.

'You're not supposed to be here,' Maquin said.

'You've been gone a long time. I was starting to worry.'

That felt strange – someone caring whether he lived or died. 'Found someone in the cabin. You should look away.'

'I've seen the colour of blood before. And he's Vin Thalun,' she snarled, looking at the rings in his beard. 'I'd be happy to watch you slaughter a whole nation of them.'

'All right then,' Maquin grunted.

'I can tell you where they are,' the warrior blurted as Maquin stepped close, knife moving.

'Where who are?' Maquin growled; his knife blade hovered at the man's throat.

'Lykos' secret. The giantess and her whelp.'

CHAPTER FIVE

CAMLIN

Camlin lay on a table in a ship's cabin, various pains clamouring for his attention. The broken arrow shaft still buried in his shoulder won.

'Bite on this and lie still,' a voice said beside him. Baird, a warrior of Domhain, thrust a leather belt at him. He was one of Rath's Degad, the feared giant-killers of Domhain. He had been assigned by Rath to see Edana to safety. In Camlin's mind there was still a way to go on that score, as they were stuck on a ship with only a handful of faithful men about Queen Edana; the rest of them were loyal to Roisin, the mother of Lorcan, young heir to the throne of Domhain.

Running again.

'Take it, you're going to need it,' Baird said. He grinned at Camlin, the skin puckering around the empty eye-socket in his face.

'Don't see there's much t'be grinning about,' Camlin said bitterly.

'It was a good fight. One to make a song about,' Baird replied, referring to the battle fought on the beach and quayside as they had made their escape. 'And we're still breathing. Happy to be alive, me.'

With a grimace, Camlin bit down on the belt.

'You'll need to hold him,' Baird said, and Vonn's serious face loomed over Camlin, his hands pressing on his chest.

'Still need t'breathe, lad,' Camlin muttered.

'How can I help?' Edana this time.

Half of Ardan is in this cabin.

'Don't think you should be in here, my lady,' Baird said. 'There'll be some blood, probably some cursing too.'

Edana snorted. 'I've seen enough blood already, and spilt some myself. As for the cursing, I've travelled with Camlin for near a year now. I don't think I'll hear anything I haven't already.'

'Well, if you're set on staying, try holding his feet.'

Baird cut away Camlin's shirt sleeve, gently probing the arrow shaft. A spike of pain lanced through Camlin, blood oozed lazily from the wound.

'Sure you know what you're doing?' Camlin growled. 'What with only one eye . . .'

'Is this the time to be upsetting me?' Baird said, grinning again. 'Done this a few times, should be fine. The arrow-head's too deep. Going to have to push it through.'

'Best get on with it, then, it's not going t'fall out by itself.'

'Agreed,' Baird said, gripping the broken shaft.

Camlin screamed.

'How does it feel?' Vonn asked.

Camlin stood on the deck of the ship, leaning on a rail, watching the dawn sun wash across blue-grey waves. To the east a line of dark green marked the distant southern coast of Domhain.

Slowly he rolled his shoulder and lifted his left arm, which had been healing nicely for the last two days.

'Feels like I've been shot with an arrow,' he grimaced. 'It's mending well,' he added at Vonn's concerned expression. *Lad's got no sense of humour.*

Be a while before I can draw my bow, though, damn Braith to the Otherworld.

Images of the battle filled his mind: Braith, his old chief from the Darkwood toppling off the quay into the ocean. Conall knocking his brother Halion senseless as Camlin escaped to the ship with Roisin's son, Lorcan. Looking back as they sailed away, Conall cutting Marrock's throat and tossing him to the waves.

Marrock. First real friend I've had in a long while. He felt the man's loss keenly, along with Halion's. They had felt like a brotherhood, friends bound by more than a common cause. *And the others – Dath and Corban, even old Brina. I wonder, have they found Cywen? Are they still even breathing?* The world was in flux, constantly changing around him. It was hard for a man to keep up. *'Specially when all I've known for twenty years is the Darkwood. Still, can't change the truth of things. Have t'bend with it. Better'n breaking.*

You should leave, the old persistent voice said in his head. *Walk away, make a life for yourself before you get yourself killed for some lordling's cause that means nothing to you. Besides, look at you – you're not the sort t'be mixing with queens and noble warriors; you're a thief, a villain.*

Dolphins leaped through waves, keeping pace alongside the ship. *Can't leave now, I've come too far, made promises.*

You've sworn no oaths.

Not out loud, no. But I need t'see this through. Besides, can't exactly walk away right now. I'm not much for swimming.

'Where's Edana?' he asked Vonn, who had settled beside him, staring silently at the coastline.

'In her cabin. Baird's guarding her.' He was silent a moment. 'Do you think we can trust him?'

'Baird? He's a good man t'have around in a scrap. Trust; now that's another matter. What d'you think?'

'I wouldn't ask me. I'm not such a good judge. I trusted my father, remember.' He pulled a sour face and looked down at the waves.

Camlin felt a wave of sympathy for the young warrior. *Evnis, betrayer of Dun Carreg, slayer of Brenin, King of Ardan. Not the best da in the Banished Lands to have.*

'Think you can be forgiven for that,' Camlin said. 'Most of us do. Trust our da, I mean. For a while, at least.'

Vonn didn't respond.

'As for Baird, my guess is he's one of those that gives his word and keeps it as best he can. Him and Rath were close, and he swore to the old man to see Edana safe.'

'He did,' Vonn agreed.

'Well, t'my mind she's not safe yet. We may be on a ship sailing away from Domhain, Rhin and Conall, but most of those aboard don't owe Edana naught, and Roisin and her boy Lorcan command a score of warriors. We won't be safe till we're off of this tub and away from them, is my thinking. Even if Edana is promised to Lorcan, I don't trust Roisin to keep her word. '

Edana. Fugitive Queen of Ardan. Initially Camlin had become part of this group through circumstance. After the fall of Dun

Carreg it had been his friendship and loyalty to a few – Marrock and Halion, the lads Dath and Corban – that had kept him with them. Now, though, they were all gone. He stayed now for Edana. At first she had seemed to be a spoilt princess, ill equipped to lead and not worth following. Over the course of their flight from Dun Carreg, through the wilds of Cambren and the mountains that bordered Domhain, Camlin had seen a change in her. A moment stuck in his mind, in the mountains when Marrock had chosen to stay on a suicide mission and delay their pursuit. Edana had stepped in. *We'll all stay, or all go. I'll not lose you so that I can run a little longer.* That's what she had said.

Took some stones, that did. And from that moment a kernel of respect for the young woman had taken root in Camlin. Over the following moons it had grown, seeing how she had dealt with old Eremon and the cunning politicking of his Queen, Roisin.

Think she might be worth following, after all.

As if the thought of her had been a summons Edana appeared on the deck and came towards them, Baird at her shoulder. Her fair hair was bound tight in what looked like a warrior braid; her face was pale and drawn. A grey cloak, the colour of Ardan, was wrapped about her shoulders, her hand resting on a protruding sword hilt.

'I'm going to see Roisin,' she said. 'Thought my shieldmen should be at my side.'

Shieldmen. Been called plenty of things in my time, but not one of those before.

'Of course,' Vonn said.

'What's this about?' Camlin asked, then felt Vonn frowning at him. *Keep forgetting she's a queen.*

Edana looked about. The ship was a single-masted trader, the steering rudder on a raised platform at the stern. Roisin and her son slept – and for the last two nights had all but lived – in a cabin beneath the steering platform. Two warriors stood by the door.

'It's time we all know where we stand. I would know if Roisin will honour Eremon's last words to us.'

She straightened her shoulders and set off, Baird, Vonn and Camlin falling in behind her. Edana stopped before the two warriors guarding the stern's cabin.

'I would speak with your lady,' she said, her voice firm.

The two men regarded her a moment.

'Get on with it, then, Cian,' Baird said good-naturedly, but Camlin could feel the threat of violence emanating from the man. He was like a pulled bowstring, always on the edge of release. One of the warriors frowned at him, but after another moment he knocked and then entered the cabin.

'And tell Roisin to pour some wine,' Baird called after him.

Edana looked at him and he shrugged.

'She will see you, my lady,' Cian said, holding the door open. Edana entered. Cian stepped between her and her shieldmen. 'Not you,' he told them.

'I swore an oath to Rath,' Baird said. 'See her safe to Ardan. I'll not be letting her out of my sight after the stunt Quinn pulled. You going to try and make me an oathbreaker?' He took a step forwards.

'Let them in,' a voice called from within the cabin.

The warrior hesitated a moment, then stepped aside before following them into the room.

The cabin was dark; Camlin's eyes took a moment to adjust. Instinctively he hung back, eyes scanning for points of exit. A shuttered window on the far wall, the door behind him. That was all. The room was small, sparsely decorated – a table, two chairs, two cots built onto the walls. Roisin sat in a chair at the table, a flickering candle highlighting her pale skin, jet black hair a dark nimbus about her. She looked exhausted, cheeks gaunt, eyes dark pools of shadow, but even under these circumstances she was still beautiful.

'Forgive Cian,' she said with a wave at the door. 'My shieldmen have been tense since Quinn's betrayal.'

That's fair enough, thought Camlin. *He caught us all off-guard. Should have trusted my instincts, though. Never liked him.*

'That is understandable,' Edana said, taking a seat and the wine that Roisin offered her.

Quinn had been King Eremon's first-sword, Roisin's champion. He had turned traitor on the beach in Domhain, when it had become clear that the ship they were boarding was too small to take them all to safety. With a handful of warriors he had attempted to snatch Lorcan and use him to bargain with Conall. Camlin had seen Halion put a sword through the traitor's heart, although Quinn's poison-tipped blade had slowed Halion enough for Conall to take him prisoner.

'I would talk frankly with you,' Edana said. 'These are dark times, and some clarity would go a considerable way to easing all our minds.'

'Dark times indeed. My husband is murdered, my kingdom stolen. My son pursued by a usurper.'

'Yes. The crimes against us both are many. But I have not come to talk of the past, but of the future.'

'Ask your questions,' Roisin said, taking a long draught of her drink.

'Your intentions. You have twenty shieldmen about you still. Do you intend to honour King Eremon's last words to me? To set me ashore in Ardan?'

'Ah, Eremon. The stubborn old fool. He should have fled with us. Should be here.'

They sat in silence, Roisin staring into her cup. With a shudder she lifted her gaze.

'And what of your promise to him? To take Lorcan with you to safety? To be handbound to him?'

Edana looked at her calmly. 'I will not be handbound to Lorcan. That agreement is dead. It was on the condition that Domhain's warband defeated Rhin and helped me regain the throne of Ardan. Domhain's warband is scattered; that hope gone. But if you wish, I will take you and Lorcan with me, give you what protection I can.' She smiled wanly. 'It may not be much. I hope to return to Ardan – as Eremon said, there is rumour of resistance gathering in the marshlands around Dun Crin – but it will be dangerous. Rhin rules there, with Evnis as her puppet. I do not know how many, if any, will be loyal to me. I cannot guarantee your or Lorcan's safety. Your other option is to sail as fast and as far away as possible, to go into a life of hiding, but I fear Rhin will hunt you, as she has hunted me. Lorcan and I are a threat to her power: we are legitimate heirs and a standard for the dispossessed to rally around.'

'There is another option,' Roisin said, slowly sitting straighter, looking at Edana from under heavy-lidded eyes. 'I could hand you to Rhin. A gift, in return for Lorcan's safety.'

She has teeth yet, the snake, Camlin thought, feeling a tension settle upon all in the room.

'That would be foolish,' Edana said, smiling tiredly. Of all of them she appeared the calmest. 'You cannot trust Rhin, whatever promises she makes. Lorcan is still a threat, no matter what gift he gives her. And she has placed Conall on the throne of Domhain – he will not suffer Lorcan to live. Surely you know that.' She stared straight at Roisin, holding her gaze. The older woman glared back, fierce and proud. Then, abruptly, like a sail with its wind taken from it, she slumped.

'I know you speak the truth,' she whispered.

'I will offer you a new deal,' Edana said. 'We have a common enemy, one that wishes us both dead and our supporters destroyed. Join me – see me safe to Ardan, help me in the fight to reclaim my home, and when it is done, I shall do the same for you. I vow on the cairns of my murdered parents, by the blood that runs in my veins and with every ounce of strength I possess: I shall see Lorcan back upon the throne of Domhain.' She stood suddenly, drawing a knife from within her cloak. Roisin tensed; her shieldmen took a step.

Edana drew the blade across the palm of her hand, blood welling, dripping, and offered her knife to Roisin.

The older woman sat and stared a moment, then stood and took the knife. She cut her palm and gripped Edana's hand tightly, their blood mingling.

'I vow to see you safe to Ardan, and to do all I can to help you reclaim your throne,' Roisin said.

More like you know where you and Lorcan are best protected, thought Camlin. *Not that sticking close to us is anything like safe, but if Rhin is going to be hunting us, the more swords about everyone the better.*

Roisin sighed, sitting back in her chair as Cian moved to her side.

'But Lorcan will be disappointed that you are not to be handbound,' she said. 'I think he is a little infatuated with you. Perhaps you could not tell him for a while, let him down gently.'

Just then the door burst open, Lorcan striding in, a warrior shadowing him. He was slim, dark-haired, fine featured, almost pretty like his mother. 'Ah, my two favourite ladies,' he said with a smile. 'My mother and my future wife.'

Edana rolled her eyes and Camlin suppressed a laugh.

CHAPTER SIX

RAFE

Rafe splashed up to his waist into the surf and grabbed the body floating in the waves. A black shaft sprouted from its chest. *That'd be more of Camlin's handiwork.* Rafe had seen the huntsman on the quay, shooting arrow after arrow into Conall's men. Half a dozen other corpses were laid out on the beach with matching arrows sticking from some part or other of their bodies. He looked out to sea, but the ship Camlin, Vonn and his companions had escaped on was long gone, not even a dot on the horizon now.

What am I doing here?

The answer to that was simple enough: he'd been ordered to come. Back at Dun Taras, when a hungry mob had opened the gates to Queen Rhin, Rafe had told Rhin and her force how he'd seen Edana and her companions flee the fortress. Conall had set about raising a pursuit, and Braith, Rhin's huntsman, had been part of that. Braith needed huntsmen, had asked for any that knew how to handle a brace of hounds. Conall had volunteered Rafe. And that was that.

So here I am, hundreds of leagues from home, on a cold beach on the edge of the world.

Rafe grunted as he dragged the corpse to shore; another warrior came to help him as he struggled onto the shingle. A hound whined and sniffed the body as Rafe and the other warrior hauled the dead weight along the beach, laying it down alongside the other dead, over a score of those who had ridden from Dun Taras with Conall.

That Halion knows how to swing a blade, I'll give him that.

As the battle had played out Rafe had been standing on a steep ridge overlooking the beach, gripping two hounds on a leash. Braith had been with him and together they'd watched as Halion's defenders had held the quay against overwhelming numbers, until Halion had toppled to the beach below. Even then Conall's brother had fought on, aided by a few who had leaped to his defence. It was only when Conall had faced him and beaten Halion unconscious that the path to the quay had been cleared. And by then it was too late: Edana and her companions were sailing away, along with Lorcan, the young heir to Domhain's throne.

One of the hounds whined and nuzzled his leg. 'There ya go, Sniffer,' he said, giving the hound a strip of dried mutton from the pouch at his belt. He crouched and scratched the grey-haired hound between the ears. 'You'll be wanting to go home now, I'm guessing,' he said.

Me too. Home. Dun Carreg, Ardan. Will I ever see it again? Memories swirled up, of long days in the wilderness with his da, Helfach the huntsman, as he taught Rafe the ways of wood and earth, of how to track prey and how to kill it.

The other hound padded over, Scratcher, seeing that he'd missed out on a treat.

'Go on, then,' Rafe said, throwing another strip of mutton. Scratcher caught it and swallowed, licked his lips.

Hooves drummed on the beach and Rafe looked up to see Conall returning, a handful of shieldmen riding behind him.

Conall was the closest thing to home now, the last remnant of his life in Ardan. Part of Rafe was scared of the warrior – quick-tempered and deadly – part of him liked the man, as swift to laughter as he was to anger. *He's risen far. Not long ago he was the same as me, just another sword in Evnis' hold.* Conall slipped from his saddle, scowling at any who dared meet his eyes.

'My brother?' he called, and men pointed. Halion was still unconscious, laid out on the beach, bound at wrist and ankle. Conall strode to him and stood over Halion's still form, staring. His face softened, then clouded, other emotions playing out across the land-scape of his features. Eventually his expression settled back into a scowl.

'Any luck?' a warrior, one of Queen Rhin's captains, asked as he joined Conall. All of the warriors who had accompanied Conall were Rhin's. Although the people of Dun Taras had opened their gates to Rhin, it was still too early to trust the warriors of Domhain.

It had not been that long ago that the men of Domhain and Cambren had been trying to kill each other.

'Not a single boat within a league of here,' Conall muttered.

'They've escaped, then,' Rhin's captain said.

'You're a quick one,' Conall snapped.

The captain frowned. 'Queen Rhin won't be happy. Glad I'm not you.'

Conall hit the man in the face, hard. He stumbled back a step, then dropped to one knee.

'*I'm* not happy, either,' Conall growled. Other warriors moved, comrades of the felled captain, a loose circle forming around Conall.

Rafe stood, took a step towards them. *He's the only link to home I have. Don't want to see him dead as well.* One of the hounds gave a low growl.

Conall turned to face the men drawing close about him. 'If any need reminding, I'm your Queen's regent, and her first-sword.' He put a hand upon his sword hilt, a reminder of how he'd beaten Morcant to become Rhin's champion.

Don't get involved, you idiot, Rafe told himself. *You don't want to die on this cold beach*, but his feet were already moving. He pushed through warriors, the dogs snarling at his heels. Rafe joined Conall; the two hounds flanked him with bared teeth.

There was a long drawn-out moment, violence in the balance. Only the roar of surf on shingle, a gull calling overhead. Then Rhin's men were turning, backing away; first one, then all of them.

'Up you get,' Conall said to the fallen warrior, offering his arm.

The man looked at him, then gripped Conall's wrist.

'No harm done, eh? Well, maybe a blackened eye for a few days. A tale for the ladies,' Conall laughed, slapping the man on the shoulder; the captain grunted and walked away.

'Saw what you did,' Conall said to Rafe. 'Won't forget that.'

Rafe shrugged.

'Where's Braith? If anyone can track a ship it'll be him.'

'He's dead,' Rafe said. 'Camlin killed him – threw him in the sea while you were fighting Halion.'

'Did he, now?' Conall said, frowning. 'Didn't expect that.'

There weren't many that could have stood against Braith.

'Me neither, but I saw it happen.'

'Shame. Don't suppose you can track a ship, can you?'

Rafe raised an eyebrow. 'Where do you think they're going?' he asked, as they both stared at the empty horizon.

'Away from me,' Conall growled. 'Somewhere far away from me.'

'He's waking up,' a warrior called to Conall. Rafe saw Halion stirring.

Conall hurried over, Rafe following.

Halion was cut and battered, a dark bruise staining his jaw. His eyes fluttered open.

'Water,' he croaked.

Conall knelt and dripped water from a skin onto Halion's lips, something tender about the act.

'Where are they?' Conall asked.

Halion's eyes fixed on the sea. 'They got away, then?'

'Aye, with your help. Where are they going, brother?'

'I don't know,' Halion whispered. 'We were just running – away from you, Rhin, Domhain. The where had not been decided.'

'You're lying,' Conall snarled, leaning closer.

'Believe what you will,' Halion shrugged. 'Either way they're safe from you now.'

Conall gripped Halion and pulled him close. 'I need to find Lorcan and his bitch-mother.' Spittle sprayed.

Halion looked at him with sorrow. 'When did you become a killer of bairns? Lorcan's your kin.'

'Do you not remember what Roisin did to us? Murdered our mam, drove us from our home?'

'Aye – Roisin, not Lorcan.'

'She's on that ship too. And Lorcan is her brood. If they're not dealt with now they'll come looking for me one day. I'll not spend the rest of my days looking over my shoulder, and I'll lose no sleep over shedding their blood. Either of them.'

'What's happened to you, Con?'

'Me? Look at you – bowing and scraping to a spoilt girl; fighting in defence of our mam's murderer. It's not me that's changed.'

'I gave my oath to King Brenin. I'll not be breaking it, not for anyone. Not even for you, Con.'

Conall paused then, just stared at Halion. A muscle in his cheek twitched. Then he drew his knife and cut the rope binding Halion's ankles.

'On your feet. I'm taking you back to Rhin. We'll see how long it takes you to tell her everything you know. She's more persuasive than you can imagine.'

Halion climbed to his feet. He saw Rafe.

'You're still alive, then,' Halion said to him.

'Aye. Hard to kill, me.' The last time Rafe had spoken to Halion was in Edana's tent, back when Rafe had been captured on the border of Domhain. The memory of it stirred a swell of anger – Corban and Dath and Farrell, all sneering at him, Edana looking down her nose, judging him.

'Things have changed since I saw you last,' he said as Halion was steered towards a horse.

'And they're likely to change some more before this is all over,' Halion said over his shoulder.

What's that supposed to mean?

'Make ready,' Conall called out. 'We'll bury our dead and then we're riding back to Dun Taras.'

One of the hounds whined, staring out to sea, his body stiff and straight.

Something was bobbing in the waves, a dark smudge amidst the foam and grey of the sea.

Another body?

Rafe waded into the surf. *Definitely a body.* He could see limbs, a shock of hair. The water was up to his waist as he reached it, then he froze.

It was Braith.

Face pale, skin tinged blue. There was a great wound between his neck and shoulder that still leaked blood, the surf foaming pink. Rafe grabbed him and began pulling the huntsman to shore.

Then Braith groaned.

CHAPTER SEVEN

TUKUL

Tukul held the severed head up high, gripping a handful of black hair. He regarded it grimly. A young Jehar warrior, female, younger even than his Gar. Empty, lifeless eyes stared back at him.

You were my sword-kin. A warrior, bred for battle, trained in righteousness, yet you ended life as a servant of Asroth, his tool. He shook his head, feeling a wave of sympathy for his dead kin, knew the shame she would carry across the bridge of swords. The emotion shifted quickly to anger as his thoughts turned to Sumur. *The prideful fool who followed a Kadoshim, who led my people into disgrace.* With a growl he put the head into a leather saddlebag, along with the heads of the other Kadoshim that had been slain during the night raid. *A reminder to us of the cost this God-War will carve from us.*

'What of these?' Gar said with a gesture as Tukul stood surveying the twisted headless corpses of the slain Kadoshim. He looked at Gar. The sight of him after so long a separation filled Tukul with deep joy. *My son, how you have grown. Strong, and with a fine measure of wisdom. Pride and humility mixed. You make my heart soar.* Tukul had often daydreamed of the man his son would grow into, but the reality was better. *Quicker to smile than the rest of us, but that is no bad thing. No smiles today, though, or for a while, I think.* Grief sat fresh and raw upon Gar's face. The death of Corban's mam had hit him hard.

Life and death, grief and joy, all part of the road Elyon has set before us. Nevertheless he frowned, wishing he could ease his son's pain. *An impossible task,* he thought, remembering the death of his own wife, Daria, a faint echo washing over him of the long despair that he had felt upon her death. *Keeping busy is what kept me sane through those dark days, and if that is the case, then Gar will be fine. We are entering the time of the God-War and that should keep us all busy enough.* He looked back to the corpses strewn upon the ground. 'I was thinking we should leave something that would serve as a reminder to those who follow, to Calidus and his ilk. A warning to them.'

Tukul gazed about, saw a cluster of windswept trees close to the stream. 'Over there,' he said, and they set about carrying the bodies to the trees. They passed Corban sitting by his mam's cairn, staring into nowhere.

He has much to think about, and not least is what he's going to do with this unusual warband that has grown up around him.

Tukul had seen Corban's dismay when he'd realized that all were waiting on his decision.

Since their meeting in the dungeons of Queen Rhin's fortress, Tukul had watched Corban with the intensity that a lifetime of expectation had nurtured. *He is the Seren Disglair, the Bright Star, Elyon's chosen avatar to stem the tide of Asroth and the legions of his Black Sun. How can any man bear such a burden?* And yet Tukul had a confidence in the young man, born not only from faith, but also from what his eyes and instincts told him. *He does not want to lead, and that is a good start. Only the vain and foolish crave such a responsibility. He is loyal to a fault, marching half a thousand leagues into a giant's fortress to find his sister and rejecting Meical's advice in doing so. That cannot have been easy, disagreeing with a warrior-angel.* Tukul liked that.

'Is he all right?' Tukul asked Gar.

His son shrugged. 'Yes,' he said simply. 'He has lost much, learned much. I trust him.'

'Good enough for me,' Tukul said with a smile. He was looking forward to hearing Corban's decision. *It will tell me more of this man that I have sworn to follow. He'd better make his mind up soon, though. We cannot just wait here for the Kadoshim and Benothi to fall upon us like a hammer.* About him the camp had been stripped down, horses saddled and ready, packs loaded, the fire kicked out, the giants grouped together, waiting, some of the bairns wrestling with one another upon the heather.

'Help me here,' Tukul ordered, lifting the corpse of a dead Kadoshim beneath the branches of a tree. More Jehar came to help.

Eventually he stood back and surveyed his and his kins' handiwork. *It will serve.*

A murmuring spread about him and he turned to see Corban leaning down to pick a purple thistle. He pressed the flower to his lips and placed it tenderly on the cairn, whispered something. Then he stood straight and strode to his stallion, his sister Cywen holding the bridle for him.

'And where are we going?' Meical asked Corban as the young warrior swung into his saddle.

Corban took a deep breath, looking at all those gathered about him. His eyes came back to rest upon Meical.

'I don't know.'

A silence settled.

Not the answer I was hoping for.

'You have counselled me to go to Drassil,' Corban said. 'As I thought of your advice, which is probably good advice, though I don't understand anything about prophecies and old forests and fortresses, my heart whispered to me. It said, you swore an oath to Edana.'

'I counselled riding to Drassil for a reason,' Meical said, speaking slowly, controlled. 'The prophecy. You must go there.'

Tukul saw Corban's eyes flicker to Gar. *He is unsure, searches for reassurance.*

'We have already lost much time and accomplished little,' Meical said, seeing Corban's hesitancy. 'And all the while Asroth is moving.'

'Accomplished little?' Corban eyes snapped back to Meical. 'It may not seem much to you, in the scheme of things, but I have accomplished what I set out to do. My sister is safe.'

'She is not safe. No one is safe. You should know that better than most – you stood before Asroth himself. You must know what is at risk.'

Corban nodded. 'I do. And you saved me from that, plucked me from Asroth's throne room before his very eyes. He was going to cut my heart out. And then you followed me north, helped me save Cywen from Nathair and Calidus.' His eyes searched out his sister. 'You will always have my thanks for that.'

'I do not seek thanks or praise,' Meical said. 'I seek victory. We are at war with a foe more powerful and evil than you can hope to imagine. I fear that another delay in the south will spell our defeat.'

'I know what you have counselled. Because of the prophecy, about these times, about me . . .' He trailed off. 'As you say, I have seen Asroth, and I know that a terrible evil is stirring. I have witnessed it, and it must be stopped.' He glanced north, towards Murias. 'I do not possess great wisdom . . .'

Tukul heard a cough, saw Brina staring at Corban, a smile twitching her lips.

'But there are things that I do know,' Corban continued, 'things that I have clung to through the dark times that I – we – have already faced.' He waved a hand at his friends. 'Family. Friendship. Loyalty. These things have been my guiding star, my light in these dark times.' He looked to his mam's cairn beside the stream.

He stopped then and met Meical's gaze.

'Edana sent the raven Fech to find me, to tell me of what had happened in Domhain, how she was fleeing back to Ardan. She asked that I find her, if I can.' He shrugged. 'My heart tells me that I should do that. I swore an oath to her.'

Tukul glanced at Gar and nodded. *I like this young man.* He had felt his spirit soar at Corban's words, even though it sounded as if he was building up to rejecting Meical's advice, and in Tukul's experience that had never ended well. *But I like what I hear. If it were me, I hope I would have said exactly the same. Although the fact that Corban seems to be taking counsel from a scruffy old raven over the high captain of the Ben-Elim is a little worrying.*

'This time, Corban, your heart is misleading you,' Meical said. 'Passion, emotion, those are Elyon's blessings upon your kind, but they can blind you as well as guide you. You must go to Drassil.'

'A question,' Corban said. 'Our journey to Drassil. How would we get there?'

'We would ride south, until we reach the river Afren, then we would turn east into Isiltir. Beyond that is Forn and Drassil.'

'The river Afren, which runs through the Darkwood, marking the border between Narvon and Ardan?'

'Aye.'

'That's what I thought,' Corban said. 'Then for a hundred

leagues our journey would be the same, whether our destination was Ardan or Drassil.'

'Aye, it would.'

'Then let us do that. Ride south. The decision about our final destination can wait awhile, be thought upon.'

Meical frowned at that.

Meical wants him to lead us, Tukul thought. *To be decisive. But it is a lot to ask in one so young, and one so unused to leading. Maybe he needs some time to adjust to the weight he now bears.*

Meical considered Corban for long, drawn-out moments, his expression as flat and unreadable as any of the Jehar. 'We shall ride south, then.'

Corban smiled, relief spreading across his face. He touched his heels to his stallion and rode over to the giants, stopping before Balur.

'If we ride south it does not mean we are running away from Nathair and the Kadoshim, running away from this war.'

'It is the God-War. There is nowhere to run,' Balur said with a shrug of his massive shoulders.

'The God-War – aye. I am not running. Nathair killed my da, burned my home, and now my mam . . .' He gritted his teeth, grief mingled with anger washing his face. 'Nathair and those he rides with are a plague that will sweep the land unless they are stopped. I mean to fight them, with all that I am. I have never met a giant before, nor do I understand your ways, anything about you or your people, except that we were once enemies. But now you are the enemy of my enemy. I would value your company, should you choose to come with us.'

Balur looked to the giantess at his side, Ethlinn, then at the rest of his group before turning back to Corban.

'It has been a long time since we have seen the southlands. I think we will come with you, at least for a while.'

To Tukul's surprise, Corban, sombre-faced, held his arm out and offered Balur the warrior grip. The giant blinked, then took Corban's arm, engulfing it with his massive hand.

'Fine. Then let us ride,' Meical cried out and suddenly all were in motion, the Jehar mounting horses, giants making the ground tremble.

'Coralen,' Corban called. 'Scout ahead, take whoever you wish.'

Coralen stared at Corban with one eyebrow raised.

Then she nodded. 'I'll take Dath,' Coralen said, eliciting a look of shock from Dath and a frown from Farrell. 'Enkara,' Coralen called to one of the Jehar, one of the Hundred that had ridden forth from white-walled Telassar with Tukul all those years ago. 'And Storm, if I may.'

Corban muttered something and his wolven padded over to Coralen. 'And your crow,' Coralen added to Brina.

'*Tired*,' the bird croaked from Brina's shoulder.

'Get on with you,' Brina snapped, shooing Craf into the air.

Tukul looked back as they rode away, saw the flattened ground of their campsite, the stone cairns by the stream, and above it, like ragged banners swinging in the breeze hung a score of headless bodies, suspended from the cluster of trees, slumped, empty sacks of skin and bone.

A reminder to those who follow. That we are not so easily cowed, not even by the dread Kadoshim.

CHAPTER EIGHT

CYWEN

Cywen rode beside Corban, close to the head of their strange warband, Buddai loping along beside her. It was highsun, the sky above was a cloudless blue, a cold breeze blew out of the east. She glanced at Corban. *Is this really my little brother? He had just taken his warrior trials and sat his Long Night, the last I saw him, and here he is, giving orders to a warband including Jehar and giants. So much has changed.* He was taller, wider about the chest and shoulders, relaxed as he sat upon Shield with the easy grace of a warrior.

Even his face had changed; thinner and sharper, the stubble of a short beard shadowing his jaw. And he was pale, dark hollows beneath his red-rimmed eyes evidence of his grief. A shared grief.

Mam.

At the thought of her Cywen felt the dark wave of sorrow that lay beneath all else in her soul. She reached a hand up to the belt of her mam's throwing knives strapped across her torso. It was the only thing she had of her.

So long apart, only a few moments together before . . . The image of Calidus cutting her mam down filled Cywen's mind, grief and rage swelled inside, a physical thing that stole her breath away.

So many things I wanted to say to her, stolen from me by Calidus. She remembered crouching, stroking her mam's face, trying to wipe away the blood that trickled from her mouth.

It is my fault she died. She would be alive now if she had not come to free me. She swiped at tears as they spilt onto her cheeks and she clenched her eyes shut.

Free. Thank you, Mam, I'll not squander your gift.

She looked about, surrounded by a bleak, rolling countryside of purple heather and gorse and breathed in a deep lungful of air. *Free.* Even Cywen's guilt could not suppress the relief she felt at having escaped the constraints of Nathair and Calidus. She shivered at the memory of them.

She felt a prickling sensation and realized that Corban was looking at her.

'We have much to talk about.'

'We do,' she agreed. *I have so many questions. Where to start . . . ?*

'Did they harm you?' Corban asked, worry, concern and fear creasing his face.

'Harm? Not really. Lots of threats. My wrists were bound at first – because I tried to escape; or kill people.'

Corban grinned at that. 'Who?'

She had to think about that for a moment. It all seemed so long ago. 'Morcant. Conall. Rafe.'

'All good people to kill,' Corban said. 'But they didn't harm you?'

'No.' Her thoughts slipped to her guards, Veradis and then the troubled giant, Alcyon. Veradis' face hovered in her mind, so serious and determined, and she remembered one of the last times she had seen him. He'd told her of the bodies in the mountains when she had been sick with worry that Corban or her mam were amongst the dead. *Heb and Anwarth*, Veradis told me. *Not Corban or Mam.* Telling her that was an act of kindness.

'Heb died,' she said.

'Aye, he did,' Corban replied, his features twisting. 'Brina took that badly.'

'Looks like you did, too.'

'I liked him,' Corban said. 'We became close. All of us did, on the road together. How did you know?'

'Veradis told me – he was my guard, for a while. Along with Alcyon; they treated me fair,' she said.

'Veradis and Alcyon?'

'Nathair's first-sword, and his giant companion.' *I hope Alcyon is all right.* She frowned at her own thoughts. *He was my captor. But he did free me, cut my bonds at the end and hid me from Calidus.* Alcyon and Balur had fought, Balur sending Alcyon crashing to the ground and taking the black axe from him.

Corban raised an eyebrow. 'I think I met this Veradis too. In Domhain. He wanted to fight me.'

Cywen felt a stab of . . . something . . . at that thought. *Worry? For Corban, of course.* But there was more than that. She chose not to think about it.

'We're starting in the middle,' she said. 'Tell me from the beginning. From Dun Carreg. Were you with Da, when . . . ?' Even now, after witnessing so much of war, pain and death and worse, she could not bring herself to say the words.

'I was with him. Rafe and Helfach stopped me from helping him,' Corban said, his expression grim. 'Nathair killed our da.'

Nathair. And Calidus slew Mam. 'One day,' she said to Corban, a hand going to her knives. He nodded, understanding her meaning.

Corban spoke for a long while after that, of his flight through the tunnels beneath Dun Carreg, sailing away to Cambren and all that befell him and his companions. He told of seeing Rafe amongst the prisoners in Domhain, how Rafe had told them that Cywen was alive. How he and a few others had set out to rescue her. When Corban spoke of his capture by Braith and how he was taken to Queen Rhin at Dun Vaner he hesitated.

'What happened there?' Cywen prompted.

'I was rescued,' he shrugged. 'Meical and Tukul were tracking me, came to Dun Vaner, although Farrell was the one who knocked my gaol door down with Da's hammer.' He grinned at that.

'And Tukul is Gar's da,' Cywen said. She was still getting used to that.

'Aye. Can you believe it – Gar, one of the Jehar?' Tukul and Gar were riding a little further ahead, with a score of the Jehar spread either side of them.

'The Jehar. They're wonderful with horses. Akar helped me, healed Shield – he was shot with an arrow during the battle where Rhin defeated Owain.'

'I don't think he and Gar get along too well,' Corban said as he leaned forward in his saddle, running a hand across the scar on Shield's shoulder.

'The Jehar – they look at you, a lot.' Cywen had noticed many of the Jehar with their eyes on Corban, something like awe on their faces. She had discovered that Corban was the reason Nathair and

Calidus had dragged her halfway across the Banished Lands; she was Corban's sister and they suspected that she could be used as bait. *They were right, come to think of it. But why? Why did they want Corban so badly?* 'Who do they all think you are, Ban? And who is Meical? They all act like you're their leader.'

He looked away, appearing embarrassed. 'This is going to sound very strange to you. Meical is one of the Ben-Elim.'

Cywen found it hard not to look sceptical. 'An angel of Elyon. One of the Faithful?'

'Yes.'

Two days ago she would have laughed at that. But since then she had seen Kadoshim boil out of a cauldron. The world was a different place now.

'All right,' she said, carefully. 'Go on, then.'

'And the Jehar call me the Seren Disglair. You remember the prophecy Edana told us about? Feels like a thousand years ago.' *Elyon and Asroth, their forthcoming battle, the God-War, their champions . . .*

'Yes.' Cywen nodded dubiously wondering where this was going.

Corban looked even more awkward and refused to meet her eyes. 'Seren Disglair is the Jehar's name for the Bright Star. The prophesied champion of Elyon, enemy of Asroth. And apparently that's me.'

Cywen gazed at the flames of the fire.

The world has gone mad. My brother, the champion of Elyon. She snorted with nervous laughter, remembering a host of moments with Corban while growing up – the day he ripped his cloak in the Baglun, when she'd attacked Rafe to defend Corban. Corban sneaking into Brina's cottage, bringing home Storm as a pup, hitting at each other with sticks in their garden, seeing him amongst the rescue party in the Darkwood, watching him as he took his warrior trial and Long Night. And yet now they were sitting in a foreign land, Benothi giants sitting to her left, elsewhere Jehar warriors were tending to their weapons.

'How have we reached this place?' she said to Buddai, the hound spread beside her, his big head resting on her legs.

Figures loomed out of the darkness and sat beside her – Dath and Farrell, another with them – the red-haired girl, Coralen. She drew her sword and ran her thumb along its edge, then pulled a whetstone out of her cloak and started running it along the blade.

'You look familiar,' Cywen said to Coralen. There was something in the set of Coralen's jaw, the confidence in her walk, the way she held herself.

'She's half-sister to Halion and Conall,' Farrell said.

'I can talk for myself,' Coralen snapped at Farrell.

'That would be it,' Cywen said. 'Conall was my guard for a while. We didn't get along too well.'

Coralen just stared at her, her face a cold mask.

'He tried to kill me. Twice,' Cywen continued, not sure why. Something about Coralen's emotionless expression annoyed her. 'But, to be fair, I was trying to kill him. Pushed him off a wall the first time. Put a knife in him the second.'

A flicker of emotion, respect perhaps, crossed Coralen's face, then it was gone. 'You're lucky to be alive,' Coralen said. 'Not many live to tell the tale once Con decides they're for the grave.'

'You haven't seen what Cywen can do with a knife,' Dath said, and Cywen liked him a lot more at that moment. Coralen looked at Cywen, then went back to sharpening her sword.

Dath passed Cywen a skin of something. She sniffed it suspiciously – *mead*?

'Where'd you get this?'

'Rescued it from Rhin's stores in Dun Vaner,' Dath said with a grin. 'That's the last of it, now.'

'It's good stuff,' Farrell said. 'Especially on a cold night like this.' He unslung the war-hammer from his back and laid it on the grass beside him. Unconsciously he patted its iron head.

That's Da's war-hammer, Cywen realized, felt her grief swell in her chest. Again. She took a sip of the mead, the taste of honey combining with a pleasant heat in her belly.

'It's good to have you back with us,' Dath said to her, reaching out and squeezing her wrist. She fought the urge to pull away, felt tears threaten her eyes.

She took a deep breath.

'It's good to be here,' she answered. Her eyes drifted about the fires that dotted their camp. She saw Corban emerge from the darkness with Gar and Tukul at his side. He sat beside Meical, who was talking to Akar. Behind them, at the edge of the firelight's reach, Storm prowled.

'Corban told me some strange things today. What the Jehar are saying about him.'

'Gar started all that. At first we thought he'd gone mad,' Dath said cheerfully. 'Then Corban gets himself captured by Rhin and a warband of the Jehar ride up and carve seven hells out of Rhin's warriors. They call Corban the Seven Disgraces, or something like that . . .'

'Seren Disglair,' Coralen corrected, not losing time with her whetstone.

'Whatever.' Dath shrugged. 'Whatever it is, those Jehar seem on the edge, to me.'

'Edge of what?' Coralen asked him.

'Insanity. It worries me.'

Coralen laughed at that, a touch of warmth melting the coldness in her face, just for a few moments.

'Do you believe it?' Cywen asked. 'That Corban is this Seren Disglair?'

'Aye,' Farrell said without hesitation. They all looked at him.

'There's more to what's going on than border disputes and a power-mad queen,' he said to their inquisitive gaze. 'Look at what we all saw back in Murias. That was the Kadoshim that came out of that cauldron . . .'

Dath shivered and made the ward against evil.

'Asroth and Elyon, the Scourging, Ben-Elim and Kadoshim, we've all heard the tales.'

'Aye, faery tales,' Dath said.

'There's usually a fire that starts the smoke,' Farrell shrugged. 'What I'm saying is: there's something big happening. You'd be a fool to ignore it.' He looked pointedly at Dath. 'So Corban's part of it. Why not? And that would explain a lot of things: like why we're here, with giants and Jehar all around us and Kadoshim a dozen leagues behind us. Besides, if anyone is going to be this Seren Disglair, I, for one, am happy it's Corban.'

'What do you mean?' Cywen asked him. She noticed Coralen was staring hard at Farrell.

'He's the best of us,' Farrell said with a shrug. 'Honest, brave, fair. Loyal. I'd follow him into any fight.'

Voices drew her attention then – Corban and Meical. Without thinking she rose and strode towards them, seating herself beside Corban.

'I'm not saying that I've decided to go to Edana and not Drassil,' Corban was saying. 'What I am saying is that *if* we went to Edana I can see us doing much good by aiding her. Rhin is our enemy, a servant of Asroth. If we can help Edana defeat her, it would be a great victory for us.'

'Rhin is an enemy,' Meical said, speaking slowly, as if he chose his words with care, 'but she is not *the* enemy. To defeat Asroth you must go to Drassil.'

'Why?'

'Because that is where the prophecy says you will go, and that the enemies of Asroth will gather about you there.'

'I have heard much talk of this prophecy,' Corban said, 'but I have yet to actually hear it.'

'I can remedy that,' said Meical. He reached inside his cloak and pulled out a round leather canister. He undid a cord that bound it and slid out a scroll. It crackled as he unrolled it; everyone gathered close to hear it.

> *War eternal between the Faithful and the Fallen,*
> *infinite wrath come to the world of men.*
> *Lightbearer seeking flesh from the cauldron,*
> *to break his chains and wage the war again.*
> *Two born of blood, dust and ashes shall champion the Choices*
> *the Darkness and Light.*
>
> *Black Sun will drown the earth in bloodshed,*
> *Bright Star with the Treasures must unite.*
> *By their names you shall know them –*
> *Kin-Slayer, Kin-Avenger, Giant-Friend, Draig-Rider,*
> *Dark Power 'gainst Lightbringer.*
> *One shall be the Tide, one the Rock in the swirling sea.*
>
> *Before one, storm and shield shall stand,*
> *before the other, True-Heart and Black-Heart.*

Beside one rides the Beloved, beside the other, the
    Avenging Hand.
Behind one, the Sons of the Mighty, the fair Ben-Elim,
    gathered 'neath the Great Tree.
Behind the other, the Unholy, dread Kadoshim, who seek
    to cross the bridge,
force the world to bended knee.

Meical paused, glancing at the faces around the fireside.

'Black Sun will drown the earth in bloodshed,' Dath whispered to Farrell, his voice carrying in the silence. 'Don't much like the sound of that.'

'There's more,' Meical said and continued reading.

Look for them when the high king calls, when the shadow
    warriors ride forth,
when white-walled Telassar is emptied, when the book is
    found in the north.
When the white wyrms spread from their nest,
when the Firstborn take back what was lost, and the
    Treasures stir from their rest.
Both earth and sky shall cry warning, shall herald this
    War of Sorrows.
Tears of blood spilt from the earth's bones, and at Midwinter's
    height, bright day shall become full night.

As Meical finished silence settled upon them, broken only by the hiss and crackle of the flames.

'Storm and shield,' Corban whispered.

'Indeed,' said Meical. 'So, you see, you are the Bright Star, our champion.'

This might all actually be true, Cywen thought. *My brother, the Champion of Elyon.* It was much easier to believe, sitting here in the dark around a flickering fire, Ben-Elim and giants for company.

'Why?' Corban said.

'Why what?' replied Meical.

'Why me? Why am I this Bright Star? Why not Edana, or some

prince or king? Me, the son of a blacksmith, a boy whose only ambition was to be a warrior and serve his king.'

'I can't answer that,' Meical said. 'I just know that it is you. The reason why does not even matter. It won't change anything. Sometimes it is just best to accept what *is*, and get on with doing.'

Corban nodded thoughtfully. 'When was this prophecy written?' he asked.

'Two thousand years ago,' Meical said.

Corban blew out a long breath. 'Two thousand years. Our fate was decided two thousand years ago. My fate . . .' He looked at Meical, his expression hovering between doubt and hope. 'So, if it's prophesied that I am the Bright Star, then we are going to win?'

'The prophecy does not say who will win, only who will fight.'

'That's a shame,' Dath muttered.

'But it does say that you must go to Drassil,' Meical added.

'Drassil is the Great Tree?' Corban asked.

'Aye.'

'It's a bit vague as to why I should go there.'

'The Ben-Elim will gather to you there. If that is not good enough reason, then there are others.'

'Such as?'

'The spear of Skald.'

'It is there still, then?' A deep voice rumbled behind Cywen, making her jump. It was Balur. He stepped into the light.

'It is,' Tukul said. 'I left ten of my sword-kin there to guard it.'

'Ten is not a great number,' Balur observed.

'No, it is not. All the more reason to return there as quickly as we can,' Meical said.

'What is the spear of Skald?' Corban asked.

'It is one of the Seven Treasures,' Meical answered. 'Skald was the high king of the giants, when there was only one clan.'

'Aye, before we were Sundered,' Balur said. 'The spear was not his. It was used to slay him, and it was left in his body; thus ever since it has been named Skald's spear.'

'It is in his body still,' Tukul said. 'Or what is left of his body. We did not move it.'

'You have spoken of the Seven Treasures before,' Corban said. 'Forged from the starstone?'

'Aye, that is right,' Balur said.

'The cauldron is the most powerful. Together the Treasures can form a gateway between the Otherworld and this world of flesh,' Meical said, locking his gaze with Corban's. 'That is why Calidus seeks them. The cauldron is one. The axe is another. To thwart Asroth they must be destroyed.'

'But we have the axe. Let us destroy it now – if Asroth needs all Seven Treasures then he will be defeated.' Corban sounded excited. 'We can end this now.'

'It's not as simple as that,' Meical said. 'To be destroyed, the Treasures must all be gathered together.'

'There's always a catch with these things,' Dath muttered. Coralen punched his shoulder.

'So Calidus has the cauldron, and we have the axe.'

'And we have the spear,' Tukul said. 'In Drassil.'

'Do you understand now?' Meical asked Corban. 'There are good reasons to go to Drassil. The spear must be made safe.'

Corban gazed into the fire. 'What you say, it does make sense. I just . . . my oath.'

'There are other options,' Meical said. 'Send word to Edana. Perhaps she will join us. The danger is wasting time, Corban. The world will not stand still and wait for you. Asroth is moving. Calidus also seeks Drassil. He has not been able to find it, yet, but it is only a matter of time.'

'I would not break my oath.'

As Cywen watched, emotions swept Corban's face: doubt, anger, pain, settling into one she recognized well.

Pig-headedness.

'Calidus has been laying plans for many years.'

'Calidus,' Corban said, the hatred he felt for him apparent to all. 'Tell me of him.'

'He is high captain of the Kadoshim, second only to Asroth,' Meical said, 'as I am high captain of the Ben-Elim. He is cunning, deadly, utterly devoted to his cause.'

'I will see him dead,' Corban said, his voice flat, emotionless.

'We could go back, slay him now,' a new voice said. Akar the Jehar, who had been sitting quietly, listening the whole time.

'Calidus is the puppet-master in all of this: Asroth's will made flesh. Kill him and the war is won.'

'And how would we kill him?' Gar asked. There was something in his tone – not quite scorn.

'With a sword in our hands, courage in our hearts,' Akar spat back.

Tukul rested a hand on Akar's wrist. 'We would fail. He is surrounded by a thousand Kadoshim clothed in Jehar bodies, all that strength and skill at their disposal. Corban would most likely be slain, and the war would be lost.'

'It can be done,' Akar insisted.

'Your shame blinds you. You were deceived and there is no dishonour in that. Sumur is responsible. As for you; master your emotions, see clearly. Meical and Corban are right. We will fight other battles first, wait for a better time.'

'And if there is no better time?'

'Then we will die then, instead of now.'

Corban stood. 'Meical, all of you, thank you for your wisdom, your guidance. You've given me much to think on. There is so much to consider . . .' He fell silent, eyes distant. 'I have not decided, but my heart whispers to me that I should find Edana. I don't say this out of stubbornness . . .'

Really?

'I gave my word, and it seems to me that our hearts, our oaths, our *choices* make the difference between us and them.' He glanced over his shoulder, northwards, into the night. His eyes came back to them, settling upon Cywen. 'And I know, if my mam and da could see me from across the bridge of swords, they would want me to keep my oath. Truth and courage, they taught me. I'd not let them down.' With that he turned and walked away. Storm appeared out of the darkness and padded alongside him.

CHAPTER NINE

FIDELE

Fidele held a knife to the Vin Thalun's throat as Maquin bound the man's hands about the trunk of a tree.

Lykos' secret, Fidele repeated the words their prisoner had uttered back at the woodcutters' cabin. *The giantess and her whelp.* Those words had kept him alive, at least for a little while longer.

'What do you mean?' Maquin had asked.

'I'll show you,' the pirate had said, refusing to comment further, even when Maquin had put his knife to the man's throat and drawn blood.

Fidele and Maquin had shared a look, both of them intrigued. Fidele had changed into the breeches and woollen tunic Maquin had stolen for her. Then they had walked into the forest, Fidele a pace behind Maquin, who held his knife close to the Vin Thalun's back, following a path that was little wider than a fox's trail. As far as Fidele could make out, the Vin Thalun led them south, which was fine by her as it was *away* from Jerolin and Lykos. They passed through rolling woodland that turned steadily thicker. Dusk settled over them quickly, the forest becoming a place of dense shadows and eerie sounds, and now darkness was thick about them. The trail ahead was almost invisible. They'd stopped for the night; their prisoner sat with his back to a tree, arms bound about it.

'No fire,' Maquin said as Fidele passed the knife back to him and started gathering forest litter. Fidele frowned. Walking through the forest she had been sweating, but soon after they stopped she felt cold, shivering despite the cloak Maquin had stolen for her. The thought of a fire had lifted her spirits for a moment. She forgave Maquin when he opened the cloak that he was using as a makeshift sack, revealing a round of cheese and a leg of cold mutton. Fidele's stomach growled at the sight of it. Maquin cut her a slice of each and she set to devouring them.

'Any spare?' the Vin Thalun asked them. Maquin gave him a flat stare but said nothing.

Starve, you animal, Fidele thought. Just the sight of the Vin Thalun, his dark beard bound with iron rings, his sun-weathered skin, even the way he looked at her, all reminded her of Lykos. A tremor ran through her at the thought of the Vin Thalun King, part fear, part hatred.

Shame and anger followed quickly. *I am a coward, pathetic. But why do I still fear him? I stabbed him, maybe killed him.* But when she thought of Lykos, she didn't see him collapsed and bleeding in the arena. No, she smelt him, his sour breath in her face, felt his hands gripping her, his will controlling her.

No! An inner scream. *I will not be ruled by him still. And even if he does still live, he no longer has the effigy. He has no power over me.* She clenched her fists, nails biting into her palms. *If I believed that, I would have walked back to Jerolin, not be sitting here, shivering and starving with a pirate and a trained killer.*

Her gaze shifted to Maquin; his face was all hard lines and shifting shadows in the moonlight, his eyes dark wells. She had seen him kill in the arena, both in single combat and against many. She was no stranger to death, had witnessed combat first-hand, seen life-blood spilt, heard death cries, had seen warriors in battle, straddling that line between life and death. None had seemed as ruthless, as devoid of emotion as the man before her. She had watched him with a mixture of revulsion and fascination, in all her years never having seen someone deal out death so efficiently. *Old Wolf, they called him in the arena. The name fits him. Lean, explosively violent, patient in combat, unrelenting.*

Maybe he sensed her watching him, for his head turned. She could not tell if he returned her gaze, his eyes in shadow. Nevertheless she looked away.

'I know you,' the Vin Thalun said to Fidele, breaking into her thoughts. 'Aren't you supposed to be enjoying your wedding night round about now?'

'Shut up,' Fidele snapped, instantly annoyed with herself at the emotion in her voice.

'Got a long walk on the morrow,' the Vin Thalun said. 'Starve me and I'll be too weak to show you the way to Lykos' pets.'

'Huh,' snorted Maquin.

Fidele regarded the Vin Thalun silently. *He is younger than he looks – twenty summers, maybe, not much more. And he is someone's son.* At that thought an image of Nathair filled her mind. *My son. Where is he? Halfway across the Banished Lands? Alive or dead? Someone's prisoner? If he is, I hope that he will at least be fed, given water.* She focused back on the Vin Thalun before her and felt a flush of shame at her earlier willingness to starve him. *I will not become that which I hate.* 'Here,' Fidele said, cutting a slice of cheese for the warrior.

'Don't know how long that has to last us,' Maquin commented, looking at the cheese.

'We are human beings, not animals,' Fidele said, the words aimed at herself as much as anyone else.

'Don't think you'd get the same treatment if things were the other way around.'

'I know I wouldn't. I have a very good idea how I would have been treated. But I will not make myself . . . less.'

Maquin said no more, just watched as Fidele offered the cheese to the Vin Thalun.

Their prisoner glanced at his bound arms, then opened his mouth. Fidele hesitated.

'I won't bite. Think your hound might have his knife out quick if I did. I've seen him in the pit and arena. Seen what he can do.'

Maquin's gaze snapped onto him at that, something predatory in the movement, threatening.

'No offence meant by that,' the Vin Thalun continued, 'made a lot of money out of you, Old Wolf. Seen you come through some pretty thin odds.'

'They were lives. Other men's lives. Not odds,' Fidele said.

Maquin's eyes shifted to Fidele.

'Aye. Well, he carved them up real good, whatever you want to call them.'

Fidele broke a piece off the cheese and put it in the man's mouth, glad that it shut him up for a few moments.

Sounds rang out abruptly, branches snapping, footfalls thudding. Voices called to one another, sounding close. Fidele's heart was instantly pounding, the fear of capture filling her mind. Maquin went from sitting to standing in one fluid movement. Fidele didn't see him draw his knife, but it was suddenly in his hand. He stood poised, listening.

There was the sound of iron clashing. Screams. *Further away? Closer? I cannot tell.* Fidele felt a moment of panic, took a deep breath to calm herself.

'Don't make a sound,' Maquin whispered, 'and do not come after me. I won't be long.' Then he slipped amongst the trees, merging with the darkness.

That's what you said last time, at the woodcutters' cabin.

Fidele counted time in heartbeats, the forest now eerily silent except for the sigh of the wind through trees, the creak of branches. Sporadically she'd hear a shout, a battle-cry, a scream, then nothing again.

'I'm still hungry,' the Vin Thalun said. She looked at him, knew that he must be weighing up whether to call out or not. She had been tempted by the same thought. But who would come if either of them cried out? Friend or foe? *Not worth the risk*, Fidele had concluded, and, judging by his silence, the pirate agreed.

'My name is Senios,' the pirate said. 'Just a man, like you said. And I'm still hungry.' Fidele gave him some more. As the cheese touched his lips he burst into movement, jerking against the tree trunk, his legs whipping round to coil about her, dragging her close. She sucked in a lungful of air to cry out, then his head was snapping forward, crunching into her cheek. Her vision contracted, an explosion of light and darkness inside her head, and she felt her body slumping. *No!* she yelled at herself, feeling her awareness flutter. *Not, a victim – never again* . . . She reached a hand down the pirate's body, between his legs, grabbing and twisting. She heard a scream, wasn't sure for a moment if it was her or the Vin Thalun, then the grip in his legs about her was gone and she was pushing away, crawling across the ground, the pirate gagging behind her, gasping for air.

A figure loomed out of the shadows, Maquin. He paused a moment, taking the scene in, then exploded into motion, a boot crunching into the Vin Thalun's head. He sagged against his bonds, unconscious, blood and saliva dribbling from his slack jaw.

Maquin was beside Fidele. 'Has he hurt you?'

'I, no, it's nothing,' Fidele said, one hand to her face.

Maquin gently lifted her, fingers touching her cheek. It throbbed.

'You'll have a bruise the size of my fist, but you'll live.' He looked at the unconscious Vin Thalun, took a step towards him.

'Don't,' Fidele said. Maquin frowned at her.

'It's not compassion. I'd happily kill him myself. But I want to see these giants.'

'It could just be a lie, to prolong his life, give him a chance to escape.'

Fidele shrugged. 'Perhaps. Give him one day – if we haven't seen these giants by dusk on the morrow . . .'

'We'll kill him. You sure you can deal with that?'

'Yes. It will be an execution, not a murder – he is an enemy of my realm.'

'Good.'

'What was out there,' Fidele nodded at the darkness.

'Death,' Maquin muttered. 'Vin Thalun chasing men of Tenebral – I glimpsed a few, running. They wore Tenebral's eagle. They were a way off, running east, away from us. You should get some sleep.'

'I don't know if I can,' she said.

'You're going to need your strength.' He paused, his face softening for an instant. 'You'll be safe.' He didn't say more, didn't need to. It sounded foolish – they were fleeing, cold, hungry, in a forest surrounded by enemies – yet, looking at Maquin, she did feel safe. She also felt suddenly exhausted.

'You'll need to sleep, too. Wake me later.'

'I will,' Maquin grunted and Fidele curled up on the ground, pulling her cloak about her. Forest litter crunched beneath her as she shifted, lumps in the ground digging into her back. Eventually she found a position that was vaguely comfortable and she tried to remain still. An owl hooted nearby, making her jump. *I may as well sit watch with Maquin, I'll never sleep out here.*

*

Something shook her and she opened her eyes to weak sunlight. A shadow hovered nearby, features pulling into focus.

For a moment she thought it was Lykos, his face dark and tanned, eyes boring into her. She gasped and jerked away.

'Sorry,' Maquin mumbled, 'didn't mean to startle you.' He stepped back.

'It's all right,' she said, her voice a croak. 'I thought you were . . .' She trailed off as a score of pains made themselves known, reminding her she'd slept on the forest floor. She groaned and hesitantly stretched, testing the pains. When she'd established that she was not completely crippled she tentatively stood, leaning on a nearby tree.

'First night in the wild,' Maquin said. A flicker of a smile creased his face.

'It's daylight,' she said, her cheek aching as she spoke, a memento of the Vin Thalun's blow.

'Aye.'

'You were supposed to wake me.'

He just shrugged and passed her a water skin. She drank thirstily, then glanced at the Vin Thalun, who sat with his back against the tree, arms still bound about it. His jaw was swollen, bruised almost black. He returned her gaze with open malevolence.

'Senios, how far to this place?' Fidele asked him. Maquin raised an eyebrow at the use of the Vin Thalun's name.

He mumbled something, grimaced, a line of spittle dribbling from the corner of his mouth. Fidele made out what sounded like 'Half-day.'

'His jaw is broken,' Maquin said. 'Don't expect too much conversation from him today.'

Senios led them on into the forest, Maquin a pace behind him. Sunlight slanted through the trees; birdsong drifted down from above.

Time passed, the sun sliding across the canopy above. Fidele heard the sound of running water, faint at first. Soon they reached the banks of a river, its waters dark, wide and sluggish. Alder and willow lined the bank, willow branches draped across their path, dangling into the river. The sun was straight above when Senios stopped.

'Bend,' he said, pointing ahead.

'What are we going to see?' Maquin growled.

'A ship. Vin Thalun. The giants.' His words were slurred.

'How many Vin Thalun?'

Senios held both hands up.

'Ten?' Maquin asked. Senios shrugged.

'We'll go together. Any noise, any movement that I don't tell you to do, you'll feel my blade.' He drew his knife, emphasizing his point.

Slowly they crept forwards. They turned the bend; reeds grew thick and tall along the bank, then Fidele heard voices.

Maquin crouched low, dragging Senios down with him, and motioned for Fidele to do the same. They moved into the bank of reeds, inched their way closer to the river's edge. Sweat stung Fidele's eyes. With every movement the reeds rustled and she expected warning cries to ring out. She could see the river through gaps in the reeds, saw the outline of a long and sleek ship resembling a Vin Thalun war-galley, only smaller. It had no mast, but a row of oars raised out of the water – *ten*, she counted. *So that's twenty oars – twenty men, double what Senios told us. And there could be more.* At the rear of the ship was a large cabin. Figures moved on the deck, others were on the far bank, where a wide fire-pit had been dug. Near them, a great moss-covered stone slab rose from the ground. Lines dissected it, too straight to be natural. *Giant runes?* Something about it was strange, unnatural. An iron ring dangled from it.

Her attention was drawn back to the ship as the cabin door creaked open and a warrior emerged. He was holding a chain, which he tugged. A female giant walked out onto the deck, tall and muscular, an iron collar about her throat. Another giant followed behind her, bound to a connecting chain at the waist. This one was male, shorter and slighter, with wisps of a scraggly moustache. *A giant bairn. I did not even know that such a thing existed.*

More Vin Thalun warriors followed behind, spears levelled at their prisoners. The giants were led from the galley onto the far bank; the chain linking them was attached to the iron ring in the great stone. One of the Vin Thalun prodded the small male with a spear, making him twist away with a pitiful whine. The female snarled, stepped in front of the smaller one and lunged as the Vin Thalun laughed and jabbed at her with their spears. They soon grew bored of their baiting and left the two giants. The giantess cupped the young male's face in her hands, the two exchanging a look both bleak and tender. Fidele felt the breath catch in her chest – something about the gesture was shockingly moving. Fidele remembered doing the same to Nathair as Aquilus was laid in his cairn, remembered the grief they'd shared in a look, intimate and unique only to them at the loss of Aquilus, husband, father.

She is his mother.

She felt Maquin's hand on her arm, saw him gesture that it was time to leave. She didn't want to go, a wave of empathy for the giant mother and child almost overwhelming her. She had been a Vin Thalun slave, just with different shackles. She wanted to help them.

There was a burst of sound close by, the reeds shuddering about them as Senios tore himself from Maquin's grip and threw himself forward. Maquin lunged after him, his knife stabbing into Senios' leg. The two men tumbled down the riverbank, splashing into the water, disappearing in a mass of white foam.

Panic exploded in Fidele. The two men rose to the surface of the river, grappling, spluttering. Senios broke free of Maquin's grasp and swam away, heading for the far bank. Maquin followed, seemingly oblivious or uncaring that the Vin Thalun warriors from the ship had noticed the commotion and were aiming their spears at the river.

'No!' Fidele yelled at Maquin. And he must have heard her, for he glanced up at her, then back across the river to where Senios was being hauled up on the ship by his comrades. Maquin scrambled back to Fidele, grasping at her hand to pull himself ashore. There was a whistling sound as a spear sank into the ground close by, another followed shortly behind.

'Quickly,' Maquin snarled, vanishing into the reeds. Fidele paused and looked back, saw the two giants staring at her. For a moment Fidele's eyes locked with the mother. *I am sorry*, she thought.

CHAPTER TEN

UTHAS

'Lift,' Uthas cried, and a dozen Benothi giants grunted as they took the weight of the cauldron on two long iron poles. For a few moments the cauldron hung suspended over the dais, its resting place for two thousand years, then they shuffled forwards, transferring it onto a huge wain that stood nearby. Its timber frame was reinforced with iron, but it still creaked as the cauldron's weight settled. Leather straps were tightened and secured to iron rings, fixing the cauldron in place. Then a leather sheet was unfurled and tied tight, hiding the cauldron from sight. The wain had taken nearly two full days and nights to construct, the forges of the Benothi belching smoke as great wheels and axles had been fashioned, using iron and weathered and hardened timber gathered from the huge doors that had hung within the fortress of Murias.

It still stinks in here. Uthas wrinkled his nose. The cauldron's chamber was still littered with the dead. The Benothi giants had tended to their own fallen, carrying their dead kin from the hall to lay them in a great cairn beyond the gates of Murias, but the stinking tangle of Jehar and wyrm corpses had been left to rot. He looked with disgust at the bodies strewn about him. *Some of them appear to have been . . . chewed upon.* Uthas looked up, his eyes meeting with Calidus, who stood beside the wain directing his Kadoshim brethren. He let out a long breath and looked away. *I don't want to know.*

Eight of the Jehar warhorses were harnessed to the wain. At his signal it moved forwards slowly, the wheels crushing flesh, crunching bone as they rolled across the cavern floor. The Benothi followed, an honour guard.

'You have done well,' Calidus said to him as they left the

chamber. 'The cauldron is not of this earth, the fabric it is made from is dense and heavy. But that wain is sturdy enough to carry it a thousand leagues.'

'The Benothi are skilled craftsmen,' Uthas said with a hint of pride.

They passed through the wide corridors of Murias, Uthas feeling a blend of melancholy and anticipation growing in his belly. He was leaving Murias, home of the Benothi for two thousand years, possibly leaving it behind forever. *I will not look back. It is the destination that is important: the end, not the beginning.*

Eventually they reached the entrance hall. A line of wains stood waiting, all loaded – most with huge barrels of *brot*, enough to provide sustenance for them for a year or more. *Though it appears the Kadoshim are acquiring other tastes.*

The Kadoshim were spread about the hall, thickest around the wains. Once the wounded Kadoshim, Bune, had been brought back to Murias and the others had heard the disastrous fate of those that had rushed after Meical and his companions, Calidus had managed to introduce a level of order to the Kadoshim. And they were adapting to their new bodies well, suppressing the spirits of their unwilling hosts and learning the *way of flesh*, as Calidus had taken to calling it. Nathair stood to one side of the open gates, the bulk of his draig making him easy to find. The giant Alcyon stood with him.

'Come,' Calidus said to Uthas, 'it is time to hear Nathair's answer to my offer.'

'What will be his choice, I wonder,' Uthas said as they strode across the wide chamber.

'He will choose life. He is no fool. He has dreams, delusions of nobility and greatness, but when life or death are only a word apart . . .' Calidus smiled coldly.

'Are you sure?'

'As sure as it is possible to be. But one thing I have learned in this world of flesh – mankind is fickle, and nothing is certain. So I have a rule: prepare for all eventualities. If he says no, then I have a lock of his hair. I need Nathair; we are too few and he has the keys to an empire within his reach. And I have worked hard to make this so; it's taken a considerable amount of time and effort to bring all of this about.'

'I can only imagine,' Uthas grunted.

'And so I would not like to see it all wasted. Nevertheless, things could go awry.' Calidus looked behind at the wain emerging into the chamber. 'Bring Salach and whoever else you think necessary if we need to dispatch Nathair's draig.'

Uthas raised an eyebrow, not relishing that thought. He remembered the creature carving a way through a mass of wyrms in the cauldron's cavern. He gestured to Salach, Eisa and another half-dozen of the Benothi. They followed.

'That would be a shame; it is a magnificent creature, and useful.'

Calidus shrugged. 'It is bonded to Nathair, would tear even me apart in his defence. If Nathair is to die, the draig must be killed too.'

'And Nathair?'

'If it comes to it, Alcyon will take care of him.'

They approached Nathair in silence. The King of Tenebral was spooning something from a bowl. When he saw them approaching he stepped closer to his draig and gave it the remnants of his meal. A long black tongue licked around the bowl, the creature nudging Nathair with its broad flat muzzle. Absently, Nathair scratched its chin and tugged on a long fang. Alcyon took a step back, his eyes fixed on Calidus.

'We are ready to leave,' Calidus said to Nathair, conversationally.

'So I see.'

'It is time for you to make your choice.'

'I'm not sure I can,' Nathair muttered, massaging his temple.

Calidus stared at him with a hint of a smile. 'You already have made it. You are just struggling with the final step. You realize if you continue on this path there can be no going back for you.'

Nathair snorted. 'You appear to know me better than I know myself.'

'I do, Nathair. We have been through much together, you and I. Risked much. Dared much. Gained much. And here we are on the brink.'

'You deceived me,' Nathair whispered. He looked intensely at Calidus, and for a moment Uthas caught a flash of real pain in the young King's eyes.

Betrayal is hard to bear. I saw that same look in Nemain's eyes when she realized the truth about me.

Calidus returned the gaze calmly.

'You know I had no choice. You would not have understood. If you were in my position you would have done exactly the same. For the greater good. Have you not done things that others would consider questionable, for the greater good?'

Nathair winced at those words, as if they brought him physical pain. 'I have,' he said, a whisper.

'And have you not withheld information, even from those you value and trust? Veradis, for example? Again for the greater good.'

'Aye.' Louder this time.

'Well, what I have done and will do is for the greater good – I am offering you a chance to fulfil your vision, to see an empire bring peace to these Banished Lands.'

'Over a mountain of bodies.'

'Was there ever going to be any other way? How many have already died for your visions of peace? This is no different. You and Asroth share the same vision: a world of order, of peace, where the powerful are able to make decisions to better lives without politics or bureaucracy getting in the way. You are stumbling over concepts – good and evil, right and wrong. Asroth has been depicted in the history of your world by his enemy – of course you will think him evil. But he is not. He is like you, a sentient creature with the ability to choose. Our base instinct is to survive, and sometimes to survive you must fight. This is not a game; it is a fight for life or death. But I promise you this, give you my oath: if we win, we will create an empire that will be everything you ever dreamed of.' Calidus paused and stared keenly into Nathair's eyes, holding him. 'Join us. I will not lie, we need you.'

'Need me?'

'You are no fool, Nathair. I will not tell you what you already know.'

'That I control the warbands of Tenebral, and that I have forged an alliance with Helveth, Carnutan and Isiltir.'

'Exactly.' Calidus nodded. 'I have the Kadoshim, Uthas and his Benothi, Lykos and the Vin Thalun. And Rhin. A powerful force, but not all-powerful. Together, though . . .'

'With me as your puppet-king, you mean,' Nathair said. His draig turned its eyes on Calidus and gave a low, baleful rumble.

'Not as a puppet. As a king, with the others as your vassals – Rhin, Lykos, Uthas. These Banished Lands are too vast for one man to conquer unaided.'

'They are,' Nathair agreed.

'So join me. Together we can crush Meical and his allies. Fulfil your dream. And afterwards you will rule. More than a king, you shall be Emperor of the Banished Lands, ruler of all you have conquered. So, you see, nothing will be changed from your dreams of old.'

'And what of Asroth? What does he want?'

'Victory. Only victory. Asroth's desire is to defeat his enemies. The Ben-Elim. Meical, his Bright Star Corban and the band of brigands they've gathered about themselves. Afterwards, when they are dead –' Calidus shrugged – 'then this world is yours.'

'Mine? Asroth would not rule here?'

'No. He does not wish to rule – bureaucracy and administration hold little attraction for my master. All that he wishes for is to see his enemies destroyed, once and for all. To see their blood and bones ground into the earth. To make Meical and his Ben-Elim nothing but a stain upon the ground.' Calidus' mouth had constricted into a sharp line, eyes narrowed to slits.

He is remarkably convincing, thought Uthas.

'And to achieve that victory Asroth needs you. He needs about him those who share his vision, whom he can trust. And, remember, Asroth chose you, above all others.'

Uthas was studying Nathair, ready for any indication that there would be defiance. *He wants to believe Calidus, longs to be the hero of his own story, and Calidus is telling him what he wants to hear. Flattery blended with a measure of truth.*

'Your dreams, which you have been having for years,' Calidus continued. 'They are true. Asroth picked you out, chose you from countless others. You, Nathair, have the qualities to see this through. To make a difference. To rule. The only error in your dreams was the name that you chose to give Asroth.'

'And myself,' Nathair said, the earlier bitterness still in his voice, but weaker now, diluted by something else.

Hope.

Calidus shrugged.

'My dreams,' Nathair said, a distant look in his eyes. 'They made me feel different. Special, chosen.'

'And you are. All you need do is change your perspective on Asroth. I will not lie, he is angry. Angry at Elyon, the Great Tyrant, his hubris nothing but a cloak for his betrayal.' Calidus' face twisted with a flicker of rage, like lightning on the horizon. 'Asroth had the audacity to question Elyon, and then to challenge his wisdom. Elyon is proud, arrogant.' Calidus smiled and shrugged. 'Questioning him did not go down too well. Asroth was betrayed and cast out, along with those of us who stood beside him, we who had the impudence to wonder, to ask, to question. We were all betrayed by Meical and the Ben-Elim, with their piety and zeal, their lack of interest in the affairs of mankind. They are callous and cruel.'

'Your words, they are convincing,' Nathair frowned. 'But, how can I trust you, now?'

'Would Veradis trust you, if you confessed to your past deceptions as I am confessing to mine?'

'I don't know. Perhaps. Not immediately, but if I proved myself to him . . .'

'As I shall prove myself to you. Join me and you will see. You can trust me, Nathair – there is nothing hidden between us now. Ask me anything.'

'What is your plan – the next step in this war?'

'To consolidate what we have. The cauldron is the greatest of the Seven Treasures; it must be kept safe. I would take it back to Tenebral, where we are unassailable. And the other Treasures must be found. They are needed to break the barriers with the Otherworld.'

'So you would bring Asroth into our world?'

'Aye. That is the goal. To crush our mutual enemies. That is the only way we can win.'

'And I would continue to rule Tenebral now, and be high king in your new order?'

'Yes. More than that. You would be this world's emperor. Those who help me will be rewarded. You. Uthas. Lykos. Others beneath them – Rhin, Jael, Lothar, Gundul. Together we will conquer these Banished Lands and bring about a new order.'

He is wavering. Only the final step remains.

'All that you have to do is say yes.'

They stood there in silence a long while, Nathair and Calidus locked in a gaze that excluded all else. Eventually Nathair sighed, passing a hand over his eyes.

'Yes,' he breathed. 'I will join your cause. Though I would tell you, the trust between us must be rebuilt.'

Calidus smiled. 'Do not trust in me. Trust in Asroth.'

'What do you mean? I have just given you my word.'

Calidus paused and stared at him, then he laughed. 'Oh, Nathair, your sincerity, it really is quite inspiring; I can understand why Asroth singled you out. But trust must run both ways and you must forgive me if I have a suspicious mind. How do I know that you have not given your word to prolong your life, to buy yourself time until you are reunited with Veradis and a thousand eagle-guard at your back? I wonder, will you feel as committed to this cause then?'

'Of course.'

'You will understand if I take steps to guarantee your integrity?'

'What steps?'

'You will see, in just a few moments.' Calidus strode to a pot suspended over a fire, emptied its contents and drew something from his cloak: a vial, dark liquid within it.

'What is that?' Nathair asked.

'The blood of an enemy. A powerful enemy; it is the blood of Nemain, once-Queen of the Benothi. Give me your hand.'

'Why?'

'It is time you met your new master.' Calidus stepped closer, gripped Nathair's hand and lifted it, then turned it, looking at the palm. 'You have made an oath before.' His finger traced a white scar.

'Aye. With Veradis.'

'You are about to make another.' He turned and poured the blood from the vial into the pot.

Pale morning sunshine and a chill wind filtered through the gates of Murias as Uthas stood and waited.

'Make ready,' Calidus cried, his voice filling the chamber, and for a few moments all was chaos.

This is it. The moment that the Benothi march to war alongside the Kadoshim. He took a deep breath, an effort to calm the mix of fear and excitement that coursed through him.

A hand touched Uthas' arm and he turned to see Eisa standing before the surviving fifty Benothi warriors.

'You are our leader, now. Lord of the Benothi,' she said, offering him an object.

Uthas looked closer, saw she held a necklace fashioned from wyrm fangs. They were threaded on an iron chain, bound with silver.

I am not worthy. A betrayer. A murderer.

He bowed his head, allowing her to slip the necklace onto him. It was a pleasant weight upon his neck and shoulders.

'I thank you,' he said as he raised his head. 'I will lead you to glory and a new age for the Benothi. We will hide in the shadows no more.'

Voices bellowed their approval and then they were moving out.

And not just the Benothi. I will reforge what was Sundered. The clans will join behind me. They must.

With a deep roar from Nathair's draig they left Murias, the cauldron on its great wain rolling into the spring sunshine, a dozen other smaller wains strung out behind it. A thousand of the Kadoshim marched around them. At the warband's head Nathair rode upon his draig, Calidus mounted on a Jehar stallion beside him. Uthas and Alcyon marched alongside them. Above, ravens cawed and circled, leaving their nests in Murias' cliffs, shadowing them like a dark halo.

They know death will be our constant companion.

They followed the road that led from Murias, down a slope from the mountain and into a land of rolling moors and purple heather. Calidus lifted a hand and beckoned to Uthas.

'I do not like the thought of Meical out there. He has too few numbers to defeat us, but he could still be plotting some mischief. I'm going to follow his trail, make sure he's not being cleverer than I give him credit for.'

Soon after, Calidus left their warband with a hundred of the

Kadoshim. Uthas accompanied them, his shieldman Salach at his side. Nathair was instructed to keep the column moving along the road. The King of Tenebral nodded, a bloodstained linen bandage wrapped around one hand. Uthas felt a wave of pity for him, remembering how Nathair had collapsed to his knees as Asroth had scoured him, searching his soul for any hint of treachery.

'Lead us to their camp,' Calidus ordered Bune, the only Kadoshim that had survived the rushed attempt to regain the starstone axe. He had recovered from his injury, his severed wrist bound with leather. He raised his head, sniffing, then took off at a loping run eastwards towards a line of low hills. Calidus kicked his horse into a canter and the small host followed.

'They can run, these Kadoshim,' Salach said to Uthas after they had covered three or four leagues. Uthas grunted his agreement. The Kadoshim had settled into their new bodies now, and they ran with a supple power, their stamina seeming to match the giants'.

They moved into the hills; Calidus, ordering the pace to slow, sent a dozen of the Kadoshim fanning out ahead.

'He is teaching them,' Salach observed.

'Aye, and they are quick learners.'

They crested a low hill and Calidus reined in his horse.

A dell spread before them. The grass had been flattened by many people, a section burned by a large fire. A row of cairns sat close to the stream, Uthas counted sixteen and saw that three of the cairns were bigger than the others – cairns built for giants.

Asroth below, let Balur lie in one of those.

Beyond the cairns was a stand of trees, bent and twisted by the wind. Headless corpses dangled from their branches like the tattered banners of a defeated foe.

Calidus watched as the Kadoshim spread through the camp, scratching at the ground, sniffing, some snarling and growling like animals.

'They are gone,' Calidus said as Uthas reached him. 'Probably the day after the battle, two days ahead of us. Where will Meical take them, though? That is the question.'

'Let him run,' Salach sneered. Calidus frowned at him. Some of the Kadoshim reached the cairns and began pulling away the stones.

'You have outmanoeuvred him every step thus far,' Uthas said.

'Aye, thus far. We must never underestimate Meical, though. I never have, and that is why we are ahead. That is why this will end with his wings sheared and his head on a spike.' Calidus looked up at the corpses dangling from the trees, heads severed. 'But we must not forget that Meical is no fool, and he has some powerful allies.'

Balur One-Eye not least amongst them. 'And he has the starstone axe,' Uthas said. 'So what now? Where has Meical gone with his rabble?'

'It does not matter.' Calidus shrugged. 'He has too few about him to challenge us for the cauldron. And we cannot change our course. The cauldron must be taken to a safer place. We will continue to Tenebral, and Meical will continue to plot and scheme, but he is undone. His more powerful allies are dead, his attempts at power blocked, thwarted. The war is won, as long as we keep our heads.'

Literally, Uthas thought, glancing at the headless corpses swaying above them.

Calidus looked up, Uthas following his gaze to a dot in the sky. A bird, high above. It circled lower, huge wings spread, riding the current until it was close enough for Uthas to see the curve of its beak.

I recognize that bird.

Calidus held an arm out, and with a beat of its wings the great hawk alighted on his forearm. Calidus scratched its chest.

'Kartala,' he said. 'Your master is dead, then.'

The bird stared at him, its head cocked to one side.

'Bune – share your meal.'

One of the Kadoshim that was taking bites out of a Jehar corpse threw Calidus a chunk of rotting flesh. Calidus ripped off pieces and fed them to the bird.

'Kartala was my link to Ventos. The man who tracked Corban, who told us of his coming north.'

'I remember,' Uthas said. 'You sent Alcyon south to waylay Corban on the information from this Ventos.'

'Yes. Unfortunately something happened between Ventos' last message and Corban's arrival at Murias. Involving a hundred or so Jehar warriors and Ventos' death, I'm guessing,' Calidus said sourly. He shrugged. 'Such is the way of war. Things change, people die, information often travels too slowly. You can help us with that, though,' he said to the bird. 'Meical is leading Corban and a band of miscreants about the countryside, and I need to know where he is going. You understand, Kartala? Meical and Corban. That is their trail.' He pointed to the wide path of trampled grass that led southwards through the hills.

Kartala beat her wings and lifted into the air, the power of her departure making the corpses sway and creak in the trees.

'That should go a long way to avoiding any more unannounced interruptions,' Calidus said.

'Indeed.'

The Kadoshim had now uncovered the giant cairns and Uthas looked in, scowling when he didn't see Balur amongst the dead.

Calidus held up a hand as one of the Kadoshim reached the cairn he was standing beside. He leaned over, picking up the purple flower of a thistle that was resting upon it and sniffed at it like a hound. Calidus nodded for the Kadoshim to proceed and it tore at the cairn, heaving stones and hurling them with a strength even more prodigious than its companions'.

'He's a strong one,' Salach remarked.

'When the starstone axe was taken from Alcyon the cauldron's link with the Otherworld was broken; my kin felt it happening. Many of them sped through the veil in those last moments, swarmed into one body before the gateway was severed. That is the body.'

'What's his name?' Uthas asked.

'His name is Legion, because . . . well, it's self-explanatory, really.'

Uthas raised an eyebrow.

In short moments a body had been uncovered – a woman, dark hair, skin waxy in death. 'Ahh,' Calidus said, smiling. 'I recognize her. She put a knife or two in me during the battle.' He looked at the thistle between his fingers, twirled it, then slipped it inside his cloak. 'Take her head,' he ordered Salach. He gestured to the Kadoshim already sniffing at the corpse. 'And they can have the rest.'

CHAPTER ELEVEN

MAQUIN

Maquin ran through the trees, the sound of Fidele's footfalls just behind.

Running away, again. This is becoming a very bad habit.

They had been running a long time, Maquin's lungs burning with each breath. Evening was not far off.

The sight of the giants had aroused his curiosity. *What does Lykos want with them? How long has he kept them prisoner? Why are they so heavily guarded?* Lykos was a sly, cunning strategic man. There must be some purpose for him to invest so much in guarding these giants. *Do not ask. I do not want to know, do not care. My life has become complicated enough already. Those giants are another distraction that I do not need. There is only Jael. Getting involved here has already led to Vin Thalun on my trail and a woman slowing me down, when I could have been leagues closer to Isiltir by now.* Nevertheless he was finding it hard to not think of the two giants. There had been something pitiful about them, something broken. *They are slaves*; he knew how that felt. It had stoked his hatred of the Vin Thalun, and he felt that hatred still, a white-hot glow that threatened to consume him. *They are following us.* He'd heard their calls as they'd crossed the river, occasionally heard them crashing through the forest – *they are seafarers, not woodsmen* – and he'd wanted to stop, to turn back and hunt the hunters, see their blood spilt, lives ended, but he knew he could not. Responsibility drove him, made him flee. Behind him Fidele's breaths were laboured, ragged. He slowed his pace, then stopped.

She was flushed, sweating, dark hair plastered to her face, clearly exhausted. *And yet she has not asked to stop.* Not what he would have expected from a pampered queen. *There is a strength in her. Pride and determination.*

'Do not stop . . . on my account,' she breathed.

There was a rumble overhead – thunder – and a raindrop dripped onto Maquin's nose.

'Senios will have told them of you. They will continue following us,' Maquin said.

'And he'll have told them about you. They may think twice about chasing us.'

'No, they'll just send enough to make sure the job gets done.'

'How many is enough? I saw you in the arena – against four.'

Maquin looked away. He remembered that day, remembered seeing the four warriors appear through the arena gates. Remembered each individual as they bled out in the mud.

'Depends how good they are,' he shrugged, banishing the memory. He looked about the forest. 'They are seafarers, not at home in a forest. Me, I lived in Forn. They should send at least seven, to be sure, and there were more than enough of them to do that.'

'How do you know?'

'I counted twenty-two at their camp. They'd need at least ten to guard the giant and her bairn, probably a few more than that. Two would have left to take word to Lykos. That leaves around ten, depending on how many stay with the giants.'

She nodded resolutely. 'What should we do?'

'Keep running, until it's too dark for them to track us at least. Then we'll go on some more, to be safe.'

Fidele nodded wearily and they set off again.

It was raining harder now, water dripping constantly from the canopy above. They were following a narrow trail; the undergrowth about them was dense and impenetrable. Maquin had considered leaving the path, forging into the forest, but that would only make them easier to track and slow them down as well. *Speed is what we need.*

Something changed around them. Maquin sniffed the air; an earthiness rose above the other scents of the forest. He slowed, then stopped. Fidele stumbled into him, knocking him a step forward.

The ground shifted beneath him and his foot sank into the

ground past his ankle, black mud bubbling up around it. His first reaction was to heave backwards, but to his horror it felt as if some creature had gripped and pulled at his foot.

At a quick glance the ground appeared normal, covered in lichen and vine, but as he looked closer he saw it shift, a ripple spreading about his boot. *A sinking hole.* Panic bubbled in his gut. He'd seen them in Forn, seen a giant trapped and sucked below the surface in a matter of moments.

'Take my hand,' Fidele said, stretching out to him. He gripped her wrist and very slowly leaned backwards, resisting the urge to heave with all his might. Slowly he felt his foot move, pulling free of the sucking mud. With a squelch and a popping sound his foot appeared and he was free. He nodded thanks to Fidele and drew his sword, prodding at the ground to negotiate their way around.

After that they proceeded more slowly. Visibility dropped steadily until shapes began to blur around them. They spilt into a clearing where dark shadows were heaped on the ground. Maquin saw the dull gleam of metal, heard a groan. He drew his knife, hissing at Fidele to stay back, then made his way forwards.

Thunder cracked overhead, lightning flashed, for a heartbeat illuminating the glade as brightly as highsun. Warriors were strewn upon the ground. The first he reached bore the eagle of Tenebral upon a battered cuirass, dead eyes staring, throat opened. Others were Vin Thalun. The last he approached still lived, a warrior of Tenebral; his breathing was laboured and uneven.

A shadow loomed behind Maquin and he tensed, but it was only Fidele. She crouched and stroked the wounded warrior's forehead. He was a young man, his face pale and eyes wide with pain. He stared at Fidele, recognition slowly dawning.

'My . . . lady.'

'What is your name?' Fidele asked him gently.

'Drusus,' the warrior breathed.

'What happened here, Drusus?'

'We fled the arena—' He grimaced with pain. 'Peritus' orders. Split up, regroup in half a ten-night. But the Vin Thalun followed us. We could not shake them.'

'You fought well,' Fidele said. Maquin grunted his agreement.

Five eagle-warriors were scattered about the clearing, eleven Vin Thalun.

'Peritus still lives, then?' Fidele asked.

The warrior nodded.

'And Lykos?'

'I do not know,' the warrior said. 'All was chaos.' Pain racked him, and he gave a gurgled hiss. Maquin checked him over. Superficial wounds everywhere. Two were more serious. A deep wound in his thigh, and one in his back, a hole punching through the lower section of his cuirass. Blood made black by the twilight pulsed rhythmically. Fidele looked at Maquin, a question in her eyes.

Will he live? Maquin shrugged his answer, tore a strip of linen from his shirt and tied it tight around the warrior's thigh. The wound in his back was another matter. *If it hasn't hit a kidney or his liver he may live. He's already lost a lot of blood, so who knows? But he's most likely dead anyway. The Vin Thalun on our trail will find him.*

'Help me lift him,' Maquin said to Fidele.

Together they raised the warrior up. He was unsteady, standing only a moment unaided before his knees buckled.

'Over here,' Maquin said, half-carrying the young warrior into the undergrowth.

'What are you doing?' Fidele asked.

'Hiding him,' Maquin grunted, pushing through a thicket.

'We can't leave him – the Vin Thalun following us . . .' Fidele said.

'I know.' Maquin shrugged. 'He can't walk. We can't carry him, or stay. Staying means dying, and I'll not be dying for him.'

Fidele's face shifted. A look of horror swiftly replaced with determination. 'No,' she said. 'I'll not abandon him. He is one of my people.'

Maquin laid Drusus down. 'This is war, not wishful thinking. We stay and we'll die. Simple as that. He's a warrior, knows the life he's chosen. Don't you, lad.'

'Aye,' Drusus gasped. 'You *must* leave, my lady.'

She looked between them.

'No.'

'Don't be a fool.'

'He is a man of Tenebral, has risked his life for this realm, for me. I'll not just walk away from him, abandoning him to certain death.'

'Your dying too won't keep him alive any longer. It's not brave, not noble, just foolish. You're throwing away his sacrifice – their sacrifice – by dying yourself.'

Fidele looked pale, but he recognized the stubborn set of her jaw. 'I said no. And you should remember, I am queen of this realm.'

'Not my queen,' Maquin growled, anger at her bubbling up. 'Fine. Stay and die if you wish.' He stalked away, gathered up some weapons from the dead warriors and returned to Fidele. She was sitting beside Drusus, speaking quietly to him. The warrior lay with his eyes closed, his breathing shallow.

'My offer to you was to help you stay alive, not sit and die with you. You should come with me.' He held out his hand.

She just shook her head. 'I swore an oath to protect my people.'

Another bound by an oath. I am not alone, then. 'Take these.' He laid a spear on the ground beside her, put a knife in her hand. He kept another knife for himself. 'If they find you, use the spear first. Keep the butt end low and push up, hard, like this.'

'I will.'

Maquin stared at her again, wishing she would relent and come with him. The expression on her face told him otherwise. Determined, resolute. *Stubborn.* With a scowl, he turned to walk away.

'Maquin,' Fidele called after him.

'Aye.' He paused but did not look back.

'Thank you. For all you have done for me.'

He walked away.

The forest was dark now, ruptured by sporadic bursts of lightning. *Idiot woman, to fight so hard for life, only to throw it away for a dying man. Still, what point freedom if you cannot decide what you will die for?* Deep down he felt a stirring of respect for her. *Walk on, man. You are free. Free to leave Tenebral, free to hunt down Jael, free to finally seek your vengeance.* He blinked rain from his eyes.

Damn her. He stopped. With a snarl he turned and strode back the way he had come. Soon he was back amongst the dead warriors. He passed through the glade like a ghost, not knowing or caring if Fidele was aware of him retracing their steps along the forest trail.

Voices sounded ahead, and then he saw the flutter of torchlight.

He stepped away from the path and nimbly climbed a tree, its branches hanging thick and low. He drew one of his knives, the heaviest one with a wide blade and a round iron pommel, the handle carved from bone.

Then he waited.

Men emerged from the gloom. He counted four, six, seven.

Too many.

A few held torches, including the first, an older warrior with the familiar iron rings bound into his beard. He paused as he passed the tree Maquin was in, crouching to study the ground. His torch hissed as rain dripped upon it.

'They came this way,' the old warrior said.

'We should make camp, continue in the morning. We could miss them in the dark,' another said, a younger man gripping a spear. He was standing at the back of their column, his eyes nervously scanning the darkness of the forest.

'We could, but I doubt we'll lose them,' the older man said. 'They've stuck to this trail so far, and leaving it would be slow going.' He waved his torch at the thick undergrowth. 'And my guess is they won't be stopping, not for a while. They'll want to put as much space between us and them as they can.'

'Don't know about you, but I don't like the idea of bumping into Old Wolf in the dark.'

Other warriors muttered agreement.

'There's seven of us, damn you,' the older warrior growled.

'Aye. Still, I've seen what he can do . . .'

Maquin gave a feral grin. They didn't know the half of it.

'Lykos won't thank us for letting them escape. Who are you more scared of?'

'I'm not scared of anyone,' the young warrior snapped. 'Just being realistic.'

'We'll go on a little further . . .'

The old warrior stood and moved on, treading slowly, carefully, his eyes scanning the ground. The seven men filed off, the last one hesitating, glancing behind him. The others were further ahead now, on the edge of sight.

Maquin snapped a twig and leaf, the sound masked by the rainfall, then stretched his arm out, holding his knife by its pommel, blade hanging down. He let the twig and leaf flutter down, landing upon the path immediately in front of the last warrior, who stared at the leaf, then looked up.

Maquin let go of his knife.

It smashed into the warrior's face, slicing through the warrior's eye, piercing his brain. He dropped without a sound, one leg twitching.

Maquin slipped from the branch and landed on the path, tugged his knife free and set off after the other warriors.

Six left.

Maquin was surefooted and light on his feet, his training in the Vin Thalun pits having raised his strength and stamina to new levels, his reactions faster than they had ever been. He ran quickly, the flicker of torchlight ahead guiding him, and in a handful of heartbeats the Vin Thalun were in sight. They were moving in single file, the trail constricting them. Maquin slowed as he drew closer, focusing on the last warrior, who gripped a spear and was using it as a staff, his head down, concentrating on where he was putting his feet. Maquin caught up with him, silent as mist, slipped a hand about the man's face, clamping over his mouth, in the same breath sawing his knife across the warrior's throat. Blood jetted, the man slumped, Maquin holding him upright and lowering him gently to the floor.

Five. His heart pounded in his head as he waited for the warrior in front to turn, but the man continued walking.

A cry went up from further along the column, bringing the Vin Thalun rippling to a halt. Maquin saw the last warrior turn; this one held a flaming torch. He saw Maquin looming out of the darkness just in front of him and let out a cry as Maquin's knife slammed into his belly. Both of them tumbled to the ground, Maquin using his momentum to rip the knife upwards, slicing the Vin Thalun from belly to ribs. They both screamed, crashing to the floor, blood exploding in Maquin's face.

Four.

Maquin rolled to his feet, came up running, snatching at the burning torch.

'It's the Old Wolf,' a cry went up. Maquin saw fear-filled faces but knew that these men were warriors. They were not so easily defeated. They turned to face him, drawing swords, levelling spears.

Surging forwards he hurled the torch at the man trying to circle to his left, sending the warrior stumbling into the undergrowth. Maquin drew his other knife, a blade in each hand, and then he was amongst them.

He ducked a sword swing, punched one knife into a thigh, left it there, powered on. He swayed away from a spear thrust, grabbed the shaft and pulled the warrior off balance, putting his knife in the man's eye, the blade sticking.

Three. Then he was through them, one dead, one injured, maybe bleeding out. Both his knives gone, he drew his sword.

The older warrior was stood before him, short sword in one hand, torch held like a weapon in the other. The man Maquin had thrown the torch at had extricated himself from the undergrowth but was keeping his distance, eyes glancing between Maquin and the old leader. The warrior with Maquin's knife in his thigh was upright; it didn't look as if Maquin had hit the artery that would have put him down. They all stood, frozen for a dozen heartbeats, then thunder crackled overhead and Maquin was moving again.

He went for the leader, covered the distance in a few strides and swung at the man's head. His blade was blocked and he swerved right, avoiding a torch in the face. Instead it caught his shoulder, pain searing through him. He grunted, spun away, saw the warrior from the undergrowth closing in, the one with the knife in his thigh stumbling after them.

Not good. I need to finish this quickly. The old Vin Thalun clearly had other ideas. He backed away, sword and torch raised, making time for his comrades to close on Maquin.

Can't just stand here waiting to be killed. Gritting his teeth, Maquin charged at the old warrior, who stepped forward to meet him, sword high, torch low.

Knows what he's doing. Maquin skidded, leaning back. The torch whistled over him, a trail of sparks streaming past his eyes and then Maquin's feet were crashing into his opponent, the two of them going down together, rolling. The torch went spinning through the air, both warriors trying to bring their swords to bear, snarling and grappling. The old Vin Thalun gouged a thumb into Maquin's burned shoulder. Maquin grunted and headbutted the man. The pressure on his shoulder disappeared.

Wish I hadn't left my knives in other men.

Footsteps thudded; the other two Vin Thalun were close.

'Hold him still,' one yelled.

'Trying to,' the old man grunted.

Maquin glimpsed a warrior standing over him, sword raised. With a burst of effort, he rolled away, dragging the old man with him. Maquin felt his sword slip from his grip. They punched, kicked, bit and clawed at each other, then a knee landed in his gut, knocking the breath from him, his limbs weakening for a moment. The old man slid away, staggering to his feet. Pain lanced along Maquin's ribs and he saw the glint of iron. Blood sheeted his side.

Get up, or you're a dead man. He pushed, made it to one knee.

'Finish him,' the old man yelled at the Vin Thalun standing behind Maquin. His sword was stained red.

'MAQUIN!' a voice screamed. They all paused, looked up the trail. Lightning exploded overhead, for a heartbeat transforming the forest into a place of light and shadow.

Fidele stood twenty paces away, spear in hand. 'Finish him,' the old Vin Thalun said, 'I'll fetch Lykos' bitch.' He grinned and strode towards Fidele. Then he staggered, stumbled forward, sinking into the ground. He looked back, twisting at the waist, a look of terror on his face. With a jerk he sank deeper, as if someone were tugging at his feet from beneath the ground.

The sinking hole.

Maquin heaved himself upright, grabbed the sword-arm of the warrior over him. They wrestled back and forth. Maquin twisted the man's wrist, the sword dropping from his grip. They slammed against a tree. Maquin wrapped his fingers around the man's throat and started squeezing.

The Vin Thalun lifted his knee, connected with Maquin and suddenly he couldn't breathe, was fighting the urge to empty his stomach. Still he would not loosen his grip. The Vin Thalun's eyes bulged, his fists punching into Maquin's ribs again and again.

Then a spear stabbed into the man's chest. Fidele stood with the spear in her hand. She stared at the dead man, her eyes fierce, breathing hard. Then she flung the spear down as if it had burned her.

Maquin glanced about, remembering there had been another,

the one with Maquin's knife in his thigh. He saw him half a dozen paces away, lying twisted on the trail, face pale, eyes staring. *Knife clipped his artery, then.* Maquin gripped his blade and pulled it free.

He put his hand to his ribs – a sword cut, not deep but bleeding heavily.

'Thanks,' he said to Fidele.

'You came back,' Fidele said to him.

'Aye. Well, seems you're not the only fool in this forest.'

She smiled weakly at him, then twisted away and vomited.

'Help me,' a voice cried. The old warrior in the sinking hole. He was submerged to his chest now. Maquin and Fidele walked to the hole's edge and stood silently watching him. He begged and pleaded, offered money, his oath, safe passage through the forest. Maquin and Fidele kept their silence, just watched him as he sank deeper. They did not move or speak until his head slipped beneath the mud.

CHAPTER TWELVE

CYWEN

Cywen rose to the sound of sparring, swords wrapped in leather to protect their edges and mute the noise of a few hundred Jehar warriors sparring with one another.

They were camped in the fringes of a wood nestled in a wide, steep-sided valley. Mountains surrounded them, their peaks wreathed in cloud. They marked the border between Benoth, the giants' realm, and Narvon to the south, once the realm of Owain, now ruled by Rhin – as were all the kingdoms of the west.

Buddai lay beside her until he saw Storm, a shadow in the woods, and bounded after her. She smiled at them tumbling together, a flash of fur and teeth.

'They act like pups around each other,' Brina said from behind her. Cywen looked to see Craf was perched on her shoulder and another shape fluttered out of the sky to land on a branch close by. *Fech.*

'Some bonds can never be broken,' Cywen told her. She turned back to watch the sparring, nearly three hundred warriors in a meadow, but her eyes picked out Gar and Corban almost immediately, the two of them moving in a blur, too fast to track individual blows. By some unspoken agreement they stopped, all those around them doing the same, then moved on to new opponents. Corban turned, and Coralen, the girl from Domhain, was standing in front of him. They shared a brief smile and set at each other. It was as fast as the combat with Gar, though with more kicking and punching, Coralen always moving close, using elbows and knees to gain any advantage. It still ended with Corban tripping her and his sword at her throat.

Cywen could relate to that, more often than not she had been in the same position when she had practised with Corban back at Dun Carreg. *I remember that feeling. It's annoying.* That was until Dath had joined them, and she had started putting *him* on *his* back. But here even Dath was sparring as if he knew what he was doing. She saw him partnered against Farrell, using his size and speed to swirl around his larger friend. And Farrell was holding his own, confident blocks merging with smooth attacks. *The last time I saw him he was a clumsy auroch. What's happened to everyone? I spend the year with my hands tied together, and everyone else has become a warrior.* She felt her face creasing in a scowl.

A ten-night had passed since they had escaped Murias, each day falling into a similar routine. She had wanted to talk more with Corban, but it seemed that everyone wanted to talk to Corban. And everyone else seemed to have a role, a task that they performed in this fledgling warband. Everyone except her. She was starting to feel useless. She daren't even spar with the rest of them, although part of her was desperate to take part. *I'm not good enough. Even the worst are better than me.* She felt her scowl deepening.

'Careful, girl: if the wind changes, your face might stick like that,' Brina rasped beside her.

Cywen smiled wryly. 'My mam used to say that to me.'

'Have some of this.' Brina held out a skin and Cywen sniffed it and wrinkled her nose. *Brot. The giants' food. Food is too generous a term.*

'*YUK,*' Craf squawked, eyeing the skin disapprovingly.

'*Tasty,*' Fech reproved.

The giants were gathered in the woods, just darker shadows amongst the trees. Mostly they kept themselves separate. Whilst the warband travelled they took the position of rearguard each day, always grouped together, rarely mixing with the Jehar. Sometimes the younger ones would run alongside the column, racing and tackling each other to the ground, wrestling and even laughing. The sight of it had made her smile, feeling like a taste of normality in this world gone mad.

'Just a mouthful,' Brina said, poking Cywen with a bony finger, and Cywen swallowed some brot, figuring it was easier than trying to argue. It was like porridge, but chewier, with all the pleasure taken out. It filled her stomach like a stone, but it did its job. Cywen had consumed just a mouthful each morning and had not felt hungry until the next day.

Brina took the skin and replaced it with an empty linen bag. 'Come help me,' the old woman said. 'I saw some foxgloves and elder in the woods.'

'Me?' said Cywen.

'Yes, you. My old apprentice seems to have become too busy lately to help me gather plants.'

Cywen followed Brina silently into the woods, frowning at Craf, who along with Fech flapped from branch to branch above them.

'Here,' Brina said, pointing at a bush dotted with clusters of white flowers. They'd stopped in a small glade, wildflowers opening about them in response to spring's pale sun.

'That is elder,' Brina told her. 'Too early for the berries, but the flowers are useful. Everything on an elder is useful, the bark, the roots.' She pulled out a knife and started cutting stems of flowers, skinning some bark and gesturing impatiently for Cywen to hold her bag open.

'We're a long way from Dun Carreg,' Brina said, peering over a branch at Cywen.

'We are,' Cywen agreed. *A long way from home, all of us different people now. Changed by what's happened.* She felt a moment of frustrated, helpless rage, aimed mostly at Calidus and Nathair.

'I don't just mean the distance,' Brina said.

'I know,' Cywen grunted. She looked up and saw Brina staring at her.

'He's still your brother. Just . . .'

'Busy?' Cywen finished with a sigh.

Brina grinned at that. 'Yes. Very busy. But he's a good boy. A big heart, a rare loyalty to his kin and friends. And quite a good brain inside that thick skull of his, when he bothers to use it. Don't tell him I said that,' she added.

'Your secret is safe with me,' Cywen said.

'*Safe secret*,' Craf commented from above. '*Trust.*'

It was disconcerting to have a crow joining in with the conversation. More so when it made astute observations.

'I was sad to hear about Heb.'

Brina blinked at that, sudden pain washing her face. With an obvious effort she smoothed it away.

'Corban told me how he . . . about the battle in the mountains of Domhain, against giants and wolven.'

'Uthas,' Brina said.

'*Bad giant*,' Craf muttered.

'*Peck out his eyes*,' Fech added, vehemently.

'What?'

Something dark contorted Brina's features, her eyes narrowing. 'Uthas is the name of the Benothi giant that killed Heb. I've been talking to Fech.'

'*Yes, she has*,' Fech confirmed.

'I know Uthas,' Cywen said. 'He joined Rhin and Nathair. He is in league with Rhin.' *I hate him, as I hate all of my captors.* Other faces swam in her mind – Alcyon, Veradis. Faces that had shown her some measure of kindness amidst the bleak horror of it all. *Maybe not all.*

'*He is a traitor to his kin*,' Fech muttered.

'He killed my Heb. I'm going to kill *him*.' There was no humour, no kindness in Brina's voice now.

'*We*,' Fech corrected.

'Sorry, we,' Brina smiled, a cold thing.

'*And then I will eat his eyes*,' Fech added.

'Good,' Cywen said fiercely. 'Heb was very brave, standing against a giant.'

'He was a fool,' Brina said, 'but he was my fool, and I miss him.' Her expression softened. Craf fluttered down and landed on Brina's shoulder, began running his beak through her hair. Brina absently scratched Craf's wing. 'The only other person I've told that to is your brother.' She smiled at Cywen. It was very out of character.

'Why are you being so nice to me?' Cywen asked suspiciously.

'I can be nice,' Brina snapped. 'You've been through a lot. And now you're here, back with kin and friends, and yet you feel . . .'

'Out of place,' Cywen finished for her. 'Useless.'

'*Useless, useless, useless*,' Craf repeated. Cywen shot a glare at him.

'You're not, you know. Useless, or out of place,' Brina said to Cywen. 'You're in the only right place – around people that care for you. You just need to find your feet again.'

'Are you feeling sorry for me?'

'Aach, you're a proud one, and no mistake.'

'*PROUD*,' Craf screeched from Brina's shoulder. She shooed him off, rubbing at her ear.

'Not *sorry* for you, Cywen, I'm just one of the few that care about you, that's all. And it just so happens that I need a new apprentice.'

'What do you mean?' Cywen asked.

'As you've pointed out, Corban is busy. He was my apprentice – I've taught him much of the art of healing. But he is busy, and that's not likely to change. I need help – my guess is there's going to be a lot of blood spilt before this is all over. Someone has to try and patch the wounded up. And I can't do it on my own.' She shrugged. 'I'm asking you to help me, and as you've just told me that you feel useless, I'm thinking you should be saying yes to my proposition. You need something to do; I need someone to do things for me.' She smiled, a little too sweetly for Cywen's liking.

Cywen felt as if she'd been neatly manoeuvred into this position, but as she thought about it, the idea of being Brina's apprentice did not seem so bad. Apart from one thing – or two.

'On one condition. I'll not be told what to do by two crows.'

'*Raven*,' Fech corrected.

'By a raven and a crow,' Cywen shrugged.

'You'll have to work that out with Craf and Fech,' Brina said.

'*Craf. Orders,*' the crow cawed, then clacked his beak repeatedly.

'Is he laughing at me?'

'Yes, I believe he is.'

Hooves sounded then, growing closer.

'*Uh-oh,*' Craf squawked and launched himself into the branches above them, merging with the shadows.

Cywen turned to see a handful of riders coming through the woods towards them. Coralen was at their head. To one side a Jehar warrior rode, a female with a thick white streak in her black hair. On Coralen's other side was Dath, his long bow strung and strapped to his saddle. He flashed a grin at Cywen as they drew up in the glade. Storm and Buddai loped up behind them, Buddai padding forward to nuzzle Cywen's hip.

'Corban was looking for you,' Coralen said. She wore a wolven pelt for a cloak, a sword at her hip, a knife beside it. Another knife hilt jutted from her boot, and Cywen saw a gauntlet hanging from her saddle pommel, three iron claws protruding from it. *Like Corban's.* 'He wants you back at the camp.'

'He's my brother, not my lord,' Cywen snapped. Something about Coralen's tone irritated her.

'Camp is broken. They're ready to ride,' Coralen said. 'All are waiting on you.'

'We'll leave when Brina is done,' Cywen said, knowing she was being childish.

Coralen shrugged, which annoyed Cywen even more.

'We are done here,' Brina pronounced.

Storm growled, Buddai as well, looking at a cluster of trees at the far end of the glade. A twig snapped. In a heartbeat Cywen had a knife from her belt and threw it. It stuck quivering in a trunk. Dath had his bow in his hand, arrow nocked, Coralen and the Jehar had drawn their blades.

'Come out, if you know what's good for you,' Coralen said.

There was a drawn-out moment, then a figure emerged from behind the tree. A giant, but slimmer, gangly limbs, and with no hair upon its face, not even straggly wisps of a moustache, like the other giantlings Cywen had seen.

A giant bairn, a girl.

She had her hands raised, palms out, and her eyes were wide, flitting from Storm to the array of weapons lined before her.

'*Mi breun chan aimhleas*,' the young giant said.

'She means no harm,' Brina said. It took a moment for Cywen to realize that Brina had translated from giantish. *She can teach me that, if she likes.*

The giant looked at Cywen's knife stuck in the tree. She pulled it out, stared at the blade a moment, then ran, faster than Cywen would have thought possible.

'Hey, that's my knife,' Cywen shouted, but the giantling had already disappeared amongst the trees.

'The Benothi,' Coralen spat, then shrugged and looked at Cywen and Brina. 'Nice throw. Now get back to camp if you don't want to be left behind.' She looked up at the branches above them. 'Craf, I know you're hiding up there. Come with me – you've got work to do.'

'*Not fair,*' Craf grumbled.

Fech clacked his beak, the sound like laughter.

'And I don't know why you're here,' Coralen said to Fech. 'You're supposed to be flying rearguard.'

'*Talking to Brina. Important,*' Fech squawked.

'Not as important as protecting us from Kadoshim,' Coralen said. 'Go on with you.' She spurred her mount on. Dath winked a goodbye and they all rode off, Storm shadowing them. Buddai whined and Cywen rested a hand on his neck. 'Stay with me, Buds.'

'*Tired,*' Craf protested.

'*Busy,*' Fech complained, but they both took to flight, flapping noisily away.

'They're good birds, but lazy,' Brina said, a half-smile twitching her lips as she watched until they'd disappeared.

'Craf's too opinionated,' Cywen said.

'A terrible affliction, I must agree.' Brina regarded Cywen with a raised eyebrow. Cywen had the good manners to blush.

'Come on, then,' Brina said. 'Make sure that bag's tied properly, and be quick about it. Don't be ruining my supply of elder.'

Cywen sighed and rolled her eyes. *What have I let myself in for?*

CHAPTER THIRTEEN

CAMLIN

Camlin checked over his kit methodically. He'd put a fresh coat of wax on his long bow of yew and had three hemp strings rolled in wax in a leather pouch. A quiver of thirty arrows stood wrapped in oiled doeskin – the ship they were sailing upon was a trader and had a good selection of furs and tanned skins. He emptied his bag, checked over its contents again. A copper box packed with dry tinder and kindling. A flint and iron. Fish-hooks and animal gut for the stitching of wounds. Various medicinal herbs – honey, sorrel leaves, yarrow and seed of the poppy. A roll of linen bandages. An arterial strap. An iron to heat for the cauterization of wounds. A needle and hemp thread. And a pot.

I'm looking at the difference between life and death.

Most of it he'd traded or won at dice during the journey from Domhain. Some of it he'd bought. He knew it would be needed, and they would reach their destination soon: Ardan, ruled by the enemy, where they would be hunted.

A horn rang out above him, muted by timber, and shouts followed.

Land.

Camlin climbed above-decks and rolled his shoulder and lifted his arm, more out of habit than need. It had healed well. Over a ten-night had passed since Baird had pulled the shaft through his shoulder. Three days ago he'd strung and nocked his bow, tested to see if he could draw it. His muscles had protested and he'd not pushed them. He'd done the same each day, and earlier today he'd managed a full draw, a bit shaky, but nothing had snapped, so that was good enough for him.

The first person on the deck he saw was Vonn, leaning at a rail, staring at a dark line on the horizon. A coastline rose up from the horizon, dark cliffs and tangled coves. *Land.* Camlin grinned at the sight of it.

Ardan.

Around him the ship's crew were busy, climbing in rigging, securing ropes. *Doing what sailors do.* There was a tension in the air now, an excitement. The end of their time at sea had arrived, and they were about to begin something new. *Something more dangerous, most likely, but I don't care. Another night on this damn tub and I'll go mad.*

Others were gathering on the deck now, warriors preparing to disembark. Camlin joined Vonn. 'Home,' Vonn told him.

Vonn's face was a mixture of emotion – longing, fear. *It'll be hard for him. His da rules there now.*

'You ready for this?' Camlin asked him.

Vonn looked at him for a few long moments. 'I'm ready. I've always been ready. The night Dun Carreg fell I was ready. If my oath to Edana had not kept me with her, I'd have put a sword through my da's traitorous heart.'

Right now, I believe you. But words are easier spoken than deeds are done. How would you feel if you stood before Evnis? Could see him, look him in the eye, hear his words?

'Is that really Ardan?' a voice said behind them. Camlin turned to see Edana. Her hand rested on a sword at her hip. *Our warrior Queen.* Baird stood beside her. The one-eyed warrior had become her shadow, rarely leaving her side.

'Aye, it is,' Camlin said.

'There were times when I thought I'd never return.' Edana took a deep breath. 'Time to roll the dice.'

Why does she look at me whenever dice are mentioned?

They stood together and watched the coast grow closer, their ship angling towards a cove with steep-sided cliffs. The sail was furled and two rowing boats were lowered from the deck to the slate-grey sea. Roisin and Edana spoke to the captain, thanked him, and then the group of them were rowing towards the coast. They scraped onto a thin strip of shingle and clambered onto solid ground, Camlin grinning for the joy of it. *I hate the sea.* It felt strange, the ground steady beneath his feet, and he stumbled as his body still compensated for the eternal pitch and roll of a ship's deck.

Roisin stood with Lorcan, her warriors spread protectively about them, a score of men. Most of them gazed up at the cliffs. Seamen from the rowing boats deposited a barrel onto the shingle, then with a last goodbye and a wave they rowed back to their ship.

'Smoked herring,' Baird pronounced as he sniffed the barrel. 'Draw lots for who's carrying it?'

'I'll carry it,' a tall and solid warrior said. He didn't seem to have a neck. *Brogan,* one of Roisin's. Camlin had won a fine deerskin belt from him.

'No complaints from me,' Baird grinned.

'Vonn, with me,' Camlin said, and without a look back he was climbing the slope, following a narrow goat track into the cove's cliffs, twisting its way upwards. He used his unstrung bow as a staff. The calling of gulls in the air was loud, the cliffs of the cove clustered with nests; here and there were stunted bushes bent by the wind.

Camlin emerged onto a landscape of rolling moorland and hidden gullies. He could see for leagues and took a few moments to check for company, then he turned and waved to those gathered below, all looking up at him. They started their climb.

He turned back to study the land. To the east the undulating moors dropped and flattened, glistening as sun reflected on a marshy peninsula that continued into the horizon, patches of it darkened by woodland. Here and there pillars of smoke marked holds, farmsteads, a small village. None close enough to worry about, though. *And I am supposed to lead this rag-tag band to Dun Crin, ruined fortress of the giants. Is it even out there, in those marshlands?* During their voyage Edana had spoken of this with him, of how King Eremon had received word that a resistance was growing in Ardan against Evnis, and that it was based around the ruins of Dun Crin, in the marshes. *Well, there are the marshes. And if there's a ruin out there, I'll find it. What happens then, I'm not so sure. One step at a time.* Vonn climbed, panting, to stand beside him and they both looked northeast. Towards Dun Carreg.

It was too far away to see, but Camlin could make out a dark stain on the horizon. *Baglun Forest. Been there. Not my best memories.*

That had been when he was part of Braith's crew, come to the Baglun to cause some mischief in Ardan. Little had he known at the time that it was all at Rhin's behest. He'd ended up with a knife in the back, put there by one of Evnis' sworn men.

And now here he was, a refugee on the other side, playing guide to the fugitive Queen of Ardan and the fugitive King of Domhain. He peered over the cliff, saw them labouring up the twisting path behind him. He'd followed his own twisted path to this spot. *From bandit to shieldman. What next?*

Warriors emerged from the path, Edana with Baird. Camlin saw she was grinning.

'The cry of gulls, it sounds like home,' Edana answered his questioning look.

'Home is fifty leagues that way,' Camlin said, pointing along the coast. Dun Carreg was there somewhere, and between them a host of Rhin's sworn men, led by Evnis, the man who had slain Edana's father.

Edana's smile evaporated as she stood staring into the distance. Men crouched, drank from water skins. *Warriors in a strange land*, thought Camlin. They were all hard men in Roisin's company, battle-tested and loyal, hand-picked by Rath.

'Why have we landed here?' Roisin said, frowning at the countryside. She was no longer dressed in her fine velvet dresses, instead wearing dun breeches, a linen tunic and leather vest, over it a dark cloak, but to Camlin she looked just as beautiful as when draped in her court finery. *And as dangerous.*

'We are too exposed here, too close to Dun Carreg,' Roisin continued. 'We should have landed in the marshes. Less likely for us to run into Rhin's followers, and it would be harder to track us. This is a mistake.'

Is this intentional? Undermining Edana?

Edana gave Roisin a hard look. 'There are reasons why we are here. Dun Crin is our destination, a ruin somewhere in those marshes. We don't know exactly where it is. It could be twenty leagues to the south, or one league east. Camlin is a masterful scout and he will find it, I have no doubt.'

I am? I will?

'He suggested we begin from higher ground. Once we are in the

99

marshes the travelling will be slow going. It will be easier to cover ground on better terrain, skirt the marshes and choose a point of entry.' She paused and gave a moment to look at each one of them.

'This is my land,' Edana said, looking at the warriors gathered about her. 'It's been taken from me. My parents murdered. My people scattered and oppressed.' She looked at the gathered warriors, meeting each eye. 'You are all brave faithful men, and I thank you for your courage and your honour. Do not think that Lorcan and I are beaten. We have yet to begin the fight. We will win back our rightful thrones, with your help, and that starts here, today. That starts now.'

Warriors nodded, muttered their approval. Even Camlin felt his blood stirred at her words. *She's growing up.*

'Camlin,' Edana said to him. 'Take us to Dun Crin.'

Camlin sped through the village, his bow strung and arrow nocked. He kept to the shadows as much as possible.

They had walked all day, steadily descending from the moorlands towards the marshes. Now they were in a kind of borderland, the terrain dry enough for scattered woodland and roads, but dissected by a thousand streams and middling rivers. Camlin had spied the village and planned on circling around it, but something had drawn his eye. The lack of sound or movement. And there were no signs of normal village life, hearth fires, livestock, dogs – nothing. Instinct told him he needed a closer look, and so did Edana when he informed her of his concerns.

Now he was starting to regret it, though.

Probably another bad idea to add to my long list of bad ideas, he berated himself. *Why couldn't I just mind my own business and walk around?*

He looked to the far side of the street, where Baird was keeping pace with him, his sword drawn. Camlin had also sent half a dozen men wide around the village, with orders to sit and wait for him and Baird. Unless they heard trouble – then they were to come running. The rest of their crew were camped a quarter-league back, with Edana and Roisin. Lorcan had volunteered to come with them, but Camlin had told him to sit tight; he'd received a sulky glare in return.

The village was small, built on the banks of a river. Camlin had seen the tips of willow rods in the river, the tell-tale ripple of a current around submerged salmon traps, nets left out to dry along the bank. A dozen coracles, assorted river craft and flat-bottomed marsh boats were pulled out of the river. There were no more than a few score homes, and so far he had not seen a single person, had not heard a single voice.

He crossed a gap between buildings, paused to look around a corner, saw a crow picking at the carcass of a dog. He walked past it, almost certain now what he would find.

Camlin smelt it first. *Death.* The metallic hint of blood, mixed with rot and excrement. He hung his head, readied himself before he went on.

The street spilt into an open area, what would have been a market square. A roundhouse stood on its far side. About halfway between Camlin and the roundhouse a gallows had been erected, a dozen or so small figures hanging in the still air. A fury rose within him.

Bairns. He took a step forward and then halted abruptly.

The ground between Camlin and the gallows was black, uneven, and moving.

Crows. Hundreds of them. And flies.

Camlin and Baird shared a look and they both moved into the square. Crows rose up before them like a wave, cawing and screeching their protests.

Part-eaten bodies were everywhere, the stench verging on overwhelming. Men, women, children, seething with flies and maggots. Over a hundred. *The whole village?* Camlin saw the glint of iron and checked a body. A warrior in a shirt of mail. His cloak was tattered, torn to pieces, splattered with blood, but Camlin could still make out the black and gold of Cambren.

Rhin.

He felt suddenly vulnerable and turned a slow circle, scanning the surrounding buildings, the dark shadows of the roundhouse. Baird appeared in the shadow of a doorway, shook his head.

Nothing. They are all dead, or fled to the marshes.

Camlin carried on searching amongst the dead, making his way deeper into the courtyard. He found three more in Rhin's cloaks of black and gold. Reaching down he unclasped one, pulling it free, stirring up a cloud of flies in the process.

Then he heard a noise, looked over at a building with wide, open doors. He heard it again, coming from within. The whicker of a horse.

Stables? Why are there horses alive, when every other man, woman, child and beast has been slain?

More movement, this time from the roundhouse at the far side of the square. Figures emerging. Warriors – five of them – cloaks of black and gold, swords in hands. Eyes fixed upon him, they were striding purposefully towards him.

He dropped the cloak in his grip and drew an arrow, nocked and released in less than a few of their strides. It took the first warrior through the eye, dropping him like a felled tree. The others began to run at him.

Not the effect I'd hoped for.

He drew and released again, the arrow hissing between warriors as they spun out of its way.

Camlin cursed as he released the next arrow, this one punching low, into a man's belly. He dropped to his knees.

Then a figure crashed into the three still running at him. Baird, sword rising and falling. One of their enemy screamed, his belly open and guts spilling about his feet. Another had grabbed Baird, whose head lunged forward, butting the warrior's nose even as his sword stabbed into the warrior's side. Camlin stood and stared a moment, frozen by the ferocity of his companion. Then his eye was drawn to the roundhouse. Three more men burst from the doorway, two running towards Baird, the other sprinting around the edge of the courtyard, making for the stables.

Before Camlin realized it he had another arrow nocked and was sighting at one of those charging at Baird. It slammed into the warrior's shoulder, spinning and dropping him. The other was too close to Baird for another shot. Camlin glanced between Baird and the warrior sprinting towards the stables, drew his sword and ran to Baird's help.

He almost didn't need to. By the time he reached them Baird had put one man down and was trading blows with the other, backing the warrior up. A panicked glance from the warrior at Camlin was all Baird needed, his sword opening the man's throat.

Hooves thudded and the last warrior burst from the stables, kicking a horse hard into a gallop. Camlin dropped his sword and drew an arrow, tracked the warrior, who was bent low in the saddle, almost hugging the horse's arched neck. Camlin's arrow took him in the throat; the warrior sagged, slumping from the saddle to be dragged by the still-galloping horse.

Camlin and Baird just stared at one another, chests rising and falling.

They both turned together to the sound of footsteps approaching from behind.

Edana and a dozen others, including Roisin and Lorcan. Quickly, Camlin moved to intercept them. *She doesn't need to see this.*

'You were supposed to wait for my signal,' Camlin said, hurrying forward to stop her reaching the square.

Some truths are best not seen.

'We heard screams, the clash of iron. I was worried for you,' Edana said with a wave of her hand as she pushed past Camlin into the square.

She stood there a moment, eyes scanning about her, body rigid. Then she stuttered into motion, picking her way through the square, eyes sweeping the ground until she reached the gallows. She faltered, looked up at the children, their bloated corpses swinging in a gentle breeze. Ropes creaked.

She saw the black and gold of Cambren upon the dead warriors' cloaks. 'Rhin, even here.'

Camlin came and stood beside her, saw tears running down her cheeks.

Lorcan pushed forward and took her hand. 'Come away now,' he said.

'These are my people,' she snapped, yanking her hand out of his grip. 'I am not some innocent girl . . .' She trailed off. 'Not any more.'

'But, why do you stare so? You do not need to be here. We have seen, now let us go.'

'I stare so that I will not *forget*. This is my land, these are my people. Rhin and her ilk have slain them. Slaughtered *children*. They will not be forgotten. There will be a reckoning.'

Lorcan looked into Edana's face, then nodded.

'What happened here, Camlin?'

Good question. And why were there warriors still here? He glanced at the roundhouse where the enemy had appeared from. *Something's wrong. We need to get out of here.*

'What happened here, Camlin?' Edana repeated.

'Hard to say. Rhin has warriors down this way, for some reason. Maybe the word that there is a resistance based in the marshes is true? Looks to me like they were making some kind of example.' He nodded to the gallows. 'My guess is it didn't go down too well, got out of—'

'Over there,' Edana blurted, pointing behind Camlin. To the stables. 'Something moved . . .'

I'm an idiot. These buildings need checking.

'You should leave,' he muttered to Edana as he set his bow down and drew his sword, Baird following him as he entered the stable. Camlin waited a moment for his eyes to adjust, then started skewering the straw in each stable. He got to the last partition, saw a lump in the straw.

'If you don't want an extra hole in your body, you'd best be standing up now.'

There was a moment's silence.

'All right, I warned you,' he said, stepping in.

The straw exploded upwards. He saw a flash of red hair as a small figure darted past him.

'Got it,' Baird shouted, hoisting the figure into the air. 'I mean *her*,' he suddenly bellowed as the child squirmed in his arms and bit his hand.

'Enough, girlie,' Camlin said. He made a point of sheathing his sword for her to see. She slowly calmed, then went limp in Baird's arms.

'We're not going t'hurt you. What's your name?' Camlin asked. She just looked at him, big dark haunted eyes in a dirty face. *She can't be more'n eight, nine summers old. What's the poor little mite had to witness to put such fear into her?*

When Edana saw the child she held her arms out, but the child only stared, her face full of fear and suspicion. Baird put her on the ground.

'We're not going to hurt you,' Edana said, crouching down to look her in the eye. 'We're friends, not enemies. What's your name?'

More silence.

'If we were going to put a blade in you, we'd have done it by now,' Camlin told her.

The child looked at him. 'Meg,' she whispered.

'How old are you, Meg?' Edana asked with an encouraging smile.

Just a silent stare.

Camlin's eyes were raking the buildings around the courtyard, his skin prickling. He wanted to take a look inside the roundhouse, but he also wanted Edana out of the village.

'You need to get away from here,' he said.

'Soon,' Edana said with a frown, stooping close to the girl. 'It's all right,' she said. 'We'll not hurt you.'

Meg just stared at her.

Need to hurry this along.

'How old are you, Meg?' Camlin asked.

'Eight.'

'How long ago did this happen?' Camlin gestured at the square.

She frowned, as if unsure. 'Two nights?' she said hesitantly. Then her bottom lip trembled and she started sobbing.

'We know it was Rhin's men,' Camlin said, feeling sorry for her – no child should have to go through this horror. 'They wear the black and gold. Don't know why they did it, though. And it'd be real helpful if you could remember how many.'

'That's enough for now,' Edana said to him as Meg continued to sob – days of pent-up emotion and fear obviously released.

'There were lots,' Meg suddenly blurted. 'And their chief was called Morcant.' She spat his name.

'Morcant,' Edana whispered. Camlin sucked in a breath as they shared a look. Back when Camlin had been part of Braith's crew in the Darkwood Morcant had joined them and led the raid that had captured Edana and her mam, Alona, Queen of Ardan. Soon after Camlin had found himself drawing a blade against Morcant and switching sides. Camlin loathed him.

He looked at the square, at the bodies swinging from the gallows. *Not a surprise that he's behind this. But what's he doing this far west. Hunting rebels?*

Something nagged at Camlin and he looked about, feeling suddenly vulnerable.

Then he saw Vonn and the others burst into the far side of the square, Vonn waving desperately. Camlin crouched down, placing a palm flat on the ground. A slight vibration. Steady, rhythmic.

Horses.

CHAPTER FOURTEEN

VERADIS

Veradis marched forwards, stepping in time with a dozen warriors spread either side of him, over two score more at his back. They were advancing upon a squat stone tower surrounded by a village of thatch and wood. The sun sat low in a blue sky, the air fresh and sharp as they continued their approach through green meadows carpeted with wildflowers.

A beautiful day.

To the west, behind a low hill, he saw a cloud of dust appear, marking Geraint's horsemen as they circled the village. *Hidden from the rebels inside.* The plan was that they would go round the village and wait for Veradis' shield wall to flush the rebels out of the town into the open meadows beyond, a killing ground for Geraint's mounted warriors.

Veradis had spent over a moon hunting down the remnants of King Eremon's resistance. The realm was still not stable, and that would not change while its newly appointed vassal king Conall was away chasing after Edana. Domhain had been conquered, the citizens of Dun Taras throwing open the gates in surrender, in acceptance of Conall, one of their own, with the blood of a Domhain king in his veins.

Even if he is a bastard. But Rhin sitting upon the throne in Conall's absence had not gone down well. Unrest had escalated into violence, and the streets of Dun Taras had run red. The rebels had notched up a string of minor victories, and even when Veradis and his shield wall had entered the fray it had been hard, bloody work. The shield wall had not been designed for enclosed spaces and back-alley fighting. But eventually the rebels had been defeated and fled. Rhin had ordered her battlechief, Geraint, to give chase, and had asked Veradis to lend his support.

Better to crush them now, put an end to the leaders, than allow them to spread their poison. It will only fester and rear up again, she had said to him.

Veradis knew she was right. The stability of the realm meant peace and less bloodshed.

They reached a field of barley, trampling through the green unripened stalks. A wide street of hard-packed mud opened before them. Veradis heard the bass lowing of a herd of auroch in the distance. He gave his commands and the warriors' shields snapped together, a concussive crack as they marched forwards, no one breaking stride. Veradis peered over the rim of his shield. It was an improved design, oval instead of round, giving more protection to his head and ankles, while making it easier to stab his short sword around its edges. He'd spent much of the winter thinking on his shield wall, considering strategies, strengths and weaknesses, seeing where injuries were most common, and the new shields were one of a few innovations he had made.

They marched into the village, their iron-nailed boots thumping on the ground like a drum beating time. A narrow street angled away, and Veradis gave more orders. The back row of twelve men broke out of formation and establishing a new compact wall, three men wide, four deep, who took this new street. This was how he'd learned to fight in the city streets – smaller, more compact groups.

The tower reared over rooftops ahead of them, its unshuttered windows like dark eyes in its granite face. *They are here somewhere, could not have slipped away in the night.* He saw a flash of movement in one of the windows. *Holed up in the tower, then.*

A sound seeped into his awareness, more a vibration at first, travelling into his boots, up his legs. It grew louder by the heartbeat, and then a cloud of dust was roiling down the street towards them. He stood, gaped open mouthed for long moments before he realized what was happening.

'Auroch,' he bellowed, leaping to the side, pulling men with him.

The huge cattle stampeded down the street, swinging their long horns from huge, shaggy-haired heads. Tall as giants, they were mountains of muscle and fur. The ground shook beneath their hooves.

Veradis slammed against a wall, other men with him, some crashing through doors and shuttered windows. One of his warriors stumbled in the road. Veradis reached out a hand, but the auroch were already upon them. One moment the warrior was there, the next he was gone, blood splattering Veradis' face as a seething, stinking mass of cattle surged by, the thunder of it almost overwhelming.

And then they were past, stampeding down the street, out into the fields of barley. He called out to his men, his voice a croak choked by the dust, and he saw shapes scattered on the ground, knowing they were his sword-brothers and that many would never stand again.

For the first time in an age he felt a deep, mind-numbing fear fill him. The shield wall had been dominant for so long in his memory, crushing any opponent with overwhelming regularity, that to see it broken and scattered so easily was shocking. Not since the very first battle, when he had stood in the wall and faced a charge of draig-riding giants had the shield wall been so easily destroyed.

Then he heard voices, battle-cries, saw shadowy figures emerging from the settling dust. *The rebels, come to finish any survivors before we can regroup.*

Somehow he was still holding his shield. He drew his short sword. 'To me,' he managed, more a choking whisper than the battle-cry he was hoping for, then again, louder, the act dissolving the fear that had frozen him, transforming it into anger. His eagle-guard would *not* fall like this. He glimpsed a handful of his warriors moving towards him. Then the rebels were on them, screaming their defiance.

Veradis took a blow on his shield that reverberated through his arm. He swept his shield wide, opening his foe's defence, and plunged his sword into the man's belly, wrenching it free in a spray of blood. He snarled and kicked the collapsing man away, strode into the chaos, a hot rage filling his veins.

Bodies littered the ground, mounds of trampled meat. The rebels were all warriors, stalwarts of Eremon and Rath, not pitchfork-wielding farmers. They attacked with a controlled fury, knowing this was their last, and also their best, chance of defeating

Rhin's notorious ally. Veradis looked around wildly, trying to find men to regroup the shield wall, but they were fractured, embroiled in scores of solitary battles.

'So be it,' Veradis growled. *They'll see there's more to us than just the shield wall.* He blocked an overhand swing that was about to take a stumbling comrade's head off, twisted and back-swung, opening his attacker's throat. He reached down, pulled his sword-brother to his feet and moved on. Smashed his shield into an enemy's side, stabbed hard, his sword-tip breaking through a shirt of mail to slide across ribs. His opponent cried out, pulled away, was hacked down by another eagle-guard. A spear was thrust towards him; Veradis deflected it with his shield, the spear-tip bursting through layers of ox-hide and beech, punching through a handspan above his wrist. He dropped his shield, wrenching the spear from his opponent's hands, and hacked his blade down into the man's skull. Veradis switched his short sword to his left hand, drew his longsword and fought on.

A horn blew to his left, two short blasts, one long. He grinned fiercely. It was one of their signals: regroup. The eagle-guard that had left the shield wall before the auroch stampede appeared from a side street nearby, a dozen men in formation, their shields locked. He started cutting his way towards them.

Others did the same, merging into the wall, swelling it, and before Veradis reached them it had grown, six men wide, four rows deep. The resistance started to fall before it.

Other sounds emerged over the din of battle – the thunder of hooves and the blowing of horns, growing rapidly louder.

Geraint and his warband. They must have heard us. Thank Elyon. He saw Geraint riding a black warhorse at the head of a host of mounted warriors. He skewered a rebel with his spear, let it go, drew his sword and started cutting down rebels as if they were stalks of wheat. It was a matter of heartbeats before the rebels were broken, fleeing in all directions. *No one can stand with a shield wall before them, cavalry behind.* Veradis stood there, panting, both swords bloody.

'Well met,' he said to Geraint as Rhin's battlechief pulled his horse up beside him. The warrior leaned over and gripped Veradis' forearm.

'Think you might just have saved my life,' Veradis said to him.

'Good.' Geraint grinned. 'I've been meaning to return that favour.'

Dun Taras came into view as the road wound between two hills, the fortress' dark walls a brooding shadow against the countryside. Veradis rode beside Geraint, their warriors spread in a column behind them. A cluster of prisoners walked at the centre of the line, hands bound and heads bowed. Thirty men, survivors of the uprising, heading towards Rhin for her judgment.

Which is unlikely to be merciful, judging by her mood when I left Dun Taras.

Geraint, however, was in fine spirits, laughing and joking as they approached Dun Taras.

Veradis was in the grip of a dark mood, the deaths of his men weighing heavily upon him.

Thirty-eight men dead. And what honour in that death? Slain by overgrown cows. More men lost than in the battle of Domhain Pass, where we fought against a warband ten thousand strong.

He looked at the pouch hanging from his belt, filled with the draig teeth he had collected from a dozen of the fallen. *Men who stood with me from the beginning, who stood against the draigs and giants of Tarbesh. Nathair's first battle, his first victory. Nathair's Fangs, we called ourselves. It was my fault. I should not have marched them into that village unprepared. I should have sent scouts first. I have become over-confident, arrogant, thinking my men and shield wall are unbeatable. This proves we are not.*

Rhin was waiting for them in Eremon's old chambers. Veradis remembered the room all too well; it had been where they had fought the old battlechief Rath and his shieldmen, where his friend Bos had died. He avoided looking at the flagstones where Bos had fallen, scrubbed of blood now, but there was still a faint outline, if you looked hard enough. *Blood always leaves a stain.*

'Well, Geraint, I can tell by your grin that my problems with rebels are ended,' Rhin said coolly. Her silver hair was braided with gold thread, spilling across one shoulder, the paleness of her skin enhanced by her sable gown.

'Yes, my Queen,' Geraint said. 'The rebellion is finished. None escaped – a few hundred dead, and thirty prisoners await your justice.'

Rhin raised an eyebrow at that. 'Something to look forward to, then. Come, celebrate with me.' Veradis was handed a cup by a servant and was pleasantly surprised to see that it was a cup of wine, not the mead or ale that was so popular in this part of the world.

'To strong men that will *always* do my bidding,' Rhin said, lifting her cup, chuckling. Veradis wasn't sure he wanted to drink to that, but the wine smelt good and his throat was dry after their long ride.

Rhin enquired of the battle, shrewd as always, asking about tactics and the decisiveness of the conflict. How many dead on both sides, how many survivors? Were the leaders dead? Her eyes bored into him as Veradis told of the auroch stampede.

'Always adapt,' she said when he'd finished. 'War is wits, Veradis. Strength, courage, skill, these are all valuable assets in combat, but wits are what win a battle, and a war. Your shield wall has served us well, but our enemy are not mindless animals. They will study, analyse, adapt. You must be one step ahead, always, or you will stagnate and be outwitted.'

'Aye, my lady,' Veradis said. *This I have learned.* 'And how go things here, my lady?'

She sighed wearily and rubbed at her temple. 'I am spending my life organizing, administrating and advocating between petty grievances, Veradis, and it is *boring*. I find myself in a position where I command four realms – all of the west, in fact – and it is tedious. There is a lot to do, and I am stuck here in Domhain, waiting for Conall to return to us.' She smiled ruefully. 'It would appear that I prefer to conquer than to rule!' She shifted in her seat, scowling. 'Not to mention that this chair is uncomfortable; no wonder Eremon killed himself.'

'I thought he was assassinated, my lady.'

'Yes, but we'll keep that between us. Took his own life is better, less likely to turn him into a martyr. A cowardly act, suicide. Couldn't face me.' She winked at him.

I would not like to face you as an enemy, either.

'And what would my orders be, my lady, now that the resistance against you is crushed?' *I do not want to spend another moon here. The God-War is happening, out there, while I play at peace-keeping on the edge of the world.*

'Getting a scratch in your boots?' Rhin asked.

Can she hear my thoughts?

'Aye,' he nodded.

'I feel the same,' Rhin said with a shrug. 'Once Conall returns I plan on leaving Domhain. Nathair is on my mind.'

'And mine too, my lady.'

'Of course he is. And there are other concerns I would attend. I sent a warband north, after this Corban and his companions – the ones I had trouble with in Dun Vaner.' She pulled a sour face. 'I have not had any news from them, and I am impatient. So I will travel north. I would like you to accompany me, and we can see if I can reunite you with your King.'

'That would be good,' Veradis said. 'How do you know where the boy has gone?'

'He told me,' Rhin said. 'He came to Dun Vaner chasing after his sister. She was with Nathair, riding to Murias with him. I forget her name.'

'Cywen,' Veradis said, her face filling his mind as he spoke her name.

'That's the one. Her brother seemed to have a strong sense of family loyalty. Foolish child. It's an overrated quality in my opinion – I've spent most of my life plotting how to kill off my kin, not rescue them.'

'So you've sent a warband after him?' Veradis asked. 'I'm surprised you have the men available, spread throughout four nations as you are.'

'I've spent many years raising my warbands in preparation for these days. Even so, you are right, things are a little stretched. I've had to send men who were stationed in Narvon. They should be at the border with Benoth soon.'

Booted feet echoed from the corridor; a guard entered.

'Lord Conall has returned, my lady.'

'Excellent,' Rhin said. 'Where is he?'

'His company approaches the gates as we speak, my lady.'

'Come, then,' Rhin said, rising. 'I could do with stretching these old legs.'

They found over three score warriors dismounting from horses in the courtyard beyond Dun Vaner's keep. Veradis knew in a heartbeat, from the averted faces and the stoop of shoulders, that Conall and his men had failed to capture Edana and Lorcan, Eremon's heir. Veradis saw Rafe dismount, the blond lad from Ardan, two hounds circling him. One jumped up at him, sniffing a pouch on his belt. He cuffed it good-naturedly and went to another horse and helped a grey-faced warrior dismount. The man looked close to collapse, a wide bandage strapped around his neck and shoulder. Spots of blood had leaked through.

'Braith?' Rhin cried out as she strode down the wide stone steps into the courtyard. She stroked the huntsman's face and for a moment it was as if the two of them were the only people in the courtyard.

'Get him to a healer,' Rhin snapped at Rafe. 'I'll be along as soon as I can,' she called over her shoulder.

Then Conall was there, his face set in proud lines.

'They got away,' he said.

'That much is obvious,' Rhin scowled. 'The *how* I will hear when we are somewhere more private. And I hope you can tell me something of the *where*.'

'I have a prisoner who may be able to help with that,' Conall said, stepping aside and pulling a man forward. He looked remarkably like Conall. Older, lacking the fire and mirth that seemed to war constantly for control of Conall's features, but definitely related. Serious grey eyes regarded Rhin.

'This is Halion. My brother, and Edana's first-sword.'

'Ahh,' Rhin smiled viciously. 'Your jaunt across half of Domhain may not have been entirely wasted, then.' She stood and stared at Halion a long moment, the warrior returning her gaze.

'Eremon's seed,' she laughed, 'all so proud.' Then she turned and marched back up the stairs towards the keep. 'Come on, then,' she snapped, 'bring him along and we'll see what we can salvage.'

*

Veradis leaned against a pillar of stone, watching as Rhin stirred a pot bubbling over a fire. Conall's brother Halion sat in a chair, his wrists tied to the arm-rests, a leather belt tightened about his chest, holding him secure.

'We could try the traditional method of questioning,' Rhin said as she unstrung a pouch from her belt, pulling some dried leaves from it and crumbling them into the pot. 'But I'm inclined to cut straight to the end of the hunt. With the traditional route – you know, flaying, toe crushing, hot irons, the removal of genitals, that kind of thing – there is always so much blood. And screaming. It takes time.' She smiled grimly. 'I don't really have the time to waste. I don't like it here. I need to be elsewhere, so you need to tell me what you know, and you need to tell me *now*.'

Halion watched her, his face an unreadable mask.

I'm glad I'm not him.

Bitter fumes started to rise from the pot.

'I wouldn't stand too close,' Rhin warned Conall and Veradis, 'unless you wish to tell me your deepest secrets.'

Both men took a step back.

'Now then, take a deep breath,' Rhin said to Halion, taking the pot by its chain and holding it above Halion's lap. He held his breath before the fumes enshrouded him. He bucked in his chair, trying to break free. Two warriors stood behind, holding it in place. Halion shook his head from side to side, searching for an escape from the fumes, his arms rigid, his back arched. Eventually he had no choice; he took a shuddering breath, then another. Moments passed and he slumped into the chair, tension seeping from his muscles.

'Good,' Rhin muttered. 'Now. Tell me your name.'

'Halion ben Eremon.' He looked surprised, then too relaxed to care. Rhin smiled.

'And whom do you love, above all others in these Banished Lands?'

'Conall ben Eremon, my brother.'

Conall took a step back, as if from a blow.

'And who is your lord?'

'I have no lord,' Halion corrected. 'I serve a lady; Edana ap Brenin. Queen of Ardan.'

Rhin scowled at that.

'Why are you asking him these questions?' Conall growled. 'How are they relevant?'

'I am establishing that he is telling the truth – that the drug has him fully.' She looked back to Halion. 'And where is Edana now?'

'At sea, I would imagine.'

'What are her plans?'

'To reunite with the resistance in Ardan. To take back her crown.'

'It was never hers,' Rhin muttered. Halion stared ahead.

'And where is this resistance? What is Edana's destination?'

'Dun Crin, the giant ruins in the marshes of western Ardan.'

Rhin smiled triumphantly. She reached out and stroked Halion's cheek. 'Thank you. You have been most helpful.'

CHAPTER FIFTEEN

CORALEN

Coralen looked up as Craf spiralled down to her. She drew her horse to a halt and waited for him, twisting in her saddle to check on the main company emerging from the woodlands of the mountain slopes, as small as ants from this distance.

'*Village*,' the crow squawked as he drew nearer, alighting on her saddle pommel.

'Where?' she asked.

'*Ahead. On the road.*'

Typical. She'd known it was inevitable that they would encounter other people at some stage but had hoped they'd have escaped detection a little longer than this. They had spent two nights travelling through the mountains and entered Narvon only yesterday.

Enkara and Storm approached her. Even relaxed they both radiated strength and menace. Coralen grinned, for a moment lost in the strangeness of the company she kept. *The world has changed immeasurably since I tracked half a dozen Benothi giants into the mountains between Domhain and Cambren.* That had been where she'd first encountered Corban and his company.

'What is it?' Enkara said as she rode over. She was one of Tukul's Jehar, one of the Hundred that had ridden out in search of the Bright Star nearly twenty years ago. Coralen had a healthy respect for all of the Jehar – their martial prowess and dedication was verging on inhuman, and the fact that the women amongst the Jehar ranks were easily as skilled as the men impressed Coralen. But Enkara had become more than that: a mutual respect had developed, and out of that a hesitant friendship.

'A village, not far ahead,' Coralen said. As she stared she saw faint columns of smoke. *Cook-fires.*

'Can we go around?' Enkara mused.

'If we numbered a score, yes, we would go around. Three hundred . . .' Coralen shook her head. 'There's no point. We would have to march leagues out of our way not to be spotted. And this is only the first of many villages that we are going to come across.'

'So we just go straight through it?'

'Yes. Fast.'

Enkara thought about that a moment, then smiled. 'I like it.'

The rest of the scouting party joined them.

'So what now?' Dath asked, sitting relaxed and confident in his saddle. He was starting to lose the nervousness that had seemed to cloak him like a mist. *He's found something he's good at. He's made to be a huntsman, can track, scout, has a remarkable eye for details. And he's a better shot with his bow than I am, or anyone else I've known.*

Coralen gave them her orders, splitting the crew, Enkara and two others leaving to warn Corban and the warband, the rest going with her to scout out the village. It still felt strange, giving orders. She had ridden with a hard crew most of her life, with Rath and his giant-killers, but they had numbered around a score or so, and she had grown up with them. And she'd never given them orders. Now she was responsible for three hundred lives and was making decisions that could mean the difference between life and death for them all.

If it is strange for me, how must it feel for Corban, sitting at the head of this warband, having the Jehar, Benothi giants and one of the Ben-Elim looking to him?

'*What about me?*' Craf squawked.

'Stay with me,' she said, clicked her tongue and touched her heels to her horse, spurring it to a canter.

Coralen lay hidden amongst gorse and heather, studying the village in front of her. She had led Dath and a dozen Jehar wide around the village and approached through woodland from the south, leaving the majority of them hidden in the trees. Coralen and Dath had crept closer for a better look, accompanied by Kulla, a young Jehar warrior who always seemed to be somewhere close to Dath. Coralen just ignored her.

The small village spread along the riverbank, consisting of forty or fifty buildings of undressed stone and turf roofs, a large round-house at its centre. Women were scrubbing clothes in the river shallows, bairns playing on the riverbank under their watchful eye. Men worked in fields of wheat and rye spread to the west, and to the east Coralen saw a herd of goats dotting the valley slopes, their bleating drifting on the wind.

As Coralen watched the women about their work she saw a girl – six or seven summers, maybe – creep up on one of the women and splash water over her back, then run away in a burst of spray and giggles. The water must have been icy cold, fresh from the mountains, but the woman didn't turn, just continued her scrubbing against a boulder. In time the girl crept back again with exaggerated stealth, but just before she put her cupped hands into the water, the woman turned and dashed after her, sweeping her up and kissing her repeatedly. Coralen heard them both laughing.

As she watched she felt something tighten in her chest, and to her horror she felt tears bloom in her eyes. *I can't remember one moment in all my life like that with my mam. I was never the child she wanted.* She blinked, sending a fat tear rolling down her cheek, and sniffed.

'You all right?' Dath asked beside her.

'Fine,' she snapped, swiping at her face. 'A fly in my eye.' She paused a moment, then crept back to her horse and swung into the saddle. Dath and Kulla followed her.

'Where are you going?'

'To the village.' The original plan had been to stick to their position until Corban and the warband appeared, and make sure that no one headed south from the village in an attempt to spread word of the warband's coming. Suddenly, though, the fear and panic that the villagers would feel were things she wanted to try and avoid.

'Why?' Dath asked her. 'It's dangerous.'

'You should stay here,' she said as she rode towards the village. Dath caught up with her.

'You're mad, but Corban and Farrell would have my stones if I let you go riding into that village alone.'

'Displeasing the Seren Disglair must be avoided,' Kulla said, a horrified expression creeping across her face. 'At all costs.'

Dath raised an eyebrow and Coralen scowled. 'I can look after myself,' she snapped.

'I know that.' Dath shrugged. 'But I'm still coming.'

'We,' Kulla amended.

'Suit yourself.'

They rode into the village. Dogs barked, children shouted and people gathered about them, more filtering from the surrounding fields. Coralen saw many making the ward against evil as they saw her, causing her to scowl. Strangers obviously weren't welcome and in these troubled times she could understand why. *But if they fear me, wait until they see Corban with a warband of giants and wolven.* She pulled on her reins, saw the gauntlet of wolven claws she wore on her left arm and realized she was also wearing her wolven fur, the head draped across her shoulders, jaws gaping and teeth bared.

Perhaps they have good reason to fear me.

A man stepped out of the crowd surrounding them. Dath and Kulla looked around warily, prepared for trouble.

'Greetings,' he said. 'Excuse the poor welcome – strangers are rare this far north.' Despite his polite tone he clutched a thick-hafted boar spear in his hands. With disapproval Coralen noted the blade was rusted. Other men were moving forward, most hefting woodcutters' axes. One had a battered sword sheathed at his side. She saw the mother and child that she'd watched in the river huddled together and remembered her purpose.

'You're about to see a whole lot more,' Coralen said. 'I've come to warn you that a warband is approaching from the north. They'll be here soon.'

Gasps rippled around the crowd, a hint of panic, some faces sceptical. Questions flew at her, raised voices.

'There is nothing to fear, they are peaceful and just travelling south. They will not stop, they will not attack. They want nothing from you. You'd be best going to your homes and closing your doors.'

Coralen saw expressions of doubt, disbelief, fear spreading through the crowd.

'Peaceful! When is a warband peaceful?' someone yelled.

'They mean you no harm is what I mean.' Coralen felt her temper fraying.

'Who are you?' the man who had greeted her shouted. People filtered away from the crowd's edges. A group began to hurry to the east, towards the wooded valley slopes. Some made to pass her, heading south, and she turned her horse, blocking the road.

'This isn't going well,' Dath whispered to Kulla, which didn't make Coralen any calmer.

'Go where you wish, except south,' Coralen said, then stood in her saddle. 'No one heads south.'

'They mean to slaughter us all,' a cry rose up, and hands grabbed at her bridle. She slapped them away, clenched her fist, causing her wolven claws to chime, and gripped her sword hilt. More people surged towards her.

Dath shot an arrow into the ground at the spokesman's feet and Kulla drew her sword.

'Stay back, or die,' Kulla said, her voice flat and cold.

I've managed to bring someone less gifted at diplomacy than me.

'Next man goes to lay a hand on her gets an arrow through the eye,' Dath said, loud and clear.

This isn't going as I planned.

Men were gathered in a half-circle about her, Dath and Kulla, a score at most, balanced on the brink of violence.

There was a moment's hush, and in it another sound grew, a distant thunder. Coralen looked to the north, saw figures appear on the valley's horizon, more pouring from the woodland. Mounted warriors, beside them the giants striding on long legs. Ahead of them ran a hound and wolven.

Corban.

'They are here. Go back to your homes,' Coralen shouted, and the crowd was suddenly moving in all directions. Most of them headed into the village, some broke away east and west. A handful swerved past her, heading south.

My scouts will send them back.

Coralen leaned down and reassured the woman from the river, who was standing frozen, wondering what to do, her daughter gripped in her arms.

'Trust me,' Coralen said. 'Go to your home. No harm will come to you.'

The woman looked at her, obviously torn between fight and

flight. The girl just stared, big brown eyes unblinking.

'I'll do as you say.' The woman took long strides and disappeared into the village.

Corban's warband was soon upon them, a wing of Jehar warriors a hundred strong riding west of the village, thundering across fields of wheat and rye, the rest marching down the centre of the valley and through the settlement. Corban rode into the silent village, Meical on one side of him, Farrell on the other, a huge grin splitting his face.

Corban nodded a greeting at Coralen's group.

'How are you, girlie?' Farrell winked at Coralen.

'Well enough, and don't call me girlie. I've spoken to you about that before.'

'Sorry – habit.' He winced, a hand moving protectively to his groin. Dath chuckled.

'Everything all right?' Corban asked, frowning as Coralen fell in beside him.

'Aye. Just trying to prevent a mass panic.'

Corban looked around; the village appeared almost deserted. Here and there a face could be spied peering from shuttered windows.

'Looks like you succeeded.'

'It wasn't easy,' Dath said. 'Don't think they're used to seeing even one or two new faces up here. The sight of you lot coming towards them . . .'

'What's the road ahead like?' Meical asked.

'I've sent Craf and the Jehar scouts ahead. Haven't heard anything, so it must be clear. I'm going to wait until everyone's through the village, then I'll join them.'

'Something bothering you?' Corban asked.

'No. Just want to make sure there's no harm done.'

'We've no quarrel with these people.'

'I know, but fear can lead to rash acts.'

'True enough. You've done well.'

She felt a smile twitch at her mouth, then scowled at herself. *I'm not a bairn to blush at praise.*

'I'll see you after,' she muttered, and reined in at the side of the road, Dath and Kulla silently joining her. Together they watched the warband sweep past, three hundred of the Jehar, Gar and Tukul leading them, a cluster of giants, Balur with his black axe at their centre. Brina and Cywen rode by, heads close in conversation. The bird Fech sat on Brina's saddle, his head bobbing, beak opening and closing as if he were joining in their discussion.

Craf won't be happy about Fech getting a ride while he's off working for his supper.

'You're supposed to be our rearguard eyes,' Coralen called out to the raven.

'Fech is educating me,' Brina said to her.

The last of the warband passed through, the Jehar Akar riding rearguard with a score of his warriors. Coralen waited a moment and then followed.

She rode away from the settlement and into the treeline, pausing to look back at the village beside the river. A flicker of movement drew her eyes upwards, to a bird high above. For a moment she thought it was Fech, but then she saw the bird hovering, raptor-like, and then it dived, hurtling towards the meadow and scooping up something in its talons. Coralen heard a faint squeak, a spray of blood and the hawk landed, its beak ripping into flesh.

In the village a huddle of people had emerged from their homes. One of them raised a hand to Coralen – the woman from the river. She returned the gesture with a smile and rode into the woods.

Two nights had passed since Coralen left the village behind, the warband ploughing deeper into Narvon. The terrain was similar to the north of Domhain where she had spent most of her life: leagues of rolling moor and black rock, shifting slowly towards greener vales, the horizon to the south carpeted with dark woodland and twisting rivers. Storm loped alongside, the rest of her scouts spread in a half-circle either side of her across a league or so of ground.

Domhain. Home. She felt a flash of guilt at the thought of her homeland, its warbands broken, her father King Eremon murdered. And now Rhin was sitting upon its throne. *And Conall, her puppet-king.* The thought of her half-brother ruling in Domhain would have been ludicrous, if she had not seen him at Dun Vaner, if she had not looked into his eyes and seen the rage and pain radiating from them. *What has happened to you?*

And what of Rath and Baird, of the Degad? Rath had near enough raised her. Fech had told them of Eremon's death and the fall of Domhain, and periodically guilt would rise up and consume her. *I should have been there, fighting beside Rath.*

And what would that have achieved? Me dead as well? It was Rath who had sent her from Domhain, Rath who had ordered her to guide Corban north through the mountains, but she knew that she had not been unhappy about that order. Another pang of guilt spiked at that. But somehow the guilt would always retreat, overcome by another emotion entirely. There was something about riding with this crew that felt different. As if she had been around them all her life.

And then there was Corban. She found her thoughts straying to him more and more often when she rode alone. She tried to convince herself: *It is concern, for a friend, over the choices he is being forced to make.*

A flapping from above drew her attention, Craf swooping down from a slate grey sky. He was flustered, squawking as he descended.

'*Warband, warband, warband,*' the bird screeched as he alighted on her saddle pommel.

'Where?' Coralen demanded.

'*Ahead.*'

'How many?'

'*A forest of spears and swords,*' he croaked gloomily.

CHAPTER SIXTEEN

CORBAN

Corban crawled across spongy grass, through red heather and fern, Coralen's boots just in front, Gar and Meical right behind him. After a quick discussion with Meical about Craf's sighting of the warband Corban had called a halt so he could take a look at what faced them.

'Down there,' Coralen pointed down a long slope to where the land levelled. First he saw the scouts, a score of horsemen strung out across the incline, making their way steadily uphill. About half a league behind them a warband was emerging from woodland, halting upon the banks of a wide stream to refill water skins and barrels. The broken branch of Cambren fluttered on banners, framed in black and gold.

'Rhin's,' Corban muttered.

'Who else?' said Meical. 'She's defeated every other realm within a hundred leagues.'

'At least three hundred swords,' Gar whispered as he drew alongside Corban. More warriors were still emerging from the trees, a steady flow. The first ranks crossed the stone bridge that spanned the stream. From this distance it was a slow-moving forest of leather and iron. A line of wains rumbled into view, shaggy-haired aurochs pulling them, bellowing as they climbed. Steadily they crossed the bridge, continuing along the wide giants' road.

What are we going to do?

It was one thing to lead three hundred warriors across a remote countryside, through small villages whose inhabitants hid or ran. It was another thing entirely to be marching towards an enemy who probably outnumbered you. *But they are not Jehar warriors or*

Benothi giants, a voice whispered in his mind. *If we fought them we would win.*

And how many of those who are following me would die?

Gar tapped his shoulder and signalled they should move back.

They crawled away, stood when the ridge hid them and mounted in silence.

'Craf, keep an eye on them,' Corban said to the crow.

'*Work, work, work,*' Craf muttered as he flapped into the air.

Corban looked around and saw Meical, Gar and Coralen all staring at him.

'What are you going to do?' Meical asked him.

I don't know. Fight? Flight?

Fear had settled in his gut like a heavy stone. Not fear of fighting or even of his own death – he had experienced enough battles now, and while there was always an element of fear present, he knew that he had the mastery of it. And besides, he had seen more terrifying sights recently, not least Kadoshim demons made flesh and the horrors they had inflicted.

What am I so scared of?

He touched his heels to Shield and rode away, heading back to the warband, the others following in silence.

Back to the warband. Back to my warband.

And then he realized. It was one thing choosing to enter battle yourself. And if others chose to follow you, well, that had given him some worry, but in the end it was their decision, not his. This time, though, he had led people here, to this point. He had chosen this course. He had expected resistance, to encounter the enemy, but not yet, and in his mind the resistance had consisted of minor skirmishes along the road. Part of him had hoped that they would be able to avoid any large conflict at the very least until they had reached the border with Ardan. Certainly he had not expected to march straight into a warband of Rhin's so soon, especially not one where the outcome of battle was so uncertain.

I am scared of people dying because of my decisions, my mistakes.

Gar cantered closer.

'Are you all right, Ban?'

'No.' The warband came into view, spread along the slope. Corban looked about: undulating moorland surrounded them. *If we were to fight, the terrain here is no good. Too open against an enemy that outnumbers us.* The sun glowed behind thick cloud. *It's highsun. Plenty of the day left. I need some time to think.*

Concerned faces watched him – men, women, giants. *Everyone always seems to be watching.*

He took a deep breath. 'Prepare to move out,' he cried. 'We're turning around.'

They rode hard, retracing their steps, Corban at their head. Craf had returned, reporting that the warband was heading due north, straight towards them.

He sent Coralen and a handful of Jehar back to watch the enemy, Storm loping beside her, as Craf had collapsed exhausted upon Brina's saddle and refused to fly another handspan.

He had asked Fech to scout for them, but the raven refused, which annoyed him. *Here I am, the chosen avatar of Elyon, the Bright Star; the high captain of the Ben-Elim listens to me, and yet a scruffy old raven refuses me.* Apparently Fech was explaining something vital to Brina. For once she did not overrule the bird, but sat there quietly, just nodding her head. She had the book in her hands, the one that she had been teaching him from. It lay open across her saddle.

He stared at the book. *The giant's book from Dun Carreg, full of their histories and lore. And of their magic.* Brina would have clipped him around the ear for calling it that, but that was how he thought of it. He remembered Vonn's confession that he had stolen it from his da, Evnis, and then how Brina and Heb had taught him from it. *When was the last time I even thought about that? Or Brina? I have just abandoned her.* At least Cywen was with Brina. In fact, she seemed to be spending almost every waking hour close to the healer. *I need to see more of Cywen, too. I ride hundreds of leagues to find her, and when I do, we hardly share two sentences.*

Corban sighed. It seemed that being the Bright Star meant sacrifices. 'Fine, have it your way,' Corban said to Fech. 'I'll not be forgetting your helpfulness, though.'

'*Sarcasm won't help,*' Fech squawked.

'Bribery usually works,' Cywen leaned in her saddle and whispered to him.

Corban considered. 'Fech, the next thing that Storm catches, I'll let you have its slimy bits all to yourself.'

Fech cocked his head at Corban. '*Agreed. Fly soon,*' he croaked.

'Good.' Corban kicked his horse on, annoyed at Fech and just wanting to be alone, if even for a few moments without some decision or another needing to be made. He cleared the front of the warband, where Meical, Tukul and Gar were riding, Balur and his daughter Ethlinn striding beside them. He clicked his tongue and Shield opened his stride, pulling ahead into an open space. Corban leaned forward, patting Shield's neck; the horse snorting with pleasure.

I've missed you, boy.

He looked back over his shoulder at the warband spread behind him, the bulk of giants mingled with the grim-faced Jehar. *How did I end up here? Leading a warband, hailed as the champion of Elyon? I'm not champion of anything. And why would Elyon, maker of all, choose me? It doesn't make sense.*

And yet Corban knew it was more than the mad delusions of a handful of fanatical warriors. Meical was one of the Ben-Elim. Corban had seen him in the Otherworld, transformed with white wings and eyes that blazed, but still most definitely Meical. And more than that, he had seen Asroth. Spoken with him. Asroth had been in no doubt that Corban was Elyon's chosen, had been quite prepared to cut Corban's heart out. He shuddered at the memory, a faint echo of the terror that had filled him.

Asroth wants me dead.

Hooves drummed louder and he turned to see Meical spurring his mount to join him. Gar and Tukul rode with him, Balur jogging beside them.

Corban sighed and slowed a little, dropping back to them.

Here it comes.

'What are we doing?' Meical asked him.

'Giving ourselves space – time. I would not throw us into battle without thought.'

'Time is something we don't have,' Meical said. 'Asroth is moving. He has been planning for this war for hundreds of years, and now he is striking. We do not have the time to ride back and forth like this. You *must* lead us.'

'That is what I am trying to do.'

'No, you are hesitating, undecided, and it will achieve nothing.'

Corban felt a flash of anger at Meical's words, mostly because he knew they were true. His eyes flickered across the others, all watching him keenly.

'We should turn and fight. Ride through Rhin's warband,' Meical told him.

'And how many of our own would die? It is not a decision I would lightly make.'

'Aye, well, decisions must be made, and they all have their consequences. You chose to ride south, and that means riding through the heartland of your enemy. It means blood being shed.'

'That is what I am worried about,' Corban muttered. 'Your blood? Their blood?' He gestured at the few hundred following behind them.

Meical sighed. 'Corban, this is the God-War. It is inevitable that *oceans* of blood will be spilt by the time it is over. All that matters is that Asroth is defeated. So, yes, I am prepared to see my blood shed, your blood, and the blood of *all* those riding with us to achieve that aim. It is all that matters.'

Corban thought about that a while, looking back at the faces who would follow him blindly into battle and beyond – into death – if he required it of them.

'You're wrong,' he said eventually. 'There is more to this than victory or defeat. I will not throw lives away. They matter. My heart broke when my da was slain, and it broke again in Murias when my mam died in my arms.' He paused, willed the tremor in his voice to pass. 'And it has broken for every friend that has died in between. Yet I am but one man, surrounded here by hundreds, each with kin, with loved ones. Balur – who is dear to you here? Who would you give your life to save?'

The giant looked surprised, then frowned, his already creased face wrinkling into a place of deep valleys. 'Ethlinn, my daughter,' he rumbled.

'And you, Tukul? Who would you give your life to save?'

'You,' Tukul replied without hesitation. He shrugged. 'Every soul here.' His eyes fixed on Gar. 'Most of all, my son.'

A gentle smile crept across Gar's lips.

'Every one of us here has those dear to them, hearts that would grieve at their deaths. We do fight for a cause. Against a great evil. But I also fight to save those I love. So I will not throw away their lives unnecessarily.'

'Admirable sentiments,' Meical said, though he looked more confused than understanding. 'Nevertheless, in this case, your sentiment is delaying action, and that will have a worse result – most likely all of us dead, eventually, and Asroth reigning over the Banished Lands. You are our leader. *Lead us.*'

Corban scowled. Meical shook his head in despair and dropped back, Balur and Tukul following him. Corban's thoughts churned. Eventually he looked over at Gar.

'I don't know what to do, Gar,' he said. 'I'm scared.' He remembered making a similar confession to Gar in a meadow below Dun Carreg, about his fear of having been bullied by Rafe. He almost laughed at the thought of it. *It feels like a lifetime ago, yet here I am, still scared. Just scared of something else, that's all.*

'All men feel fear,' Gar said.

You've told me that before.

'I know. It's what we do about it that counts.'

Gar smiled at him.

'This is different,' Corban said. 'I'm not scared of what may happen to *me*. I'm scared of getting people killed.'

'Fear is fear,' Gar shrugged. 'It will disable you if you let it; freeze you, crush you.'

'What would you do in my place?'

'Fight. We have no choice. Try and go around, they'll pick up our trail and chase us across Narvon. Sooner or later we'll find someone else in front of us that wants a fight. When that happens you don't want three hundred men with swords at our back.'

They rode on, the sun sinking, the mountains that marked the border with Benoth looming closer. As the sun was melting into the horizon they came upon a thick stretch of woodland, to the east a fast-flowing river, to the west a gentle hill swathed with pine and spruce. An idea started to form in Corban's mind. He stared back at the woods, remembering passing through them. A few leagues deep, and beyond them the village they had passed through. *Can't lead*

Rhin's warband onto that village. He raised his hand and reined in Shield, the warband rippling to a halt behind him.

Meical's right, I can't just lead this warband winding all across the Banished Lands. And it is a warband; warbands are for war, sooner or later we will have to fight.

He turned and stood in his saddle, staring long and hard at the terrain about them.

'We'll make camp here,' he called out, 'and on the morrow this is where we'll fight and crush Rhin's warband.'

CHAPTER SEVENTEEN

UTHAS

Uthas paused and gazed ahead. It was late in the day and the sun was sinking behind hills to the west. The mountain cliffs that had shadowed the pass they'd been marching through had gentled to pine-shrouded slopes, and beside them a white-foamed river carved a valley, widening into the green meadows of a flood-plain only half a league ahead.

'Narvon,' Calidus said beside him.

'Aye. Once it was Benoth, as were all of the western realms.'

They moved on. Before them Nathair rode his draig, the lumbering beast scattering stone and gravel with each footfall, pine cones falling from shaking trees. Alcyon marched beside Nathair, a handful of the Kadoshim spread about them. Calidus rode close behind. His eyes were never far from Nathair.

He does not trust him, yet. Nathair had given no sign of rebellion, had ridden mostly in silence every day, any conversation he did participate in was usually with Alcyon. *Time will be the judge. He will have to act upon his new oath soon enough.*

The Kadoshim and Benothi were strung behind them: over a thousand men and women lending their strength pulling the wains. It had been hard going through the mountain passes, Kadoshim massed around each wain's wheel, straining to turn them across the ancient and pitted road and through deep banks of wind-piled snow. They had made it, though, and now they were moving ever downhill, the road smoother and wider with every league.

'I was a lord of western Benoth, once, governing for Nemain from Dun Taras,' Uthas said.

'How long ago was that?'

'Six hundred years, give or take a moon.'

Uthas felt a prickling on his neck and turned to see Calidus staring at him.

'You drank from the cup.' It wasn't a question.

'I did,' Uthas said, looking away. He didn't want to talk about the starstone cup.

'You know I need the Treasures. They are vital to our plans.'

'I know.' Uthas tugged on his long white moustache, a habit when he was troubled, or anxious.

'Do you know something that could help me?'

It is too late to go back now.

'I have knowledge of two of the Treasures: the cup and Nemain's necklace. I know where they were last seen.'

'What?' Calidus hissed. His hand snaked out and gripped Uthas' shoulder. It was cold. 'Where are they?'

Uthas took a deep breath and swallowed.

'I would be king of *all* the giant clans, not just the Benothi. And I want Forn as my seat. As the new seat of the reconciled clans.'

'That is a lofty dream indeed,' Calidus said, looking at Uthas through narrowed eyes. 'Your ambition exceeds even what I expected from you.'

Uthas shrugged. 'The world is changing. Why not reforge something that was broken.'

'Indeed,' Calidus said with a calculating stare. 'In return for the Treasures you speak of I will aid you in this. You have my word.'

'I suspect your generals might disagree with you. Rhin, Nathair, Lykos – they will not be as enthusiastic to see the strength of the giant clans restored. I need to hear that assurance from a higher power than you.'

'You would bargain with Asroth?' Calidus said, raising an eyebrow.

Uthas shrugged. 'Why not. I rolled the dice when I betrayed Nemain – I don't think they have stopped rolling yet.'

Calidus laughed, a genuine warmth in it. 'What is the phrase I have heard amongst men and giants? You have some stones, Uthas. I shall arrange a private conversation for you.'

Uthas felt suddenly scared at the thought. *It's done now.*

The path led through woodland, the scent of pine strong in the air, the ground spongy with fallen needles. Cries rang out from ahead: the Kadoshim. Calidus kicked his horse on. Uthas lengthened his stride to keep pace.

They powered through shadowed woods and then burst into sunshine, Uthas blinking for a moment against the glare of daylight.

They were in a valley, the river flowing fast through its middle, meadows rolling either side into hills. Ahead of them lay a village, faint screams drifting on the breeze. A handful of the Kadoshim were running towards it, faster than Uthas thought possible.

By the time Uthas and Calidus caught up with them villagers were scattering in all directions, Kadoshim flooding the streets, crashing through doors and windows, killing anything that moved with a childlike glee.

'I need to work on their discipline,' Calidus said, glancing casually at a Kadoshim pinning a screaming man down, taking bites out of his throat.

'They must learn to control themselves,' Uthas said in horror. 'They cannot behave like this throughout the Banished Lands – the whole world will turn against you.'

'I know, but they are new to their bodies and this world. I remember the wonder when I first became flesh. And the taste of it . . .' He paused, eyes wistful. 'And besides, they have had only brot for a ten-night. A little indulgence, one last time.'

'They are animals,' Salach muttered beside Uthas.

'As are we all,' Calidus said flatly. 'Creatures of flesh and blood that must consume flesh and blood to live.'

Uthas saw a Kadoshim leap from a rooftop, land running and dive onto a fleeing bairn, roll with it, biting and wrenching. The child's high and terror-filled scream suddenly cut short.

Nathair and his draig thundered into the village. Someone burst from a shuttered window, falling into the street: a woman, a Kadoshim peering out from between the broken shutters behind her. Nathair viewed the carnage with a flat stare, his lips twisting briefly in distaste.

'There is no need for this,' Nathair called over his shoulder to Calidus. 'They are slaughtering innocents.'

'The unfortunate casualties of war,' Calidus called back.

Nathair just stared at him.

'I have neglected to teach the Kadoshim the code of combat,' Calidus said. 'They are fresh to this world. I shall rectify that soon.'

'Not soon enough for these,' Nathair said.

'Aye, but not all here are innocents,' Calidus answered. 'Look ahead.'

Other villagers were making a stand by the roundhouse, clutching weapons — spears and axes bristling. Some of the Kadoshim were learning to use their weapons, harnessing the memories of their hosts. With a last shake of his head Nathair whispered to his draig and led a handful of the Kadoshim at the villagers, the Kadoshim with swords drawn, swinging with greater speed and strength than any human could possibly manage, even the Jehar. The draig crashed into the knot of warriors, Kadoshim behind, and then limbs were spinning through the air, blood spraying and in moments the resistance was shattered.

'We shall make camp here,' Calidus declared, looking at the sun sinking into the hills to the west. Screaming drifted about them, the stench of blood and excrement thick in the air. Uthas and Salach shared a look and marched on, through the village and out the other side. Survivors were running through the fields, Kadoshim hunting them like hounds chasing down hares. A group of villagers reached woodland to the south, disappearing into the shadows, but a handful of Kadoshim saw them and followed.

'You'd better call your kin back in, before they get lost in the woods.'

'They are like bairns,' Calidus said fondly.

More screams drifted from the woods.

CHAPTER EIGHTEEN

CORBAN

Corban snapped awake, jerking to one elbow. Instinctively he reached for Storm, but she was not there.

It felt as if something had woken him. *A scream? Was it a dream?* He rubbed his eyes, stopped himself when he realized he was still wearing his wolven gauntlet, and climbed to his feet. They had made camp close to the river; the trees were widely spaced here. The ground was damp with dew, the world fresh and new for a few moments beneath the sun's first rays, yet Corban felt tired already. He had hardly slept, the weight of his decision bearing down upon him, though it seemed that the rest of the world had snored quite contentedly around him.

We will fight. He had felt sure yesterday, once he'd made the decision, determined. Now, though, he found himself hoping that Rhin's warband would turn away and march east or west, anywhere but across their path – wishful thinking. By now they would have come across the trail of Corban's warband. He was resigned to battle now.

An idea had formed in his mind yesterday when he'd seen the terrain of the land, based on his memory of an ambush that Camlin had orchestrated back in Cambren. He had consulted with Meical, Tukul and Balur, and they had agreed on his strategy. The bulk of the warband would remain within the woods where they were camped and would emerge to face the enemy warband head on. A smaller force, a score of giants and a hundred Jehar, were hidden on the slopes to the west, a flanking ambush. Meical would lead them. Between them the plan was to pin Rhin's warriors against the banks of the river and crush them.

A Jehar appeared close by – Akar, captain of the Jehar that had travelled with Nathair. He held a warning finger up to his lips.

Corban heard it again then. A scream to his left, distant, filtering through the woods. At first he thought it was a fox, the cry high pitched and childlike. Then he heard another, closer, straight ahead. Akar gripped the sword hilt upon his back but did not draw, other Jehar guards moving about them, more rousing from sleep. A figure emerged from the shadows – a Jehar running swift and silent, a guard from deeper within the wood.

'People are out there, coming this way,' he breathed to Akar and Corban.

'Who? How many?' Akar asked.

'Hard to tell. They sound scattered through the forest.'

Hooves drummed behind him and he turned to see Coralen riding into the camp, back from a night's reconnoitring to the south. Storm and Buddai were with her, Jehar riders at her back.

That's where you've been, he thought, looking at Storm.

Coralen reined in before him, opened her mouth to speak, then her eyes stared past him, deeper into the woods.

Light streamed in broken patches through the canopy above, punctuating the perpetual woodland twilight. Undergrowth crackled and voices called out. Corban could make out a group of people staggering through the trees towards him – twenty, thirty people, maybe more. Behind them shapes moved. Fast. A woman hugging a child to her chest ran stumbling into the undergrowth. Something rose from the ground behind her, blood dripping from its chin.

Kadoshim.

Corban felt a shiver of fear course through him, somewhere along the way transforming into a white-hot rage. He heard a giant bellowing in its guttural language, then he was yelling his own battle-cry, running at it, swinging his sword. Two dozen strides and he was almost upon it. His mind flickered to his last encounter with a Kadoshim; this time his rage didn't blind him, instead he focused it, the world evaporating away, leaving only the pale, black-veined creature before him. He feinted high with his sword, shifted his weight and twisted his wrist, swinging suddenly low, putting his hips into it, the weight and strength of his back and shoulder. His wolven claws caught the Kadoshim's blade as it swept high to block a blow that didn't land, Corban's sword hacking into the creature's leg, just above the boot. There was a meaty slap, Corban's blade shearing almost clear through the leg, lodging in bone, then his momentum was carrying him past the Kadoshim, one of its hands reaching out, snatching at his cloak. He staggered away with the Kadoshim lunging after him, swung his wolven claws, cutting into a hand. Severed fingers fell away and he was free, the creature stumbling as its injured leg betrayed it.

There was snarling and then Storm smashed into it, teeth ripping at its throat, hurling it to the ground. Corban yelled a command, fearful as he remembered the injuries she'd sustained from her last encounter with the Kadoshim. Reluctantly she released her grip and backed away, snarling at the fallen enemy as it scrabbled on the ground, pushing itself upright, Corban's sword still lodged in its leg.

Then the Jehar were there: Akar first, others close behind, Gar amongst them, swirling about the injured Kadoshim, their swords gleaming as they sliced and cut. The Kadoshim's sword was a blur as it blocked a dozen blows, snaking out and drawing blood. A Jehar warrior staggered back, gurgling as blood jetted from his throat, but no one could defend against a sustained attack from half a dozen Jehar at once, not even a demon from the Otherworld. Corban saw a severed hand spinning through the air, thick black blood trailing it, the Kadoshim still struggling forwards, grabbing at those around it, its face twisted with hatred.

Abruptly it was over; there was an explosion of shadow above the Kadoshim, the demon's winged spirit emptying from its headless host, a frustrated screech and then it was gone, evaporating into the morning air.

'Better that you hang on to this,' Gar said reprovingly as he returned Corban's sword. 'You won't take a head off with one swing of those claws.'

Around them small pockets of combat raged. For a moment Corban had feared that the entire host of the Kadoshim had descended upon them, but now he saw there were only a score at most, all of them surrounded by Jehar and giants. Even as he looked, Balur took the head from one with his black axe.

But why are they here? And how far behind is the rest of their host? He stared into the gloom, searching for any hint of movement, of a host hidden just beyond sight.

He watched as Coralen spurred her horse past him, towards the woman and bairn that he had seen earlier. They were still running, a dark shadow chasing them.

Coralen angled her course to head off the Kadoshim, swerving around trees, crashing through undergrowth. Corban felt a flush of fear, a weightlessness in his belly, and started running.

The Kadoshim leaped a fallen tree and was upon its prey, the three of them falling in a tangle of limbs, the child flying free, snagging in a bush of thorns. The Kadoshim and woman came to a halt, the Kadoshim on top, pinning the woman down. Its teeth sank into her shoulder, ripped away a chunk of flesh. The woman screamed.

It's eating her.

Then Coralen was upon them, leaping from her horse as it hurtled by. She crashed into the Kadoshim, rolled with it, somehow got her feet into its belly and sent it flying through the air, crunching into a tree trunk.

She rolled to a crouch, drew her blade as she rose, without pause surged forwards, her sword a blur. The Kadoshim pushed away from the tree, drew its own sword. Their blades clashed, a cascade of sparks bright in the woodland shadow, ringing out, five, six blows, faster than Corban could follow. Coralen was ducking, pivoting, slashing with sword and claws, the Kadoshim countering and striking with a force that sent Coralen reeling away. It followed, relentless, blood welling from half a dozen cuts, struck again, Coralen tripping and falling to the ground, cracking her head on a moss-covered stone.

The Kadoshim stood over her, sword raised, then staggered back a pace, an arrow jutting from its chest. Something else slammed into it, snapping its head back, a knife hilt protruding from an eye socket. The Kadoshim's remaining good eye fixed on Coralen, who was trying to stand, and it surged towards her, a bloody butchered mess that still radiated menace and power.

Corban jumped over Coralen, still on her knees, and stood before her to meet the Kadoshim, sword raised two-handed over his head. The Kadoshim's mouth shifted – smile or snarl, he could not tell – then their blades met, a crunch that numbed Corban's wrists. They traded blows, Corban forcing the creature back a step, then another.

It's weakening. He swept its sword up, turned his parry into a downward cut, chopping through its wrist, severing its sword hand, kicked it in the chest, sending it staggering back another few steps. An arrow slammed into its belly, another knife followed, and Corban was aware of figures closing all around them: Jehar, giants, Storm and Buddai snarling behind them. Farrell appeared beside him, hefting his war-hammer. It was black with blood.

The Kadoshim powered forwards; Farrell smashed his hammer into the creature's chest. Bones shattered, flesh mangled as the Kadoshim flew backwards. Then Corban's sword flashed, hacked into the Kadoshim's neck, half severing its head. It jerked, tried to turn and grab Corban. Farrell gripped its wrists as Corban's sword rose and fell again. The head fell away, black shadow-like oil pouring from the severed neck, rising to take winged shape, then drifting apart, a frayed and tattered banner.

Corban stood there, chest heaving; everyone around him stared for a frozen moment.

'Elyon's stones, but they're hard to kill,' panted Farrell.

'Too hard,' Corban agreed, feeling the notches in his sword. He patted the flat head of Farrell's war-hammer. 'You need a blade for them.'

'Aye.'

He walked to Coralen, who was on her feet but still groggy.

'Thank you,' she said. He squeezed her arm.

Cywen put her foot on the Kadoshim's severed head and pulled her knife from its eye. Brina was crouching over the woman it had attacked, staunching the blood from her injury. Corban looked around and saw the combat was over. *But for how long?* Pockets of Jehar and giants spread out amongst the woods, searching for any survivors. *Meical is right: there is no running away from this God-War. I ran from Dun Carreg all the way to Domhain, and it followed me. I travelled to the far north and walked into the middle of it. And now it finds me again. It cannot be escaped. At best I can choose where and how I fight.* He took a deep breath.

'We need to get out of here,' he said to no one in particular.

'Gather the Kadoshim heads,' Tukul yelled beside him.

They formed up on the meadow beyond the woods, gathering up any who had survived the Kadoshim attack in the woods, of which there were at least a score. Corban searched out Brina. She and Cywen were tending the wounded. Three Jehar and a young giant had died and were laid out on the grass, having cairns piled around them. Brina was applying a salve to the shoulder of the woman whom Coralen had saved. She was grimacing with pain; her child, a girl of seven or eight summers sat silently in the grass beside her. She was plucking meadow flowers, twirling them between dirty fingers.

Corban knelt beside the woman.

'What is your name?'

'Teca,' the woman said.

'Where are you from, Teca?' Corban asked her.

She stared at him. 'You helped me. You and the girl, red hair.'

'You had a lot more help than just us two,' he said. 'I need to know, where are you from?'

She told him of her village, of a host of the Kadoshim arriving, led by a warrior riding upon a great draig.

'Some stayed and fought. I ran,' she said. Tears welled in her eyes.

'You were wise to.' Corban gripped her hand. 'There is no standing against them yet. Did they all chase after you, are they close behind?'

'I don't know,' she breathed through clenched lips as Brina bound a strip of linen about her shoulder.

'Would you come with me, please?' Corban asked Brina when she was done.

'What for?'

'I wanted to talk to you about something. And I'm about to make a decision: I'd value your advice.'

She blinked at him. 'Do you have a fever?' she asked him.

'Sarcasm isn't an attractive quality, and it's also not very helpful.'

She shrugged and followed him, the sound of flapping wings accompanying them.

Corban gathered up what was becoming his war council: Meical, Balur and Ethlinn, Tukul, Gar and Brina. He noticed Cywen had also joined them. Craf and Fech were nearby.

He felt the familiar tingle of fear. *I am making plans, changing plans, and people's lives will depend on my choices.* The weight of that was huge. He closed his eyes and gathered his thoughts.

'The plan has to change,' he said to them. 'Calidus, Nathair and a host of the Kadoshim are behind us, to the north. At best they are a day's ride away, at worst . . .' He shrugged, looking at the dark wall of trees behind them.

'And what about Rhin's warband?' Meical asked him.

He paused. *When I speak it, there's no going back.* Took a deep breath. 'Can't go around, so we'll have to go through them.'

'Is that wise?' Brina said. 'You risk being ensnared with one foe while another gets to stab you in the back.'

I asked her for advice, not criticism. Though the two are often entwined where Brina is concerned.

'My da used to tell me, don't hit if you can help it, but if you have to, hit fast, and hit hard.' Corban saw a grin split Gar's face and he heard Cywen grunt. *They remember him saying that, too.*

'That makes sense,' Meical agreed. 'But how? Ride straight at them? Many will likely be lost.'

'I've had a few thoughts about that.' Corban said. 'I think I have an idea.'

CHAPTER NINETEEN

CAMLIN

Camlin peered through a crack in the roundhouse's shutters, loosely holding his bow and a nocked arrow. The sound of hooves was growing louder. He swore quietly.

I wanted them to ride around. Why the hell do they want to come back to this stinking hole? And he didn't mean that metaphorically. The roundhouse stank of death, flies buzzing in lazy circles around half a dozen corpses of villagers who had obviously sought refuge there. He'd had a superficial look around, wondering why Rhin's warriors had been in here, but a quick glance had revealed little, and the sound of hooves bearing down upon them outside hadn't helped his concentration. When the news of riders approaching had reached them, Edana had looked to Camlin. He'd been frozen for a moment, conflicting interests warring in his brain, then ordered them all into the roundhouse, pausing a few moments to unclasp a few of the black and gold cloaks from Rhin's fallen warriors.

Once upon a time it would have been a simple decision – prepare for an ambush, use the buildings around the town square. Spread our swords. If it came to it, kill and run. Regroup at an appointed spot.

Now, though, he had twenty-six lives other than his own to think of. That included a deposed king and queen and an eight-year-old girl. Meg, the bairn they'd found hiding in the stables, was sitting by his leg. She didn't talk much, but every time he moved she moved with him, straying no further from him than his shadow.

He frowned as he glanced down at her now.

The shutters started to shake, the drumming of hooves becoming deafening.

There's a lot of them. Just gets better.

So his plan had been to stick together and hide. Hide and hope they passed through.

He looked over his shoulder, saw pale, serious faces staring back at him. Roisin stood at the back of the hall, a dozen of her shieldmen tight about her. Lorcan was close to them, sitting on a blanket-covered chest, his feet dangling. He glimpsed Vonn and Baird, backs bent, digging at the wattle and daub wall with spear and sword. *Always need an escape route. If they find us . . .*

We'll deal with that if it happens.

He peered through the crack in the shutter again. It was sunset, the sky was a wash of pink and orange clouds, shadows long and wide. *That's in our favour, at least.*

He felt a presence behind him: Edana, trying to peer over his shoulder.

'You should get back,' Camlin whispered.

She ignored him.

Riders thundered into view, spreading around the edges of the market square. *No horse wants to stand on a corpse.* Camlin counted sixty, but he could hear more beyond his vision, hooves thumping on the hard-packed earth.

The warrior at their head sat tall in his saddle with an easy grace about him. He was clothed in a shirt of gleaming mail and a black leather surcoat, a sable cloak draping his shoulders.

'Morcant,' Edana whispered venomously.

Camlin shared her hatred, remembering the last time he had seen the man. Back in the Darkwood Morcant had led the ambush on Queen Alona, Edana's mam. Both of them had been taken prisoner, as well as Cywen, Corban's sister. Soon after, Morcant had ordered Cywen's death, and that had been the last straw for Camlin. He'd drawn his sword and stood in front of her.

What kind of fool am I, standing against Rhin's first-sword? Even now he couldn't explain exactly why he'd done it.

'Don't do anything stupid,' he whispered.

'He's evil.'

'I know. But let's live long enough to kill him and tell the tale.'

Edana glared, then gave a sharp nod.

Morcant turned. Camlin saw him take a deep breath and wrinkle his nose.

'Let's make this quick,' Morcant said to the warrior beside him. 'I don't want to stay here any longer than I have to. Bring them up.' He paused, looking across the square to the roundhouse. 'Where are the guards I left?'

Camlin wrapped one of the cloaks about his shoulders, threw one to Baird and the two of them stepped into the roundhouse doors. Camlin raised a hand to Morcant.

'Ah,' Morcant said. He stared a moment, but then another rider appeared, leading a line of half a dozen riders by a rope, men and women with hands bound sitting upon them. Prisoners.

'Look around you,' Morcant said to them, languidly gesturing with a hand to the corpse-strewn ground. 'This is what happens when I am defied. This could happen in your village too.' He tapped his heels against his mount, guided it through the dead to the gallows, where he pushed at the body of one of the hanging bairns. It spun lazily in the fading sun. 'Men, women, children. I will spare *no one.*'

One of the villagers on horseback bent over and vomited.

Morcant's horse picked its way back to them.

'It doesn't have to be like this. All you have to do is tell me. Where are the outlaws based?'

'We don't know,' one of the prisoners said, a white-haired woman. 'We are peaceful people, we want no trouble.'

'Neither do I,' Morcant said. 'I'd rather get my task finished and be on my way back to Dun Carreg. Marsh life is not for me.' As if to emphasize his point, he slapped at a mosquito that had landed on his neck. 'So tell me where they are. My patience is wearing, my temper fraying.'

'You're a monster,' one of the younger men snarled, 'a woman-killer, a bairn-slayer.' He spat in Morcant's face.

Morcant's expression shifted from annoyance to blind rage in a heartbeat. In a blur his arm moved, there was the ring of iron and a head was spinning through the air, Morcant's face splattered with the dead man's blood.

'I. Am not. A monster.' Morcant calmly cleaned his blade on the headless corpse's shirt. Slowly it toppled back in the saddle and slumped to the ground. He sheathed his sword and with the hem of his cloak wiped the dead man's blood and spittle from his face. 'I do, however, admit to a temper. It gets the better of me sometimes. As to what I did here – in my defence, the people of this village did more than just refuse me information. I had reason to believe that they were supplying provisions to the outlaws in the marshes.' He shrugged. 'That could not be allowed to continue.'

He rode along the line of the remaining prisoners, his hand resting lightly on the hilt of his sword. 'I do not just punish those who oppose me. I reward those who help me. I will pay well for the right information. Enough silver to feed and clothe your entire village for a year. Or you could just share it between the five of you. Our secret.'

'You're lying,' one of them muttered.

'Am I? There's a chest full of silver in that roundhouse. Bring it out.'

Camlin looked at Baird, then back into the roundhouse. He stared at Lorcan, who looked at him in horror, lifted the blanket off the chest he was sitting upon and kicked it with his heel. It chinked. Everyone in the room stared at him.

Asroth's stones. And I call myself a thief. I'm ashamed.

'Bring out the chest,' Morcant called impatiently.

'Some help,' Baird shouted back, then shrugged at Camlin.

Morcant gestured to two warriors. 'Go fetch it for me.' The warriors rode towards the roundhouse.

'Baird, Vonn, how's that bolt-hole coming?' Camlin snapped.

'Nearly there,' Vonn hissed.

They heard horses come to a stand outside the roundhouse, boots hit the ground. Footsteps.

No time now. Everyone scrambled for the dark corners of the room, hiding behind an overturned table, chairs, anything. Camlin shoved Edana behind him and drew his knife.

The wooden doors creaked open. It was dusk now, almost dark in the roundhouse. A weak wash of light filtered a little way into the room, silhouetting the warriors as they strode inside. Camlin let them take a few steps in, out of sight from the square, then leaped forwards, one hand clamping over a mouth, his knife plunging into a back, slicing between ribs, puncturing a lung. The warrior in his grip stiffened, hissed. Camlin stabbed again, and again. The other warrior was turning, sword already half out of its scabbard, his mouth open, drawing breath to yell.

A sword crunched into his neck, cutting deep, blood spurting. The sword swung again, wildly, hit him in the face, taking off half his jaw and spinning him. Teeth, blood and bone sprayed as he collapsed to the floor.

Camlin turned, saw Edana standing with her sword gripped in both hands. She was staring at the fallen warrior. Camlin peered through the shutter.

No one's noticed. Yet. He swept up his bow and arrow and ran to the back wall, where Baird and Vonn had finally cut a hole in the wall. Pale light seeped through. *We've about a fast count to thirty, if we're lucky . . .*

'Out, now,' he hissed.

Cian was first through, Roisin behind him, another half-dozen shieldmen straight after. Camlin stuck his head through the hole.

'Don't wait – head south, to the river. Saw some boats – they're our best chance.' He searched the room for the bairn Meg, jumped a little when he saw her standing beside him. 'Meg, show Cian the way to the river and boats.'

'You coming?' she asked.

'I'll be along after.'

She chewed at her lip a moment, then nodded, slipped through the hole and sprinted off into the dusk. Cian and the others hurried after her.

Edana was still standing by the door, clutching her sword. Vonn was whispering to her, but to no apparent effect. Camlin strode over, took one look at her and shook her by the shoulders.

'You've killed a man,' he hissed at Edana. 'Good. He was your enemy and would have killed you. Now sheathe your sword and get out, 'fore someone else comes and tries to kill you.'

She blinked at him, then nodded, tried to sheathe her sword but her hands were shaking. Baird helped her and hurried her through the hole in the wall, other warriors following.

Morcant's voice called out and Camlin felt his heart freeze. Hooves, footsteps.

'Move,' Camlin hissed, pushing men through the hole. 'Lorcan, you next.'

'I shall wait with you and defend Edana's escape.'

Camlin sighed.

There were only a handful of them left: Camlin and Lorcan, a couple of Roisin's shieldmen, one of them Brogan – the shieldman with the barrel of herring still strapped to his back – and Vonn.

Camlin calmly pulled a handful of arrows from the quiver at his belt and stabbed them into the ground.

Feet drummed at the doors, warriors strode in, half a dozen at least. They saw Camlin and his companions, froze a heartbeat or two and Camlin put an arrow through the first man's throat. He fell back in a spray of blood, crashing into those behind him. Draw, breathe, release, and Camlin put another arrow into them. Then they were charging, calling to their comrades outside as they came.

Vonn was through the hole.

Camlin nocked, drew, released, another warrior stumbled to the ground, tripping others behind him.

One of Lorcan's shieldmen shouted a battle-cry and ran at the warriors. He swung his sword two-handed, gutted the first man he reached, ploughed into the others shoulder first, sending them all staggering.

'Come on,' Vonn yelled through the hole.

'Time to go,' Camlin said to Lorcan, grabbing him by the shoulder and shoving him through.

'You next, big man,' Camlin told Brogan, at the same time drawing his bow and releasing. More warriors in black and gold were crowding through the roundhouse doors. Brogan grunted, stuck in the gap, as the barrel on his back wedged tight. Camlin took a step back and hurled himself at the warrior, both of them exploding through the wall. Camlin rolled on the ground, looked back, saw feet pounding towards them and caught a glimpse of the chest full of silver. He gave one last wistful look at it. *Once upon a time . . .* Then he was running. Vonn and Lorcan were just ahead of him, swerving between wattle-and-daub buildings, Brogan hard on his heels. Hooves were drumming, warriors yelling somewhere behind him, far too close for Camlin's liking.

The river, find the river. It was near dark, a bluish tinge to the air as the sun faded. Camlin heard the sound of water, ran around a hut, stopped to yank open the gate of a pig pen and then ran on. There was a stampede of feet and squealing pigs, followed almost immediately by swearing, crashing, falling. Camlin grinned and then burst out of the village onto the riverbank.

The boats were tied along the bank, Roisin and Cian already in a canoe, a dozen others sat in boats, pushing away from the bank into the wide, sluggish river.

'Lorcan,' Roisin cried out when she saw her son, and he clambered in beside her.

Baird stood over Edana in a larger flat-bottomed boat, gesturing frantically to them. Then a hand was slipping into his, Mcg, tugging him towards the boat. He didn't need much encouragement, rushed to the riverbank and boarded.

Horses thundered along the bank, warriors yelling. Spears whistled past them, splashing and disappearing into the river. Close by someone screamed and fell from a boat.

'Upriver, into the marshes,' Camlin yelled as he saw a coracle with two warriors in it start to paddle downriver.

It'll be faster going downriver, but they'll track us with no problem. Only chance is to head into the marshes.

Then Camlin saw Morcant. He burst from between two huts, saw the boats pushing into the river and snarled. Camlin nocked another arrow, drew and sighted, aiming for Morcant's chest. A spear suddenly slammed into Brogan; the big man grunted and dropped the steering pole, the boat veering. Camlin's arrow skittered wide as he tried to regain his balance. Swearing loudly, he drew another arrow from his quiver but the boat was starting to spin, caught in the sluggish current. Camlin clambered to his feet, the boat rocking; he grabbed the pole and started pushing. In seconds they were moving in the right direction, heading upstream into the marshes with half a dozen other river craft. Brogan groaned and pushed himself up.

'Thought you were dead,' Camlin said to the big warrior.

'Spear hit the barrel of fish on my back.' Brogan grinned and held up a herring from the shattered barrel. Baird laughed, the sound strange amidst the panic and fear of their flight.

'Come on, fish-man, lend a hand,' Baird said.

Morcant was leading riders along the bank, shadowing the boats.

'Meg, do you know your way around these marshes?'

'A bit,' the girl confessed.

'Appreciate it if you'd be our eyes, take us where they can't follow.'

It did not take long before Meg was guiding them off of the main river down narrower tributaries, ever south and east, sometimes pushing their way through great banks of reeds, sometimes coasting like ghosts on the liquid dark, always heading deeper into the marshes. It was darker now, the moon and stars veiled by ragged cloud. Camlin watched with satisfaction as their pursuit slowed, the terrain becoming unnavigable for the horses in the dark.

Eventually Camlin heard a splash and a horse neigh wildly. Before they disappeared into the darkness Camlin saw a rider come close to the bank. For a moment the clouds cleared and moonlight shone bright upon them, silvering the dark river and the warrior upon his mount. It was Morcant, and he stared straight at him. Camlin returned the gaze with a mocking grin.

CHAPTER TWENTY

FIDELE

Fidele watched Maquin as he gutted and skinned a rabbit, his movements efficient and practised.

If I were alone out here I would have starved to death long ago. She felt a surge of frustration as she observed Maquin, a moment of shame at how useless she was proving to be. *What can I actually do? Run through woodland, and that not very well. Rule? And I didn't prove to be too successful at that, either.* She felt a wave of shame, thought of how the world had changed in so short a time. *It was not so long ago that I dwelt in Jerolin with my husband and son. Now Aquilus is dead, Nathair gone who knows where, and I am living hand-to-mouth in the wild. Who even sits on the throne in Jerolin now? Who rules the people of Tenebral? My people.* She felt a failure, felt that she'd let down all those who depended upon her.

All of those years living a life of service, bound by duty and honour. Aquilus was almost a stranger through our last years of marriage, so consumed and driven by Meical's prophecy, and yet it all came to nothing, ended by a traitor's blade. And Nathair, my own son, left me and then chose Lykos over me. She felt a flush of anger – the two men in her life whom she had trusted wholeheartedly, both abandoning her. Neither of them taking her into their confidences. The emotion was swiftly followed by shame - *Aquilus was a good man, just preoccupied by these dangerous times. And Nathair is a good man, again, swept away by the dark times we live in.*

As I have been.

But I was betrayed. It all changed with the letter from Nathair, his orders for me to step down as regent of Tenebral and hand over the stewardship of the realm to Lykos. Why did he do that? How could Nathair side with Lykos? I fear for him. Have they bewitched him too? Or is he just misled, deceived? With an effort she focused on Maquin, wrenching her thoughts away from their dark spiral, forcing herself to watch Maquin's hands as he prepared the meat for their evening meal.

They had stopped a little earlier than usual, the sun still a handspan above the horizon as Maquin had set snares around a network of burrows that he had spied. She'd watched with fascination as he'd cut, looped and tied twine to overhanging branches, bending and pegging them to the earth, and then settled beneath a densely leaved oak a score of paces away. It had been dark when she finally heard the snap and creak of the snare tripping. Maquin had grinned at her, a rare thing, transforming his dour expression.

'Hot meat for our supper,' he'd said.

She couldn't express how happy she was about that. It had been raining all day, a soft drizzle that had soaked her through long before highsun. Maquin's hard pace had allowed no time for rest, keeping her breathless and exhausted as usual. She was glad to stop before the darkness settled about them.

'Is a fire safe?' she asked as Maquin searched for kindling that wasn't soaked through, cutting away at a rotted branch to reach the dry wood within.

'So much cloud, and it's so low, smoke shouldn't give us away, and we've gone a ten-night since we last saw any Vin Thalun. I can bank and hide the fire, keep the flames low and covered. Reckon it's worth the risk, eh? Feels like my bones are damp.'

I'm glad to hear him say that. He seems inhuman, all of him distilled down to strength and will. Maquin skewered the quartered meat of the rabbit and set it on a spit above the small fire.

They were a ten-night into the heartland of Tenebral, keeping as much as possible to the dense woodlands that carpeted the undulating landscape.

After that night in the woods when Maquin had slain the Vin Thalun – *with some help from me* – they had set out east. Fidele had still not recovered from that night – she had killed a man. She'd put her spear through his throat, and had had nightmares about it ever since. *Idiot woman. He was my enemy, would have killed Maquin and then me.*

'Teach me how to do that,' she asked abruptly, nodding at the rabbit.

'Don't think it's something for a fine lady's hands,' Maquin said.

'Well, it should be,' Fidele snapped. 'What use am I, otherwise? I am like an infant, unable to fend for myself.'

Maquin shrugged. 'We all learn what we need to,' he said. 'People like you learn how to govern, give orders. People like me, to do what we're told. To learn something useful.'

'And what is your useful trade, then?' Fidele asked him.

'Death. I deal in death.'

His gaze dropped to his hands, and her eyes followed. They were surprisingly fine and long-fingered, like a musician's hands at court, though as he turned them she saw thick calluses on his fingers and palms, the whorls of his skin marked by earth or blood.

'I'll teach you to catch a rabbit, prepare it for cooking, make a fire, if you'd like. Though there may not be another opportunity before we reach Ripa.'

If we reach Ripa.

The injured warrior of Tenebral, Drusus, had died the same night, but not before he'd told them that Peritus had set a rendez-vous point with every member of his small rebellion. Ripa, fortress of Lamar. That had made sense to Fidele, as Lamar and his eldest son Krelis had always borne an ill-concealed hatred for the Vin Thalun. *If anyone would declare openly against the Vin Thalun it would be Lamar of Ripa.*

Maquin passed her a piece of the quartered rabbit and she bit into it, burning her lips but not caring, it tasted so delicious. She realized Maquin was watching her and she wiped her mouth.

'Sorry, not very ladylike.'

'Don't mind me,' Maquin said. 'It all goes down the same.'

'Tell me, Maquin. How did a man of Isiltir end up here?'

'It's a long story,' Maquin grunted.

'And we have many dark nights ahead of us. You don't have to finish it all tonight.'

He stared silently at the fire a while, as if trying to remember.

'I was shieldman to Kastell ben Aenor. His cousin, Jael, killed him in the tombs beneath Haldis. He killed Romar, King of Isiltir as well, though he didn't hold the blade.' He spoke to the fire, not taking his eyes from the flicker of the flames. 'I fought against Jael in Isiltir. Lykos came with his Vin Thalun and turned the battle.' He paused, as if remembering. A hand lifted to his ear, which Fidele noticed was only a stump. 'I was captured. Lykos took me as part of his spoils, put me on an oar-bench, gave me this.' Maquin touched the scar on his back, where Lykos had branded him.

He speaks as if it didn't happen to him, as if he is recounting someone else's tale.

'He threw me in the pit, told me that if I lived long enough he'd set me free, that I could seek my vengeance on Jael.'

'Is that what you want?'

He looked up at her now, his eyes dark pools, a glint of firelight a spark in their depths.

'Aye, with all that I am.'

Fidele resisted the urge to recoil at the hatred she heard in his voice. It emanated from him, throbbing like the pulse of a wound. He had spoken of Lykos, and at that name she had felt her own anger stir and bubble.

'I feel the same about Lykos,' she whispered fiercely. 'I hate him. I am scared of him too. If he lives I would wish to spend my life hunting him until he were dead. But another voice within me says that I would run, as far and as fast as I could to escape him. To the very edges of the world.' She ground her teeth, fear, anger, shame, all swirling through her.

'He's high on my list of people to see dead, I'll not deny,' Maquin said. 'If he's not already dead. I saw you put that knife into him; it went deep. Wouldn't be surprised if you killed him.'

'Aye, maybe. And then again, he may still live.'

Maquin shrugged. 'Can't change that. Yet.'

'No, but it doesn't stop me being scared. Don't you feel fear?'

'Fear? I left that in the pit. I have nothing left to lose, nothing to fear for. I have lost everything – my kin, Kastell, my sword-brothers. My pride. In the pit I lost my honour and humanity. All that's left is revenge.'

'Then why are you here?'

He shrugged again. 'I made you a promise.'

'You were going to break your promise, though. You left me. You walked away.'

He stared at her. *Why did I say that?*

'I did. I won't do that again. Not until you're safe.'

The effect of those words was comforting, seeping through her like hot soup on a cold day.

'I didn't blame you for leaving. Or judge you.'

'I judged me. That was enough.'

Fidele woke to a touch, Maquin's hand on her shoulder. She half rose, then paused as she saw his face.

'What's wrong?' she said.

'Listen.'

She did.

'What is that?'

'Hounds,' Maquin said. 'We have to go. Now.'

She leaped to her feet and in moments they were hurrying through the undergrowth.

Fidele hoped that Maquin was mistaken, or that the hounds were just a coincidence, out on a hunt with a local woodsman. But all morning the sounds trailed them, becoming clearer, an excited baying. The land around them changed, the woodland growing denser, the ground rising into a steady incline. The scent of pine grew around them as they climbed higher, the woodland opening up, pine needles dense and spongy underfoot. The baying behind them was louder now, and Fidele had started looking over her shoulder, fearing to see hounds and men behind her.

'They are a league or so behind us,' Maquin said.

'They sound . . . so close,' Fidele gasped.

'Sound carries in this woodland,' Maquin grunted. 'But they were double that distance away at daybreak.'

What are we going to do? She was walking with a spear in her hand, the same one that she had used to kill the Vin Thalun. Now, though, she was using it as a crutch to keep herself upright. Her grip on its shaft tightened. Sweat ran down her face, dripping into her eyes, stinging, her lungs heaving, the aching in her legs a constant companion. They were following a fox trail. *Animals know the way through the forest better than I do*, Maquin had said to her. *Better to trust them than try cutting a new way through the undergrowth.* Blessedly, the ground levelled beneath them, to one side a cliff rising steep and sheer, pines crowding close on the other. A new sound made itself known, growing with each step. Running water.

Maquin pulled up in front of her and grabbed her about the waist as she stumbled past him, her legs not instantly obeying the order to stop. She was glad he did.

A ravine opened up in front of her, a river roaring through it some distance below. She fell to her knees, sucking in great lungfuls of air.

'What are we going to do,' she asked.

'Well. If the dogs weren't onto us I'd say we climb down this ravine and swim for a bit. Come out a few leagues downriver. It would take a huntsman a ten-night to pick up our trail again, if ever they could find it.'

'Let's do that, then.'

'No point. They'll know we've used the river, and with those hounds they'll pick up our scent and trail again within a day; we'll be back to square one.'

Hunted again. Death breathing down our necks, again.

'I am sorry to bring this upon you.'

'Well, I'll not deny, you're proving to be a great deal of trouble.'

'So what do we do?' Fidele felt that old companion squirming in her belly. Fear. *I cannot be caught. I cannot go back to Lykos.*

Maquin reached inside his bag and pulled out the ball of twine he'd taken from the woodcutters' hut.

'Got to kill those hounds.'

Fidele crouched behind a tree, peering back down the track in the twilight.

The sun was setting behind the treetop canopy, its last rays dappling the ground pink and orange. Fidele thought she saw movement.

Please Elyon, let it be Maquin.

He had set out his plan to her – if it could be called that – and left her soon after. Fear had been steadily filling her since then, like the drip of ice melting into a bucket.

No. I will not die scared. Or live scared any longer. Maquin is right. There is nothing I can do other than face it. She gripped her spear tightly.

A figure emerged out of the gloom: Maquin sprinting towards her and skidding to the ground beside her.

'Well, I think I got their attention,' he said through ragged breaths.

Men were visible on the path now, the first one straining to control three hounds, all barking frantically and straining on their leashes.

'Didn't think there'd be three,' Maquin muttered, pulling one of the many knives he carried. 'Woodsmen usually hunt with two.'

He stood and let their pursuers see him.

The first man let the dogs go, all three of them bursting along the path towards Maquin. They were big grey-coated hounds with broad heads and wide muzzles, the type she'd seen bring down boars when accompanying Aquilus on hunts. Their bared teeth glinted in the twilight.

We're dead.

One pulled ahead of the others, tongue lolling, so close that Fidele could see the muscles of his chest and shoulders bunching and flowing with each ground-eating stride. He stumbled on something across his path and suddenly the undergrowth was in motion, a long branch whipping out of nowhere, sharp spikes slamming into the hound's flank, impaling it a dozen times. It howled, squirmed, the howls slipping to a whine, then it slumped, blood dripping from its mouth.

The other two hounds paid it no attention, surging past.

'Remember, do what I told you,' Maquin hissed as he spread his feet, crouching, drawing another knife. Fidele shifted the weight of her spear, eyes focused on the nearest hound. It was thirty paces away now. A heartbeat, and it was twenty. She shuffled involuntarily backwards, heard the roar of the river behind her, set her feet.

The hound jolted to a stop, one leg wrenched into the air, its body swinging around, dragging on the branch that it was now snared to. Fidele held her breath but the snare and branch held. The other hound powered past it and leapt at Maquin. As she rushed forward, she glimpsed Maquin tumbling away, the hound slamming into him.

Finish your task, she screamed at herself as she ran forwards and plunged her spear into the snared hound's chest. Dimly she remembered Maquin telling her to stab it in the belly, that it would be softer there, at the same time feeling the spear head slide on bone. She put all her weight onto the shaft and pushed, felt the spear slip past ribs, deeper, into something softer, the hound whining, snapping and writhing. It shuddered and then collapsed.

She pulled on her spear but it was stuck; she tugged more frantically, then heard the shouts of men running towards them down the track. A hundred paces, closing quickly. She left her spear in the dead hound and turned.

Maquin lay beneath a pile of fur, the last hound slumped on him. *He's dead.* Fidele rushed to him, feeling as if her heart was lurching in her chest, and heaved the dog away. Maquin groaned and she felt a tide of relief wash her.

'Thought I was dead,' he blinked.

'So did I,' Fidele breathed as she helped him stand. 'What now?'

'Didn't think we'd get this far.' He glanced down the trail at the onrushing warriors, then over his shoulder at the river.

'Time to get wet,' he said. He gripped her hand in his and together they ran at the ravine's edge, leapt into the air and plummeted towards the river below.

CHAPTER TWENTY-ONE

LYKOS

Lykos wandered in a world of grey. Grey plains undulating into the distance, a charcoal river curling through it like some fluid serpent. Grey trees, branches swaying, slate-grey clouds boiling above him. In the distance he saw a structure, arching out of the land.

A bridge?

On its far side was a wall, stretching into the sky, merging with the clouds. Or was it a wall . . . ?

He squinted, saw that there was movement within it, a billowing, like sails in a fickle wind.

It is not a wall. It is mist. A fog bank.

He saw a rock and sat to assess the situation.

Pain spiked, in his face and back. He put his hand to the greater pain, his back, and his fingers came away red. Blood red.

'How did that happen?'

He felt a flicker of worry, but almost as soon as it had come it was gone. It was hard to care in this world leached of all colour. Of all life.

He looked about again, knew where he was.

The Otherworld. He had been here before, since he had made his pact with Asroth, summoned here on rare occasions by Calidus for some clandestine communication or other. But this time it felt different. Time was different here, hard to measure, but he knew somehow that he'd been here . . . *a while? How long?*

'Long enough. Longer than ever before.'

Is this death?

'No,' a voice said beside him, startling him. 'But near enough.'

It was Calidus, sitting upon a boulder. He looked younger, his white hair softer, less brittle, the creases in his face lines instead of grooves. He wore a coat of chainmail, dark leathery wings folded behind him. A smile spread across his face.

'You look pleased with yourself,' Lykos commented.

'I am. Things are going well.'

'So why am I here?' Lykos asked him.

Calidus' smile disappeared. 'I have not summoned you this time. You found your own way here. You are dying.'

'Oh.' *I guessed as much. I should feel scared, but I don't.*

'And that, over there?' He pointed to the bridge and the wall of mist.

'The bridge of swords, and what comes next,' Calidus told him.

'What does come next?'

'Death. Whatever that is.'

Lykos felt indifferent to it. Not even any hint of curiosity.

'I don't want you to die,' Calidus said. 'I need you to live.'

Lykos shrugged again.

'Here,' Calidus said and passed him an apple. Lykos took it in both hands, ran his fingers over the featureless skin. *A grey apple. Not very appealing.*

'Would you walk away from it all, then?' Calidus asked him.

'From what?'

'Your life.'

Lykos thought about that, maybe for a few heartbeats, maybe for a moon, he could not tell. Eventually he shook his head. 'I can hardly remember it.'

'Your heart's desire was to unite the Three Islands. To become Lord of the Vin Thalun.'

'The Three Islands?'

'Aye. Your father was a Vin Thalun corsair, and Lord of the Island of Panos. You inherited that island, though you had to fight for it.'

A dim memory stirred. The corpse of his father lying upon a bower of thorns. Flames. Blood in the firelight.

'I did.'

'You made a pact with Asroth. He helped you win the Three Islands. You united them, forged a nation out of the Vin Thalun and became their king.'

Lykos felt a flicker of emotion, an echo of the joy that had consumed him as he had sat before the defeated captains of Nerin and Pelset and heard their oaths of fealty.

'Take a bite of your apple.'

Lykos lifted it to his lips and saw there was a pink flush to its skin, faded and pastel, but there now, stark against the grey of this world. He took a small bite, tasted . . . something. Faint, bland.

'And you have done more. You rule in Tenebral, are regent in Nathair's stead.'

'Aye. But that hasn't gone so well.'

'Tell me of it.'

As Lykos spoke, he remembered: the effigy of Fidele that Calidus had gifted him, the power it gave him over her. Passion stirred in him at the memory of her, the sensation of her skin beneath his fingers, the taste of her fear. He remembered the arena, his wedding day, Fidele as beautiful and desirable as he had ever seen her. Maquin and Orgull duelling in the fighting-pit. Maquin throwing down his weapons, the explosion of eagle-guard from amongst the spectators.

Chaos.

Battle.

Fighting Maquin, Fidele plunging a knife into his back. He felt a wave of anger at that, but it soon subsided into a self-deprecating chuckle. 'I suppose I had that coming.'

'No. In your world you take, or it is taken from you.'

'I remember those words. My da spoke them to me.'

'Aye. And you have taken, and tasted.'

'I have.' He thought of Fidele again, felt a spark of anger at Maquin, the man who had taken her from him.

'Your face, Lykos. What happened to it?'

He touched his cheek, felt gouges in his flesh, blood congealing into crusted scabs.

'She attacked me, clawed me like an animal. The bitch.' He licked a drop of his blood from a finger. 'She was magnificent.'

Calidus grinned at him.

'Do you want to go back?'

'Aye.' Lykos grinned in return, took another bite from his

apple. It was blood red now, the flesh sweet, juice dripping down his chin.

Lykos' eyes fluttered open.

Where am I?

The swaying sensation gave it away. *On a ship.* He reached out, gripped the side of a cot and pulled himself up. Pain throbbed in his back but he gritted his teeth and managed to sit upright. He sat there long moments, head in his hands, fighting the pain, the swirling sense of nausea and the fact that he felt weak as a newborn pup.

A door creaked and a figure peered into the cabin, a woman. He blinked, remembering her.

Nella. She had been his woman before his obsession with Fidele. Or one of his women. Something was strapped across her chest, a lump wrapped in linen.

She put a hand upon his head, her face creased with worry.

'I'm fine, woman,' Lykos said irritably. Or at least, that's what he meant to say. It came out strangled and unintelligible. She poured water from a jug, which he drank greedily.

'Slowly, or you'll bring it back up,' Nella scolded him. He waved her away.

Others came through the cabin door – old Jayr, his ship's healer, Alazon, the white-haired shipwright, and another, a warrior bristling with hilts and iron. *Where's Deinon, my shieldman?*

Memories and dreams were starting to blur. The arena, fighting the Old Wolf Maquin, Fidele. She'd put a knife in his back. After that everything was vague. Being carried, half-dragged, from the arena. Then nothing.

No, not nothing. The Otherworld. Calidus. He gave me a task to do.

His stomach growled, complaining about the sudden influx of water or the fact that he felt half starved, he did not know. *Probably both.*

'Slow down with the water,' old Jayr said as his fingers probed at Lykos' throat, then lifted bandages from his waist, checking the wound on his back. 'You're well,' he sniffed.

That didn't mean much from Jayr, who pronounced everyone healthy until they were a handspan from death. *But that in itself is encouraging, I suppose.*

'Where's Deinon?' Lykos managed to get out, his voice a croak.

'Dead,' Alazon said.

That hit Lykos like a punch in the gut. Of course they lived and usually died by the sword, but Deinon had seemed invulnerable. And he had been the closest thing to a friend that Lykos had known, his presence always reassuring.

'The Old Wolf, so men have said,' Alazon continued. 'This is Kolai. I appointed him as your chief shieldman until you were able to choose Deinon's . . .' He didn't finish the sentence.

Lykos gave Kolai a perfunctory nod as he looked him over. His age was hard to gauge, his skin weathered and scarred, but Lykos vaguely remembered him, had bet money on him. *Another one from the pits. It always ages them on the outside. Thirty summers, maybe.*

'How long have I been out?'

'Over a ten-night,' Nella said, fetching a bowl and dipping a linen cloth into it. 'Goat's milk. Take a few drops, then stop,' she ordered. His eyes dropped to the lump strapped to her chest and he saw a shock of black hair as she leaned over him. It gave out a whimper.

'What's that?' he asked as he grabbed the linen from her.

'Your son,' she snapped.

He blinked at that, abruptly remembering that she had been heavy with child the last time he'd seen her, back on Panos. He slurped a mouthful from the linen, then took the bowl and drank it down.

Nella tutted at him.

'She's right – slow down,' Jayr said to him reprovingly.

'My son,' Lykos said, feeling a grin split his face. 'What's his name?'

'Rodas.'

Lykos reached over, pulled the linen sheet back and stroked his thumb across the child's cheek. 'Well met, Rodas,' he said, patting him on the head. That didn't go down too well, the boy's face wrinkling as he sucked in a breath and wailed.

'He's not a hound,' Nella said, slapping Lykos' hand away.

'He needs to be strong,' Lykos said as he stood. 'My sword? My knives?' The world felt as if it was moving, more so than he would expect from a ship's cabin, but he refused to lie still a moment longer.

'Report,' he ordered as he pulled on a linen shirt and a leather vest, wincing at the jolts of complaint from the wound in his back.

Alazon spoke to him of all that had happened since the uprising in the arena. He had taken control while Lykos was incapacitated, a decision which Lykos approved of. Apparently a bloody battle had raged on the meadows and streets of Jerolin for half a day. The steady influx of Vin Thalun from ships moored on the lake and others arriving by river had turned it. Since then the Vin Thalun had been going door to door, searching, burning, executing. The uprising had not spread, in large part due to the fact that many of the eagle-guard of Jerolin had stayed allied with the Vin Thalun. Fidele had been wed to Lykos, after all, so with her missing – kidnapped, Alazon had announced, by a madman and murderer – Lykos was to all purposes her representative until she was found. Slowly the unrest had died down and a semblance of peace had been restored, at least within Jerolin and the surrounding vicinity. Meanwhile Alazon had sent hunting parties out after any survivors of the uprising.

'What of the Old Wolf and Fidele? I want his head, and I want her back.'

'Got someone you might want to talk to about that.'

Lykos leaned against a timber frame in the shipyard that stood on the lakeshore before Jerolin's dark walls, resting for a moment as the sun beat down upon him.

Damn, but it's hot. Without a word Alazon handed him a skin. Lykos sniffed and drank, cool watered wine. A glance at the village on the lakeshore and Jerolin on its low hill had been reassuring. All seemed normal, people going about their everyday business. *It's as if there was no uprising.*

The only visible difference was that there were more Vin Thalun about the place. In the village, on the lakeshore, standing watch on the walls of Jerolin alongside the fortress' eagle-guard.

Alazon has done well. The situation could have polarized us.

The lake was a forest of masts and black sails, a Vin Thalun fleet settled on it like crows upon a field of corpses.

'I've had word from Calidus. A fleet must be readied for sail. War-galleys and transporters for a warband two thousand strong. Room for horses and baggage.' *And something else.*

'That's fifty ships, at least. We can do that,' Alazon shrugged.

'Good. We'll talk more of it later.'

'This way,' Alazon said, striding bow-legged through the ship-yard, and led him to the arena that still stood on the plain before Jerolin. Its earth was hard packed now, dried out by the sun. Dark stains betrayed the violence that it had witnessed.

There were cages on the far side, designed to hold pit-fighters. The cages were full. A score of Vin Thalun warriors guarded them, lounging in the sun, some sparring half-heartedly, some drinking.

Alazon called out a name and a warrior separated from the guards, a young Vin Thalun, his beard oiled and bound with only a few iron rings. He looked as if he'd seen combat recently, his nose crooked, his jaw swollen, bruises fading.

'This is Senios,' Alazon said. 'He's got something to tell.'

'I saw Fidele and the Old Wolf,' he said, eyes unable to meet Lykos'.

'Where?'

'The forest – I was guarding the timber fields, the day of your . . .' He trailed off.

'Aye. Go on.'

Senios told of his capture by Maquin, bargaining for his life and time. How he had tried to escape, fought hard with the Old Wolf, only losing because Fidele had struck him from behind.

Lykos looked him up and down. *I saw the Old Wolf kill Herak, trainer of pit-fighters. Can't see you besting him.*

'What did you offer in return for your life?' Lykos asked him.

'Information.'

Lykos just stared at him.

Senios looked at the ground, shuffled his feet. 'The giantess and her whelp,' he muttered, just above a whisper. 'I took the Old Wolf and Fidele to see them.'

Lykos felt a hot gush of rage, fear entwined about it. His most closely guarded secret. Twelve years he had kept them safe from harm and prying eyes on the island of Pelset, but things had become so fluid, danger everywhere, that he had wanted them close to him. And now Fidele and the Old Wolf had seen them.

The Old Wolf must die and Fidele must be returned to my side, where I can seal her flapping lips.

'And,' he managed to say, bottling his rage.

'I escaped,' Senios said, raising his head and meeting Lykos' gaze. 'They ran. Some of the giants' guards gave chase.'

'How many?'

'Seven, eight.'

Not enough.

'When did this happen?'

'Twelve nights ago,' Alazon said. 'Senios reached us eight nights gone. I sent a score more into the forest, hounds and a local woodsman with them.'

'Good, Alazon,' Lykos said, patting the old warrior's shoulder. He looked hard at Senios, reached a decision.

'Kolai,' he snapped to the warrior whom Alazon had appointed as his shieldman.

'Aye,' the warrior said, stepping forward.

'I need new shieldmen. See if Senios is worthy.'

Kolai drew a short sword and knife from the impressive array of weapons strapped about his body. Senios blinked and took a step away.

Kolai moved into the arena, beckoned for Senios to follow.

Senios' eyes darted about, fell onto Lykos, who was watching him like a horse trader at market.

'What are you waiting for?' Lykos said.

Senios walked hesitantly after Kolai. He drew his short sword and shrugged a buckler onto his arm.

'Begin,' Lykos said and Kolai exploded forwards. Iron met iron, sparks flying, feet shuffling on the dusty earth. Senios fought well – any Vin Thalun who reached adulthood knew how to fight, but Kolai steadily broke down his guard, Senios' blocks and lunges becoming wilder as Kolai's skill became more apparent. In a dozen heartbeats Senios was bleeding from many small wounds, blood sheeting into his left eye. He knew it was only a matter of time and decided on an all-or-nothing attack.

I admire that, at least. But he betrayed my secret.

He ended up flat on his back, Kolai's boot on his chest, sword hovering over his throat.

'Live or die?' Kolai asked, not taking his eyes from Senios.

There was only ever one outcome I wanted from this. Senios betrayed me to save his skin for an extra day.

'Die.'

Kolai's sword stabbed down, a gurgle and a rush of blood, then he was cleaning his blades and sheathing them. Lykos nodded to him as he resumed his position a few steps behind Lykos. *He knew this was as much a test for him as for Senios. Unlike Senios, he has just passed.*

'Who are they?' Lykos asked Alazon, pointing to the men crammed into the cages at the far end of the arena.

'Prisoners. A mixture. Mostly locals who got caught up in the rioting. A few eagle-guard. Pit-fighters who turned on us.'

Lykos remembered that, could see in his mind's eye Maquin and Orgull smashing the locks to the cages, the pit-fighters inside rushing out. Lykos walked to the cages, paced slowly alongside them, studied those inside. Local people, farmers, trappers, traders, a handful of battered and bloodstained eagle-guard. He stopped suddenly.

'Javed.'

Javed was a pit-fighter, one of the few who had risen up through the ranks with Maquin. He was from Tarbesh in the east – small, slim, seemingly built solely of wire-like muscle. Lykos had offered him and a handful of others their freedom, one last fight and a chest of silver at the end of it for the victor. Javed had won his bout, earned his freedom and his silver, and yet he had chosen to fight beside Maquin and Orgull. He sat with his head bowed, refusing to look at Lykos.

'I saw the Old Wolf set you free. He used you, you know. Needed some help in getting out.'

Javed looked up then, glaring, but still he said nothing.

'You could have had a chest of silver, and yet you're back in a cage.'

'I saw my chance for freedom and I took it,' Javed said.

No doubt I would have done the same.

'Not for long, by the look of things.' Lykos grinned.

'I'll earn another chest from you,' Javed said.

He always had a pair of stones on him, I'll give him that.

'Maybe, but you'll have to earn your way back into the pit first. It's an oar-bench for you.'

He saw the light dim in Javed's eyes as the horror of his fate swept him.

'That's right. Back to the very beginning. Then the first level of the pits, if you're still alive. Perhaps I'll see you back here in a year or two.' He walked on, Javed's eyes burning into his back. He counted five eagle-guard warriors within the cage, ordered that they be brought out.

'Peritus was behind your uprising. Where is he?'

None answered. He drew his sword and buried it in a warrior's belly, ripped it out, intestines spilling to the ground like a barrel of writhing snakes. The man screamed.

'Where is Peritus?' Lykos asked again.

Silence, except for the agonized screams of the man who had just been gutted.

Lykos swung at the next warrior's ankle. There was a crack as the bone broke. Lykos struck again, hacking through flesh and bone, leaving the man's foot hanging by a thread of skin. Lykos felt a sharp pain in his back, stitches pulling, tearing. He brushed hair from his face, breathing hard.

The warrior with his guts on the ground had stopped screaming, was now making pitiful mewling sounds, like a hungry kitten.

'Where is Peritus?'

Three men looked silently back at him. One grey-beard stared flatly, one glared. The third was a young man, barely past his Long Night. Urine dribbled down one leg, pooling in the dirt. Lykos left him, went to the man who glared.

'Where is Peritus?'

The warrior spat in his face. Lykos smashed the pommel of his sword into his mouth. Blood and teeth spattered the ground. Lykos punched and punched the iron hilt into his enemy; the man slumped unconscious, face a bloody pulp. Lykos swung two-handed at his neck, half-severing the head.

He paused to catch his breath and wipe blood from his face, felt something warm trickle down his back and onto his hip, knew he'd opened his wound, but didn't care.

'Where. Is. Peritus?'

No answer, the one that had soiled himself now whimpering.

Lykos took a step towards him.

'No, please, no,' the young lad pleaded.

'A warrior should not beg, it is unseemly,' Lykos said. Laughter rippled through the Vin Thalun. He took another step closer, raised his sword.

'Ripa,' a voice said. Not the young warrior, but the grey-beard. 'If he still lives, Peritus is in Ripa.'

CHAPTER TWENTY-TWO

HAELAN

'I'm hungry,' Haelan said.

'You'll have to wait for the highsun bell, like everyone else,' Tahir replied, not even bothering to look at Haelan.

They were in a huge paddock, Tahir inspecting the saddle-straps on a bay stallion. It dug at the ground with one hoof. 'I'm surrounded by impatient souls,' Tahir muttered.

Mam never made me wait, Haelan thought. He felt a pressure behind his eyes at the memory of her and blinked hard. 'I hate waiting,' he said.

'Don't we all,' Tahir grunted as he adjusted the straps, then stood and patted the animal's neck. 'Shouldn't you be at your chores?'

I hate chores. There were a good score of children living at Gramm's hold who were too young to set foot in the Rowan Field, but of an age where they could be put to some practical use.

'You could go and get me some food,' Haelan said, ignoring Tahir's mention of chores. He looked back at the feast-hall that sat at the crown of a hill, smoke from the kitchens wafting into a grey sky. His stomach growled.

'No,' Tahir said, pausing to look at Haelan, his gaze hard. Haelan knew that look, had seen it many times now, although he was still struggling with it.

No one ever used to say no to me, except Mam and Uncle Varick, and that was rare enough.

Tahir's eyes softened, responding to something that swept Haelan's face. 'There's no special treatment here, lad. You *have* to blend in. It's too dangerous for you to stand out; you know this.

170

We've spoken about it more than once, haven't we?' The young warrior looked sternly at Haelan, holding his eyes until the boy nodded.

'Now I'm going to let this lad know what it feels like to have me on his back. You should be at your chores, anyway – blending in. You're supposed to be in the timber yard, aren't you?'

Haelan grunted a response.

'Besides, it'll be highsun soon enough and you'll be filling your belly before you know it.'

I'm not a bairn, thought Haelan. *When I have my crown I'll make you fetch me food all day long.* He scowled at Tahir's back as the warrior pulled himself into the saddle, the bay dancing a few steps.

'Go on with you, then,' Tahir said. 'I'll not be going far; just around the paddocks. If harm comes knocking I'll be close enough to shut the door, as my old mam used to say.'

With a sigh he began walking across the paddock.

Gramm's hold spread before him, a sturdy timber wall surrounding a collection of buildings scattered across a low hill, the main hall standing at the hill's peak. People were busy, working on the various trades that kept the hold thriving – timber and horses being the main ones. Gramm had built this place with his own hands within sight of Forn Forest's borders, raised his sons and daughters here, and now more than two hundred souls dwelt about the hill.

Over half a year Haelan and Tahir had been here. Gramm had taken them in, looked after them, protected them. At first Haelan had thought his mam would come for him soon. After a ten-night he'd asked Tahir what was taking her so long. The young warrior had just muttered about patience – one of his annoying sayings, of which there were many. After a moon had passed Haelan asked again. This time Tahir had not been able to meet his eyes. Soon after, Gramm had come to him and sat him down.

'How old are you, lad?' Gramm had asked him.

'Ten summers; but I'll be eleven on Midwinter's Day,' Haelan had replied.

'Aye. Well, you're still a bairn, but I'll talk to you like a man, nonetheless. It's the only way I know how, and it never did my boys much harm.' He'd scratched his beard; a sadness in his eyes had stopped his words for a moment.

'We've had word from the south, from Dun Kellen. About your mam.'

Haelan's heart had beat faster.

'She's dead, lad. Or so my messenger tells me, and I've no reason to doubt him.'

'Dead,' Haelan had echoed, the word sinking in his chest like a heavy stone dropped into deep water.

'Aye. Jael's put her head on a spike. And he's looking to do the same to you.'

The tears had come then, a seemingly endless flood.

'Doubt that it helps much, but I share your grief. My eldest son died there. Orgull. He was a captain of the Gadrai, friend of Tahir. He held the door to the tunnel you escaped in.'

Haelan did remember him, the huge bald man with no neck, looked as if he could never be defeated. In blurred images he remembered Gramm trying to comfort him, then leaving the room and Tahir entering. He'd sat quietly, waiting for Haelan's tears to run their course.

'I'll look after you,' Tahir had said. 'We're two of a kind, you and me – the last of our kind. Me, the last of the Gadrai; you the last of your line. But things will be different from now on. You're hunted – Jael knows we escaped Dun Kellen and he wants you dead. You're the rightful heir to Isiltir, and Jael wants that crown – so you mustn't be found . . .'

I know I'm hunted, Haelan thought. Once a group of warriors had been spied riding towards the hold. As they'd drawn closer Haelan had made out the banner that rippled above them; a lightning bolt on a black field, a pale serpent entwined about it. Jael's banner. *They have come to kill me*, Haelan remembered thinking, the fear as he had seen them cantering along the road freezing him in the courtyard. Tahir had swept him up in his arms and run, hiding him in the cellars beneath the feast-hall's kitchens. They had stayed there together, Haelan trying to control his shaking limbs, Tahir staring at the trapdoor, one hand permanently fixed to his sword hilt. It had felt like days before Gramm had opened the door and told them the warriors were gone. That had been over four moons ago.

The courtyard was heaving with activity. A score of warriors were climbing into saddles, horses stamping and blowing. Wulf, Gramm's eldest son, shouted a call and led them clattering towards the gates. Haelan jumped out of their way, aiming for the shadows, trying to hide from Wulf's eyes – the warrior had scolded him more than once for shirking his duties around the hold.

Haelan put his head down and ran across the courtyard, heading for the timber yard, which was situated in the far north of the settlement, beside the river. He sprinted along the edge of the feast-hall, pausing for breath as he crested the hill the hold was built upon. His eyes were drawn eastwards, towards Forn Forest, the river disappearing into the endless expanse of trees that consumed the horizon. Closer on the river Haelan saw line after line of felled timber bobbing in the water, like the body of some half-submerged creature, the current and long barges speeding it towards the hold.

An open gateway in the hold's wall led to the river, and to the stone bridge that spanned it, remnant and reminder of the giants that dwelt here once. Haelan saw figures moving on the bank amongst the moored craft. He glimpsed Swain, Wulf's boy, the closest thing to a friend that he'd ever known. Back at Dun Kellen he'd had playmates, but there was always a divide between the future heir and future subjects. *I am still heir of Isiltir, but here that does not seem so important.* Sometimes he struggled to remember his mam and da's faces.

Swain was the natural leader of those who were not old enough for the Rowan Field, and from Haelan's first day at the hold had looked out for him.

Haelan ran down the hill, through the gates onto the riverbank.

'There you are,' a voice boomed, old Kalf beckoning to him, as barrel-chested as the boats he tended.

'You're late, but better late'n never, so here you go,' Kalf said as he handed Haelan a mallet and a bucket, Haelan wrinkling his nose at the hemp and pine-tar inside. 'Get cracking, then, before the day's over.'

Haelan found a barge without workers and began. He knew what to do now, having performed the same task every day for the last ten-night. Gramm's hold had grown wealthy on timber from Forn Forest, and most of it was transported down the river, great floating rafts of it tied and pulled by barges. Over a dozen of those barges had been dragged from the river and now hung suspended on timber frames in various stages of repair. All of their hulls needed caulking with the pitch in Haelan's bucket.

I can do this now. Haelan felt a flush of pride as he banged tarred fibres into gaps between the timber strakes of a barge's hull, the pine-tar sticking to everything. He managed to get most of the tar in the right place, unlike his first day, when his wastefulness had earned him more than one clump around the back of his head by Kalf. He'd felt ashamed and useless, until Swain had taken pity on him and shown him how to scoop and spread the pitch without losing half of it to the ground. Now with something resembling competence he scooped, spread, hammered and repeated, kept going until his arms were aching.

'You're getting better at that,' a voice said close by. Swain appeared with a bucket of his own, his younger sister Sif and a scruffy dog at his heels. 'I'll help you finish up.'

'I'll help too,' his sister said.

'No,' Swain said firmly. 'Last time you tried you ended up with more tar on you than the boat. You looked like a river-wraith. Mam had to cut your hair and Da nearly killed me. You sit there and play with Pots.'

Swain was half a year away from entering the Rowan Field, his limbs looking too long for his body, wiry muscles stretched upon his frame. He was all energy and ideas, always coming up with ways to brighten each day, whether it was leading stealthy night-time excursions to catch river rats or organizing raids on the kitchen ovens. Tahir had caught Haelan more than once as he was sneaking after Swain and a dozen others – *You can't go*, Tahir had said, *it's too dangerous* – but lately either Haelan had perfected his skulking skills or Tahir had decided to turn a blind eye to the adventures.

Swain climbed the scaffolding to work on the parts of the hull that Haelan couldn't reach; working together they made quick progress along the barge. The sounds of Sif giggling drifted around them as she played with the dog, a wiry ball of white fur that took a willing part in Swain's adventures, sniffing out pies that had been hidden in the kitchens or rooting out rats' nests along the riverbank. All of a sudden the dog abandoned Sif and began jumping at the scaffolding below Swain, trying to bite his dangling mallet.

'Stop it, Pots,' Swain ordered.

'Why do you call him Pots?'

'He was born in a cook pot in the kitchen, him and six others. And he kept going back after the litter was grown and given out. Maybe that's why he's so good at finding the pies.' Swain grinned conspiratorially as he climbed down from the scaffolding. He crouched low, beckoning Haelan closer, and pulled something from a pouch at his belt.

'Here's some of the last pie Pots found, keep us going till highsun.' He passed some to Haelan and Sif, then threw the rest to the dog, who swallowed it without chewing.

'Thank you,' Haelan mumbled over pie-crust. He gave his last bit to Pots and scratched him behind an ear.

'Well, it's a family business, looking after you.' Swain winked at him. 'You mean Orgull. He was your uncle? Your da's brother,' he said, steering his thoughts away from his mam and Dun Kellen.

'Aye. He left here a long time ago, joined the Gadrai in Forn Forest after killing a giant from the north.' Swain's hand dropped to a hatchet hanging from a loop at his belt, running a thumb along its edge. 'He gave me this, when he left.'

It was a perfect, smaller copy of the throwing axes Haelan saw the warriors of Gramm's hold carrying.

'What was he like?' Swain asked him, something other than his usual confidence in his face.

Haelan shrugged. 'Big.'

Swain laughed. 'I remember that. He used to throw me around like Pots with a rat. Do you remember anything else?'

Haelan thought hard. This obviously meant a lot to Swain, and Haelan was grateful to him for many things since he'd arrived here, not least the piece of pie he'd just gulped down.

'Tears,' he said at last. 'Tahir wept as we left Orgull and the other one. They were good friends, is my guess.' He knew there was a tale there, of sword-brothers. Part of him wanted to know more, another part shying away from anything that reminded him of the circumstances in which his mam died. He looked at Swain, saw a desire for more, a need to know. 'I'll ask Tahir about him.'

Swain patted Haelan's shoulder and gave him a weak smile.

A murmur of sound drifted over to them, growing quickly.

Haelan saw a dozen or so lads and lasses gathered in a huddle down by the riverbank. He and Swain hurried over, Sif trailing after them.

It was Trigg, holding a willow-trap high.

The half-breed.

Trigg was of an age to Swain, but she stood a head taller than him, her face broad and angular, limbs long and muscular. Her mam and da had been part of Gramm's hold, and part of an expedition that had rowed up the river into Forn. They hadn't returned. The barges they'd used had eventually been found, half-sunk in the river, signs of battle on the vessels, but no bodies.

A year later Trigg's mam had staggered back into the hold from across the bridge that led into the Desolation. Her belly was swollen with child and she was half-mad, babbling about being made slave to the Jotun giants.

Trigg had been born, her mam dying in the act of giving birth, so the hold had raised Trigg, not one person taking her on, but many of them. Now she was just part of the hold, although Swain and the others behaved differently around her. Nothing they said, but Haelan could see a wariness in the way Trigg was treated, like an unbroken colt. As if she were dangerous. Haelan had only spoken to Trigg fleetingly, the tall girl always standing on the edges, when she was around at all. She disappeared for long lengths of time, Swain told him that she travelled into Forn. What for he didn't say.

'What've you caught?' Swain asked, pushing through the crowd.

'Biggest rat you've ever seen,' Trigg grinned, hefting the basket. Whatever was in it was heavy, as even Trigg was straining to hold it high. As Haelan watched the basket bucked and rocked.

And angry.

'It was in the river, after the salmon.'

Swain peered through the willow slats and whistled. 'I've caught bigger,' he said, winking at Haelan.

'I don't believe that,' Trigg said flatly, no anger in her tone, no insult, just a statement of a fact as she saw it. Pots was yapping at Swain's feet, jumping up at the basket. 'Looks like your ratter wants a go. How about a wager?'

Haelan had seen Pots sniff out and kill a score of rats down by the river, and he was good at it, quick and deadly, the rats always dead within heartbeats.

'No,' Sif said. She tugged at Swain's hand. 'Don't do it,' she said.

Swain peered back into the basket and frowned. 'Old Kalf'll catch us, then we'll be scrubbing these barges till midwinter.'

'There's an empty barn over there.' Trigg smiled, sensing a victory over Swain. 'Are you scared for your pup?'

Swain snorted. 'What's the wager, then?'

'My knife for your axe.'

'No chance.'

'Don't have much faith in your dog, do you?'

Swain was silent a moment, then he nodded and they were all rushing to one of the timber barns. As he hurried with the others, Haelan glanced across the river. Beyond a strip of green vegetation the land to the north quickly changed, turning into a wasteland, barren and pitted, punctuated by a scattered range of mountains receding into the distance. The Desolation, it was called, a peninsula of land where the Scourging had raged hottest, so Tahir had told him. The battleground where Asroth and Elyon's hosts had met, the Ben-Elim and the Kadoshim. The land was still scarred and broken from the outpouring of Elyon's wrath, a place of rock and dust, of ruins and bottomless chasms. Haelan often looked out at the northlands, imagining the clash of angels and demons filling the landscape. He shivered. Now only giants were supposed to roam the wasteland, occasionally raiding across the river on their great bears. A huge war-hammer and a bear pelt hung in the feasthall to remind Haelan that the giants and their bears were more than just tales.

Once inside the barn Swain and Trigg threw together a circle from hay bales while others started shouting wagers. Haelan was holding Pots.

'Kill it quick,' he whispered in Pots' ear; the dog gave his face a quick lick.

Swain came and took Pots, holding him by the scruff of the neck as Trigg placed the willow basket on the far side of the makeshift ring. Pots growled, his hackles standing, and Trigg opened the basket.

Something black and sinuous leaped out, a collective gasp issuing from the small crowd. It was a rat, but bigger than any that Haelan had ever seen before. *From snout to tail it must be as long as my arm*. Yellow incisors gleamed in a malevolent face, thick bristly hair coating its body, and suddenly Haelan was scared for Pots.

Pots was surging towards it, all fur and snarls.

The rat didn't try to run, it just bunched up, then leaped.

They collided with a meaty thump, Pots twisting, trying to get his jaws at the rat's neck. They rolled on the dusty ground, teeth snapping, spittle flying, then parted, skidding in different directions, Pots' feet scrabbling for purchase.

The rat found its balance first, darted forwards, and the two animals were a swirling mass again. Abruptly there was blood spattering the ground, an animal whine. Haelan closed his eyes, scared, saw a memory of blood flying in a dark tunnel and quickly opened his eyes again. The fighting animals crashed against a hay bale. Haelan saw the rat's jaws clamped around Pots' shoulder, the dog squirming frantically, teeth snapping, head twisting as he tried to get to the rat.

Pots shook violently; the rat flew off with a ripping sound, bouncing off of a hay bale.

The two animals stood staring at one another, Pots holding a front paw in the air, blood pulsing from a ragged gash in his shoulder.

He's going to die, Haelan thought, knowing Pots killed with speed. That was gone now.

'Help him,' he whispered to Swain.

'I can't,' Swain said, looking on in shock.

Sif buried her face in Swain's breeches.

The rat approached Pots, slower this time, nose twitching. Pots lunged forward, teeth snapping and stumbled, the rat leaping aside, then it was on Pots' back, teeth gouging, Pots crying out, high-pitched. Haelan screwed his eyes shut, clenched his fists, trying to blot out the sound. Memories surged, Pots' screams becoming deeper, morphing into something else, something worse; the sound of men dying in a dark tunnel, blood flowing. He grabbed his head, fingers squeezing, trying to stop the sound, but Pots' cries of pain filtered through everything. Distantly he realized he was moving, a hand grabbing at him, but he shook it off, voices shouting at him, then his arm was rising and falling, faster and faster, warm liquid spraying his face, in his mouth, blurring his vision.

Then silence; only the heaving of his breath, a dog whining.

He wiped blood from his eyes, saw Swain's hatchet in his hand, slick with blood. The rat was a twitching mess on the floor, hacked into savage ruin, intestines spilling about Haelan's feet. Pots had crawled away, watching him.

He looked up, around the ring, saw faces staring back at him, mouths open. Sif was crying.

'Not fair,' Trigg said. 'My rat was winning.' Swain stepped into the ring and picked Pots up.

Haelan felt tears bloom, leaving tracks through the blood on his cheeks. His shoulders started to shake.

'Come on,' Swain said, putting an arm around Haelan. Sif came and took his hand.

'Look at my rat,' Trigg said, frowning. 'I would have won. You put him up to it.'

Swain stopped and turned, then took the hatchet from Haelan's grip and threw it at Trigg's feet.

'Your prize,' Swain said.

'No, you can't,' Haelan blurted. 'Orgull gave it to you.'

'That is fair,' Trigg said. 'I'd have won it anyway.' She stooped and picked up the weapon, wiping its shaft clean on a hay bale.

A horn call echoed through the barn, all of them looking to the entrance. Swain strode away.

They stood outside, the horn call ringing out again.

'What's that about?' Haelan asked.

'Look,' Swain said, pointing north, across the river towards the Desolation.

Haelan stared, frowning. In the distance a cloud hovered low over the land.

'What's that?' Haelan asked.

'Dust. Look to the land beneath it,' Swain replied.

At first Haelan saw nothing, then he caught movement. A line of riders emerged from the wasteland, approaching Gramm's hold, metal glinting in the sunlight.

CHAPTER TWENTY-THREE

ULFILAS

Ulfilas felt a wave of relief fill him as he saw the river come into view, a dark, shimmering vein winding across the land. Beyond it was Isiltir. *And goodbye to this pox-ridden land of ash and stone. And giants. And bears.*

'It is always good to return home, after a long journey,' King Jael said to him as they cantered down a gentle slope, the hooves of two hundred mounted warriors raising a cloud of dust behind them.

'Aye, my King.'

'And a successful one,' Jael added, quieter this time.

The meeting with the Jotun had gone well enough. No one had died, and King Jael's spirits had seemed much improved on the return journey. Ildaer, the Jotun's warlord, had appeared most impressed with the gift of ancient weapons that Jael had given him. *Impressed enough to hunt down a runaway princeling, though?* Ulfilas wasn't so sure about that. And he couldn't shake the sense of wrongness about the situation. Giants were the enemy, as they had always been, for time without end. Ulfilas had grown to manhood beneath the shadow of Forn Forest, where the threat of giant raids had been very real – admittedly the Hunen, a different giant clan from the Jotun but giants were giants, warlike, savage and not to be trusted. So making deals with them was just wrong.

But who am I to judge? These are strange days . . .

'What's wrong?' Jael asked him.

'I was thinking on the wisdom of making alliances with giants,' Ulfilas said.

'A polite way of saying I'm a fool,' Jael replied. He smiled, but there was a sharpness in his features, no warmth in his smile.

'Never, my King.'

'I hate giants,' Jael said. 'And wish every giant clan dead, have dreamed that since the Hunen slaughtered my mam and da, burned out my home.' He paused, the flare of his nostrils giving away a measure of his anger. 'But I wish to be king more.'

'The greater good, then,' Ulfilas said.

'*My* greater good, at least,' Jael said with a grin. 'And who knows, my dream may yet come true. We have seen the Hunen of Forn broken, destroyed. That is one less giant clan. But I need the Jotun.'

'Do you think they'll find the child?' Ulfilas asked Jael.

'Maybe –' Jael shrugged – 'if he has reached this far. He may be dead. He may be alive and still in Isiltir, hiding in some woodsman's shed. Many would help him, out of misguided loyalty to a dead king. Or he may have escaped north into the Desolation. I do not know, but I will not rest until I see his dead body at my feet. While Haelan is out there, alive or dead, there is a challenge to me. He is a rallying point for every naysayer. He must die, and be seen to be dead by all.'

Warbands had been set to scouring Isiltir, circling ever wider after the fall of Dun Kellen. Ulfilas guessed that Jael was probably correct when he said that Haelan was already dead. *Probably lying in a ditch somewhere, food for crows.*

'We'll find him,' Ulfilas muttered.

'Aye, we will. Us or the Jotun. Little travels through the Desolation without their knowledge.'

I believe that. Ulfilas glanced back at the hills they were finally riding out of. At the edge of his vision, far beyond the column of Jael's shieldmen, there was a flicker of movement, a shape outlined against the horizon for a moment. It looked like a bear.

Making sure we leave their lands.

He turned his eyes forwards. To the east the bulk of Forn Forest loomed, dark and brooding. The river was closer now, dark shapes of boats appearing upon it. To the south-east was a bridge, beyond it a hill with a timber hall at its crest, a palisaded wall circling it. Buildings sprawled down the slope, almost right to the river's banks.

'A desolate and dangerous place for a hold,' Jael remarked.

'Aye. Who would be mad enough to build here? Forn Forest to the east, the Desolation to the north.'

Dag the huntsman dropped back to join them. 'That is Gramm's hold. He's been here a good long while: twenty, twenty-five years.' Dag had a set of scars down one side of his face that stretched from skull to jaw, looking like the raking of claws. Part of one ear was missing and the hair on that side of his head only grew in patches.

'Has he, now?' Jael said. 'Perhaps he needs reminding who really is king.'

Hooves clattered on stone as the warband crossed the bridge, the river's dark waters clogged with dressed timber, cut and ready to be shipped downstream. Faces peered over the palisaded wall as Jael and his shieldmen cantered onto a road that skirted the wall, taking them past the usual array of boats beached for repair, smokehouses, tanners' yards and grain barns, eventually bringing them around to the southern approach to the hold. Ulfilas noted the glint of sunshine on iron along the wall. *Ten armed men, at least.*

'More like a village than a hold,' Jael said to Ulfilas and Dag.

'It is, my lord.'

They rode alongside sweeping fenced meadows where herds of horses ran. *Impressive, powerful horses*, Ulfilas noted, remembering now the reputation Gramm's hold had for more than just timber. Ulfilas eyed them covetously. *They would make fine warhorses.*

'Magnificent. They are wasted up here,' Jael said with a grin.

'Just what I was thinking,' Ulfilas replied.

The road sloped up the hill, the hold's gates open and they cantered through the gateway into a wide courtyard. Guards with long spears stood on the palisade's walkway, a handful more around the courtyard's edge. *Well-equipped guards*, Ulfilas thought, taking in their coats of mail and weapons – all of them with swords hanging at their hips, spears in their hands. *And all with an axe strapped across their back. Unusual. A dozen guards that I can see around the gate. Five more in the courtyard. Must have been another ten on the palisade wall as we passed. How many more here? Is this all of them, a display intended to impress us? They would have seen us coming, had time to prepare a welcome.* Ulfilas smiled as Jael's shieldmen filled the courtyard, which was big, but nevertheless hard-pressed to contain two hundred of the King's shieldmen, all on proud warhorses. *I think we will impress them more.*

A figure emerged from the feast-hall and stood at the top of wide steps. He was thick muscled, though with a large belly as well, tall and fair, streaks of grey in his hair and braided beard. He wore plain breeches and a woollen tunic tied at the waist.

'Greetings,' the man shouted. 'I am Gramm, lord of this hold, and I bid you welcome.' He looked at the banner carried by one of Jael's shieldmen, snapping in a stiff breeze from the north. A lightning bolt on a black field, a pale serpent entwined about it.

'You are Jael's men, then. I say welcome again. Come, enter. I will find you some food and drink.'

Ulfilas dismounted and climbed the steps, dipping his head to Gramm.

'We are more than King Jael's men,' Ulfilas said, accenting the word *King*. 'We are his chosen shieldmen, guarding him on this journey to the north of his realm.' Ulfilas swept a hand to Jael, who sat tall on his stallion, wrapped in a sable cloak, looking as regal as any king that Ulfilas had ever seen.

Gramm stood frozen for a moment, something sweeping his face. Ulfilas felt the hairs on his neck prickle, the possibility of violence suddenly thick in the air. Then the expression on Gramm's face was gone.

Ulfilas frowned, disconcerted.

Slowly, clumsily, Gramm dropped to one knee.

'You do me honour,' he said. 'Be welcome in my hall, King Jael.'

Jael dismounted and climbed the steps of the hall, resting a hand on Gramm's shoulder, bidding him stand.

'Welcome to my hall,' Gramm repeated.

He looks flustered, but then it is not every day that a king comes calling.

'My thanks,' Jael said.

'If I had known of your arrival I would have prepared a feast and fine beds worthy of a king and his company.'

'It is not a planned visit,' Jael said. 'In truth I am riding the northlands of Isiltir in pursuit of rebels and brigands. We came upon your hold by chance. It seemed to be a good opportunity to meet someone I have heard much talk of.'

'You honour me,' Gramm said.

'My apologies for descending upon you unannounced,' Jael said.

'We will not be staying long, but something to wash the throat and fill the belly would be welcome.'

'My mead and meat is yours,' Gramm said the guest-greeting. 'Food and drink for our guests,' he shouted, waving his arms in the air.

All was chaos for a short while as warriors dismounted, a swarm of children appearing from nowhere to take reins and tend to horses. Gramm put his arm about one lad and bent to whisper in his ear. The boy cradled a dog in one arm, a ratter. It was bleeding from a gash on its shoulder.

'Go fetch your da,' Ulfilas heard Gramm say.

'Yes, Grand-pa,' the lad replied and scurried off across the courtyard. Ulfilas caught Dag's eye and nodded after the disappearing boy. Dag slipped away through the crowded courtyard.

Gramm barked orders as he led Jael and Ulfilas into his hall, other warriors following.

The hall was big, two long tables running down the sides, leaving a path down the centre. Embers still glowed in a fire-pit. Another table ran the length of the back wall. Hanging from the wall above it was a huge bear pelt, its mouth open and snarling. A giant's war-hammer was mounted above it.

It's obvious that the relationship with their Jotun neighbours is not that friendly.

The food that came out of Gramm's kitchen was good – simple but hot and lots of it. A fair-haired child offered Ulfilas a jug of mead but he refused it, taking cold water instead. As Jael's shieldman he was always on his guard, but here that sense was heightened. He felt unsettled.

'That jug looks too heavy for you, child,' he said to the girl with the mead.

'Grand-pa says we should lift more than we can handle,' the girl said, freckles wrinkling as she concentrated. 'He says it makes us strong, inside and out.' Her eyes flickered to Gramm.

'A good lesson,' Jael said, smiling good-naturedly.

'Life's hard in these northlands,' Gramm said. 'Now run along, Sif,' he added to the child.

'You have children, then?' Jael asked.

'Aye,' Gramm muttered.

'And grandchildren,' Jael added, his eyes following the girl as she took her jug of mead to a table full of Jael's shieldmen.

After Gramm's initial surprise at meeting the King it seemed that his nerves had calmed. Jael was courteous and charming, as Ulfilas had seen him on countless occasions. Now Gramm was telling Jael of how he had built the hold with his own hands, braving close proximity both to Forn Forest and the Desolation to take advantage of the timber and the river.

'A bold endeavour,' Jael remarked.

And one that has paid off, Ulfilas thought as he looked at the size of the hall.

'You have carved out a fine living for yourself,' Jael said. 'Profits must be high indeed to provide for so many.'

Jael is no fool – he has no doubt seen all that I have seen, and more.

'Trade is good, I'll not deny,' Gramm said.

'And your warriors – I've not seen so many in a single hold, and uncommonly well equipped,' Jael commented.

'Life is dangerous this far north.' Gramm pointed to the bear pelt and giant's hammer hanging on the wall. 'They are not there for decoration, but as a reminder. We are close to the Desolation and to Forn Forest. A cold winter is often all that's needed to lure giants across the river or entice creatures from the forest with more legs and sharper teeth than is entirely good for us. Warriors with sharp swords are a necessity here, not a luxury. And besides, what with all the goings on further south –' his eyes flickered to Jael – 'there has been an outbreak of lawlessness and thievery the likes of which I have never seen before. Brigands seeking to take advantage of Isiltir's upheaval. My lands have been raided more than once.'

'That will all end, now. I will see to it. Isiltir has a new king, and I mean to bring peace to the land. These brigands' days are numbered.'

'Glad to hear it,' Gramm said.

'And talking of the *goings on in the south*, where do your loyalties lie?' Nothing about Jael's tone changed, but the hall seemed to quieten, an indrawn breath waiting upon Gramm's answer.

Gramm looked at Jael with an undecipherable expression. 'We are a long way from anyone here. Isolated. Priorities change when you live on the edge of the wild. In truth I have little interest in the goings on in Isiltir. Family. Food on my table. Trade. That the giants stay on the north side of the river. Those things are highest on my list. But if a choice had to be made, then I am a man of Isiltir, and my loyalties lie with its King. Of that you need have no doubt.'

'That is good to know,' Jael said. 'I thank you for your honesty.'

'It's all a man has,' Gramm shrugged.

'Indeed.'

Ulfilas saw a shadow appear at the hall's open doors: Dag the huntsman. The man nodded to him and then stepped from view.

'And let me return the favour and be honest with you,' Jael said to Gramm. 'It would please me greatly if we could work together.'

'What do you mean?' Gramm asked.

'I need information. If I know where my enemies are hiding, then I can end these dark times that you speak of. We would both benefit.' Jael stopped eating and stared at Gramm.

'Hiding?' Gramm said, pausing as he ripped a chunk of bread from a loaf. Slowly he looked at Jael, returning his gaze.

'Aye. These northlands are vast, with countless places that a cunning enemy may hide. But you are well placed to hear of them. If you could send me information of the whereabouts, the movements of these brigands that you speak of, it would be helpful information. And I always reward those who are helpful to me.'

Gramm remained silent.

'There is one in particular that I speak of, who I am searching for,' Jael continued. 'One enemy who may be hiding somewhere in these northlands. A boy and a warrior.'

'They don't sound so dangerous. Hardly a band of brigands,' Gramm said with a smile.

'No, but nevertheless, it is important that they are brought to me. I *will* catch them. The boy is eleven summers, red hair. The warrior young – no more than twenty summers. A survivor of the Gadrai.'

'I thought the Gadrai were servants of Isiltir, loyal to the King,' Gramm asked.

'Not this one. For the most part the Gadrai fell in Forn Forest, slain in combat with the Hunen. Not as skilled at giant-slaying as their reputation would have you believe.' Jael chuckled at his joke, as did some of his shieldmen. None of Gramm's people did.

'But this one still lives, or did, when Dun Kellen fell. He is a traitor, a renegade. Have you seen anyone matching their description, or heard any news of two such roaming the land.'

'No,' Gramm said.

'I would appreciate it if you would help me find them.'

'I will do what I can,' Gramm said, going back to his bread.

'Of course you will. You seem like an honest man, so I should take you at your word. Unfortunately my experiences of late . . . Well, let us say that I find it difficult to trust anyone. My own fault, granted, but I often suffer with feelings of doubt, mistrust. I am feeling them now.'

'I can only give you my word, my assurance—' Gramm began, but Jael cut him off.

'Assurance. Yes, just what I was thinking.' Jael touched Ulfilas' arm.

Ulfilas launched himself over the table, scattering bowls, food, jugs, as he lunged forwards. There was a high-pitched yelp and then Ulfilas was holding the serving-child, Sif. He drew his knife and put it to her throat.

A woman screamed, tried to reach Ulfilas, but Jael's shieldmen stood, forming a wall about Ulfilas and the child.

'No,' Gramm yelled, standing, his chair falling behind him. Other men were shouting, the sound of swords leaving scabbards.

'I wouldn't,' Jael said, standing too, slowly, wiping food from the corner of his mouth. He walked calmly to Ulfilas.

'She is your grandchild, and family are your first priority, as you have just told me. I think she will come with me. My guest. She will be looked after, not harmed, so long as you do as I ask. An assurance. Do you understand me?'

Gramm just stared at Jael, muscles bunching in his face, his fists.

'Do you understand me?' Jael repeated. 'I'll not ask you a third time.'

'I understand you,' Gramm said flatly.

'Good.' Jael looked at Sif. 'Stop snivelling, child,' he said. 'She is dear to you, I guess. But just one amongst many, and only a girl. I think I need more assurance than this.'

'If you think I will parade my grandchildren before you, you are a fool,' Gramm snarled.

'True, I would be. Far better to just take another.' Jael called out and figures appeared in the doorway – Dag, holding the lad that Gramm had sent off earlier. The boy was bleeding from a swollen lip, still clutching his ratter under one arm.

'Swain,' Gramm gasped, and the woman who had run to the girl cried out and sank to her knees, sobbing.

'Good,' Jael said with a smile. 'Now I am confident that I have my assurance.' He strode from the hall into the pale sunlight and mounted his horse.

Ulfilas was behind him, followed by all in the hall. Sif struggled as Ulfilas climbed into his saddle and he shook her.

'Be still, girl, or you'll get a slap,' he snarled.

The boy in Dag's care lunged for him but Dag grabbed his tunic and clumped him across the back of the head with his knife hilt. The boy collapsed to the ground. His dog stood protectively over him, growling at Dag.

Jael laughed at the sight of it. Dag kicked the dog, sending it rolling away with a whine, then hoisted the lad up and slung him across his saddle.

'You are now my eyes in the north,' Jael cried. 'The boy and his guardian. Bring them to me, or send me word of them, and your kin will be returned to you unharmed.' With that Jael turned his horse and cantered out of the courtyard.

Ulfilas caught up with Jael on the long road that skirted the paddocks.

'Think you made an impression.'

'Aye. Gramm won't be forgetting his new king.'

'Didn't get a new horse, though,' Ulfilas said as he looked into the paddocks.

'Next time,' Jael replied.

'Do you trust Gramm now?'

'I don't trust anyone, Ulfilas, not even you, though you've been my shieldman since before I could hold a sword.'

Nor I you.

'But trust is overrated, as are love, loyalty and devotion. Fear, Ulfilas. That is what is important to me. As long as he fears me, all will be well.'

Ulfilas looked back at Gramm's hold, ringed by its stout wooden walls. Ulfilas had not seen fear on Gramm's face when he'd first greeted the new King. No. What had swept Gramm, only for an instant and quickly masked, had been something else entirely.

It was hatred.

CHAPTER TWENTY-FOUR

TUKUL

Tukul sat close to Corban, patiently waiting as the warband pre-pared to leave. Idly he leaned forward and rubbed one of Daria's ears; she whickered quietly. All were gathered and waiting upon Corban, who was in close conversation with Brina and Ethlinn. They parted, and Corban pulled himself onto Shield's back, the stallion stamping a hoof and snorting, making Daria whicker in response next to him.

Something has changed within him. Yesterday he was unsure, worry leaking from him. Now he looks . . . resolved.

Corban looked about at the faces watching him.

'Foes ahead and foes behind,' Corban yelled. 'The only choice to make is who do we fight first. We'll head south, see what Rhin's warband thinks of us. The only running we'll do is at them.'

Tukul felt a thrill go through him, part fear, part excitement. He welcomed it. Corban stood tall in his saddle, Storm pacing around Shield. 'We'll leave the Kadoshim for another day.' Laughter rippled through them at that. Corban raised a fist. 'Truth and courage, and I'll see you all on the other side.'

Tukul heard his voice joined to many others in a shared battle-cry.

'Craf, Fech, I need you both now,' Corban said.

Both birds were perched on Brina's saddle and regarded Corban suspiciously with their beady eyes.

'Please.'

'*Fech will fly. You asked nicely.*' The raven dipped his head in what looked like a mock-bow.

'Thank you,' Corban said, lips twitching. 'Fech, you fly ahead, give us warning of Rhin's warband. Craf, see if you can spot Nathair and the Kadoshim.'

Craf and Fech flapped into the air, spiralled upwards together, then separated – one heading south, the other north.

The warband jerked into motion, Corban leading a central column along the crumbling road. A number of the Jehar horses now bore an extra rider – the villagers who had escaped the Kadoshim in the woods.

Only a score or so.

Meical had counselled to leave them, but Corban had steadfastly refused.

'They will slow us,' Meical had told him.

Corban had looked horrified. 'I cannot abandon them to the Kadoshim.'

'Leaving them is not a death sentence; they will likely survive here, all they need do is hide until the Kadoshim have passed by.'

'And what if the Kadoshim find their trail? What if the Kadoshim are hungry?'

They had all seen how the Kadoshim in the woods had started feasting on those they caught, and the survivors were telling similar tales from the attack on their village.

'This is war, Corban. Hard decisions must be made – they can make the difference between victory and defeat.'

Corban had asked the villagers if they would rather accompany the warband or stay and hide. Not one of them wanted to stay behind.

'I'll not leave them,' Corban said stubbornly, and that had been the end of that. Meical shook his head but said no more.

Our Ben-Elim is finding his Bright Star less compliant than he expected. Tukul had just shrugged. *An extra score we can absorb. And besides, we may have some spare horses soon. Those of our own dead or of our enemies.*

They'd been travelling a little while when a squawking drew Tukul's attention. There was something frantic about it. He turned and looked back, saw a black dot in the sky, growing larger.

Is that one of ours? He could not remember which bird had flown north – *Craf or Fech?* Something was in the sky higher above it, another black dot, suddenly streaking downwards.

'Craf!' Brina shouted, and she was riding back. Corban followed her, the warband slowing, rippling to a halt. Tukul wheeled his mare around and galloped after Corban.

Craf had just reached the woods when the hawk hit him.

Brina screamed.

There was an explosion of feathers and the two birds spun together, Craf squawking in terror, the hawk's talon's snatching at the smaller bird.

The whole warband watched helplessly as the birds fought and twisted through the air. Dath had his bow strung and an arrow nocked, but it was impossible to take a clear shot.

Then another bird crashed into them.

Fech.

There was another explosion of feathers and one of the birds dropped straight down, plummeting into the tree canopy. There was a crashing and snapping of branches, then a black form fell to the ground. It flapped feebly, one wing twisted and not moving.

'*Craf hurt*,' he squawked as Brina rushed to the crow, sweeping him up in her arms.

Above the trees Fech and the hawk twisted, separated. An arrow whistled through the air, missed the hawk by a handspan, then they were together again, surging past the trees, over the meadow, hurtling towards the river. They were low now, skimming the meadow grass. The ground rumbled as Balur broke into a run, chasing after the two birds.

They crashed into a flat-topped boulder at the river's edge, the two birds rolling apart. The hawk righted itself first, and with a flap of wings leaped upon the still-tumbling Fech and with another beat of its wings it was airborne, rising, gripping Fech tight. An arrow skittered off the rock, just missing it.

More arrows sliced the air as it rose – and the hawk veered, Fech wriggling feebly in its grip. The hawk hovered overhead a moment and gave a savage twist of its talons. Tukul heard the crackle of tiny bones snapping. The hawk's beak slashed down, came away trailing droplets of blood and it dropped Fech. The old raven plummeted like a stone to the ground, hitting it with a dull thump.

The hawk rose swiftly, more arrows sailing past it. In moments it was out of range, flying north. Balur reached Fech and scooped him up, wings dangling. The giant's face twisted and Tukul knew that Fech was dead.

They rode in silence along the crumbling road, a grim mood hovering over the company after the death of Fech.

He was only a bird, and three of my sword-kin died this morning fighting the Kadoshim. Yet Fech's death still seemed to affect them all.

Corban had said that he'd recognized the hawk, had sworn that it had belonged to a trader who had betrayed him in the mountains near Dun Vaner. He called it Kartala. *A servant of the enemy. That would make sense. And now we are no longer the watchers, but the watched.*

Tukul shrugged to himself.

No use worrying about things I cannot change. A battle is ahead of us. That I can do something about.

It was highsun now, and they had made good time. The terrain was shifting from wooded hills to rolling moorland. *We should be upon them soon.* He felt the reassuring weight of his sword strapped across his back and his hand dropped to the axe at his side, gifted to him by Wulf at Gramm's hold. It had served him well so far, split more than one skull. *And there will be more to come.*

To Tukul's left Corban called out, glancing down the slope of the road's embankment to the white-foaming river.

It is time, then. Tukul liked Corban's plan; there was a simplicity to it that appealed to him. The only issue he had was the part that Brina and the giantess had been asked to play. Things could go drastically wrong where the earth power was concerned.

Brina was riding close by, Ethlinn the giantess striding beside her. They shared a look and started to chant, long rhythmic sentences in a language Tukul did not understand. Meical added his voice to theirs.

Ahead of them the river began to churn, a white mist boiling out of it, spreading across the meadow, creeping up the embankment and across the road, covering the warband. Tukul looked across to his son, riding just behind Corban. The mist swirled about their horses' hooves like cords of silk, rapidly expanding, creeping higher until it engulfed them.

Riding in the mist was strange. It limited Tukul's vision, Gar and

Corban becoming fleeting shadows. He risked a glance behind him, at the handful of Jehar and giants he saw staring grim-faced back at him, then focused on the space in front of him, straining his ears for any hint of their enemy.

There was a scream to his left, a crash and a wild neighing, then silence. In front of him a shape loomed, solidifying in heartbeats into a warrior on horseback, his face twisted in panic, clutching at a horn hanging at his belt.

One of their scouts. We are close, then.

With a hiss, Tukul drew his sword and took the warrior's head, blood jetting startlingly bright against the white mist. Sounds rang out along the line of the warband – similar encounters. Tukul felt a wave of exultation sweep him. *Riding into battle with my son, behind the Seren Disglair. Praise be to Elyon, Lord of Hosts, that I lived to see this day. May our hearts stay pure and our swords sharp.* He laughed, long and loud, adrenalin pumping through his veins. Now they were moving at a canter. Tukul yearned to kick his horse into a gallop, but he held back. The mist started to thin about them, evaporating. A horn blast rang out nearby, roughly where Tukul judged Corban should be.

'With me,' Tukul yelled, guiding his horse right, sweeping out from the warband. A hundred warriors followed him. They left the dissipating mist behind them, the sunlight suddenly bright, making Tukul blink.

The enemy were there, spread along the wide road, a mix of mounted warriors and men on foot, those mostly gathered about the wains that brought up the rear of their column. *Three, four hundred swords.* Tukul could see expressions of shock and horror upon his enemies' faces as their warband emerged from the mist, wolven and giants snarling and yelling battle cries.

I think even I would be scared at the sight, Tukul thought.

A moment later there was a great crash as Corban and the bulk of the warband smashed into the front lines of the enemy. He saw Storm leap high, tear a rider from his saddle. Tukul's eyes searched for Gar, thought he saw him, a curved sword rising and falling. Fear for his son fluttered in his belly. *He will live or he will die*, he told himself, dragging his eyes away.

He touched his reins, guiding his horse into an arc that led back towards the road, fixed his eyes on a pocket of warriors who seemed to be organizing quicker than the rest. They were gathered about the wains, were spreading along the embankment of the road, moving to flank around Corban's arrowhead that had punched into the heart of the enemy. He glanced behind him, saw the Jehar and Benothi were following him, spreading either side. They would be a wall when they hit the enemy, not a point. He saw Akar's face, the man nodding grimly to him. Tukul had mixed both groups of the Jehar, having noticed a polarization occurring between the Hundred that had followed him from Telassar and the survivors of those who had followed Sumur. *That is not good. We are kin. What's done is done and there should be no grievance between us. And nothing binds like battle.*

Tukul was two hundred paces away when he urged Daria to a gallop and let her go. She did not need telling twice, exploding forwards. Wind whipped his face. He looped his reins around his saddle pommel, pressing his knees tight against her flanks, flicked open the leather catch on his axe's saddle holster.

A hundred and fifty paces.

The ground was drumming to their charge, hooves and iron-shod giants. He pulled his axe free, drew his sword from his back in one long sinuous move. All about him he heard the Jehar echoing him.

A hundred paces.

Battle was raging further along the road, Corban and his followers carving deep into the warband, their progress slowing, horses jostling and heaving in a mass of flesh. Closer to Tukul men amongst the enemy were screaming orders, moving to meet Tukul and his hundred.

Fifty paces, and Tukul fixed his eyes on a trio of warriors standing together, braced, shields raised, spears dipped like stakes. *Elyon above, I give you my sword and my soul.*

He charged them, Daria not slowing as she hit the embankment, powering up the small slope. Heartbeats before collision Tukul threw his axe, at the same time nudging Daria to the left. He saw the axe smash into a face, the warrior falling back, blood erupting, and he slashed at another with his sword as he pounded past, felt the blade cut through leather and flesh. Then he was beyond them, hooves clattering on the stone of the road. A mounted warrior appeared from amongst the wains, saw him and charged. Tukul raised his sword two-handed over his head. Sparks flared as their blades clashed, the momentum of their mounts carrying them past each other, Tukul back-swinging, decapitating his enemy. The horse carried on, disappearing down the embankment, its headless rider slowly slipping off its back.

There was a thunder of hooves; he looked to his left and a horse crashed into him, its rider slashing at his head. Pain exploded in his leg. He blocked, a part of his mind disapproving his technique. Daria neighed wildly as she was bludgeoned backwards, hooves slipping, scrabbling, almost falling. She bit the enemy's horse in her frustration and Tukul grabbed his opponent's wrist, pulled and stabbed his sword up, into the man's armpit, piercing chainmail and sinking deep into flesh. He fell away, Tukul ripping his sword free, blood spraying his face.

Daria righted herself and with a grimace he sent her plunging deeper into the battle. He slashed either side, great looping strokes, left a trail of blood and dying men in his wake. Blows came at him but the stark clarity of battle had taken him – everything bright, sharp, every blow seen as if in slow motion. Men came at him and they died.

Abruptly Daria was sliding, plunging downwards. Tukul felt a moment of disorientation, then realized they had cut their way across the wide giant road and were sliding down the embankment on the far side. For a moment Tukul could see the river, the meadow before it heaving with battle. Then they were hurtling towards a press of warriors looming before him, mostly men on foot. Daria collided with a solid wall of flesh, their momentum stalled, and then Tukul was hurtling through the air, thrown from his saddle. He fell into a warrior, bones crunching – *not mine* – he thought, then he was on the ground, rolling clear, somehow still clutching his sword.

He came to his feet, his left leg throbbing, sword held in the stag's guard, met a surge of blows, his blade parrying and striking faster than he could think, his years of training and discipline taking over, counteracting more rapidly than conscious thought. In a matter of heartbeats half a dozen men lay dead or dying about him. He stood frozen, sword raised, breathing hard.

I am getting old.

Other men appeared – four singling him out. They spread around him in a half-circle. Then one in the middle hurtled forwards in a spray of blood, knocked down by Daria's hooves as she reared behind him and lashed out. Tukul was moving before the others could understand what had happened, sidestepping to the right, his sword sweeping left to right, opening a throat, following through with his momentum to slash downwards, his blade ringing against a rushed block. He rolled his wrists, shifted his feet and his sword was slashing across a face, his enemy reeling back, screaming, hands reaching for his ruined eyes. A lunge and the screams stopped.

One man was left of the four. He looked at Tukul, then turned and ran.

Daria trotted forward and nuzzled his shoulder.

'Good girl,' he said as he swung back into the saddle.

Silhouettes loomed on the road above him, one clearly a giant, others on horseback, instantly recognizable as Jehar. More appeared as Tukul looked, and they swept down the embankment to him. A Jehar rider pulled up beside him – Akar.

'Regroup?' the warrior asked him.

'No,' Tukul said. He blinked away sweat from his eyes, felt the battle joy spreading through his veins, overwhelming the pain in his leg and a dozen smaller wounds.

'We press on, give them no respite.'

The road above looked clear, the bulk of the fighting appearing to be happening on the meadow before him. Tukul didn't know if the plan had worked or not, he just saw the black and gold of his enemy before him, servants of those who had set themselves against Elyon, who had already attempted to cut the heart from his Bright Star. A dark anger swelled in him, bubbling hot through his veins.

'Control it, lest you be controlled,' he murmured the Jehar mantra, then he raised his sword and charged into the meadow, ignoring the shafts of pain jolting up from his leg, yelling a battle-cry that was taken up by a wave of Jehar and giants behind him.

'TRUTH AND COURAGE!'

*

Tukul sat on the roadside. He'd found his axe and was busy cleaning blood from his weapons, then using a whetstone to work out the notches.

His body ached everywhere, but particularly the leg that had been slammed by the charging horse. He'd cared for Daria, checking her wounds, taken her to a spot upriver where the water wasn't flowing pink and washed her down, did the same for himself, discovering a dozen or so cuts on his body that he hadn't known were there.

The battle was done, an overwhelming victory made all the more joyous when Tukul had seen Gar striding through the dead. They had hugged fiercely, only their eyes betraying their secret fears for one another. The body count so far was fifteen dead Jehar and three giants, against three hundred or so of Rhin's warband. In the end the enemy had broken and scattered, many leaping into the river rather than face the Jehar swords and Benothi hammers and axes. A score of prisoners had been rounded up and were kneeling in the grass before Corban and Meical. Along with a handful of Jehar guarding them, Storm was prowling a circle about them, her jaws bloodstained, Buddai lying in the flattened grass, watching.

I don't think any will be stupid enough to try escaping.

Further along the meadow Brina and Ethlinn were treating the wounded, Cywen helping, as well as a handful of the Jehar and some of the giantlings. The smell of burning flesh wafted on the breeze to Tukul as wounds were cauterized.

'I'll not murder men that have surrendered,' Tukul heard Corban say, his voice rising. Meical just stared implacably back at him.

Tukul shared a look with Gar, and with a sigh he rose, his muscles complaining, already stiffening, and strode to join them.

'This is war, Corban,' Meical said as Tukul reached them. 'It is not murder; it is the execution of an enemy that fights on the side of Asroth. There is no moral dilemma here. Let them live, they will join with Nathair and Calidus behind us, swell their ranks, give them information, and fight against us again.'

Corban pinched his nose.

Leading is a hard task, Tukul thought. *And he is bowing beneath the weight of it.*

'They are warriors following orders from their Queen. Not innocent, but not knowingly Asroth's servants,' Corban muttered. 'I understand your points, and they are practical.' He sighed. 'But there is no *honour* in killing helpless men.'

'This is the definition of honour,' Meical said, frowning. 'They chose a side. They were not helpless when they made their choice, or indeed half-a-candle ago, when they were set on separating our heads from our shoulders. They fought. They lost. And they have failed their lord. There would be more dishonour for them if they lived.'

I do not think they would agree, Tukul thought, looking at the captives.

Corban looked at the prisoners kneeling in the grass, many bloodstained, wounded.

'I cannot kill them.'

'Break some bones,' Tukul said.

'What?'

'Break the thumb and a finger or two of their sword hand. Break an ankle. They'll not be able to hold a weapon or move in combat. They'll not face you in battle any time soon. And they'll be alive.'

Corban thought about that a few moments. A relieved smile spread across his face and he squeezed Tukul's shoulder.

'See that it's done,' he said. 'And quickly. We need to move out before the Kadoshim decide to join us.'

Tukul organized the task, asking Balur and a few giantlings to do the deed.

Involve each group in this warband – the Benothi, my Jehar, and those who joined us in Murias. We need to become one.

Balur chuckled as the first man fainted at the sight of a giant raising his war-hammer, but he only brought the butt-end down on the unconscious warrior's hand. Bones smashed.

It was over quickly enough, most of the prisoners knowing that it could have been their heads lying on the grass.

Soon the warband was ready to ride.

Corban was already mounted, eager to leave. A string of horses was roped to take with them, spoils of the battle, and that was after the rescued villagers had each been given a mount. The spare horses were loaded with more spoils from the battlefield – cloaks, boots, leather jerkins, a few good coats of mail, bundles of spears, swords and knives as well as barrels of salted meats and mead.

It won't last long, but it'll make a welcome break from brot.

The auroch that had been yoked to the supply wains were cut loose and set free on the open moors.

Corban spoke again to the handful of villagers who had joined them, gave them a choice of staying with the warband or riding out on their own. They discussed it briefly and then Teca, their chosen speaker, told him that they would stay with the warband.

And with that Corban called out and they set out, moving down the old giants' road in a wide column, Coralen and her chosen scouts riding ahead.

Our first real battle with the Bright Star leading us. He has done well.

CHAPTER TWENTY-FIVE

CAMLIN

Camlin woke with a stiff neck. They'd slept in their boats, tied in amongst a thick bank of reeds. A gentle current had tugged Camlin's boat out into the marsh stream, where dawn's rays painted the world in a golden sheen. Meg was sitting by his feet, staring at him. She offered him a piece of . . . something – *bread, maybe?* He looked closer, saw it had a spongy texture, like a mushroom. He shook his head.

The others were still asleep, Edana and Baird at the far end of their flat-bottomed boat, Brogan propped in the middle, his snoring rocking the boat, sending waves lapping. Amongst the reeds he could make out the tips of boats. Eight in total, and beyond them the shadowy figures of those on the last shift of night's watch. He spied Vonn's straw-coloured hair leaning against a willow.

They had rowed or poled their way deeper and deeper into the marshes, long after all sounds of Morcant's pursuit had faded, eventually grouping together in this reed bank. Camlin groaned as he moved. His neck wasn't the only part of him that ached. He scratched at a lump on his neck, and another, then looked at the back of his hand, saw more red bite marks trailing up his arm. *I've been dinner for a warband of mosquitoes.*

'Don't recommend sleeping in a boat,' he muttered.

Edana stirred and Baird opened his one good eye. Instantly he was awake, sitting up, hand straying to his sword hilt. Brogan let out a snore as loud as a horse and Baird kicked him. He sat up too quickly, the boat almost tipping.

'Morning,' he said with a grin as he scratched his arse.

*

They gathered on the marsh bank.

Three men had died in the escape from the village. A few were wounded, though nothing seemed imminently fatal.

'So where is this Dun Crin?' Roisin said, looking between Edana and Camlin.

'I don't know,' Edana said.

'A giants' fortress, how can you not know where it is?' Roisin snapped.

Apparently a night spent sleeping rough in a boat in the marshes doesn't improve her mood.

'This whole marshland covers an area of fifty leagues or more, and the fortress is rumoured a ruin. Who knows what little is left of it. But Eremon received word that a resistance has taken root here, and what we saw and heard from Morcant would confirm that. They must be here somewhere.'

'So your plan is to row around these stinking marshes until we bump into them?'

Yes, thought Camlin, *though that's not the most diplomatic answer, right now.*

Edana stared at Roisin for a few moments, their gazes locked. 'Yes,' she said.

Oh dear. Even princesses have an end to their patience.

'I can't believe what I'm hearing.'

'If you don't like it you can always go back to Domhain. Or back to your ship.'

Looks as if Edana isn't so polite after a night as food for mosquitoes, either. Camlin tried not to laugh, but he could see ripples of anger flickering through their group, Cian and some other of Roisin's shieldmen. *Not a good sign. They're obviously not used to hearing their Queen spoken to like this. I've seen men start putting knives into each other for little more reason than that they were tired and hungry. This could all turn ugly right quick.*

Camlin was still trying to think of something to defuse the situation when Lorcan broke the sullen silence.

'No point squabbling,' he said. 'We should be rejoicing in our glorious escape from Rhin's henchmen. And I must say that to hear my two favourite ladies exchange such harsh words is almost more than I can bear.'

More silence. And this time Camlin could not stop the grin spilling across his face. Edana scowled at the young warrior, while Roisin looked surprised.

'Isn't it best if we work together?' Lorcan continued, finding everyone looking at him. 'Perhaps there is a better way of finding our allies than wandering aimlessly around.'

'Agreed,' Vonn said, who was sitting against a thick-trunked willow. 'Arguing won't help us find them, and we're here now, so no point regretting it. At least we know that they are definitely here, somewhere – else why is Morcant here? He's hunting them – we all heard what he said to those village elders.'

'They are in these marshes somewhere,' Edana said, her eyes hovering over Camlin.

She wants me to say something.

'That they are,' Camlin said. 'It's just the finding them we have to master now.' He looked carefully at everyone in their group, finally settling upon Meg, the girl from the village.

'Meg, can you help us?' Camlin said. 'You know who we are searching for?'

'Aye,' Meg said, chewing her lip. 'The people my kin were slaughtered over.'

'That's right,' Camlin said. 'I'm not promising anything will happen quickly, but those warriors back at the village – Morcant and the others, that did . . .' His words failed, the image of a child swinging from a gallows filling his mind. 'They're our enemies. We are here to fight them. We'd see some justice done for your kin, but we can't do it alone.'

She looked at all the faces staring at her, finally settled back on Camlin.

'They used to come to the village, trade for goods. And news. They had coin – some gold. Never seen gold before.'

'Can you find them, child, in these marshes?' Roisin asked her. Meg wouldn't look at her, instead sidled closer to Camlin.

'Do you know where they're based, girlie?' Camlin asked her.

'Maybe.'

'And what does that mean?' Roisin said, throwing her hands in the air.

'Mother,' Lorcan muttered.

'Can you help us, Meg?' Camlin said, crouching down to look her in the eyes. 'It'd mean a great deal to us.'

'I can't take you to Dun Crin, don't know where it is. But I know roughly where they came from, the direction they took when they left my village – followed them for a while once, for the fun of it.'

Camlin nodded. It wasn't much. But it was better than nothing.

They spent three days making their way through winding streams, some dead ends, others choked with reeds or dense with willow branches that draped the water like lazy fingers in a stream. Camlin's flat-bottomed boat led the way, Meg sitting upon the steering oar as the others took shifts in poling the boat deeper into the marshes. They ate through Brogan's barrel of herring in two days, but after that Meg taught them how to weave willow traps and set them in the stream for the night. Each morning they were wriggling with life – mostly eels, but other things as well, frogs and toads, the odd trout and roach. Camlin could tell that some of this new crew didn't care too much for the food, but he was accustomed to living off of the land.

This is easy. Food's a bit slimy, and a bit smelly, but slimy food's better than no food at all.

And as Camlin poled, he thought. Thought about how he'd gone from being part of Braith's crew to here, with Edana. *How did I get here? Poling through a marsh with a renegade queen looking to me for direction.* In his mind it all went back to one moment: in the Darkwood, when he had stood in front of Cywen as Morcant ordered her slain. And since then he had felt as if he was involved in something greater than him, something more than just living to line his pocket. He had made, and lost, real friends. Marrock, Corban, Dath . . .

I hope they are well, that they found Cywen and are safe.

And Halion.

Was he slain defending the steps on the beach? Or taken prisoner by Conall? Never did like that Conall – now King of Domhain. Everyone has a temper, but him, he was ruled by it, unpredictable. Wouldn't trust him in a fight, whether he was on my side or the other.

Camlin's mind drifted back to the village, to the corpses hanging from the gallows, to the conversation Morcant had had with the captives he had brought to the village. And he thought a lot about the chest of silver in the roundhouse. *A chest of silver right under my nose. What kind of thief am I?*

'I'll take a go at that, now,' a voice said, Baird moving along the boat.

'I'm all right for a while more,' Camlin said.

'Please, I need to do something. Can't just go to sleep at the drop of a cap like our big friend.' He pointed at Brogan, who was stretched out in the boat, snoring peacefully. 'And his snoring is making me want to kill something.'

'All right,' Camlin said and passed him the pole. Behind them boats twisted in single file, the stream they were travelling too narrow for anything else.

'Think she knows where she's going?' Baird asked him, nodding towards Meg.

'Don't think she's lying,' Camlin said. 'But following someone for a while and then turning back doesn't mean we're going to find them. They may be moving around – sensible thing to do when you're in a crew that's hunted.' He shrugged. 'What are your plans, once we find them?'

'If we find them,' Baird corrected.

'Aye, if.'

'Cross that bridge when I reach it,' Baird said. He shrugged. 'I swore I'd see Edana safe. Not sure leaving her in a marsh with a bunch of hunted rebels is safe.' He grinned, looking slightly insane. 'Besides, I've got nothing better to do, and sticking around with Edana is likely to see me crossing blades with Rhin or her arselings eventually. I want revenge. Rath was a good man, and my friend. Most likely he's dead now, on Rhin's account.'

They turned a bend in the stream, its banks widening a little, passing through a copse of willow and dogwood. Camlin felt the hairs on his arm prickle.

Something's wrong. Something was missing. He frowned. *Noise. It is silent.* Abruptly there was no birdsong, the constant drone and buzz of insects startlingly absent. The only sound was Brogan's basal snoring and the lapping of paddles in water. Baird was staring ahead, a frown creasing his brow.

'Be ready,' the one-eyed giantkiller from Domhain whispered.

Camlin reached for his bow, making the boat rock. Brogan's snoring spluttered and then evened out again. The last of the boats behind him came into view around the bend. Camlin slowed his movements and tried to string his bow calmly, eyes scanning the banks ahead.

Before he had a string out of its pouch the banks exploded into life. Thirty, forty men, all armed, most with spears aimed their way. Camlin put a restraining hand onto Baird's arm as the warrior reached for his sword.

'No point dying here,' Camlin whispered. 'They've got us cold.'

Is this them? The rebels we've been seeking?

Others in the boats behind Camlin were of a different mind, drawing weapons, yelling.

A warrior stepped forward on the riverbank, older, red hair streaked with silver spilling from beneath an iron helm. He wore a coat of mail and a leather vest, held a thick spear.

'Put up your arms or you'll be food for the fish. Bring your boats to the bank, nice and smooth, and get up here where I can see you.'

No one moved.

Edana's voice rang out. 'Do as he says. I'll have none of you die here.' She stood in the boat, the hood of her cloak drawn over her head. 'And who are you, that waylay us?' she asked.

The red-haired warrior opened his mouth, appearing to be about to answer, then frowned. The first boats reached the bank, Cian and Vonn jumping ashore, then Lorcan, who turned and helped his mother to disembark. More than a few of the warriors stared openly at Roisin.

'I'll be asking the questions here,' the red-haired warrior said. 'And my first question is: who are you?'

Don't do it – let's at least find out who these men claim to be. Could be scouts of Morcant's, or lawless men, or mercenaries, Camlin thought.

Edana stepped onto firm land and pulled her hood down.

'I am Edana ap Brenin, Queen of Ardan.'

Oh well. Camlin winced. He stepped ashore, bow finally strung, hand reaching beneath his cloak for his quiver of arrows.

There were at least a dozen heartbeats of silence, then the red-haired warrior was stepping forward, staring hard at her, eyes narrowed. Baird and Camlin moved either side of her, Vonn moving along the riverbank. Spear-points were levelled at them.

'Maybe you are,' Red Hair said quietly. 'I saw Edana – in Uthandun. It was years ago, though, and only from a distance. Any of you lads recognize her?' he cried. Voices murmured along the bank.

To be fair she doesn't look much like a queen right now. Edana's hair was tied tight to her head, its natural blonde dull with sweat and dirt. Her cloak and clothes were torn and mud-stained.

'I think it's her,' one voice said.

'No,' another cried – 'too old.'

'It is Queen Edana,' Lorcan shouted, standing in front of her. 'And the next one to call her a liar will feel my sword.'

'Lorcan,' Edana hissed. 'Why would I lie?' she said to Red Hair.

'This world is full of snares and traps, my lady. It's of no matter, I know someone who will be able to tell me for sure.' Red Hair stepped forwards. He waved something in front of Edana, a hemp sack. 'All of you, put one of these over your heads and I'll take you to someone who'll tell me if you're queen or liar.' He gripped Edana's arm.

'Take your hands off her,' Lorcan snarled, grabbing Red Hair's wrist. The warrior punched Lorcan in the face; the lad staggered back a step, then dropped to the floor, unconscious. Roisin screamed and swords began to leave scabbards.

'No,' Edana yelled, at the top of her lungs.

Brogan woke at that – until then he had still been snoring in the boat. He staggered upright on unsteady feet, the boat rocking beneath him, and he fell over the side with a splash. He managed to get his feet under him and stood, spitting water.

'What's going on?' he spluttered.

Men on the riverbank laughed.

'If you are Queen of Ardan, I think you need a new shieldman,' Red Hair said, smiling.

Edana caught Camlin's eye. *What should I do?*

He shrugged imperceptibly. *Go with them. What else can we do? I think they're our rebels, and if they're not – well, we could put up a fight, but the outcome is clear.*

He looked down and saw Meg was standing close to him.

'Get out of here,' he whispered. She ignored him, only shuffled closer to him. *Stupid bairn.* He tried to kick her but she sidestepped.

Edana took the sack from Red Hair. 'We'll go peacefully. But I'll have your name before I put this on my head.'

'My name is Drust, and I was shieldman to Owain, King of Narvon. Now get on with you.'

It didn't take long for them all to be blindfolded in some way, and soon they were being led along the riverbank, with much stumbling, tripping and swearing along the way.

Shieldman of Owain – what's someone who served Owain doing here? An enemy of Rhin, no doubt, but also a man who must have fought Ardan's warriors, played a part in the sack of Dun Carreg. He can't have that many friends in Ardan.

Camlin felt the sun on his back and his throat was dry when hands grabbed him, forcing him to stop. The bag was pulled from his head and he blinked in the fading sunlight.

A slope led down to a lake that spread before him, wide and dark, calm and flat as a mirror, its far banks a shadow on the horizon. Towers and walls protruded from the dark waters of the lake, a labyrinth of criss-crossing stone slick with weed and moss. On the ground before the lake was an encampment, tents and more permanent-looking structures, fire-pits, and people – lots of people. Warriors, but also a mixture of others: women, the elderly, bairns running in groups.

'Welcome to Dun Crin,' a voice boomed; a large figure was striding towards them. A warrior, tall and barrel-chested, old but not ancient, lots of grey in a long beard tied with leather that draped down to his belly. 'What have you brought me, Drust?' His eyes scanned them all, pausing momentarily upon Camlin.

I know you.

Then the big warrior's eyes fell on Edana and he froze. His mouth opened and closed. 'Edana? It cannot be,' he said, then he dropped to one knee before her.

Edana gasped and she flung her arms around him, smothering his face with kisses.

'Pendathran,' she cried, 'I thought you were dead.'

CHAPTER TWENTY-SIX

RAFE

Rafe trekked along an old fox trail that wound through green mead-ows. He was a league or so north of Dun Taras, the fortress a dark shadow on the horizon behind him. A ten-night had passed since he'd returned with Conall and Braith. Word of Halion's capture and imprisonment had spread and, within days, the unrest had begun again. It seemed there was a rebellious element that wanted Halion as king, rather than Conall. Grain barns had been burned, the camp of Veradis and his eagle-warriors had been vandalized, and last night an attempt had been made to rescue Halion. It had failed, but the mood in the fortress was grim and Rafe had decided he needed a break from politics, people and stone walls, to be somewhere green, with only sky above him.

So here he was. The plains to the north of Dun Taras reminded him of Ardan, an undulating landscape of wood and meadow. As he walked he thought of his days back home with his da, when they would head out on hunting trips with just a small bag with rope, flint and tinder, some bread and cheese, never enough to last the dura-tion of their outing – *You'll have to catch us something to eat, Rafe my lad*, his da would always say to him, *else we'll starve to death* – and slowly but surely his da had taught him the way of the wild. How to track anything that moved, to read the signs, to be cunning, patient when necessary, and fast as a striking adder as well.

Out of habit he'd packed a bag just as his da had taught him. He liked the weight of it across his shoulder, familiar as the weight of a knife on his belt.

I miss my da.

And now he's dead. Ripped apart by that devil-wolven, Corban's pet.

I hate them both. He looked at the landscape around him, imagined hunting them through it, wearing them down, eventually forcing them to turn at bay. And then he would kill them. The wolven first, so Corban could watch. And then Corban, in a repeat of their Court of Swords in the feast-hall of Dun Carreg. Except this time Rafe would win. *He cheated. Lunged at me before I was ready. It'll be different this time.* And in his mind it was, Corban begging for mercy before Rafe slowly pushed his blade home, into Corban's heart.

He was smiling when one of the hounds started barking.

He'd brought Scratcher and Sniffer out of habit. He saw Scratcher's hind end disappear into a cluster of shrub, saw the familiar streak of a hare as it burst from the far side of the undergrowth, weaving across an open meadow, leaping a narrow stream. Sniffer went around the shrub that Scratcher was wading through and was bounding after the hare in great, ground-eating strides.

'Oi,' Rafe called, 'here now!' But he knew it was too late for Sniffer; he had the scent and was for the time being deaf in the joy of his euphoric chase. Scratcher broke through the shrub as Rafe reached him and, being closer, was called to heel.

'Come on, boy, we'll catch them together.'

They hurried across the meadow, Rafe splashing across the stream, Scratcher crossing it in a single bound. The ground became spongy underfoot, more streams dissecting the land, thick clumps of marsh grass appearing.

Don't like this much – soon we'll be wading into a bog. The thick smell of peat and stagnant water was filling the air. Rafe put his fingers to his lips and whistled, high and shrill. He paused and listened.

Nothing.

He whistled again; this time heard a bark. Looking about, he saw that the ground rose. He headed towards it and climbed a slight incline, realizing that it was an old road, wide, crumbling stone worn and broken by years of attrition, frost and thaw, root and rain. *Must be giant-made, like the giantsway back home.* He whistled again, walking on, keeping to this high ground. He saw a streak of grey, Sniffer weaving back to him, something lolling between his jaws.

He caught the hare, then. Good boy.

Rafe stood on the old road with Scratcher and waited, Sniffer making his way through a landscape of glistening streams and pools, edged by strips of blackthorn and dogwood. Willows grew here and there, great curtains of branches draping the ground. In a pool a heron stood tall and still, silhouetted by the sun.

Sniffer was almost back to them when he seemed to stumble and fall. Beside Rafe Scratcher whined.

Sniffer tried to climb to his feet, but couldn't, as if something had reached out from beneath the ground and had gripped him in a fist of iron.

A bog. He's fallen into a bog.

Rafe ran down the embankment, stumbling, almost falling, saw the shift from solid to marsh just in time. Black mud was erupting about Sniffer as he thrashed, his great bulk heaving and bucking in the viscous soil, but the more he struggled, the quicker he sank.

'It's all right, boy. I'm here, I'm here,' Rafe called out. Not surprisingly the words didn't have any effect on Sniffer as he writhed, only his head and shoulders visible now, eyes rolling white in panic. Scratcher paced the edge of land and marsh, whining frantically.

What to do? What to do? Rafe forced himself to be still, then threw his bag from his shoulder and pulled out the rope. *Thank you, Da.* He ran back to a stand of blackthorn and tied one end around the thick, twisted trunk, cutting his hands on the thorns, checked the knot, then tied the other end around his waist. He looked back to Sniffer and was horrified to see his muzzle sink out of sight; he took a run up and leaped into the bog.

He fell in with a great splash, the marsh somewhere between water and mud. It was thick, black, and it stank. He thrashed his way closer to where he thought Sniffer had been, with each move sinking deeper. He reached down, arms feeling like they were pushing through porridge, felt something solid brush his finger tips.

Fur?

He hesitated for a moment, thought about pulling himself back up onto solid ground, but the thought of Sniffer, scared and drowning, filled his mind. He took a deep breath and let the bog take him, digging his way down, doing everything that his da had told him not to do in this situation. With each move of his arms and his legs he felt the bog suck him down, deeper and deeper. His lungs started to hurt, and still he went deeper. He could hear his pulse pounding in his head, his heart thumping in his chest. His lungs burned now, and still he went deeper. Then he felt it, something solid; fur and flesh. He wrapped one arm around it, felt his fingers dig into a thicker level of mud, scrape along something hard and cold. Instinctively he gripped onto it with his fingertips, pulled his arm tight about the hound's body, with his other hand pulling on the rope stretched taut above him.

He didn't move. Panic surged through him, combined with the screaming in his lungs into an overwhelming urge to open his mouth and breathe. By an immense act of will he didn't, instead just kept pulling on the rope.

He moved. Just a fraction at first, then more, half an arm's length. The hound was a huge weight, anchoring him down, and he was tempted to let go. *No. Not now, not after this.* He reached higher up the rope, pulled again, this time moving easier, pulled again and now he was moving through honey, not tar. He pulled again and his head burst out of the bog, his mouth opening to suck in a huge lungfull of air. He pulled again, dragged the limp weight of the hound clear, onto his shoulder, started heaving himself towards the bank.

Scratcher was going berserk on the bank, leaping, barking and howling at them.

Rafe crawled onto solid ground, the body of Sniffer flopping beside him. He realized he was gripping something in his other hand, a handle attached to something caked in mud. He dropped it on the ground, ran his hands over Sniffer, Scratcher licking the hound, pushing him with his muzzle.

The hound wasn't breathing; viscous mud clogged his nostrils, dripping from its mouth.

No! Rafe put his ear to the hound's deep chest. Nothing. Hot tears came to his eyes and he shook the dog. Its head lolled drunkenly.

'No!' he yelled and slammed his fists onto the dog's chest. Again, and again.

Suddenly the hound jerked, started choking, legs kicking, coughing up great clumps of black earth. Scratcher leaped about them both, barking and licking.

'Good boy,' Rafe said as he flopped down beside Sniffer, draping one arm over him. Sniffer lifted his head and looked at Rafe. 'Good boy,' Rafe said. 'Good boy.'

Sniffer licked his face.

Rafe trudged wearily through the gates of Dun Taras, headed for his room, a barrack that he shared with a score of other warriors. People were staring at him.

Can't blame them, I suppose. He was quite a sight, the mud of the bog drying black, caking him from head to foot. He'd tried to wash, but it didn't seem to want to come off. Sniffer was the same, grey fur spiked with dried mud. He didn't seem to care, though.

Why did I do that? I'm a bloody idiot, could have got myself killed. My da would've given me such a hiding.

As he approached the keep he saw a familiar face sitting on the steps of a fountain. Braith.

He was much recovered from his wound, just a slight stoop to his shoulder that gave away the weakness where the muscle had been cut.

'What in the Otherworld happened to you?' Braith asked him as he approached. Rafe thought about telling the truth, but then thought better of it. *Risking death to pull a hound out of a bog. He'll think I'm touched.*

'I fell in a bog,' he said. 'Scratcher pulled me out.' *A good lie is best mingled with the truth, my da always told me.* He sat next to Braith, dropping his bag at his feet. It clunked and he remembered the box he'd pulled out of the bog. It had been locked so he'd put it in his bag, thought he'd have a look at it later.

'How're you feeling?' he asked Braith. He liked the woodsman, respected his skill in the wild. And there was something about Braith; when you spoke he made you feel that he listened. Really listened, as if you mattered.

'Well enough,' Braith said. 'My legs aren't what they were, yet. That's why I'm sitting here; had to stop for a breather.' His mouth twisted in a rueful smile. 'But nothing a few good meals won't change. Don't think my aim'll ever be as good, though.' He rolled his shoulder and grimaced. 'Something I'd like to thank Camlin in person for.'

Rafe nodded. He had a few scores of his own that he'd like to settle.

A noise rose up beyond the archway to the keep, a crowd gathered. Many were marching through the gates.

'What's that all about?' Rafe asked.

'Rhin's making an announcement at sunset,' Braith said. He glanced up at the sky and stood. 'Lend me your shoulder and let's go and see what she has to say.'

Rhin was standing at the top of a dozen steps before the gates to the keep. She looked regal and imposing in her sable cloak edged in rich embroidery, a torc about her neck and golden thread wound through her silver hair. Conall stood one side of her, glowering at the crowd, Geraint the other. Rafe saw Veradis standing lower down, on a level with the crowd, but apart. A dozen or so of his eagle-guard were with him, looking fine in polished cuirasses of black and silver.

'I'm not one for grand speeches so I'll make this quick,' Rhin began, the crowd quietening almost instantly. 'There are unsavoury forces at work in this realm that are determined to stay rooted in the past, and in the process cause me some irritation. The past is not always good, by the way. In the case of Domhain the past involved a senile, lecherous old King and his selfish bitch of a young whore wife.'

Mutters rippled around the crowd, some laughter as well.

'I like to say things as I see them – something you will no doubt become accustomed to. Anyway, this unsavoury element that I speak of amongst you: it has come to my attention that they are keen for Halion ben Eremon to sit upon the throne of Domhain. Now, you already have Conall, the brother, and a very fine King he is proving himself to be, too. So why be so greedy?'

Some more laughter.

'You malcontents out there will have to make do with Conall, for two reasons. First, because, in case you have forgotten, I have conquered Domhain. Defeated its warbands, seen your King take his life rather than face me, and so I get to choose who I put on your throne. That's the victor's right.

'Secondly. Halion will be unable to sit upon your throne, because as of this time on the morrow, his head will no longer be connected to his body.'

There were gasps at that, some widespread muttering, and still some laughter. Conall took a step back, eyes wide, but he quickly composed himself.

'Think that was as much news for Conall as it was the rest of us,' Braith said in Rafe's ear.

'That's all I have to say,' Rhin said and disappeared into the shadows of the keep. Conall stood there a moment, head bowed, then he strode after her.

The crowd dispersed slowly. Rafe decided it was time to find somewhere to wash the mud from his body, when a warrior of Cambren pushed through the crowd and called to Braith.

'Queen Rhin wants to see you,' the warrior said.

'Come with me,' Braith said, bending to massage a leg.

Rafe shrugged, though he didn't much like the thought of being too close to Rhin. She scared him. They followed the warrior and he escorted them into the keep.

Rhin was waiting beside a fire-pit, shadows rippling across her face. She raised an eyebrow when she saw Rafe.

'Legs are still a bit weak under me,' Braith said by way of explanation.

'Are you well enough for a long journey?' Rhin said to Braith, no preamble.

'I am,' Braith said. 'Long as I'm sitting on a horse, not walking. How far?'

'To Ardan. Tracking. Hunting.'

'I could do with some help.'

Rhin looked at Rafe. 'You're a huntsman, I believe.' She looked him up and down.

'I . . . I am,' Rafe stuttered.

'Good. There's your help, then, Braith.'

'What would you have me do?' Braith asked.

'Come ready to my chambers tonight, seventh candle. And be ready for the road.'

Rafe followed Braith hesitantly into Rhin's chamber. It was late, the only light coming from a low-burning fire and a candle or two dotted around the room.

'Sit,' Rhin said, waving them to two chairs pulled close about the fire. She poured them both a cup of wine and then reclined, her eyes shining in the firelight. Shadows clung to the deep grooves of her face.

She looks exhausted, worse than normal.

'What is the mission, my Queen?' Braith said.

'Ahh, Braith. My faithful Braith. You have served me well. I'm glad you didn't die on a cold beach in Domhain.'

'I'll drink to that,' Braith said as he raised his cup.

'As to your mission. Well, it is based solely on a prediction, at the moment. It may not happen. Though I am usually right. If there is one thing I know well it is the hearts of men. But I will not speak of it yet. We must wait, and see if my suspicion is founded.'

'I'll just drink some more of this fine wine, then,' Braith said.

'As long as you are able to ride, you can drink all you like,' Rhin smiled.

Rafe took a sip and settled back into his chair. For a while he listened to the low murmur of Braith and Rhin's conversation, but in time his eyes drooped.

He came awake with a start. Rhin and Braith were still in their chairs, though they were no longer talking. They were looking at the fire. Rafe stared too, and as he watched, fresh flames curled up, wood crackling, a spark spitting out onto the stone floor.

'What—' Rafe began.

'Quiet,' Rhin snapped.

A figure formed in the fire, like the thread of a tapestry being sewn upon a fabric of flame. Slowly it became clearer: a figure sitting upon a stone floor, a chain of iron about its wrists.

The figure spoke, a crackle of flame. 'What do you want?' Then Rafe recognized him.

Halion.

Witchcraft. Rafe felt his body prickle with goose-bumps. He wanted to get up and run, as far and fast as he could, but his feet seemed to be frozen, his arms pinned to the leather chair he was sitting in.

Another figure appeared, moving quickly. It bent over Halion, then the shackles were falling away, clanging on the stone.

'What are you doing?' Halion asked.

'Get up,' the other figure said, a man, his back to the flames.

'I don't understand,' Halion muttered.

'Rhin's had enough of you being alive. She's putting your head on a spike, on the morrow.'

'Thought that would suit you. You've made your choices,' Halion said.

'Don't be a fool, Hal.' The figure held out his arm for Halion. 'You're my brother. I can't see that done to you.'

Conall.

'So what is this, then?'

'It's an escape, you idiot what did you think?' Rafe could almost see the grin on Conall's face.

Halion gripped Conall's arm and stood slowly.

'Come with me,' Halion said.

'No. I don't want to see you dead, but that doesn't mean I want to go back to life on the run, in a saddle. And besides, I don't like those whom you serve.'

'The feeling's mutual there,' Halion said.

'So, I'll take you to the tunnel in the stables, give you a horse. You're on your own from there. Where you go is your business – and don't tell me, I don't want to know.'

'But Rhin'll have your head for this.'

'She'll never know.'

Rhin snorted at that.

Then they were moving, disappearing from the flames.

Silence settled in the room. Rafe stared at the fire. The flames died down, shrinking back to glowing embers.

'How did you do that?' Rafe whispered.

'You don't really want to know,' Rhin said. 'Suffice to say that it involved the freshly flayed skin of an enemy and some blood. Actually a lot of blood. It wasn't easy. But then, if it was, everybody would be doing it, wouldn't they.'

Rafe swallowed, feeling his gut churn. *Wish I'd never asked.*

'Never did trust that Conall.' Braith muttered.

'No. It's a shame,' Rhin sighed.

'Did you know he would do this?'

'I suspected.'

'So will it be Conall's head on a spike alongside Halion's on the morrow?'

'No. Not yet, at least. I need him for the moment. I have to go – pressing needs elsewhere, and I really don't like it here. So I'll let him think he's deceived me, leave him to rule Domhain for a while, see whether he can tame the dissenters. He may just get himself killed, of course, which will save me a job in the long run.' She shrugged. 'I can't worry about everything.'

'Better get moving,' Braith said. 'Else Halion'll get away.'

'I want him to get away. And you're going to follow him.' Rhin said with a slow smile. 'All the way to Edana.'

CHAPTER TWENTY-SEVEN

MAQUIN

Maquin crawled through the long grass, breathing in the scent of meadow flowers. Abruptly the grass parted and a wide plain dissected by a forked river opened up in front of him. *We're going to get wet. Again.*

The grass rustled behind him and Fidele crawled up.

'It's big,' she said.

'Aye.'

'I have ridden past it many times, and it never looked so daunting before.'

'That's because you and your honour guard could ride across a bridge that wasn't guarded by Vin Thalun then.'

Beyond the river a forest followed the skyline into the east.

'That is the forest Sarva, and beyond it is Ripa.'

Ripa. Our destination, and safety, according to Fidele.

And now we are nearly there. Just a river and a forest to cross.

They had been travelling for over two moons now, shadowing the main river most of the way from Jerolin. After the hounds and the jump into a river they had been carried a few leagues south. They'd hauled themselves out, shivering, battered and bruised but still alive, and gone to ground, hiding in a cave for a ten-night as they let the Vin Thalun pass them by. Since then they had avoided all pursuit, though they had glimpsed Vin Thalun corsairs patrolling the great river that flowed from Jerolin to Ripa.

Maquin scanned the plain below them. There was no bridge crossing the river, but he spied a ford. Movement on the river drew Maquin's attention.

It was a ship's prow, oars rising and dipping.

He recognized it as a Vin Thalun war-galley. He had spent enough time breaking his back rowing one all the way from Isiltir to the island of Panos. As he watched his hands itched, the memory of pulling at an oar triggering a host of feelings and memories. All of them unpleasant.

The Vin Thalun galley reached the ford in the river, a gangplank appearing and men swarming down it. Some carried great lengths of timber, half a dozen stripped trunks and spare masts. With an efficiency that Maquin grudgingly respected they set about portage of the ship across the ford, placing the lengths of timber in front of the ship's prow, at the same time ropes were hurled down for men to haul the ship over the masts, warriors running to the stern of the ship to collect the timber as it rolled over it and carry it back to the prow, repeating the process until the ship was back in the water on the northern side of the ford. Then they boarded the ship and set to rowing again.

The sun was low in the sky when the Vin Thalun galley disappeared over the horizon, heading north-west.

'They are going to Jerolin,' Fidele said.

'Most likely. And we're going to Ripa. Come, let's go get our feet wet.'

Maquin watched Fidele as she skinned a rabbit, the first rays of dawn dappling her skin through the canopy above. Her cuts were economical and precise, first gutting the dead animal, dumping the offal in the river, keeping the heart and liver, slicing a neat line all along the underbelly, then ripping the skin free in a series of fluid tugs.

She's not useless now. Not that I thought she was before. Stubborn, pigheaded, maybe, but not useless. Over their time together Maquin had learned a quiet respect for her. She was a lady of rank and clearly not capable of surviving in the wild – *well, not when I met her* – but to her credit she had refused just to rely upon him. She asked more questions than an inquisitive bairn, and slowly built up a set of skills that would look after any woodsman in the wild.

The rabbit was skinned and quartered now. She pierced each piece on a long knife and set it over their small fire, a luxury Maquin would not normally have agreed to, but they were half a day from

Ripa now. Fidele was focusing on turning her makeshift spit, face set in lines of concentration so as not to burn any of the meat. The last two moons had taken their toll on her. She was pale, her face gaunt, dark shadows beneath her eyes, streaks of grey in her otherwise jet hair. Yet something else had changed about her. When Maquin had led her from the arena at Jerolin there had been a rage within her, something cold and hard. Brittle. Over their journey that had changed, gradually melting away. She was relaxed in the wild, appearing more comfortable than Maquin had ever witnessed her in Jerolin.

And now I have taken her almost to safety, to Ripa. The first promise that I have not broken in a long time. He felt something at that thought, a warmth deep in his chest. The satisfaction of a task completed. *I'd forgotten what it is to feel . . . good. To have honour.*

And he felt something else, an echo of his life before Lykos and slavery, before Jael's betrayal and Kastell's death, when life had been more than just a consuming need for vengeance or survival. *She has reminded me what it is like to be a man, not just a trained killer. That feels good, too.*

She looked up at him, perhaps feeling his eyes upon her.

'What?' she said, a smile warming her face.

'Nothing,' he muttered and looked away.

They stepped out of the forest; the road and river left a gaping hole amongst the trees that reminded Maquin of the dark entrance to the catacombs beneath Haldis. Ripa appeared before them: a stone tower on a high hill overlooking the sea. It was guarded by a stout wooden fortress, a town of wood and thatch spilling from the hill's slopes and down into a bay. Columns of smoke rose up into the sky. The river curled languidly towards the sea through a plain of tall grass, the smell of salt and sound of gulls in the air.

They walked on the road, which was built upon an embankment, beside them fields of tall grass swaying in a strong breeze. Maquin felt exposed and self-conscious now that they were out in the open. Vulnerable. *Been in the wild too long.*

As they followed the road from the forest that led to Ripa something nagged Maquin.

Where are the people? The children?

'Something's wrong,' Maquin said.

As they crested a slight rise they saw what. Black-sailed ships dotted the bay – lots of them.

A blockade. Maquin stopped walking, pointed to the bay. Fidele stared, her brow creased with worry.

'That smoke doesn't look right,' she said.

She was right. Even as Maquin watched thick black columns of smoke appeared, close to the harbour.

Ripa is under attack.

'We should get back to the forest,' Maquin said.

They turned, hurrying back. Before they'd gone a dozen strides a shape appeared in the darkness that enveloped the river's entrance to the forest. A sharp prow emerged like a spear bursting through a body. A lean hull, low to the water, oars rising and falling in constant rhythm.

Maquin grabbed Fidele and dragged her down the embankment into the long grass that edged the road. Once under cover Fidele pulled Maquin to a halt.

'I must see,' she hissed at him.

'We should leave, get away,' he said, all his instincts screaming to run, to survive.

'Go where? There is nowhere else to go. This is the only safe place.' There was a tremor in her voice.

She thought her running was over, that she was safe.

He allowed her to lead him to the edge of the grass. They peered out, saw the Vin Thalun galley sail past them, sleek and fluid, others emerging from the darkness of the forest. They were close enough to see faces on the first galley's deck, Vin Thalun warriors gathered there, staring at Ripa. Maquin's eyes were drawn to one – dark-haired, an oiled beard. Maquin knew him just by the way he stood.

Lykos.

Fidele's hand gripped his forearm, nails digging in as she hissed. She took a step forwards, one hand reaching for the knife at her belt. Maquin grabbed her and dragged her back, the grass around them swaying. A cry of alarm went up from the galley's deck. He risked a glance back, saw Lykos staring hard. Lykos shouted an order and the galley swerved towards the bank. The oars were pulling out of the water, being drawn back through the oar-holes. A gangplank appeared, warriors crowding behind it.

Maquin looked to the forest, then up to Ripa on the hill. *In the forest we'll be hunted. In the fortress we'll be trapped.*

Fidele made the decision for him. She bolted away from him, through the long grass towards Ripa.

Maquin caught up with Fidele. He could hear the sound of pursuit, feet drumming on the road, the change in sound as they hit the long grass. It was hard going, the grass weaving about them as they powered through it. All Maquin could hear was his own breathing, the sound of their passage as the grass rustled and swayed. He risked a glance back, to his horror saw Vin Thalun running along the road, tracking them. And they were gaining.

Got to do something.

He grabbed Fidele and burst out of the grass and dragged her up the embankment to the road, shoved her forward, yelled for her to keep running as he turned, pulling a knife from his belt. A score of Vin Thalun were pounding up the road towards him – forty paces away, thirty – galleys alongside him flowing down the river, and to his right the long grass was rippling in the wake of those who had followed them. He flipped the knife in his hand and threw it at a warrior on the road. The man swerved and the blade punched into his shoulder instead of his neck. 'Old Wolf,' he heard someone call out from the river as he turned and ran, other voices taking up the cry. He didn't stop to look.

He caught up with Fidele and together they hurtled along the road, buildings streaming past them. Sounds of battle drifted on the breeze from the bay, clouds of black smoke billowing across the road.

'Hold your breath,' Maquin grunted as Fidele slowed before the thick smoke. He sucked in a deep breath, grabbed her hand and plunged in. A dozen heartbeats and there was no change, his eyes stinging, forty heartbeats and he could feel the veins pounding in his head, felt like his heart was thumping out of his chest. Fifty heartbeats and the smoke thinned, and then suddenly they were through it. Fidele staggered into him, coughing, her eyes streaming.

'Can't stop,' he rasped. Blurred images fought on the road

ahead. He turned to his left, pulling Fidele into a huddle of buildings, led her through a twisting maze of alleys and paths. Eventually Maquin stopped, leaning against a wall. Fidele collapsed to her knees, chest rising and falling violently as she struggled for breath. Maquin realized he was still clutching a knife in one hand.

'Got to keep moving,' he muttered. He glanced up, saw the tower of Ripa looming above them.

'One hard climb and we're there,' he said. Dragging Fidele to her feet they stumbled on, turning a corner and almost falling into a running battle, Vin Thalun trading blows with warriors of Ripa in the black and silver of Tenebral. The Vin Thalun were fewer in numbers, but more were emerging from the streets and alleys all the time. Maquin looked up the hill, saw that the gates of a tall wooden wall that ringed the tower were open – people streaming through them.

These men are the rearguard, buying time for the people of Ripa to reach safety.

'Up the hill,' Maquin yelled at Fidele over the din of battle. Together they ran, swerving around combat, over bodies. Two men crashed in front of them, punching, kicking, stabbing. Fidele hurdled them and stumbled on, but a hand grabbed Maquin as he leaped over them. He crashed to the ground, rolled to his feet, brandishing his knife. A Vin Thalun was climbing from the ground, short sword blooded and buckler still in his hands. Maquin didn't wait for him to find his balance and lunged forward with his knife, at the same time drawing another. His first blade scraped along the Vin Thalun's buckler, his second slicing low, beneath the rim of a battered cuirass. Blood and a tangle of intestines gushed out of the wound. Maquin kicked the screaming man over and turned back to Fidele a dozen paces ahead. He waved her on, sprinting after her.

The men of Ripa were trying to form a wall against the Vin Thalun, but there were too many, more surging up the hill, others flowing out of side streets, flanking the beleaguered rearguard.

They have no chance.

Then Vin Thalun were spilling into the road above them, two score at least, more appearing, blocking the road and falling on the men of Ripa.

Fidele looked at him despairingly.

There was no way back. The side streets were swarming with Vin Thalun, and besides, running that way would only delay the inevitable.

The tower gates were still open, a hundred paces up the road.

Only chance is to get through those gates.

He stared at Fidele a moment, the worry etched upon her features, moments from their journey flashing through his mind. Strangely, he found himself smiling, remembering snippets of conversation and silence.

I think you're worth dying for. He knew making the gates was unlikely – just too many Vin Thalun in the way, and more arriving by the heartbeat.

Death is only ever a moment away.

'What now?' Fidele asked.

I carve us a way to those gates, or die trying.

'Stay behind me,' he grunted, stepping in front of her.

The first men saw him too late, his knives bringing sudden death upon them. In a dozen heartbeats three Vin Thalun were dead, another slumped upon the ground, bleeding out from a deep gash in his groin.

Maquin pressed forward, felt Fidele behind him, knew she would have her knife in her hand.

The Vin Thalun saw him coming now, a handful moving on him together, spreading into a half-circle.

Don't give them time. He knew from the pits that to hesitate against many was to die. With a snarl he swept forwards and to the left, one knife high, the other low, cutting, blocking, slicing, always moving. Time slowed, each heartbeat a lifetime. He felt cuts appear on his arms, his thighs, thin lines of pain burning like flame as his attackers managed to get past his guard. He stabbed, hands slick with blood. A blow high on his back staggered him and he fell to one knee, rolled forwards from it, a sword slicing a handspan from his face. He had no idea where Fidele was now. Could only hope that she was still close. He kept stabbing, every face he saw superimposed with the features of Lykos or Jael. He killed them both, countless times, a feral grin on his face. One of his knives stuck between ribs, was ripped out of his hand as his victim fell away. He pulled another blade from his boot, powered on, blood splattering his face, blurring his vision, the taste of iron in his mouth. Someone grabbed his arm; he spun on a heel, sliced a hamstring, the man falling, still clutching him, pulling him down. A blow crunched into his gut, low, above his right hip, felt like a punch. He snapped an elbow into a face, heard cartilage snap, took a step forwards and suddenly he was falling, his right leg numb, the ground rushing up to him, his head slamming onto the blood-slick ground, his knives skittering away. He pushed at the ground, tried to rise, but his legs weren't working properly; he just managed to roll onto his back. He sucked in air, the sky a bright blue above him. Numbness pulsed out from the blow to his gut. He reached there, fingers coming away dark with blood.

Is this death? He felt no pain, just weariness settling upon him like a heavy cloak, his limbs suddenly filled with lead.

A face loomed over him, blotting out the sky, a Vin Thalun beard thick with iron rings, face twisted in a snarl, iron glinting. He thought about moving, fingers twitching to find one of his knives, but it was all too much effort. Then the face was falling away, Fidele replacing it. She dropped to her knees, shook him, face contorted with fear.

'Run, you idiot,' he said, though he wasn't sure how loud he said it, or even if the words had passed his lips at all.

Hands gripped his head, Fidele lifting him onto her lap. Tears stained her cheeks, dropped onto his face. He tasted the salt on his lips. Her fingers brushed at his hair, wiped blood from his eyes. Her mouth was moving, her voice filling his head, but he couldn't distinguish the words.

'It's all right,' he tried to say. His eyes fluttered closed.

'Live, damn you!' she screamed at him, a fist pounding his chest. His eyes snapped open. He heard that.

I'm trying, but it's not as easy as you'd think. In truth just staying focused on her face was proving difficult; a dark nimbus formed around the periphery of his vision, the urge to close his eyes overwhelming. *So tired.*

A noise grew, filling his head: pounding, rhythmic, growing louder. *Hooves?* Shadows were all around him now, a flash of hooves stamping. Arms reached down and grabbed Fidele, pulling her away and his head thumped onto the earth.

She fought them, shouting, reaching out, pointing at him.

Then hands were gripping him, lifting him high. A new face appeared, a man, thick black beard on a weathered face. He grinned, which Maquin thought was strange at a time like this.

'Welcome to Ripa,' the face said, and then the darkness surged in and Maquin knew no more.

CHAPTER TWENTY-EIGHT

LYKOS

Lykos stood on deck and stared up at the tower of Ripa. Gulls circled and screeched and absently Lykos spied a sea-eagle, sailing the currents high above the flocks of gulls.

He is like me. Striking without warning. But I did not strike quickly enough. The tower still stands, its walls and gates closed against me.

He tried to focus on strategy, on finding a way to end this, but his mind kept looping back to Maquin and Fidele. For a moment he had not believed his own eyes, not believed that his fortune could be quite so good. Two moons he had waited for word of their capture, had become increasingly frustrated with every passing day. Eventually word reached him that their trail had been found, only for them to disappear again. And then, nothing.

Until today, when he saw them staring straight at him from a sea of undulating grass.

And again they have escaped me.

'Your boat is ready,' a voice behind him said. Kolai, his shield-man. Lykos had hand-picked another dozen men, a mixture of pit-fighters and corsairs, more than he had ever felt the need for before. But a knife in the back had convinced him of his mortality. *Better too many than too few.*

Lykos made his way across the ship's deck and swung nimbly over the side, climbed down a rope net into a rowing boat bobbing on the swell. The wound in his back was as good as healed, though he could sense a weakness there, an ache when he exerted himself. His twelve shieldmen were already in the boat, half of them sitting at the oars. Each one of them had a grapple hook and rope wound about one shoulder. Kolai dropped into the boat behind him and they set off, cutting across the bay to the harbour.

They skirted the burning galleys of Ripa, larger, heavier and slower than any Vin Thalun galley. Lykos smiled at the sight, knowing how many ships the Ripa fleet had cost him while defending their coastline against Vin Thalun raiders before the pact with Nathair and Aquilus. It was very satisfying.

They moored the boat and climbed stone steps to the harbour. A group of Vin Thalun was standing on a pier, a hundred men, maybe more. Lykos walked up to one who stood before them, black-haired, beard oiled and clinking with iron like any self-respecting Vin Thalun. A scar ran from the corner of his mouth to his left ear.

'Demos, it is good to see you, you old pirate.' Demos was the closest thing to a friend that Lykos had. He had no interest in politicking, or in power, just lived for the thrill of riding the waves, of hunting on the deep blue. He was a shark, a predator, and a friend.

'Less of the old,' Demos grinned, 'I'm younger than you.' He held Lykos by the shoulders and stared at him. 'Being a lord is taking its toll, I think.'

'Aye. That and being stabbed in the back,' Lykos said grimly.

'Think you can do this?' Lykos asked him, looking at the cliffs that Ripa's tower was built upon.

'Only one way to find out,' Demos grinned.

'I'll go and draw their eyes,' Lykos said. They gripped forearms and then Demos was jumping into a long rowing boat, one of five that were moored beside the pier.

Lykos strode into the town. He did not rush. Dead littered the streets, warriors of Ripa stripped of anything useful – weapons, armour, boots, cloaks. Vin Thalun gathered about him as he passed through the town, until a few hundred were massed at his back. As he climbed the hill to the tower he looked back out over the bay.

Vin Thalun galleys filled it, at least a score used in this strike on Ripa. Most had sailed around the coast and blocked the bay, burning the ships that were moored in Ripa's harbour. An attacking force had landed as Lykos had sailed his own men down the river, another ten shallow-draughted galleys. Fifteen hundred swords, and another thousand crew on the ships, reserves if need be. His sources told him that old Lamar had no more than eleven hundred men at his disposal, and judging by the corpses on the street a good few of them wouldn't be lifting a sword against him.

So I have the manpower to finish this. Lykos felt a worm of worry burrowing through his belly. He was overstretched and he knew it. He'd sent a fleet north-west at Calidus' request: fifty ships, including a score of transporters for horses and wains, all under the command of Alazon. Calidus had not expressly ordered Lykos to sail with the fleet, although he knew it had been presumed. But for Lykos only one thing dominated his mind, filling it, which was why he was here now.

Fidele. He had never felt like this about a woman before, always took what he wanted, with rarely a second thought. No doubt he had enough bastards scattered about the Three Islands to one day crew a galley. But Fidele was different. *She's the only one who's stabbed me, for a start.* He chuckled to himself, Kolai glancing at him. *I will have her back.*

Besides, this rebellion needed to be crushed before it spread. *Peritus is in Ripa and so he has Lamar's backing, and Lamar commands the largest warband in Tenebral after my own.*

And he did not want Calidus finding out what level this rebellion had escalated to, at least not until after Lykos had dealt with it.

The road steepened and he saw the tower looming above him, black gates closed before it. The walls bristled with men and iron. *No matter. A fortress is only as strong as its weakest man.* Bodies were thicker upon the ground now, and to his annoyance Lykos saw a number of Vin Thalun faces amongst the dead. He paused again, turning; his position gave a fine view of the surrounding countryside. To the north and west the forest of Sarva stretched, a green, undulating ocean of bough and leaf. In its fringes a hill reared, broken walls and towers jagged on the horizon. *Balara, the giant ruin.* He had been there only yester-eve, making sure that his secret was guarded and safe.

Not so secret now, since Fidele and Maquin saw them. He had considered sending his giants back to Pelset, but decided in the end that keeping them close was the safest answer. He faced the tower and gates, stepped over the last of the dead that clogged the road and walked on a dozen paces, stopping within hailing distance of the barred gates.

'Close enough for a good spear throw from their wall,' Kolai observed.

Lykos shrugged. He was more careful since his injury, but some things smacked of cowardice, and he had not become Lord of the Vin Thalun by being a coward. Or by being cautious.

He gave his orders and shortly a few warriors returned carrying a wooden table and a chair. They positioned it in the road before Lykos. He sat, theatrically nonchalant as bread and cheese were placed before him, a cup of wine. He began to eat. Men were led before him now, warriors of Ripa roped together. With kicks and punches they were forced to their knees on the road before Lykos.

'Kill them,' Lykos said, crumbs of cheese spilling from his mouth. He washed it down with wine as the prisoners' throats were cut.

The row of warriors upon the wall watched it all in stony-eyed silence.

'Should have their attention now,' Lykos said as he stood and the table was carried away. He belched.

'You up there,' he shouted. 'Anyone worth talking to?'

His voice rebounded from the black walls.

'I don't expect someone my equal – no deities amongst you, I would guess. But Lamar, maybe even Krelis, or Peritus the cowering worm, of course. Any of you will do.'

'I'm going to enjoy killing you,' a voice called back, a large man appearing above the gate. Very large, towering at least a head over any others around him. Lykos recognized him. Hated him.

'Well met, Krelis,' Lykos called back. 'A beautiful day, no?' Krelis was Ripa's beating warrior-heart. He had led the shipbuilding and then defence of the bay and coastline surrounding Ripa. His ships had not been as sleek and deadly at sea as Lykos' own galleys, but they were big enough and fast enough to consistently spoil Vin Thalun raids on villages along the coast.

'It'll be a better day when your head no longer graces your shoulders.'

Lykos pulled a face. 'A little too aggressive a start for a peace talk, I think.'

'This is no peace talk. Look what you've done to my town.'

As if to prove Krelis' point, black smoke billowed across the road, obscuring the view for a few moments.

'Wine,' Lykos called, and Kolai passed him a skin. He drank deep and smacked his lips.

When the smoke cleared, Lykos spread his arms.

'There is nothing damaged that cannot be repaired. I needed to make a point.'

'And how will I repair my slain warriors? My murdered people?' Lykos could hear the hatred in Krelis' voice, barely contained.

Good. Anger is always the best enemy. It blinds, cloaks, distorts.

'You are harbouring an enemy of the realm. Peritus. He is guilty of treason. Murder. Inciting rebellion.' Lykos shook his head, tutting. 'To protect such as he, well, there are consequences.'

'You are not the law-giver in Tenebral. You are a pirate, usurping power. And Peritus is battlechief of Tenebral, a better man than you could ever hope to be.'

'He is an outlaw, stripped of his titles and sentenced to death by Fidele, Regent of Tenebral in Nathair's absence. And incidentally my wife, by the way.'

'She is *not* your wife.'

'I think she is. I was there. Any who says different is a liar.'

'*She* says different,' Krelis called out.

Lykos froze at that. *She is in there, then.* He felt something cold clench in his belly. 'Will you give Peritus up to me?'

'I will not,' Krelis said.

'Is he brave enough to talk to me? Or will he continue to hide behind you, his puppet?'

'Krelis is no puppet,' a voice called out, older.

Ah, Peritus; good. I did not think you would keep yourself from this.

'So, you have found someone stupid enough to take you in,' Lykos called. 'And I cannot help but notice that you are all scared to meet me in combat, else you would not be hiding behind your walls.' He was starting to enjoy this now. 'What say you, Peritus? Care to test your blade against mine?'

'I'd like nothing more,' Peritus called down. 'But I do not trust you – I've tasted your justice and hospitality before, remember. I think if I came out to fight you that your shieldmen would fall upon me. You are a liar, a man of no honour.'

'I am hurt,' Lykos said, putting a hand to his heart. 'Well then, it would appear we have a problem to resolve. How would you suggest we go about that?'

'Nothing springs to mind,' Peritus called back. 'This is the end for you now, Lykos. To openly attack Lamar – you have made a mistake, after your years of schemes and lies, to be so impulsive at the end. I thought you a more worthy adversary. The other lords of Tenebral will act now. Your farce of a marriage will aid you not one bit.'

'It was no farce,' Lykos screamed, spittle flying, venting a sudden rush of rage. He was taken aback by it and had to take a few moments to control his breathing and wait for the red mist to fade a little. *He plays me at my own game.*

'We have only to wait here, let word spread,' Peritus continued. 'That tower behind me is dug deep into the rock, has huge supplies of grain, fresh water. If your plan is to starve us out you'll be waiting a very long time. You could always try to take us by storm. Please do. That way we may still get to test each other's blades. I think I'd win.'

So confident. I'll cut the smile from his face. He has a point, though. I can't afford a long siege, even beyond the fact that I hate waiting.

Shouting drifted from beyond the tower walls, the clash of arms somewhere behind it. Movement rippled through the warriors above the gates, sudden and startled.

Good job then that I have a plan of my own. He drew his sword and charged forwards, a thousand Vin Thalun roaring as they followed behind him.

CHAPTER TWENTY-NINE

FIDELE

Fidele splashed water on her face, then dipped her hands into the bowl before her. The water turned pink. Events since her rescue by Krelis were a blur.

In a seeming hurricane of movement she had been swept through the gates and into a hard-packed courtyard, hands lifting her from a horse's back to others that checked her for wounds, half-dragging her up wooden steps into a feast-hall, through it into the giant's tower. She remembered cold stone beneath her feet. Eventually she had pulled herself from the gripping hands and demanded to see Maquin.

It turned out they were being taken to the same place. A series of rooms on a lower level of the tower that were being used as an infirmary for the injured from the town.

Well, she *was* wounded – a score of cuts and bruises all over her body – but nothing serious. Maquin, however, was a different matter. He had been stabbed, slashed, kicked. A memory filled her mind – him striding forward into the massed Vin Thalun, carving his way through them like some untouchable demon, always moving, always striking. She had seen the blow that felled him, seen him kill the attacker – his body failing as even then he tried to force a path for her to the tower – saw him collapse. She'd killed the Vin Thalun standing over him, recalled the sensation with a shudder: she had plunged her knife into him, punching through leather into the body beneath. *Twice, now, I have killed in Maquin's defence.* Her hands shook as she put them back into the bowl, scrubbing at them with a hard-bristled brush.

'Will he live?' she asked as she turned away from the bowl.

Maquin lay upon a cot in a stone room with white walls. A row of large windows were open, shutters flung wide, letting in streaming sunshine and a strong breeze that diluted the cloying scent of blood and sweat. Other beds filled the room, the injured or dying groaning as they were tended by a score or so of healers. Tables were being carried in, more injured stretched out upon them.

A man was bent over Maquin, white-haired and thin. Alben was the swordsmaster of Ripa and, ironically, one of its most skilled healers.

'A man can die of many wounds,' he murmured. Maquin was still unconscious, his breathing shallow. Alben cut away the prone warrior's leather vest and linen shirt, revealing a dark wound above his hip. It pulsed blood rhythmically, with every beat of Maquin's heart. Alben probed it, fingers pushing around the wound. Maquin stirred and groaned.

'Knife or sword?' Alben asked.

'What?' Fidele asked, eyes still fixed on Maquin's face.

'What made this wound – knife or sword? It will tell me how deep the wound is.'

'Knife, I think. I'm not sure, it was so quick.'

'Hmm.' He reached out to a rack of tools, pulled out a metal rod with a flat iron head and placed it alongside other similar tools heating in a fire that burned in a wide pot. He left it there a while, gathering what he needed. A salve that smelt of honey, some leaves, gut twine, a curved needle, a roll of linen bandages. He placed them all on a table beside Maquin, then went back to the iron rod, checked its end.

'Hold his legs,' Alben ordered one of the healers.

'I'll do it,' Fidele said, stepping forward.

'He may kick out, my lady.'

'Alben, this man has saved my life many, many times; he has kept me alive for two moons, brought me through the wild, slain Vin Thalun hunting parties against all odds. All for someone that he could have walked away from.' She was going to say more but the words died on her tongue. 'This is the least I can do.'

Alben studied her a moment, then nodded. 'Hold them like so,' he said, demonstrating for her.

She gripped his ankles and leaned all her weight upon them.

Alben asked an attendant to hold Maquin's shoulders while he rinsed the wound. There was so much blood Fidele wondered how Maquin could survive – but he had to. Alben took another long look at the gaping cut, then pressed the heated iron head into the wound. Maquin's feet kicked, his body jerking, and he groaned. There was a hiss, the stench of cooking meat and Fidele felt her stomach lurch – she refused to look away. Alben pushed the rod a little deeper, then with a twist took it out, dropped it into a bowl of water. He cleaned up the wound, stitched it closed, then applied the honey-like salve and covered it over with a leaf. Finally he bandaged the wound.

'Thank you,' Fidele said, feeling suddenly weary beyond measure.

'It's a gut wound,' Alben said. 'If it's pierced his intestines, he will most likely die, in agony.'

She felt something twist inside her, a cold fist clenching around her heart. *No. Not after coming so far.*

'If they are not cut then he may still die – fever and the like. I have seen people live, but only a handful out of hundreds. He may wake at any time – there is seed of the poppy for his pain. No food, only water for the next day. Now, let me take a better look at you.'

'I am fine, just scratches.'

'They need to be cleaned. A scratch can still kill.'

A hand touched Fidele's shoulder and she spun around. At first she thought it was a patient, a sickly-looking man staring at her, pale with lank hair, his frame gaunt, almost withered.

'My lady,' he said, his eyes touching her face.

Ektor, Lamar's son.

Without thinking she reached out and hugged him. He was a strange man, reserved and introverted, but Fidele had spent some time with him the previous year, poring over manuscripts in his library buried deep in the tower's bowels, and she had come to see another side of him.

'It is good to see you, Ektor,' she said as they separated. He was standing stiff and blinking.

'And you too, my lady,' he managed. He looked around the room. 'My father, he is waiting for you in his chambers. You should go, now.'

'Lady Fidele has been injured, Ektor. She will be along as soon as she has been cared for,' Alben said, his hands guiding Fidele to an empty cot. 'If you could pass that on to your father, I'd be grateful.'

'Send a messenger, I'm busy,' Ektor said, retreating.

'We'll talk, soon,' Fidele said to Ektor, who nodded as he turned and left the room, disappearing into a corridor.

'That boy is always busy, in his mind,' Alben remarked.

'A boy?' Fidele smiled. Ektor was the youngest of Lamar's sons, around twenty summers.

'When you reach my age, my lady, all whose sleep is not interrupted by the need to empty their bladder are boys.'

Fidele sat there as Alben checked over her wounds, a myriad of cuts and scratches, washed away some blood.

'Have you had word from your son, my lady?' Alben asked as he cleansed her wounds.

'No.' *My son. Where are you, Nathair?* She felt a knot of worry bloom every time that she thought of Nathair, which was every day. Every night before sleep took her she whispered a prayer to Elyon for his safety. Lykos had hinted at terrible things . . .

'So no news of Veradis either, then,' Alben said.

'Veradis. No,' Fidele said. For a moment she had had to concentrate to pull his face into memory. *So much has happened since Nathair sailed away.* 'In my last correspondence from Nathair . . .' *The letter that stripped me of my regency, my son replacing me with Lykos . . .* 'Veradis was at Nathair's side, in Dun Carreg, Ardan. Elyon willing, they are still together. Veradis is the one man I trust with Nathair's life. He has been most faithful, a true friend to my son.'

'He is a good boy,' Alben said, a faint smile touching the corners of his mouth. 'I taught him his weapons.'

'And taught them well.'

A groan drew Fidele's attention. Maquin was stirring on his cot. His fingers moved and his eyes flickered. They opened, searching. He made to sit up.

Alben was there, holding his shoulders. 'No,' he said.

Fidele squeezed Maquin's hand, leaning over him. Recognition swept his face and he relaxed.

'You're safe,' Fidele said. 'Rest.'

His lips moved but only a whisper came out.

She leaned forward, putting her ear to his mouth.

'You are a great deal of trouble, my lady,' he whispered, then his eyes closed and his breathing steadied.

She jumped suddenly – a loud bang, a grating sound. She turned, saw a grapnel hooked about the edge of the window's stone sill. A rope dangled from it, disappearing over the sill's edge. A hand appeared, then a head, shoulders, and in a heartbeat a Vin Thalun corsair was crouched on the wide sill, breathing hard. He drew a sword. All along the room grapple-hooks appeared in other windows.

Alben was the first to move, powering forwards, sword appearing in his hand. A flick of his wrist and it was buried in the Vin Thalun's throat. The warrior fell backwards with a gurgle, spinning into nowhere.

Screams echoed through the hospice as more Vin Thalun appeared, leaping into the room, stabbing at healers and wounded alike.

'Out of here,' Alben snapped at Fidele. Even as he said it another figure was appearing in the window behind him. Before Alben could turn the Vin Thalun was leaping forwards, crashing into the old swordsmaster, both of them tumbling to the ground. They came to a stop, the Vin Thalun on top of Alben, a knife in his hand.

Fidele grabbed one of the iron bars heating in the fire-bowl and rammed it into the corsair's face. He screamed, flesh sizzling as he rolled away from Fidele, from the pain, clutching at his face. Alben rose, sword flashing, and the Vin Thalun stopped screaming.

'Come on,' Alben said as he gripped Fidele's shoulder, steering her to the door.

'Maquin,' she breathed, pulling free and staggering back into the room.

Vin Thalun were everywhere, slaughtering those about them like wolves in a sheep pen. Maquin was still lying on his cot, though he had pushed himself up onto one elbow, sweat and pain staining his features. She reached him and wrapped an arm about his torso, helping him to stand.

He grunted with pain but got his feet under him.

'Thought you'd—' His face twisted in a grimace. 'Gone.'

Then Alben was there and they both had him, half-dragging him into the corridor. The sunlight failed to reach here, torches illuminating the hall in a sequence of light and shadow. Screams drifted down the corridor, echoing from other rooms. A figure crashed into them, sending them smashing into a wall. Alben's sword was at the man's chest before his panicked cries told them it was Ektor. A handful of Vin Thalun were just behind him.

'Run,' Alben said as he stepped into the corridor. Ektor ran on, calling for them to follow. Fidele grunted under Maquin's weight as Alben stepped away on light feet, his arm straightening to skewer the first Vin Thalun. He kicked him back into his comrades, slashed across the eyes of one that avoided the dead man, and then the corridor was momentarily jammed with the dead.

'Alben,' Fidele cried as she struggled down the corridor with Maquin's arm about her shoulders. Alben glanced back at her, hovered, clearly on the brink of decision, then sprinted after them.

They reached a staircase that spiralled both up and down. Alben began to lead them up but Ektor grabbed him.

'No, they are loose on the floors above us; listen.'

The sound of combat, screams drifted down the stairwell.

'The Vin Thalun behind us will head up, to the gates,' Ektor said. 'We should go down, to my chambers. They won't go that way.'

Alben nodded sharply and they were running downwards, feet slapping on stone, sconced torches sending their shadows flickering on damp stone walls. Fidele and Alben stopped Maquin from tumbling down the stairwell. Even so he was drenched with sweat and breathing hard when they reached Ektor's chamber.

'Torch,' Ektor said to Alben, who reached up and took one from a wall sconce. Ektor rattled a key in a lock, threw the door open and ushered them in, closing it hastily and locking it again. The only light was from Alben's torch, but Ektor quickly used it to light a few lanterns, then he doused the torch in a bucket.

'Can't be too careful,' he said, gesturing into his chamber. Fidele remembered his fear of naked flame and the thousands of scrolls that were kept in this room.

It didn't seem to have changed from when Fidele had seen it last. The first half looked as if battle had raged through it: chairs overturned, bed sheets strewn on the floor, half-eaten trenchers of food left to rot. Beyond this wreckage was the library, a great curved stone wall with a thousand alcoves carved into it.

She helped Maquin into the chamber and he collapsed onto a long table, rolling onto his back with a moan.

Ektor shrieked at Maquin and none too gently started pulling him upright.

'Ektor, he is injured,' Fidele said, something in her tone giving Ektor pause. He looked at Maquin, saw the wound low in his belly. 'My maps,' he said. 'He's crushing my maps. And he'll be more comfortable on my bed.'

Fidele and Alben helped Maquin to a huge bed on one side of the chamber. Alben went back to the door and put his ear to it, listening for any sound of the Vin Thalun.

'You need to stop saving my skin,' Maquin said to her through gritted teeth. 'This way I'm never going to be out of your debt.'

You saved me from something far worse than death. From a living hell. No matter how many times I save you from a knife through the heart you will never be in my debt.

'You need to learn how to keep out of the way of sharp iron, then.'

He started to grin at that, but it shifted into a pained grimace.

'Quiet,' Alben hissed and they all froze.

A hundred heartbeats went by; eventually Alben turned back to them.

'There were footsteps on the stairwell, but they have not come this way.'

'How did they scale your walls?' Fidele asked.

Alben shrugged. 'It has never been done before. We are a long way up from the bay.'

'And what now?' Fidele asked.

'We wait,' Ektor said.

'For what, the Vin Thalun to overwhelm the tower?' Fidele said.

'What would you suggest we do?' Ektor snapped. 'You, no offence intended, are not exactly warrior-born. Your friend, on the other hand, looks as if he could carve his way to the Otherworld if he had a mind to.' It did not sound like a compliment the way Ektor sneered as he said it. 'But he is clearly injured and unable to stand unaided, let alone fight. And the oldest swordsmaster in the Banished Lands.' Alben scowled at that. 'And me.' He smiled ruefully. 'Not the greatest band of heroes ever mustered.'

'He's got a point,' Maquin grunted.

Fidele thought about it. *To go charging into the unknown would be foolish.* The thought of Vin Thalun out there, though, possibly taking the tower, opening its gates to Lykos. It was terrifying, all the more so for the not knowing.

I will cut my own throat before I let him touch me again. She found herself pacing about the chamber, searching for a distraction. Ektor was tidying his table, a worried frown on his face. *He seems more worried about his maps than the fact we're possibly being overrun by invaders.*

I remember studying them with Ektor – how long ago was that? A year? Two?

She had spent a long day in this chamber with Ektor, listening to his wealth of knowledge on the history of the Banished Lands, trying to unravel clues in the ancient writings of the giants. She had been unsettled by what they had discovered, rumours about the Ben-Elim and Kadoshim walking the earth clothed in bodies of flesh and blood. There was reference to the high king's counsellor being Kadoshim, a servant of Asroth. The question had been which high king? Aquilus or Nathair? Meical or Calidus? *I think I know now, if Lykos' association with Calidus is anything to go by.*

'Did you ever find the answer?' Fidele asked Ektor.

'Not exactly,' he said quietly, as if guarding some great secret. 'But I narrowed it down to two conclusions.'

'So did I,' Fidele whispered.

Ektor nodded at her, smiling. 'You really show a great deal of potential, you know.'

'Thank you,' she murmured.

'Footsteps,' Alben hissed, drawing his sword. Fidele pulled her knife from its sheath. The latch lifted, rattled as someone tried to open the door. A fist pounded on the thick oak, dust puffing from the hinges. Fidele felt a knot of fear squirm inside her. She gripped her knife tightly.

'Ektor,' a voice shouted, 'are you in there, you pasty-faced book-worm?'

Fidele's fear melted away. *Only close kin can be so personal and insulting.*

Alben unbolted and opened the door, revealing the bulk of

Krelis standing in the doorway, a dozen warriors filling the corridor behind him.

Ektor came forward and glowered at his brother. 'You took your time.'

CHAPTER THIRTY

CAMLIN

Camlin stood in the shadows, leaning against a wall. They had rowed into the lake to a tower that protruded from the dark waters like a spear, disembarked and entered a huge round chamber, ivy growing up its walls and birds nesting in its eaves. Edana sat in one of many chairs around a long table, Baird stood a step behind. Pendathran was there, and Drust, the warrior who had brought them here, as well as Roisin and Lorcan.

News of Edana's arrival had spread through the camp like sunlight in a dark room, people thronging to see her. She had happily wandered amongst them for a time, Baird and Vonn keeping a watchful eye over her.

She was not the only one to cause a stir. Roisin seemed to have made a big impression, if the way Pendathran's eye kept settling upon her was anything to go by.

'An unusual place for a meeting,' Edana said, looking around the room.

'Aye. Dun Crin is an unusual place altogether,' Pendathran replied. 'A giant's fortress that stood in a valley, is my guess. The histories tell of the world changing shape after Elyon's Scourging.' He shrugged, a rippling that made his chair creak. 'We'll never know how it came to be like this. But it is hidden well, and if discovered is defendable. Towers like this one are linked by old battlements that are easily defended by only a handful. And there is little chance of surprise out here when the only way across is swimming or a boat.'

'You have chosen admirably,' Roisin said, 'A better-defensible place I could not imagine.'

'Thank you, my lady,' Pendathran said gruffly.

Is he blushing?

Camlin glanced out of the window he was standing beside. *A good spot to defend, Roisin's right. But not much of a line of retreat. Or escape.* Something sinuous rippled in the waters close by and Camlin pulled a face.

Don't much care for the wildlife, either.

A movement in the shadows near his feet drew his eye and he saw Meg sitting there, knees hunched up to her chest.

She's as quiet as a wraith.

'So, I think there's a need for us to swap tales,' Pendathran said, smiling at Edana.

Edana nodded and told them of the flight from Dun Carreg to Domhain. Pendathran and the others about him listened with surprise creeping across their features as Edana told of the battles fought as they clawed their way through Cambren and into the mountains of Domhain.

'Wolven and giants,' Pendathran muttered, 'and you fought them all off.' Camlin saw something kindle in Pendathran's eyes – *respect?*

'Not without loss,' Edana acknowledged sadly.

The old battlechief lowered his head when Edana spoke of Heb's death. He had been well known and well liked amongst those who dwelt in Dun Carreg. Many of them nodded and grunted as she spoke of Eremon's support and first the elation and then the despair of the following battles. Finally Edana told of the flight to the coast and their journey by ship to Ardan. Pendathran growled when he heard of Conall slaying Marrock.

'Ach, how many of my kin will fall in this war? Is there no end to the hurt our family must bear?' He wrung his hands as if he was squeezing on someone's neck.

I forgot, Marrock was Pendathran's nephew.

'And then we sailed here,' Edana said. 'With the help of Roisin and a score of Eremon's finest shieldmen.'

'Aye, and I'm grateful for that. Both for your presence and that of the extra swords.'

'We are glad and grateful to be here,' Roisin said, managing to look both sad and happy at the same time.

She has more talents than I realized.

'And you, Uncle?' Edana said. 'I thought you slain in the feast-hall of Dun Carreg.'

'It was a close thing,' Pendathran said. He shifted a dirty scarf tied around his neck to reveal a white scar. 'I must have come close to bleeding out in the hall. Don't know how I didn't. All I can tell you is that I woke up in a stinking hole – turned out to be Evnis' cellars.' He could not stop his eyes flickering to Vonn, who stared fiercely back.

Just the mention of his da seems to set a cold flame burning in the young warrior.

Pendathran explained how Evnis had tortured him, and then how he had been rescued by Cywen. After escaping through the tunnels below the fortress he had travelled south from Dun Carreg, ended up wandering around the marshes for over a moon before he had been found by the fledgling resistance.

'Turned out I wasn't the only one who fled here – there were men from my son's warband . . .' He paused, a shadow crossing his face at the mention of his son.

I remember watching from the walls of Dun Carreg as Dalgar led his warband against Owain's host. They were sorely outnumbered. Pendathran had led a force out of Dun Carreg's gates, but the bridge to the mainland had been blocked by Owain's men. The battle was hard fought, but eventually Pendathran's relief force had been turned back and Dalgar's warband routed. Dalgar's corpse had been delivered to Dun Carreg's walls. Camlin could still see Pendathran carrying his son's broken body across the bridge.

Pendathran rubbed a hand across his eyes and carried on. 'Warriors who survived the defeat of my son's warband fled here, many bringing their families with them. Even some of Owain's have come here.' He nodded at Drust. It turned out that he had been telling the truth when he claimed that he was a shieldman of Owain.

'We share the same enemy,' Drust said with a shrug. 'Rhin betrayed Owain as much as she did Brenin. And I would say to you, for all the harm that Owain did to you and your realm, he was acting out of a desire for vengeance, for the murder of his son. He was mad with grief when he thought that Brenin had Uthan slain.'

'That is a lie,' Edana hissed.

'I know that now. Rhin played him, played all the kings of the west.'

'The game is not done, yet,' Edana said. 'So, tell me how you came to be here.'

Drust told of the battle between Owain and Rhin, Nathair's and Evnis' betrayal on the battlefield. Once again glances flickered towards Vonn. And Drust also spoke of Cywen helping him to escape.

'She saved my life,' he said.

'Ha,' Camlin laughed at that. All eyes swept to him, half-forgotten in the shadows.

'That girl and her brother,' he said to their enquiring glances. 'Always in the right place for some action.'

'Sometimes the wrong one,' Vonn said, not much louder than a whisper.

A silence settled over the room; the sound of lapping waves drifted through the stone windows.

'Well, hard tales, of that there's no doubt,' Pendathran said. 'But we are gathered together now. Reunited. And your arrival will lift spirits here – Ardan's princess back amongst her people.'

'I am Ardan's Queen now,' Edana corrected.

'Aye, that you are, lass,' Pendathran said. 'We shall celebrate tonight, and welcome our royal guests from Domhain.' He dipped his head to Roisin and Lorcan. Then he stood.

'Where are you going?' Edana asked him.

'There is always work to do here, lass.'

'But there is more we must speak of.'

'Such as?' Pendathran frowned.

'Such as, what is the situation here?' Edana's smile had gone. 'Numbers, strategies, what is your plan? Has it been successful thus far?'

'Survival is the plan,' the big man said, pausing half out of his chair. He looked a little surprised at Edana's questioning. 'The rest is boring details for you.'

'Not boring for me, I assure you,' Edana said. 'Please, sit and tell me.'

Pendathran stayed hovering above his chair a moment, then sat. *He thinks of her still as the frightened girl he last saw in Dun Carreg.*

'As I said, survival is top of that list. There are over four hundred of us here now, and we're still growing, and less than half of them are warriors. They're families, mostly, seeking a safe haven from Evnis and his *justice*.' He paused and sighed. 'It's not easy trying to feed this many people; do you know how many fish need to be caught every day?' He smiled ruefully. 'Could be worse, though. Fish is the one thing we're not short of in these marshes, and we've managed to trade for grain and the like from villages beyond the marshes.'

'That may be coming to an end soon,' Roisin said. 'We passed through one of those villages on the way in. They'd been slaughtered – every last man, woman and bairn. Made an example of.'

'It was Morcant,' Edana said.

'That's not the best news,' Pendathran rumbled. 'There's not one of them that could give away our location, but if we can't trade . . .'

'And other than survival?' Edana asked again. 'What is your strategy against Evnis and Rhin?'

'We take the battle to them, when we can.' His bushy eyebrows knotted together.

He doesn't like being questioned like this. Doubt that he's used to it, and definitely not by the spoilt princess he still thinks Edana is.

'I'm sure the tales of valour are too many to recount,' Roisin said.

'Go on,' Edana prompted.

Pendathran picked at a nail. 'We've killed a few men in Cambren's black and gold, those who have ventured into the marshes. A few raids further afield. We're not strong enough to take the fight to Rhin yet. And everyone here, we've all lost kin, loved ones . . .'

'Dun Carreg fell over a year ago,' Edana said.

They're scared, Camlin realized. *They've been beaten and bullied and just want to hide away from it all for a while. Scared of another defeat, and nowhere left to run.*

'It is the same throughout the west,' Roisin said. 'Domhain's king has been slain, its warbands broken, its warriors scattered. But not all of us. Wherever we stand together, there is hope. I escorted Edana here because she told me of the warriors of Ardan. Told me they had courage and would fight.' She looked around the room.

She makes it sound as if it was her idea, and she's not mentioned that she considered using Edana as a bargaining piece with Rhin for her precious son. Still, if she can light a fire under their arses then I'll not complain.

'But this is not fighting,' Edana said. 'This is *existing*.'

Pendathran's face coloured, dark blotches appearing on his cheeks. A silence hung in the air, charged with tension, like clouds bloated with thunder.

'You do not understand, my lady,' Pendathran said through gritted teeth. 'This is war-making, and there's more to it than notions of bravery and glory.'

'I understand well enough,' Edana snapped. 'I have seen enough bloodshed to rectify any misconceptions I may have once entertained.' She looked at her hands and Camlin remembered them shaking, spattered with blood, back in the village roundhouse.

'As have I,' Roisin added. 'And I understand caution, was its strongest advocate in Domhain. I was wrong, I should have listened to Edana. Victory usually has to be claimed, not observed. Look, here in this room three realms are represented – Ardan, Domhain, Narvon. And who is our enemy? Rhin. And she is weak, her warbands stretched thin over four nations. Now is the time to strike, not sit back and watch her grow strong again.'

Pendathran sat straighter at that.

'Roisin is right,' Edana said, not quite keeping the scowl from her face.

'We have done some of that,' Drust growled. 'The band I led, which found you, we were heading to the borderland with that intention. But you must understand, there are practicalities. Four hundred is a lot of mouths to feed. And we are not just warriors here, who would be more inclined to risk all. There are women and bairns – families.'

Edana shrugged. 'We can't make a life here hidden away from Evnis and Rhin. They are searching for you even now; eventually they will find you. Better to act now, while they're still off balance. And besides, I didn't come here to catch fish and eke out a life in the marshes. I came here to fight back. I've had enough of running and hiding. It's time that Rhin's tide was turned.'

'I agree,' Roisin added.

Camlin looked from Pendathran to Drust. It was clear that those two had been running things here – Pendathran the chief and Drust his captain. *And they don't look to appreciate two women wandering in, throwing their weight about, despite them both being queens.*

'That's all well and good,' Pendathran said. 'But fight back how? Morcant patrols the marshes' border with more men than we can take, and there's plenty more where they came from. Evnis has a warband of Rhin's at his disposal, and whatever else I'll say about him, he's no fool.'

'No, Evnis isn't, but Morcant?' Edana said. 'I spent some time in the Darkwood with him. He's arrogant, conceited. Perhaps we can use that.'

'I think you're onto something there,' Camlin said. 'Prod him and he'll get angry.'

'And angry people make mistakes,' Edana finished, with a smile twisting her lips.

'Just so, my lady,' Camlin said with a dip of his head.

'How do you know so much about Morcant?' Pendathran asked Camlin.

Camlin looked at him, didn't want to say, *because he was my chief, for a while. I took orders from him, helped him kill your Queen's shield-men, your King's first-sword, capture your Queen and your Princess.*

Edana filled the growing silence. 'Camlin helped to rescue me from Morcant in the Darkwood. He drew his sword and stood between us.'

'Of course, I remember now,' Pendathran said, eyeing Camlin suspiciously. 'You were one of the brigands that we hunted down in the Baglun.'

'I was,' Camlin said. *Can't deny that.*

'And I recall taking you back to Dun Carreg as a prisoner.'

Aye, that's true enough. Eighty men after twelve of us. And things were different then. I'd rather run and live than fight and die.

'So if we were to try and prod him, how would you suggest we go about it, Edana?' Roisin asked. Pendathran and Drust shared a look.

Edana and Roisin have swept in here like a summer gale. The two men don't know what's hit them.

'Camlin is a master huntsman and tracker; during my escape to

Domhain he masterminded a number of ambushes against over-whelming odds.'

Camlin almost blushed at that, feeling heat flush his neck. *Don't think anyone's ever spoken about me like that before.*

Then he realized that all eyes in the room were upon him.

He blinked.

'Well?' Pendathran said.

Good question. What should we do? He remembered Morcant upon his warhorse in the village square, tall and proud, his words to the village elders. A mixture of threat and bribe.

'Someone needs to take that chest of silver from Morcant,' he said.

Camlin blinked as the blindfold was removed from his eyes. Drust stuffed the rag into a hemp bag and moved on to the next person beside Camlin, lifting their blindfold too. It was Vonn.

'I don't see the need for that,' Vonn muttered as Drust carried on down the line, pulling blindfolds from another dozen men.

'Makes sense to me,' Camlin said quietly to him. 'Less that know the way to Dun Crin, the safer it is. A tortured man will talk in the end, no matter how brave he thinks he is, but you can't tell what you don't know.'

'Just feels like we're not trusted,' Vonn muttered.

Camlin raised an eyebrow at that. *Something I'm used to. Can't blame Vonn for feeling like that, though, the way everyone looks at him as soon as his da's name is mentioned.*

'It's not just us,' Camlin said nodding down the bench, where warriors who had been at Dun Crin before them were having blind-folds removed.

Vonn looked but didn't comment.

They were sitting in a long barge with about thirty warriors, now standing and clambering onto the riverbank, a force picked to go and get Morcant's chest full of silver.

If it's still there. And if it's not, we need to find it. Otherwise it'll be the end of Dun Crin and Edana's resistance. Only takes one tongue to wag, and there's altogether too much silver in that chest for everyone to resist. Loyalty only goes so far . . . He'd explained as much at the council meeting. Edana had backed him completely, and Pendathran had grudgingly agreed that the silver posed a danger that should be investigated.

He stood and stepped onto dry land, gave himself a moment for his legs to adjust.

Camlin had planned most of this incursion, but Drust was clearly in charge here, Camlin recognizing most of the warriors as Drust's crew. A few of Roisin's shieldmen had volunteered as well, though – Brogan one of them. He looked over at Camlin and smiled cheerfully.

You'd think he was still at the feast night.

They had had quite the celebration at Dun Crin on the evening that they'd arrived, three nights gone now, a lot of sore heads the next morning. Edana and Roisin had been all business, though, pulling him to one side the next day.

'What is it?' Camlin had asked them.

'Much rides on this,' Edana had said to him.

He nodded. 'Some objections to your right to lead?'

'I had not expected more politicking,' Edana sighed. 'Here, amongst my own people, my own kin.'

'Huh,' snorted Roisin. 'Family *is* politics, the hottest forge you'll find.'

Aye, and some come out sharp as iron, others bent and twisted. Some a little of both.

'So my little trip needs to be successful,' Camlin said.

'Exactly. Eyes are watching, and judging.'

'I'll do my best.' Camlin mustered a smile he didn't feel.

'You always have,' Edana said, and then walked away.

So here he was, three days later, standing on a riverbank, nominally leading thirty men into enemy-infested land in search of a chest of silver that was probably no longer there.

Beats sitting by a lake eating frogs. Besides, it's my fault I'm here, nobody else's. No one made me open my big mouth.

He reached inside a pouch and strung his bow.

'You ready?' he said to Drust as the warrior approached him.

'Are you?'

'Course.'

Drust gestured for him to lead the way, then leaned in close as Camlin was passing him.

'Don't go getting my lads killed, or me, for that matter.'

'Do my best,' Camlin said with a sour twist of his mouth.

They crept single-file along the riverbank, Camlin's eyes and ears working ceaselessly. When the village came into view he hadn't heard or seen anything that set his hairs tingling. Birds were singing, insects buzzing.

Buzzing a little too much, he thought as he paused behind the last cover between them and the first buildings.

Camlin raised his hand and the group split, more than half of them looping away east with Drust, setting a perimeter. Camlin waited a while, giving them time to reach their marks, then with a nod to those behind him he moved quick and silent across the open ground to the first buildings.

By the time he reached the central square he knew they were alone. The village was as they had left it, inhabited by a horde of flies and maggots, the bodies of the dead a little more decayed, a little more chewed upon. He threaded his way through the putrefaction, trying not to breathe any more than he needed, then reached the roundhouse doors. They were still wide open, fresher dead littering the floor amongst the more seriously decomposed. Camlin saw one of his arrow shafts poking from a throat.

The chest was gone, a depression in the ground where it had sat.

A lot of silver in there to leave that kind of dent.

He sent a warrior to tell Drust; the red-haired warrior returned with the messenger soon after.

'A waste of time, then,' Drust said as he strode into the courtyard, pausing and doing a double-take at the scattered dead.

'Elyon's bones,' he muttered.

'Not Elyon's,' Camlin said.

'Back to Dun Crin, then,' Drust whispered, not able to tear his eyes away from the heaps of tattered flesh and bone.

'There's another option I'd advise,' Camlin said.

'What?'

Camlin pointed to wheel tracks in the dirt. He bent down, picked at a pile of horse dung close by.

'They took the chest out on a wain, no longer than a day ago. This dung's fresher'n your breath.'

'So?'

'We should follow it. See if there's a chance of snatching it.'

Drust shook his head.

'Risks are too high. And we can't move across this open ground – no horses. Morcant catches us, we'd be ridden down.'

'True enough, but I'm not suggesting we stroll through the meadows. Most could stick to the waterways, just a couple of us out keeping an eye on the trail.'

'If the trail follows the marshes.'

'Aye, again, true enough. But I've more'n a hunch that Morcant is taking his silver through the villages around the marsh.'

'I'll not risk my men's lives on a hunch.'

Camlin sucked in a breath, biting back an angry response. 'You're not understanding,' he said slowly. 'Morcant will use that silver to bribe the villages surrounding these marshes. I heard him say as much. No matter how loyal a soul, there's not many that'll choose torture closely followed by death over a bag of silver. Even if no one knows your whereabouts now, once the population around here gets a sniff of that silver there'll be eyes on you, searching for you. It'll only be a matter of time before Dun Crin is betrayed. Eventually someone somewhere will offer to guide him and a lot of sharp iron to Dun Crin – it's just too much silver. If we don't find and take it from him, you and all your men are dead. Just not yet, that's all.'

Drust frowned at him, the silence growing.

'We don't know these marshes well enough. We're as likely to get lost as find this chest of silver.'

'I might have a solution to that.' Camlin looked around the edge of the courtyard. 'Meg,' he shouted. There was a silence, then a shadow emerged from a building, Meg stepping into the sunlight.

Least she's got the manners to look guilty.

'Thought you might follow us,' Camlin said.

Drust scowled.

'She's only a bairn, but she's also part water rat. No chance of Morcant or his lads ever catching her. And she knows the marshland. Ready-made guide.'

Drust thought some more, scratched his beard, blue eyes narrowed.

'You need to take that silver,' Camlin said. 'It's self-preservation.'

'Think you might be right,' the ageing warrior said, frowning down at Meg. 'All right then. We'll follow your marsh rat.' He gripped Camlin's arm before he could stride away. 'Pendathran told me what you were – a brigand from the Darkwood. Edana may be convinced of your worth, but I'm not. I've bitten too many rotten apples in my time. I'll be watching you.'

'Didn't expect anything different,' Camlin said. He pulled his arm free and walked away.

CHAPTER THIRTY-ONE

HAELAN

Haelan gripped the boulder and heaved, wobbling as he stood upright, almost toppling back into the stream that the boulder had been hauled from. He looked into the meadow, at the piles of rock spaced around it at regular intervals. He took a deep breath and started into the meadow, Pots running circles around him, enjoying the game.

It's all right for you. You're not carrying a rock.

Pots seemed to have adopted Haelan since he had saved the dog from the rat. Haelan was puffing and panting when he reached the pile of rocks and dumped his on the top. His hands throbbed and upon inspection he found three blisters.

'Thanks, lad,' Tahir said to him, sweating as he picked up a boulder from Haelan's mound. He'd stripped his clothes off to the waist: shirt, leather vest and sword-belt laid in a pile. Men all along the meadow were taking boulders from the mounds made by children and repairing an old wall.

'Why are we doing this?' Haelan asked Tahir.

'Because a wall's no use if it's got holes in it,' Tahir said.

Haelan sniffed, looking at his blisters.

When I am king I shall get you to carry my rocks for me.

'But why is the entire hold going to so much trouble? Haven't they got better things to do?'

'Wulf thinks it's best to tighten his hold's defences. I'd agree with him there, and I think you would too.'

'Where is Wulf, then?' Haelan asked sullenly. 'He comes up with the idea, gives the order and then is nowhere to be seen.'

'I don't know where Wulf is,' Tahir said. 'On business for

Gramm, no doubt. But you'd do things here differently, would you?'

'Aye. Lead by example. That's what my mam said to me.' He felt a lump in his throat and picked at a fingernail.

'Well, that's good advice. But whether Wulf's here or no, this wall still needs fixing. Don't want Jael just wandering in, if he comes back, do we?'

No. Haelan remembered the sight of Jael's warband as it rode bold as brass into Gramm's courtyard.

'A wall won't stop Jael, though.'

'No, right enough. But it would slow him, if the road was blocked too, and a wall's good for other things, as well. Surprises, traps, stopping people getting out, once they're in. Now stop flapping your tongue and bring me some more rocks.'

Haelan sighed, looking across the meadow. Every man, woman and bairn had been split into work groups of about a score and fanned out to this outer wall. His group was now leagues away from Gramm's hold, closer to Forn Forest than Haelan had ever been. Its trees were huge, towering high into the sky, trunks thick and knotted. *I don't think a dozen men could link their arms around those trees.* For some reason, though, Haelan liked to look at Forn. *It's like another world, away from Jael and all of his hurt. Somewhere safe.* He drifted off in a daydream that involved carving a house inside the trunk of one of those great trees and living out his days in safety, hunting by day with Pots at his side, reclining at night in his hall in the trunk's heart.

'Sore hands?' a voice said behind him. It was Trigg, the half-breed. She glanced at Pots as she put a rock on the pile, bigger than anything Haelan could hope to lift, let alone carry a hundred paces.

And she doesn't even look to be sweating.

'That dog should be dead,' Trigg commented matter-of-factly. 'And you killed the biggest rat I've ever caught. Could've made me rich, that rat.'

Haelan glanced at Trigg's belt, at the axe that hung there.

Swain's axe, which I used to kill the rat.

A fresh wave of guilt rose up in him at the thought of Swain. His friend, taken by Jael. *Because of me.*

Gramm had raged like a madman when Jael had led his warband from the hold, taking Swain and his sister Sif with him. Gramm had grabbed a long-handled axe and hacked away at the feast-hall wall. No one had tried to stop him, just watching Gramm until his arms had drooped with exhaustion. It had taken a long time. Just before sunset Wulf had ridden in at the head of thirty men, the patrol that travelled daily the boundary of their land. One look at his wife Hild and Gramm and the colour had drained from his face.

That night Gramm had summoned the entire hold into the feast-hall, more than two hundred souls. Around eighty of those were warriors, men who walked the hold's wall, patrolled Gramm's land, kept out predators from Forn and bandits from the lawless lands round about. The rest were those who worked the lifeblood of the hold – timber and horses, as well as all that went along with it, smiths and tanners, leatherworkers and weavers and trappers. And most had families, wives and bairns. Even so the hall had been silent when Gramm spoke.

'Two of my grandchildren were taken from me this day,' he had said. Hild started sobbing again, Wulf sitting straight-backed and red-eyed beside her.

'Taken by a tyrant. An evil man who would rule us because he can.' Grumbling had rippled around the room at that.

'And I could have my grandchildren back, if I would do but one thing.' He had beckoned to Haelan, called him to his side. Haelan had stood with eyes downcast.

'If I hand this boy over to Jael, I get my grandchildren back, and gold besides.' Silence had settled again. Gramm let it stretch, looking around the hall slowly, at every face there.

'I'll not do it. It's wrong, simple as that. You all know who this lad is. Haelan, rightful heir to Isiltir's throne.' There had been no point trying to hide that information, as Haelan had announced himself, full title and all, upon his arrival at Gramm's hold in front of a full feast-hall. *In hindsight, not the most sensible thing to do.* But Gramm had been adamant that none would betray him. *These people are closer than kin to me. None would betray you, for betraying you they would be betraying me.*

'His da's been murdered by Jael, and his mam. Our rightful Queen.' Gramm had continued. 'When he came here I promised him sanctuary, gave him my oath. I'll not break it. I'll stand my ground. We'll stand our ground.' He'd put a big hand on Wulf and

Hild's shoulders. 'We'll get them back, somehow. On my oath, we'll get them back.'

Something prodded Haelan's shoulder and he blinked. It was Trigg, poking him with a finger.

'You listening to me? I said you owe me for my rat, some kind of recompense.'

'I don't owe you anything,' Haelan said. 'You've got Swain's axe. That was the bet.'

Pots growled.

'Well, it wasn't fair, was it? I think you should give me something for my loss.'

'No,' Haelan said.

Trigg stared at him, then nodded, humour in her eyes. 'Fair enough – worth a try, but I don't want you getting angry with me. I remember what you did to my rat.'

Haelan snorted, looking Trigg up and down, cords of muscle twisting about her arms. This was the most he'd spoken to her, the most he'd heard her ever speak to anyone.

Pots was still growling. Haelan thought the dog had been growling at Trigg, but he was looking the other way, towards Forn Forest. Haelan looked too, past the stream and the first line of undergrowth, deep in amongst the thick trunks. It took a few moments for his eyes to adjust, to discern shadow from bush. He was about to look away when he saw something move, deep amongst the trees, a hulking shadow that moved differently to the branches around it.

Haelan shivered, squinted as he stared harder.

It's too far away.

A breeze blew across him, out of the forest. Pot's nose twitched and he growled louder. Behind them horses whinnied.

'Something's in there,' Trigg said, staring too. 'Something big.'

Then there was other movement, blurred shapes, shrubs undulating, and suddenly the forest was seething, branches shaking, undergrowth crashing. A great roaring shattered the silence, followed by growls and snarls, thuds and screams. Everyone in the meadow froze, staring. Then Haelan felt a hand on his shoulder and Tahir was stepping in front of him, moving to where he'd stripped his shirt and vest, his belt and sheathed sword lying on top. He buckled on his belt and drew his sword.

The noise from the forest continued, a cacophony of roars and growls, punctuated by the sharp crack of timber snapping, then it faded. The sound of an animal whining drifted on the breeze, then nothing. Finally a great bellow roared from the trees, making branches quiver and leaves fall. Haelan covered his ears with his hands and closed his eyes, the sound reverberating in his chest. Behind Haelan horses neighed, some breaking their tethers and bolting. Abruptly the roaring stopped, replaced by the sound of undergrowth crashing, fading quickly.

Tahir threw on his clothes and ran to where his horse was still standing, one of only a few that had not bolted. He swung into his saddle, others about the meadow doing the same, and trotted towards the forest.

'Take me with you,' Haelan shouted, running alongside him.

'It could be dangerous,' Tahir frowned.

'Better than leaving me here. What if whatever it was comes into the meadow while you're in the forest?'

Tahir reined in for a moment, then nodded. He pulled Haelan up into the saddle. 'Hold on,' he said and kicked his horse on, Pots running along beside them.

Other riders joined them as they approached the forest until they numbered a dozen, all men with iron in their hands, sword, spear and axe. Haelan peered around Tahir's waist as the forest closed in about them. It was like walking from full day into the cool of the evening, twilight falling about them like a shroud. Branches scratched Haelan's arms as the undergrowth became denser. He looked back over his shoulder, saw the meadow bathed in sunshine, the wall shrinking, and a figure running after them, gaining. It was Trigg, her long legs eating up the ground. She caught up with them and fell in quietly.

They spilt into a glade, the undergrowth trampled and flatted. Pots froze, growling. Tahir hissed an indrawn breath. The smell hit Haelan first, warm and cloying. It brought back memories. *I know that smell. Death.*

'Elyon save us,' someone said. That scared Haelan, for he knew that these were all hard men, used to the wild, living within sight of Forn and the Desolation.

Haelan squirmed behind Tahir, peered around him. At first he couldn't make sense of what he saw. Blood was everywhere, staining the ground in great pools, spattering bark and leaves. Here and there were mounds of fur. Four, five of them. He looked closer, still didn't understand what he was seeing.

'What are they?' he whispered to Tahir as the warrior slipped from his saddle.

'Wolven.'

Tahir crouched by one of the dead creatures. It lay in a pile of its own intestines, great claw marks carved across one side of its head. Trigg joined him.

'They're young,' Trigg muttered, lifting a paw and checking the dead animal's claws.

'What did this?' Haelan said.

'This did,' Trigg said. Even though Haelan wasn't sure what he thought of Trigg, whether he trusted her or not, he didn't doubt her on this matter. All knew that she spent much of her absences from the hold in Forn Forest, and to do that and survive meant you knew a fair bit about the ways of the forest, including its inhabitants. Trigg was standing beside a huge paw print, as big as a pewter plate, claw marks gouging the earth.

'What does that belong to?'

'A bear,' Trigg said with a frown. 'They don't often wander south of the river.'

'This one did,' Tahir said, crouching beside another dead wolven. 'What happened here?'

'Think a wolven pack set its sights on the wrong meal,' Trigg muttered. 'They're smaller than usual. Maybe a young pack that made the wrong choice?'

Haelan slipped from his saddle, something compelling him to take a closer look. His hand fumbled at his belt, reaching for his eating-knife. Trigg chuckled and held out her hatchet – Swain's hatchet.

'That's yours,' Haelan said.

'I know. Which means I can loan it to who I like.' She offered it again. 'It would be more use than that pin.'

Haelan took it with a nod, liking the weight of it in his hand.

'Looks like the bear ran off this way,' one of the other men said.

He was standing before a gaping hole in the underbrush, taller and wider than a large man. It led into darkness.

'Should we hunt it?' someone suggested.

'Don't be a fool. Five wolven tried that. Best off getting back to the women and bairns,' someone else said.

Haelan was looking at each wolven, just piles of flesh, bone and fur now. They all bore great rents upon their bodies, marks of claw and tooth.

'Come on, lad,' Tahir said, lifting Haelan back onto his saddle.

'Think you should look at this,' Trigg said. She was squatting beside one of the dead wolven, claw marks exposing its ribs.

Tahir strode over to her and crouched to inspect the wound.

'Not that,' Trigg said. 'This.' She lifted the wolven's head, exposing a huge cut in its neck, the head almost severed.

'That's a clean cut. Tooth and claw didn't do that,' Trigg said. 'Looks more like an axe-blade to me.'

The feast-hall was full that night. A summer storm had swept in from the north and Haelan's cloak was soaked through. Outside, wind howled and thunder rumbled. Haelan heard the phrase 'dark omen' muttered more than once as he sat with Tahir and a few other warriors. Pots was begging for scraps by his feet. He dropped a chunk of bread to the dog, his hand wandering to the hatchet at his belt – Trigg had told him to look after it for him. *I don't understand Trigg. She's confusing.*

As if his thoughts had summoned her, Trigg came and sat next to Haelan with a trencher full of meat and gravy, the bench creaking as she sat upon it.

'Got something for you,' Trigg said with her mouth full and pushed something across the table. It was a tooth, a long, curved fang, a hole drilled in the wide end, a leather thong threaded through it.

Haelan just looked at it.

'Go on, take it. It's yours. A reminder of your first steps into Forn.'

Haelan lifted it up, fascinated.

'My thanks,' he stuttered. 'How'd you get it?'

'Ripped it out as everyone else was getting back on their horses and leaving. Before the others came back and skinned them wolven.

I've got one too,' she said, pulling her shirt open to reveal another fang hanging about her neck.

Gramm stood at the head of the table. Haelan's gaze flickered to the giant hammer and bear skin nailed to the wall above him. The skin was huge, twice the size of a horse. *Is that what was in Forn today?* He shivered at the thought of it. *Maybe the wolven pelts will be hanging there soon.*

'You'll all have heard by now: strange things have been sighted in Forn today. A wolven pack attacked by something, most likely a great bear. And there were other signs . . .' Gramm paused, looking around the room. 'It looks like the Jotun have crossed the river. One at least, but where there is one giant, there are usually more. On the morrow I'll be tracking them.' His eyebrows knotted in a frown. 'These are dark times, and I'm hearing many of you say what happened in Forn today is a dark omen. Well, you're right. Dark times are here, the night is upon us, and we must all be vigilant if we want to see dawn rise again. You all know what I believe is coming, have heard me talk of the God-War. I'm not going to repeat myself. But I'll tell you this. It's here. It's happening. What was found in Forn today, that was no coincidence.' He looked around, letting the silence stretch. Goose-bumps prickled Haelan's skin.

Am I part of this God-War? As if I didn't have enough to worry about already. Are we really the puppets of Elyon and Asroth, playing out their war with our lives? My mam's life? He felt a frustrated rage bubbling inside him at that thought. *I want them to just leave us alone.*

Gramm raised his cup. 'So keep your eyes open and your blades sharp,' he said, then drained his drink to the last drop.

The hall echoed him, even Haelan and Trigg lifting their cups and muttering the oath.

Just then the doors banged open, rain sleeting in. Three men stood outlined by the firelight. Lightning crackled behind them as they strode into the hall.

Two were warriors whom Haelan recognized from the hold, both older men with grey in their beards, men high in Gramm's confidences. The man walking between them was Wulf. He looked none too happy.

They walked the length of the feast-hall, stopping before Gramm.

Gramm stood, resting his big fists on the table.

'We have brought him back to you, lord,' one of the men beside Wulf said.

'Where did you find him?' Gramm asked.

'Where you said. Dun Kellen. Looked as if he was just about to have a go at storming the gates on his own.'

'Ach, Wulf, my boy, that was a foolish thing to attempt,' Gramm said.

'They're in there, my Swain and Sif. I heard shieldmen of Jael's talking about them,' Wulf said, staring up at Gramm. His expression drifted between anger and abject misery.

'Whether they are or not, you wouldn't be able to bring them out. You'd just end up in a cell alongside them, or your head separated from your shoulders. Why'd you do it, lad?'

'I had to do something,' Wulf said. 'The thought of them in that fortress, scared, cold, alone . . .'

'We'll get them back, somehow,' Gramm said.

'How? When?' Wulf asked.

Gramm sighed, his shoulders slumping. 'I don't know,' he said.

Haelan was sitting in his chamber with Tahir. He had shared a room with the Gadrai warrior since the night they had arrived at Gramm's hold.

There was a quiet tap at their door and then it creaked open. Wulf came in. He nodded to Tahir and pulled a chair up, poured himself a cup of mead.

'I need your help,' he said when his cup was empty. His eyes were red-rimmed.

Tahir just looked at him.

'I'm going to Dun Kellen to get my children back.'

'You've just come back from there. And besides, that's suicide,' Tahir said. 'A fool's errand. Listen to your da.'

'You know a way into Dun Kellen. The secret giant tunnel you escaped by.'

Tahir looked hard at him. 'It's not a secret any longer. Your brother Orgull stood in front of it and made a mountain of the dead there.'

'Doesn't matter. Jael will not be expecting anyone to try and sneak into Dun Kellen. The tunnel is my best hope.'

'It is no hope.'

'I'm going. Will you help me?'

Tahir gave him a long look, eventually sighing.

'I cannot go. I'm sworn to Haelan.'

Wulf poured himself another cup of mead and drank it down. 'You owe us. You owe my family. You would both be dead now, if not for this hold.'

'Aye, that's most likely true,' Tahir said. Haelan could tell he was uncomfortable, did not want to be having this conversation. 'And I am grateful. More grateful than I can ever express—'

'Deeds, not words, show the truth and depth of a man's gratitude,' Wulf interrupted.

'My old mam used to say that,' Tahir muttered, looking into his empty cup.

'Please go with him,' Haelan said. 'I want you to go. Swain is my friend. I've never had a friend before. Not a real one.'

Tahir turned his gaze upon Haelan.

'Neither of you understand,' he said. 'I swore an oath. To Maquin and Orgull, my sword-brothers. We were the last of the Gadrai, we three. Now *I* am the last. To leave you here, go off on a task that risks me never coming back . . .' His shoulders slumped. 'I'm not afraid,' he growled, 'in fact, I like the idea. It's suicidal enough to earn its own song. But to break my oath when there is no one left to take it up for me.' He shook his head.

'You'd not be breaking it,' Haelan assured him. 'I'm safe as I can ever be here, whether you're here or not. I don't mean any insult, Tahir. I saw your bravery, on the walls of Dun Kellen. I saw you, Orgull and Maquin keep Jael's men from taking the walls, time after time. But you are one man. If trouble comes here, Gramm has warriors aplenty. You would make little difference.'

'Nicely said.' Tahir's lips twisted in a brief smile. 'But you are wrong. Every man here serves Gramm as his lord, has given their oaths to him. Gramm would be their first priority. Whereas me, I swore an oath to protect you; not Gramm, or Wulf, or any other soul living in these Banished Lands. You. And I would give my life to do it. Can any other say such a thing?'

Haelan was moved by Tahir's words.

'Will you be my shieldman when I am king?' Haelan asked.

Tahir smiled. 'Aye, lad, if we get that far, I'll be your shieldman.'

'Do you mean that, or are you just humouring a bairn?'

Tahir looked at him seriously. 'I mean that, Haelan.'

'Then swear it now. I'm likely to die, I know. Probably before I see my twelfth nameday. But just in case.' He shrugged.

Tahir regarded him a good long while. 'Do you know what is involved? It's not just words. Blood seals it,' he eventually said.

'I've seen many an oath sworn to my mam and uncle. I know my part,' Haelan said. He felt a lot older than his eleven years, suddenly.

'We would need a witness.'

'Wulf could bear witness.'

'Aye,' Wulf agreed. 'An oath is no small thing,' he added.

The silence stretched again.

'I'll give you my oath,' Tahir said and drew a knife from his belt, laid it on the table between them. 'Wulf, will you say the words?'

'Aye, if you're sure.'

'I am.'

'Tahir, will you bind yourself to Haelan ben Romar, become his sword and shield, the defender of his flesh, his blood, his honour, unto death?'

'I will,' Tahir said. There was a tremor in his voice. He gripped his knife's blade, cut his palm and let blood drip from his fist onto the iron hilt.

'Haelan, will you bind yourself to Tahir ben Davin, accept his fealty, swear to provide for and protect him to your utmost ability, unto your dying breath?'

'I will,' Tahir said. He picked up the knife, regarded it a moment, then squeezed its blade. He winced as blood welled from his hand, but he still felt brave, grown up. Blood dripped from his cut and he let it flow over the knife hilt, mixing with Tahir's blood.

'It is done,' Wulf said.

Haelan handed the knife back to Tahir.

'So you are my shieldman now?'

"I am,' Tahir said.

'Good. Then my first request to you is that you help Wulf get Swain and Sif back.'

Tahir sat back in his chair, blinking. Then he threw his head back and laughed.

CHAPTER THIRTY-TWO

MAQUIN

Maquin recognized Krelis, like a memory from a dream.

He was the man who lifted me from the street and carried me through the gates of Ripa.

'The Vin Thalun?' Alben asked.

'Some are still scurrying about the tower,' Krelis said with a shrug of his massive shoulders. 'Think we've dealt with the worst of it. Either way, we need to get you out of here.'

'We're safer down here,' Ektor said.

'Not if any Vin Thalun decided to come poking around. I haven't come to debate it with you, brother. You're coming with me.'

Ektor looked sullen but he said no more.

Krelis' men closed about them as they filed out of the room, Maquin walking behind Fidele. He made it as far as the spiral steps before his legs began to shake. A dozen more paces and he began to sink. Fidele turned and saw him, grabbed him before he hit the floor.

'Help,' she called.

'Didn't realize it was you,' Krelis said as he put an arm around Maquin and lifted him upright. 'You should be dead, not walking around,' he added good-naturedly.

Maquin grunted, 'There's still time.' With Krelis one side of him and Fidele the other, he managed to climb the stairs. Distant sounds of combat drifted along a corridor as they passed its entrance, but nothing that sounded close.

'Krelis, what is the situation, with the Vin Thalun?' Fidele asked as they made their way upwards.

'It was a coordinated attack,' Krelis said. 'A force approached the gates, drew our eyes and waited for their men to scale the cliffs. Then they assaulted our walls. We beat them back, though it was too close for my liking. The ones in the tower are mostly dead – they tried to get to the gates.' He shrugged. 'They failed. There's a few still running around the tower's corridors, but they won't be breathing for much longer.'

Eventually they left the spiral staircase and stepped into a hall, the cold stone disappearing, replaced by timber. Maquin was helped to a bench beside a long table and he realized they were in a feast-hall. He reached for a jug of water, his throat drier than he could ever remember, and began to drink.

'Only sips,' Alben said beside him, placing a hand on his wrist.

A tall man stood nearby, ringed by warriors. He was old, grey-haired, his face lined and weary.

'Father,' Krelis said as he approached the old man, 'Fidele has been found.'

So that is Lamar, then. As Maquin studied him he saw an echo of his friend, Veradis. Not so much in the features, more the set of his shoulders, a certain conviction that he radiated, a resolution in the line of his jaw.

'Good,' Lamar said, turning to take Fidele's hand and bowing his head.

'Welcome to Ripa, my lady.'

Another figure appeared, shorter, whip-cord slim, each muscle a defined striation of fibre. Maquin had seen this man before – the last time chained in the arena at Jerolin, ready for execution.

Peritus, Aquilus' battlechief, Fidele's friend. It had been Peritus who had begun the uprising against the Vin Thalun. He dropped to his knees before Fidele and kissed her hand.

'My Queen, I thought we had lost you, that I had failed you.'

'You lit the spark that set me free,' Fidele said, gently tugging him to his feet. To Maquin's surprise he saw tears staining Peritus' cheeks.

As Maquin sat there the throbbing in his belly began to grow, becoming impossible to ignore. It pulsed rhythmically with his heart, an organic drumbeat.

I have a gut wound. It will most likely kill me. He felt a wash of anger at that, because death meant he would not get to put a knife through Jael's heart. As he sat there watching Fidele, though, the desire to destroy Jael burned less brightly than it usually did. His vision dimmed at the edges, painting a dark border around Fidele.

I am glad that I didn't leave you in the forest, he thought abstractly, watching the bones in her face move as she spoke, the curve of her lips as she smiled, a pattern of fine laughter lines that stretched from her eyes. *You were worth saving. Worth dying for.* He saw her face turn towards him, her smile evaporate, replaced by concern. He tried to say something, to tell her not to worry, but somehow his mouth refused to work. His hand moved to his sword hilt – for some reason it was important that he feel the hilt in his hand. But his fingers were numb, and suddenly he realized he was cold, shivering, a chill spreading through his bones. He slipped from the chair, as if the strings holding his body upright had been cut.

Maquin was standing before a stone bridge. It arched over a wide chasm, deep and dark, the bottom, if there was one, lost in shadows. The far side was blurred, a mist infused with a nimbus glow, like the last light of day, pale and golden.

I need to cross over. He didn't know why, he just knew he should, as if someone pulled upon a cord tied about his waist, so he took a step onto the bridge, realized he was holding his sword. Nothing had ever felt more natural to him. He took another few steps, the bridge feeling strange underfoot, uneven. He looked down and saw the stone was merged with sword after sword beneath his feet. He paused halfway across as a figure took form and approached him through the mist.

It was man-like, but taller. Not like a giant, all slabs of muscle, but finer, more elegant. And it had wings, great wings of white feather that spanned the width of the bridge.

One of the Ben-Elim.

It held a sword in its hand, wisps of flame curling up from the blade.

The wings flexed, a rush of air buffeting him and the creature was airborne, landing gracefully a dozen steps before him. Maquin strode towards it.

'Are you ready to cross the bridge of swords, child of flesh?' the Ben-Elim asked him.

Maquin felt a shock go through him at that.

I am dead, then. He did not feel anything, just a cold detachment. Possibly an echo of disappointment.

The Ben-Elim stooped a little, regarding Maquin with dark eyes. It held out its sword, the tip glowing, hovering a handspan before his heart. 'Hold, something is . . . different.' He sniffed the air, reached out with one hand and touched Maquin's face.

Maquin tried to open his eyes but the light was blinding, painful. He gave up.

Where am I?

He moved his hands, or tried. A finger moved, slightly. Maybe.

I'm lying down.

The sound of gulls filtered through to him, a gentle breeze upon his face.

Ripa. I'm in Ripa.

Slowly he became aware of a presence close by, the sound of breathing. A stirring in the air. A hand touched his face.

A door creaked, footsteps getting louder.

The hand on his face disappeared.

'My lady, how is he?'

'The same. His fever burns.'

I know that voice. Fidele. It felt nice to hear her, a comfort.

Footsteps approached, a cool, dry hand on his brow. Fingers probed the pulse in his neck.

'Alben, how long can he survive like this?'

'He should be dead, my lady. I have not seen anyone cling to life through a fever this severe or that lasted this long.'

'I've done all you said – water, goat's milk, the herbs you mixed – all dripped through linen into his mouth.'

'Others can do this, my lady. Lamar has been asking for y—'

'No. This is where I choose to be.'

'As you say. But . . .' He fell silent.

Wise man. No point arguing with her.

'The good news is his gut wound seems to be healing. It is rare, but it can happen. Now, if he could just beat this fever.'

'He can.'

An indrawn breath.

'My lady, you should prepare yourself.'

'No. You told me that a ten-night gone, and yet he is still here.'

'But look at him. There is little more than skin and bone left of him. He has fought hard, but unless this fever breaks . . .'

'He is the strongest man I have ever known. In flesh and in spirit. He *will* beat this.'

'Perhaps. If he is as strong as you say then he has a chance. But I must warn you, my lady, it is very slim. If he is a fighter . . .'

Fidele snorted. 'He is the definition of the word.'

'I shall call in before sunset.'

'Thank you, Alben. I do not mean to sound ungrateful.'

'You do not, my lady. You stand vigil over a friend who straddles the line between life and death.'

The door closed, footsteps receding.

A hand closed about his. Squeezed.

'*Live*, damn you.' A soft breath brushed his ear.

The Ben-Elim was staring at Maquin; it felt as if he was staring *into* him, viewing his soul.

'You have a choice to make,' the Ben-Elim said. 'Most who reach this place have no choices left to them. A rare few do. You are one of them.'

'What choice?' Maquin breathed.

'Go forward, or go back.'

Something moved behind the Ben-Elim, beyond the bridge, a figure forming in the mist. Maquin frowned, something familiar about it. He froze, not believing his eyes.

It was Kastell. He was as Maquin remembered him, a shock of red hair, face pale, freckled. They stared at each other.

The sight of him set a flood of memory loose within Maquin, coursing through his body like heady mead in his blood. The day he had sworn his oath to Kastell, so many years ago, standing upon a palisaded wall within sight of Forn Forest. Carrying him from his father's hold as it went up in flames, giants chasing them, bellowing their war-cry, silhouetted by flame. Joining the Gadrai. Walking into the catacombs of Haldis, fighting side by side. Maquin felt tears wetting his cheeks.

He called out, dropped to his knees. 'I am sorry, my friend. I have failed you, Jael still lives.'

Kastell stared at him, head cocked to one side.

'It was not your fault,' Kastell said, the words sounding like wind rustling through dead leaves.

'I swore an oath to you,' Maquin said, tears blurring his vision.

Other figures appeared around Kastell – the first bent and twisted, like a wind-blasted tree. He had not seen him for a score of years, but Maquin knew him instantly. His da. Beside him there was a woman, a warm smile upon her face; his mam. Another man, broad and red-haired. Aenor, his first lord, Kastell's da. They all stood at the bridge's edge, watching him. Maquin felt his heart lurch, a longing flow through him to be with these people.

'Join us,' they said. 'There is peace here.'

'Peace?' Maquin breathed.

'Have you tired of the world of flesh?' the Ben-Elim asked him.

'Tired? Aye, I am tired. Of the pain, of fighting, always, of the blood, the misery. I am tired of failing.'

'Is there aught you would return to the world of flesh for?'

Maquin opened his mouth, lips forming the word 'No,' but then he hesitated. He closed his eyes, images forming in his mind. He saw Jael plunging his sword into Kastell's belly, the moment frozen forever, seared into his brain. He remembered being taken by Lykos. Being branded, forced into the pits, his humanity stripped incrementally away. Jael and Lykos, their faces floating in his mind's eye, merging, separating. Rage coursed through him, cold yet burning.

And then another face, a woman, hair of jet flecked with silver framing pale, milky skin, a warm smile from red lips. *Fidele*. Somehow she had made him feel human again, something more than a trained animal. A voice echoed through his mind. *Live, damn you*, it said, and something else rose up within him, battling with the rage that consumed him, warring for his soul.

He opened his eyes.

The Ben-Elim towered over him, flaming sword held loosely, wings flexing.

'You must choose,' it said. 'Go forwards or go back.'

He climbed to his feet, wiped the tears from his eyes. Kastell and the others were standing as still as the stone carvings in Haldis, watching him.

'Peace,' Maquin breathed. Then louder, 'I shall see you again. One day. But not yet.'

He turned and strode back across the bridge.

Maquin opened his eyes, blinking in the light. He moved his head. He was alone. Slowly he grew accustomed to a flood of sensations. His fingers tingled, his back ached. *Everywhere aches.* His throat was dry, constricted. He opened his mouth, felt his lips tighten, skin pulling close to cracking. After a while he tried to sit up and managed it on his second attempt. A jug of water sat on a table beside him and he poured half a cup and sipped, the effort draining him. He looked about, saw that he was sitting on the only bed in a spacious room. A single chair rested beside the bed. It was dark; a window opened onto the bay of Ripa, stars flickering into life on a velvet canopy.

The door creaked open and Alben entered. He paused when he saw Maquin sitting up, then looked over his shoulder and said something. Footsteps echoed, fading quickly.

'Welcome back to the land of the living,' Alben said with a smile.

'How long?' Maquin said, his voice a dry croak. He sipped some more water.

'Twenty nights. You should be dead.' Alben put a hand upon Maquin's forehead, then held two fingers to the pulse in Maquin's wrist.

'Lykos?' Maquin asked. The Vin Thalun was suddenly all that Maquin could think about. He had an overwhelming urge to find a knife and sheathe it in Lykos' heart.

'We are under siege. You remember the attack on the tower?'

'I do.'

'We fought them back. They have ventured a few sorties against our walls since then, but nothing has come as close to success as that first attempt.'

Fidele appeared in the doorway. She froze when she saw him sitting there. She smiled at him, and he smiled in return, feeling a flutter in his belly as he did so.

'I knew you wouldn't die,' Fidele said, crossing the room to him as Alben left. Tentatively she reached out, her fingertips brushing the back of his hand.

Memories flowed, sharp and vivid. Standing on a bridge, one of the Ben-Elim before him. *You have a choice to make.*

'I was standing upon the bridge of swords,' he breathed. 'One of the Ben-Elim stood guard upon it.'

'You have been racked by fever for almost a moon. You have had many dreams,' Fidele said. 'Fever dreams.'

'It was no dream. The Ben-Elim, he gave me a choice. Go forward or go back. I wanted to cross over, to be with my kin, my friends. To find peace.'

'Why did you come back, then?' Fidele asked him.

'Three reasons. Three people. Jael. Lykos. You.' He paused and looked up into her eyes. 'Two for vengeance. One for love.'

She stared at him a long, timeless moment, then she leaned forwards and kissed him.

CHAPTER THIRTY-THREE

RAFE

Rafe stared across the river at the wall of trees on the opposite bank.

'The Darkwood,' Braith said beside him, with something close to real affection in his voice.

And beyond it Ardan. Home.

It had been a long journey, two moons of hard riding on Halion's trail.

And now they were just a few leagues away. It was a strange feeling after being away so long.

The dogs were down by the bank, worrying at the mud and silt that edged the estuary.

They'd follow Halion's trail right into the water if they could. Best scent hounds I've ever known.

'He crossed here, then,' Rafe said. It wasn't a question. Hoof prints had churned the mud, then led off north. Halion hadn't ridden the horse, though. His footprints led right up to the water's edge. And even if they hadn't been there, Scratcher and Sniffer's behaviour was enough for Rafe.

'Aye,' Braith said.

'Why did he turn his horse free?' *Still got a long way to go once he gets to the other side, if Rhin was right. Better to swim his horse across.*

'He must know the Darkwood. Too dense and overgrown to take a horse through. Nearer to the giantsway it's easier going, more open. But not here. He could've crossed further upriver, but every step takes you closer to Uthandun, and that's one place he'd want to stay clear of. They'll have patrols out. He made a decision, chose caution over speed. Besides, he can always steal another horse once he's in Ardan.' Braith shrugged. 'It's what I'd have done.'

I thought my da was a good huntsman, but Braith, he lives it.

Rafe looked dolefully at the river. It was wide and slow, only a league or so before it spilt into the sea. 'We're going to get wet, then.'

'Ah, that's where you're wrong,' Braith said with a grin. 'Follow me.'

They rode only a short way east along the riverbank before Braith dismounted and made his way down to the river. He disappeared where the bank was eroded into an overhang.

'Come lend a hand,' Braith called.

Rafe found him tugging at what looked at first glance to be the broken branch of a willow. It turned out to be a cleverly made screen that was draped over a dozen coracles.

'Used these to cross the river, back when I was a brigand in the Darkwood,' Braith said with a grin to Rafe's questioning look. 'Best get the horses stripped down and turn them loose.'

Soon Rafe was paddling across the river, and it wasn't long before he was wading onto the far bank, the muscles in his shoulders and back feeling as if they'd been filled with lead. Sniffer splashed ahead of him and gave Braith's hand a lick; he'd already dragged his coracle into a worn-out overhang. He helped Rafe do the same and then they were up the bank and stepping amongst the first trees of the Darkwood. It took less time for the dogs to find Halion's scent again than it had taken to cross the river.

'Good boys,' Rafe whispered as they slipped into the twilight of the forest.

Rafe pulled a strip of salted pork from his pouch and chewed, the meat tough and stringy.

Looking forward to a fire and some hot food.

They had followed Halion's trail deep into the Darkwood, eventually making camp beside a stream when the light forced them to stop. The dogs were curled at Rafe's feet now, though their ears were twitching at every sound from the forest, of which there were many. It was very different from camping out in the open. In the distance something howled.

'How far ahead of us do you think he is?' Rafe asked once they were settled.

'No more than a day. Maybe a little less.'

'You don't think he knows we're following him?'

'No, lad,' Braith said. 'I've tracked others and been tracked myself more times than I remember. He doesn't know we're here. At first he knew he'd be followed – remember how he flew hard and fast from Dun Taras and headed straight for the border with Cambren. He knew his only hope was speed. After that – in the mountains and then in the woodlands of Cambren – he tried a few tricks that would've thrown most huntsmen. Not that I'm bragging,' he smiled. 'And he's taking his time now. Caution, not speed, so as not to be spotted by locals. He's not worried that there's anyone on his tail that might catch up with him.'

'So you think Rhin was right – that he's heading for Edana?'

'Aye. He told Rhin that Edana was running for Dun Crin. By the looks of it, that's where he's headed.'

'Why would Halion *tell* Rhin where Edana's going. Halion's not the type to talk, even if he's losing body parts.'

'Rhin can be very persuasive. And she has *other* methods.' Braith didn't need to expand on that. Rafe remembered how he had sat in Rhin's chamber and watched Conall freeing Halion through the flames of a fire. *By flayed skin and blood, Rhin said.* He shivered at the memory of it.

'So if Halion told Rhin where Edana is, why do we need to be following Halion?'

'Because Dun Crin is in a marshland that covers fifty leagues, more or less. You should know that. Could take a while to search a marsh that big, whereas Halion will lead us straight to her.'

'Does he know where Dun Crin is, then?'

'No one knows exactly where Dun Crin is,' Braith replied. 'Only that it's somewhere in those marshes. But Halion has as good an idea as anyone. He'll have discussed it with Edana and Camlin; he'll have some idea where they're headed. If anyone can take us straight to Edana, it's Halion.'

Straight to Edana. Can't believe she's survived this long. She never seemed strong enough for times like this. Mind you, she'd changed a bit when I met her back at the battle for Domhain. Lording it over me in her tent, along with Corban and the rest of them. Bet she's not so high and mighty now.

'So what do we do then? Kill them all?' Rafe asked. He didn't actually like that thought, but he'd come to admire Braith and wanted to show him he wasn't scared of anything.

'That'd be a tall order for even you and me.' Braith grinned. 'No, we'll pick up some help along the way. Evnis is sitting on his arse in Dun Carreg – he'll be glad of something to do.' He stared straight at Rafe, his smile gone now. 'Got to do this right – can't have Edana escaping again. Or Lorcan, Eremon's whelp. We take their heads to Rhin. If we can't do that then we'd better build our own cairns. Rhin's big on rewarding success and punishing failure.'

I bet she is.

'You've known Rhin a long time?'

'Aye. All my life, it feels like. When I was a bairn my kin were killed in one of Owain's raids,' he waved his hand. 'Rhin found me when she rode out in response. I was curled up on my mam's dead body, all cried out. Just about ready to die. Anyway, Rhin took me in, gave me a home. All I've ever wanted was to repay something of her kindness.'

Kindness? Can't say that's the first word that comes to mind when I look at Rhin.

'And have some revenge against Owain, of course.'

'Well you've had that,' Rafe said. He had been there, at the battle where Owain was defeated. He'd fought in it, part of Evnis' retinue.

'Aye, that I have,' Braith said. 'Just one more score left for me to settle.'

'Who's that?'

'Camlin. Bastard nearly killed me on that beach in Domhain.' He reached up and rubbed his neck. 'But I can forgive him that, I suppose. This is war, after all, and we've chosen our sides. We all know our end may be a sharp blade, don't we, lad?'

'Not really thought about it like that.'

'Well, it's the truth, no point hiding from it. Camlin, though . . . he betrayed me. We had Queen Alona and Edana all trussed up and were leading them off to Rhin. He stood against me. Next thing I know, those brothers – Halion and Conall – are hurtling out of the shadows with iron in their fists and men of Ardan behind them. And that lad with his wolven.'

'Corban,' Rafe said. His lips twisted over the name.

'Not your favourite person, then?' Braith asked him.

'No. His wolven killed my da. Tore his throat out. Did this to me.' He lifted his shirt sleeve and showed Braith a ragged white scar that stretched almost from wrist to elbow. 'And Corban put a sword in my leg.' He shrugged. 'He's my score to settle.'

Braith stared at him in the darkness. 'Think you might want to walk away from that one,' he said after a while.

'Why?'

Braith shook his head. 'Just take my word for it – a bit of advice from one friend to another.'

'He's nothing special,' Rafe spat. 'I will see him dead.'

Braith gave him a measuring look. 'I've crossed paths with him a few times now,' he said. 'Most recently I took him prisoner in the mountains near Dun Vaner.' He fell silent, eyes distant. 'Me and my crew almost didn't make it to Dun Vaner, on account of that white wolven of his and his friends. They chased us to the gates of the fortress. Then they found a way in and killed just about every sword Rhin had. They had some help, granted, but still, storming Rhin's fortress; took some stones, that did.'

'You sound as if you admire him. Them,' Rafe said accusingly.

'Suppose I do,' Braith said. 'Takes a rare person to inspire his friends to try and drag him out of an enemy fortress. Nothing wrong with a bit of respect for your enemies. Won't stop me from killing them if I get the chance.'

'That wasn't the first time you've seen Corban, then?'

'No. First time was in Dun Carreg when, me being the fool I am, I decided to rescue Camlin. Somehow Corban became mixed up in it, with his sister and the wolven – not much bigger than a pup, then.' He laughed. 'He had some stones on him, even then. I saw him again – here in the Darkwood; like I said, he was part of the rescue party that came after Queen Alona and Edana. I think him and his wolven are the reason they found us.' He grimaced at that. 'You're best off just walking away from him. He'll meet a bad end, eventually, but I don't think it'll be by your hand.'

Rafe stared sullenly into the fire.

Walk away from my vengeance? Never.

*

Dun Carreg was a dot on the horizon in the east, the Baglun spread before him. They had followed Halion for another ten-night, three days through the Darkwood, another seven through the moors and valleys of Ardan. They'd stopped at Badun for as long as it took to buy two horses and then set off south, Halion's trail skirting away from the giantsway and heading south through empty moorland towards the eastern fringes of the Baglun Forest.

'We'll have to part ways for a while now, lad,' Braith said to him.

Rafe reined in his horse, so surprised he nearly lost his balance. 'What do you mean?'

'Halion is heading south-east, looping around the outskirts of the Baglun. My guess is that he's avoiding Dun Carreg and the giantsway so that he can approach the marsh from the east – a much safer route for him.'

'Aye, that makes sense.'

'Whatever his reason, when he finds Edana, you, me and two hounds aren't going to be enough to finish this. Chances are she'll have more than a few swords around her. Ride to Dun Carreg, tell Evnis to come, personally, with enough warriors to end this. Take Sniffer with you, he'll find us quickly enough.'

Rafe nodded.

'Ride hard,' Braith said, 'otherwise they'll go to ground and we'll have a much harder job, worming them out of the marshes.'

'I won't let you down,' Rafe said to him, leaning in his saddle to grip Braith's forearm.

'I have no doubts in you, lad; no, it's Evnis that I'm worried about.' He reached inside his cloak and pulled out two things. A silver chain with a stone pendant and a vellum scroll, sealed with red wax. 'The pendant will get you through the gates and in front of Evnis quickly enough, and the scroll – give that to the old snake – it's a letter from Rhin. If your words don't move him this should put a fire up his arse and get him in a saddle.'

Rafe grinned at Braith, put the scroll into a pack strapped to his saddle and then he was off, Sniffer bounding along beside him.

It took over half a day of hard riding to reach the giantsway, memories flooding back to Rafe – hunting countless times with his da in and around the Baglun, his warrior trial and Long Night, the night Dun Carreg fell, marching to battle against Rhin.

And now I'm back. Almost a year to the day that I left on a ship for Cambren.

He reined in and dismounted, quickly unstrapped his kit bag from his saddle. There wasn't much of worth in there – a coat of mail he'd taken from a dead warrior in Domhain the most valuable thing, and the box from the marsh, of course, not that that was worth anything. He still hadn't had a chance to open it – he'd tried briefly, wiggling his knife in the lock, but to no avail. Since then he'd been on the road with Braith and something had stopped him from getting the box out in front of the huntsman. He thought about having another go at opening it now, but his excitement at seeing Dun Carreg was mounting, so he took the coat of mail out and quickly put it on. He adjusted his warrior torc, checked his warrior braid and straightened his sword-belt. He didn't want to look like a bedraggled huntsman when he rode across the bridge and through the arch of Stonegate.

Havan, the fishing village at the base of the hill that Dun Carreg sat upon, appeared as it always had: wood and thatch buildings, smoke rising from the roundhouse at its centre, figures moving about their daily work. As he passed through and began the winding climb up the hill to Dun Carreg he recognized faces, some pausing to stare at him. He ignored them. Halfway up the hill he stopped and looked out over the village and bay, the sea glittering blue and green, fisher-boats dotting the waves. As he gazed out beyond the bay, black sails caught his eye. Lots of them, coming up the coast from the south like a great flock of black-winged birds. They sailed past the bay, disappearing north around the cliffs of the headland. Rafe just sat there and watched, counted at least fifty ships, and remained there staring for a while after they'd disappeared.

They look like the ships we sailed on to reach Cambren.

When he was sure that they weren't coming back he rode on.

His hooves clattered on the bridge that spanned the chasm between the mainland and Dun Carreg and then he was reining in before Stonegate. He showed the pendant Braith had given him to a handful of guards in the black and gold of Cambren, and soon after was dismounting in the courtyard before Dun Carreg's feast-hall. A stable-boy came to take his mount and Rafe threw some strips of meat to Sniffer and ordered him to stay, a few moments later finding himself standing in the feast-hall waiting for Evnis. The hall was empty, the fire-pit dark and cold. Rafe's eyes wandered, saw black scorch-marks scarring timber pillars and supports, testament to the night Dun Carreg had fallen. Rafe's eyes searched out the spot where his da had died.

A door behind the King's dais opened and Evnis walked in, followed by a handful of warriors, all in sable cloaks edged with gold.

Evnis looked older than the last time Rafe had seen his lord. He still walked with purpose and energy, but there was a stoop to his shoulders that hadn't been there before, the lines of his face deeper, and silver streaked his dark hair.

'By Asroth's stones, if it isn't Rafe returned to us,' Evnis said, a grin splitting his face. As he came closer Rafe saw rings of gold and jet on Evnis' fingers, his warrior torc wound with gold wire.

Rafe blinked. *He seems genuinely pleased to see me.* Without thinking, Rafe dropped to one knee and bowed his head.

'Stand,' Evnis said. 'We have much to talk about, not least your adventures with Queen Rhin and the conquest of Domhain, but I think there is more to your arrival here than a yearning for home. Am I right?'

'You are, my lord,' Rafe said. He fumbled inside a pocket and produced the scroll that Braith had given him.

Evnis broke the seal and read.

Evnis was close enough for Rafe to smell his breath – it was sour, a hint of mead upon it; spidery veins spread across his cheeks, there was something bloated about his face. He had the look of a man who spent too much time in his cups. Rafe's gaze drifted to the warriors behind Evnis – most he didn't recognize, but then his eyes fell upon a familiar face – Glyn with his twisted nose, broken by Tull in the sword-ring. He winked at Rafe, and he grinned in return.

Evnis looked up and stared at Rafe; his eyes still held all their wit and cunning.

'So,' Evnis said. 'News indeed. Glyn, muster a hundred swords, we are riding south.'

'Aye, my lord,' Glyn said and strode from the room.

Evnis put an arm around Rafe's shoulder and steered him towards the doors. 'We shall make ready and you can tell me your news. First, though, if you don't mind, I have one question to ask of you.'

'Of course, my lord.'

'Have you seen my son?'

CHAPTER THIRTY-FOUR

CYWEN

Cywen sat with Brina against the trunk of a broad oak. It was late in the evening but still light, both sun and moon sharing the sky above; dusk was settling about them.

'Again,' Brina said.

'*Lasair. Uisce. Talamh. Aer.*'

'Good,' Brina said.

Good! That's the first time she's used that word and aimed it at me. Cywen couldn't keep the smile off her face. She'd been officially titled as Brina's apprentice for over two moons now, spring turning to summer as they travelled through the realm of Narvon.

After the battle with Rhin's warband in the north they had encountered little resistance. An occasional skirmish, but even then only between Coralen's scouts and small bands of Rhin's warriors. No one chose to stand against the whole warband, mostly in Cywen's opinion because their warband consisted of Jehar, Benothi giants and a wolven. *No one in their right mind would willingly choose to fight us, unless we were actively threatening their hearth and home, or they numbered in the thousands.* Also, most of the villages were stripped of warriors of fighting age – most had gone to Owain's summons and ridden to war against Ardan.

Some had even joined them. After seeing what the Kadoshim had done to the survivors of the village in the north, Corban had insisted on riding into each village that they passed to warn them. If it was a fortified town he would ride to its gates under the truce of a rowan branch and tell those gathered on the walls of what followed behind them. Corban had told Cywen that it was to give them a chance. *Knowledge is power, Cy. At least, that's what Brina always told me, and she's usually right.*

Many distrusted and disbelieved. Some didn't. Corban offered them the opportunity of riding with his warband, much to Meical's disgust. Over the course of their journey through Narvon the warband had swelled, numbering now around four hundred.

'You've a gift for language, I have to say,' Brina interrupted her thoughts. 'You're learning this much quicker than your brother ever did.' The healer was sitting with her book open across her lap.

'Can I see that?' Cywen asked Brina.

'Why?' Brina asked.

'I like letters,' Cywen said with a shrug. It was true. When her mam had taught her and Corban, back in their kitchen in Dun Carreg, letters had always been Cywen's favourite subject, while the histories had been Corban's. She'd always thought Corban just liked hearing about ancient battles.

'Here, then,' Brina said, a little reluctantly. 'Be careful – it's very old, many of the pages are brittle. And only look at the first half – that deals with what concerns you.'

The cover was thick leather, dark and cracked. She opened it carefully, each page inside a waxy parchment filled with giant runes. Sometimes it was clear that more than one hand had written in the book, the writing changing from spidery scrawl to firm, broad strokes and back again. There were many words that Cywen recognized, some from her lessons with her mam, others from her recent teaching with Brina. *Teaching me to be an Elemental. Who'd have thought?* The idea excited Cywen and she had taken to it well enough. Already she had made a spark appear, on her first attempt only yesterday. Admittedly it had fizzled out almost as soon as it appeared, but Cywen put that down to her own shock at seeing it appear as much as anything else, and Brina had been exceptionally pleased.

'You see, there is so much to learn before you can really start to put the theory into practice,' Brina said. 'Basic commands are simpler – like the one for fire that you tried yesterday. But if you want to shape your commands, exercise some kind of real control – like when we summoned the mist from the river – a mastery of the language is essential. We didn't just make mist from the river, we directed it across a meadow and *up* an embankment onto the old giants' road. That wasn't easy.'

'*Mist scary,*' Craf croaked mournfully.

He was sitting beside Brina, every now and then his beak darting into the ground and coming back up with a wriggling worm. His wing was healed now, fully recovered from the attack by the hawk, but he was a different bird. He was forlorn all the time, his mischievous comments replaced with melancholy. And he never flew; Cywen saw him often looking nervously to the skies. A ten-night or so after the attack Corban had asked Craf to help in the scouting, but Craf had become a trembling wreck at the mention of it. Corban had obviously felt so sorry for the bird that he had let it go, and not asked again. Now Craf always stayed close to Brina, usually perched on her saddle. *He misses Fech. So do I, strangely enough. And I think if I was him I'd be scared too.* She had often seen a winged shape riding the currents high above them. It looked suspiciously hawk-like. *It would make sense for Nathair and Calidus to track us, so it could well be the hawk that killed Fech.*

Brina leaned forward and scratched Craf's neck.

Farrell appeared and sat down with them, throwing something to Craf as he did so. Something slimy, judging by the noises Craf made as he consumed it.

'*Tasty,*' Craf croaked by way of thanks.

'You're welcome,' Farrell said. He unslung his war-hammer and placed it on the ground beside him, patting its iron head lovingly, a habit that Cywen had noticed he did almost every evening. Farrell had taken to spending his nights with them – Dath was always out scouting, and Corban was permanently busy.

It's funny how we all group together – the Benothi giants are always together, the Jehar, though they seem to be in two camps – Tukul's lot, and those who rode with Nathair, led now by Akar. And us, a small remnant of Ardan. Perhaps Farrell takes some comfort in being around us – we are as close to home as he can find in this patchwork warband.

Pages passed and Cywen turned them quicker, until about halfway through the book something changed. A new hand took over the writing, for one thing, the runes taking on an elegant flow. Also diagrams started appearing, strange designs, and the giant runes changed from flowing sentences into something more fitful,

appearing almost like lists. Cywen saw the giantish word for blood
– *fuil* – and further down the page *namhaid*.

She felt her eyes drawn to the pages, almost as if she was sinking
into them.

'What does *namhaid* mean? Is it enemy?'

'Hey,' Brina snapped, making her jump. 'I told you not to go so
far.' Brina snatched the book back. Cywen held on a moment, then
thought better of it and let go.

'What's wrong with looking at that part?' she muttered.

'First of all, because I told you not to,' Brina said acerbically,
'and secondly, I don't say things without good reason. I'm too old to
start wasting my breath.' She scowled at Cywen.

'*Too old*,' Craf muttered.

Brina's scowl gravitated to Craf.

'Sorry,' Cywen and Craf said together.

'Apology accepted. Just don't do it again.'

'I won't,' Cywen said. *Not when you're sitting right next to me,
anyway.* She was already desperate to have another look.

'Is that Vonn's book?' Farrell asked. 'The one he took from his
da?'

'It is,' Brina said curtly.

'Can I have a look at it?' Farrell asked.

'What, with your big sausage-fingers. Absolutely not,' Brina
snapped.

'All right,' Farrell muttered. He sounded hurt. Cywen caught
him snatching a glance at his hand. He wiggled his fingers.

Cywen stood and stretched. The camp sprawled about them,
nestled between the fork of two streams. There were no fires, there
had been none since they had fought the warband in the north, and
with the supplies of brot and the summer nights they didn't really
need one. *It would still be nice, though.* Brina had occasionally set a fire
and boiled a pot of water. When Corban or Tukul had reminded her
that they were in enemy territory and not lighting fires she had told
them it was for making poultices and informed them that if they
didn't want anyone to know where they were, to kill that damned
hawk hovering above them all the time. They went away shame-
faced – it wasn't as if they hadn't tried, but even the most skilled
archer couldn't shoot that high. Brina had always managed to make

her and Cywen a mug of tea whenever she boiled a pot, though. Cywen wasn't complaining. Or telling.

Cywen could see Corban skirting the horses' picket line with Meical and Tukul. As she watched a handful of riders cantered into the camp, heading for the makeshift paddocks by the stream. Coralen rode at their head, Storm pacing silently beside her. Further out Cywen could just make out the shadowy figures of Jehar and giants circling the camp, over a score on guard duty at all times.

Since Brina had asked Cywen to become her assistant Cywen had stopped feeling so useless – mostly she helped Brina in the tending of ailments, ranging from the severely battle-wounded to mundane injuries incurred during the day-to-day of a small host on the march. Sprained ankles, headaches, stomach upsets, stung by something unpleasant, usually with roots or wings.

Cywen liked it. She was kept busy, which was important; spare time usually ended up with her brooding on the death of her mam. And Brina was a good teacher.

As long as I learn something the first time she tells me. Apparently she doesn't like repeating herself.

Sometimes Brina's abrasiveness just became too much. At times like that Cywen liked to throw her knives at something.

Today is one of those days.

She walked a few steps into the undergrowth that surrounded them and was abruptly enveloped by a stand of ash and elm. Brina was still close by, within earshot. She drew one of her knives from the belt across her chest and sighted at a tree. She pulled the blade back to her ear, held her breath and threw. It connected with a satisfying *thunk*. Without thinking she pulled another knife and buried it in the trunk a finger-span from the first.

She sensed a presence and looked around, saw a tall figure half-hidden behind a bush. She blinked, realizing it was a giant. *Not quite big enough for a fully grown giant.* A giantling. She stared, and hesitantly the giantling stepped out from behind the bush and took a step towards her. 'You do that well,' the giantling said, her speech faltering, almost clumsy.

'It's just practice,' Cywen shrugged, then put another knife in the trunk beside the other two. 'I'm Cywen,' she said.

'I know. The Bright Star's sister.'

Something about that made Cywen scowl internally.

'I am Laith,' the giantling said. She took a few steps closer, reaching inside a leather vest and pulling out a knife. Cywen's knife.

'I thought it was you,' Cywen said.

'Aye. Balur told me to return it and to ask your forgiveness.' She stopped beside Cywen, holding the knife out to her. It looked very small in her flat palm.

'Why did you take it?'

'You threw it at me,' Laith said defensively. Then she smiled. 'I like things that have been made – it is a good knife. A bit small –' she shrugged – 'but unusual. The balance is different.'

'My da made it for throwing,' Cywen said. 'The weight is concentrated in the tip.'

'Ahh, made for throwing. That explains it.' She held the knife close to her eyes, examining it with fresh interest. 'I thought that. Your da is a smith?' she asked Cywen.

'Aye.' *Was.* She threw another knife, imagining the trunk was Nathair.

'I am a smith,' Laith said with pride, standing straighter and puffing her chest out. She took up a lot of room. She turned Cywen's knife between thick fingers. 'Your da is good. Is he here?'

'He's dead,' Cywen said and drew and threw another knife.

'Oh.' Laith hung her head. 'My da is dead, too.'

Cywen paused and looked at Laith. In the twilight of dusk she looked more like something carved from stone, her limbs long, muscles striated like rope, though not slab-thick like Balur and the other adult Benothi.

'Keep the knife,' Cywen said with a smile. 'Though it looks a little small for you.'

'I cannot. Balur would . . .' She looked wistfully at the blade in her palm.

She looks like a bairn with a present on her nameday.

'You are a smith – keep it to use as a pattern – make another; bigger. More suited to you.'

'You would have to teach me to throw,' Laith said. 'I cannot do that.' She nodded at the tree trunk, now studded with half a dozen throwing knives.

'I'll teach you. It's not as hard as it looks, especially when the knife is made right.'

'Yes, it is,' Farrell said from behind them.

'That's because you're impatient. And you've got sausage fingers,' Cywen said.

'Oh, and the giant hasn't,' Farrell muttered.

'Look, like this,' Cywen said. She gave Laith a demonstration, breaking down the action. Grip with two fingers and thumb. Arm loose, back to the ear, sight, breathe, throw, snapping the wrist. Laith tried it and threw the knife in her hand. It *tinged* off of the trunk, spinning into the undergrowth. With a gasp of horror she ran to find it, trampling undergrowth as she searched in circles. The look of relief on her face when she found it was immense.

'You did it wrong,' Cywen said. 'Look. The blade strokes your ear – not too close, don't draw blood.'

Laith stood next to her, set her feet as Cywen had, gripped the knife and pulled it back to her ear.

'No. Like this,' Cywen said. She walked around the giantling and moved her arm to the correct position, having to stand on tiptoes to reach it. Cywen stepped away and saw that Farrell was standing close by.

'I always wondered how you did that,' he said.

'You could have just asked.' To Laith she said, 'Try it now.'

Laith's arm sprang forwards, and before the knife had connected with the trunk Cywen knew she'd thrown well.

Laith grinned and ran to the tree, Cywen and Farrell following.

'Oh,' Laith said.

The knife had almost disappeared, only a finger's width of the hilt protruding from the trunk.

Laith tried to pull it out, but couldn't get a grip on the hilt. Farrell tried. He did manage to get a hold of it, but it was stuck fast.

'Short of chopping the tree down, you'll not be seeing that blade again,' he declared.

Laith hung her head unhappily.

'Here,' Cywen said, working one of her other blades free. 'Take this one as your pattern. When we find a forge, make some of your own. Until then try not to bury it in something inanimate.'

Laith smiled, her mood turning like a summer storm.

'Though I don't know when we'll ever get to use a forge again.'

'There'll be a forge at Dun Crin. Or Drassil,' Farrell said. 'Wherever we're going.'

'Balur One-Eye says that we will see the Darkwood on the morrow,' Laith said quietly.

'The Darkwood,' Cywen breathed. She remembered it none too fondly. It was where Ronan had been slain. They had been courting. And he had been slain by Morcant.

'Aye. Time for the Bright Star to choose our way,' Laith said.

'What's going on here?' a voice said. The three of them spun around to see Coralen approaching, wrapped in her wolven pelt and claws as usual. A few of her scouts followed behind her – Dath and two Jehar, both women, one young, one old.

Coralen's band of scouts had grown to thirty or forty the deeper they had moved into Narvon; even some of the villagers that had joined them in the north had become part of Coralen's wolven pack, as they had taken to being called.

'Cywen's giving a lesson in knife-throwing,' Farrell said. 'You're looking fine this evening, by the way,' he added.

'I look like an unwashed wolven,' Coralen snorted, then ignored Farrell, looking between Cywen and the tree trunk as Cywen pulled her knives free.

'That's something I'd like to learn,' Coralen said.

'I'd be happy to show you,' Cywen told her. The two girls had not spoken much since travelling together. Cywen had thought Coralen aloof and disdainful. And in truth she was also a little jealous of her – she was so capable with a blade, could best many in sparring and hold her own with most of the others.

'What would you like in return?' Coralen asked her. 'A trade.'

'Teach me how to use that,' Cywen said, pointing to Coralen's sword.

'All right then,' Coralen said and held her arm out. They gripped and shook forearms.

I like her a bit more, already.

'Brina, I've a message for you from Corban. He says he would like to speak with you.' Coralen paused.

'Oh did he now,' Brina snapped. 'Wasn't so long ago I was teaching him what end of a broom to use, and now he's *sending for me*.'

'He asked me to say please,' Coralen said, smiling. 'He was very insistent that I didn't forget that bit.'

'Ahh, well then. Maybe I will go and see him. Cywen, come on.'

'Me?'

'Of course. You are my assistant, so come and assist.'

Corban was sitting beside one of the streams with his boots off and his feet in the water. Coralen turned to go but Corban called out to her.

'Stay a while, Coralen, if you would.'

She hesitated a moment, then muttered, 'I can spare a few moments, I suppose.'

'You'll kill the poor fish doing that,' Brina said to Corban as she sat beside him, pointing at his bare feet in the stream. Craf appeared beside Brina and hopped up onto her leg.

'Ahh, Brina, I've missed you.'

'Missed me? I've been no more than a hundred paces away from you for the last two years.'

'You know what I mean,' he said, wrapping an arm around her shoulders and squeezing her tightly. He kissed her on the cheek. Cywen thought she saw the edges of Brina's mouth twitch.

I'd be too scared to do that to her. Dark shapes appeared on the far side of the stream, Storm taking form first, her bone-coloured fur seeming to glow in the last rays of dusk. Buddai ran beside her, a brindle shadow. Cywen was shocked at how much bigger than him Storm had grown. Buddai was tall, his back as high as Cywen's waist, but Storm was a head taller than that, and broader and longer besides. They tumbled in meadow grass together, nipping at each other's fur.

'You wouldn't think we were knee-deep in a God-War, looking at them,' Corban said.

'Ignorance is bliss,' Brina agreed.

Coralen snorted.

Storm leaped the stream in a single bound, circling then pushing in tight against Corban. She folded her legs beneath her and laid her big head across his lap. He grunted with her weight but didn't push her off, instead tugging absently at one of her fangs. It was about as long as one of Cywen's knives. Buddai followed, not quite clearing the stream and splashing them in ice-cold water. He curled up against Cywen.

'Dun Cadlas, the capital of Narvon, is only a half-day's ride ahead. Balur One-Eye tells me the border of Narvon and Ardan is close, Uthandun and the giantsway only two days' ride from Dun Cadlas,' Corban said. 'Coralen saw the fringes of a great forest during her scouting. It can only be the Darkwood.' He turned and reached a hand out to Cywen, squeezing her hand.

He remembers Ronan, too. They were friends.

'In many ways it feels like the place this all started. When Rhin sprung her trap, ambushing Queen Alona, kidnapping you and Edana. Uthan being murdered, Brenin blamed for it.'

'*And Craf found you, lost in the trees,*' Craf muttered.

'That you did, Craf. You saved us,' Corban agreed.

'*Yes, Craf did. Clever Craf.*'

Corban stared at Craf a while. 'I miss Fech,' he said.

'*Craf miss Fech too.*'

'That bird,' Corban said. 'It was Kartala, Ventos' hawk.'

Of course, Cywen thought.

'You're right,' she said. 'It brought a message to Calidus about you.'

'It's been following us, ever since Fech,' Corban said. 'We need to do something about that. Calidus and Nathair cannot know our every move.'

'Unless you can fly I don't know what you're going to do about it,' Brina said.

'How's your needlework?' he asked her.

'I stitch my clothes,' Brina shrugged. 'How's yours?'

'The same. Mam and Da taught us both to sew – Mam our clothes, Da leather – boots and the like.'

'Why?'

'I'll talk to you about it after. First, though . . . It's time for me to choose which way we're going to go. Dun Crin or Drassil.'

'Well, what's it to be?' Brina asked him.

'That's what I was hoping to ask you,' Corban said.

'Oh no you don't,' Brina said. ' Usually I'd be more than happy to tell you what to do – it's often safer that way. And of course I don't mind advising you until all our skin wrinkles and turns to dust. But it's your decision that counts here.'

'I know,' Corban said flatly. 'I'm still struggling with why.'

'Me too,' Brina and Cywen said together.

'I've thought a long time over why I have been chosen for this,' he waved his hand vaguely towards the warband. 'Why me – a blacksmith's son, no particular ability or influence in our world.' He shook his head.

'I'm still confused about that,' Brina said. 'But Meical is convinced, and he is one of the Ben-Elim. You should probably listen to him.'

'I know. And I do. I've asked him *why me*, but that is the only thing he doesn't want to tell me. He usually likes telling me what to do – he reminds me of you like that.'

'I've always liked him,' Brina said.

'I wish it wasn't me. Not that I don't want to fight. Back in Murias I saw evil enter our world, and there's no running from it. We tried that, eh?'

'We did,' Brina sighed.

'No, I understand that, and I will fight Calidus and Nathair until my last breath. But what I don't want to do is lead. So many consequences from every decision. So many lives at stake. I wish it wasn't me.'

Cywen felt a wave of guilt. *Poor Ban. And most of the time I've been sulking that he isn't spending every moment with me.*

Brina nodded. 'But it is you. There are times when we cannot understand something, don't know the reason for a thing and have to leave it at that – I know that that goes against every fibre in your very being . . .'

Cywen and Coralen both snorted laughter at that.

'But on these occasions we just have to accept that they just *are*.'

'That's the conclusion I've reached,' Corban said glumly. 'When Gar started saying similar things to me, when we were fleeing Ardan, I just thought him mad. But I can't really argue against it now. Things have happened.'

'You mean apart from seeing Kadoshim boil out of a cauldron?' Brina said.

'Aye. Other things.'

'What things?' Cywen asked.

He took a deep sigh. 'When I was held captive by Rhin – in Dun Vaner – something happened. She did something. Witchcraft. I woke up with her . . . somewhere else. It was the Otherworld. She brought me before the throne of Asroth.' He paused here, staring at the stream a long time. Eventually he shivered and carried on. 'He told me he'd been hunting for me. And that he was going to cut my heart out.'

And I thought my time with Nathair was hard. What kind of a world are we living in?

'If it was true, not a dream, or a hallucination, I mean, how did you escape from him?' Cywen asked.

'Meical and a host of the Ben-Elim smashed their way in and saved me. I saw Meical as he truly is. He's got wings.'

'Strange and terrifying times we live in,' Brina said. She reached out and squeezed Corban's hand. He smiled at her.

'Yes, they are,' Corban agreed.

'But you still have a decision to make,' Brina said.

'I know, but I was hoping for some advice. There are times when I feel I am going mad with it all.' He rubbed his temples. 'So. Advise me. Please.'

'That I'll happily do,' Brina said. 'The way I see it, there are good reasons to go to both places. Ardan because, we hope, Edana is there, with warriors about her. Combine them with this warband that is gathered behind you, we could make a considerable force. And Rhin must be stretched thin, ruling four realms so suddenly. It could be a good opportunity to take Ardan back.'

She paused, running a bony finger through Craf's feathers. 'And Ardan is our home – it would be nice to be back there. Familiar and comforting.'

'Aye, it would,' Corban murmured.

'And it's closer. Much closer than Drassil.'

'Aye, it is.'

'As for going to Drassil. Meical says you should go there. He is Ben-Elim, he should be listened to. Also, this prophecy says you should go. I am usually suspicious of fate and divine control, but in this case, you should listen. And one of the Seven Treasures is there.

We will need them all if victory against Asroth is to become vaguely possible, so we should go and get it.'

That's a better assessment than I could have made. When Brina says it like that, it seems that we should go to Drassil.

'So there you have it, Corban, the fors and againsts of both choices. The question is, which one will you choose?'

'My head tells me to choose Drassil,' Corban said. 'For all of the reasons that you state. Mostly because Meical tells me to, and, as you say, he is Ben-Elim, so he should know. But my heart whispers to me of my oath to Edana. I can't get her out of my mind.'

There was a loud crack. Coralen was sitting with two halves of a stick in her hands. She was glaring at it. They all stared at her. After a few heartbeats she must have felt their eyes, for she looked at them. With a snort of disgust she threw the two halves of the stick into the stream, then rose and stalked away.

'What's wrong with her?' Corban asked.

Brina laughed.

CHAPTER THIRTY-FIVE

FIDELE

Fidele stood in Lamar's chambers situated at the very top of the high tower of Ripa, gazing out of the window onto the landscape beyond – limestone cliffs, the horseshoe of the bay and the wide sea beyond. Black sails studded the waters, settled about the bay like a murder of crows.

The Vin Thalun. Will we ever be rid of them?

Over a moon now she had been here, surrounded by the enemy. Lykos was out there somewhere, she knew that. Once, not so long ago, that thought would have filled her with rage, and with fear. Now, though, something else consumed her thoughts.

Someone. Maquin.

I feel . . . happy. A ten-night had passed since Maquin had awoken, since she'd found him awake and kissed him.

He did tell me that he'd returned from death for me. Truth be told, though, he hadn't needed to say anything. When she'd seen him collapse in the feast-hall she thought she'd lost him – and something in her had died. The feelings of relief when he had awoken had overwhelmed her like some dark, powerful wave. *It's ridiculous.* And yet, she felt happy, for the first time since . . .

Since before Aquilus died. I should feel guilty about that. My dead husband. And yet a lifetime has passed since then.

'My lady?' a voice said behind her.

She turned. Peritus was standing beside their council table, maps strewn across it, platters of food and jugs of wine.

'Yes?' she said.

'We have much to speak on; are you ready to begin?' Peritus said.

'Of course.' She turned and sat at the table. Lamar was there, flanked by his sons Krelis and Ektor, as well as Peritus, once battle-chief of Tenebral, until Nathair had replaced him with Veradis.

'The messenger told me you had news?' Fidele said.

'That is true,' Lamar said. He looked older than the last time she had seen him, his skin sagging like melted wax upon the frame of his skull. His eyes were sharp, though. And hard.

'Marcellin marches,' Peritus said. 'He has gathered his warband, and the eagle-guard that had been sent on fool's errands when . . .' He paused, looking into his cup. 'Sent to the kingdom's borders by Lykos.'

Fidele took a deep breath at that. When Lykos had controlled her through his witchcraft he had governed Tenebral through her. She had signed letters, orders written by him that sent the most loyal of her eagle-guard to the fringes of the realm, on the pretext of giant raids or supposed sightings of lawless men. All untrue, part of Lykos' scheming to ensure that the balance of power in Jerolin remained in favour of the Vin Thalun. She knew that she had had no control of the matter, but that didn't stop her feeling shame for it.

'That is good news,' she said.

'Your letter to him must have convinced him, my lady,' Peritus said.

Marcellin, Baron of Ultas, had barred his gates to Lykos and the Vin Thalun, but equally he had seemed unmoved to take any action in defence of Tenebral. He lived to the north-east of the realm, on the edge of the Agullas Mountains, a long way from Jerolin and the events and politics of Tenebral.

'I am glad to have contributed something of use,' Fidele said. 'How many men march with him? And how long before Marcellin reaches us?'

'We don't know the numbers for sure. Marcellin can raise a war-band at least two thousand strong, and if he has gathered all those who were sent on postings from Jerolin –' Peritus shrugged – 'three and a half thousand swords at least, most likely more. As for time, it will take them a moon at least to reach us.'

'Another moon for us to hold out here.'

'We can do that,' Lamar said. 'We have the supplies.' He looked to Ektor for confirmation, his son nodding.

'Part of me says we should march out and show these Vin Thalun what the men of Ripa can do,' Krelis growled. 'We don't need Marcellin to come and save us.'

'We must wait,' Peritus said to Krelis. 'You have eight hundred swords under your command here. The Vin Thalun ranks have swelled, more ships arriving. They must have at least two thousand men out there. With Marcellin's reinforcements we will crush them, give them the lesson they deserve. Unless, of course, our King Nathair returns to us unbidden.' He turned his eyes to Fidele.

Nathair. Once, not so long ago I yearned for his return, thought that he would set me free of Lykos' spell, give me justice. Now I am not so sure . . . Her gaze flitted to Ektor, who was watching her. Ever since he had told her of the prophecy, read to her from the giant scrolls in his chambers, a gnawing seed of doubt had taken root in her belly. *What if Calidus is not Ben-Elim? What if he is Kadoshim?* If that were true, then Nathair was in great danger. *And the things Lykos had said, insinuated about Nathair. That he had troubles of his own.* She did not hold out for Nathair's return any time soon, and part of her did not want him to come back, for fear that her foreboding might turn out to be more than just the paranoid fears of a mother long parted from her child.

'I fear that Nathair's quest will keep him from our shores for a good few moons yet,' Fidele said. 'You must be patient, Krelis.'

Krelis lifted a cup and drained it. 'Patience,' he growled as he slammed the cup down. He sighed. 'I know, you're right. I've had enough of sitting on my arse, though. It wasn't so bad when Lykos kept sending sorties against the walls. Kept me busy . . .'

'Perhaps there is something we can do,' Peritus said. 'I spoke to your scouts earlier.'

'The ones returned from Sarva?'

'Aye. They said they saw Vin Thalun in the old ruins of Balara.'

'Perhaps they are setting up a base of command there,' Krelis offered.

'That would make sense,' Fidele said. 'That is where we discovered the fighting-pits, is it not?'

'Aye, my lady,' Krelis and Peritus said together.

Fidele could remember it still – the stench of death, the haunted looks in the eyes of the pit-fighters they had saved. *What they must have been through*. Her thoughts returned to Maquin. *How has he survived such a thing?* She knew, though. *You just do. You dig deep into your soul. Endure. But not without cost.*

'You said we could do something?' Krelis said to Peritus.

'I think it is time that we took the initiative, instead of sitting in here, drinking wine all day long.' He looked pointedly at Krelis.

'Sounds good to me,' Krelis said, sitting up straighter. 'What exactly are you suggesting?'

'Night raids. Nothing big – plans easily go awry in the dark. Kill some Vin Thalun on the night watch, break some axles in their baggage trains, maybe burn a ship. And perhaps we should take a closer look at Balara, see what mischief we can perform there.'

'Is this wise?' Ektor asked. 'As you said, plans in the dark easily come undone. We cannot afford to lose more warriors. And who would lead these raids?' He raised an eyebrow, looking at Krelis.

Krelis raised his cup and grinned.

'That is a bad idea,' Ektor said. 'As much as I know that you are just the brawn in Ripa, your death would devastate our warriors. You cannot go.'

'Ahh, brother, I didn't know you cared.'

'I don't, really. But I care about Ripa falling, and you are the cornerstone that our warband's morale rests upon. Cut you out and it would come toppling down.'

'I'm going,' Krelis said.

'That would be foolish – the rewards do not outweigh the risks.'

'Ektor's correct, Krelis. You cannot go,' Lamar said.

Krelis' mouth twisted but he held any retort in.

'Help us plan the raids,' Fidele said. 'Whatever Ektor says, I know that you have a gift for strategy.'

'Aye, and you have a gift for diplomacy, my lady.' Krelis smiled at her.

Fidele passed through torchlit corridors, her footsteps taking her to Maquin's door. She paused outside, a flutter of excitement in her belly, then opened the door.

Maquin was standing gazing out of the open window, his back to her. A ten-night of recovery had put a little meat back on his bones, his frame not quite as gaunt and skeletal as it had been. He wore a plain linen tunic, belted with rope at the waist.

She walked up behind him and he turned, a smile softening the sharp lines of his face. They embraced silently, melting into each other. Footsteps sounded in the corridor and they parted. The footsteps passed by.

I feel like a guilty maiden. Maquin smiled ruefully at her, a twist of his lips.

'There is not much to see out there,' Fidele said, looking out into the night. Far below lights flickered on the bay, pinpricks marking the Vin Thalun ships. She knew what he'd been watching.

He pulled an oar on a galley like those down there. Perhaps even one of them.

They had talked much during the ten-night since he'd woken. He'd told her of his youth in Isiltir, of his kin and friends, of Kastell, the Gadrai, of Jael and Lykos and everything in between. He had wept when he spoke of Kastell and she had held him, felt his sobs rack his body. And she had spoken of her life, growing up in Jerolin, of Aquilus, how he had lived and died, a man of principle. Of the council, the proposed alliance. She had spoken of Nathair, of her hopes and fears for her son, and of Lykos. How he had controlled her, eventually marrying her, on the day that Maquin had fought Orgull, the crowning celebration.

'How did the council go?' he asked her.

'Well enough.' She told him of the news that Marcellin was marching to their aid, and of the plan to begin raids against the Vin Thalun. He seemed more interested in that.

'When?' he asked her.

'Soon,' she shrugged. 'A few days, maybe a ten-night. Peritus suggested that a number of raids be carried out on the same night – three, four groups with different targets. He said if they did one at a time that the Vin Thalun would be alerted after the first raid, and their security would tighten.'

'Makes sense,' Maquin muttered. He stretched as he spoke, rolled his neck and shoulders. 'It is time for me to start doing – some sparring, maybe. My body is aching more from lying in this room doing nothing than it did from running through the forests of Tenebral with you.' He smiled at her, both of them remembering.

It had been often terrifying, always hard, physically and mentally, but now Fidele could not help but look back at their journey from Jerolin to Ripa with a sense of . . . nostalgia. It had been simple, then, just the two of them. She was happy now, more so than she could remember, but something was growing in her, a sense of foreboding.

There was a tap at the door, a pause, then the door opened.

Alben stepped in, the old warrior looking tired, but graceful as always. He dipped his head at them both.

'And how is my miracle patient?' he asked, moving to check Maquin as he always did – his temperature and pulse, then the wound in his belly, just a slight bump and the silver knotting of a scar upon the skin now.

'Restless,' Maquin said.

'I am not surprised,' Alben said. 'Men such as us, a lifetime of routine and training, it does not just go away. And it is a good sign, your mind and body telling you that they are ready. We best get you into the weapons court.'

'Will you spar with me?' Maquin asked him.

'You will have to go easy on me.'

'Ha, I think it will be the other way round,' laughed Maquin.

Alben smiled at him. 'In the morning, then.'

He walked back to the door, hesitated before he opened it.

'You should know, people are talking of you both,' he said.

Fidele felt her breath catch in her chest.

Alben turned and looked at them. His expression was sadness mingled with concern.

'Go on,' Maquin said.

'War does things to people. Our mortality becomes clear. Will we die today, or on the morrow? These questions become foremost in the mind.'

'I have lived in that state for more years than I can remember,' Maquin growled. 'This is no passing fancy.'

Alben shrugged. 'I am not your judge. But you should know, talk is spreading, of the Queen and the pit-fighter. You have scarcely left this room, Fidele.'

'I am not a queen,' Fidele breathed.

'You are to them,' Alben said, gesturing vaguely about him. 'The people of Ripa, the survivors, they see you as their queen, at least in Nathair's absence.'

Fidele drew in a deep breath, standing taller. 'I have lived in misery, thought that my life was ended – a living hell. And yet, here I am.' She felt her hand searching for Maquin, just wanted to touch him. 'I will not deny myself this. It came to me unsought, but I cannot deny it.'

'You do not have to explain or defend yourself to me, my lady. I am both warrior and healer; I exist in a place where life and death cohabit; where they are bedfellows, only a breath apart. Life should be lived, and what is life without heart and passion?' He shrugged. 'I thought you should be aware, that is all.'

'Thank you,' Maquin said.

The swordsmaster left the room. Maquin just stared at Fidele.

'I'll not give you up,' she said fiercely.

'I returned from death to life for you. Rumours aren't going to scare me,' Maquin grinned.

CHAPTER THIRTY-SIX

CORBAN

Corban hoisted his saddle onto Shield's back and buckled the girth. Shield looked round at him and nudged him as he went through his routine.

When he had finished he put his arm under the stallion's neck and laid his head against Shield's shoulder. He stayed like that a while, listening to the rhythm of Shield's heart, the steady flow of air expelled from nostrils. Eventually he stepped back, began picking a knot from Shield's mane.

'Big day today,' he said, 'and I'd rather be here seeing to you than over there.'

He glanced towards a group that had gathered at the head of the warband, waiting for him. Meical was at their head.

Shield regarded him with his dark liquid eyes and whickered. He stamped a hoof.

'I know – truth and courage,' Corban whispered as he swung into his saddle and trotted towards Meical.

The sun was rising, a finger's width over the rim of the world, the sky clear of cloud. There had been no sword dance or sparring this morning. Meical had suggested that at this point speed was more valuable than training, and Corban was inclined to agree.

I want to be out of Narvon.

He saw a dark speck circling high above them and frowned. *Kartala – we need to do something about that bird.* He glanced at his fingers, the tips sore and throbbing from all the stitching he had done last night.

He pulled up before Meical, Tukul and Balur One-Eye, the rest of the warband gathered behind them. All were ready to travel, watching him.

'Balur, will you lead us to Ardan?' Corban said. He waited as the meaning of his words settled upon them. Meical sat tall and straight in his saddle. He gave nothing away except for a tightening around his lips, perhaps a rigidity in his shoulders. They locked gazes for what felt like a hundred heartbeats.

Meical nodded, a sharp, controlled movement, and Corban let out a breath he hadn't known he'd been holding.

'To Ardan,' Balur said, striding off on his trunk-like legs. Like a creature rousing from sleep the warband followed him.

'Dun Cadlas lies to the east,' Balur said to Corban as they travelled through a green-sloped valley. 'It was Owain's fortress, his seat of power. Rhin will likely have a strong garrison there.'

'I thought the same,' Corban said. *So we need to avoid them.* Coralen had already gone ahead with a score of scouts, Dath amongst them. Corban had asked her to search for a specific location for their evening campsite. She had scowled at him as she'd ridden away.

Did she want to go to Drassil?

'We will loop wide around the fortress, then rejoin the old road – it is the fastest route to the border,' Balur continued. He didn't usually offer information, speaking only when Corban asked questions of him.

Hooves drummed and Meical rode up beside them. He nodded at Corban but didn't say a word.

Thank Elyon for that.

The leagues passed quickly and soon after highsun Balur led them back to the giants' road that they had followed virtually all the way from Murias.

'Dun Cadlas is ten leagues behind us, the bridge into the Darkwood forty leagues ahead,' Balur said. The road was in better repair now, and there were more travelling upon it. Ahead of them Corban saw shapes fleeing down the embankments and heading for cover as they thundered down the road. No one stayed on the road to challenge them. Frequently Corban looked up at the sky. Every time he found the winged shadow trailing them. He swore under his breath.

Amazingly they encountered no opposition throughout the entire day. As the sun began to merge with the horizon they crested a ridge and Corban saw to the south an ocean of green boughs spreading across the landscape.

The Darkwood. It was still some distance away, most of a day's ride, the land between dotted with woodland and undulating meadow. To the west Corban saw hills rolling into mountain peaks. *We will not make it today.*

A black dot appeared on the road ahead, quickly growing larger. Soon individual riders were visible – three of them, and a wolven loping beside them.

Coralen.

She'd found a place for camp that suited Corban's request and led them to it, a patch of woodland upon the slopes of a gentle hill, a stream curling along its base. The sun painted the sky pink as they saw to their mounts and secured the area.

While all were at their tasks Corban went to see Craf.

'Now, Craf,' Corban said, and with a flapping of wings Craf took to the air. It wasn't elegant, the first time that Craf had become airborne since the death of Fech, but it was flying.

'*Craf won't fly,*' the crow had said when Corban had sat and begun talking to him.

Higher Craf spiralled now, at the edge of the trees, level with the first boughs, then higher, cresting them and bursting into open skies. He circled there a moment. Corban was sure that the bird was looking back down at them, at him.

Don't ask him to do this, Brina had said. *It's not fair. He's old, he's been through enough.*

'He's going to come back down,' Corban said to no one in particular.

Craf didn't. He winged higher, angled his course to the north.

I don't want to ask him, Corban had said. *But I see no other choice.*

Corban put a hand above his eyes and peered into the sky, tracking Craf as he shrank to a black dot.

We are in a foreign land, enemies all about us. Coralen and our scouts have saved our hides a hundred times, but we need eyes in the sky.

Craf passed out of sight and Corban slipped into the treeline, looked back to check that no one was left out in the open. Only

Brina was still standing on the grassy slope, her face pale and anxious.

'Brina, come on,' Corban called, holding his hand out to her. She gave him a foul look but hurried under the cover of the trees, refusing to take his hand.

Corban looked, saw Balur standing by a tree trunk to one side, another giant to Corban's left. The trees either side of him formed a kind of gateway into the woods. He looked behind, up at the tallest tree, saw Dath's boots dangling down from the highest branches. Dath had the best eyes in the whole warband.

'Anything?' Corban called up to him.

'Nothing,' Dath called back down.

Corban swallowed.

'*Craf won't do it*,' the crow had said. '*Craf scared. Too dangerous. Might die.*'

'I know it is dangerous,' Corban had said to Craf, 'but it is necessary. Please help us, Craf. Be brave and do it for us. And you will get first pickings of everything that Storm catches.'

'*Everything?*' Craf had asked.

'Aye, everything.'

'*First pickings, not last?*'

'Aye. You have my word.'

Craf had bobbed his head, thinking.

'*First pickings no good if Craf dead*,' the bird had eventually croaked.

'You won't die, Craf.'

'*Corban can't say that. False promise.*'

'I don't think you'll die,' Corban had corrected.

'Anything?' Corban called up to Dath again now.

'N— . . . wait, I think I see something. Yes. He's coming.'

'Just Craf?'

'No. The other one's after him.'

Corban's heart rose into his throat. Brina edged closer to him. Corban wasn't sure if it was for comfort or so that she would be nearer to kill him if Craf got hurt. Heartbeats passed.

'Nearly here,' Dath called down. 'The other one's almost on top of him.' The creaking of branches signalled that Dath had started to climb down.

It was just as before, Craf setting off on a scouting mission, the hawk spotting him and swooping down from above, Craf dashing for the safety of the warband.

Please. Elyon, don't let it end like last time.

Craf burst over the edge of the canopy, cutting tight to the trees and looping steeply down the slope. The hawk appeared, just moments behind, talons outstretched, wings tucked tight in a steep dive. Somehow Craf turned, a sharp bank in the air that brought his path around to face towards Corban beneath the trees. Wings flapping furiously, he powered towards Corban. The hawk turned too, with greater control and agility, hardly breaking pace.

Come on, Craf. Corban willed himself not to move, prayed that no one else would. Craf was close to the first branches now, with a rush of beating wings passed under the first boughs, the hawk half a dozen heartbeats behind. Craf hurtled over Corban's head.

'Now!' Corban yelled.

Balur and the other giant tugged on the ropes they were holding, each one looped over a branch of the tree they were standing beneath. The same rope had lain slack upon the ground beneath the two trees. Now it shot into the air, pulling up beneath it half a hundred cloaks that Corban, Brina and Cywen had stitched together the previous night. This wall of cloaks appeared in the air so fast and sudden that it appeared to be magic, a sorcerous barrier between Craf and the hawk.

With a thud the hawk crashed into the cloaks, almost tore through them, its speed so great. The giants let go of their ropes and the huge tapestry of fabric tumbled to the ground, dragging the hawk with it. There was a powerful flapping of wings as the hawk tried to right itself. It spun in the air, wings beating furiously, scraped the ground and rolled. For a moment it stood upon the ground, then its wings unfolded, beat once and it lifted off.

An arrow slammed into a wing, spinning it, sending it crashing back to the ground. Corban glanced back, saw Dath reaching for another arrow. Coralen stood beside him, her own bow bent. Her arrow pierced the hawk's body, and another from Dath impaled the bird to the ground. It screeched, shuddering.

There was the sound of beating wings again. Craf glided down onto the dying hawk, pinning it with his talons. Even now the hawk's beak lashed out, trying to strike Craf, but there was no power and Craf brushed off the blow. He raised his head and struck down with his own beak, straight into the hawk's head. Again and again. When he stopped the hawk lay still.

'*For Fech*,' Craf squawked, looking up, his beak dripping red.

'For Fech,' Corban echoed.

Cheers rang out behind him.

Corban walked into the trees, Storm at his side. Dimly he was aware of Jehar standing guard, a shadow too straight here, a movement there. He sat with his back to a tree, Storm curling at his feet. It had been good, taking Kartala out of the skies, and the relief that Craf had not been hurt was a physical thing. The whole warband had celebrated a little, as much as was possible whilst in the heartland of their enemy, anyway, and broken out the last few barrels of mead left from the battle in the north. Now, though, Corban had a headache and he just wanted to be alone for a while, away from the questions.

Footsteps sounded, soft on the woodland litter. It was Meical. He sat beside Corban.

'To Ardan and Edana, then,' Meical said to him.

I thought I'd got away too lightly with it.

'Aye.' Corban sucked in a deep breath. 'I mean you no insult, Meical. You have saved my life, snatched me from the throne room of Asroth, followed me through the wilds of the north, advised me, fought beside me. I could not have saved Cywen if not for you. I am more grateful to you than words can express. And you are Ben-Elim. But . . .'

'Yes. I know, your heart tells you to keep your oath.' He sighed, but some of the tension that Corban had seen in him that morning was no longer there.

'Yes,' Corban said simply.

Meical had two cups in his hand and offered one to Corban.

He took it and sipped some mead.

'At first, I was angry with you,' Meical said. 'But I have thought about it all this long day, and now I am merely annoyed, and anxious.'

Corban said nothing, just waited, a trick he'd learned from Brina.

'We have had a few disagreements since Murias, you and I,' Meical continued. 'Elyon cut us from different fabric, I think – mankind and the Ben-Elim, I mean. Duty drives me, my duty to Elyon in his absence, unclouded by passion or emotion, whereas in you and your kind I see emotion lurking beneath each and every decision. Fuelling every decision.' He rubbed his eyes. 'Whether that is good or bad, I know not, but that is the way Elyon made you, and so I must accept it. Sometimes that is not easy for me to do.' He glanced at Corban, the flicker of a smile touching his lips.

This is the most human he has sounded since I met him.

'Thank you, for not disagreeing with me in front of them all,' Corban said.

'What point me declaring that I will follow you if I won't? Or only when you do as I want you to do? Perhaps I have lessons to learn.' He shrugged. 'I will follow you to Ardan, Corban. I wish we were going to Drassil, feel that our hope is best served by going there. But, I am not Elyon. I do not know all things.' He shrugged and drank from his cup.

'Do you think we will win?' Corban asked, voicing the thought that dominated most of his waking life.

'Win? I don't know. I have laboured for more of your years than I can remember in preparation for these days, and many of my plans have come to nothing, or been thwarted by Asroth and Calidus, his servant. I thought I had sought out the best of men to fight Asroth and his Black Sun, from kings to ordinary men. But so many of them are now dead – Aquilus of Tenebral, Braster of Helveth, your own King Brenin. Many others.'

'Brenin knew you?'

'Oh aye, he was one of the first to swear his oath to me. A good man, and he was one of the few that knew about you. Another one murdered by Asroth and Calidus' schemes.'

All that time, as I grew up in his household, and this God-War was already happening.

'I dreamed of you, last night,' Corban said.

'Of me,' Meical said.

'Aye. In the Otherworld.'

'You know that the Otherworld is no dream,' Meical said, looking concerned now.

Corban nodded.

'And what happened, in your dream?'

'I was in a valley. It was beautiful, not like the Otherworld I remember; this had vast cliffs and waterfalls. You were there. I saw you, flying. You landed upon a high ridge, greeted your kin, and entered a cave.'

Meical frowned. 'This happened. I returned to the Otherworld last night. It is dangerous, even for me, but I longed for a moment of home, to speak to my kin.'

I can understand that.

'I wanted to follow you, but I was afraid, so I just, wandered . . .' Corban tried to remember, but it was all blurred images now.

Meical grabbed his arm, the grip like iron. 'You must not do it again, do you understand? Asroth is looking for you there. If he finds you . . .' Meical shook his head.

'I don't know how to make it stop.'

'Then promise me if you find yourself there again, that you will hide, do not move. Asroth's Kadoshim fly high, like the hawk you caught today. They will see you before you see them. And they are not the only dangers in the Otherworld. There are creatures, rogue spirits that would do you harm if they found you.'

'Rogue spirits?'

'Aye. Kin that went their own way, would not side with Ben-Elim or Kadoshim. They took on new forms, a reflection of their spirits. Some have become . . . savage.' He closed his eyes a moment. When he opened them he gripped Corban's wrist. 'Promise me that you will hide.'

'I promise,' Corban said.

'Good,' Meical muttered, calming a little.

'How is it that you and Calidus are here? Made flesh?'

Meical looked into his cup, swirled it around. 'It is part of the prophecy; one Ben-Elim, one Kadoshim. Part of Elyon's fairness, I suppose. Though Calidus hasn't entirely embraced that aspect.' He barked a laugh, then sipped some more mead.

They sat in silence a while, then Meical sat straighter. 'So what I wanted to say to you is this: I have made mistakes, thinking they were the right thing to do, and been outwitted by my counterpart, more than once. So, perhaps doing something that I consider a mistake will turn out right.' He smiled at Corban and drank some more mead.

'I'll drink to that,' Corban said and raised his cup.

They set out the next morning with the rising sun, though thick cloud made dawn a grey, shadow-filled place. There was an air of anticipation about them all.

We will reach the Darkwood today, if no one bars our way. And then Ardan.

They knew Uthandun was the test, the fortress built by Uthan, Owain's son, overlooking the stone bridge that crossed the river Afren, serving as the gateway to the Darkwood and Ardan beyond.

If word has travelled ahead of us, then Uthandun is where the resistance will be gathered. I pray that we have moved fast enough to outpace all news of us.

Highsun came and went, with only a short break to rest and water horses. The road was becoming busier, traders with loaded wains, trappers with piles of skins, sometimes a family travelling to the market at Uthandun. All moved off of the road and sought to hide as the warband thundered past.

The sun sank lower.

They passed into a region of low-lying hills, to the south-east they occasionally glimpsed the Darkwood, bringing back a multitude of memories to Corban. Walking into a glade full of the dead, feeling a gut-wrenching fear for Cywen, discovering that she'd been captured along with Queen Alona and Edana, and finally the exhausting hunt through the night, deep into the heart of the Darkwood as Storm led them unerringly on the trail of the kidnappers.

Tukul's voice drew Corban's attention back to the world about him. A rider was galloping towards them. It was the Jehar Enkara.

'Warriors of Rhin ahead,' she said as she reached them. 'About a score – we let them through. They'll run when they see you, and Coralen will pick them off.'

Corban nodded, felt a spike of worry for Coralen and the others. *Nothing to be done about it.*

Figures appeared on the road ahead. Warriors, by the glint of metal and the way they rode. No sooner had they become visible than they were turning and galloping back down the giants' road.

Corban saw them stop, saw figures topple from horses – *Dath and his bow* – Jehar appearing from woodland on either side of the road as Storm surged into view, leaping upon a rider and dragging him and his mount crashing to the ground.

Corban kicked Shield on, breaking from a canter to a gallop, the warband increasing their speed with him. Even so it was all over when they reached them. Storm greeted him, running up and circling about Shield. Her jaws were sticky with blood. Dead men and horses littered the road.

'Two got away,' Coralen said when she saw him. 'I'm sorry.'

'How far are we from Uthandun?' Corban asked.

'A few leagues,' Coralen said.

'Then we're too close now for it to matter.'

They rode on.

Soon after, they crested a low hill and suddenly the Darkwood lay spread before them, Uthandun a few leagues away, sitting upon a gentle hill before the forest. Corban reined Shield in, just sat in his saddle and starred.

The meadows surrounding the fortress were filled with tents. Hundreds of them, men moving about like industrious ants. But that wasn't the worst of it. Corban's eyes were drawn to the river Afren, glistening between the meadow and the forest. It was full of ships with black sails.

CHAPTER THIRTY-SEVEN

VERADIS

Veradis stared out of a window high in Uthandun's keep. It was sunset, the day's last rays washing the land in golden hues. And in the distance, far along the curving line that was the giantsway, Veradis saw a dark smudge appear upon it. The smudge glittered with sunshine on iron, like a dirty jewel.

'How far away are they?' Veradis asked Rhin, who was standing at his shoulder.

'Three or four leagues.' She looked sideways at him. 'Too far away for a battle this night.'

'And you are sure it is the Black Sun?'

'Aye. Did Calidus not say so in his messages. That Meical and his puppet, this Corban, would be arriving at the gates of Uthandun within the next day or so.'

'Aye, so you have told me, although I have not seen these messages,' Veradis said, trying to keep the annoyance from his voice and not entirely sure that he had succeeded.

'Do you doubt me?'

Not now I don't.

'No, my lady. Of course not.' He paused, straining his eyes to see the gathering warband in the fading light. 'How many did Calidus say?'

'Three hundred swords, or thereabouts.'

'It looks to be more to me.'

Rhin shrugged. 'Three hundred, four hundred, six hundred. It matters not. You have close to a thousand men. I have double that. We have our Vin Thalun friends on the river, another five hundred

313

swords. And Calidus and Nathair are four days north of here, another thousand men. The Black Sun cannot win.'

'They have giants and wolven.'

A remnant of the warband that Rhin had sent north had trickled into Uthandun over the last ten-night, a score of men. All of them told a similar tale – of magical mists, of giants and wolven and warriors silent and deadly.

'They do. Forgive me, but you sound . . . scared.'

Veradis bridled at that. *Am I? Maybe a little, but not of them; only of failure.*

'I have faced giants and magical mists before, wolven and worse,' Veradis murmured, 'but I have been taught caution since then. Courage does not always equal victory.'

'No, of course not.'

'It feels almost *too* easy.'

'More wars are won by errors of planning than great valour on the battlefield, or at least that has been my experience. Plan well. When it is time to strike, do it hard and fast.'

Never, ever, underestimate this woman.

'And think, the God-War could be won in a single day. A single battle.'

'Indeed. How far did you say they are?'

Rhin laughed. 'You cannot bring them to battle this night. By the time you reached them it would be full night. On the morrow . . .'

'The morrow,' Veradis said, the words falling from his lips like a long-awaited promise. He could not suppress a smile. 'This is all that I have dreamed of, for so long now. To take to the field against the Black Sun.'

'And to win, I hope,' she said with a sidelong glance.

'Aye, and to win.'

'Good. Then it would seem that your dream is about to come true.'

A smile spread across his face.

The sun disappeared behind hilltops, the sky turning to dark velvet as they stood in silence and watched. Campfires blinked into existence where the Black Sun's warband had been, undulating across a far slope like a cluster of stars.

'They may attempt to slip around us on the morrow,' Veradis

said, imagining being one of them, seeing his warband and the Vin Thalun ships arrayed before them.

'They might,' Rhin said, 'and that would be a shame. Perhaps we should do something to ensure that battle is joined with the rising of the sun.'

Veradis marched along the hard stone of the giantsway. It was cold and dark, the heart of night wrapped tight all about him. There was no sign of Rhin's scouts that were apparently ranging ahead, fifty of them leaving the fortress ahead of him, a protective screen picking methodically over the ground for any sign of the enemy.

I hope.

The tramp of his warband's feet on the giantsway behind did a good job of obscuring his hearing, the only sense that was of any use in this inky darkness. Nevertheless he strained his ears, trying to pick out sounds from ahead, not an easy task.

This was a mistake, he thought, not for the first time since leaving Uthandun's walls. Walking into an ambush was not a pleasant thought.

It had seemed like a wonderful idea when Rhin suggested it, full of deep cunning: a forced march before dawn, not seeking battle, but to be close enough to give the enemy a surprise and no room for retreat when the sun rose.

No room for escape.

Now, though, all the dangers and potential disasters loomed tall in his mind.

What if they can hear us coming and are flanking us even now? He glanced down at his feet, boots wrapped in lamb's wool, the same as every other warrior behind him. It made a remarkable difference; usually the tramp of two thousand warriors on a stone road would have been close to deafening. Still, they were not silent, and every sound seemed magnified in this darkness.

We will still win. Cannot lose. Too much is riding on this. And we are meant to win. This is not just another battle, it is the fate of the world. He shifted the shield on his arm, shrugged the weight of his chainmail shirt, loosened his sword in its scabbard and kept marching.

It had taken them almost three moons to journey from Dun Taras in Domhain all the long way to Uthandun, travelling through three realms. Rhin had paused along the way, gathering warriors, sending others off to enforce her new sovereignty upon her new-born realm. They had reached Uthandun a ten-night ago, Veradis putting the time at camp to good use. His eagle-guard had drilled hard every day, working on horn signals from the back to signal front-line switches, or flank-strengthening and a myriad of other manoeuvres, working on the weaknesses of the shield wall, not that there were many. And Veradis' excitement and anxiety had grown daily in equal measure as Rhin reported to him of messages that she had received from Calidus.

They are close, so close. It will be good to see Nathair again. And he has been successful, captured the cauldron, one of the Seven Treasures. He must be overjoyed. Veradis had felt a worry lift from his shoulders that he had not realized was there.

It is only a shame that Nathair will not be here to witness the defeat of the Black Sun. He will be disappointed at that.

Something drew his attention, a flicker in the corner of his eye, just for a moment. A bone-grey blur. His senses strained as he stared into the darkness.

Nothing. He looked back over his shoulder as he continued marching, could make out an embankment that dropped steeply away from the road, but beyond that he saw nothing to confirm that his eyes had seen anything more than a trick of starlight. He marched on, the distant campfires of the enemy growing as they got nearer.

Dawn was a sliver of light in the east, the land a uniform grey, punctuated with deep, impenetrable pools of shadow. Muffled hooves drummed behind him; even they had been bound with fur. Rhin drew up before him, Geraint riding at her side.

'It is time,' she said, her eyes wide and bright with excitement. He felt the same, a night's march doing little to dampen his enthusiasm for the coming battle.

'Proceed as we planned,' Rhin said to him, then leaned in her saddle, reached down and stroked his cheek. 'We'll soon toast our victory over a cup of wine.'

He shivered, and not in anticipation. He knew that Rhin had a thing for younger men and he had no idea how he'd be able to reject her and live. She pulled on her reins and was gone before his mouth could work. His cheek felt hot where she'd touched him.

Geraint lingered a moment. 'Keep your head down,' the older warrior said, then he was riding away too, back down the road to Rhin's warband – close to two thousand swords spreading wide behind him, a mix of mounted men and foot soldiers.

This is it, Veradis thought, emotion swelling within him.

'Give the signal,' he said, and a warrior blew on a horn, two crisp notes. Before they had faded his eagle-guard was spilling from the road, forming into three blocks facing east. He would lead the first one, the other two behind, and together they would become a spearhead of iron and wood, flesh and bone. He marched towards his front rank, glanced at the shield wall to his left, warriors milling, forming lines. He saw Caesus, his captain, leaning out of the front line, looking towards him. They shared a glance and Caesus touched his fist to his heart, a salute. Veradis returned the gesture, then strode along the front line of his wall.

Faces stared back at him, grim and resolute. Many of them he recognized as having stood with him from the beginning, faced the charge of giants and draigs on that hillside in Tarbesh. Nathair's Fangs, they had called themselves, named after the draig teeth Nathair had given to each and every one of the survivors. Veradis' hand slipped to his sword pommel, where his draig tooth had been carved into the wood and leather hilt.

'Victory or death!' he cried in a loud voice and tugged his helmet on, hefted his shield and took his place in the wall. His cry was echoed, a thunderclap in the dawn as his men slammed tight around him.

The enemy were camped about half a league away, tents sprawled upon a gentle slope to the east of the giantsway, disappearing over the crest of the hill. Their fires were dimming as the sun rose, washing the earth with a pastel glow. Horn blasts rang out and the shield wall slipped into motion, smooth and practised, not a misstep that Veradis could tell. They had all removed the fur from their boots and now their progress was marked by a rumble as they marched forwards.

His heartbeat and the marching of feet kept time, helping to calm nerves, giving a discipline to their advance that somehow helped to keep in check the surge of emotions that accompanied battle – rage, fear, doubt. They passed across open meadows, the enemy growing ever closer.

Veradis' eyes scanned the hillside but it was still cloaked in great patches of shadow, the sun rising behind it, making silhouettes of tents and figures, and making him squint. Figures stood tall, silently waiting for them.

Wise, making camp with the rising sun at your back. But sunlight will not save them. Not this day.

Cywen must be up there. As soon as he'd heard the news of this warband's approach Veradis had suspected that Cywen must be with them. He had asked Rhin before he had thought.

'I do not know,' Rhin had said, regarding him with a puckered frown.

The next time she'd told him of a message from Calidus she had walked away, paused at the doorway and told him that Cywen lived, had been taken by Corban and his companions during battle in the halls of Murias.

Veradis had been surprised at the relief he'd felt to hear that she was still alive.

Corban found her. Rescued her. And she is up on that hillside now. I hope her brother tells her to stay out of this battle, or she's likely to get herself killed. He chuckled at that, the thought of Cywen taking orders from anyone, even the Black Sun, seeming like an impossibility.

His feet hit the beginnings of the slope, a gentle incline. Behind him he heard the rumble of hooves, neighing, sporadic battle-cries as men summoned their courage.

Still there was no movement from above. He'd expected a charge. Everywhere he'd fought, warriors attacked in the same way. The old way. A wild surge with the blood up, then the singling out of opponents, the distilling of battle down into single duels, the winner moving on to find his next opponent, the loser food for crows. And so on, until the battle was done.

Not us. The shield wall had torn apart all that came against it. *Except a charge of draigs, and a stampede of auroch. Here, though, it is against men and giants we fight. We will not lose.*

He felt his heartbeat thumping in his chest, his mouth dry, palms sweaty, and everything seeming enhanced, sharper. The grating of iron-rimmed shields as they rubbed together in the advance, the smell of grass wet with dew underfoot, the sound of wood pigeons complaining as they abandoned branches nearby. This was the precursor to combat, the process his body went through before imminent violence. He was almost used to it now, even welcomed it. He loved the simplicity of battle. All the doubt of the night's march was gone, as if evaporated by the rising sun. He felt alert, confident, focussed.

This war will be won today.

They were a third of the way up the hill now, the first fires a hundred paces away. Still no movement. The hairs on Veradis' neck prickled, his eyes searching over the rim of his shield for the enemy. For any sign of movement.

Something is wrong.

'Sound the halt,' he grunted to the signaller stationed behind him. A horn blast rang out. The shield wall rippled to a standstill, the other two on his wings doing the same, only heartbeats behind. Veradis stared at the clusters of figures before him, standing straight-backed and static, a breeze tugging at their cloaks, a fluttering of fabric.

He lowered his shield and stepped out of the shield wall, cursing himself for a fool.

He strode forwards, past a guttering fire, drawing the longsword at his hip as he approached the first group and hacked at a figure. It collapsed to the ground, the sound of sticks splitting, others in the line tugged to the ground where they were tied and stacked together.

He kicked at the form at his feet – sticks bound together and wrapped in a cloak. Cries from the woodland on his flank rang out: Rhin's horsemen moving through the open trees, discovering the true nature of their foe. Caesus reached him, eagle-guard at his back.

'Search the campsite,' Veradis ordered, already knowing what they would find. Or not find.

Rhin cantered up the hill to him, Geraint and a dozen shieldmen about her.

'A trick, my lady,' Veradis said bitterly, lifting a tattered cloak from the ground as she drew near.

'That I can see,' she snapped, her face tight with rage. 'The question is: where are they?'

Just what I was thinking.

A cry sounded from his warband, spreading, taken up by others. From the slope they were standing on they had a fine view of the surrounding countryside. Veradis saw men pointing back towards Uthandun. A sick feeling flowered in his belly, the aftermath of a punch to the gut. He stared hard at Uthandun, walls bathed in the light of dawn as the sun fully crested the hill at his back. At first he could see nothing wrong, then a flicker drew his eyes. Not Uthandun, but close to it. The Vin Thalun ships.

Their sails were burning.

CHAPTER THIRTY-EIGHT

TUKUL

Tukul ran up the boarding plank onto the black-sailed ship, his sword dripping red, Corban and a score more following behind him. All along the riverbank his Jehar were doing the same, killing guards and boarding ships. Thus far there was little clamour of battle – the defenders having been taken by surprise.

That won't last much longer.

They'd chosen eleven ships to board, eight of these sleeker galleys and three fat-bellied transporters. Enough to hold their entire warband, and their horses as well, if all went to plan.

But I've never known any plan to go smoothly.

To his right there was a burst of brightness and a wash of heat. He glanced, saw a furled sail burning fiercely, fire feeding greedily on fabric, saw the flicker of arrows, flames trailing incandescent in the sky and in moments more ships were on the way to becoming crackling torches.

The thud of running feet, more warriors emerging from the gloom. They saw him and slowed, came at him hesitantly, circling – hard-looking men with wiry muscle and weather-beaten features, all with dark, oiled beards, iron rings tied into them. For the most they gripped bucklers and short swords. Then Corban and others were spreading out from behind him. Tukul slipped his axe from its holster into his left hand and charged, blades swirling.

Men died.

Tukul left his axe buried in a skull, surged on, wielding his sword in great two-handed strokes. Blades stabbed at him, but he sent them all spiralling away. He carved his way down a narrow deck, an unstoppable force, his sword-kin spread either side. Soon the planks were slick with blood and gore. A shadow reared up on his left but then a mass of fur and teeth crashed into it. A glance showed Storm standing over a still form, her jaws dripping. On his other side Corban swept past him, dressed in his wolven cloak and claws. He blocked an overhead blow with his sword and opened his opponent's throat with a slash of his wolven claws, kicked the dying man aside and ploughed on.

A hand touched his arm, Gar. Their eyes met for a moment and then they were following Corban, cutting into a retreating knot of warriors. A dozen heartbeats later and their enemy, those who could, were leaping over the sides. Tukul looked about for the next man to kill and realized the deck was clear of any resistance.

Is that it? Tukul thought. *Not so hard to take a ship, then.*

He glanced over the side at the ships moored close by. Combat still raged on them, battle-cries and the clash of weapons ringing loud in the still dawn, echoing back from the wall of trees on the far bank. On one deck he watched giants, war-hammers and axes swinging, saw one giant lift and hurl an enemy into the river.

Corban disappeared down an entrance in the deck and Tukul ran after him, fearing more enemy hidden below-decks. He almost gagged as he climbed down the steep steps, the stench of ordure almost overpowering. He blinked at the bottom, eyes adjusting to the darkness, the only light leaking in through oar-holes.

Men were chained in rows to benches, or what resembled men, all of them skeletal thin, pale and scarred. Most of them were slumped where they sat, regarding him and Corban with flat, empty eyes.

Corban lifted his sword and the nearest man flinched, then Corban swung his blade down and sparks flew, shattering the chain that bound the first bench of rowers.

'I've taken this ship, killed those who enslaved you.' He worked his way down an aisle between the benches, hacking at the chains, splashing through liquid that Tukul suspected wasn't river water. 'You are free to go, if you wish, or row a little longer and be set ashore somewhere else.' He glanced out of one of the oar-holes. 'This is not the safest place to be stranded. Tukul, make sure they understand what I have said,' Corban muttered as he turned and climbed back up towards the light.

Tukul ordered barrels of water brought down and made sure the rowers all had their fill, though slowly. One man gripped his wrist. He was short and wiry, with skin that was olive dark, like the men from his homeland in Tarbesh. His eyes burned brighter than the others'.

'What's your name, brother,' Tukul said to him.

'Javed,' he whispered after a long pause, as if he were struggling to remember.

'Some water for you,' Tukul offered a jug from the barrel. Javed drank noisily.

'Is this a Vin Thalun jest?' Javed said, water dripping from his beard. 'Another entertainment?'

'No. You are free, as my lord said.'

'What's the catch? You'll kill us if we try to leave?'

Tukul shook his head. 'Leave if you wish, there will be no punishment from us.' He peered through the nearest oar-hole, heard horns ringing from the nearby fortress. 'Though I cannot guarantee the reception you'll receive from them.'

The man peered through the hole.

'You're welcome to stay.'

'Where are you going?'

'East,' Tukul said.

'East is not the ocean,' Javed snorted. 'Now I know you are playing with us.'

'I speak the truth,' Tukul replied calmly.

Javed stared into Tukul's face. 'Think I'll stay a while,' he said.

East to Drassil. How quickly plans can come undone.

Corban had turned pale when he'd seen the warband and fleet arrayed about Uthandun. They hastily made camp and Corban had summoned his war council – Meical, Tukul, Gar, Balur, Ethlinn, Brina and Coralen.

Corban sat in a camp chair with his head in his hands. Craf flapped down from the sky and perched on the arm of Corban's chair.

'*Cheer up,*' the crow squawked. He had taken to following Corban everywhere since the plan against Kartala the hawk had succeeded.

'Options,' Brina had snapped at Corban, making him jump and lower his hands.

'What?' Corban said.

'There are always options,' Brina answered.

With a deep indrawn breath he visibly gathered himself. 'What are they?' he asked.

'Fight.'

A humourless smile. 'Not a good idea. There are thousands of them. We are outnumbered.'

'Run away.'

'Better for us. I'd like to, but where? All routes to Edana are blocked.'

'Run north – retreat, in other words,' Brina said.

'And run into Calidus, Nathair and a thousand Kadoshim,' Tukul pointed out.

Corban shook his head. 'We've tried that already. Not appealing.'

'West, then,' Brina said.

'West is Cambren and Domhain. What is there for us?'

'Nothing,' said Brina, 'but I'm going through the options.'

'So what does that leave?'

'East,' Brina said.

'And what is east? The Darkwood, then marshlands.'

'Drassil is east,' Meical said.

Corban looked at him.

'He's right,' Brina added. 'Much further east, granted. But you've just said we can't go south, north or west.'

'And what of Edana?'

'Even if we could break through those ahead of us,' Gar said, 'and I for one am happy to try, and avoid those behind, they would be on our trail, would follow us straight to Edana.'

'Would Nathair and Calidus not follow us to Drassil?'

'Perhaps,' Meical said. 'Though somehow I doubt it. I suspect that Calidus' focus is elsewhere.'

'What do you mean?' Corban asked.

'If he wanted to bring us to battle, he could have. They are not so far behind us, could have caught us with a handful of forced marches.'

'Then why hasn't he?'

'I cannot say, for sure, but I suspect he is fixated upon the cauldron. To catch us he would have to leave it behind, under a smaller guard.' Meical shrugged. 'I am guessing, but I do not think they would be as quick to follow us all the way to Drassil. The journey is many leagues longer, and takes us far from the relative safety of Rhin's realms.'

Corban stood and paced for a while. He eventually stopped before Balur and Ethlinn.

'What would you do,' he asked them both.

Balur shrugged his massive shoulders. 'My heart says fight, my mind says run, live, fight another day. When there's a chance of winning. Here, there is no chance.'

'To fight now is to die, to run aimlessly is a longer death,' Ethlinn said, her voice a rustle, autumn leaves on the air. 'But to run somewhere that has meaning, hope. Drassil is the wisest choice.'

Corban bowed his head for long moments, then sucked in a long breath and looked around at them all, his gaze coming to rest on Meical.

'We will try for Drassil,' he said quietly.

He was silent a while, eyes staring into the south. Eventually his eyes dropped back to the fortress in the distance, a dark shadow now before the glitter of the river Afren in the twilight.

'They know we're here. Come sunrise there'll be a warband after our blood, whatever direction we decide to move in,' Corban murmured.

'We should leave before sunrise, then. Steal a march on them,' Coralen said. She'd been standing silently in the shadows until now.

'Marching in the dark is no easy task,' Gar said. 'There's a risk of getting lost. We could end up in more trouble than we started in.'

'We'd not get lost with Storm. She's better than the north star,' Coralen replied.

'That river,' Corban said. 'How far east does it go?'

'To the marshes that border Narvon and Isiltir. From there we could follow it to the northern sea,' Meical answered. 'If we had ships we could sail all the way to Gramm's hold.'

'Who is Gramm?' Corban asked.

'A friend,' Tukul said.

'An ally that dwells on the fringes of Forn Forest,' Meical said. 'He has helped us before, and will join us, now that the God-War has begun in earnest.'

Corban had nodded, eyes fixed on the black sails dotting the river Afren. 'Looks like we need some ships then.'

Tukul looked up at Dath, who stood on the raised cabin deck at the rear of the ship.

'We must leave *now*,' Dath yelled, and Tukul echoed the cry, standing atop the boarding-plank, beckoning to Balur and those still gathered upon the riverbank. All was chaos, ships burning, waves of heat and smoke billowing across the river. Many of the sailors who had fled from the flaming ships were trying to put the fires out, but more than half of the enemy galleys were blazing hotter than a forge. Tukul suspected there had been some Elemental assistance to the fire. As more of the sailors gathered upon the bank they launched a fierce counterattack on the ships that were being stolen. Horn blasts rang out from Uthandun, the sound of hooves and battle-cries drifting down from the fortress.

Balur was pushing warriors onto the boarding-plank, giants and Jehar both, sending them stumbling up the ramp and onto the ship's deck, then he turned, swung his black axe about his head and launched himself into a knot of enemy warriors surging towards him.

Tukul saw the first warrior chopped in half, legs and torso flying in different directions, the second taking the iron-spiked butt of Balur's axe in the face, a third losing his head, then smoke billowed about them, obscuring them from Tukul's sight.

All else had boarded now, Dath yelling for the ramp to be pulled in and the mooring rope cut, but still Tukul hesitated. He took a few steps down the ramp, yelled out to Balur, glanced back onto the boat, the faces staring at him.

I'll not leave the living behind.

He drew his sword from his back, began to stride purposefully down the ramp, ignoring the voices behind that called his name, then Balur burst from the roiling smoke, blood-spattered, a limp figure slung over one shoulder. He hurtled towards the ramp, other forms appearing behind him, chasing him. Giant boots thudded onto the ramp, wood creaking, and Tukul saw Balur carried a giantling across his shoulder, blood flowing from a gash across its scalp.

Balur heaved past him, Tukul stepping to the edge of the ramp, a straight lunge impaling the first sailor chasing after Balur. Tukul kicked him off his sword, sent his corpse falling back into the others following. He stepped forwards, his sword slashing twice, took off a hand at the wrist, opened a face and then the enemy were staggering back, tangled, falling as they tried to get away from him. He turned and sprinted back up towards the ship, Balur dragging the boarding-ramp in as he leaped to the deck, another Jehar slicing the rope that moored them to the bank. Oars rose and dipped; sluggishly at first, the ship pulled away, quickly picking up speed.

All along the river behind them others were following suit on different ships. Ten more followed, seven sleek-hulled, like the one Tukul was aboard, three wider, deep-hulled transporters with pot-bellies. The horses had been loaded on them.

A weight fell on Tukul's shoulder, staggering him, and he looked round to see Balur, his big hand coming down again to pat Tukul on the back.

'My thanks, little man,' the giant said.

Tukul nodded. 'Your companion?'

Balur pointed and Tukul saw Ethlinn, Brina and Cywen bent over the gangly form of the giantling Balur had carried aboard. A female.

'She is in good hands,' Tukul said, then climbed onto the rear deck, where Dath stood wrestling with a steering oar, Kulla the Jehar standing close to him, watching what he did with a raised eyebrow. Corban and Meical were standing at the rail, eyes fixed on the smoke-hazed riverbank. Farrell and Coralen were there, Storm sitting and licking blood from her claws.

'You sure you know what you're doing?' Farrell asked Dath.

'He is a skilled seaman,' Kulla said.

'Course I do,' Dath grunted. 'It's a little bigger than Da's fisher-boat, but the principle's the same,' He wrestled with the oar a moment.

'You need to be stronger,' Kulla pointed out. Farrell laughed.

'She's got a point,' Dath admitted. 'You may be a better choice for this job.'

'Here you are, then,' Farrell said, striding over and taking the steering oar from Dath.

'Try not to ground us on a bank,' Dath said.

Farrell gave him a flat stare.

Tukul strode to Corban's side and leaned on the rail. He noticed his hands were dark with blood and grime.

The cries of those trying to put out the flaming ships faded, further away.

'Not all of their ships are burning,' Corban said. 'They could follow us.'

'Perhaps, but not until they've cleared the way. That will be no easy, or speedy, task.'

'Aye.' Corban rubbed his eyes. 'Well, then it would appear that we did it,' he said to them both.

'Aye. Fortunate for us that the bulk of their warband marched during the night,' Meical said.

'Someone on their side has a mind for strategy,' Tukul added.

'Aye. And fortunate for us that we do too.' Corban was staring into the distance, where the smoke had parted to give a view of the surrounding land. They could see the hill they had camped upon, fires still a pale flicker, their stick men and cloak-wrapped crow-scarers facing down a warband thousands strong.

'I'd like to see the look on Rhin's face just about now,' Dath said.

Tukul laughed. It had been a close thing, that march through the night to reach the ships before dawn. Especially when Storm sniffed out an enemy warband marching along the giantsway towards them.

That wolven has saved our lives more times than I can count.

'Coralen, you're a genius – your ruse worked,' Corban called.

'It always has done,' Coralen said proudly. 'Distraction,' she continued. 'Rath taught it to me, and I'm sure you know the rule well enough; the blow that ends the fight is the one your opponent doesn't see coming. Make them look somewhere else, then make your move.'

I know that rule very well.

Tukul saw Meical nodding approvingly.

'You rode with Rath?' a voice grated behind them: Balur, the steps creaking as he climbed onto the deck. Brina followed behind him, small in his shadow. Her hands were red with blood. Craf fluttered down from above, perching on a rail.

'I did,' Coralen said. 'He was my uncle.'

Balur's white eyebrows bunched. 'Did he use that trick against the Benothi?'

'Yes,' Coralen shrugged.

There was an uncomfortable silence, Balur glowering down, Coralen scowling up.

'We have put old grievances behind us,' Meical said quietly.

The silence continued, then Balur sighed.

'Aye,' he rumbled and walked away.

The ship turned a bend in the river; Uthandun disappeared from view.

Corban turned and looked ahead, the river winding beneath the trees of the Darkwood.

'Craf, will you do something for me?'

'*Anything*,' Craf croaked. Brina raised an eyebrow at that.

'Find Edana at Dun Crin, tell her we tried, but it was impossible to reach her. Tell her we are going to Drassil. Tell her . . .' He paused, shoulders slumping. 'Tell her my oath still stands.'

Without a word of complaint Craf launched himself into the sky and winged southwards, disappearing beyond the trees.

'What have you done to my crow?' Brina muttered.

Corban stared after him a while, then looked at their course ahead.

'So. To Drassil,' he said, though Tukul thought he may have been speaking to himself.

Indeed. To Drassil.

CHAPTER THIRTY-NINE

UTHAS

Uthas stepped into a cavernous room, massive pillars rising high to a domed roof far above. A nimbus of light filtered through, as if the material the ceiling was carved from was thin, translucent.

Asroth's throne room. He felt a surge of fear coursing through his veins, paralysing him.

Why have I done this? What kind of fool am I?

'Remember, this is what you asked for,' Calidus said to him, still bound in his human form, appearing small and frail amidst the might of Asroth's Kadoshim.

And they were everywhere. Thousands of them, beyond counting. Not the shadowy wraiths he had witnessed emerge from the cauldron in Murias, but solid, grey-skinned creatures of scale and fang and wing. They wore coats of dark mail and bore spear and sword, regarding him with curious stares. The air crackled as one close by stretched its bat-like wings.

Uthas wrenched his eyes away from them and paced down the aisle before him, focusing on Calidus' back. He had walked what felt like a long way when a sound drew his eyes.

A scream.

He looked to his left, saw a figure chained to a post. A winged man, or what was left of a winged man.

He is Ben-Elim.

Uthas stopped and stared.

One wing of white feathers, stained with blood and grime, hung broken and useless from his back. The other wing was gone altogether, all that was left of it a frayed stump protruding from the Ben-Elim's back. He was chained to the post, suspended by iron collars about his wrists, head slumped, dark hair hanging. Another collar of iron was fixed about his neck, the chain secured to an iron ring embedded into the ground. As Uthas stood and stared, the Ben-Elim raised his head, dark eyes fixing him.

'Help me,' the Ben-Elim whispered through cracked and swollen lips.

'Why do you not just kill him?' Uthas asked.

'Where would be the fun in that?' Calidus replied. 'Besides, life and death are not the same, here in the Otherworld. It is nigh impossible to slay one of Elyon's Firstborn. They have tried.' He shrugged at the Kadoshim nearby. 'So we settle for pain.'

Uthas could not take his eyes away. As he stared, a Kadoshim approached the Ben-Elim, buried a spear-blade into his belly, twisting it; the Ben-Elim screamed in agony.

'Onwards,' Calidus said and they carried on, the screams fading behind them.

Eventually they came to wide steps that stretched the entire length of the chamber. Uthas climbed, at their top saw a figure sitting upon a throne that resembled the looping coils of a great wyrm. The figure was reclining, a leg draped across one coiled arm of the throne.

Asroth.

He radiated power, silver hair bound into a single, thick warrior braid. He wore a coat of oil-dark mail, leathery wings curled tight behind him. Kadoshim stood about him, some were guards holding bright spears, others were in conversation with the Lord of the Fallen. They fell silent as Calidus and Uthas approached.

'I bring an ally, my King,' Calidus said, more reverence and fear in his voice than Uthas would have thought possible. 'Uthas of the Benothi clan.'

Black eyes in a milky-pale face that could have been carved from alabaster regarded Uthas.

Asroth rose from his chair and paced forward. The ground smoked and hissed with each footstep, leaving behind a blackened imprint.

'Welcome to my home,' Asroth said, smiling through blue-tinged lips.

'My lord,' Uthas said. He stood a hand taller than Asroth, but still his legs were suddenly weak and he slid to his knees.

Asroth crouched before him, a broken-nailed finger tracing Uthas' chin, lifting his head so that their eyes met. The ground lurched beneath Uthas' feet, he felt as if he was falling. He did not much care for the sensation.

Asroth licked his lips with a black tongue, as if tasting the air. 'I know you,' he said. 'You are mine.'

'I am,' Uthas heard himself say, voice dry as gravel. He remembered vividly when Rhin had conjured Asroth through spells and flame. At the time it had been terrifying and exhilarating both. This time it was mostly terrifying.

'Why are you here?' Asroth asked.

'Uthas has information of value to our cause,' Calidus said. 'He knows the whereabouts of two of the Treasures.'

'That will be most helpful,' Asroth said. 'They are vital to our campaign. Which Treasures?'

'The cup and the necklace, my lord,' Uthas said.

'Nemain's necklace,' Asroth said quietly. He closed his eyes, dark veins tracing his eyelids. 'I remember seeing it about her neck as she fought me.' He smiled, opening his eyes. 'She had spirit. And you slew her.'

'I did,' Uthas said, feeling both shame and pride flow through him.

'So where are these Treasures?'

'I am aware of their last known locations,' Uthas said.

'Not quite the same as where they are now,' Asroth said.

'No, my lord, but it is unlikely that they have been moved.'

Asroth nodded. 'So. Where are these last-known locations?'

Uthas paused, fighting the urge to speak, to spill the information from his mouth. He clenched his teeth together.

'Uthas would ask a reward of you, for this information,' Calidus said.

Thank you, thought Uthas. Never had he felt more grateful to someone for speaking for him.

Asroth frowned, his alabaster skin creasing like old parchment.

'You would bargain with me?'

'No, my lord,' Uthas uttered. 'A reward . . .'

'Ahh.' Asroth stood and strode back to his chair, his leathery wings wrapping around him as he sat. 'It is true, I reward those who serve me – successfully. And punish those who fail me. What reward do you wish for?'

'To be King of the giant clans – and to rule from Drassil, our ancient home. When the war is won.'

'But your giants are Sundered. Even I cannot change what is already done.'

'I ask that they be given the choice, in this God-War. Those who join your cause have me as their lord, your vassal king. Those that refuse, back to dust.'

Asroth smiled. 'That does not seem unreasonable. I agree. If you are successful in your part of the bargain. Calidus must have these Treasures in his possession before your part is deemed fulfilled. Agreed?'

'Agreed,' said Uthas.

'Good. Now, where are these Treasures?'

'The necklace is in a tomb in the tunnels beneath Dun Carreg. The cup was lost in the marshes around Dun Taras. I know the location, but I have never been able to search there because it is in sight of the walls of Dun Taras. The men of Domhain would have fallen upon us. But now, Domhain belongs to Rhin, so I would have the freedom to search.'

'Can you find them? Bring them to Calidus?'

'I believe so,' Uthas said.

'You can, or you cannot. Which is it?' Asroth's voice was a deep basal rumble, filling his senses like a vapour.

Uthas licked his lips, which were abruptly dry. 'I can. I will.'

Asroth grinned. 'Good. I am pleased.' He held his arm out, black veins mapping it. He pressed a long, broken nail against the pale flesh, drew a line, dark blood welling.

'A bargain must always be sealed in blood, no?'

Uthas nodded and Asroth gripped his wrist, pulled his arm out and dragged a sharp nail across the inside of his forearm. His flesh parted as if cut with the sharpest iron, feeling as if Asroth had lit a fire in his veins, but he clenched his jaw, refusing to show any weakness.

Asroth wrapped long fingers about Uthas' forearm in the warrior grip, their blood mingling. Within heartbeats Uthas was feeling dizzy, intoxicated.

'Bring me the cup and necklace,' Asroth growled as he released his grip.

Dimly Uthas was aware of Calidus leading him from the great chamber, walking out into the pale light of the Otherworld.

'You must return to the world of flesh now,' Calidus said to him.

'What of you?' Uthas said. He blinked, trying to focus. He was aware that he did not want to leave Calidus. He had come to find the old man's presence comforting in this grey world.

'I have another ally to meet,' Calidus sighed. 'My work is never done.'

Uthas woke to the sound of Calidus screaming.

He staggered upright, reaching for his spear. His arm throbbed and he looked down to see a scab of black blood. He blinked and shook his head, for a moment a vision of Asroth's pale face and dark eyes consuming his mind.

Moonlight shone upon Salach, who lay close by, seemingly reaching full alertness before Uthas. Eisa was curled beside him.

Uthas felt a pang of jealousy, but quickly buried it.

We find comfort where we can, and in these end days it is rare and often short-lived.

More screams rang out, magnified by the darkness. Uthas followed the sounds, Calidus' voice distinct, even in rage. And the screaming was soaked with it – not fear, not pain, not even anger, but pure, undiluted rage. As Uthas drew closer he heard the rasp of a sword drawn, the thud of iron cutting flesh, a wild neighing, then Uthas saw him.

Calidus was standing amidst the paddocked horses that pulled their wains. He was hacking at a stallion, the beast already fallen to its knees, eyes rolling white, blood spurting black in the night from a great rent in its neck. Even as Uthas stood and stared, dumbstruck, the animal crashed onto its side, legs kicking as if it were running. With a shiver it lay still.

He has gone mad.

'Calidus,' Uthas called out, striding over to him. He was dimly aware of footsteps behind him, Salach, no doubt, as well as a growing number of Kadoshim. Uthas dipped beneath a rope bound between trees. Calidus turned his eyes upon the giant, blazing with malice, and Uthas froze, deciding that getting too close to Calidus with sword still in hand might not be the wisest move.

'What is wrong?' Uthas asked.

'Incompetent. Fools,' Calidus hissed, then turned and swung his sword overhead, chopping into the dead horse, wrenching his blade free in a spray of blood and bone.

'Who?' Uthas asked.

'Rhin. Veradis.' With each name he hacked into the horse again. Then once more. Finally he pulled his blade free and leaned upon it, chest heaving, head bowed. After a while he wiped his blade clean on the horse's carcass and strode to Uthas, saw a crowd of faces staring back at him.

'Meical and his puppet have escaped,' Calidus said, all calmness and composure now, although somewhat ruined by the streaks of blood splattering his pale face and silvery hair. 'And the Vin Thalun fleet is burned, sunk or stolen.'

'What! How can that be?'

'They attacked the Vin Thalun fleet moored at Uthandun, stole some ships and sailed east, burned the rest. The details are vague. We shall have to wait until we see Rhin face to face for the finer details. I met her in the Otherworld and must confess, I became . . . a touch irritated. She fled from me.'

I can understand why.

'Meical is behind it, of that I have no doubt,' Calidus said.

'We could change course, pursue them, perhaps catch them before they leave the Darkwood.'

'No,' Calidus snapped. 'The opportunity was too great to resist – to catch them between our two warbands. But to change course, chase them across the Banished Lands. No. I cannot lose sight of the task I have been set.'

'What do you mean?' Uthas asked.

'I was not clothed in flesh to destroy Meical's Bright Star,' Calidus snarled at him. 'My task is to make Asroth flesh. To bring him across the divide, from the Otherworld to this world of flesh.' He shrugged. 'Once that is accomplished, Meical and his Bright Star will die. It will be inevitable. Though this was still an opportunity missed, and causes me to doubt those I have raised about me.'

Uthas reached inside his cloak and drew out a leather flask. He pulled out the stopper, the oaky scent of usque drifting out, and offered it to Calidus.

'A good idea,' Calidus muttered, taking a long drink from the flask.

A glow in the east heralded the coming of dawn.

'Make ready,' Calidus called. 'I will see Uthandun today.'

Figures melted back into the darkness, Kadoshim seeing to their packs, going about the tasks of breaking camp.

Uthas looked at the humped shadow of the butchered horse.

The cauldron's wain will move slower, not faster, with one less horse pulling.

Calidus followed Uthas' gaze over his shoulder to the dead animal.

'Tell Nathair he can give that to his draig.'

Uthandun appeared as they crested a hill, the Darkwood a solid wall behind it, between fortress and trees a river glittering in the sunlight. Even from this distance Uthas could see the blackened hulls of ships half-submerged in its waters. Beside him Calidus hissed an expelled breath, the extent of his rage now. A vent to the deep ocean of fury that no doubt still surged within him.

He must have been angry indeed. I have never known Calidus to be anything but calculated control.

They rode down the slope, Calidus looking either side at the remains of fires, here and there were branches tied in the loose shapes of men, wrapped in cloaks. His mouth twisted in disgust. Behind them the wain carrying the cauldron rumbled over the crest of the hill, pulled by seven horses and a dozen giants. Uthas had ordered Benothi strength to replace the dead horse and ensure that they reached Uthandun before nightfall. Surrounding the great wain were the Kadoshim. They had changed over the course of their journey from Murias. Calidus had taught them a measure of self-control – they still had a taste for flesh, but Calidus had instructed them how to cook and eat like normal men, and also how to use and care for their host bodies of flesh and blood, like a treasured weapon. Now they looked comfortable in their skins, no ungainly jerks or spasms, and they had learned to use their hosts' voices, as well as harness their skills. They had learned discipline.

A fearsome combination – the skill of the Jehar and the strength of the Kadoshim. They exuded power, almost a physical thing, like waves of heat rippling about them on a hot summer's day.

Calidus spurred his mount on, speeding up to ride alongside Nathair, who rode at the head of their column. He sat straight-backed upon his draig, the beast's belly swollen and swaying with its recent meal. Alcyon was striding beside Nathair, as always.

This will be a test for our young king, Uthas thought. He had been mostly a silent travelling companion. *That is understandable, he has had much to think on, and grow accustomed to. Not least selling his soul to Asroth.*

Occasionally Nathair had asked Calidus a question – usually on the subject of the new order that Calidus had hinted at, sometimes about a strategy for the coming war. He had always seemed, if not submissive, then at least resigned to the stark realities of his new world.

But he will see Veradis soon. Then we will see where his loyalties truly lie.

'You are ready for this?' Calidus asked Nathair.

Nathair looked at Calidus, his face stern, otherwise emotionless. *He is learning to mask his feelings.*

'Of course,' Nathair said. 'I have made my choice, and sealed that bargain.' His lips twisted briefly.

Though he still has some way to go with that.

'You need not worry, Calidus.'

'I always worry,' Calidus said with a shrug. 'It is why I am still alive, and why we are winning this war.'

'I will perform my task. Play the king, the figurehead.'

'You are far more than that, Nathair. You are my supreme general, and unlike Rhin, you have never failed at a task.'

I would not wish to be in Rhin's cloak when they meet. Nathair straightened at that.

How fickle are these men, who are swayed so by a little flattery.

'And you remember what to say, in our war council?'

'I do. Certain things must be made to happen.'

'Indeed. And Veradis,' Calidus probed. 'You are prepared for meeting him?'

'I am,' Nathair said with a sigh. 'He is a good man; he is my friend.'

Alcyon grunted beside Nathair, the first sound the giant had made.

'He will not understand . . .' Nathair trailed off. 'He will not understand the complexities of our situation. Yet. But in time I hope to be candid with him. Bring him into your, our, circle . . . ?' It was a question more than a statement, Nathair looking almost pleadingly at Calidus.

'Of course,' Calidus said. 'I am fond of Veradis.'

Alcyon looked at Calidus, brows furrowed.

Uthas watched the giant suspiciously. 'And Veradis is a great asset,' Calidus continued. 'Skilled, more loyal than a faithful hound. A fighter and a tactician. I have many plans for Veradis.'

'Good,' Nathair said with a curt nod.

From Alcyon's expression, the giant was not as convinced.

Uthas sat in a chamber high in Uthandun's keep. Unlike most of the fortresses that served as mankind's seats of power in the Banished Lands, it was not giant made, nor stone, just timber and thatch, and so it was cramped and uncomfortable, doors too narrow, ceilings too low. There were no chairs suitable for a giant, and so Uthas and Alcyon stood behind Nathair and Calidus. The Kadoshim Sumur was also there, stood a pace behind Nathair, his eyes dark pools in a pale face.

The door opened and Rhin walked in, warriors behind her. With a wave of her hand she ordered them to remain in the corridor. Rhin shut the door and sat. She looked tired, dark shadows beneath her eyes. Uthas felt a wave of sympathy for her. She had been many things to him over the years – his enemy, his captor, torturer, saviour, and finally, strangely, friend. But he knew he could not help her now. Calidus glowered at her in her chair. Slowly she raised her eyes and met his gaze. A silence grew. She did not look away.

'Well?' Calidus eventually said, his voice breaking the quiet like a whip-crack.

'We were outmanoeuvred,' Rhin said. 'A battle lost, not the war.'

Calidus slowly stood, the leather of his surcoat creaking. With deliberate steps he walked around the table to Rhin and stood beside her. He laid a hand on her shoulder. She twitched.

'You have made a mistake,' Calidus said, a whisper that filled the room.

'Yes, I ca—'

'No,' Calidus said. 'Do not shame yourself with excuses. There are no pretences amongst us, Asroth's inner circle.'

Rhin's eyes darted to Nathair.

'Yes,' Nathair said with a cold smile. 'I have been enlightened.'

'That is . . . good,' Rhin whispered.

'It is,' Calidus agreed. 'What is not so good is letting Meical and his Bright Star slip through your fingers, and allowing my fleet to be *destroyed*. Ships that were to take us, take the *cauldron*, to Tenebral.'

After a long silence Rhin finally spoke.

'I am sorry.' Rhin said. Uthas saw her shoulder twitch again beneath Calidus' hand.

'I am sure that you are,' Calidus said, his voice calm, matter-of-fact. 'But good intentions alone will not win us this war.' He muttered, his hand upon Rhin's shoulder moved, fingers contracting, a black mist flowing from his palm, slipping about Rhin's throat like a dawn mist, heavy and slow. Rhin gasped, her mouth opening wide.

'Do not try to speak,' Calidus said, calm as before, 'you'll only find that you cannot. Only listen.' He bent close, lips almost brushing her ear. 'Asroth rewards, but he also punishes. Faithfulness is good. Faithfulness and success is better. Failure, on the other hand . . .'

He took his hand away from Rhin's shoulder, the black mist coiled within his grip, looped about her neck. He clenched his fist, the mist contracting. Rhin's hands grasped at her throat, passed through the mist, clawing her own flesh. Her eyes bulged, flesh turning red, then purple. She threw herself about in the chair but Calidus wrenched her back, put a hand in her hair and twisted, holding her still.

'Never. Ever. Fail.'

There was a knock at the door and Calidus stepped away from

Rhin, opened his palm and with a hiss the black mist evaporated. Rhin collapsed to the table in a fit of coughing.

Calidus walked back to his seat, adjusted his cloak, then sat.

'Compose yourself,' he said to Rhin, who pulled herself upright in her chair, dragging in deep breaths. Slowly the rise and fall of her chest calmed. 'Enter,' Calidus called out.

The door opened and Veradis stepped in. He looked solemn, almost guilty.

He feels the shame of defeat, also, Uthas realized.

Nathair stood as Veradis entered the room. At the sight of Nathair a grin broke across Veradis' face and Nathair smiled in return, the expression looking out of place on his face.

That is a deep and genuine friendship. I have not seen Nathair smile since before Murias.

Veradis took a few long strides and dropped to one knee before Nathair.

'My King,' Veradis said.

Nathair stood there, looking down at his friend in silence, his smile slowly fading. A shadow crossed his face. He glanced at Calidus, adjusting his expression to cold inscrutability, and then he put a hand on Veradis' arm.

And now we shall see how deep your oath to Asroth is rooted.

'None of that, old friend,' Nathair said, pulling Veradis upright. The two men embraced; Veradis took a step back, looking into Nathair's face. He frowned.

From the corner of his eye Uthas saw Calidus' hand slip to the hilt of a knife at his belt.

CHAPTER FORTY

VERADIS

'What's wrong?' Veradis asked.

At first Veradis had been focused only on Nathair, consumed with the sense of relief that always flooded him whenever he was reunited safely with his King. But as that started to melt away he became aware of something else. There was a tension in the room, the air heavy with it. Rhin was sitting with eyes downcast, Calidus straight-backed, lips a tight line beneath his close-cropped silver beard. Sumur and Uthas the giant were shadows outlined by sunshine through an open window. And Nathair. He looked gaunt, a strain in his features that spoke of more than weariness at the end of a long road.

'Wrong? Nothing,' Nathair said. 'We have the cauldron, a dream of many years fulfilled.' He smiled, but to Veradis' mind it looked weak, somehow. Empty.

'The cauldron, after so much – the dreams, the planning, the hardship,' Veradis smiled in return. 'I have known for a while – Rhin has received messages. It is wonderful news.'

'Aye. It is,' Nathair said.

And yet, I expected something else. What? He should be overjoyed. This does not seem like the focused, determined man whom I left on the borders of Domhain. 'You look weary, Nathair, but there is more, I think.'

Uthas shifted behind Nathair.

'We have endured hard battles, a long road,' Nathair said. 'And I find that I have completed a quest only to realize that it is the beginning of another one.' He looked about the room, eyes lingering on Calidus before they returned to Veradis. 'I *am* weary, but you are right, there is more.' He paused again, just stared at Veradis for long, silent moments. 'I am disappointed in you, Veradis. You had a chance to end this. The Black Sun with only a few hundred swords about him. And you let him escape. This is the first time that you have failed me. And now it feels like the battle against the Black Sun is only just beginning, a long road with the end far from sight.'

Veradis felt each word like a blow, a knife punching into his belly and twisting with each new syllable.

Veradis dropped his eyes, shame coursing through him. 'I know. It could have been over.' He shook his head, eyes filled with shame. 'I let them get away.'

'You did.'

'We expected more from you,' Calidus said.

'But it is done now, Veradis, no changing it,' Nathair said. 'An opportunity missed, aye. We will fight on.'

'Replace me,' Veradis said.

'*No*. That is the coward's way out.' Nathair's voice was harsh, harder than Veradis had ever heard, and more painful than lashes across his back. He gripped Veradis by the shoulder. 'You've made a mistake. Do *not* make another.'

'Never. Death first,' Veradis assured him.

Nathair nodded curtly and returned to his seat. Veradis sank into a chair besides Rhin, for the first time seeing Alcyon's bulk standing in the shadows. He smiled ruefully at the giant.

'Well met, little man,' Alcyon said, a smile twitching his moustache.

'Not so well, I'm afraid,' Veradis said.

'You live, that is well enough, by my reckoning,' Alcyon grunted.

'Very touching, but enough of that. Time for greetings later,' Calidus snapped. He turned his hawk-like gaze upon Veradis and Rhin. 'I need to know – what happened?' There was something in Calidus' voice, an edge that whispered of rage well concealed, enough leaking through to fill Veradis with a sense of dread.

This is worse than my childhood weapons training, when Krelis would beat me black and blue, and then Alben would make me tell him what I did wrong.

'We were concerned that the enemy would flee, once they saw how outnumbered they were,' Veradis said, reciting the strategy emotionlessly. 'So we marched at night and crept up on their camp in the dark. I thought, if we were close enough come sunrise that we would be able to bring them to battle, give them no time to flee.'

'And you agreed with this?' Calidus asked Rhin. She lifted her chin and met Calidus' gaze.

'It was *my* idea,' Rhin said.

'It seemed like a good plan, at the time,' Veradis added weakly.

'They usually do,' Calidus said flatly, leaning back and folding his arms. 'So what happened?'

Veradis explained about the march and the deception that they had fallen for.

'So they crept around you, stole my ships and burned the rest.' Calidus leaned forwards in his chair.

'Not all of them,' Rhin said.

'Ah, that's something.'

'How many left?'

'Fifteen.'

'A transporter? We need a transporter to carry the cauldron.'

Veradis shook his head. 'No, only the galleys.'

Calidus frowned.

'We could take the fifteen ships and sail after them,' Veradis offered.

Calidus tugged at his short beard. 'They number three to four hundred, mostly Jehar, also Benothi giants, Corban and his followers – who almost single-handedly decimated the garrison at Dun Vaner . . .' Calidus shot a withering glance at Rhin. 'The maximum you could sail with would be a thousand men – your warband. You would lose.'

'My shield wall has faced giants before, draigs, wyrms,' Veradis said.

'Aye, but not a warband commanded by one of the Kadoshim and his Black Sun. Or the Jehar.'

'Or Balur One-Eye,' Uthas muttered. 'He is a formidable foe.'

I have heard his name in the tales my nan used to tell me.

'The answer is no,' Calidus continued, frowning at Uthas' interruption. 'You will not pursue them. When it was our combined forces against them then the answer was beyond doubt. I will not take risks, you and the eagle-guard are too valuable. And I cannot spare men who are guarding the cauldron to swell your numbers. Besides, I know their destination – they are going to Drassil. We shall follow them there in our own time, when all is ready and the cauldron is safe.'

Veradis bowed his head, defiant but resigned. 'Where is the cauldron?' he asked. 'The story of its taking is something I'd dearly love to hear.'

'It was a hard battle,' Nathair said. He looked out of the window, eyes distant. 'A tale I'll tell you another time, over a jug of wine. And now a great weapon is in our hands.' He looked back to Veradis. 'Our plan was to transport it by ship to Tenebral, and for all of us to sail with it.'

Veradis hung his head.

'All is not lost,' Calidus said. 'Correct me if I am wrong, Nathair, but your plan was to summon our allies to Tenebral: the kings of Isiltir, Carnutan and Helveth, for a council of war?'

'It was.'

'Well then, if we march the cauldron back we could travel through Isiltir, send messengers ahead and summon Jael, Gundul and Lothar to meet us at some practical location; say, Mikil.'

'Good,' Nathair said, nodding slowly. 'We would need to move fast, to reach Mikil before winter comes.'

'Aye. It could be done.'

'A good plan,' Veradis said.

'You will not be coming, I'm afraid,' Calidus said.

'What?'

'I have heard news from Lykos in Tenebral. There is trouble brewing – a rebellion. He claims he can deal with it, but he is Vin Thalun, born to fight on the seas. Land war is not his speciality. I think he needs some help. Take the galleys and your warband back to Tenebral. You can put down this rebellion and then meet us in Mikil.'

'What?' *No. How can I be parted from Nathair, again. What kind of first-sword spends his life fighting hundreds of leagues apart from his king?*

'And you want *me* to go?'

'Yes,' Nathair said. 'There is no one else whom I would trust with such a task.'

'But I am your first-sword, I should be at your side,' Veradis said pleadingly to Nathair.

'And you are also my battlechief. Do this for me, redeem yourself for yesterday's failure.'

Veradis sighed, feeling his heart sink. 'Who leads this rebellion in Tenebral?' he asked.

Nathair looked at him sorrowfully. 'Your father.'

Veradis walked through the corridors of Uthandun in search of Nathair.

Two nights had passed since Nathair had arrived, and he had hardly seen his friend and King, and then only amidst a press of voices all clamouring for Nathair's attention. Even then Calidus would always appear and send him off on some other task.

And now it was the day of leaving and so Veradis had left his chambers while it was still dark, determined to find Nathair, only to find that his King's chambers were unguarded and empty. Muttering curses Veradis marched through corridors, flickering torchlight fading as the corridors became pale with dawn.

Eventually he found Nathair on the meadows beyond Uthandun's walls. He was standing in a shallow dell, an area roped off into a paddock sheltered by a line of trees that edged a stream. The King of Tenebral was standing with his draig, throwing the great beast quartered sections of an auroch. Alcyon was standing a few strides away, a dark silhouette in the pale dawn.

'I have been searching for you,' Veradis said as he approached. Nathair looked up but said nothing, just went back to pulling chunks of meat and bone from a sack and throwing them to his draig.

'I did not think *I* was that hard to find,' Alcyon said.

'Surprising, I know,' Veradis grinned at Alcyon.

Another thing that is even more surprising is how I have come to value a giant as a friend. The first time they'd met, Alcyon had broken Veradis' nose, but then Veradis had just hurled a spear at the giant. Since then, though, they had travelled and fought together, saved each other's lives many times, and slowly the barriers had melted and a friendship had formed. They stood together a moment in companionable silence, Nathair with his back to them.

'I have heard talk of the battle of Domhain Pass, and your name is always mentioned,' Alcyon said.

'Aye. It came as a pleasant surprise that I can manage to survive a battle even if you are not there to save me.' Veradis looked up at Alcyon with a smile, saw the hilt of a longsword arching over the giant's shoulder.

'Where is your black axe?'

Alcyon scowled. 'It was taken from me, in battle.'

That axe was one of the Seven Treasures.

'So two of us out of favour, then.'

Alcyon looked down at Veradis with a frown. 'More than you could ever imagine,' he said.

'Who took it?'

'An enemy.' Alcyon rippled, a tree shrugging off snow. 'I will meet him again.'

Veradis did not doubt it. He glanced sidelong at the giant, at his tattooed thorns swirling around the slabs of his forearms to disappear beneath chainmail sleeves, his long drooping moustache bound with leather cords, dark eyes in a pale, angular face. *Different, and yet not so different, after all.*

'Who are you?' Veradis asked him.

'Huh?' grunted the giant.

'You are of the Kurgan clan, are you not?'

'I am,' Alcyon agreed slowly.

'Where are they from?'

'We lived once in your Tenebral, our realm stretching further north and east, all the way to what you call Arcona, the Sea of Grass.'

'And within your clan, who are you?'

'What do you mean?' Alcyon asked suspiciously.

'You see how our people are divided – king, shieldman, warrior, blacksmith, horsemaster, shipbuilder, and so on. What were you?'

Alcyon's brows jutted, a frown creasing them. 'I am nothing,' he growled.

Veradis shrugged. 'It's your business. But for my part, I don't agree that you are nothing, now. If nothing else you are my friend.'

Alcyon turned his gaze upon Veradis for long moments. Then he nodded. 'As you are mine,' he said.

Nathair turned and walked over to them.

'I am sailing for Tenebral today,' Veradis said, remembering why he came here. 'I wished to speak with you, before I left. As we once did.'

Nathair nodded. He looked pale, much as he had after taking his wound when Aquilus had been murdered. 'I have wished to speak with you, share that jug of wine. But . . .' he spread his hands.

'I know. The days are too short,' Veradis finished for him. There was a change in Nathair. Veradis recognized it. The same aura surrounded Alcyon, always had.

Melancholy.

'Aye, they are,' Nathair agreed.

'We have now, though, at least.' Mist drifted around their feet, evaporating with the rising sun. Behind them Uthandun was a hazy shadow, the sounds of its waking distant and muted. All seemed still and silent. Veradis pulled a wine skin from his shoulder and pulled out the stopper with his teeth. 'Good wine from Ripa,' he said, grinning.

Nathair smiled at that, took the skin and drank deep. For a moment Veradis thought he'd drain the whole skin. He passed it back, a drop of dark red wine running into his short beard.

Veradis offered some to Alcyon.

'So, tell me of Murias,' Veradis said to Nathair.

Nathair grimaced, a twist of his mouth. 'The Benothi were fierce, fought harder than I imagined possible. Wyrms guarded the cauldron, many. Three, four score of them. Near a thousand of the Jehar fell.' He recited the facts with little to no emotion.

He speaks as if he is reading it from the histories, not as if he were there, in the thick of it.

The Jehar were the most accomplished and deadly warriors Veradis had ever witnessed. He could not imagine a foe strong enough to slay a thousand of them.

'How many Benothi were there?'

'A few hundred,' Alcyon said. 'But many sided with Uthas.'

'Survivors?' Veradis asked.

'Uthas has fifty or so Benothi with him,' Alcyon answered. 'Of those who stood against us, they have joined with Meical and the Black Sun. Maybe thirty.'

'And what of Cywen?' That was a question he'd wished to ask since Nathair had arrived, but felt somehow foolish asking it when the others were around.

'Cywen,' Nathair raised his eyebrows and Alcyon looked at his feet.

'She escaped,' Alcyon rumbled. 'Another failure that I am held accountable for.'

'Corban took her. He appeared when the battle for the cauldron was at its most fierce,' Nathair said. 'I saw them flee the hall together.'

Good. Veradis did not know why, but it was important to him that Cywen lived. That she was safe. She had seemed to be an innocent swept up in dark times. *Not that she is safe while in the company of the Black Sun.*

'I met Corban, the Black Sun,' Veradis said. 'He was at the Battle of Domhain Pass, led a night raid on Rhin's warband. He wore a wolven pelt, he and a few others.'

'He has a wolven,' Nathair said. 'Storm, he calls it. It was at Murias.'

'Aye. Between them they scared the living hells out of Rhin's men. Many fled during the night.'

Nathair shrugged. 'I'm not surprised, if they thought wolven were fighting against them.'

'He called for you – Corban, when he saw the eagle-guard and our shield wall.'

'Called for me?' Nathair raised an eyebrow at that, for the first time looking more than mildly interested.

'Aye. He called you out, declared you coward, claimed you slew his da.'

'I did,' Nathair whispered.

'He challenged you to the court of swords.'

'He did? Brave of him.'

'Aye. I went to fight him in your place, but . . .' He trailed off, remembering Bos dragging him back, because of the Jehar who had stood beside Corban, the one that had single-handedly slain Rauca and near a dozen other eagle-guard. He closed his eyes, the chaos and panic caused by the night raid coming back to him in vivid detail, could hear the crack of the shield wall closing up tight before him.

'He got away,' Veradis shrugged.

'Aye, well. He seems to have a knack for that.'

Veradis dropped his eyes.

'It was meant to be, I suspect,' Nathair said, his voice softening. 'We shall meet someday, he and I, of that I have no doubt.'

'Aye. As long as I am with you when that day comes. We should face him together. That is my dream – our warbands gathered behind us, facing the Black Sun and his allies, the war to be decided in one fell battle.'

'That is how I imagined it, once.'

'You don't think it will happen like that?'

'Perhaps,' Nathair sighed. 'The Black Sun,' he whispered, speaking the words as if for the first time.

'Aye.' Veradis frowned. *What is wrong with him? It is as if he suffers with some malaise.* 'We will hunt him down,' Veradis repeated, trying to stir up some spirit in his friend. 'But first I must deal with this rebellion in Tenebral.'

'Aye. It is a delicate situation,' Nathair said. His face became stern, angry, more fire in his eyes than Veradis had witnessed since they'd been reunited. 'But it is Tenebral. How can I lead an alliance or rule an empire if I cannot keep my own realm in order. You must be my hand of justice, Veradis.'

'I know,' Veradis said, fear edging his voice. Not fear of battle, of death, but fear of what he may have to do. *My father. My brothers.*

'It is your kin, I know,' Nathair said, his face softening. 'I suspect your father's hatred of the Vin Thalun is at the heart of it.'

'And my brother's,' Veradis muttered. 'Krelis despises the Vin Thalun.'

'If that is the root of the problem then I think you can repair the damage that has been done. It will require some diplomacy, which is not your strongest point, but it could be done.'

'Aye. If that is the problem, then I will solve it.' *But what if it is more? What if it is deeper than that? I remember how my father spoke to Nathair. Dismissing him as an arrogant boy. I chose whom I would follow that day.* He took a deep breath, swallowing his worry. *All choices have consequences.*

Nathair put a hand upon Veradis' shoulder. 'Perhaps I should send someone else, it is unfair to ask you to do this.'

'No,' Veradis said. 'You can trust me in this.'

'Trust you to do what?'

'Whatever is right. To enforce your will. You are King, your will and word is law.'

Nathair smiled, but even that was a faded shadow of its former self. His eyes narrowed as if he were in pain. 'If you judge that force is necessary . . . tread carefully. Keep your blade sheathed until all other routes are exhausted. He is your father . . .' Nathair looked at the palm of his hand, where he traced a white scar. Veradis had one of his own, made the night he and Nathair had sworn their oaths to one another, become brothers bound by blood. Alongside Nathair's old scar was a new cut, pinked now, healing but obviously fresh.

'What's that?'

Nathair stared at the new scar, then looked up at Veradis, emotion heavy within his eyes.

'Someone comes,' Alcyon said.

'There you are,' a voice called, Calidus and Sumur appearing over the crest of the dell. They marched quickly towards them.

Nathair leaned close to Veradis. 'It marks a new oath,' he whispered.

'A new oath? To whom?' Veradis asked.

Nathair's face shifted, emotions crossing it like clouds on a windswept day. 'Remember what I said, about your father.'

'Of course,' Veradis said. 'Nathair, you are troubling me. What is wrong? What new oath?'

'It is nothing,' Nathair said. He turned away, back to his draig, then glanced back over his shoulder. 'Keep a close watch on the path you follow, my friend, else one day you will look about you and not know where you are,' Nathair said quietly.

'Veradis,' Calidus said as he reached them. 'I have been looking for you. There are many last arrangements to speak of, before you sail.'

'Of course there are,' Veradis sighed. He was frowning, still looking at Nathair. 'I was just . . .'

'What?' Calidus asked, his wolf eyes boring into Veradis.

'Saying goodbye,' Nathair said for him.

'Ahh.' Calidus looked between the three of them – Nathair, Veradis and Alcyon.

Veradis looked behind Calidus to Sumur. He had seen little of the Jehar since they had arrived, so busy had he been with the organizational duties of the journey to Tenebral that he had not even had time to go and view the cauldron, something that he had dearly wanted to do.

Seeing Sumur now he blinked and swore.

'What has happened to you?' he gasped. Sumur was clothed in his usual dark chainmail, his curved sword arching across his back; he was eating a chicken leg. His tanned skin had paled, though, veins clear beneath the skin. More striking though were his eyes. They were black, no pupil, no iris, just dark, inky wells.

'A token of the battle for the cauldron,' Calidus said. 'Witchcraft was used by the Benothi, and the Jehar bore the brunt of it. Many died, and those who survived now bear this memento. Think of it like a scar. A badge of honour, of their bravery.'

'This has happened to every one of them?' Veradis asked.

'Aye. Every last one who survived.'

'What of your vision?' Veradis said to Sumur, peering closely at the Jehar. 'Is it hindered?'

'No,' Sumur replied, his accent thick.

Veradis frowned, not quite believing him.

Sumur threw his chicken leg into the air; faster than Veradis could track he drew his sword from his back and left a silver blur as the blade hissed through the air.

The chicken leg fell to the ground, in two portions, neatly chopped in half.

'See,' Sumur said, sheathing his sword smoothly.

Veradis shrugged. 'Clearly your vision is fine.'

Calidus put an arm around Veradis' shoulder and steered him away.

'I wanted to talk to you,' Calidus said. 'Of the rebellion in Tenebral.'

'We have just been speaking of it,' Veradis said.

'No surprise, it must be on your mind.'

'Aye, it is.'

'Kin, eh. You can choose your friends, but not your kin,' Calidus said. 'My kin have had a habit of getting me into trouble. Try and find the middle ground. Avoid bloodshed if you can.' Calidus steered him back towards Uthandun. 'Of course he is your kin so a peaceful solution must be sought, but even putting sentiment aside, we need your father, Ripa, and his swords. Only remember, most of all you must support Lykos, not undermine him. And let your support for him be seen.'

'I will. Nathair has already asked as much.'

'Good. There is more, though. The situation in Tenebral is delicate.'

'What do you mean?'

'Fidele is involved.'

'Fidele, how?'

Calidus sighed a deep breath. 'There is no easy way to say this. I suspect that her mind is unhinged.'

'What?'

'She has behaved most strangely, I fear there is no other explanation. You remember when we met with Lykos at Dun Carreg, he told us of how the barons of Tenebral were manipulating Fidele, how she was proving unsuited to ruling.'

'Aye. Nathair thought that she was still grieving for Aquilus.'

'Yes. Well, upon Lykos' return Fidele began behaving in ever more erratic ways. She divided the eagle-guard and sent them to the four corners of the realm on meaningless errands. She arrested Peritus and Armatus.' He stopped walking and looked back at Nathair, checking that he was well out of earshot. 'She wed Lykos.'

'What!' *I cannot believe that. Regal, cultured Fidele and that corsair.*

'It is true, and Nathair cannot know. Not yet. He has too much to focus on. I need you to bring her to me, discreetly. And by that I mean secretly, in chains if needs be.'

CHAPTER FORTY-ONE

RAFE

Rafe threw Sniffer a strip of dried meat, the animal seeming to swallow it without chewing.

'Go on, boy, after them,' Rafe said, pointing into the distance with a flick of his wrist. Sniffer turned and loped ahead, his nose low to the ground.

'How far ahead, do you think?' Evnis asked him.

Rafe squinted into the distance. 'Half a day,' he said. The Baglun Forest was a solid wall to their right, curling away westwards as they rounded its eastern fringes. Behind them a hundred warriors sat upon their horses, a mixture of men from Ardan and Cambren, though all wore Rhin's colours.

Rafe sucked in a deep breath, the air fresh and clean with dawn.

I am riding at the head of a hundred shieldmen, beside Evnis my old lord and new King; it is good to be home. Good to be alive. He had not felt like this for a long time. *Ever? Certainly since Da died.* He felt happy. But Evnis had been so full of praise for him, had treated him so well since they had ridden out from Dun Carreg, that he found it almost impossible to feel any other way. The only blight in the ten-night since they'd left had been on the first day, when they'd ridden down the winding slope of the hill that Dun Carreg was built upon, past the wind-choked copse of trees where he had had his arm ripped open by Corban's wolven. Memories of that day had flooded him. Idly he ran a finger down the scar on his forearm, running near enough from elbow to wrist.

There'll come a day of reckoning, mark my words.

He knew why Evnis had been so full of praise for him.

Vonn.

Rafe had brought the news that Evnis had wanted to hear. His son was back in Ardan. Not with absolute certainty, of course. But he knew that Edana had intended to flee to the marshes in Ardan, and that when Rafe had last seen her, standing upon a ship's deck as it sailed away from a beach in Domhain, Vonn had been standing beside her. And that pleased Evnis.

'Let's be after them, then,' Evnis said and kicked his mount on. With a clatter of harness and the drumming of hooves the hundred-strong honour guard lurched into motion. The sun rose steadily in the east and soon Rafe was sweating.

'You were a friend to my Vonn,' Evnis said after they'd ridden some leagues in silence.

'I was, my lord,' Rafe said.

'We can dispense with the "lord", I think,' Evnis said. 'At least when we are alone, anyway. I have known you since you were a bairn clinging to your mam's skirts.' Evnis smiled good-naturedly at Rafe. 'What kind of friend was Vonn to you?'

'I always looked up to him,' Rafe said automatically. 'He's a couple of years older than me, seemed like a hero. He was the best out of us all with sword and spear, always knew what to do, no matter the problem.' He thought a bit harder. 'He always tried to do the honourable thing.'

'Hmm, yes,' Evnis muttered. 'That was becoming a problem.'

'What do you mean?'

Evnis shrugged. 'It's no secret that we argued. That's why he's been wandering about the Banished Lands, instead of riding beside me now. He was – is – young, his head still full of tales of noble warriors and deeds of valour. The world was black and white to him – good and evil. And he was in love, which didn't help matters.'

'Mordwyr's girl,' Rafe said.

'Aye. I thought it was their secret.'

Rafe shrugged. 'I'm born and bred a huntsman's son. Been used to watching, observing, reading signs.' *Spying.*

'I wish I'd spoken to you sooner,' Evnis sighed. 'As you know, I had plans. Brenin stopped me from saving my wife Fain . . .' He fell silent, mouth twisting. 'That is avenged now. But Vonn did not understand.'

'You have to be realistic,' Rafe said.

'Exactly. Perhaps some time in the world has helped to teach that lesson to Vonn.' Evnis sighed and shook his head.

'If he is with Edana still, we will get him back,' Rafe said.

'We will, one way or another.'

They rode on in silence.

Highsun came and went, the sun sinking ever westwards, sending their shadows stretching towards the first trees of the Baglun. A few hundred paces ahead a figure emerged from a copse of rowan, one man upon a horse, a hound at his side. Sniffer bounded up to them, began leaping playfully about the hound.

'It is Braith,' Rafe said to Evnis.

'We are close, then,' Evnis said.

'Well met,' Braith said as they drew near. The huntsman flashed a grin at Rafe, then dipped his head to Evnis.

'Well met,' Evnis replied, riding close and offering his arm to Braith in the warrior grip.

'Halion. Where is he?'

'Less than half a day ahead.' Braith pointed into the distance, along the southern fringes of the Baglun. 'The marshlands of Dun Crin are south and west of here, where Halion is headed, but he is keeping to the edges of the Baglun for now – more cover, is my guess.'

'After him, then,' Evnis said.

'Not so hasty,' Braith said. 'You should lead your warband into the forest and follow along under better cover – it's open woodland, easy enough to ride through, but it'll hide you from prying eyes.'

'Can he see us, then?' Evnis asked, peering into the distance.

'I saw you,' Braith shrugged. 'We don't want to get too close or we'll spook him, then we'll never find Edana.'

Evnis nodded and led his warriors into the fringes of the forest.

'Not you,' Braith said to Rafe. 'You can ride with me.'

They set off again, Scratcher and Sniffer leading them unerringly west, skirting the edges of the forest.

'Anything to report?' Braith asked him.

'Evnis is desperate to find his son, Vonn. I saw him on the ship with Edana.'

'I know,' grunted Braith. 'I was there.'

'Thought you might have been too busy getting kicked off of the pier by Camlin to notice.'

'That's enough of your cheek, now.' Braith's expression shifted, a dark cloud. 'Anything else?'

'There is a resistance based in the marshes. There have been raids; nothing of any real impact yet. There is a warband down here hunting for them. Morcant leads them.'

'Ahh. Not the best man for a task like this.'

'How so?' Rafe asked him.

'To catch rats you need patience. Morcant is proud, impatient, spontaneous. Though I'd not tell him that to his face.' Braith grinned. 'He's a rare talent with a blade.'

'I know. I saw his duel against Conall. He lost, but then, so would most against Conall.'

'He's that good, Conall?'

'Oh aye.'

Braith nodded, looking thoughtful, but said no more.

To the south the land dipped, spreading into a wide bowl of water-dappled land, dotted with patches of woodland. They passed a few villages, columns of smoke and tilled land marking them out. Rafe saw the occasional tower standing lonely on a rare hill, large pyres beside them built up high and silhouetted against the skyline. Sometimes there was a palisaded wall about the tower. It was hard to tell from that distance, but something about them suggested to Rafe that they were recent constructions.

As the sun began to sink behind the Baglun the hounds came to a sudden stop. They both stared into the distance, still as statues, their hackles rising.

Rafe stared too, saw distant figures materialize in the fading light: riders, lots of them. 'It's Morcant, or at least a large portion of his men,' Braith said. 'See the banner – Rhin's broken branch.'

Hooves drummed behind them and Rafe turned to see Evnis approaching.

'What is it?'

'Morcant, I'm guessing,' Braith said. 'Do you want us to go and fetch him?'

Evnis just sat and stared a while. 'No,' he said eventually. 'I don't want him charging in head first and scaring Halion off. We'll likely only have one chance at this.'

'I agree,' Braith said. 'We may as well make camp here. The dogs won't lose Halion's scent now. They've tracked him half a thousand leagues already.'

And Vonn. That's who Evnis really wants to find. Thing is – what will he do once he finds him?

CHAPTER FORTY-TWO

CAMLIN

'How're we going to get in there?' Vonn asked Camlin.

They were lying on a slope amidst long grass and wildflowers, staring at a palisaded tower that was built upon a low hill, a massive pyre of wood piled high about a hundred paces from the gates. The setting sun was hot upon their backs.

'The wall's not more'n two men high. Two or three of us with a lift over'll get those gates open.'

'Is that possible? There are men on the wall, at the gates. And how many more inside?'

I've done it before. Many times. The last time had been at a hold south of Dun Carreg. He'd been leading the crew then, as well. It had gone smoothly at first – over the wall and gates open. Then they'd been heard and blood had been spilt. He felt a flush of shame as he remembered the women and bairns.

Feels like a different life. A different man.

'There's not many left in there. Most of them rode out with Morcant.'

They'd caught up with the chest of silver yesterday, after almost a ten-night of tracking it, Meg leading them through a confusing network of waterways that edged the marshes. Unfortunately, when they caught up with the wain carrying the chest, it had been surrounded by Morcant and a convoy of over two hundred swords. When Morcant had stopped in the open and made camp for the night Camlin had considered attempting to snatch the chest, but there had just been too many guards and Drust had refused to commit his men. So they'd followed Morcant and his chest of silver the next day to this tower.

Camlin and the three of them had spent half the day creeping closer to the fortification. When the sun was a shield of fire shimmering above the Baglun the gates had opened, Morcant riding out at the head of at least two hundred warriors. They had headed east, the sound of their horses hooves fading like distant thunder.

'We should strike just before dawn,' Camlin said, looking at Drust.

The ageing warrior stared at Camlin. 'I'll not risk my men's lives for nothing. You are sure the chest is in there?'

'Aye. We saw it carried in there upon a wain, and it hasn't come out. And Morcant just left with his warband. No wain.'

'He'd have left men to guard it, though.'

'Of course, but not many. I've counted six on this watch – there'll be double that, then maybe a dozen others to keep the place running, no more'n that. Remember, Morcant's a proud, arrogant bastard and the chest's in his tower, behind a wall and a score of men. He doesn't think anyone'd have the stones to try and take his silver.'

Drust smiled at that. 'Put that way it's a hard challenge to resist.'

'Now,' Camlin whispered and ran, stooping low to the ground, his eyes never leaving the palisaded wall he was approaching. He heard the thud of Vonn's footsteps behind him, Baird, Brogan and a few others as well.

They approached from the south-west in the dim of false dawn, the tower a solid blackness amongst the shadows. They headed for a dark patch of wall between two torches, Camlin picking up his speed as he neared the wall, twenty paces, his heartbeat loud as a drum in his ears.

Almost there.

The slope was gentle but Camlin was still breathing hard when his back finally touched the wall, the timber planks smelling sweet and leaking amber.

Other figures reached the wall about him and he searched out Brogan, nodding to the big man from Domhain. Brogan cupped his hands, Camlin put a foot in them, and then he was being hoisted into the air, hands gripping the wall's rim and he was over. For a horrifying moment his slung bow snagged on the wall. He wriggled, trying not to snap the string, then he was free. He dropped to a walkway with hardly a sound, hand searching for the hilt of his knife.

Baird appeared heartbeats later, the one-eyed warrior grinning like a fool, Vonn and three more following shortly behind.

Camlin closed his eyes and listened. Heard the deep lowing of auroch nearby, further off the whinny of a horse. Nothing else.

Place like this should always have a hound or two. Or a wolven. Or a crow. He missed Corban's company, and the reassurance of Storm and Craf.

He rose to a crouch and moved along the walkway, Vonn following him, Baird and the other three dropping to the hard ground and shadowing them.

The torchlight over the gates grew quickly closer, two men standing within the circle of light. On the ground there were two more guards, and nearby the window of a small guardhouse bloomed orange with firelight.

Another in there, most likely. He gestured to Baird, then, a handspan from the edge of the light, he put one knee on the walkway, pulled and nocked an arrow, drew and released.

The first warrior toppled and fell with hardly a sound, until he hit the ground with a thud. Vonn had surged past Camlin the moment his arrow had left the string, his sword scraping from its scabbard, the second guard turning weary eyes their way. With a flash of red in the torchlight Vonn's sword ripped the guard's throat open.

He saw Baird pausing for a moment in the doorway to the guardhouse. Camlin leaped to the ground, regretting it as he felt the impact in his knees. Vonn ran down the stairs to stand beside him.

I'm getting too old for this. He winced at the throbbing in his knees.

Vonn looked to him, the young warrior's face all dark pools of shadow and flickering torchlight. Together they shouldered the bar from the gates and pushed them open.

Brogan's grinning face greeted them, standing at the head of fifteen warriors, Drust amongst them.

Camlin held a finger to his lips and led them into the hold.

Between scaling the wall and killing the gate guards true dawn had arrived, and now buildings were materializing out of the uniform shadow. The men moved methodically, checking the buildings as they went. All were empty apart from one – a naked man and woman wrapped around one another in a cot.

Wife or whore? Probably whore, as there seem to be no families here, no bairns or other women, no signs of permanent settlement.

The man was snoring. A helmet and leather cuirass hung over the end of the bed, scabbarded sword leaning against a chair. His eyes flickered open and he opened his mouth to cry out but Camlin's sword-point at his throat silenced him.

Kill him, move on. Time is short.

Camlin drew his arm back, tensed for the killing thrust, the warrior on the bed frozen. Yet he hesitated.

For a moment he felt as if he was back in Braith's crew, knew he would have cut the warrior's throat without a second thought.

I'm not that man now.

The door creaked and Vonn entered, eyes moving from Camlin to the two upon the bed.

The moment stretched.

'Bind them,' Camlin said, holding his sword ready as Vonn tore strips from the warrior's cloak and bound and gagged the two on the bed.

They moved on, past a small smithy and a stable; beyond them was the tower that the fortification was built around. An open space ringed the tower and Camlin stopped in the shadows of the stable, gestured to Drust and the others to do the same, then nocked an arrow and waited.

It only took a few moments for the tower doors to swing open, revealing a small feast-hall. Warriors emerged, three of them, others clustered behind. Camlin's first arrow hit one through the eye and he collapsed bonelessly; his second arrow punched into a warrior high in his chest, piercing leather vest and woollen shirt beneath, sending him stumbling back into someone behind. Others came out, shields raised. Camlin sent another arrow into an exposed thigh. Another dinged off an iron helm, the man staggering, and then Drust's men were amongst them. Camlin dropped his bow and drew his sword.

Vonn was ahead of him. He had no shield and so was sending controlled strokes at ankles and heads. Beside him Brogan roared into the fray, face twisted like a madman, swinging an overhead blow crashing into a shield with such force that the rim crumpled, his blade carrying on to crush a helm. The warrior collapsed, dead or unconscious. Brogan leaped over him as he roared a battle-cry.

With his left hand Camlin pulled a knife from his belt and joined the battle.

Baird was retreating before a man who knew how to use his shield. Camlin stepped in close on the man's flank and stabbed his sword behind the shield, felt it scrape along knuckles and flesh.

The warrior lowered his shield, blood dripping from the rim and lunged wildly at Camlin. Baird punched his sword-point into the warrior's face and he collapsed in an explosion of bone and brains. Two of Drust's men were battering at an enemy, pushing him back into the doorway of the tower. There was a hissing noise and suddenly a spear sprouted through one of Drust's warriors, dropping him. Camlin glanced behind, searching for the spear-thrower. He was standing on the walkway of the palisade, over a hundred paces away, three or four other warriors in black and gold about him.

Hell of a throw, that.

The battle here was moving inside the feast-hall, only a handful of Morcant's men left. Camlin grabbed Vonn, Brogan and Baird and pointed to the men on the wall. With only a fierce grin from Brogan they set off running, Camlin stooping to retrieve his bow.

A hundred paces closer and Camlin saw the warrior who had cast the spear take his comrade's spear. Camlin skidded to a halt, drew an arrow as he saw the warrior aim for Camlin's comrades. Camlin sucked in a breath, held it, drew back the arrow until the feathers brushed his cheek, then released.

Camlin's arrow hit the man at the base of his throat, just above the rim of his cuirass. He crashed back a couple of paces into the wall and toppled over it. Then Brogan and Baird were charging up the stairs, Vonn right behind them. Camlin launched another arrow before they clashed, sending another warrior in black and gold reeling. He slung his bow and ran, drawing his sword as he reached the stairs. By the time he made it to the top the remaining enemy were dead, Vonn, Baird and Brogan all blood-spattered and breathing heavily.

The sun had risen fully now. Inside the hold the clash of arms still rang out, but it was the sound of only a few men.

It is done. We've taken it. Camlin gave his friends a savage grin. 'We've done it, lads.'

He told Vonn and Brogan to put on black and gold cloaks and patrol the walkway. 'Keep an eye out, just in case Morcant forgot something,' he grinned again.

'Aye, chief,' Brogan said. Camlin quite liked the sound of that.

He headed back to the tower with Baird, found Drust putting his men to work, dragging the dead out into an open space before the tower.

'Twenty-one of Morcant's dead,' Drust said as Camlin approached.

'There's another six dead on the wall,' Camlin said with a jerk of his thumb over a shoulder. 'Five more at the gates.'

'Thirty-two, then. More than you guessed. Bad odds for my men, bad guess from you.'

'How many dead of ours?' Camlin asked.

'Three,' Drust said.

'Don't know what dice you've been playing but that sounds like good odds to me,' Baird said.

'A risk worth taking,' Camlin added. 'We need that chest of silver.'

They found the chest in a room at the back of the first floor. Camlin just smiled when they opened its lid, the silver glowing in reflected torchlight.

Half a dozen men carried it out while others found the wain it had arrived in and harnessed an auroch up to it. When Camlin emerged from the tower the day was bright, all of the enemy warriors stripped of their useful items – weapons, boots, armour, warrior torcs.

'Take their cloaks,' Camlin said to Drust. 'Anything else with Rhin's colours or sigil.'

'We'll not be wearing Rhin's black and gold,' he spluttered.

'Might come in handy,' Camlin said with a shrug. 'This is the second newly built tower we've passed in the last ten-night. My guess is they're in your – the resistance's – honour. Might have to do something about that.'

'What do you think they're up to?'

'Flushing you out. Morcant wants results. Did you see the pyre piled high out on the hill? Looks suspiciously like a warning beacon to me.'

Drust nodded thoughtfully. 'Let's get that chest onto a boat.'

They left the hold behind; the ground levelled as they approached the marsh. Meg came scampering out from a tall bank of sedge.

'There's someone over there, on the north slope in the long grass. He's watching you. Best not look – don't think he can see us from where he is, but better safe than sorry.'

'How many?' Camlin asked.

'Just one that I saw,' she shrugged. 'Could be more. Saw him hobble his horse and sneak closer. He was good at it.'

'Better get this chest loaded,' Drust said. 'I'll send a few swords to poke him out of the long grass.'

'Best not kick the nest till you know how deep it goes,' Camlin said. 'I left Vonn and Brogan walking the walls in black and gold; that should buy us some time. Get everyone out of that hold and into the marshes, but calmly. No rushing. I'll go and take a look at our uninvited guest.'

Drust caught his arm and stared at him. 'You did well, Camlin. I may have judged you wrong.'

'Too early for back-slapping,' Camlin said gruffly. 'We're not out of this yet.'

Camlin left them to it, slipping into a bank of tall sedge, Meg at his heels.

'Best stay here, lassie,' he said to her. 'Don't want you getting hurt.'

'I can look after myself,' she sniffed. 'And you don't know where he is.'

Camlin took a moment. 'All right, come part of the way. Stop when I tell you.' He held her eyes until she nodded.

They looped wide around the hill, following the sedge and willows that grew thick on the marshland's border, eventually replacing that cover for tall witch-grass. Camlin stooped low, following narrow trails through the grass that spoke of foxes and weasels, curling slowly north-east around the base of the hill.

'Over there,' Meg eventually whispered to him, pointing towards a gnarly old elm that grew in the meadow on the north side of the tower.

'All right, lass. You get on back to your boat, now.'

She nodded, flashed him a grin and disappeared back into the meadow grass.

It was highsun when he saw the horse tied on the far side of the elm, a dapple-grey mare. He edged closer, saw it was fitted with what looked like good-quality but travel-sore kit, the saddle-blanket fine wool but mud-spattered and its edges fraying. He scanned the area between the elm and the tower, eyes methodically running over every patch of ground.

There.

A shadow in the grass, a flicker of movement. Slowly he pulled an arrow from his quiver, quieter than the sighing of the grass, then crept closer, eyes flitting between each new space for his feet and the shadow up ahead.

At the edge of his vision he saw a figure walking along the tower wall, knew without having to focus that it was Brogan. Closer and closer he inched, until the whole figure was outlined in shadow through the grass, now only twenty paces ahead.

Close enough that I won't miss, too far for a dash with a sword.

He straightened and drew his bow, the wood creaking.

The man in front of him froze, hearing the sound. He held his hands out, showing they were empty.

He knows what a drawn bow sounds like.

'Nice and slow, turn around now.'

The man turned.

Elyon's stones, it cannot be. Then Camlin was blinking, lowering his bow, rushing forwards to embrace the man before him, caught up in a bear hug in return.

It was Halion.

CHAPTER FORTY-THREE

EVNIS

Evnis rode amongst the wide-spread trees, dappled sunlight slanting in from the east. His eyes constantly drifted out onto the meadow to where Braith and Rafe rode, the two grey hounds ahead of them. Beyond them sunlight glistened on a thousand waterways, the marshlands opening up like a jewel-crusted spider web of streams and rivers, fragmented by drab, impenetrable clusters of woodland.

Is Vonn truly out there? When Rafe had walked into the feast-hall and told him that Vonn was most likely back in Ardan it had hit him like a punch in the gut.

What will I say to him? Will I ask him for forgiveness? Will I scold him for a fool? He recoiled at that thought. *No, I will not drive him away. Not again. I will reason with him. He has had a taste of the real world now, surely his notions of honour and glory have been doused with a good dose of reality.*

'My lord,' Glyn said close by, startling him from his reverie.

'What is it?' Evnis asked, more irritably than he had intended.

'Rafe's coming.'

Indeed he was. Evnis raised his hand, his warband stuttering to a halt amongst the shadow-drenched woods.

'Braith thinks you should join us,' Rafe said as he entered beneath the first branches.

'Why?'

'Dogs are acting strange, and there's something up ahead, in the distance. Looks like a tower.'

'It may be one of Morcant's. I received a message from him some time ago that he was considering building a series of watchtowers around the marshes. I told him to do whatever he liked, so long as it ended in rebels swinging from a noose.' Laughter sputtered fitfully through the warriors at his back.

'Maybe it's one of them, then. But still, the dogs. Think we're getting close to Halion.'

Evnis sat there a moment, felt a lightness in his chest, excitement and fear mixed.

'Glyn, send two men with a change of horse. Tell them to ride and bring Morcant back. Quickly.'

'Aye,' Glyn grunted.

'And give me that,' Evnis said, pointing at a horn hanging from a hook on Glyn's saddle.

'Come on, then,' Evnis said as he kicked his horse into a trot. Rafe caught up with him and they rode into the meadow.

Evnis crept through the long grass, occasionally catching a glimpse of the tower.

My back aches. He'd joined Braith and ridden through the meadows for a while, but then the hounds had become excited, so agitated that they had been forced to dismount and creep through the meadow grass, crouching low. It felt as if they'd been walking for a ten-night, but in truth it was only a little past highsun. *Long enough to cripple my back. I am a king now; I should not be slinking through the grass like a snake.* Not for the first time he reminded himself why he was here. *Edana, a threat to my crown. And Vonn, my son. Just a little more patience and all will be well. Edana dead, Vonn back at my side. And I can do patience. There have been years of waiting, and now my dream is reality. I rule Ardan.* At first it had been the most overwhelmingly euphoric feeling, just *knowing* that he was king. Lord of all he surveyed. Crossing Stonegate as the lord of Dun Carreg, walking into the feast-hall as king. *Not king*, a voice whispered in his head. *As Rhin's regent.*

That does not matter. The reality is that I rule.

Rafe stopped in front of him and Evnis almost collided with him. He slipped to the side, saw the two hounds a dozen paces ahead, their whole bodies trembling, tense as drawn bowstrings. They were staring straight ahead. Rafe put a hand on each one and they seemed to calm, marginally.

Evnis saw the tower, part of a larger hold with a palisaded wall around it. A figure moved along the wall, even from this distance the black and gold of his cloak catching the sun. Closer, about a hundred paces to the left, stood an old thick-trunked tree. A horse was cropping grass before it. It was saddled, but riderless.

Evnis opened his mouth to speak but Braith put a finger to his mouth, then pointed.

Something was moving in the long grass ahead of them, a ripple that went against the breeze.

They sat and watched, the sun sliding across the sky. Sweat dripped into Evnis' eyes. His back muscles burned, slowly began to scream at him.

Just when he thought he could stand it no longer a man stood in the long grass, back to them. He raised a bow, pointing it ahead and drew an arrow.

Braith gasped, a name hissed venomously as quiet as the breeze. 'Camlin.'

Evnis saw the huntsman reach for his own quiver of arrows, at the same time slipping his strung bow from his back. Evnis reached out and gripped his wrist.

Braith stared at him, and for a moment Evnis saw murder in the huntsman's eyes.

Evnis shook his head. He mouthed a word.

Edana.

Slowly, incrementally he saw the commitment to violence leave Braith's face.

Then Camlin was moving forwards, another figure emerging from the grass a little further ahead. Evnis recognized him instantly.

Halion. He had changed. Looked exhausted. Leaner, definitely, his face all sharp bones, his beard ragged, but still he had that *look*. Those grey eyes that could stare you down, calm, terrifyingly so, in the face of fury. That was why Evnis had determined to turn his brother against him. Together Halion and Conall were unstoppable, two parts of the same whirlwind, the calm and the fury. Separate, they were just men. Dangerous, still, but not unstoppable.

Halion and Camlin embraced, a silent camaraderie passing between them that stirred up anger in Evnis' belly. He could not say why.

They parted, grinning like fools at one another. Words were

exchanged, too low for Evnis to hear, and then Camlin was dragging Halion through the long grass, up the slope towards the tower shouting at the guards on the wall.

What are they doing? They'll be seen.

Then the word Camlin was shouting coalesced inside Evnis' head, finally making sense.

Vonn.

A man in a black and gold cloak was leaning over the timber wall. As Camlin and Halion climbed the hill the man on the wall vaulted over, landed agilely with knees bent.

Suddenly, like a candle lit in a dark room, Evnis knew him.

My son.

He was tall, a shock of golden blond hair on his head, a neatly trimmed beard with streaks of red amongst the gold. He ran the dozen strides between him and Halion and hugged the older warrior, grinning and laughing.

Evnis stood up from his hiding place in the grass, shook off grasping hands from Braith, cupped his hands to his mouth and yelled his son's name.

'*VONN.*'

The three men on the hill turned and looked at him, and for a frozen moment the world dimmed, seemed to form a tunnel to the exclusion of all else between Evnis and Vonn as they stared at one another. Then Braith swore and stood beside him, his bow drawn.

'Damn you to hell,' the huntsman spat at Evnis, then loosed. His arrow sped towards the three men, Camlin moving first, shoving the other two so that Braith's arrow slammed thrumming into the timber wall.

A heartbeat later an arrow came back at them, Rafe dragging Evnis to the ground, the arrow hissing by frighteningly close. There was shouting from around the tower wall, figures appearing from the south. Figures with swords and spears in their hands.

Braith and Camlin were launching arrows at one another. Evnis caught fleeting glimpses of Halion and Vonn running along the wall, away.

Away. At the same time other warriors were moving closer, a dozen at least, some of them already wading into the long grass on the hill slope.

Evnis reached for Glyn's horn that he'd tied to his belt and put it to his lips, blew hard, a long wavering blast issuing from it. Men paused all over the hill.

A sound filled the silence, a distant rumble. Heads turned, staring northwards to see Glyn and a hundred warriors riding out of the tattered fringes of the Baglun. Then an older warrior with rust-coloured hair spilling from an iron helm was shouting, giving orders to those on the hill. They retreated, heading southwards. Before Evnis knew what he was doing his feet were moving and he was running, up the hill, wading through the long grass. Voices called after him but he ignored them, eyes fixed on the back of his fleeing son.

Behind him the rumble of his approaching warband was growing louder, but not loud enough to reach him in the next hundred heartbeats. For a moment he considered stopping, retreating, the sensible part of his mind screaming at him to listen, but then he caught another glimpse of Vonn, staring back at him briefly.

He drew his sword and carried on.

Two warriors came at him, and a small thread of fear squirmed through his belly. In a few heartbeats he appraised them – both younger men, lean and hungry for glory, their armour consisting of little more than leather vests and thick armbands, whereas Evnis wore a coat of mail that hung almost to his knees. It was making him sweat but he was glad of it.

They probably do not know who I am, or more of them would have turned to take my head. I am a fool. He started to regret his decision.

One came straight at him, the other circling to his left. Evnis blocked an overhead blow, deflecting it so that his opponent's swing pulled him off balance. Evnis turned his block into a cut, one of the first moves he'd been taught in the Rowan Field, and to his surprise he felt his blade connect. It cut into the back of his opponent, not deep, the leather vest taking the brunt of the blow, but nevertheless there was blood on Evnis' blade and he felt a rush of elation. The young warrior stumbled forwards.

I will do this.

There was movement at the edge of his vision and Evnis twisted to see the other warrior swinging at his neck. Evnis staggered clumsily, partially catching the blow on his blade. A pain lanced through his wrist and his opponent's blade crashed through his defence, glancing off his shoulder, the chainmail turning it, his arm going numb. Evnis attempted to pivot, desperately trying to summon the sword forms he'd learned with so much dedication from the Field, so easily done when someone with sharp iron in their fist wasn't trying to kill you. The hard grin on his enemy's face didn't make him feel any more confident. Somehow he managed to avoid the next blow, grabbed a wrist and then their limbs were tangling and they were falling, rolling down the slope. They came to a halt with Evnis on his back, his opponent sitting on his chest.

This isn't going as I'd imagined.

They'd both lost their swords in the tumble, but the man sitting on his chest had at some point pulled a knife from his belt. He raised it high, Evnis struggling futilely, his arms pinned.

An arrow slammed into the throat of his attacker and he was thrown backwards, a spray of blood misting across Evnis' face. Evnis pushed up to his elbows, saw the other man bearing down upon him, sword raised.

My sword, where's my sword? His hand scrabbled around in the grass. *I'm going to die. Should have waited for the warband.*

The man standing over him with his sword raised paused, his expression shifting from a victory grin to fear, then he was thrown backwards by a mass of fur and snapping teeth. Hands reached down to help Evnis stand, Braith glaring at him. Rafe ran past, his sword stabbing down into the body that was wrestling with two hounds. Rafe's sword came away bloody, the warrior's feet drumming on the ground, then falling still.

'My thanks,' Evnis said as he retrieved his sword. Braith nodded curtly, his face still tight with anger. They were alone on this side of the hold; their enemy had fled southwards. Behind them Glyn thundered up, a hundred warriors following. He dragged on his reins to stop before them.

'Horses,' Evnis shouted and in short moments he was mounted and leading his warband around the curve of the hold's wall. Ahead he saw men running down the hill onto flatter marshland. He glimpsed a river, boats upon it.

'After them,' he yelled, pointing his sword and kicking his horse onwards.

They galloped down the hill, a summer storm; a few of those they were chasing were overtaken and ridden down. The ground rapidly turned to sucking mud, though. One horse fell, screaming as its leg broke. Swearing, Evnis dismounted, picking his way carefully through the spongy ground. Ahead of him men were leaping into boats, pushing away from the bank with long poles and oars. A few paces away one of his men fell with an arrow in the face.

Evnis paused, slipping behind the cover of a draping willow. He was calmer now, had a grip on the emotion that had overwhelmed all reason earlier. *Think. Don't repeat your mistakes, rushing in and nearly getting yourself killed.*

His warriors were following him, dismounted and threading their way through the marshes. Some had forged ahead and reached the riverbank, swords clashing with a few stragglers. Another arrow sent one of his men spinning. Rafe appeared beside him, the two hounds flanking him. The fur of their jaws was matted with blood. Braith was a shadow further away, his back to an alder, stepping out to shoot an arrow at the retreating warriors. A man on a boat screamed and toppled into the water.

A new sound grew, rising above the cries of battle along the riverbank. Evnis looked back to see riders crest the slope, sunlight glinting on iron. He felt a moment of panic.

This is not a good place to be trapped, between horsemen and marshland.

Then he saw the black and gold, Rhin's banner of the broken branch whipped by the wind. Morcant rode at their head, taking in the scene and riding hard for the marsh. Even as Evnis watched, he saw Rhin's disgraced ex-first-sword rein in his mount and slip from his saddle, drawing his sword without breaking a stride. Grudgingly Evnis felt some admiration for his skill.

Not like me, rolling in the grass and losing my sword. He determined then and there to resume his sword training in the Rowan Field.

Morcant was yelling orders, pointing, a few score riders peeling off to ride back up the hill and through the tower wall gates. Then he saw Evnis.

'What's going on?' Morcant called out to him above the din, striding over.

No 'my King', no bend of the knee? 'Your hold appears to have been attacked,' Evnis said, not wanting to talk about Halion and Vonn right now. An arrow whistled through the air, skittering off Morcant's helm. He staggered a step, then joined Evnis behind the cover of the willow. His eyes glanced along the riverbank, then he froze.

'My *SILVER*,' he screamed, eyes bulging.

Evnis followed his gaze, saw a flat-bottomed boat quite a way down the river, a large chest sat within it. Another boat drifted between them, a handful of warriors rowing frantically. One was kneeling, bow drawn. An arrow leaped from the bow, thudded into the chest of one of Evnis' men.

Camlin.

Behind him Vonn stood, staring back at him. Evnis scanned the riverbank, chose a route and stepped out from the willow tree, began to zigzag across the marshy ground. He reached a firmer patch and began to run, heard footsteps behind him, but his eyes were fixed upon Vonn. His son returned the gaze.

Evnis reached the riverbank, leaped over fallen bodies, swerved past two men locked in a knife-fight and then the way was clear, but the bank was blocked by a snarl of osier and sedge. His face twisted in frustration, staring at the last boat in the convoy rapidly disappearing around a bend in the river.

Camlin, Halion and Vonn were in it, as well as a couple of other warriors, one of them the biggest man Evnis had seen since Tull. But he only had eyes for Vonn. He stood and watched him, eyes pleading. Vonn gazed flatly back. Dully he saw Camlin nock another arrow and draw its feathers to his ear, aiming straight at Evnis. He just stood there, exhausted, heartbroken, for a moment not caring if he lived or died.

'Do it,' he whispered.

Then Vonn reached down and put a restraining hand on Camlin's arm.

They shared another few heartbeats, then Vonn disappeared around the bend in the river. Evnis just stood there, staring, the world numb around him. Distantly he heard Morcant screaming in something close to apoplexy.

CHAPTER FORTY-FOUR

MAQUIN

Maquin slipped over the wall and climbed down the rope. Muscles in his stomach clenched and he felt a dull ache begin to pulse from the wound in his belly, knotted and scarred now. *A reminder of the Otherworld.* He wasn't concerned as he felt well now, had sparred in the weapons court and resumed something of his old training as a pit-fighter, and although he knew that he wasn't back to pit health, he was close. He knew his body, knew his limitations. His feet touched the ground and he crouched, adjusted the kit bag strapped across his back, gave the rope a shake to tell the warrior behind him that it was safe to follow, then padded across the road to an abandoned building. Alben and three other warriors were already there, waiting.

It was a dark night, no moon, clouds a thick veil before the stars. *A perfect night for sneaking about.*

Another warrior crept across the deserted road towards them.

It was a ten-night since Fidele had told him about the suggested night raids. He'd volunteered at once. Alben had been chosen to lead them. At first Maquin had been uncertain about that choice; Alben seemed old and frail, but a few moments together in the weapons court had disabused Maquin of that notion. Old he was. Frail he was not. He'd touched a blade to Maquin's throat more than once, and yesterday put him on his back. Of course, Maquin had returned the favour triple-fold, apart from the throwing. He liked the old warrior and so held back for the most part. He suspected Alben knew, just by the occasional raised eyebrow. But it was training, no more, and he was well past having to prove himself to anyone. Unless Fidele was watching, then he found himself behaving like a warrior just come fresh from his Long Night.

What has happened to me?

He had never felt like this, never felt so many things as a result of just one person. Calm, even serene when he was with her, as if the world stopped when she entered the room, an ache in his chest when they were apart, excited when he knew he was close to seeing her. Anxious when he thought of the future.

Out of control. That is how I feel. Unable to control my feelings, and from when I could first walk my da taught me to take command of my emotions. Taught me that is the way of the warrior. He'd seen forty-two summers come and go, and this was the first time he'd ever experienced this. He grinned in the darkness. *I like it, though it scares me.*

They waited in silence, another warrior joining them, then one more. The last one.

They huddled close together.

'We go now, a long road. Silence until we reach the forest. Any questions?' Alben whispered.

They set off in single file, Alben leading the way, Maquin taking rearguard, eight men slipping through the abandoned town of Ripa, giving wide berth to the bonfires that marked Vin Thalun guard posts. If the fires had not been burning Maquin would still have been able to find and avoid most of them by the drunken singing.

We are under siege, but these Vin Thalun are not made for such things. They are too savage, bred to strike hard and fast, win or retreat. A siege requires patience, planning, organization. Lykos is up to this task, maybe, but the rest?

Soon they were out of the town and into the long grass that undulated all the way to the Sarva forest. A breeze off the bay soughed through the grass. Maquin was sweating when they reached the first trees of the forest. They paused here, drank from water skins and rested a few moments. Maquin looked back, the lights from Ripa's walls and tower twinkling like starlight in the distance. He thought of Fidele in that tower, remembered their parting, could still taste her lips.

I feel alive again, as if I've woken from a long sleep. From a nightmare. He grinned again. He found he'd been doing that a lot since he'd woken from his fever. *Although in this new world some of the monsters from my nightmare have followed me.* He thought of Lykos, a dark rage bubbling up from the place where it always simmered deep within him, growing as he thought of the pain the Vin Thalun had brought Fidele.

Alben put a hand on his shoulder and he had to stop himself reaching for a knife.

'You'll see her again,' Alben whispered to him, too quiet for anyone else to overhear.

'How far to Balara?' Maquin asked.

'Half a day's ride. So for us a day and a half of hard walking.'

'We'd best be off, then,' Maquin said.

'Aye. Fidele tells me you're accustomed to forests.'

'You could say that. I served with the Gadrai in Forn.'

'Well then, join me at the front, and let's see if we can make Balara in a day.'

With that they set off into the forest, the trees engulfing them like a dark cloak.

'There it is,' Alben said, pointing. Balara was visible through a gap in the trees, a crumbling stone ruin built upon a tree-shrouded hilltop by ancient giants.

In another lifetime, when the world was a different place.

It was a little past dawn, sunrise gleaming upon the eastern wall of the ancient fortress. All eight of them stood and stared for a while. Maquin saw a wain slowly roll up a track to the east, pulled by auroch, six Vin Thalun riding with it. They were not good horse-men. No one said a word as the wain and riders disappeared within the broken archway of what had once been the grand entrance to the fortress.

'We didn't come all this way for nothing, then,' Alben murmured.

They'd near enough run the whole way, taking them just over a day. Maquin's body ached in a thousand places, but it felt good to be out in the wide open, no walls, only trees and sky. 'Get some sleep,' Alben said to them all. 'I'll take first watch. We'll move at sunset.'

Maquin dipped his fingers into black mud beside a stream, wiped streaks across his cheeks, rubbed the rest across the pommel and cross-guards of his sword and knives. The others were performing similar acts, going through their own rituals that reassured them before the prospect of battle. Maquin reached inside his leather jerkin and pulled out a piece of red velvet. Fidele had given it to him when they parted, cut from the hem of her dress.

'Ready to move,' Alben said close by. 'We are to investigate the ruins. Our orders are to find out why the Vin Thalun are here. No killing.' He shrugged. 'Not until I say so.' Men grinned around him.

They hate the Vin Thalun almost as much as I do.

Alben drew a circle in the mud with a stick. 'This is Balara.' He drew a smaller circle at its centre. 'This is the heart of the fortress, a tower and foundations where we found the Vin Thalun fighting-pits.'

That made Maquin snarl, an involuntary reaction.

Another line from the outer wall to the tower. 'This is the main route in, most likely the bulk of the Vin Thalun will be contained within this area.' He drew a line circling the area between the gates and the central tower.

'That's all we know about the fortress.' He shrugged. 'We will search first. Perhaps that is all we'll do. We may leave without drawing blood. That decision will be made later, and by me alone. Do you understand me?'

Alben looked around the half-circle of men, held each one's gaze a few moments.

'Good. Then let's move.'

They followed Alben up the slope. The trees thinned and the men broke out into open meadow, the weak light of a new moon and stars gilding the hillside and ruin towering above them in silver.

The main gateway, where they had seen the wain enter, lay to the east. Alben led them in a wide loop, eventually ending up beneath the western stretch of crumbled and ruined wall.

As they climbed across huge boulder-sized blocks, a scattering of rock dislodged and fell, rattling loud in the dark. They paused – ready for an alarm to be raised – when none came, they went on.

They entered the ruins, slipping from building to building, the flicker of firelight ahead. They edged closer, fires burning in iron-wrought bowls edging a wide flagstoned street. At the end of it a broken tower loomed, an orange glow pulsing from a wide-open doorway at its base. Vin Thalun stood guard about the tower, four that Maquin could see. The wain they had seen arrive earlier was sitting in the shadows, the auroch nowhere to be seen.

Alben moved towards the tower, Maquin and the others following. They circled wide again, approaching the tower from the north side. Creeping up to one of the windows, Alben beckoned Maquin to join him.

Inside, the tower consisted of one huge circular room, a broken stairwell spiralling upwards about its edge. A fire-pit burned in its centre, the remains of a spitted carcass crusting black. Vin Thalun were scattered about the room, eating, singing quietly, drinking. A score maybe, no more. Alben pointed. Maquin squinted, not seeing anything at first, then he noticed the iron spike hammered into the ground. Two thick chains were attached to it, trailing off into the shadows beneath the stairwell. Two hulking figures crouched in the darkness, barely visible, but Maquin knew them in an instant.

Lykos' giants.

Alben tapped his shoulder and they stole away from the window, back to the others grouped in the darkness. Alben whispered an explanation of what he and Maquin had just seen.

'Are they the giants that Fidele spoke of?' Alben asked Maquin.

'Aye. A female and a bairn. They are Lykos' giants.'

'Why are they here?'

'Why does he have them?'

The questions started to snowball.

'It does not matter,' Maquin interrupted. 'All that matters is that they are precious to Lykos and that they are within our grasp.'

'What are you suggesting?' Alben asked him.

'That we take them from him.'

'Eight of us against thirty, near enough,' Alben said. He was looking at Maquin with his head cocked to one side.

'It can be done,' Maquin said, returning his gaze. 'The guards, by stealth – that's six, evens the odds a little.'

'And the score in that tower?' Alben said.

'I'm thinking you have a plan for that already.'

Alben stared at him a moment longer, lips twitching.

'How would we get the giants back to Ripa?' someone asked.

'The same way they were brought here – under guard,' Maquin

said. 'We would need to kill every man here. Word cannot reach Lykos. It would be a difficult journey back to Ripa, but there are enough of us to guard them, and you know the forest paths. We would slip back into Ripa as planned, under cover of darkness.'

'And if the giants do not cooperate.'

'They are mother and child. I saw with my own eyes that she will do anything to protect her bairn.' Maquin shrugged, a ripple in the dark. 'All we must do is convince her that it is better for her bairn's health that she cooperate rather than fight us.'

Alben stared at him long moments, then he nodded.

Maquin crouched below the tower window. Alben had left one warrior with Maquin – Valent, one of Krelis' men, a veteran of many sea battles with the Vin Thalun before the peace of Aquilus – and taken the others into the darkness.

'I will deal with the guards. Wait for my signal,' Alben had said as the shadows claimed him. Maquin had not bothered to ask what the signal would be.

I'll know it when it happens.

So Maquin and Valent waited, listening to the murmur of conversation filtering out of the window. Someone was complaining of the plunder that they were going to miss out on when Ripa fell.

A loud shout, the signal Maquin had been waiting for, followed closely by the clash of iron. Inside the tower twenty Vin Thalun leaped to their feet, drawing swords and rushing to the tower's wide doorway.

Maquin shared a look with Valent, who reached for his sword hilt. Maquin shook his head. 'It'll be knife-work first, close and bloody.' Valent nodded and then Maquin was climbing through the window into the tower.

No one saw them, all eyes were fixed upon the main door where shadowy figures fought. No one except the giantess. Her eyes met Maquin's, small and dark in a shadow-haunted face. She made no sound, no movement, just watched him as he slipped behind a Vin Thalun warrior. Maquin ripped his eyes away from her, though he felt her gaze still upon him as he grabbed the Vin Thalun, one hand clamping across a mouth, the other sawing his knife across the warrior's throat.

Close by Valent slipped his knife between a Vin Thalun's ribs.

379

Maquin slew another before they were heard. Men peeled away from the doorway, where bodies crammed the entrance, already corpses snaring feet.

Alben is holding them in the doorway, confining them where their numbers will be useless.

Half a dozen men at least came at him and Valent. Maquin strode forwards to meet the attack, leaving Valent to protect the giants.

He kicked at the blackened carcass spitted above the fire-pit, sending it crashing into a Vin Thalun, knocking him to the ground, saw one of the others hesitate.

'It . . . it's the Old Wolf,' the Vin Thalun cried, a flash of doubt sweeping his face, his cry loud enough for others to hear. There was a pause amongst them and Maquin took advantage, hurling a knife which buried itself with a dull crack up to the hilt in another Vin Thalun's forehead.

Maquin drew his sword.

The Vin Thalun circled around the fire-pit, slowly.

Mistake. Should have rushed me.

He moved to the right, sidestepped a hesitant blow, and hacked at the man's ribs, felt bones break, ducked the sword-swing of another warrior, kicked the first into the fire-pit in an explosion of flame, pivoted, took the next sword blow overhead with his own blade, stepped in close, iron grating sparks, and punched his knife through leather into a belly, ripped it sideways as he pulled away, intestines spilling into a steaming heap in his wake. The recent wound in his belly began to throb, an ache deep within.

A quick glance saw Valent standing before the giants, giving ground to three Vin Thalun. Maquin saw the warrior he had kicked the spitted carcass onto push it away and begin to rise from the ground. The main doorway was empty, bodies piled across it, the clash of iron telling of battle in the road outside. There were no others left within the tower. In two long strides Maquin was upon the man trying to rise, kicked him back to the ground and stabbed his sword into the soft flesh of his throat.

Valent went down, a gaping wound between his neck and shoulder. His attacker stood above him, sword-arm rising and falling into Valent's skull, an explosion of blood and bone. Another Vin

Thalun stood close by, one arm hanging limp at his side, blood dripping from his fingertips. The third one was approaching the two giants, their bulk still huddled beneath the spiral staircase.

Maquin ran at them.

He hamstrung the one with the injured arm, heard him drop to the ground with a thud as he threw himself into the warrior that had slain Valent, buried his knife to the hilt in the man's armpit, left it there, spun away and staggered on towards the man now attacking the two unarmed giants. He was hacking at the giantess, who was crouching before the bairn, her teeth bared in a snarl, using the chain she was shackled with to block his sword blows. Maquin saw she had not been entirely successful, blood running from a gash in her forearm, another from her calf.

The Vin Thalun heard Maquin's approach and turned, swinging his sword, sending Maquin's stabbing thrust wide, and they crunched together, wrestling, Maquin trying to break free, make room to swing his blade. They tripped over the giant chain and crashed to the ground, rolling on the stone floor. Pain spiked in Maquin's body, his old wound screaming a complaint.

No time for pain. He ground his teeth.

Maquin lost the grip on his sword, butted his head forwards, felt something crunch. The grip about him loosened and he reached for the last knife in his boot. A punch in the kidneys took his breath away, pain exploding in his back, then an arm was around his throat. He bucked, writhed, threw his head backwards but nothing changed the iron grip around his neck. He clawed at the arm, feeling his strength fading, a dark nimbus seeping into the fringes of his vision, white dots exploding in his head. Something gripped one of his boots and he saw the warrior he'd hamstrung dragging himself across the floor, leaving a trail of blood. *I will not die.*

Panic swept him and gave a last burst of adrenalin. His body spasmed, every muscle and sinew straining, his face purple, tendons thick as rope bulging in his neck, but still the grip about his throat held.

He slumped, feeling the strength flowing out of him, somewhere distantly realized with mild surprise that this was the end.

Fidele . . .

His body jerked suddenly, shook like a straw doll, then the grip around his throat was gone and he was choking, sucking in great, ragged breaths. Behind him a man screamed.

The warrior gripping his ankles stared up at him, then let go and reached for a sword.

Too late.

Maquin kicked him in the face, pulled his last knife from his boot and stabbed the man through the eye. He spasmed, legs kicking, then went slack.

Maquin rolled over, saw the warrior who had almost killed him caught by the giantess. She'd wrapped the length of her chain about his throat and was pulling tight. The man's face was a grey-purple explosion of veins, bulging eyes and swelling tongue. There was a popping sound, vertebrae in his neck snapping, and his head suddenly lolled, eyes glazing. The giantess continued to pull, muscles bulging, rippling along her forearms like snakes in a sack. With a tearing sound Maquin saw the flesh about the chain begin to fray, then tear, blood seeping, then exploding in a violent jet as the giantess gave one last savage wrench and the man's head ripped free.

She stepped away, her eyes fixed on Maquin, letting the Vin Thalun's corpse flop to the ground, and sitting beside her son, who gripped her hand tightly.

Maquin backed away, picked up his sword, still watching the giants, then headed for the tower doorway, stopping to retrieve his knives on the way.

Alben stepped into the room. Blood sheeted his forehead and his sword was red to the hilt. 'The giants?'

'Still alive.' Maquin pointed to the shadows beneath the stairwell.

They stood and stared a long while at the giants, who returned their gaze with wariness.

She saved my life. The thought left Maquin feeling uncomfortable. *But then, I saved hers.* She was still bleeding from her wounds.

Alben offered her a flask of water.

'Drink, and clean your wounds,' Alben said. The giantess stared unblinking back at him. Alben tried again. '*Deach agus glan do gortuithe.*'

Giantish.

The giantess frowned, then reached out and took the water skin.

She sniffed it, took a tentative sip, then gave it to her bairn. He took a deep drink, then poured water over his mother's wounds, washing the blood away.

'I can tend your wounds, bind them for you,' Alben said.

'*Cad ba mhaite leat?*' the giantess said. Her lips twisted in a sneer.

'*Me troid ar son an realta geal. Sbhilt anois. Ach ni feidir liom a leagtar t' saor in aisce – mo namhaid stor. Ni mor duit teacht liom,*' Alben replied.

'*Ni feidir liom,*' the giantess growled, her voice a basal rumble. '*Bhaineann me go dti an aingeal dorcha.*'

'*Sin deireadh leis. Ar m'anam tar liom go sÌoch-nta agus beidh t' sln. NÌ dhÈanfar aon dochar duit,*' Alben replied.

Maquin did not know what they were saying, but he saw Alben's gaze shift to the giant bairn, then back to the giantess.

She stood suddenly, her body hard and ridged as a slab of granite. Men behind Alben reached for their swords, but Alben did not flinch.

'*Tiocfaimid, ach is eagal dom go bhfuil gealltanas tugtha agat nach fÈidir leat a chomhllÌonadh,*' the giantess said.

Her voice resonated in Maquin's chest.

'Time will be the judge,' Alben said. He drew his sword and struck the chains on the post, shattering them.

'We are moving out, now.' Alben turned and strode away. The giantess and her bairn followed.

'What did you say to them?' Maquin asked.

Alben did not look at him as he marched from the tower.

CHAPTER FORTY-FIVE

CORALEN

Coralen pulled on the oar, feeling muscles contract in her back and shoulders, her torso swaying forwards and back with the motion. It had been like learning to ride all over again, the rhythm of it at first strangely alien, the dip and lift of the oar, pulling against the resistance of the Afren's dark waters, using the sway of her body to help not hinder, and on top of that, to do it in perfect time so as not to snare her oar in another rower's.

I've got it now, though.

The first night after their escape from Uthandun Corban gathered all of the oarsmen from the eleven ships they had stolen, over three hundred men. He had repeated the offer he'd made during the raid – told them that they were free. He suggested that they row both for Corban and for themselves now, away from the pirates who had made them slaves, and be put ashore at a safer location.

Some had demanded their freedom then and there. Corban had let them go, no more than a score of them, staggering into the gloom of the Darkwood. The rest had stayed.

Many were close to death, weak and emaciated, but Coralen had been surprised to see the effect a mouthful of brot had upon most of them.

Corban had asked one other thing from them and, more than anything else, that seemed to convince them of his sincerity.

He asked them to train his own warband up as oarsmen.

She'd received a lot of strange looks when she'd volunteered. She'd ignored them. Her body could cope with it, strong and supple after year upon year of sparring, though in truth after the first shift she'd spent at an oar her hands were blistered and weeping, and her back and shoulders were in agony. When she woke the next morning it was worse. By the third day she was getting used to it.

The veteran rowers had accepted her presence quickly, especially when the Jehar started filling benches as well, at least half of them women. They had attacked rowing as if it was an enemy, with stony faces and determined stoicism. Harder to get used to, though, were giants sitting on the oar-benches. Balur had been the first to try. The bench had creaked when he sat upon it, and the first time he and a few of his kin pulled at their oars the ship had listed so heavily the decks had taken water. It had taken some careful re-arrangement of seating to balance the ship out.

'We're leaving the forest behind us.' It was the small, dark-skinned man named Javed sitting on the bench across from her. His head was shaved clean, dark stubble shadowed his jaw, and he had more scars on his body than Coralen had ever seen. He was small framed, but his musculature had a wiry strength that Coralen recognized and respected, and he moved with a grace reminiscent of the Jehar that spoke of explosive power.

'Aye,' Coralen grunted. She'd not really mastered the art of talking and rowing yet.

'Where exactly are you all going?' Javed asked her.

'Forwards,' Coralen grunted. Everyone within the warband knew that they were travelling to Drassil, the city of tales, until recently something she'd thought of as exactly that: a tale. Now, though, it was just accepted. Coralen was aware that other people would not view it in the same way.

'Strange company you keep,' Javed observed.

I suppose it is. Coralen didn't think of it that way any more, much as she no longer viewed Drassil as a strange destination.

A bell rang behind her, signalling the end of her shift on the bench. Smoothly she raised her oar, pulled it through its hole and shelved it. Javed gave her a mock-bow as she stood and filed along the aisle to the stairs that led to the top deck. She blinked in the sunlight and nodded to Farrell as he passed her to take his place at an oar. The deck was narrow, dominated by a single mast and furled sail, beyond it a raised deck where Dath stood helming the steering oar. Coralen walked to the ship's rail and leaned out, looking down-river. More ships followed them, their small fleet.

Four nights they'd been rowing up the Afren, away from Uthandun, each morning expecting to see ships appear on the river behind them, or hear the pounding of hooves as a warband swept along the riverbank.

That wouldn't be so easy, though; most of the time I haven't even been able to see beyond the riverbank. It had been choked thick with coppiced woods and undergrowth, trailing willow and black alder. Although now the banks were mostly clear, trees and undergrowth thinning, flat meadows visible through them. *Why have our enemy not come after us? We were outnumbered, within their grasp.* Whatever the reason, Coralen was starting to think that they were not being followed, that they had escaped.

It was a good plan, I can't deny. Corban's leadership skills had gone up in her estimation, coming up with the plan, and keeping a cool head to see it through. It had been well done, she had to admit, and she felt a swell of pride at her own contribution to it – the straw men and fires to draw the enemy's eye.

Aye, it had worked a treat.

And now, to all appearances, they were free of pursuit and on the borders of Narvon and Isiltir, almost out of enemy territory. It was a strange feeling. Relief. It still didn't stop her looking over her shoulder, though.

And now we are sailing to Drassil, instead of travelling south to Ardan. To Edana. She wasn't sure how she felt about that.

A hand touched her on the shoulder.

'You ready?'

It was Cywen, twirling a throwing-knife between her fingers and grinning.

During the first day upon the ship, after the heat of battle had left her veins and general tasks had been finished – clearing the ship of the dead, tending the wounded and mourning fallen comrades – Coralen had found herself in an unusual situation. Every day for as long as she could remember she had been in her saddle before dawn, riding out with her growing band of scouts, always active and contributing. But as the ships had rowed further and further away from Uthandun she had started to feel useless, obsolete.

Cywen had saved her, requesting that she teach her blade-work. Coralen had been more than happy to oblige, and asked for a lesson in knife-throwing in return. She wasn't sure that learning to throw a blade whilst standing upon a moving, swaying ship was the best way to begin, but it was too late by the time she thought of that.

Since then Dath had filled the inactivity gap, giving orders to anyone whom he saw standing around – any small task to ensure the smooth running of the ship. Even now if Coralen stood still long enough she knew that she'd hear him calling her name.

'Of course,' Coralen said.

They stood and faced the raised deck at the rear of the ship. Upon its timber wall Cywen had painted a human outline, arm raised and brandishing a sword. Someone had, humorously, given it small horns and titled it a Kadoshim. Cywen handed her a knife.

Having been witness to previous sessions, Jehar, giants and off-duty oarsmen scattered from the rear half of the deck. Coralen had not taken to knife-throwing like the natural she'd expected to be. From the corner of her eye she saw Javed lean against the ship's rail to watch them.

She took aim, setting her feet as Cywen had taught her, bringing the blade back to her ear, then—

A sword slammed into the wooden outline, almost exactly where Coralen had been aiming.

'Hah, Laith is getting better,' a voice laughed from just behind her, deep and almost deafening her.

'Stop boasting,' Cywen said, smiling up at the giantling. Laith's head was bandaged from the wound she'd received during the battle. It didn't seem to dampen her enthusiasm, though.

'I'm speaking truth,' Laith said with a frown. 'Look.' She pointed at her handiwork. 'And it's not stuck, see,' Laith said, bounding over to the sword and tugging it free. 'Laith has been thinking,' she said, puffing her chest out. 'I listen to Cywen – skill not strength.' She tapped the side of her head. 'And a bigger blade.'

Despite herself, Coralen laughed, then shook her head. *Laughing with a Benothi giantling; me, who rode with Rath and his giantkillers. How things change.*

'Where'd you get that sword?' Cywen asked Laith.

'From the dead,' Laith replied. 'They do not need them now.'

Coralen looked closer, saw that it was one of the short swords that the Vin Thalun favoured. The giantling lifted a leather coat to reveal another half-dozen of them secreted about her body.

Cywen shook her head, still smiling. She grasped it, testing its balance.

'It's weighted wrong,' she said. 'When we get to Drassil I'll ask Farrell to make you something this size and weight, but balanced and weighted for throwing.'

Laith grinned. 'I am a smith, too,' she said, 'but I've only made bigger things – wheels, axles for wains.' She shrugged. 'Will Farrell do it?'

'If he says no to me, we can always get Coralen to ask him,' Cywen said.

Coralen scowled at that, well aware of and unimpressed by the smith's feelings for her.

'Drassil?' Javed said loudly. He sauntered closer. 'Did you say Drassil?'

Cywen looked at him, frowning. They'd all forgotten he was there. She ignored him and turned away.

'Hey,' Javed said, reaching out and grabbing Cywen's shoulder.

A huge hand clamped around Javed's wrist and wrenched him off of Cywen.

'You do not touch her,' Laith said. Her playful, cheerful expression was gone, replaced by jutting brows and flat eyes. Javed's face twitched and he exploded into movement, faster than Coralen could see. Javed's free hand lashed out, his feet shifting, a flurry of movement, and then Laith was falling like a felled oak. She crashed to the timber deck, Javed crouched above her, a knife in his hand, hovering over the giant's throat.

How did he do that?

'Bigger they are, harder they fall,' Javed muttered.

Everything froze for a moment, Coralen dimly aware that all on the ship's deck were staring at them. Something warred across Javed's face, emotions fighting for supremacy. His jaw spasmed, like a spark setting something in motion, followed by a contraction in the striated muscles of his shoulder, a drawing back of his wrist, and then Coralen was lunging forwards. She kicked out, caught Javed's wrist as the knife began its descent, sending it spinning out of his hand. With a snarl Javed was turning, launching himself at her. A dozen blows flew between them, some blocked, some landing, then they were crushed together, spinning, still punching. Coralen's back slammed into the wall of the cabin.

Blood dripped from Javed's nose.

They froze, staring at each other, both breathing heavily.

Then another sound filtered through the fog of Coralen's focus. Growling. Deep, vibrating through the timber deck into Coralen's boots.

'You should let her go and step away,' a voice said, cold, angry but controlled.

Javed stared a moment longer at Coralen, his face twisted with anger – no, something deeper than that, a berserk, consuming fury. Then, slowly, muscles shifted, loosened. He blinked, let go of her, stepped away.

Corban stood behind them, a look on his face that was a far cry from his usual amicable smile.

'I'll not see a hand raised against my friends, or tolerate them being hurt,' he said to Javed. 'So do we have a problem here?' Corban did not move, had no weapon in his hands, but Javed took a step away from him. Storm's growl shifted, became deeper somehow. Saliva dripped from her bared fangs.

'I – I am . . . sorry,' Javed said. And actually looked as if he was. He wiped a hand across his face, then turned and staggered away.

As the sun sank into the west it bathed the flat land of glistening marsh spread before them in its orange glow, myriad waterways and stagnant pools glistening like liquid amber. Behind them the bastion of the Darkwood stood stark and silhouetted, fading into the distance, and along with it the realm of Narvon.

Ahead is Isiltir, and beyond it Forn Forest and Drassil. Coralen stood with Farrell by the gap in the rail where the boarding ramp would be lowered, waiting for Dath to yell his orders. He was on the riverbank, telling Laith where to secure a mooring rope. Her lip throbbed, a reminder of her earlier encounter. The fight sat heavy in her mind, the look in Javed's eyes as he fought her. It had been as if he'd become another person. *We all do that when we fight for real, to some degree.* But still, what she had seen in his eyes . . .

And how he had reacted to Corban. There had been something

new about Corban, in his voice and also in his eyes, something commanding. She hated that he had come to her rescue, that he had felt the need to step in. She scowled. *I can look after myself. A few moments more and I would have had him.* She thought about that a while, in all truth not sure if she would have. Javed was so fast, so committed to each move, with nothing held back, as if life and death were of no consequence.

'Come on, then,' Dath yelled up to them, 'we've not got all day.'

Coralen made to shout something abusive but then grimaced as her lip pulled.

Farrell caught her wince. 'I will call him out,' he snarled from the other side of the boarding-ramp as they lowered it to the bank, their end hooking onto a timber lip.

'What?' Coralen said, having no idea what Farrell was talking about.

'That oarsman,' he said. 'If only I'd been there.'

'Good job you weren't,' Coralen said. 'He put a giant bigger than you on her back.'

'It's not about size,' Farrell said, looking offended. 'I've seen more combat than Laith.'

'Don't be an idiot,' Coralen snapped at him. 'It was nothing.' *And he might have killed you, you big oaf. Much as you get on my nerves, I'd rather you alive than dead.*

'And besides, I can look after myself. Don't need anyone to fight my battles for me.'

Farrell looked as if he wanted to say something but chose not to. *Not as much of an idiot as I thought.*

'Everyone off,' Dath yelled, cupping his hands to his mouth. Laith copied him, her voice booming across the river.

They were sitting along the riverbank and spread in a half-circle around a row of fire-pits. Real meat was turning on spits – auroch, boar, deer – all found salted and hanging in one of the large transporters they'd stolen. Close to seven hundred souls sat curving around the fire-pits, stomachs growling and mouths watering at the smells, a murmur of anticipatory conversation thrumming amongst them.

Coralen sat with Farrell, Cywen and Dath. Also Kulla the Jehar, who seemed to have become Dath's shadow in recent days. A few oarsmen that Farrell had befriended from his shift joined them, a father and son.

'Atilius and Pax,' Farrell introduced the two men.

Conversations with the oarsmen had been hesitant at first, so many of them on the verge of death, emaciated, withdrawn and insular. More of them were beginning to mix with Corban's warband now, though, probably helped by the fact that they were sharing shifts on the oar-benches.

'Where are you from?' Dath asked them.

'Tenebral,' Atilius, the older man, said. He had the look of a warrior about him, close-cropped hair and beard, darkly tanned skin, solid and stocky, not an ounce of excess fat on his frame. There was something about him that looked familiar to Coralen.

'How did you end up . . .' Dath said, glancing back at the ships moored along the river's edge.

Always tactful, Dath.

The two men exchanged a glance, a look of fear flitting across the younger one's face.

'Prisoners of war,' Atilius said with a shrug.

'War against who?' This time it was Farrell asking the question.

'The Vin Thalun,' Atilius said. 'The pirates you stole those ships from.'

'Damn them to hell,' Pax murmured. 'Damn them to hell.' He had a furtive, jumpy look to him.

Atilius patted his son's leg, pain washing his features.

'You're warriors, then,' Cywen said.

'He is,' Kulla said, nodding at Atilius.

'We both were,' Atilius said. His son looked away.

'The warriors of Tenebral are our enemy,' Farrell said, frowning. 'Nathair is your king?'

'Aye,' Atilius said slowly, looking about at them. Cywen and Dath were sitting straighter, and Coralen was remembering the warriors she had fought and killed during the night raid on Rhin's forces back in Domhain Pass. They had been men of Tenebral.

'Eagle-guard,' Cywen said.

'Aye. That is what they called the best of us,' Atilius said. His son was looking nervously between them.

'Veradis. Do you know him?' Cywen asked.

'He is Nathair's first-sword. A good man, or so I hear.'

'Yes, I thought that, too,' Cywen said, a distant look in her eye.

'Are we your enemy, then?' Atilius asked them.

A straight talker, at least. I like that.

'To my mind, no,' Cywen said. 'But it is for Corban to decide. Should I consider you my enemy?'

'No,' snorted Atilius. 'Nathair gave Tenebral's rule to a madman – Lykos of the Vin Thalun – and then walked away on some mad quest. He abandoned his people to a lunatic. I want no part of such a king. If I were to fight, it would be against the Vin Thalun, whether they are allied to Nathair or not.' He looked at his son. 'But I don't want to fight.' He said it almost reassuringly. 'I just want to find us some peace.'

Good luck with that. We're marching knee-deep into the God-War.

Just then Javed walked past their group. He saw Coralen, his steps faltering for a moment as she met his gaze, then he walked on.

'Heard about earlier,' Atilius said.

'Do you know him?' Farrell asked, his voice dangerous.

'Aye. He was a pit-fighter.'

'What's that?'

'A form of entertainment for the Vin Thalun. Slaves they capture – they break them in on the oars; if they survive that then they throw them in the pit, a dozen, more. Last one alive gets to come out. Gets to fight another day. Some fight all the way to their freedom. He was one of them – almost.' He looked at Coralen. 'Heard you held your own with him. You'd have won a fortune in silver if you'd have done that back in Tenebral.'

'He's fast,' Coralen said wryly, touching her lip.

'He's an animal,' Pax said. 'And touched.' He tapped a finger against his temple. 'They all are.'

'Are there more like him on the oars – pit-fighters?'

'Pit-fighters, aye,' Atilius grunted. 'Many. Like him, though? None. Not here, anyway.'

Coralen noticed a change around them, the murmur of conversation dying down. She looked up to see Corban vault onto a wide, low branch of an old elm. Storm lay at his feet, Meical, Gar, Tukul and Brina arrayed about him.

'Looks like your brother has something to say,' Dath said, slapping Cywen's arm.

CHAPTER FORTY-SIX

CORBAN

Corban stood on the branch of an old elm, looking out at the sea of faces staring back at him.

For a moment his mind went absolutely blank. He took a breath. 'I'm not much for speech-making,' he said, his voice falling into the silence like a stone in a deep pool. 'But there are some things that need saying.' He looked around again, his mouth dry, feeling a little overwhelmed.

'Get on with it,' Brina muttered under her breath. Corban scowled at her. Speech-making was all well and good for those used to it – but he wasn't one for rhetoric and flowery talk. All he could do was speak from the heart and hope it was enough.

'When I took these ships I promised you freedom,' Corban shouted. 'I also asked you to row us all to safety. Well, you have. Narvon lies behind us, Isiltir ahead, so I say to you again, you are free.'

Someone cheered, more voices adding to it, rippling through the crowd, surprising him, and also making him feel less self-conscious.

Maybe I'm not making a huge fool out of myself after all.

When it quietened he carried on.

'But where is *safe* in this land of ours now? I'd like you to think on that. Of Rhin's armies conquering nation after nation. Of the Vin Thalun enslaving our people.' There were hisses at the mention of the hated pirates. 'And of the Kadoshim, slaughtering men, women, bairns – innocents.' A mass of faces gazed at him in silence. Corban sighed wearily, for a moment lost in a blur of memories – the Kadoshim in Murias, afterwards in the woodland of Narvon, one of them biting into the flesh of a terrified captive. He shook his head, forced himself to concentrate on those in front of him. 'Tonight is for feasting, for celebrating our escape.' He gestured to the fire-pits and the spitted meat. 'And tonight is for making a choice. To join us or go your own way.'

'Where are you going?' someone shouted.

Corban frowned. *How many will flee at the mere mention of our destination? They will think us mad. But I'll not start our journey with a lie.*

'We are going to Drassil in Forn Forest.'

More silence.

Corban rubbed his eyes and sucked in a deep breath. 'Some of you will believe. Others will think we talk of myth and legend. But we have seen things – things that can leave us in no doubt. The God-War has begun. Sides are being chosen . . .' He paused.

'You must tell them,' Meical had said to him earlier. Corban had looked pleadingly at Brina.

'Might as well.' She had shrugged. 'Get it all over with in one go. Besides,' she added. 'It's true.'

He sighed now and searched the faces in front of him. 'I am the Bright Star spoken of in prophecy. I fight for Elyon, against Asroth and his Black Sun.' He paused, the words sounding strange even to him.

Fighting a god – how can I do that?

'I don't want to fight,' he said. 'But what choice do I have? What choice do any of us have? I will fight to protect those I love. My kin. My friends – I fight for my realm. For our people. And for myself. Rhin, Nathair, the Vin Thalun – they will not stop until every one of us is dead or enslaved.'

Another silence, somehow deeper and denser than any that had preceded it.

'So we get to fight the Vin Thalun if we stay with you?'

'Definitely,' Meical said quietly beside him.

'Yes,' Corban said loudly.

'Good enough for me,' someone yelled. There was a smattering of quiet laughter at that.

'I cannot guarantee victory.' Corban's voice was rising now, echoing back from the ships moored along the river. 'We may lose. We may all die.'

How can I ask this of them? Is this what leaders do – ask their followers for everything and offer them nothing in return?

He looked at the gathering spread before him and knew that if they had any chance against the armies that were coming they needed to unite. And it was on his shoulders to make them see that.

'I have *seen* the evil that comes against us, and it is terrifying. If we do not stand against it, who will? There is only one promise that I can make to you . . .' He felt a lump in his throat as he saw familiar faces staring back at him – Cywen, Dath, Farrell, Coralen, Balur One-Eye, Gar – people he cared for. People he may lose.

What choice do we have?

He put his hand upon his sword hilt.

'I will be beside you every step of the way and I will *fight* until my last breath.'

He shouted those last words, feeling passion swell in him like a dark wave. As he stepped down from the branch he was battered by a deafening roar from the crowd. Jehar and giants were brandishing their weapons in the air, cheering at the top of their lungs. And so were most of the others. The faces of oarsmen that had looked close to death only a few days ago, empty and listless, were now alive with passion.

And so it begins.

The marshlands were a flat, stinking, mosquito-infested wasteland. The river curled through it like a lethargic serpent, taking their eleven ships slowly eastwards. The oarsmen that remained all set to their shifts, and the ships moved ever closer to Drassil. Tukul and Meical had spoken to him, warned that such broken men could not be trusted and would need watching. But Corban disagreed.

They were men – warriors – once. It was not their fault that they were enslaved. I believe there must be honour left among them. And while I may only offer an uncertain future – it's at least better than the certain death they faced before. Besides, I know what a driving force hatred and revenge can be . . .

Corban stood upon the raised rear deck of the lead ship, Dath at his side with one arm hooked around the steering oar. Kulla his shadow was loitering nearby.

'We couldn't have done this without you,' Corban said to his friend.

'I know.' Dath grinned. 'And I may remind you of those words.'

'Dath is gifted in many ways,' Kulla said. Dath blushed at that; Corban suppressed a smile.

'But what would you expect,' Kulla continued, 'from one of the Bright Star's closest friends?'

Corban blushed this time, and Kulla beamed with pride at Dath.

'We will have to leave this river soon,' Meical said. 'It flows through the south of Isiltir, almost to the doors of Mikil, Isiltir's seat of power. Jael holds Isiltir, now, and Mikil is his. We cannot go that way. To reach Gramm's hold we need to join one of the rivers that flows north, to the sea.'

'And how exactly are we going to do that?' Corban asked. 'Pick up the ships and carry them across land?'

Meical and Dath just smiled at him.

With a huge splash and a spray of water that soaked him and a few hundred others, the first ship slid into the river. Corban didn't mind; he was already soaked through with sweat. He stood on the bank, bent over with his hands on his knees and sucking in deep breaths. And he was grinning. They had managed to haul the first four ships out of the river and into the marshes. The horses had been unloaded from the three transporters and roped into teams, used to help pull the ships onto land. Then they'd begun the long portage across the spongy ground towards another river, rolling the ships across three or four masts like giant rollers, running them from back to front. The oarsmen taught them the most efficient technique for this, as they had been forced to do it many times by their Vin Thalun masters. Every man had helped, taking it in turns, a bizarre convoy of four ships rolling across the flat landscape. Benothi muscle had added considerably to their teams and the ships rolled across land surprisingly well.

It was a journey of about two leagues.

Not so far to walk, normally, but when you're pulling a ship . . .

They made their way back to the remaining ships and began the process all over again.

'We've got a problem,' Dath said to Corban. 'Those transport-ers aren't coming out of the river.'

'Why not?'

'Their hulls are too deep. These galleys like the one we've been sailing upon, they're shallow draughted – not much sits below the water. Those transporters, well, a third of the ship sits below the water. That's fine in a wide, deep river, but we'll never get them out. And even if we do, we won't be able to roll them two leagues across land.'

Corban put his head in his hands.

They were sitting in a big circle, Corban surrounded by his growing council: Meical, Tukul, Brina and Gar, Balur One-Eye and Ethlinn, Dath, Cywen and Coralen – who seemed to be in each other's com-pany whenever Corban saw them – and two others had joined them, representatives of their new recruits. Javed and Atilius. Storm and Buddai were lying in the shade of a willow. Corban watched Javed, remembering the way he had fought Coralen. That had set a rage burning in Corban and it had taken all his will not to draw his sword and cut him down.

Can I trust him? Someone so close to rage and violence?

The honest answer was that he didn't know, but the oarsmen had chosen Javed and Atilius as their representatives, so for now Corban chose to trust their choice.

And I shall keep a close eye upon Javed.

They had been discussing options. Corban was listening to Gar as he suggested dismantling the transporters and rebuilding them beside the new river.

'Have you ever built a ship before? Sailed one?' Javed asked Gar.

'No. I was born in a desert,' Gar said.

'Hah,' Javed barked a laugh, throwing his arms in the air.

'It will not work,' Dath told Gar glumly. 'Apart from not having the tools to do the job without punching holes in the hull, the timbers would have to be caulked – sealed – or the ship would sink as soon as it sat in the water.'

Voices spoke out at the same time, offering equally impossible solutions.

'There is only one solution,' Tukul spoke out, loud and commanding. 'We must split up. One group takes the horses and rides through Isiltir to Gramm's. The other group sails round the coast.'

Corban frowned. That was the one answer that his mind kept on returning to, but he did not like it.

'It would be dangerous,' Cywen said.

'What isn't in these Banished Lands?' Tukul snorted. 'Besides, we did it before. We rode from Gramm's, through Isiltir into Ardan to Dun Carreg. Then all the way to Dun Vaner. We rode like the wind, and the Jehar are hard to stop once they are in the saddle.'

'The ships would reach Gramm's a long time before the riders,' Meical said. He sounded as if he was thinking out loud, rather than posing problems.

'Maybe, maybe not,' Tukul said with a proud grin.

'Two horses a rider,' Coralen said. 'Ride one horse, rest the other.'

'That would speed things up.'

The conversation went on for a while, but eventually a silence fell and all heads turned to Corban.

'It is the only workable answer,' he said. 'Though I don't like the thought of us splitting up. All that is left is to decide who rides and who sails.'

'The Jehar are the best riders,' Brina said.

'I will not leave Corban,' Gar said automatically.

'I will not ask you to,' Tukul said, resting a hand upon his son's shoulder. 'But it should be mostly Jehar. Brina is right. We are the best riders, best equipped to get to Gramm's quickly. I would ask that Coralen ride with us,' Tukul said.

'Why?' Corban asked, not really liking that idea. Coralen frowned.

'Because she is the best scout I've ever seen, and you won't need that skill while you sail upon the northern sea.'

Corban could not fault the logic, and he also knew that it was an immense compliment to Coralen. But still, it would be dangerous . . .

He looked at Coralen. She was staring at him.

'It makes sense,' he said.

'I shall go, then,' Coralen snapped.

'Only if you want to,' Corban said.

'I do. Why would I not?'

Because I want you to stay.

Corban shrugged and looked away.

'Best get the last galleys shifted across this marshland then,' Dath said, looking up at the sun.

The next morning saw one hundred and fifty Jehar mounted and ready, horses stamping and restless, happy to be on solid ground and full of energy. Balur had taken a handful of Benothi and holed the hulls of the three pot-bellied transporters, sinking them into the depths of the river.

Better that than the Vin Thalun reclaim them, thought Corban.

Corban stood on the riverbank with Storm and Shield. He stamped his feet and blew warm breath into his hands. It was cold, a new chill to the air.

Summer is waning. We need to reach Drassil before winter finds us.

Shield nudged him and snorted.

'Sorry, lad,' Corban said, rubbing the stallion's nose and patting his muscular neck. 'I'll miss you. Behave for Tukul. And enjoy your run.' Shield had pranced off of the transporter like a coiled spring, full of life and energy, eager to gallop. Corban felt jealous that he would not be riding him across Isiltir to Gramm's hold.

Tukul was embracing Gar. He stepped back and held Gar's face in his hands.

'Look after our Bright Star while I'm gone.'

'I have done so for close to eighteen years,' Gar said indignantly. 'I'll not be stopping now.'

Tukul flashed a grin. 'My beloved son,' he said and kissed Gar's cheek.

Corban turned away, memories stirring of his da. He came face to face with Coralen, who was checking her mount's saddle girth.

'Be careful,' Corban said to her.

'Huh,' Coralen grunted.

They regarded each other, Corban noticing the emerald of her eyes, the pink flush of her freckled cheeks in the chill dawn air.

Footsteps thudded and Farrell appeared, Cywen and Dath with them.

'I could come with you,' Farrell said.

'And why would you do that?' Coralen snapped.

'You might need me?'

Coralen just sighed and shook her head. She swung gracefully up into her saddle.

That's remarkably reserved for her. She must be going soft.

'Here, this is for you,' Cywen said, grinning as she held out a throwing-knife in a fine sheath and wrapped in a belt.

Coralen drew the knife and smiled, pale sunlight glinting on the iron.

'I'll practise every day,' Coralen said.

'See that you do.'

'And make sure no one's standing close by,' Corban added.

Coralen scowled at him.

'Time to go,' Tukul called out. He leaned in his saddle and he and Corban gripped arms.

'Ride fast, and I'll see you after,' Corban said.

'Aye. This side or the other.'

'No,' Corban said. 'At Gramm's. That's my first order to you. Stay alive. All of you.'

'We'll do our best,' Tukul said with his wide grin. 'And see that you all return the favour.' His eyes lingered over Gar. 'We'll be sitting in Gramm's feast-hall warming our toes long before you get there,' he said, then he was turning his mount and cantering along the riverbank, the host of Jehar flowing out behind him.

Coralen nodded to Corban and then she was gone, cantering to the head of the column, riding ahead to pick their route through the marshlands.

'You going to miss her?' Dath said.

Corban had opened his mouth to answer when he realized that Dath was talking to Farrell, not him.

'I will,' Farrell said.

Corban just watched them ride away. Finally in silence he strode back up the boarding-plank and onto his ship.

CHAPTER FORTY-SEVEN

FIDELE

Fidele walked up the wooden steps of Ripa's outer wall, her doeskin boots hardly making a sound. When she reached the walkway that edged the high wall she stopped, making sure that she stayed out of reach of the torchlight that crackled in an iron sconce close by, spreading a circular glow across the wall. Further along she saw the dark shadow of two guards, but they were both facing outward and had not heard her.

Below her the town of Ripa was a dark shadow, here and there fires and torches marking the tiers of its flow down the hill that Ripa's tower was built upon. Occasionally voices lifted in drunken song drifted up, borne on the sea breeze. Vin Thalun voices.

Further out, she gazed at the wide meadows that surrounded Ripa, a huge black shadow, like a sable cloak spread across the land. And beyond that, the forest Sarva, and somewhere within it, to the north, lay Balara, that ancient giant ruin.

And Maquin. Where is he?

It was the eleventh night since Maquin had left with Alben and six others, heading to Balara to investigate the reports of Vin Thalun activity there.

Eleven nights. They were supposed to be gone no more than four. Maybe five. A trickle of ice dripped into her heart, taking her breath away.

Is he dead?

Others were saying so, or thinking it at least.

No. He has survived too much. But she knew that was ridiculous, as if life held a weighing scale to balance fair with unfair, right with wrong. *But he came back from the bridge of swords . . .*

She gripped the timber wall, knuckles white.

Nought but a fever dream, though I believed him, at the time. Wanted to believe him. And it doesn't matter if it was a dream or truth. It does not change how I feel.

Footsteps sounded on the stairs behind her, the creak of timber, and she turned to see Peritus approaching. He came and stood beside her, looking out into the empty street beyond.

'It is dangerous out here,' he said quietly.

She lifted her cloak and tapped the hilt of a knife. She'd taken to the habit of being armed at all times. It had been Maquin's idea.

Peritus grunted, no doubt thinking her knife would make little difference against a Vin Thalun. *Maybe he is right, but I feel better for it. And I am not afraid to use it.*

'You have come here every night.'

She didn't answer.

'They are long overdue,' he said.

'That means nothing.'

'It means something. Maybe not the worst.' He looked at her. 'You were Queen of Tenebral . . .'

There was a question in there, hesitant, voiceless. It said: *What are you doing? How can you consort with a pit-fighter?*

Because I love him. 'Do not worry,' she said coldly, 'I know my duty.' *Duty has taken so much from me. My pride, my dignity, almost my life. I will not let it take Maquin from me as well. Just a little longer – I will do what I must for Tenebral, for my people. And then . . .*

She reined her thoughts in, the possibility that Maquin could be lying out there dead returning to her.

A long silence grew between them, like a wide space. She felt Peritus shake his head, a ripple in the air.

'You should not be alone,' he said eventually.

She didn't answer. A silence fell between them.

'Marcellin will be here soon,' Peritus said into the quiet.

'Has there been any word of him?'

'None. But he cannot be far away. We shall have justice.' He looked at her. 'And our revenge.'

Peritus had suffered much, seen Armatus, his oldest friend, beheaded by Lykos. And he had seen Fidele in Jerolin, with Lykos at her side. She had condemned him to death, her friend, because of Lykos' spell. Peritus knew why.

'I am sorry,' she whispered.

He reached out a hand and squeezed hers. 'You were not yourself,' he said.

A Vin Thalun voice raised in song drifted on the breeze from the town.

'Why are they not attacking?' Fidele said.

Peritus shrugged. 'They have tried to storm the walls, and they have tried stealth. Easier to starve us out.'

'But what of Marcellin? They must know he is coming.'

'Aye.' Peritus' face creased in a frown, moonlight picking out ridges and making deep valleys of shadow on his lined face. 'That troubles me, too.'

A shout suddenly went up from the darkness beyond the wall. A clash of iron, a scream.

Feet drummed on the stairwell as more warriors took to the wall. Peritus had his sword drawn. Krelis suddenly loomed over them, a dozen warriors filling the stairs behind him.

'What's going on, then?' he asked them. 'An attack?' He sounded hopeful.

'Don't think so,' Peritus murmured, eyes scanning the shadows. 'Hard to tell, too dark.'

'We'll see about that,' Krelis said. He grabbed a torch from a warrior behind him and hurled it over the wall. It spiralled through the air, trailing a tail like a shooting star and thumped to the ground, sputtered but stayed lit. Darkness retreated around it, an orange glow illuminating the road and first buildings. Shadows appeared at its edge, figures lurching into the light, the first one silver-haired.

'It's Alben,' Krelis boomed. 'Ropes,' he cried.

Men spread along the wall, Fidele pushing her way through them to see.

Alben stopped, pulling the man behind him on – a big man, tall, gangly, his limbs looking oddly stretched and out of proportion, somehow. Alben shoved him on, then turned and faced the darkness. The man he'd helped staggered out of the light, across the street and slammed into the wall, Fidele feeling the vibration of it. A handful of Alben's men appeared running to the wall, shouting up at the onlookers.

Krelis unfurled a rope over the side and tied it off. It creaked as someone began to climb.

Other figures spilt from the alley, Fidele searching desperately for Maquin. One man staggered and fell to his knees, was grabbed and pulled up and on. Two men, three. A dark shadow blotted out the torch for a moment and Fidele blinked.

What was that? Then it was gone.

Hands appeared over the wall, Krelis grabbing an arm and pulling one of Alben's warriors up. He was soaked with sweat, breathing hard, clothing torn, blood welling from many cuts, but he did not pause, instead leaned back over the wall, calling to the figure behind him.

A head appeared, a shock of jet hair upon a pale face, all sharp angles, flat planes and small black eyes. Wisps of a straggly beard grew from his chin.

It is a giant.

Men swore around her, swords grating, spearpoints lunging.

'No!' Alben's warrior yelled, stepping before the emerging giant with his arms wide, protective.

'He is our prisoner. Alben ordered that he is not to be harmed.' He helped the giant over the wall. *I recognize him.* Then she remembered where from. *The riverbank; Lykos' prisoner.*

'Where is his mother?' Fidele said into the shocked silence.

'Down there,' the warrior said.

Fidele stared back into the street, then she saw Maquin. He was standing with his back to her, though she recognized his form, the way he moved. He had stopped with Alben on the far side of the street, both of them trading blows with enemies in the shadows. Sparks grated, then Maquin and Alben were retreating, moving deeper into the street, Vin Thalun spilling out of the alley about them. Three, four, five of the enemy, more voices yelling beyond the torchlight. Fidele's heart lurched in her chest.

Alben's men were starting to reach the top of the wall, one flopping over, another close behind.

'Spears,' Peritus called.

Maquin and Alben were standing before the torch now, legs

bent, a weapon in each hand. Vin Thalun were circling them, at least half a dozen, hanging back. Bodies littered the floor. Then Maquin did the unthinkable. He charged them. Fidele heard herself shout his name, saw him wade into the warriors, who were instinctively flinching away from him. He spun amongst them, leaving in his wake trailing arcs of black blood. For a moment Alben stood frozen, then he followed Maquin and hurled himself at the enemy.

For a few heartbeats she thought they were going to do it. Men were falling or staggering away, Maquin and Alben in constant movement, death-dealing wraiths, but then more Vin Thalun appeared from the alleys. The sound of marching feet sounded in the street, yet more running up from their fires by the main gates. Maquin took a blow on the shoulder, staggering him. Alben was hit in the back and he dropped to one knee, another blow sending him sprawling to the ground. Maquin stood over his fallen comrade, sword and knife black with blood, for a few moments holding back the enemy.

Fidele watched, praying to Elyon, her fist tight around the hilt of her knife. Peritus sighted with his spear and threw, his aim true. His spear struck a Vin Thalun through the chest, sending him crashing back. It did little good, though, more Vin Thalun crowding in upon Maquin and Alben.

Then another figure appeared from the darkness, broad and hulking.

The giantess.

She swung something in her hands, long and sinuous. A chain. It smashed into the figures crowding around Maquin and Alben, sent them flying like straw targets on the weapons court. Then the giantess was throwing Alben over her shoulder and running for the wall, Maquin retreating behind her.

Vin Thalun swarmed after them, but as soon as they were in range a hail of spears from the guards on the walls lacerated them. Those that didn't die scurried back to the shadows. Maquin was shouting from below and then Krelis and a dozen men were tugging on the rope. The giantling loaned his strength and weight, pulling with all his might. The rope creaked, strained and moved.

Alben appeared first, still slumped across the giantess' shoulder. Hands pulled him onto the walkway, then the giantess was over,

Maquin behind her. Fidele pushed her way through the milling warriors to Maquin. He was close to Alben, shouting for help. At her voice his eyes snapped onto her. His hand reached out and squeezed her tight.

'Told you . . . I'd come back,' he said, still breathing hard.

More Vin Thalun were in the street, but they kept a healthy distance. Then a face appeared amongst them that she would never forget.

Lykos.

He stood there as still as stone, looking at the wall. His eyes fixed on the giantess, a combination of rage and fear twisting his features. Then he saw her.

Her blood felt as if it turned to ice as terror struck her, her freedom, the escape, all she had endured and conquered during her flight to Ripa suddenly forgotten. A hundred memories flooded back, jumbling her mind, all of Lykos, his voice, his eyes, his breath, his touch. Then a hot rage swept through her. They stood there staring at one another, then he stepped back into the shadows and was gone.

Fidele marched through the corridors of Ripa's tower, Maquin at her side.

He had told her of Balara, of finding the Vin Thalun and giants. Of the decision to take them. And of their flight through Sarva.

'I don't know how the Vin Thalun found us so quickly. Perhaps someone escaped Balara, or they visited there soon after we'd left. Whatever it was, we knew we were being tracked by sunset of the next day. Alben led us deeper into the forest. We tried to lose them,' Maquin had said.

'How did you manage to do that with two captive giants?'

'They cooperated,' Maquin said, something in the tone of his voice shifting.

'I saw that. The giantess helped you save Alben – fought beside you and carried Alben to safety.'

'Aye.'

'That's unusual.' She looked at him.

'Aye, it is.' He shrugged. 'Alben spoke to them in giantish. He would not tell me what he said. Whatever it was, he must have been very convincing.'

'Indeed. Giantish? That doesn't sound like the Alben I know.'

'There's more to him than herbs and poultices.'

'Yes, clearly. I think I'm going to pay these giant prisoners a visit.'

'I'll come with you.'

'You should be resting,' Fidele had said.

'If you think I'm letting you walk alone into a room with two giants in it then you're mistaken.'

'I have guards,' she had said, adding, 'when I request them.'

He had just ignored her and finished slipping his knives into their various homes about his body.

Two guards stood outside Alben's chamber in the belly of the tower, only a floor or two above Ektor's rooms. They did not try to deny Fidele entry to the giants' chamber, one of them dragging a huge deadbolt open and unlatching the door. They nodded respectfully to Maquin as he walked behind Fidele.

He is gaining a reputation amongst the warriors of Ripa.

The chamber was large, a row of shuttered windows high along one wall, chiselled through the rock to allow sunlight and fresh air in. Candles flickered in the salty breeze, the cry of gulls was loud and mournful.

Alben was there, sitting in a chair before a wide table. The two giants were with him, the giantess sitting on the far side, her son lying upon a thick-mattressed cot. They all looked at Fidele and Maquin as they entered the room.

'I am Fidele,' she said to the giants, ignoring Alben, 'once Queen to Tenebral's King, and now regent in my son Nathair's stead.'

The giantess regarded her impassively with small dark eyes. Her face was pale with a sharp nose and high angular cheekbones. She was muscular beyond belief, wearing a mixture of leather and animal skins. Her wrist was red and scabbed, and Fidele remembered the iron chain that the giantess had wielded in the dark, bound at her wrist with an iron collar. *Gone now.* Tattooed thorns spiralled about her right wrist, curling around her forearm and disappearing into a sleeve.

'Can you speak the common tongue?' Fidele asked.

'I speak a little of your tongue. Enough.' Her voice was like gravel sliding across granite.

'You are mother and son?' Fidele asked, looking at the giantling, who was still lying upon his cot, but he had propped himself up on one elbow and was watching with interest.

'Yes.'

'What are your names?'

The giantess' eyes flickered to her son, then back to Fidele.

'I am Raina. My son is Tain.'

'And what clan are you?'

'We are of the Kurgan.' As she said it, something crossed her face. *Longing?* It was hard to read. Her son tugged at his wispy moustache. It was a surprisingly old gesture on his young features, like an infant copying his grandfather.

'Why did Lykos hold you prisoner?'

At the mention of the Vin Thalun's name Raina snarled, fists bunching, and for a moment she was savagely feral, more animal than human. She did not answer, just glared at Fidele.

Fidele sighed, recognizing some of that pain and rage. 'How long have you been his prisoner?'

The fire dimmed in Raina's eyes. She shook her head. 'I do not know. A long time. I tried to count the moons, but they faded, blurred into one another.'

'Eight years,' another voice said. Tain, from his cot. His voice was flat, emotionless, a rasp to its edges.

'Alben tells me that you are our prisoners. Yet I see no chains of iron, no collars or bonds. And last night, you seemed willingly to climb our wall and enter this fortress. You *fought* beside our warriors.'

'For which I thank you,' Maquin said, nodding to Raina. He was leaning against a wall where he could see both Raina and Tain.

'You are welcome, little man,' Raina said with a twitch of her lips. 'Ones that fight so fearlessly should not be left to die in the street.'

'I thank you for that, too,' Fidele said. 'But my question still stands. How is it that you are not bound? That you did not take advantage of the flight to Ripa and flee your new captors? How is it that you fought with us?'

'Your healer is persuasive,' Raina said.

Fidele turned her stern eyes upon Alben. 'You speak giantish, then. How is that?'

'I am a healer, which required that I also became scholar. There is much to learn, and more is written in the scrolls I have read than how to make a poultice or boil a herb.' He shrugged.

'So what did you say to them, that so convinced them to become such willing prisoners?'

Alben looked from Raina to Tain.

'I told her that if she did not cooperate I would kill her son.'

Fidele blinked at that, then looked at him long and hard. He returned her gaze flatly, displaying no emotion.

I don't believe you. She did not think the Alben she knew would resort to threats, but more than that, there appeared to be something between Alben and the giantess, not quite a familiarity, but they both seemed . . . comfortable with each other.

The door suddenly slammed open, Krelis bursting in, Ektor in his shadow. Raina and Tain leaped to their feet, Raina stepping in front of Tain.

Krelis looked from face to face, paused with his mouth open.

'We've been looking for you,' Ektor said to Fidele. 'Marcellin is come.'

CHAPTER FORTY-EIGHT

ULFILAS

The feast-hall of Dun-Kellen rang out with the clack of wooden swords. Ulfilas sat at a long table beside King Jael, who was leaning forward in his chair, head propped upon a fist. They were watching a pair of men swinging hard blows at one another. They were good: fast, strong, both veterans and evenly matched.

'Are they better than you?' Jael asked him.

Ulfilas shrugged. 'Maybe. They are skilled, no doubt. Sword-crossing in practice is different from a real fight, though.' *In the sword-crossing ring not only do you have to win, but you have to make it look good. You can't bite a nose off, or twist someone's stones. In a real fight, though, all that counts is walking away alive.*

It had been Maquin who had told him that, shieldman to Kastell, Jael's cousin. He'd liked both of them, Maquin a little more than Kastell. They'd both been good men to share a cup of ale with. That hadn't stopped him from standing by and doing nothing as Jael had put a sword through Kastell's belly, though. Or made him feel bad about it.

We all choose the life we lead. We all know it'll likely end in blood. Don't see so many grey-haired warriors as you do smiths or tanners or fishermen.

'Aye, that's true. Perhaps I should take away their wooden toys and let them fight with iron.'

'You'd end up with dead shieldmen, my King, and in these days good shieldmen that are sworn to you are better alive than dead.'

'Huh,' Jael grudgingly agreed. 'I need a first-sword. Are you not tempted to enter?'

Ulfilas shrugged again. 'If you wish me to, my King. I am happy as your shieldman and captain of your honour guard.'

'That would not change, if you were to win this little tournament,' Jael said. 'You'd just be busier.' He flashed a grin. 'But I need the best sword in Isiltir at my side. I have enemies, and they will try to bring me down.'

'Most of your enemies are dead, my lord.' Ulfilas glanced out of the open doors of the feast-hall. Late summer's heat was lingering. He could just make out the iron spikes that decorated the courtyard, a series of heads in various degrees of decomposition adorning them.

'I wish that were so,' Jael said. 'My enemies fill the shadows, biding their time.' He pinched the bridge of his nose, squeezed his eyes closed. 'I dream of them,' he said quietly. He shook his head. 'Enemies are like rats, Jael: leave them alone too long and they will breed and multiply. Enemies don't need culling, they need exterminating, to the last bairn of their bloodlines.'

A philosophy you have committed yourself to wholeheartedly.

'Which is why I need the best sword in Isiltir at my side, not hired by my enemies and coming for me. So, if you are the best sword in the realm, I would like to know.'

'Then I shall enter your tournament, my King.'

Jael nodded, eyes fixed on the two men duelling in front of him. One was retreating before an onslaught of looping blows. The one retreating stumbled; his opponent, sensing victory, stepped in quickly.

Too soon, Ulfilas thought.

The warrior who had stumbled dropped to one knee, straightened his arm and drove the wooden sword beneath the raised weapon of his opponent letting the man run onto his blade.

Even the most skilled can be defeated by a well-timed ruse.

'Hah, nicely done,' Jael cried out, clapping.

Beyond the open doors hooves clattered on the flagstones of the courtyard. A few moments later Ulfilas and Jael were approached by a messenger from King Nathair.

The rider appeared travel stained and weary, the eagle of Tenebral upon his leather cuirass dusty and faded. He presented Jael with a scroll and stood quietly by as Jael opened it and read.

'We will have to finish my tournament in Mikil,' Jael said. 'Tell your King I shall be honoured to host the meeting there. A moon from this day.'

The messenger nodded.

'Tell me, to whom else has this request gone out?'

'Gundul of Carnutan and Lothar of Helveth, my lord.'

'Very good. You are welcome to eat and drink with us, stay and rest.'

'My orders are to return to King Nathair with your response, my lord, but some food and a fresh horse would be welcomed.'

'Of course,' Jael said with a wave of his hand and watched as the man was led away.

'Mikil?' Ulfilas asked.

'It appears that our high king wishes to hold a council of war with his allies. He has asked that we meet him at Mikil.'

'High king,' Ulfilas grumbled. 'There has been no high king in the Banished Lands since Sokar and the fleet of Exiles set foot upon these shores.'

'I must go,' Jael snapped.

Ulfilas frowned. *What hold does Nathair have over him?*

'High king is a tradition more than a reality, true,' Jael said, calmer. 'But Nathair is an ally. Without him I doubt that Isiltir would be mine, or in fact that I'd still be breathing. Or you, for that matter. It was a close thing, that day on the bridge. Nearly ended with our heads out there, not Gerda's and her cronies.'

Ulfilas remembered. They had been hard pressed, close to breaking, and then he had seen the black ships on the river.

'Aye. But still. We need him no longer. Best he keep his nose out of Isiltir's affairs.'

Jael laughed. 'Hah, you are a true patriot, Ulfilas. But I will not make more enemies when there are already so many of them to choose from. No, we will go to Mikil, and see what our high king has to say.'

A hand touched Ulfilas' shoulder and he jumped, half-standing from his chair and reaching for his sword.

It was Dag, Jael's huntsman, and rapidly becoming Jael's spymaster, as well. He was clearly good at creeping.

'Don't do that,' Ulfilas muttered.

'You must come,' Dag said to them both. 'It is urgent.'

'What is it?' Ulfilas asked.

'A messenger has come.'

'It is the season for them, it would seem,' Jael remarked. 'What messenger?'

'A giant. One of the Jotun. He has news.'

Jael stood without another word and followed Dag to the rear of the hall, Ulfilas following and gathering a dozen shieldmen along the way. He knew Jael's talk of enemies was more than just paranoia.

They wound down a wide spiral staircase into a twilight world of flickering torches and damp, dripping walls. Dag led them through the bowels of Dun Kellen. Ulfilas glanced down a side corridor, recognized it as the one that led to the cell where Gramm's grandchildren were kept under guard.

Dag led them on until they stood before the thick iron-banded door that opened into the escape tunnel, the one that Haelan had fled through, leaving Maquin and Orgull to hold it. He remembered that sight, the two of them gore-spattered, a mound of the dead clogging the corridor. Dark stains still patched the cold stone.

Dag pulled a huge key from his belt and unlocked the door, opening it with a rusty creak. Jael and the others filed through, lighting torches from a burning sconce, only the echo of their feet and the sound of their breathing magnified in this ancient tunnel.

They walked a long time, the silence about them suffocating.

'How did you come by those scars?' Ulfilas asked Dag, more to break the oppressively monotonous silence than out of any real desire to know.

'Wife,' Dag grunted. 'She came off worse.'

Ulfilas couldn't imagine much worse than Dag's disfigured features.

'I wouldn't want to meet her in the dark, then.'

'Not much chance of that,' Dag said. 'I killed her.'

Ulfilas stopped asking questions after that. His mouth was dry and his belly rumbling by the time they came to a set of stone steps. Night had fallen when they emerged into a ruined room, crumbling stone all about them, apparently held together by a thick tapestry of cobwebs.

Dag led them through an archway and into woodland, the treetops swaying and rustling in a breeze, making shadows dance. Then something moved in the darkness, an impenetrable shadow, huge, like a tree come to life. It growled, and Ulfilas reached for his sword, stepping in front of Jael as the other warriors spread protectively around their King.

'Peace,' Jael said, resting a hand upon Ulfilas' arm, then Ulfilas realized what it was.

A bear, a giant sitting upon it in a high-backed saddle.

'Well met, Ildaer,' Jael said.

The giant swung a leg and slipped to the ground, his blond braided hair and thick moustache appearing like silver in the starlight. He gripped a long spear in one hand, a double-bladed axe was strapped to his saddle. Two other forms shambled out of the darkness – more bear-riders, one of them female, her chin and lip hairless, appearing strangely fine-boned amidst all the lumps of muscle and bone. The three giants repulsed Ulfilas. He tried to keep his face impassive as he looked at them.

'We have found your runaway bairn,' Ildaer grated. He glowered down at Jael.

'Where?'

'What is this information worth to you?'

'All that I promised. Every Jotun artefact found within Isiltir.'

'That is not enough.'

Jael tensed at that. Ulfilas doubted that anyone else could tell, but he had known him so long. An inflection crept into his voice, a shift in his posture.

'What else do you want?'

'Land. South of the river.'

Jael looked up at Ildaer, the giant taller than any man there.

'How much land?'

'Enough for three hundred of my kin, and our bears.'

'That's a lot of land.'

'Your Isiltir has a lot to spare.'

'Agreed,' Jael said. 'Though I will choose the land.'

'We must both agree,' Ildaer said.

Jael looked between the three giants, then slowly nodded.

'Where is Haelan?' he asked.

Ildaer looked over his shoulder, at the female giant.

'Ilska and her bear found him. He is at Gramm's hold.'

Jael stood silent a moment.

Gramm's! And we have his grandchildren. How did he not give the child up? He will regret that more than ever, now.

'You are sure?' Jael asked, his mouth a straight line.

He is angry now. If true then Gramm has played him for a fool. Gramm will not die quickly.

The giantess whispered something and her bear lumbered forwards. Ulfilas resisted the sudden urge to take an equal number of steps backwards.

'I saw him,' the giantess said. 'Creach smelt him.'

'Creach?'

She patted the thick neck of the bear she was sitting upon. It raised its head, making a deep rumbling sound. 'Creach,' she repeated.

Jael shook his head. 'Old fool,' he muttered. 'Gramm's time is over. Help me take the boy from him, and his hold is yours, if you want it.'

Ildaer made a strange noise, like two boulders grinding, his shoulders shaking. Ulfilas realized he was laughing. 'Agreed, little King.' He grunted something in giantish to the giants behind him and their laughter joined his. It was unsettling.

'Wait here one day for me. I will make arrangements.'

Ildaer grunted and Jael turned and walked away. Ulfilas took one last look at the giants and then followed his King.

They walked in silence back to the ruined building in the wood. As they passed into the embrace of the crumbling stone Ulfilas voiced the question that had been on his mind since they'd left the giants.

'Why do they want it?'

'Want what?' Jael asked.

'Land.'

'Fertile land, perhaps. The chance to grow, to sow and reap. You've seen the Desolation. It's . . . desolate.' Men laughed at that. 'In truth, Ulfilas, it doesn't matter. I get Haelan, and in return they get something that is no hardship to give. And better. The Jotun will now be gathered where I can see them. Keep your friends close . . .'

And your enemies closer.

Dag paused at the trapdoor to the tunnel. He was frowning.

'What's wrong?' Jael asked him impatiently.

Dag knelt and studied the ground before the trapdoor. 'Someone's been here.'

They drew their swords and stepped into the corridor cautiously. The torch was still burning. Dag took it from its sconce and studied the ground again.

'Men have passed this way – see, footprints overlying ours.'

'How many?' Jael asked him.

'Hard to tell. Not many. Maybe only one. No more than three.'

They sped along the corridor, buckles and shirts of mail clanking, Ulfilas' breath loud in his own head. Finally they reached the doorway into Dun Kellen and slowed, Dag still leading.

Further along they found blood trailing into a side corridor. Ulfilas had a sick feeling in the pit of his stomach and knew what they were going to find before they saw two dead guards and the door open to the cell of Gramm's grandchildren. The guards were stripped of their livery – cuirasses with Jael's sigil and red cloaks.

Jael's face whitened, first with fear, then a cold rage.

'Dag, take a score of men and find them,' he said, fury lurking in the depths of his voice. 'Ulfilas, take two hundred swords and ride to Gramm's. Take Ildaer with you.'

'What of you, my King?'

'I cannot come. I have to be in Mikil in less than a moon. It would take almost that to ride to Gramm's hold. You will have to do this work for me.'

Ulfilas went to hurry away but Jael reached out and grabbed his arm.

'You understand the import of this?'

'I do,' Ulfilas said.

'My crown rests upon finding that child.'

'I will find him, my King. What would you have me do with him – bring him in chains before you?'

'The only part of Haelan that I am interested in seeing is his head. Bring that to me so that I can display it beside his mother's; leave the rest of him at Gramm's, the crows are welcome to him.'

CHAPTER FORTY-NINE

CAMLIN

Camlin smiled at the reunion between Edana and Halion. They hugged as tightly as kin, Edana laughing, then crying, and then laughing some more. Halion's grin was so wide it looked as if his face would split. Camlin left them to it. *I need to talk to someone.* He took himself for a walk around the perimeter of the encampment, though calling it that was over-generous. Disorganized and sprawling was closer to the truth.

Won't be good if Braith leads a few score warriors in here. Pendathran had guards spread around the camp and deeper into the marshes, but the encampment was becoming unguardable. Shacks had been made out of anything handy – walls latticed out of willow and alder, packed with mud. But they were everywhere, along the lake's shore, amongst stands of trees, spreading up the banks of streams. And there were dozens of those feeding into the lake. Any one of them could become a line of entry for Braith. He looked around with a growing tension filling his chest. *It'd be a bloodbath.*

Braith. The time at the tower had been a day of shocks, and no denying. *Didn't think I'd be seeing him again. Last time I saw him he was poisoned, had a hole in him and was falling into the sea. How did he survive?* He felt a worm of fear wriggling deep in his belly. Braith was a formidable enemy, a fine woodsman and a man who made it his business to resolve all grudges. *Those qualities combined do not make the future that attractive.*

You could leave. Run. As far away and as fast as you can. You know he's going to be coming for you. He sighed at the voice in his head. *I'm long past running from this crew. But we found our way back easy enough, and that was rowing blind, and like madmen.*

They'd rowed and poled and rowed like Asroth was snapping at their heels when they'd fled Evnis and Morcant, roping their boats together and carrying on well after dark. Meg said she knew the general direction of Dun Crin if not the exact waterways, and Camlin trusted her enough, while Drust was too exhausted to care. Five days later they'd rowed into the lake that covered most of Dun Crin, and Camlin noted that Drust had not bothered to insist on blindfolds.

Probably because none of us knew where we were, but there it is. Maybe there is some trust growing after all.

He heard a rustling in the undergrowth.

'Might as well come on out, Meg.'

There was a silence for a moment, while Meg thought about it, most likely. Then her red hair appeared and she skipped up to him.

Can't say that I'm too fond of bairns, but this one's been handy. And she's not such bad company. Doesn't talk a lot, at least, which I'll count as a blessing.

'What's going t'happen?' Meg asked him.

He thought about lying to her, but then he remembered where he'd found her, and what she'd already seen.

'They're going to kill us, or we're going to kill them. Can't see any other answer to it than that.' *And there's a lot more of them than us. Maybe I won't tell her that bit.*

'Morcant's going to find us.'

'If we stay here he will.'

She chewed her lip and shuffled her feet.

'He'd have killed me already, if it wasn't for your help, girlie. Think I owe you one.'

She grinned at that and he ruffled her hair. Then he saw who he'd been looking for.

'Be a darling and go and get me something to eat,' he asked her. As she scampered off he called after her. 'Nothing too slimy – grilled fish'll do me fine.' Then he turned and strode after Vonn.

They'd shared a boat for two days but it had been too cramped to talk. *Too many ears for what I've got to say.*

Vonn was standing in the shadows of a draping willow, looking at the lake.

Looks as if he's thinking about the same things as I am.

Vonn heard Camlin coming and turned to wait for him.

'Why'd you do it?' Camlin asked him. *No point beating about the bush.*

'Do what?' Vonn said after a long, indrawn breath.

'You know what. Evnis. I had a clear shot. Could've ended a world of trouble; could've ended him, and bought some well-deserved vengeance for Edana. He killed her da, remember? We all saw it.'

Vonn stared at him angrily, Camlin almost hearing a host of different answers lining up and being tried out in the young warrior's head. In the end Vonn's shoulders slumped and he dropped his eyes.

'I don't know,' he whispered.

Honest? Maybe.

'I don't believe you,' Camlin said, making sure his voice was cold, hard.

Vonn's head snapped up at that. A tear streaked his cheek.

'Believe what you wish,' Vonn hissed. 'As I looked at him I wanted to leap out of the boat and put my sword through his heart . . .' His face twisted between anger and pain, another tear rolling down his cheek. 'He betrayed everything I loved and valued. He's the reason my Bethan's dead. I *hate* him.'

Camlin stared at him a long time, willow branches stirring about them. *You don't sound as convincing as you did in Domhain. In fact, you sound as if you're trying to convince yourself.*

'That so?'

'Aye.'

'Then I'll ask you again. Why'd you stop me?'

'I don't know,' Vonn whispered. 'Maybe I want to be the one that does it. Maybe I had a weak moment – he is my da. Maybe . . .' He shook his head. 'I just don't know.'

Another silence stretched between them.

I'm inclined t'believe him. Either way, I'd not want him at my shoulder in a fight against Evnis. He doesn't know his own heart. How can I trust him when he doesn't trust himself?

Meg pushed her way through the trailing branches of the willow and offered a wrapped leaf to Camlin. He took it and sniffed. Then smiled. Grilled trout. He took a bite and realized how hungry he was.

A voice hailed them from the lakeshore – Baird, helping Edana into a boat.

Time for another meeting.

Camlin gave Vonn one last look.

'Are you going to tell Edana?' Vonn asked.

Don't know yet.

Camlin said nothing and walked away.

Camlin assumed his customary place in what he'd come to think of as their council chambers, though it was decorated with creeping vines and birds' nests in the broken rafters. Halion now stood behind Edana, back in his position as her first-sword. Baird and Vonn stood beside him and Camlin eyed Vonn suspiciously.

Drust and Pendathran were there, as well as Roisin and Lorcan, whose eyes kept drifting to Edana. Roisin sat beside Pendathran and, as Camlin watched them, Roisin leaned close to the battlechief and whispered in his ear. He laughed.

'Congratulations on a successful mission,' Edana said. 'And I am overjoyed to have my first-sword back at my side.'

Halion dipped his head at that. Camlin had been surprised at the depth of emotion he'd felt at seeing Halion alive. It felt good to have a friend back, and also it was nice to have something good happen, a balance for the trail of the dead they seemed to leave along the way.

Having Halion back filled Camlin with a new sense of hope, but the other edge to that blade was the knowledge that Braith was alive and had tracked Halion almost all the way to Dun Crin.

Probably would have, if Evnis hadn't stood up and started shouting. Won't stop Braith finding us, though, will only slow him down a little. And give me a chance to prepare a welcome for him.

'It's good to have you with us,' Pendathran said. 'I for one would like to hear your tale.'

Halion spoke of all that had happened to him since the beach in Domhain. Of Rhin's questioning and Conall setting him free.

Roisin snorted at that. *Doesn't like the thought of Conall on her lad's throne.*

The rest was one long journey from Domhain to Ardan.

'You were followed,' Camlin said.

'I know that now,' Halion said with a shake of his head. 'I am ashamed to have led the enemy here. I don't know how they managed it – I am no stranger to the huntsman's arts, and did much to avoid pursuit.'

'Nothing you could do about it. It was Braith, and he could track a bird. He'll be here soon enough, with Evnis at his side.' Camlin looked at Vonn as he said the last part.

That set things off, like throwing fish oil on a fire. Voices all talking at once, some panicked, some planning. In the end Pendathran thumped a fist onto the table, making it jump.

'Let's talk this through right, or we'll still be clamouring when Rhin's warriors start shoving swords up our arses.'

'Let's have the facts,' Roisin said.

Good place to start.

Camlin stepped forward. 'The facts are that Evnis and Braith, who happens to be the best huntsman that draws breath, are out there, along with Morcant and a warband. They've built towers and beacons around this marsh. Put it all together, looks like they're going about ending this resistance sooner rather than later.'

More raised voices. Eventually Edana stood.

'There's only one chance for us,' she said. 'We have to leave.'

'And what? Just keep running?' That was Drust.

'No. It's time to gather allies. There are more loyal warriors in Ardan, Narvon and Domhain than are here with us right now. We must give them somewhere to rally to.'

'Aye, and how are we going to do that?' Pendathran asked in his gruff voice.

'We're not as strong as our enemy, don't have their strength of numbers, so we have to be cleverer than them.'

'Pendathran,' Roisin said, 'your experience of battle is greater than any other here. What do you say?'

'Makes sense,' Pendathran said. 'This war won't get won by sitting on our arses. Options are few, as they're going to be coming in here and stabbing us.' He nodded thoughtfully. 'Time to move out.'

'We don't have to make things easy for them, though.' Edana looked at Camlin as she said that.

I'm liking this girl more'n more.

There was a fluttering from above and a big black bird crashed onto their table.

'*Edana*,' it squawked. '*Edana, Edana.*'

There was a moment's silence, all of them looking on in shock and surprise.

'Craf!' Edana cried.

CHAPTER FIFTY

CYWEN

'Drink this,' Cywen said to the man sitting before her. His name was Gorsedd and he was on the ship's deck, back to a rail, pale-faced and gritting his teeth against the pain. His arm was purpling already, a shard of bone poking through flesh a handspan above his wrist. With his good hand he sipped at Cywen's flask. Buddai lay against the rail, snoring through the whole thing.

He was one of the villagers who had joined them during their flight through Narvon; he'd been stacking barrels below decks, unused to the pitching of a ship at sea. There'd been an accident. Pax the oarsman – Atilius' son – had heard him screaming and helped him onto the top deck.

Where's Brina? The old healer had told Cywen to prepare Gorsedd for resetting his broken bone, which mostly meant filling him up with seed of the poppy.

'Another sip,' she said to Gorsedd, and with a wince he complied.

Pax was standing to one side, watching. He looked almost as pale as the man with the broken arm. Cywen swayed as the ship rode another swell, the one huge sail tight and snapping in the wind. They'd been at sea for two days now, early the first day leaving the sluggish marsh river behind and entering a wide bay that they'd continued to row through, the sea tame and relatively docile. The second day they had rowed into open sea, skirting the coast. A strong wind had almost immediately caught them and Dath had yelled for their sail to be unfurled. The wind had freed them all from the oar-benches, at first everyone relieved and thankful, but after half a day on the open sea over a score of people had lined the ship's rails, vomiting into the slate-grey and foam-speckled waves. Cywen had been one of them. She'd sailed across the straits between Ardan and Domhain with no problem, but this sea was another beast entirely, as different as a wild horse from one broken to ride. She'd hardly seen Dath as he hadn't left his post on deck since they'd left the wide-mouthed river estuary and entered the sea. Fortunately a good dozen of the oarsmen had worked on a ship's crew before, and so Cywen was vaguely confident that they had the skill required to avoid sinking by incompetence. That was something.

'Come on, then,' Brina said, appearing suddenly and squatting down beside Gorsedd, one hand on his shoulder, the other about his elbow. She looked into Cywen's eyes.

'You ready for this?'

More than he is, Cywen thought. She took a deep breath and nodded, then wound a leather cord around Gorsedd's wrist. She gritted her teeth and pulled.

Gorsedd screamed.

No amount of poppy milk can dull that pain.

The bone sank back into flesh, like a shattered ship sinking into the sea. *Why am I thinking of ships sinking.* Cywen tugged harder, waiting for the click that Brina had told her would signal that it had settled back into its proper place. Sweat dripped into her eyes. She glanced up at Brina, willing her to say that it was done.

Brina didn't, just held on to Gorsedd's elbow.

The leather cord slipped in Cywen's hand, the bone poking through flesh again.

'Rest a moment,' Brina said. 'Dry your hands. Try again.'

Cywen released the cord as gently as she could, Gorsedd howling, eyes rolling.

'You could lend a hand, as you've time to stand around watching,' Brina snapped at Pax. He winced but nodded, looking more scared of Brina than the blood and bone oozing from the injured man's arm.

'Can I help?' a grating voice said above and behind. The giantling Laith looked curiously over her shoulder at the wound. Buddai wagged his tail at Laith's voice, though he seemed to otherwise still be asleep.

Cywen smiled and Pax looked relieved. Brina explained to Laith what she had to do.

Laith gripped the cord and looked to Brina for the nod.

'Don't pull his arm off,' Brina said. 'Slow and steady.'

'Slow and steady,' Laith repeated. Then she pulled.

The bone disappeared, sliding smoothly back into the wound. Laith made it look as easy as stretching dough for bread.

'You have to go further than the break,' Brina said, 'then it should slot into place. You'll feel it.'

Laith's face was knotted with concentration. She continued to pull, then she smiled.

'I felt it,' she said and let go of the cord.

Gorsedd sagged in their arms.

'You know what to do,' Brina said, then stood and walked away. Her hand was pressed tightly to her side, the outline of the giant book clear under her cloak.

Cywen frowned as she watched Brina leave, then groaning from Gorsedd drew her attention. She washed out the wound, drizzled it with honey, gave him some more poppy milk, then pulled out her fish-hook and thread ready to stitch the wound. She couldn't hold his arm still for the rocking of the ship. She looked to Laith but she was playing with Buddai, completely oblivious to Cywen now.

She has a short attention span.

'Here,' said Pax, and he took Gorsedd's arm.

Cywen began her work, stitching it loose to allow it to drain, then bandaging it. As she did, her eyes wandered to Pax. He was fine featured, high cheekbones on a tanned face, close-cropped hair and stubble for a beard. And bright blue eyes. There was something in them, a haunted look that seeped from them. Something niggled at Cywen about him. Something missing.

'Where's your warrior braid?' Cywen asked him.

His eyes touched hers and then looked away.

'Lykos cut it off.' His hand rose to a ragged tail of hair.

'Why?' Cywen was horrified at the thought.

'Did it to all of us on our first day at the oar-bench. Said we were less than men, let alone warriors. He gave me this, as well.' He pulled up his linen sleeve and twisted to show her a circular lump of sliver flesh, a burn-scar. Part of it was scabbed and weeping a mixture of blood and pus. 'His mark, to show me as his property.'

'Why's it bleeding?'

His face twisted, part shame, part embarrassment. 'I tried to cut it off. I couldn't; it hurt too much.'

Laith laughed at that from over with Buddai. 'I am not surprised,' she said, laughing some more.

This giant lacks any sense of sympathy.

Pax scowled.

'Here, let me clean it for you.' Cywen asked Laith to take Gorsedd to his cot.

'After,' she said. 'I like your puppy.'

Puppy! Buddai's big as a pony. The hound did look smaller, though, beside Laith. The giantling was on her hands and knees, hiding her face in her arms. Buddai was slapping at Laith's arms with a paw, then digging to reveal Laith's face. The giant laughed and rolled onto her back, Buddai licking her face.

Cywen dabbed at Pax's wound with salt water. He winced but he did not pull away.

'You're sister to Corban, aren't you?' Pax said.

'Aye,' Cywen muttered, scrubbing the scab away, applying pressure to squeeze all of the pus out of the wound, and then bathing it in a salve that Brina had prepared. 'What of it?' She glanced up at Pax and saw a new look creeping over his face. Awe.

'He's going to kill Lykos.'

'Is he?' Cywen asked.

'Aye. Lykos is evil, sure as the sky is blue. If there is an Asroth then Lykos serves him. And Corban's the Bright Star – everyone says it. And look around: giants – Balur One-Eye stepping out of the faery tales. Jehar – they are the greatest warriors that have ever lived. A wolven as his guardian.' He shook his head. 'And he set us free.' Something like adoration was in his eyes now. 'Lykos tried to break me, made me less than a man.'

Are you old enough to be a man?

'At first I did not believe we were free, thought it some twisted ruse for Lykos' pleasure. Then, when I knew we *were* free, all I wanted to do was find somewhere to be alone, to live in peace, away from it all. To hide. But now, after listening to what your brother said, who he is. He will kill Lykos, he will win this war, and I will follow him.' He was grinning at Cywen now, nodding fervently.

'Well, I'm glad to hear that,' Cywen said, not really knowing what to say.

He's talking about my brother. Ban, whom I used to push into puddles. 'You're done,' she said, standing. 'Keep it clean. And don't try to cut it off again.'

Laith laughed at that, then she hoisted Gorsedd to his feet and carried the injured man to his cot. Pax nodded his thanks to Cywen and stood, hovering.

'Tell your brother . . .' he mumbled. 'Tell him us oarsmen, we owe him. And love him. He set us free.'

'Tell him yourself,' Cywen said. 'Here he is now.'

Corban was walking along the deck, his wolven pelt pulled across his shoulders.

It is colder, suddenly, and this wind finds every gap there is.

Storm padded at Corban's side. Her coat was slick with sea-spray, the markings that streaked her torso darker now they were wet. Thick muscle rippled along her chest and flanks as she walked beside Corban, her head almost as high as his chest.

She's still growing.

Storm padded over and nuzzled Cywen, almost pushing her over. Pax took an involuntary step back. Cywen stroked the coarse fur of the wolven's muzzle. As she looked closer she noticed a host of scars latticing Storm's head and body, silvery stripes where fur no longer grew, one ear ragged and frayed. *The last few years have given us all scars, of one nature or another.*

Storm saw Buddai and bounded over to him, a cub again.

'Cy,' said Corban, smiling. He looked to Pax. The young man mumbled something unintelligible and left.

'He thinks you a hero,' Cywen said.

'Then he's wrong,' Corban replied. 'I'm sure you told him.'

Cywen grinned. 'I'm starting to think of you as a bit of a hero, myself. Even if it wasn't so long ago that I used to tell Mam on you for wiping your nose on my cloak.'

'I can always count on you.' He smiled. 'Walk with me.'

The two of them picked their way along the deck, a companionable silence settling between them.

'I'm sorry – I've wanted to see more of you,' Corban said.

Cywen shrugged. 'There's a lot to be done, I imagine.'

'Huh.' Corban snorted.

'You have to learn to delegate. Learn from Brina.'

He laughed at that, something that he'd done rarely of late, she realized, seeing him.

'I've done better, I've asked her to delegate for me.'

'I know.' She paused, wondering whether to speak her mind. Then she did. 'I'm worried about Brina,' she said.

'What?'

'She's different.'

'What, you mean grumpier?'

'No, not really. If anything, less grumpy, less sarcastic.'

'And that's something to worry about?'

'Aye. She seems less *interested*.'

'That doesn't sound like her. If anything she's too interested in everyone else's business.' He said it with an affectionate smile.

'Exactly. It's out of character. At first I thought she was ill, but it's not that. She just has no interest in anything. Except her book.'

'The giant book?' Corban asked.

'Aye. She doesn't know I've seen her, but she sneaks away to read it. And she won't let me look at it any more.'

Corban frowned. 'I don't like the sound of that. After Heb . . .' He fell silent, lost in a memory. 'She grieved hard. But I thought she came through it, in the end. As much as any of us do.' He glanced at Cywen. 'I'll try and do something . . .'

Laughter rang out from above and they both looked up. Figures were climbing in the rigging about the sail. After a moment Cywen realized it was Dath and Kulla.

'I think she likes Dath,' Cywen said.

'I think so too. The only person that doesn't seem to have noticed is Dath.'

Ha. Cywen laughed to herself. *I could say the same about you, brother.*

They watched Dath climb through the rigging, swinging between ropes, moving like a monkey through the treetops.

'For a coward he can be ridiculously brave,' Cywen observed.

'Dath's no coward,' Corban said. 'He just screams louder than the rest of us, that's all.'

Another silence settled between them.

'Where are we sailing to, Corban?'

'Drassil.'

'And then what?'

'War. An end to all of this.'

Aye. But whose end?

'It seems to me a great deal is being asked of you, little brother.'

'Asked of us all,' Corban said. 'And I agree. If ever I meet Elyon the All-Father face to face, I'll have a few things to say to him.'

Me too.

They stared out over the ocean. The sea stretched into the horizon, a foam-flecked world of grey and green, shimmering beneath a hard blue sky.

'We're leaving summer behind us,' Corban observed.

'Aye. And sailing into winter.'

'It feels like that.'

Corban, I'm scared,' Cywen said.

He gripped her hand and squeezed. 'So am I,' he replied.

Cywen crept through undergrowth, looking back at the rows of sleeping forms along the riverbank, framed by the dying embers of a dozen fires. Further off in the darkness their moored ships creaked in current and breeze.

Can't go too far, or I'll walk into someone on first watch.

She eventually sat with her back to a wind-twisted tree, sharp-thorned bushes shielding her from the eyes of anyone not sleeping at this late hour. She concentrated on becoming completely still, even trying to slow her breathing, and listened. When she was convinced that no one had followed her she opened her cloak and pulled out Brina's book, opening the pages to the bright moon above.

What is Brina so obsessed with?

For a ten-night they had sailed east and north, while the weather turned colder and sullen black clouds hid the sun. Dath made sure they never lost sight of the coast, a line of dark cliffs and shattered coves, each night searching for an inlet or bay, sometimes just a strip of beach to shelter. They had moored in a cove for two days while a storm lashed the coast, the eight ships bucking and rearing on the waves like wild stallions. On the thirteenth day, soon after sunset, Dath had sighted the estuary of a great river flowing into the sea that Meical confirmed would take them to Gramm's hold. Another two days they'd rowed against the current, the wind still helping them, and earlier this day, as the sun was setting, they'd turned a bend in the wide river and Meical had pointed out Gramm's hold, a pinprick upon a distant hill. Behind it had been a dark stain on the land, as far as Cywen's eyes could see.

Forn Forest. Cywen had felt a dread settle upon her looking at it.

Dath said it was half a day's rowing, at least, so the decision was made to make camp and approach the hold in daylight.

And so here she was, sneaking off in the dark to take a look at the book that seemed to be leaching Brina's enthusiasm for life.

Carefully she turned pages, knowing how fragile it was, moving steadily to the back of the book. The part that Brina had forbidden her from looking at. In the moonlight the pages took a silvery hue, the writing like black shadows crawling across the pages. Things began to change, as she'd seen before, more diagrams and runes. Occasionally words she recognized.

She paused, mouth working, brain aching as she tried to translate what she was seeing.

'*An dorcha sli*,' she breathed. She blinked and stared harder, the words seeming to be clawing out of the page at her, the flesh on her arms and neck goose-bumping as the words appeared in her mind.

'The dark way.'

Suddenly she felt scared, a creeping terror filling her, as if eyes were watching her, crawling over her. The darkness around her abruptly felt ominous, the silence malefic.

Almost against her will she turned more pages, eyes glued to the runes scrawled before her.

'*Ghloigh gheasa*,' she murmured. 'The spell of summoning. *Fuil de namhaid*, blood of an enemy.'

This is not Elyon's way of faith. What is this? And why has Brina been spending so much time poring over this?

A twig cracked behind her and as Cywen was turning she felt her ear gripped and pulled, hard enough that she either had the choice of following the ear or having it ripped off.

She staggered upright and came face to face with Brina, angrier than she had ever seen her before. Her lips were twisted, noises spluttering from her mouth, but rage seemed to have taken her beyond the use of speech.

Cywen felt truly terrified.

'I'm sorry,' she blurted.

'Not as sorry as you're going to be, you thieving, back-stabbing, soft-footed, plotting little witch,' Brina hissed. Cywen tried to take a step back, but found that unfortunately in her anger Brina hadn't loosened her grip on Cywen's ear.

Escape was out of the question, so Cywen resorted to the next option.

She screamed.

Immediately footsteps were thumping and voices calling.

Brina grabbed the book from Cywen's hands and tugged it out of her grip, slipping it into her cloak just as the first people reached them. Two guards from the first watch – Cywen recognized one of them as Akar, the Jehar captain.

Close behind them but from the other direction Meical and Corban appeared, Balur striding out of the darkness from another direction.

'What is going on?' Meical asked.

Cywen looked at Brina, then Meical. She wanted to tell Corban about the book, ask Brina what it was that she'd just read, and what exactly Brina was doing, but something stopped her. Deep down she felt something horribly wrong was going on, like an infection in a wound that ends in gangrene, but Meical and Balur's looming faces served only to keep her mouth closed.

'She was sleepwalking,' Brina said. 'I woke and saw that she was gone – found her and woke her. She screamed.'

Sleepwalking! Is that the best you can do?

She looked to Corban, saw the question in his eyes and on the tip of his tongue, but for once he kept it firmly behind his lips.

If Corban can keep his mouth shut, then so can I. Besides, Brina may not wish to remove my intestines with her bare hands if I keep her secret – is it a secret? – a little longer. I'll talk to Corban alone.

'You were sleepwalking?' Meical asked her, one long finger prodding Cywen.

'I – I don't know,' Cywen said. 'I was asleep, and then . . .' She gestured around her. She stopped her eyes from flickering to Brina.

If anything, Meical's frown bunched deeper.

'Is this a regular occurrence with you?'

No.

'What's that?' Akar the Jehar said, pointing away from Cywen, into the darkness.

They all stopped and stared. A flicker of light appeared in the distance, like a distant candle. As they watched it grew and spread a little, blazing brighter in the darkness.

'What is that?' Corban repeated.

'Elyon, no,' Meical gasped. 'We need to rouse the camp and move. That is Gramm's hold, and it is burning.'

CHAPTER FIFTY-ONE

HAELAN

Haelan crouched in the darkness and cuddled Pots.

He was sitting on a barrel of apples in the cellars beneath Gramm's hold, a single candle burning, Pots at his side with ears pricking at every strange sound that filtered down from above. And there were a lot of those.

Why did I send Tahir away? I wish Tahir and Wulf were here. They had left a few days after the bear-hunt, riding away one cold morning towards Dun Kellen. Wulf had given Haelan a note to pass to Gramm. *When the time is right*, Wulf had told him.

Gramm had read the letter, stared at it a long time, then crumpled it in his fist. His gaze had shifted to Haelan, who'd stared back at him, or tried to.

'They'll be back,' Haelan had whispered weakly.

'I hope so,' Gramm had said and walked away. Haelan had not heard him mention Wulf or Tahir since that day, but he saw him each evening standing on the wall staring into the south as the sun faded into the horizon.

Shouting drifted through the cracks in the boards above his head, sometimes a distant scream, making him jump and sending fear jolting through him. His hand searched out the shaft of the hatchet Trigg had given him and he pulled it from his belt, gripping it tight, imagined becoming a grown warrior and standing on the wall besides Gramm, the man who was risking all to help him.

The warband had been sighted in the pale blush of sunset, approaching from the south-west. It hadn't taken long to see Jael's banner held above them. Gramm had ordered the gates barred; everyone from the houses beyond the hold's wall was herded inside, and every warrior in the hold dressed in his war gear and manned the walls. Eighty men in all. Haelan had climbed the wall and hidden in the shadows by the gate tower, waiting along with Gramm and his men.

The warband had reached the gates soon after sunset, three hundred strong at least. A tall warrior approached the gates in gleaming mail and a horsehair plume trailing from his helmet.

'I am Ulfilas ben Arik, come in the name of Jael, King of Isiltir,' the warrior cried out, his warband gathering like a storm cloud behind him, bristling with iron and malice.

'Give up the child. I know he is in there. Give him up, and be rewarded by your King with more silver than you could spend in a lifetime. Continue to protect him and every last one of you will be dead by this time on the morrow.' His horse had fidgeted, stamping and dancing on the spot. He'd turned it in a tight circle. 'Talk on it; I will return soon.'

'You can have my answer now,' Gramm yelled, looking more like a giant than a man in his war gear of leather and mail, a great axe clenched in his fists. 'Jael's no king of *mine*, and you can tell him from me to shove his silver up his arse.'

Chaos had erupted then, spears flying, Jael's men attacking the gates with an iron-shod ram. Gramm's men on the wall had hurled spears and rocks down upon them, a great cauldron of oil heating over a fire-pit above the gates. Gramm had been yelling orders and suddenly spied Haelan crouching in the shadows.

'To the cellars with you,' he'd growled at Haelan. 'One stray spear and you make all this worthless.' The look on his face had both scared Haelan and made him feel ashamed and so he'd gone running for the cellars, an old healer giving him a candle, opening the trapdoor for him and shutting him in.

And here he was still, what seemed like days later. It was full dark, Haelan knew that, as there was a grate at the back of the cellar that opened onto the world above. Moonlight shone through the bars, and wisps of smoke occasionally drifted down, bringing the smell of burning timber. Other noises filtered down to him through the gaps about the trapdoor. From the feast-hall came the sounds of injured men being tended to, or comforted as they died. *Or not comforted. Just watched. Maybe holding their hands.* He remembered his mam telling him sometimes that was all you could do.

Footsteps sounded above, dust shaken loose from the cracks in the floorboards, then the trapdoor opened. Light flooded in, making Haelan blink. Gramm stood there, silhouetted. He strode down the steps, ducking his head. Haelan saw blood on his axe, caught the smell of woodsmoke and the sharp tang of metal. *No, that's blood. I remember it from Dun Kellen.* He squeezed his eyes shut, trying to stem the flood of memories that surged up.

Gramm sat on the bottom steps and rested his chin on his fist.

'I can't get you out,' he said.

Haelan frowned at him, not understanding.

'They've surrounded the hold, lit a ring of torches. I was thinking to sneak you over the wall and into Forn while it is dark, but . . .' He shrugged.

'They're not attacking, then?' Haelan asked.

'Not any more.' Gramm chuckled. 'They tried that and it didn't go so well for them. We've given them reason to stay back, at least.' He patted the head of his axe. A waft of smoke curled down the steps.

'What's that smell?'

'They're trying to burn us out. The gate tower's in flames.'

'They did that at Dun Kellen,' Haelan said morosely.

They sat in silence a while.

'Thank you,' Haelan whispered. He felt tears welling in his eyes at what Gramm had sacrificed to help him. 'For all that you have done for me.'

Gramm nodded. 'I'll not lie to you, lad, I've always spoken straight. Things don't look good. There's over three hundred of them, all proven swords, eighty of us in here. Hard men and brave, and a wall between us and them, but . . .' He shook his head. 'I expected more. All my years I've been waiting for these days – the God-War. To be taken out of it before it's hardly begun.'

'Life's not fair,' Haelan said.

'No. It's not.' Gramm sighed. 'If they find you . . .' His hand dropped to the hilt of a knife at his belt.

'I know. My head will be on a spike.'

'Aye. And maybe more.'

Haelan swallowed at that. He wasn't sure what Gramm meant, but the edge in his voice and the look in his eye spoke louder than any words.

Gramm drew his knife from his belt, turned it in his hand, the candle flame shimmering on the iron.

Haelan felt afraid.

I'm used to that, he told himself. He felt a small flicker of anger in his belly, at Jael, the author of his fear, the man that had hounded and hunted him. In his mind's eye he saw Jael's face, remembered him from court visits, always with a smirk twisting his lips.

'We're not dead yet,' Haelan muttered. 'And, as Tahir is fond of saying, every path has its puddle.'

Gramm stared at him, then he threw his head back and roared with laughter.

I didn't think it was that funny.

Gramm stood, towering over Haelan, wiping his eyes.

'It's as safe down here as anywhere. I'll have the trapdoor covered with something heavy when I leave. Just stay quiet. There's food, drink, more than enough to last you a moon. You never know . . .'

They might not find me. Can't see that happening.

'And if they do find you, take this.' He gave Haelan his knife. It was heavy in his hand, the iron cold.

Is this to use on the enemy that come through that trapdoor, or on myself? He was not brave enough to ask.

Gramm ruffled his hair and walked up the stairs, the trapdoor thudding closed. Then there was the sound of grating above as something heavy was dragged, men grunting. Then fading footsteps.

Haelan lay down on the floor, shivering, curling around Pots, and closed his eyes.

He woke with a start, Pots licking his face. He'd been dreaming, about the hunt for the bear in Forn, the one that had killed the wolven. Tahir had still been here, then, and he had gone on the hunt with Gramm and Wulf and a few score others, leaving Haelan at the hold. They'd not found it, but Tahir told him they'd followed its tracks into Forn and then north to the river. Huge paw prints had led down to the dark waters, and all had concluded that the bear and its rider had swum back across to the river's far side, to the Desolation. Haelan hoped so, though from that night on he'd had the same recurring dream of being lost in the forest, wandering alone and terrified, and then finally becoming aware that he was no longer alone. That he was being followed. Hunted.

I've been hunted for as long as I can remember.

And now they've found me.

He realized his candle had gone out but he could still see, faintly. *Dawn has come, then.*

It was quiet, no sounds of battle, or anything, come to that. He remembered his conversation with Gramm, picked over it, looked at the knife Gramm had given him, lying on a flagstone beside his hatchet. The prospect of staying in this cellar for a moon or more made him shiver. Another day was too much.

'Pots, what am I to do?' He stroked the wire hair of the dog, wanting to leave the cellars, too scared to move.

Even if I wanted to leave, the trapdoor's been blocked and hidden. I'd never get it open.

A crash echoed from somewhere above, making him jump. Sounds drifted down, men shouting, behind it a dull thud, repeated, like a heartbeat.

They're attacking the gates again.

Another crash, this time much louder, and closer.

Are they inside the walls? Have they found me?

He clutched the hilt of the knife that Gramm had given him. More crashing, and Haelan realized with a start that someone was pounding on a grate high in the cellar. It shook in its foundations, buckling under the pressure as it was repeatedly thumped, then it was falling into the cellar, a face filling the space it had occupied.

Haelan brandished the knife, waiting for the enemy to come slithering through the man-sized hole in the wall. Instead he saw a face staring down at him.

Trigg.

The half-breed smiled grimly and stuck her arm into the cellar.

'Think you better come with me – they'll be through the gates soon.'

'Gramm said this is the best place to hide,' Haelan said.

'I'm not going to put you somewhere to hide,' Trigg said. 'I'm going to get you out of here.'

Haelan paused a moment and then his feet were moving.

He dragged a barrel over, found that when he stood on it he could reach Trigg's hand. All of a sudden he jumped down from the barrel, retrieved his hatchet and knife, threading them both through his belt, held Pots under one arm and climbed back onto the barrel. He lifted Pots up and Trigg took him, hoisting him out. The dog turned and poked his head in through the gap beside Trigg's broad face, looking down at Haelan, then Haelan was being heaved through the hole, wriggling out, fingertips digging into the dark soil. Pots growled and pounced on his arm, began tugging on his sleeve as if it was some game. And then Haelan was out.

'Where are we going?'

'This way,' Trigg said.

They headed towards the main gates, slipping into the deep shadows along the feast-hall, Pots trotting at Haelan's heels.

'Shouldn't we be going the other way, finding somewhere dark and small to sneak through?' he asked, though part of him was glad that Trigg was leading him towards the gates, maybe the knowledge that this was all happening because of him, and the very least he could do was not hide from it.

Mam never hid from anything.

'It's madness at the gates, easier to slip through,' Trigg hissed down at him. Then they were around the corner of the hall and looking at the gates.

They stood frozen for a moment, then Trigg gestured and they ducked behind the wheel of a wain, both of them peering through it at the scene before them.

Dark silhouettes of warriors strode the walkway on the wall, more of them appearing through thick smoke. One of the gate towers was on fire, flames crackling into the sky, clouds of smoke billowing across the courtyard. People were running, a chain of them passing buckets of water in an attempt to douse the flames. The gates were still closed and barred, though there were cracks in the thick timber and the bar across them was twisted and buckling. They shuddered at another impact. Warriors stood in a line before it, shields and spears ready.

Haelan saw Gramm on the wall, above the gates, bellowing, pointing with his axe-head. As Haelan watched he saw Gramm and a few others lift the cauldron hanging suspended over the fire and empty its steaming contents over the wall. Screams rang out. The crashing against the gate stopped.

There was a loud crack, and part of the flaming tower collapsed, charred wood tumbling into the courtyard, pinning someone beneath it. Their shrieks of pain made Haelan cover his ears.

Then something strange happened.

Everyone on the wall stopped moving.

They were staring, out beyond the wall. Then Gramm turned and bellowed.

'GIANTS!'

There was a rumbling from beyond the gates, like the pounding of drums, marching, and then an unmistakable sound, one that Haelan had heard before, that day in the meadow close to Forn when he'd been helping to repair the wall. A roar, ear-splittingly loud, the vibration of it reverberating through his chest.

Something colossal crashed into the gates. The wood cracked, the bar bucking in its rests, hinges screaming protest. Gramm was yelling himself hoarse, throwing another spear over the wall, ordering the cauldron filled and back on its spit, shouting at a few huntsmen with their bows nocked to shoot faster.

Another impact on the gates. There was another crack as the bar bowed in its rests. In the courtyard before the gates warriors yelled and shuffled closer together, spear-points wavering.

Then the gates shattered, a huge explosion of splintered timber and iron, a cloud of dust and smoke blown into the courtyard, smothering everything, billowing as far as the steps of the feast-hall.

Haelan covered his mouth, blinking. Beside him Pots growled.

The dust slowly settled, revealing the open gateway, one door hanging from snapped hinges, the other gone entirely.

A huge shape came shambling through, all teeth and claw and fur, eyes glaring, a giant sitting astride it bellowing a war cry, brandishing a war-hammer.

Pots whined and tucked his tail between his legs.

Trigg hissed beside Haelan, her whole body tensing.

All became chaos.

The warriors lined before the gates spread out in a half-circle, over a dozen of them. Haelan saw them all drop their spears and shields, reaching to their backs for their axes.

Then the axes were spinning through the air, crunching into the giant and his bear. The giant toppled from his saddle, his face a red ruin, axe-blades buried deep in his chest. The bear bellowed, two axes in its skull, staggered on half a dozen steps and crashed to the ground, sending up a fresh cloud of dust.

The men of Gramm's hold have fought giants before.

Another bear appeared in the gateway, surging through it, the giant upon it yelling a battle-cry and brandishing a spear as thick as a small tree.

A giantess, Haelan thought absently, noting the lack of moustache.

She flung her spear at the warriors gathered before the gates as they scrabbled for their own shields and spears. The giants' spear struck one and sent him crashing backwards in a fountain of blood. The bear powered forwards, as broad as two stallions and taller, and smashed into the clustered warriors, raking one paw through them, leaving a trail of gore. Some still standing stabbed with their spears, piercing the bear's thick coat. Haelan saw blood flow from a handful of wounds, but the bear ignored them, tore the head from a warrior with its powerful jaws, the giant on its back swinging a war-hammer, turning another warrior to bloody pulp. More shapes appeared behind the giant and bear – warriors on horseback surging in upon either side, the unmistakable sound of more bears roaring beyond the wall.

Something fell from the wall above, hurtling towards the bear and its giant-rider in the courtyard.

Gramm. Not falling. Leaping.

He was yelling, swinging his great axe. With a wet crunch it slammed into the giantess' head, blood, bone and brain erupting.

The bear roared, standing on its hind legs and flinging Gramm and the dead giant to the dirt, the surviving warriors before it cringing back. With a concussive *boom* the bear fell back to all-fours and sniffed the giant. It lifted its head and roared again, spittle spraying from its jaws. Gramm staggered to his feet, swaying, and the bear raised a huge paw and swiped him, sending him flying through the air to land and roll to a stop at the feast-hall steps. He did not move.

Haelan ran to Gramm, Trigg trying to grab him and missing. He dropped to his knees beside the big man's head, wiped hair and blood from Gramm's face and the man's eyes flickered open.

Gramm looked at Haelan, his lips moving, and Haelan put his ear to Gramm's mouth.

'Run,' the big man whispered.

Haelan hesitated. He looked over at Trigg, still behind the wain, and she pointedly looked from him to the open gates. Then he was off, sprinting to the outer wall, then zigzagging across the courtyard, spinning around fighting warriors, ducking through horses' legs, avoiding bears, until he was at the gates. They were empty now, the enemy warband had passed through, fighting within the courtyard or riding people down beyond the feast-hall. More fires were springing up.

Haelan stepped hesitantly through, looking out at the meadows beyond, huge pastures undulating into the distance.

Where do I go? Not that way – they'll see me from a dozen leagues away.

He looked east, to Forn, and shivered, remembering his dreams. *Hunted.*

Horses neighed in the paddocks, Gramm's legacy, a lifetime of breeding. Haelan felt fresh tears spring to his eyes at that.

I need one of those horses, else I'll never make it to Forn.

He was a good rider, had been trained by the best since he could walk, and even the prospect of riding bareback didn't put him off too much. He looked about, then dashed away from the gates. Almost immediately he heard the sound of hooves, behind and to the left, closer with every heartbeat. He dived forwards, rolling away from hooves that thudded about him.

The horse was reined in, a warrior in chainmail leaning in his saddle to snatch at him.

'Come here, you little brat,' the warrior snarled, 'or I'll put my spear through you and we'll see how you squirm then.'

Haelan rolled away and then Pots was standing over his head, snarling, teeth snapping and fur bristling at the horse and rider. If he had not felt such overwhelming terror Haelan would have laughed.

'Have it your way,' the warrior said, hefting his spear.

Then a sword-point burst through his chest and blood exploded, showering Haelan and Pots.

A hand shoved the dead warrior from his saddle and a man took his place, long arms reaching down for Haelan, a familiar face staring grimly at him.

Tahir.

Haelan just stared at him, not sure if he was dreaming.

'Take my hand, Haelan,' Tahir said, and he did, was swung up into the saddle, and Haelan was hugging his shieldman tight, then they were riding, Pots running alongside them. There were other riders about them, warriors from the hold who had ridden with Tahir and Wulf in search of Swain and Sif. Haelan caught a glimpse of Swain and Sif in the saddle of another horse, and Wulf, leaping from his saddle, staring at the shattered gates of his home, tears streaking his cheeks. Wulf looked back at his children as they rode away from the hold, then he turned and strode through the smoke-wreathed gates. Haelan tried to tell Tahir, but all that came out was a sob, then everything became a blur for him, the wind whipping tears of his own from his eyes.

CHAPTER FIFTY-TWO

ULFILAS

Ulfilas kicked his horse on, sword arm rising and falling, the man running from him crashing to the ground in a tangle of boneless limbs. All about him his warriors were swarming, the courtyard seething with combat, riders spilling around the sides of the feast-hall where Gramm's men were starting to break and run. Behind him a bear bellowed, making his head rattle inside his helmet.

Would I stand against such a foe? He was glad that he did not have to find out, and respected these men of Gramm's who stood against such overwhelming odds. That didn't stop him killing them, though.

He saw a knot of them rallying about a bear, the one whose rider Gramm had killed. Six or seven men were forming a crude half-circle, one stepping in to stab with his spear, the bear lunging at him as he jumped away, another moving close on the other side, bloody-ing the animal again, enraging it.

That is the way to kill a bear, usually. Wear it down, bleed it until it's weak. But not bears like this – it would take a moon to weaken that beast.

Ulfilas spurred his horse on and rode at the men about the bear, slashed one across the skull, the warrior's iron helm ringing as he dropped, dead or unconscious. They turned on him and Ulfilas dragged on his reins, his horse rearing, hooves lashing, sending men stumbling back into the range of the enraged bear. A paw whistled through the air and a man fell, eviscerated, another caught in its huge jaws, ripping flesh and crushing bone. The survivors broke and scattered. Ulfilas allowed himself a satisfied grin, until he saw the bear lumbering towards him.

He felt his horse panicking beneath him, shying away, and he had to yank on the reins to bring it under control, the bear looming closer.

Then another bear filled the gap between them, the Jotun warlord Ildaer upon it. He shouted words in giantish at the enraged bear. It seemed to calm, marginally.

'He is mad with grief, his rider slain,' Ildaer said to him.

Do bears feel grief? Ulfilas rode towards the feast-hall, passing another giant who knelt upon the ground, cradling the corpse of the giantess that Gramm had slain.

Another brave deed. Songs would be sung about that leap, tales told around the campfires this night.

The courtyard was less frantic now, full of the dying rather than the fighting, combat drifting around the edges of the hall and amongst the outbuildings. More bears and their giant riders disappeared behind the feast-hall, part of the dozen more Jotun who had arrived with Ildaer at dawn.

'No mercy,' Ulfilas cried to his warriors. 'Find the child.'

He dismounted, warriors falling in behind him, and approached the broken form of Gramm, who lay where he had fallen. Ulfilas stood over him, knew that the man was finished. Blood dribbled from his mouth and nose, his skin was ashen and pale. Broken ribs poked through the ruin of his flesh and leather war gear.

That was where Ulfilas kicked him.

Gramm screamed, eyes snapping open.

'Where is he?'

Gramm's eyes took a moment to focus. Ulfilas pulled his helmet off, hair sweaty and plastered to his head, but he saw recognition dawn in Gramm's eyes.

'Jael's dog,' Gramm whispered.

Ulfilas kicked him again.

'Where is the boy?'

Gramm just stared at him.

Ulfilas turned to Ildaer, sitting upon his bear.

'Ildaer, this is the man who killed your kin – Ilska was her name, if I remember right.'

'You do,' Ildaer growled, small eyes fixing on Gramm.

'He was lord of this hold, and if anyone knows where the child is, it is him. Would you help me here?'

'I will.' Ildaer swung a leg over his saddle and slipped to the ground, pulled his war-hammer from a leather sleeve and strode over, his blond warrior's braid swinging.

'Inside this hall a giant's war-hammer and the skin of one of your bears are nailed to the wall,' Ulfilas said.

Ildaer's eyes narrowed at that. He laid his war-hammer upon the ground, grabbed one of Gramm's hands and heaved him from the ground, slamming his body against one of the broad columns that flanked the feast-hall's steps. A cry of pain whistled from Gramm's lips. Ildaer drew a dagger from his belt, as long as a short sword, and slammed it into Gramm's forearm, halfway between wrist and elbow, impaling him against the column. He left him dangling as he searched the ground for another weapon, lifted a spear and impaled the other arm beside the first, hanging him like a snared hare.

'Feel more inclined to tell me where Haelan is?' Ulfilas asked, climbing steps to look Gramm in the eye. Gramm spat blood in his face.

Ildaer punched Gramm in his broken ribs, sending him swinging. Gramm screamed, loud and long.

'Where is he?' Ulfilas asked again.

Gramm squeezed his eyes shut.

'Speak, giant-slayer,' Ildaer grated, 'and the hurt will end.' He pulled his arm back for another blow.

'NO!' someone screamed from behind them. At the same time something whistled past Ulfilas' ear and slammed into Ildaer. The giant staggered forwards a step and dropped to one knee, a single-bladed axe buried in his back, high, between his shoulder and spine.

Ulfilas turned and saw a man running at them, pulling another axe from a strap on his back. He was wrapped in fur and leather, with dark hair and eyes, body knotted with thick muscle.

Gramm's son, Wulf.

Wulf threw the second axe as he ran, this one at Ulfilas, but his warriors were moving protectively about him. One stepped in front of Ulfilas, at the same time raising his shield. He was too slow and took the axe in the face, collapsing in a twitching ruin.

Ulfilas snarled and drew his sword, beside him Ildaer plucking the axe from his back and calling out in giantish, his bear moving to him.

Other warriors converged on Wulf, two reaching him at the same time. Wulf ducked, a sword and another smaller axe in his hand. He hamstrung the first warrior with his axe, slit his throat as he fell, swirled around the next one, burying his sword in the man's belly, ripping it free as his momentum carried him on, eyes fixed on Ulfilas. He was thirty paces away, powered on, blocked a sword blow with his blade, buried his axe in a neck. Fifteen paces away.

Ulfilas felt a ripple of fear, welcomed it as an old friend, set his feet and lifted his blade.

Then someone crashed into Wulf, one of Ulfilas' men, wrestling him to the ground, another appearing, clubbing him across the back with a spear-butt. More swarmed upon him.

'Don't kill him,' Ulfilas yelled as Ildaer strode over, blood streaming from the wound in his back, tossing Wulf's axe away as if it were a child's plaything. He grabbed a fistful of Wulf's hair and dragged him to the feast-hall steps, lifting him to look in his eyes.

Wulf was semi-conscious, eyes flickering, a cut on his scalp sheeting blood. Ulfilas slapped his face and his eyes snapped open.

'Say hello to your father,' Ulfilas said.

Wulf stared at Gramm, impaled to the feast-hall column, blood drenching his arms. He was looking back at his son, tears in his eyes.

'My boy,' he whispered '. . . shouldn't . . . come back.'

Wulf kicked and writhed in Ildaer's grip, spat and cursed. The giant held him tight, only laughed.

'Perhaps you should join your father,' Ildaer grunted, pinning both of Wulf's wrists together with one huge fist. He strode up the far side of the steps to its opposite column, bending to pick up a spear as he went, and in one blow pierced both of Wulf's palms, stabbing the spear into the column. Wulf stood with his arms raised overhead, blood running down the column, eyes fixed on his da.

'Now,' Ulfilas said, 'I shall ask you both. Where is Haelan? Hiding in some bolt-hole? Where is he?' He looked between the two men, father and son, could see the defiance in their eyes. He sighed.

I am a warrior, not a torturer. Where is Dag when he's needed? Nevertheless, Ulfilas knew his duty, and he knew that he could not return to Jael without Haelan's head, or else there was a high chance he'd lose his own, and that was not an option.

'I am going to torture one of you until the other speaks. This will bring me no pleasure. It will be best for you both to speak now and avoid the unnecessary pain.'

Neither answered him. He drew his knife and walked up the steps to stand halfway between them. 'Who shall it be?' he asked.

'I know where he is,' a voice shouted, someone stepping out from behind a wain. A youth, tall, fair-haired and long-limbed.

A girl?

The youth walked towards them, something in her stride seeming wrong, somehow, different. As she drew closer Ulfilas saw that her arms were corded with thick muscle, her face flat planes and sharp angles.

Like a giant.

'What are you?' he asked, frowning.

'My name's Trigg,' the youth said. 'I'm a half-breed.'

Ulfilas noticed Ildaer cocking his head to one side, studying this new arrival with interest.

I didn't know such a thing was possible.

Trigg reached the wide steps and stopped.

'Why would you offer up this information?' Ulfilas asked, himself as suspicious as the girl appeared to be, half expecting some kind of trap.

'They have mistreated me all my life,' Trigg said, pointing at both Gramm and Wulf.

Fair enough.

'We gave you a home, treated you well,' Wulf yelled at her.

'You mocked me, scorned me, beat me,' Trigg said, her face cold, holding Wulf's gaze.

'Where is Haelan, then?' Ulfilas asked.

'Trigg,' Gramm breathed, 'don't.'

Ildaer cuffed Gramm across the head.

'He's in the cellars, I saw Gramm go down there, heard them talking.'

'You traitorous half-breed, curse you, I'll kill you,' Wulf yelled.

'Take me to them,' Ulfilas said. Trigg strode up the steps into the feast-hall, Ulfilas and Ildaer behind her, Wulf's screams following them. They passed through the hall, dead men lying on tables, others between the tables, through a wide door into the kitchen, ovens cold. A pile of barrels were massed in one corner and Trigg pointed at them.

'Trapdoor's under them.'

Ildaer tossed them aside in a few heartbeats to reveal a trapdoor. Ulfilas threw the bolt and lifted the door, hefted his sword and walked down steps into a dark, musty room, pale light leaking in from some kind of grille at the far end of the room.

'There's no one here,' he snarled after searching it thoroughly. Then he saw the open grate and a barrel underneath it and ran back up the steps two at a time. The half-breed girl was nowhere to be seen.

'He must be close,' he snarled at his men as he ran out into the courtyard. 'Tear this place apart.'

He strode to Gramm. 'Where would he go?'

'He's . . . gone, then,' Gramm breathed. He had the gall to smile. Ulfilas felt a rush of frustrated rage, edged with fear of failing his task.

'Ildaer, your giant-kin's bear – he grieves for his rider?'

'Creach, aye, he does,' Ildaer rumbled. 'We raise our bears from cubs, our bonds are strong.'

'Then have some vengeance for your bear.' He pulled his knife from his belt and punched it into Gramm's gut, ripped it across so that intestines spilt about his boots like writhing snakes. He stepped away to the sound of Wulf and Gramm's screams mingling.

Ildaer barked something in his guttural tongue and the riderless bear shambled forwards.

'*Feasta*,' Ildaer said and the bear sank its jaws into the pile of intestines, eating them with a disgusting slopping, sucking sound that turned Ulfilas' stomach.

Gramm screamed louder, again and again, Wulf weeping and cursing.

'Lord Ulfilas,' a warrior called down from the wall. 'There is something you should see.'

'What? It better be to do with the child,' Ulfilas growled as he strode to the steps. The heat of battle was fading and he felt a chill wind now.

Ulfilas reached the walkway and looked where the warrior was pointing.

It was north-west, beyond the pastures and outbuildings of the hold, towards the river that separated Isiltir from the Desolation. A ship had appeared, sleek-hulled and shallow-draughted, rowing hard, even as he watched a black sail being furled and the mast coming down for the ship to slip beneath the stone bridge that spanned the river. More ships appeared behind it – four, six, until they numbered eight in total.

I recognize those sails, and those ships from the battle at Dun Kellen. The Vin Thalun, servants of Nathair. Why have they been sent here? Has Jael communicated with Nathair, said that I need help? He felt a stab of anger at that, followed by a flush of pleasure that the hold was all but conquered. *They are too late. We need no help.* Distant sounds of battle drifted up from the slopes beyond the feast-hall, edging through the buildings and warehouses that led to the river. *It will take some time to flush all resistance out from this rats' lair, but their back is broken. Only the child to find.*

Gramm's screams still rose up from the courtyard, rising now to a hoarse, high-pitched shriek. The bear had worked its way through the piled intestines, had followed their trail up and was sticking its jaws into the wound in Gramm's belly. Wulf hung limp as he watched. Ulfilas winced. I should go down there and put him out of his misery. He regretted his moment of anger.

The child. Where is he?

'Ildaer,' he called down from the wall. 'Your bear, could he find Haelan's scent?'

Ildaer nodded, climbed back into his saddle, and then his bear moved off, disappearing behind the feast-hall.

Ulfilas' thoughts shifted to practical details and he thought of setting up a perimeter around the hold to prevent the chance of Haelan slipping away in any confusion. *Perhaps I could use these Vin Thalun newcomers.* He looked back to the ships, saw the first one docking against a quay, a boarding ramp sliding across. Figures began to disembark, too far away to determine details, but something niggled at his mind. Two hounds leaped from the first ship as the other ships began to thud against other quays. One of the hounds was enormous, white furred and exuding power even from this distance. He stared harder, eyes narrowing.

Are there giants amongst them? Jael had mentioned to him that Nathair had giants amongst his allies. But why are they here? He felt a seed of doubt squirm in his belly.

'Lord Ulfilas,' the warrior beside him said.

'I know,' Ulfilas murmured. 'A strange shipload.'

'Not the ships, lord. To the south-west – there are riders approaching. A lot of them.'

Ulfilas turned away from the ships and looked to the south-west. The warrior was right. A cloud of dust hovered above a smudge on the land, and now he could hear the faint rumble of hooves.

Who are they?

'Blow your horn; gather the warband,' he said as he tugged his helmet back on.

CHAPTER FIFTY-THREE

TUKUL

'Looks like we're in for a fight,' Tukul said to Coralen and Enkara, the three of them riding at the head of their column. He glanced over at Coralen and saw she was buckling on her wolven gauntlet with her teeth. He grinned.

I like this girl. She will be a fine match for Corban, and they will have strong children. Well behaved, unlikely; wayward, perhaps; fiery and stubborn, definitely. He had said as much to her on their journey across Isiltir, but she had blushed as red as her hair and threatened to cut his tongue out with her wolven claws if he said such a thing to her again.

Fiery.

He smiled at the memory of it.

As soon as he'd seen the smoke rising from Gramm's hold he'd known something was wrong. He had a hasty conversation with his sword-kin.

'Do you want me to scout the hold out?' Coralen had asked him.

'That would be sensible,' Enkara said.

'Sensible be damned,' Tukul said. 'Gramm is my friend, and he may need help.' He shrugged. 'We will go and help him.' He'd ordered the spare horses that they'd alternated riding across the length of Isiltir left in the pastures before Gramm's hold, giving Shield a fond rub on the nose.

You'd make a good warhorse, my friend, but Daria and me, we know each other, like you and Corban, eh? So I shall ride her into battle, and she can tell you of her glory later. Shield had snorted at him and stamped a hoof.

And then Tukul was leaping into his saddle and kicking Daria into a ground-eating canter. Not a gallop, he didn't want her blown if there was going to be a fight at the end of this last dash to the finish line.

They crested a rise in the road and saw the hold before them, black smoke billowing from the gate tower. From this distance Tukul could see figures on the wall, hear the blowing of horns, behind it all the faint din of battle. He thought of the last time he had been here, of Gramm's friendship and hospitality, of learning to throw an axe and being gifted one by Wulf. He thought of Gramm's huge laugh and crushing embrace.

I hope I am not too late, my friend.

They rode on, Tukul loosening his sword in its sheath, fingertips brushing the haft of the axe strapped to his saddle, then they were on the road that sloped up to the gates, meadow pastures to either side.

All-Father, may my sword stay sharp and my body swift.

He could see the gates had been smashed in.

Whoever did that will be regretting it, now that they cannot shut us out.

Horns blew from above the wall and riders issued from the gates, forty, sixty – more all the time. Tukul grunted his respect for whoever had made the decision to meet them in the open.

Better to keep us out than in, and brave not to hide behind their walls.

Tukul raised a fist and a hundred and fifty Jehar spread to either side of the slope, forming dark wings about him.

'Should we be doing this?' Coralen shouted to him.

'Doing what?'

'Charging uphill against a mounted foe.'

'Probably not,' Tukul called back, then laughed with the joy of it. *Strategy be damned, nothing will stop me reaching my friend.*

Then something huge strode through the gates. For a moment Tukul did not know what it was, then his eyes focused on the enormous jaws and hammer-like paws, tipped with thick-curved claws. A giant rode upon its back, dark-haired and brandishing spear and battle-axe. Another bear and rider filled the gates behind it.

Except perhaps that.

Tukul grinned. *Now this is a fight worthy of the Jehar.*

'We'll make a song out of this one,' he yelled to Coralen,

laughing, wind whipping his hair. She grinned back at him, raised an arm and clenched her fist, wolven claws chinking.

Attacking uphill, against a mounted enemy, giants and the great bears of the north. Madness.

He drew his sword, all about him the Jehar doing the same, a flash of lightning in the pale sunshine. He whispered to Daria, urging her into a gallop, holding his sword two-handed above his head, using foot, ankle, knee and thigh to guide his mount.

'TRUTH AND COURAGE!' he cried, the battle-cry taken up and echoed back at him by Coralen, Enkara and the others, a thunder-clap of voices.

Then they were crashing together, two waves of flesh, blood and bone, leather and fur and tooth and iron. Tukul had ridden Daria straight for the great bear and its rider, but warriors had flowed into the space between them.

I will carve my way to it, then.

With his first blow Tukul took a head from its owner's shoulders, sending it spinning, blood jetting. He swerved Daria away from a spear lunge, deflected the spear-point, ran his sword down its shaft and severed the fingers that clutched it, then he was riding past, back-swinging his blade into the warrior's neck. Daria slammed shoulders with the next horse; a roll of Tukul's wrists, and he opened the rider's throat, Daria stretching her neck and biting chunks of flesh from horse and rider.

Then he was through the line, blinking at the speed of it, a stretch of turf and dirt road before the gates to the hold. Behind him battle raged, and even at a glance he could tell the Jehar were cutting more of the enemy down with every stroke. To his right loomed one of the giants. As he watched, the bear it was riding crushed a horse's skull with a swing of one huge paw, the giant lunging with his spear and skewering one of his Jehar, lifting the man from his saddle and flinging him through the air.

Tukul kicked Daria at them, raising his sword, yelling a war cry.

A horse and rider crunched into them, Daria staggering, almost falling, the warrior swinging at Tukul's head. Tukul blocked the blow, irritated at being delayed from reaching his intended foe. Rotating his shoulders, he turned his block into a downward chop, but he was parried, the enemy swaying in his saddle and turning his own defence into a stab at Tukul's throat.

Tukul flicked the sword-point away, nodded and smiled, acknowledging the skill of his opponent. He took a heartbeat to study him – an ornately etched helmet with horsehair plume and mail tail protecting the back of the neck, shirt of mail, single-handed sword and an iron-rimmed shield – fine, solid equipment, better than most around him.

A leader of men, then. A captain, perhaps even lord. Because of the man's skill Tukul gave him the respect of his full attention.

He touched his heels to Daria's ribs, urged her to the left and forwards, sending a combination of blows at his enemy as he rode at him, a series of swooping chops and short lunges, splinters and sparks flying from the warrior's shield and blade. His opponent blocked most of them, though ever more wildly, each time pulling him more and more out of position, blood welling from a cut to his thigh and another on his forearm. Daria bit his mount's neck, causing it to pull away, for a heartbeat spoiling the rider's balance. Tukul struck again, opened a cut across the warrior's bicep, slicing deep into muscle just below his mail sleeve, slashed at the reins, severing them, a short backswing, sword crunching into the man's mail shirt, bruising if not breaking bones, then pulled back and chopped down once, twice, three times, the third blow glancing off of his opponent's helmet and slicing into the gap between mail shirt and the helmet's mail tail. Blood spurted, though Tukul knew instinctively that the wound was not deep.

Nevertheless the combination of blows sent the man reeling in his saddle and, without his reins to balance himself, he toppled from his mount, crashing to the ground, where he lay, winded and bleeding.

Tukul hovered over him, looking for a space to lean down and finish the man, then he heard a scream from his right, saw a Jehar sent flying from his mount by a bear-swipe.

That beast needs to stop killing my sword-kin. He whispered in Daria's ear and she leaped away, found some open ground and launched herself at the bear and its rider.

There was a pile of corpses about the bear and giant, horses and Jehar massed like a tide-line of the dead. Tukul mastered his anger, guiding Daria along the bear's flank, and he sliced into the animal's rear leg, pulling away, knowing it had been a good blow, cutting through muscle and chipping bone.

The bear bellowed in pain and stumbled back, its leg giving out, the giant lurching in his saddle, seeing Tukul and lunging at him with his spear. Tukul swayed back, hacked and splintered the spear-shaft. He guided Daria away from the bear's front claws, felt the wind of their passing as he rode out in front of the bear, turning Daria in a tight circle. Tukul sheathed his sword in its scabbard across his back.

The bear was twenty paces away, stationary now, wounded, enraged and savage. It roared at Tukul and Daria, spittle spraying from its great jaws, the giant lending his voice, bellowing at them and brandishing its battle-axe. Tukul snarled back at them and kicked Daria straight at it, unclipping his axe and hefting it. He slipped his feet from his stirrups, in one smooth move bringing them up to the saddle, and then he launched himself into the air, flying over one swiping claw, bringing his axe down two-handed with all his strength to crunch into the bear's skull. Bone and brain splattered his face, and he heard a horse screaming. The bear collapsed in a spasm of fur and muscle, Tukul losing his grip on the axe-shaft, spinning through the air to land with a bone-jarring crunch. He tried to get up but couldn't draw a breath, his lungs burning, his back screaming at him to lie still.

Dimly he was aware of a hulking form rising out of the ruin of the bear's slumped carcass, heard the grief-edged bellow of the giant.

Get up and live, stay here and die, he told himself, jolts of agony stabbing through him as he rolled onto his front, pushed himself onto one knee. The giant towered above him, his axe pulling back, and Tukul reached for his sword, drew it, stood on unsteady feet, face raised in defiance.

Then the giant staggered and roared in pain, arms flailing. It turned away and Tukul saw a figure clinging to its back, legs wrapped around the giant's waist, punching one fist into its side, time and time again, the fist coming away red, sharp claws splattering blood.

Claws?

Tukul blinked, still dazed from the fall. Then he realized.

Coralen.

The giant sank to its knees, arms reaching for Coralen. She grabbed a fist full of its hair, yanked its head back and raked her wolven claws across its throat. Then she dropped from its back and kicked it face down into the dirt.

'This battle's growing into a fine song,' she said as she put a steadying arm on his shoulder.

'That it is, lass,' he said, looking at the dead giant and bear, doubting the song would mention his aching back. He turned to look for his horse, thinking he'd feel more stable back in a saddle, then saw Daria a dozen paces away, lying on her side. Half her flank was ripped open to the bone, and Tukul remembered the claw swipe that he'd leaped over.

He ran to her, staggering, and she raised her head at his voice, whinnied at him, pink foam frothing from her mouth and nostrils as she tried to stand, legs kicking. She got her front legs under her, then toppled back on her side, eyes rolling white with pain.

'Easy, my brave girl,' he soothed, tears welling in his eyes. He patted her neck, the battle about him dimming to a dull roar.

You'll not be getting back up to run again, my faithful friend.

For a moment his voice alone seemed to soothe her pain and she lifted her head and looked at him with dark, liquid eyes.

Resting his head on her muscular neck, he breathed a prayer, kissed her and then put his sword through her throat, the last act of a faithful friend. He crouched beside her as the battle passed him by, only a few footsteps away, stroked and whispered to her until her eyes glazed and her legs stopped kicking.

He stood, a dark rage swelling in his chest, and looked about. Coralen was gone. Out here on the slope the battle was almost done, the enemy retreating back into the hold. His Jehar were pressing after them, sounds of battle ringing out from the courtyard beyond.

He stalked through the gates, the courtyard he remembered transformed, full now with heaving battle, the stench of blood and death, billowing smoke. He looked to the feast-hall, saw a great bear standing guard on the steps, two men behind it spiked to two thick columns.

Gramm. Wulf.

The bear swatted at anyone that came close, but did not move from the steps, a beast defending its kill.

Tukul ran across the courtyard, ignoring the pain in his back, past Coralen and Enkara fighting back to back, swerving around another dozen acts of combat, his grip tightening on his sword hilt. The bear saw him coming and roared, fur bristling, swung at him with one great paw. Tukul skidded under the blow and hit the ground, his body rolling before coming up underneath the bear's snapping jaws and ramming his sword up, through fur and flesh, the blade going deeper still, through the lower jaw and on, blade almost to the hilt now, into the bear's brain.

It spasmed, a mountain of muscle and fur, blood gushing from its mouth as its head jerked, a convulsion that tore through its body, one last violent paroxysm and then it was collapsing, Tukul taking the weight of the beast's head upon his shoulders. He stood there, chest heaving, covered in blood, then ripped his blade free and shrugged the head to the ground.

He pounded up the stairs. One look at Gramm and he knew the man was gone. His belly was one great wound, looking as if the flesh had been chewed, not cut. Tukul grimaced and looked away, saw Wulf, unconscious, pale from loss of blood, his chest rising and falling weakly.

Tukul grabbed the spear that pierced Wulf's wrists, jerked it free and Wulf sank into his arms, eyes fluttering open.

'My da . . .' Wulf whispered.

A sound filled the courtyard, overwhelming the din of battle. A pounding roar. Tukul looked up to see bears with giants upon their backs come lumbering around the side of the feast-hall. Two, three, four of them. Upon the first bear sat a blond-haired giant, war-hammer in his fist dripping gore. He looked at the steps, saw the dead bear; his face twisted in rage.

Then he saw Tukul.

CHAPTER FIFTY-FOUR

CORBAN

Corban ran up a gentle slope, weaving amongst half-repaired boats suspended on timber scaffolding as he followed Meical deeper into a maze of grain barns and boatyards, tanners and smokehouses.

They had rowed through the night until Corban felt that his heart and lungs would burst. With the coming of day he'd heard the sounds of battle echo down from the hold upon its hill, seen the fires spreading. Meical had urged them on, until they had turned a bend in the river and seen a row of jetties and boathouses lining the bank. At a glance it was clear that the battle was not over, but also that it wasn't going well for Gramm, great columns of black smoke punctuating the pale blue sky, figures fighting on the hold's walls.

Corban had ordered all armed for war, he'd arrayed himself in his wolven pelt and claws, as had Farrell and Gar. The ship had barely scraped against the jetty before the boarding-plank was lowered and Meical was leaping to shore, Corban and the rest of them surging after him.

Briefly they paused on the riverbank, waiting for numbers to gather, and then they were off, Meical leading the way, Corban following close behind.

He heard the thumping rhythm of Storm running at his side, behind that Balur One-Eye's thunderous gait and the sound of other ships grounding, his warriors pouring from their decks. The plan was simple: to gather on the riverbank and follow Meical to the top of the hill where Gramm's feast-hall stood, where the fighting had seemed fiercest. He'd ordered Cywen to stay on the ship with Brina, Buddai and a handful of others, though that hadn't gone down too well. Giving Cywen orders never went well.

Meical slowed before him and they spilt out of the lanes between buildings into an open space, a high wall looming above them. A bonfire crackled close by, red-cloaked warriors with black cuirasses, a white lightning bolt and coiled serpent upon their leather breast-plates were gathered around it – Jael's men. Open gates stood to the left, bodies strewn about. Gramm's folk. Meical saw them and charged for the gate, seemingly in a berserker rage.

Corban followed without thinking, blocked a hurried blow from a rider, Storm leaping and tearing the attacker from his saddle, rip-ping his throat out before they'd hit the ground.

Balur roared a battle-cry, a handful of his Benothi kin surging forwards swinging their black axes, and suddenly blood was foun-taining. In heartbeats the enemy before the wall were dead or fleeing and Corban was following Meical through the open gates.

Ahead of them towered the rear of a long timber feast-hall, an open space before it of hard-packed earth. To either side of the hall were wide lanes, edged with long stable-blocks and all manner of outbuildings, and amongst them battle raged. Here and there clusters of what must have been Gramm's warriors were holding against overwhelming odds. At the slope's crest, before the feast-hall, Corban caught a glimpse of riders in black mail with curved swords.

Jehar.

'Tukul is here,' Corban cried, turning to Gar, then he was raising his sword and charging into the fray, the thought of his comrades on the far side of this feast-hall fighting alone filling him with a cold fear.

Where is Coralen?

He chopped into the leg of a rider, dragged him from his saddle and let Storm finish him, ran on, slammed into a knot of warriors that had more of Gramm's men backed into the gates of a stable-block. He didn't stop moving – sword and wolven claws raking, stab-bing, chopping. The *battle mind*, as Gar often referred to it, settled upon him, when everything about him seemed slow, as if his foes were moving through water and he could see every blow before it began. A man on foot with sword and shield came at him cautiously and Corban stepped in close, swept a stabbing sword aside and punched his wolven claws over the shield's rim. They came back bloody, the warrior collapsing. He moved on, deflected a spear lunge, stabbed his sword up into an armpit, pivoted away from another horseman who had moved in to attack, Storm leaping at the horse, making it rear and throw its rider to the ground. Corban stabbed him through the throat before he could rise. To his right Corban glimpsed Farrell crush a skull with his war-hammer, to his left Gar took someone's head off. In front of him a rider toppled from his saddle, an arrow through his throat.

Dath. A quick glance showed Kulla with him, the young Jehar protecting Dath's flank.

A deafening roar reverberated around the hold. From the corner of his eye he saw something disappear around the far side of the feast-hall, something huge. He glanced at Gar, but he was concentrating on pulling his sword from someone's chest. Corban continued forwards.

He'd moved closer to the feast-hall, the slope levelling, but still the way was blocked by a heaving mass of combat. He snarled in frustration, desperate to reach Tukul, Coralen and the others. Glancing about, he saw stairs running up the hold's wall and without thinking ran towards them, bounding up two at a time, footsteps following him – Storm and Gar, Farrell, Dath and Kulla.

The walkway was empty of the living. He paused at the top a moment to look about.

The hold was full with seething battle, horses rising and plunging, men screaming. There were more of his warriors pouring through the open gates, numerous Benothi giants amongst them. Further back, he saw Javed leading scores of oarsmen – many of them veterans from the Vin Thalun fighting-pits. Down below him Meical was carving his way through the enemy, behind him Balur and a handful of Benothi moving forwards like a floating island.

A faint sound caught his ear, drifting from the far side of the feast-hall. A battle-cry. Words he'd first heard from his da's lips. He whispered it now.

'Truth and courage.' *Tukul. It is Tukul.*

He ran on, leaping over dead men, the timber planks of the walkway drumming. As he drew closer to the front the gate tower came into view. It was burning, waves of heat and smoke rippling outwards, beyond the wall corpses littering the meadow and entrance.

Then he was above the courtyard before the feast-hall's entrance.

Combat still raged here just as fierce, but not as dense and close-packed as elsewhere. Corban caught a flash of red hair and felt a rush of relief, but before he could shout or even think, his eyes were drawn to the feast-hall steps.

Tukul stood upon them, his sword drawn and held high. Before him a blond-haired giant was sitting astride a monstrously huge bear. Other bears with giants upon their backs roamed the far side of the courtyard – three more of them – killing anything that stood in their way.

Even as Corban and the others stared, frozen for a few moments in shock and disbelief, the bear rumbled forwards, jaws snapping at Tukul, the giant leaning in his saddle to swing a war-hammer. Tukul slipped to the far side, the giant's left, hindering his reach, at the same time slicing at the bear, leaving a red line across the beast's snout. It roared in pain and rage, half-reared and leaped forwards, catching Tukul with a paw, sending him flying up the stairs.

Then Dath was nocking an arrow and drawing, sending it thumping into the great bear's flank. The arrow sank deep but the bear only gave a twitch, as if shrugging off a mosquito. Dath drew and released, and then again, each arrow finding its mark. The fourth one he aimed at the giant, but it skittered off of leather armour as the giant swung his hammer again at Tukul.

'Truth and courage,' Gar bellowed as he leaped from the walkway, landing with a thud on the stable-roof below, then rolling and jumping into the courtyard. Corban echoed the war cry and followed him, Storm leaping after him gracefully. Warriors in the courtyard turned at the sound of their voices, and distantly Corban heard a wild neighing.

Shield?

An arrow hissed over Corban's head, thumping into the bear's belly. This time the bear paused and looked at the feathered shaft protruding from its side.

Tukul took advantage of the lull and darted in, chopping into the creature's shoulder, darting out again, backing up the stairs.

Corban sprinted across the courtyard, swerving amongst mounted Jehar locked in combat with red-cloaked warriors, then he glimpsed Coralen's red hair, fighting back to back with Enkara, four or five enemy closing on them. Corban changed direction, barking a command at Storm. She sprang forwards, smashing one of the red-cloaks to the ground, a scream cut short, and then Corban was there, chopping into a neck, yanking his blade free as that man collapsed, gurgling, Corban spinning and punching his claws into another's thigh. The warrior stumbled back and toppled, his leg giving way, Coralen finishing him. There was no time for words. Corban's eyes met Coralen's for a heartbeat, and then he was running again, towards Tukul. Tukul was at the top of the steps now, standing before two injured men. The bear was wounded, favouring one leg, blood dripping from sword cuts and arrow wounds. The giant upon it was yelling guttural commands. Behind them the other bear riders had formed a half-circle, protecting the blond giant, who was clearly their lord, while he made his kill.

Corban increased his pace as he saw Gar and Farrell ahead of him, a blur of wolven pelt and dark mail. Gar ran straight for the feast-hall steps, a giant seeing him and shouting warning. The giant threw a spear, Gar swerving, the spear-blade slamming quivering into the hard-packed dirt, then Gar was between two of the bears, rolling beneath a paw, leaping onto the steps, trying to reach his da.

At the same time Corban saw the bear on the steps lumber closer to Tukul, who it was clear would retreat no more, standing guard before the injured men. The bear swung a huge paw, Tukul ducking underneath, then standing, fluid as silk, sword rising and falling in a mighty blow, severing the bear's paw.

The bear's roar of pain was deafening, staggering Tukul, and the blond giant took advantage, hurling his war-hammer into Tukul's chest, knocking him backwards, slamming him into the feast-hall doors. He slid to the floor.

Gar screamed, reached the top of the stairs, hurdled the injured men and ran to his da.

Storm was next to reach the steps, leaping onto the bear's neck, sinking her fangs deep into its flesh. The bear reared, throwing the giant on its back from his saddle to crash down the steps into the courtyard. The bear swiped its maimed leg at Storm; with a ripping sound the wolven was torn free, sent flying into one of the pillars with a crack.

Corban and the others reached the steps, swerving around the maimed bear's thrashing limbs. It swiped at Coralen but she ducked and Corban leaped in and buried his wolven claws in the bear's soft belly, raking them and ripping them free, blood gouting from the wound. Then the others were there: Coralen, Enkara and Kulla stabbing and chopping, Farrell swinging his hammer. It crunched into the bear's skull and it spasmed, went rigid, reared up and toppled back down the stairs.

The other giant bears lumbered into motion, closing on the stairs, the fallen giant rising and glowering up at them, reaching for his war-hammer.

Corban ran to Storm.

She rose groggily, whined when he touched her ribs, then growled at the approaching bears.

The others had formed a half-circle about him, bristling with iron. The blond giant knelt down beside his bear, now a bloody ruin of fur.

'I nursed her from a cub,' he said, his voice harsh, grating. He gripped his war-hammer, with a roll of his shoulder twirled it in his hand like Cywen could twirl a knife. Two of the giant bears closed in behind him, the other one clashing with Jehar in the courtyard, holding them back.

Corban braced himself. *Never fought a giant before. Can't be as bad as the Kadoshim.* He gritted his teeth.

'I am Ildaer, warlord of the Jotun,' the giant said. 'You should know the name of your killer.'

'You're welcome to come and try,' Coralen snarled.

An arrow hissed and punched into the giant's shoulder, staggering him.

A strangled cry rang out behind them and Gar pushed past Corban, leaping down the stairs, sword raised, Ildaer raising his war-hammer and catching Gar's blow on the iron-banded hammer-shaft. Gar crashed into him and they tumbled back down the stairs, fell apart, Gar rolling to his feet, surging forwards, the giant rising almost as quickly. Gar's blade sang as it flashed through the air, the giant gripping his war-hammer two-handed, iron sparking and screeching as he blocked a barrage of blows, retreating step by step.

The giant towered over Gar, but he pressed on, unrelenting, striking too fast for Corban to follow, high and low, loops and straight lunges, feints and combinations, a savagery and power in Gar's blows that Corban had never seen before.

The giant was fast, faster than something of that size had the right to be, blocking each sword strike, jabbing with the hammer-shaft, a step back, another jab, but as fast as he was, he could not contain the storm that Gar had become. As Corban watched, a red line opened up on the giant's thigh, another across his forearm, a razor cut across his cheek.

The giant took another step back, Gar pressing on, and Corban frowned. Something was wrong, a repeat in the pattern of blows, something Gar had always told him never to do.

He remembered Gar's advice to him, so long ago, it seemed.

Anger is the enemy.

Abruptly Ildaer stopped retreating, blocked Gar's next blow, sweeping his blade wide, and kicked Gar in the chest. Corban heard bones crack and Gar tumbled head over heels backwards. The giant strode after him.

Corban ran down the stairs, leaped and stood over Gar.

'Where is your honour?' Ildaer sneered. Blood sheeted the giant's cheek, ran down one arm, slicking the spiralling tattoos, soaked the wool of his breeches.

'Honour be damned, he is my friend,' Corban snarled, 'and you'll have to kill me before you touch him again.' He heard Storm growl behind him.

Ildaer looked at him, at his friends on the steps behind him. The giants and their bears stood like stone, tension thick as storm clouds.

A voice rang out from the left and Corban looked to see Balur standing with Meical at the far end of the courtyard, scores of the Benothi and Jehar at their back.

'Ildaer, you whelp,' Balur growled, raising his black axe.

'Balur One-Eye – it cannot be,' Corban heard Ildaer whisper, suddenly going as pale as alabaster.

Then Ildaer was turning and running to the closest bear-rider behind him, swinging up onto the bear's back and fleeing through the gates. Balur charged after them, the Benothi following and screaming insults. Corban knelt beside Gar. He was conscious, breathing in short, controlled breaths.

'Help me, to my father,' he whispered.

Farrell was beside him and between them they carried Gar up the steps, past the two injured men that Tukul had been protecting – one alive but unconscious, one very obviously dead – and then they were beside Tukul, his body twisted where he'd fallen.

Tukul was still alive, his breaths coming in ragged wheezes.

Gar grimaced in pain, took his father's hand.

Tukul opened his eyes, for a moment unfocused. Then he saw his son.

'My Gar,' Tukul wheezed. Blood speckled his lips.

'Corban, where is Brina?' Gar said, voice cracking. 'Get Brina.'

'Peace, Gar, it is . . . too late for that,' Tukul said. He looked past Gar and saw Corban, other faces pressing in.

'I told you . . . I would be here . . . first,' he said to Corban.

'Aye, you did,' Corban said with a lump in his throat.

'And we made a fair song of it, eh, Cora?'

'We did,' Coralen said, a tremor in her voice. 'You did. You weren't content with one bear. You had to kill two.'

A smile fluttered at the edges of Tukul's mouth. 'Remember what I said to you.'

She smiled softly at him.

Tukul coughed, went rigid with pain, blood dribbling down his chin.

'My sword,' he whispered, voice faint and thin.

Corban put the hilt in Tukul's hand, closed his fingers around it – he looked away to hide his sorrow. He was Tukul's Bright Star and he would stay strong for him in his last moments. No matter what it cost him.

Footsteps sounded on the steps behind. Meical was standing silent, looking down upon them.

'Gar, my beloved son,' Tukul whispered, 'you are my *joy*.' Tears dripped from Gar's nose. 'Never forget that. I'll see you again, on the other side,' Tukul breathed, then with a sigh he was gone.

CHAPTER FIFTY-FIVE

VERADIS

Veradis stood at the prow of the ship and watched the coast of Tenebral pass him by.

I grew up on this coastline. He closed his eyes and thought of sailing with Krelis, dolphins chasing their ship as it cut through the water. Krelis laughing. *Krelis is always laughing when I remember him.* Of swimming in the bay of Ripa, sunning on rocks, drinking wine, sparring on the beaches that ringed the bay. *Krelis always laughed at that, too. How I'd not give up until I was on my back, him a giant and me little more than a bairn.*

He opened his eyes as the ship shifted beneath him. Alazon was yelling commands; ropes on the sail tightened and loosened, and then the dip and bite of oars. Before them a bay opened up in the coastline, deep and wide, high cliffs dipping towards sandy beaches.

The Bay of Ripa.

Home.

They passed from the open sea into the bay's sheltered embrace, behind them fourteen black sails following their course.

There was already a host of black ships in the bay, clustered about the port of Ripa, more spread throughout its waters. Veradis spied other ships amongst them. *More like the corpses of ships.* They were ruined and fire-blackened, hulls upturned and wallowing. *Ripa's ships.* He frowned at that. Beyond them, rising high upon gleaming limestone cliffs Veradis saw the tower of Ripa, built by giants, conquered and claimed by men, now the home and symbol of the Lord of the Bay.

My father.

What am I doing here? The weight of his task came crushing down upon him, the sun-tinged, halcyon glow that had filled him turning to iron-grey clouds, heavy with impending doom. His mind returned to Calidus pulling him to one side on the banks of the Afren in Narvon, just before he had set sail.

Bring me Fidele, in chains if needs be.

Veradis had not believed it, or that she had wed Lykos, and he had said as much, had questioned Calidus' information, but the silver-haired counsellor – *and Ben-Elim* – had been adamant.

I was as shocked as you,' Calidus had said. 'But it is true. By all accounts Lykos is infatuated with her. But that is not the end of it. She arrested Peritus and Armatus, sentenced them both to death. That seems to have been the touchstone of this rebellion. There was rioting, Lykos and the Vin Thalun attacked by an angry mob. And now, moons later, Fidele has reappeared, in Ripa where the rebellion is centred. Now she is denouncing Lykos and the Vin Thalun, and inciting the whole of Tenebral to rise up against them.'

Veradis shook his head, eyes fixed on the tower. Fidele, my father and brothers. How can I fix this? I am a warrior, not a diplomat.

'What do you want me to do?' he had asked Calidus.

'Try to reason with them. Peace is what we need, with Lykos in control. If that is not possible.' He shrugged. 'A decisive victory, show them the strength of your shield wall.'

'All warbands in Tenebral have been learning the shield wall. It would be a bloodbath, and a waste of men.'

'Aye, but your father and Krelis – they are not progressive. I doubt they would fight with it, and even if they did, you have faced giants, draigs, warbands numbering thousands. You are battle-hardened, veterans of a score of battles. You will not lose.'

'How can I fight my kin?' Veradis asked the waves now.

'Whoever leads this rebellion must be put down. Fidele, Peritus, your father or brother, without sentiment. Whoever they are, they must be cowed, that is all. Taught that opposing Nathair is pointless. You can teach that lesson. Fidele you bring to me, the rest, deal with at your discretion. Bring them to me, execute them, exile them, do as you will,' Calidus had said.

'Deal with them at your discretion,' Veradis murmured.

*

The port of Ripa was empty and silent. Veradis' fifteen ships docked and his men disembarked, near a thousand men in iron helms and coats of mail, black cuirasses polished, silver eagles gleaming upon their chests. They were dressed in the modifications Veradis had implemented over the last two years: iron-banded boots instead of sandals, breeches of charcoal wool instead of leather kilts, longer, oval shields instead of round ones. They all wore two swords at their hips – short and long, and held spears in their hands, lighter and longer than the traditional hunting spears.

Lykos was waiting to greet him, a few hundred Vin Thalun about him, looking more like a rabble than a warband beside Veradis' disciplined ranks.

They look dangerous enough, though. Especially him. Veradis was looking at a warrior beside Lykos, of average height, lean and scarred, but his eyes were cold and hard, grey and bleak like a stormy sea. They stared flatly back at him. *Dead eyes.*

'Well met,' Lykos said, grinning at Veradis. They greeted one another with the warrior grip. Things had not gone well for Lykos in Tenebral, and not so long ago Veradis might have taken a little pleasure in that, probably because of his own deep-rooted prejudices against the Vin Thalun, but since Veradis' failure to catch or kill Corban he felt mostly empathy for Lykos rather than anything else.

'Nathair sends his greetings,' Veradis said, 'and he sends you this.' Veradis reached inside his cloak and pulled out two scrolls, checked the seals on them, gave one to Lykos and put the other back in his cloak.

Lykos took it and slipped it into his belt.

'Not going to open it?' Veradis raised an eyebrow.

'Later,' Lykos said, linking his arm with Veradis'. 'Right now we need to go and join a battle.'

'What?'

'Your timing is excellent, my old friend,' Lykos said, his breath smelling of wine, 'but any tarrying here and we'll miss the fun.'

Old friend?

'Three warbands are arrayed on the fields beyond Ripa, all of them eyeing each other with bad intentions.'

'With all haste then,' Veradis said and he led his warband through the streets of Ripa.

*

Veradis stood and surveyed the field. He was standing to the south-west, at the foot of the slope that Ripa was built upon. To his left, filling the meadows right up to the eaves of the forest Sarva, were the Vin Thalun, numbering well over three thousand men, at a glance. Upon the slope to the east stood the warband of Ripa, fewer men but appearing more formidable, all wearing the black and silver of Tenebral, though without Nathair's eagle.

And to the north another warband, again men of Tenebral, the banner of Marcellin of Baran rippling above their formed lines. From this distance it was hard to reckon their numbers, but easily in the thousands.

Lykos wasn't joking; he is fortunate I have arrived.

'Lykos, I need a horse,' Veradis said, 'saddled and ready.' The Vin Thalun frowned but barked at a warrior and sent him off running.

'Caesus, you know what to do.' Veradis' young captain nodded to him and marched off with two dozen eagle-guard in tow.

It was not long before a white mare was presented to him, dancing with energy. Veradis adjusted the harness for himself and swung into the saddle, patting the mare's neck. He reached out and an eagle-guard handed him a banner.

He cantered first up the hill towards his father's warband, holding the banner high. It was white linen, the black branch and red berries of a rowan stark upon it, symbol of truce. As he drew closer he began to see faces he recognized – these were by and large men whom he'd grown up around for the first eighteen years of his life.

A murmur spread along their ranks, rippling ahead of him as he rode along their front line, nodding to those he knew. When he reached the centre of the line he reined in before a man a head taller than any other gathered upon the slope. His brother Krelis.

They just stared at each other, silence settling about them, between them.

'Didn't expect to see you here,' Krelis said in the end.

'We need to talk,' Veradis said. 'Bring Father, down there.' He nodded into the centre of the field, where a white tent was being erected by Caesus and two dozen eagle-guard.

'This has gone past talking,' Krelis said.

'If we don't talk lives will be lost for no good reason.'

Behind the tent being raised Veradis' eagle-guard were marching in shield-wall formation. For a moment Veradis just sat and admired them, pride washing over him. The crash of their shields as they turned and stood behind the tent echoed about the field.

Krelis watched too.

'It's a trap – I don't trust that bastard Lykos.'

'Trust me. It is a rowan-meet. My men will guard all who set foot there.'

He looked at Krelis again, noticing lines around his eyes and across his forehead that had not been there the last time Veradis had seen him.

'You've changed,' Krelis said to him.

Veradis smiled. Krelis had always made him smile.

'You've changed too, big brother. You look old.'

'Cheeky pup.' Krelis grinned.

Veradis kicked his horse into motion. 'Down there, bring Father, and anyone else who you think should have a say.'

He rode away from the warband, towards the north of the plain, where Marcellin was camped.

More than four thousand, Veradis thought as he approached Marcellin, *closer to five.*

Marcellin hailed from Baran, a fortress carved out of, and into, the Agullas Mountains. He was a big, gruff man of somewhere between fifty and sixty summers, and he had a pair of bushy eyebrows that dominated his craggy face.

Bos came from Baran, grew up there, I remember. He felt a stab of sadness at the memory of his friend. Good friends were hard to find.

'Who are you?' Marcellin asked him as he reined in before him.

'Veradis ben Lamar, first-sword and general of King Nathair, and I speak with his voice.'

'Oh, do you now?' Marcellin asked, eyebrows bunching as he stared up at Veradis.

'I do, my lord.'

'Well, don't think to try and persuade me against kicking that arse Lykos out of my country. He is a disease, and I mean to cut him out. There's nothing you can say to sway me.'

'I am not going to try,' Veradis said. He reached inside his cloak and suddenly Marcellin's shieldmen were pointing a lot of sharp iron his way.

'I am no assassin,' Veradis said, trying to keep the anger from his voice, and not entirely sure he was successful.

'Go slowly, then,' Marcellin said. 'My lads are fond of this old man.'

Veradis pulled out a rolled scroll, sealed with red wax.

'From Nathair,' Veradis said.

Marcellin took it, frowning bad-temperedly at it.

'Read it, and if it is to your liking, join me for a rowan-meet with Lamar and Lykos in that tent.' Without waiting for an answer, he rode away.

CHAPTER FIFTY-SIX

CYWEN

Cywen wrapped bandages around Gar's chest; it had started to bruise already but he didn't so much as wince as she pulled the cloth straps tightly to bind his ribs. He sat upon a bench in the feast-hall of Gramm's hold, eyes downcast. Once she'd tied off the bandage she squeezed his hand and he looked at her, eyes red-rimmed and hollow.

I remember that pain, can feel it still, though it is buried deeper now than it was. Da, Mam, Heb, Tukul – how many more people we care about will we lose before this is over? She wished she could do something to ease his pain.

'You've some cracked ribs,' she said. 'The bandages will give some support, help them heal, but the fact is anything you do is going to hurt, and that includes breathing.' He nodded and she helped him back into his coat of dark mail. 'Take this with you,' she said, offering him a vial.

'What is it?'

'Poppy milk, it will dull the pain.'

'I do not want it dulled. I deserve it,' he muttered. He picked up his scabbarded sword and walked away.

The feast-hall had been turned into an impromptu hospice, and bodies were everywhere, filling long tables, the metallic tang of blood thick in the air. Cywen had stayed on the ship during the battle, ordered by Corban to help in the organization of unloading the provisions they'd need from ship to shore. She'd been annoyed at first but had seen the sense of it. She was not Corban with a blade, or Gar, or even Farrell for that matter. And the ships needed unloading by someone with more than half a brain, so she'd set to it, with Brina snapping orders at her and Cywen delegating the heavy lifting to Laith and a dozen other giantlings – who had also been forbidden by Balur and Ethlinn to join in the fight.

Added to the giantlings there were over two score of the villagers who had joined them during the journey through Narvon, as well as a few score oarsmen who had rowed the last sprint to the hold and had been too exhausted to move, let alone fight, so Cywen and Brina had quite the workforce at their disposal. All eight ships were close to unloaded when Cywen heard a great rumbling and ran to the raised deck at the back of the ship to get a view of what was happening. The hold on the top of the hill was wreathed in smoke, but the din of battle had faded, only the occasional muted rumble. Now, though, that rumble grew, a cloud of dust rising beyond the hold and swirling eastwards. Brina and Laith had come to stand beside her, then other giantlings.

The dust cloud had veered north, down the hill, then Cywen had seen what looked to be animals, running, small from this distance, but still clearly bigger than horses, three or four of them, with figures riding upon their backs.

'Are they auroch?' Cywen mused.

'They are the war-bears of the Jotun,' Laith said beside her, something in her voice hovering somewhere between awe and loathing.

Then Cywen saw what the bears were running from: a mass of horses, Jehar, and giants. Amazingly the gap between the bears and those chasing them widened. The bears ran with surprising speed once their momentum was up, straight to the river and without a pause leaping in, sinking beneath the surface for a moment before reappearing and swimming steadily to the far bank. Cywen watched them cross the river and climb out upon the far side, bears shaking themselves dry. A giant had dismounted and walked back to the river's edge, stood there staring across at his pursuers, who had reached the riverbank now and stood ranged along it, Cywen seeing the silver of Balur One-Eye's hair. The giant across the river had raised his arm, holding an axe or war-hammer – Cywen could not tell from this distance – and shouted. No one gave a response and the giant turned, climbed onto a bear's back and the three bears had shambled away.

After that, word had come down to them that the battle was over and Brina and Cywen were needed at the hold.

And here she was still. She watched Gar walk from the feast-hall, the bright light of highsun beaming through the open doors about him. There were many working on the injured: Cywen and Brina, Ethlinn and Laith, as well as healers from the hold itself, chief of them a woman named Hild, the wife of Gramm's son, Wulf.

The far end of the hall was being filled with the dead, Jehar, Benothi giants, men of the hold laid out upon tables. Cywen looked back at Tukul's corpse, wrapped in his cloak now and lying alongside Gramm's body.

So many dead. She felt a hot flush of rage, aimed mostly at Calidus and Nathair. *All of this goes back to them, eventually. Calidus most of all, by whatever webs he has woven and pulled the threads; he is the author of this ill.*

She turned and walked for the doors, suddenly feeling suffocated by the cloying stink of blood.

Fresh air, I need fresh air.

She walked out onto a balcony before wide steps; Buddai uncurled from the spot he'd been lying in, tail thumping on wood. Cywen made her way to one of the columns bracing the overhanging roof and leaned against it, taking long, deep breaths. There was a cold wind blowing through the hold, but right now it was refreshing, setting her skin tingling and easing the taint of death that was thick in the feast-hall. She looked at the bloodstains on her hands, under her fingernails, saw stains on the column she was leaning upon, pooled about her feet.

Blood, everywhere.

She forced herself to look away and saw that she was not the only one who had been busy.

The courtyard was clear of the dead, instead filled with a score of wains and a herd of horses, all being laden with goods – barrels, chests, clothing, weapons tied in bundles – harvested from the dead, no doubt. At the edges of the courtyard long stable-blocks rang with life, familiar sounds of saddling up, horses neighing, harness jangling that reminded her with sudden and sharp clarity of Dun Carreg, so much so that it almost took her breath away. Closer she saw Corban at the bottom of the steps. He was standing with Meical and

Balur, in conversation with Wulf, now lord of this hold. Gar stood behind Corban, his eyes fixed grimly on the carcass of a great bear that had been dragged aside. Corban saw Cywen and beckoned to her.

'The wounded, Cywen,' Corban asked her when she reached them. 'Can they travel?'

Brina should be asked this question. Where is she?

'Most,' Cywen said. 'There are a few who could not sit on a horse, probably for at least a moon.'

'How about a wain?'

Cywen looked at the wains in the yard. 'Aye, that should be fine. Stitches will need to be kept an eye on, fevers and so on, but I'd say there's none amongst the living unfit to travel.'

'Good,' Wulf said with passion. 'I would be gone from this place.'

'Agreed,' Meical said. 'We need to leave. Word will spread of what has happened here, and we need to be long gone before Jael sends a larger warband, or Ildaer braves the river with the full strength of his clan.'

Balur grunted at that.

'There are so many of us, so much to bring . . .' Hild said.

'There is plenty of room in Drassil,' Meical said. 'But we must travel light – we will most likely be hunted. We must make it to Forn with all haste.'

'The horses,' Wulf said. 'My da spent a lifetime breeding them, I cannot just abandon them.'

'Bring them,' Meical said. 'Drassil is colossal. There are no stables, but there are bear pens the size of this hold that could be easily converted. And meadows have been cleared for a league all about the fortress – your da did not rest idle at Drassil for sixteen years,' Meical said to Gar.

Coralen approached them, the first that Cywen had seen of her. She'd been sent to oversee the sinking of their ships, Corban determined that nothing be left for their enemy's use. Her red hair was dark with sweat, her face was soot stained and tight with grief. She was carrying an axe in her hands that she offered to Gar.

'It is your da's. I found it in the skull of a dead bear, beyond the wall,' Coralen said.

Gar took it. 'His sword I leave with him,' he said, voice hoarse. 'But I would be glad to carry one of his weapons. It feels . . . right. Especially one that he was so fond of.' He frowned, looking down at it. 'But I have never used an axe before . . .'

'I will teach you,' Wulf said, then his mouth twisted as he looked at his bandaged hands. 'If I can.'

'He spoke highly of you,' Gar said. 'And of your da.'

Grief swept Wulf's face. 'He tried to save my da – pulled him down from . . .' His eyes flickered to the column, to his bandaged hands. 'He stood over us, before that bear . . .'

A warrior ran up, one from Gramm's hold.

'Has the half-breed been found?' Wulf said to the man, a cold rage in his voice.

'She is not amongst the dead,' the warrior replied.

'Fled, then,' Wulf snarled.

'Who?' Meical asked him.

'A half-breed traitor. We gave her a home, raised her, yet she chose to betray Haelan to the enemy. It was only thanks to the boy's quick wits that he'd fled his hiding place before Trigg revealed it to our enemies.'

'Sometimes it feels that this world is full of traitors,' Meical said.

'Aye.' Wulf nodded. 'But I vow, if I ever see this one again, it will be one less amongst the living.'

'We should raise cairns—' Corban said, looking at the blood-stained hold.

'Too long,' Meical said. 'We would still be here when Jael came riding up with a thousand men.'

'Burn them,' Wulf said grimly, 'burn the entire hold, leave nothing for our enemy.'

Cywen stood beside her brother, facing the feast-hall, a host gathered behind them. Beyond the gates a long column of wains and horses loaded with provisions was waiting for them.

A silence fell over the courtyard and Brina sang the first lines of the lament, the melody stark and pure, Gar and Wulf adding their voices first, then more joining until the whole host sang the song for the dead, their voices rising to deafening crescendo, filling Cywen's heart with a tide of emotion. As the last notes died, Wulf and Gar stepped forward and threw burning torches at the feast-hall steps.

The steps and hall had been doused with oil, and flames roared skywards, hungry and crackling. In short moments the hall was ablaze, heat rolling at them in great waves.

Wulf turned and left the courtyard, followed by Corban and then all of the others. As Cywen mounted her horse she saw Gar standing before the gates, outlined by flames, still staring at the hall.

Cywen glanced sidelong at Brina.

Should I talk to her, about last night, about the book? After all that's happened it seems almost unimportant . . . Still the memory of the giant words she'd seen had haunted and swirled about her mind throughout the whole long day. She'd wanted to talk to Corban about it, but there had been no opportunity thus far.

'You might as well come out and say it,' Brina said acerbically. 'Holding your tongue suits you just about as much as it does your brother.'

They'd ridden leagues across rolling meadows, their convoy now close to a thousand souls, heading steadily towards what looked like an ocean of trees that filled the horizon in every direction. Behind them the hold still burned, a flickering beacon upon its hill.

'The book,' Cywen said, talking quietly, even though they were riding between two wains full of the injured and semi-conscious.

Brina sighed, lips pursing, but she said nothing.

She's not going to make this easy.

'It scared me,' Cywen said.

Brina was silent, again. Cywen thought she would not answer. Then Brina spoke softly.

'It scares me, too.'

'It is a book of spells, isn't it?'

'Aye, some of it is.'

'I don't understand. I thought the book is about faith, that being an Elemental is simply believing it and speaking it. That's what you told me – that's what the book says. I read it myself.'

'Aye, that's right,' Brina said. Her wrinkled face twitched.

'So why the need for spells, when faith is all?'

'Faith is *not* all,' Brina snapped. 'That is the point. Faith can be strong, then weak, then gone, all in the same person, all in the space of a hundred heartbeats. That's why Heb died. His faith wavered.' She was silent a moment, abruptly her breathing laboured. 'So the book explains the alternative. The other way. Spells give the wielder more control, more consistency.'

'So they're easier?'

'Not exactly. With faith, there is no cost, no price to pay. But spells are . . . different. Firstly they are harder to perform, in one sense – there is the gathering of ingredients, how to prepare them, knowing the words of power and so on.'

'Like a poultice, or medicinal potion?'

'Exactly.'

I knew she wanted to talk about this, would not be able to stop once she started.

'Although from what I can see, the ingredients are not so easy to come by as meadowsweet or foxglove, or as pleasant.'

'What do you mean?'

'I mean, the ingredients for these spells are often hard to come by, and by and large unwholesome.'

'Unwholesome?'

'Yes. For example, blood is often an ingredient.'

Cywen was silent. She didn't like the sound of this, just talking about it was making the hairs at the back of her neck stand on end.

'But there is also another cost.' Brina stopped there, looking around to check that no one was listening.

'What other cost?' Cywen prompted.

'I'm not sure,' Brina said. 'The book hints and alludes, but –' she shrugged – 'I need more time to work it out. It is appealing – could be useful in this God-War. To go into battle *knowing* what you are capable of, having confidence in what you can do. Not like my poor Heb . . .'

'I don't like it,' Cywen muttered.

'I don't like it either,' Brina retorted. 'But that doesn't mean you don't use it. I don't like swords or spears, or fire when it's used to burn a person. There is much in life I don't *like*. But should I throw away or choose not to use a weapon that could help us *win*?'

'I don't know,' Cywen said begrudgingly.

'I know you wish to speak of this with Corban,' Brina said. 'I am asking you to wait. There is more I have seen – hints and riddles about the cauldron, about the Seven Treasures. I am trying to understand it.'

'We could ask Balur, or Meical,' Cywen said.

'No,' snapped Brina. Then, calmer: 'Please. Let me try. Just a little longer.'

I guess I owe her that much. If spells can help us then we should probably take every opportunity. Still, I don't like it . . . and if she doesn't tell Corban soon then I will.

Having reached a resolution with herself, Cywen slipped into silence again until she saw a group of riders cantering towards them from the east, a score, maybe a few more.

Brina kicked her horse on.

'Where are you going?' Cywen asked her.

'One of the benefits of being a counsellor,' Brina said over her shoulder, 'I get to be nosy.' She cantered down the column towards Corban.

Cywen thought about that a moment.

Well, I am Brina's apprentice, or assistant, or whatever she likes to call me. So I should assist her. She kicked her horse after Brina.

Corban raised an arm and Dath blew on his horn, the whole column rippling to a halt. The riders approaching them were mostly warriors, dressed in leather and fur, with iron helms, straight spears and strong shields, their war gear looking similar to that of the surviving warriors from Gramm's hold. Then Cywen saw the bairns – two riding together on one horse, a lad and lass, and another sitting before a thickset warrior with long arms and no neck. A small white dog ran along beside them.

They are from Gramm's hold.

It was a good guess because Hild, sobbing and smiling, jumped down from the wain she was driving and ran to meet them, the lad and lass slipping from their horse to run into her arms.

Wulf and Hild's children, then. The ones Jael had been holding hostage. But who is the other child?

Corban stopped before the warrior with the child sitting in front of him. The white dog ran around Shield, barking excitedly, then he saw Storm, tucked his tail between his legs and hid behind the horse. He stuck his head out from behind a leg and growled.

Storm looked disdainfully at him, then looked away.

'Wulf tells me that you are Haelan,' Corban said to the lad, who was dirt stained, and looked exhausted and scared witless, but he managed to sit straighter in his saddle, and when he spoke he looked Corban in the eye and his voice had conviction.

'I am Haelan ben Romar, rightful King of Isiltir,' the lad said.

'Well met, Haelan,' Corban said, speaking solemnly. 'I am Corban ben Thannon, and I am prince of nowhere and king of nothing, but I do lead these people, and we are sworn to fight the man who has usurped your throne, because he serves Asroth and the Black Sun. So you would be welcome amongst us and, I suppose, as safe as it is possible to be in these times of war.'

Haelan looked up at Corban, then down at Storm, and finally along the column that stretched back almost out of sight, full of Jehar, Benothi giants, pit-fighters and so many others.

'You are going to fight Jael? Going to defeat him?'

Corban smiled. 'I cannot promise you a victory, only that I'll fight him and win, or die in the trying.'

Haelan nodded, not looking like his eleven or twelve summers at all.

'That is good enough for me,' Haelan said. 'I will gladly join your warband, Corban ben Thannon.'

Corban held out his hand and took Haelan's arm in the warrior grip. The lad looked momentarily taken aback, then pleased. And then Corban was riding back to the head of the column, Dath blowing on his horn again, and the warband stuttered into movement, the newcomers joining them. Buddai left Cywen's side and loped over to the small terrier, who jumped all over him as if they had been friends forever. Buddai slapped the dog gently with a paw, then rolled in the grass.

Cywen smiled at the sight, seeming so natural and ordinary in these most unnatural of times. She took one last look behind her, the sun sinking into the horizon, the fires on Gramm's hill guttering low. Then she turned her head to the east and rode on, towards the endless green that was Forn Forest.

CHAPTER FIFTY-SEVEN

EVNIS

Evnis sat by the tower gates with his head in his hands. He felt a lot of things right now. *Foolish, most of all. I cannot believe that I just stood up in the middle of a field and called Vonn's name.*

The emotion of seeing his son after so long had been over-whelming. *Clearly.* But it was fading now, a distant blend of joy and fear. In its wake was the realization that he had ruined an excep-tional plan. It didn't help that Braith was pointing that out to him, repeatedly.

And Morcant was furious about his silver. *It's not his silver. It was given to him by Rhin, and she will expect to see it used wisely or returned to her. Perhaps that is why he is so angry. Or scared.*

The sun was setting, and Evnis' hundred shieldmen had arrived. Morcant had ridden in with two hundred swords, so the tower and hill was suddenly a very busy place with horses being put out to pasture, tents going up and food being cooked.

Before him the marshlands shimmered, glittering like a many-faceted jewel in the fading rays of the sun. With a deep sigh he stood and walked down the hill to where Braith and Morcant were stand-ing, close to where the enemy had escaped. Glyn followed a few paces behind.

I cannot believe that I stood in the open and allowed an enemy to aim his bow at me.

Evnis had never been an impulsive man – emotional, yes, deeply so, but he never acted on that emotion. Not immediately, anyway, certainly not impulsively. *Except today.*

And there had been one high spot, one good moment in the midst of all of the irrational behaviour and shame.

Vonn saved me.

Evnis had played that moment over and over in his mind; Camlin with an arrow aimed at his heart, and then Vonn's hand resting on the archer's arm, stalling him.

What does that mean? The one thing for sure is that at that moment he didn't want me to die. That gives me much hope. If only I could have talked to him. He ground his teeth. *It will happen, and when it does, he will come back to me. If he does not – I cannot have my son fighting for my enemy.* He stopped himself from thinking that . . . he would not allow it to come to that.

He reached Braith and Morcant. Rafe, a little apart, was squatting with the two hounds and looking down the waterway that had been used so effectively as an escape route. Morcant had tried to follow, hell-bent on recovering his chest of silver, but within a few hundred paces the ground became impossible to ride a horse upon, and soon after that was too treacherous to walk upon. Maybe with time, men picking their route, but not fast enough to keep the boats within sight.

'We need to talk,' Evnis said, the sight of Morcant's petulant face both annoying him and focusing him.

'We need to do more than talk,' Morcant muttered, but Evnis pretended he hadn't heard him and walked on towards the riverbank.

'So. Let us decide,' Evnis said. 'How, exactly, are we going to kill Edana?'

'Starve them out,' Morcant said. 'I've been building towers around the marshland, they won't be able to leave without my seeing them. And I'll either buy the local villages' loyalty, or raze them to the ground. Either way they won't be able to trade for food.'

Evnis looked at him as if he was mad.

'They live in a marsh. It's not farmland, where crops only come in the right season. Look in that river and you'll see a hundred fish. They are not going to come out because they're starving.'

Morcant scowled at him but didn't reply.

Intelligence is not a necessary pre-requisite for skill with a blade, then.

'We either lure them out, which I imagine will be impossible, or we go in there after them,' Evnis said.

'I'm going to go in there and find them,' Braith said. 'Then I'll send someone back to get you.'

'You can do that?'

'Aye. That's what I was going to do anyway – would've been easier if I'd had Halion to follow . . .' He looked pointedly at Evnis. 'And now Camlin knows I'm here, he won't make life any easier for me.' His hand drifted up to the scar between his neck and shoulder. 'But I can still do it. It will take longer, and I'll need a few more men – huntsmen, preferably. If that's not possible then men who are good on their feet, quiet. Observant.'

'You shall have them. But, once you find Edana and send word to me, how do you suggest I bring a warband in there?' He looked at the marsh, lip curling in disgust.

'Buy boats. Build boats. Steal boats. That's how they're getting around in there, and it's the only way you'll move a significant amount of men.'

There's a forest a few leagues behind me, and every village situated about this stinking mosquito-infested latrine will have fisher-boats.

'We can do that,' he said.

'You'll need a lot of boats for that lot,' Braith observed, looking back up to the tower.

'I don't think even that will be enough,' Evnis said. 'I'm sending a messenger back to Dun Carreg for more warriors. We don't know how many are in there – fifty, a hundred, three hundred, five? I don't want to go to all this hard work, get our warband in there only to find out that we're outnumbered.'

'Makes sense,' Braith said. 'And you'll want to leave Morcant's towers manned, in case they decide to bolt and run. Not enough for a fight, but enough to track them if they go running.'

'Aye. Good,' grunted Evnis. *For all of his arrogance he is a good man to have around in a situation like this. And whatever arrogance he has, it is as nothing to that preening peacock over there.*

Morcant had just stood and listened, glowering every now and then into the marshland.

'Long as I get that chest of silver back,' he muttered.

'You might never see it again,' Evnis said, enjoying seeing him squirm a little.

'If I don't I'll be telling Rhin you're the reason it's gone,' Morcant snapped.

'Ha, that silver was gone before I arrived. You wouldn't even know about it for another ten-night if I hadn't been here.'

Morcant stalked up to him, his blade in his hands, and Evnis fought the desire to take an involuntary step back.

'I will have it back, or I'll have blood,' Morcant snarled.

'I can promise you one of those,' Evnis told him, glaring.

'And what if you see your son again?' Morcant sneered. 'Will you betray our position again? Perhaps you should not come.'

'You do not make the decisions here,' Evnis said, cold and hard now. 'And I promise you all, I shall not act again as I did today. The next time I see him, my son will join me, or he will die.'

CHAPTER FIFTY-EIGHT

VERADIS

'I do not think this is a good idea,' Lykos said as he leaned back in his chair and tipped more wine into his mouth.

'Why not?' Veradis asked him.

'Because none of the people that you have invited to this party like me.'

'That is probably true—'

'Definitely,' Lykos interrupted.

'You are safe enough for now, this is a rowan-meet; it is sacred.'

Lykos raised an eyebrow. 'You'd be surprised how far some people will go, once they have begun a course. And, as I said, they *really* don't like me.'

What damage have you caused in Tenebral? Whatever you have done, it ends now. Veradis felt an overwhelming anger at Lykos and the trouble he had caused. If it were up to him he would have slapped him in chains and given the regency back to Fidele, or to Peritus if the rumours of her unstable mind were true. *But it is not up to me. I have been given clear orders where Lykos is concerned, more's the pity.*

'We must try and reach some compromise.'

'Surely. As long as it doesn't involve me being separated from any of my body parts.'

'Nathair values you most highly. That is not an option.'

'You reassure me,' Lykos said with a smile, then drank some more wine. 'Not as much as having Kolai standing at my back, perhaps, but enough to convince me to stay and see what happens.'

All were allowed one person to accompany them, again, out of tradition more than any real fear of danger. The rowan-meet was sacred, a deep-rooted tradition brought with the Exiles from the

Summer Isle. Kolai, the cold-eyed warrior whom Veradis had noticed on the harbour, stood implacably behind the chair Lykos was sitting in. Veradis had brought Caesus with him.

The tent flap was pulled back and in walked Lamar, Lord of Ripa.

Da. Veradis felt the breath catch in his chest. His da had aged, far more than the two years that had passed since last they'd seen one another. He was gaunt, a stoop to his frame that had never been there before, and the skin on his bones was loose and waxy. His eyes met Veradis' and he stopped, just stared at his son. Those eyes still held all the wit and intelligence that Veradis remembered.

'Father,' Veradis said.

'You have grown,' Lamar said solemnly, looking him up and down.

Veradis shrugged, not knowing what to say. Suddenly he felt like a little boy in his father's presence.

'Gods, but you look like your mother,' Lamar said with a sigh.

Veradis blinked at that. Others had said much the same. Many others, but never his father.

'Please, sit,' was all he could think of to say.

A table had been set out, with a jug of wine and cups. Lamar sat opposite Lykos. He regarded the Vin Thalun lord with what most would have considered an emotionless gaze, but Veradis could see the cold hatred behind his father's eyes. Then there were more figures entering the tent. Ektor came first, looking completely unchanged, dark hair stuck across his forehead, face pale and sallow. He met Veradis' eye and nodded to him, no words of greeting.

They had never been close.

Behind him came Peritus and Alben, both men he respected, one whom he loved. Alben had been his weapons-master, and more than that, had shown him more kindness than his father ever had. He smiled at the old man, silver hair tied tight at the nape. Alben returned the smile, warm and open, and then they were both sitting.

Marcellin entered then, with one shieldman at his back, a warrior almost as tall as Krelis. He sat with a nod to Lamar and Peritus and poured himself some wine.

'Welcome,' Veradis said, moving to a chair.

'Not all are here yet,' Lamar said, holding a hand up.

Then Fidele stepped into the tent.

She paused at the entrance, her eyes fixing on Lykos with clear hatred and scorn.

Hardly the loving wife, then. She was as beautiful as she had always been, though different. There was something hard about her, the bones of her face harsher, muscles shifting in her forearm as she gripped the tent pole. And stronger. She had seemed frail when Veradis had left Tenebral, brittle with grief. Now that was gone. She tore her eyes away from Lykos, who was not looking happy at her presence, and walked to an empty chair.

'She should not be here,' Lykos said. 'She is unhinged, has brought this realm to the brink of war.'

'I will not leave,' Fidele said. She looked at Veradis as she said it, not Lykos.

She does not look unhinged to me.

Behind her a warrior entered, not overly tall or muscular, but his presence filled the room, a melding of grace and menace. He was old for a shieldman, streaks of iron in his hair, heavily scarred, one ear just a lump of flesh, and he was not dressed as a warrior of Tenebral, only in a plain linen shirt and leather vest. And knives. Two at his belt besides his sword, a hilt poking from a boot, and Veradis suspected more were secreted about his body. Then the warrior looked at Veradis.

'Maquin,' he whispered.

'Well met,' Maquin said, his face a cold mask.

The last time I saw him was in Forn. He was wounded, bloody, had been chased to exhaustion, but I still recognized him. Now, though, this is not that man . . .

Maquin stood behind Fidele.

'So you have tamed the Old Wolf, then,' Lykos said.

'Do not speak to her,' Maquin said.

'Or what?' Lykos said good-naturedly. 'This is a rowan-meet, remember.'

Maquin said nothing, just stared unblinking at Lykos.

'Perhaps I should speak to you, then,' Lykos said to Maquin. 'I see you have grown your warrior braid back.'

'Hair grows,' Maquin shrugged.

'Aye, and can be cut again.'

'Many things can be cut,' Maquin said, his gaze radiating hatred as palpable as heat from a fire.

What is going on here?

'Enough,' Lamar said. He looked at Veradis. 'We have come at your request, though I hold no hope for reconciliation here. Lykos has done too much, gone too far.'

'That is yet to be seen,' Veradis said with a sigh, taking his place at the table, opposite his father. He had thought he was ready for this, prepared. He realized that he wasn't. He poured himself some wine.

I must resolve this. Redeem myself to Nathair for my failure in Narvon. He took a slow sip from his cup and focused, just as he did in the shield wall, when the shields cracked together.

'There *cannot* be war in Tenebral,' Veradis said. 'We must find another way, and the fact that you have all come here shows me that you are willing to try.'

'We are here out of respect for Nathair, the King,' Lamar said.

'That is a good place to start,' Veradis said.

'How is my son?' Fidele asked him.

'He is well, my lady. Weary. He has fought a long campaign, and come through many trials and battles. He has forged alliances, as Aquilus began before him.'

'He has abandoned Tenebral to this lunatic so that a foreign king or two can put their names on a piece of parchment,' Lamar said with a snort, gesturing at Lykos.

Veradis took a deep breath.

'No, Father. He has done much more than that. He fights the God-War, is the Bright Star spoken of in prophecy, and he has captured a fearsome weapon, the starstone cauldron, one of the Seven Treasures.'

Lamar frowned at that.

'He has it, then,' Ektor said. He glanced at Fidele.

Fidele reached over and gripped Veradis' wrist.

'I fear for Nathair,' she said, 'I suspect he is in terrible danger. The company he keeps—'

'Of course he is in danger,' Lykos interrupted. 'It's not easy being the champion of Elyon. Instantly you have a very long list of enemies.'

This is heading away from the discussion. I must bring it back on course.

'Nathair is well, and fighting hard not only for Tenebral, but for all of the Banished Lands,' Veradis said. 'But what you are doing here threatens to undermine all he has achieved. You must see that there cannot be open rebellion in his own realm.'

'This is not rebellion,' Fidele hissed. 'This is saving Tenebral. Lykos—'

'Lykos is Nathair's chosen regent. You all know this. Nathair spoke those words to me not two moons gone. What you are doing here is treason.'

'Well said,' Lykos whispered.

Shut up. You are not helping.

'Veradis,' Peritus said, making an effort to keep his voice steady. 'You do not know what has happened here, what Lykos has done. He killed Armatus—'

'On whose order?' Veradis asked. Had Calidus been mis-informed? Surely it could not have been Fidele.

'That is . . .' Peritus glanced at Fidele.

'On whose order?' Veradis repeated.

'Mine,' whispered Fidele.

'Not Lykos'?' Veradis asked. *It is true, then.* He almost could not believe it, even hearing it from Fidele's own lips, had been convinced that Calidus had been mistaken.

'No doubt you have heard many things about me, Veradis,' Fidele said, holding her chin high.

'I have,' he said. *You married Lykos. You ordered the execution of Armatus and Peritus. You sent the eagle-guard to the four corners of Tenebral on pointless errands.*

'They are all true. But, I did them against my will. Believe me or not, Lykos cast a bewitchment over me.'

That surprised him. He had not expected Fidele to accept the charges in the first place, but to then accuse Lykos of *sorcery* . . . Veradis had doubted Nathair's judgement in choosing Lykos as his regent, he had many faults in Veradis' opinion – but a sorcerer? *He is too drunk, most of the time.* His first reaction was to laugh, the accu-sation seemed so ludicrous, but one glance at Fidele's face convinced him that she believed what she said. Or that she was mad.

Show her some respect. She was the high king's wife, is mother to Nathair.

'How did he bewitch you, my lady?'

'I do not know how or where he learned his infernal talents,' Fidele snapped. 'All I know is that he had a doll, a clay figure, a strand of my hair set within it. When Maquin fought him at the arena it was crushed underfoot, destroyed, and immediately the chains within my mind were broken.'

'So there is nothing left of this doll?'

'Obviously not, or I would still be under his spell.'

Genius and insanity are separated by a hair's breadth.

'Lykos has committed countless atrocities,' Peritus said.

'He has burned Ripa, sunk our ships,' Lamar said.

'I told you they don't like me,' Lykos said in a mock-whisper.

Shut. Up. Nathair is right, politicking is like parenting a horde of bairns. He took a deep breath.

'Veradis,' a new voice said. Alben. He had stayed silent and listened, thus far. He leaned forward now, his gaze intense. 'Lykos is false.'

What is that even supposed to mean? And what do they expect me to do? Hand them Lykos' head on a platter?

'Even if he is, Alben, I am not here to judge any man's character,' Veradis said. 'I am a King's messenger. Nathair has a proposal. A command.'

A silence settled over them, angry glares criss-crossing the table.

'Let us hear it, then,' Alben said, leaning back in his chair.

'I will state the facts. You have grievances, that is clear. There has been a breakdown of government in Tenebral to the point of civil war. That is also clear. The next step here is battle, where many people will die.' Veradis gestured to the tent entrance, through which gathered warbands could be glimpsed.

'Many have already died,' Fidele said.

'What is the alternative?' Marcellin asked, speaking for the first time and startling a few of them. 'What is Nathair's proposal?'

'That you come with me to Mikil in Isiltir. Nathair will be there – he is holding a council of the alliance. You can put your grievances before him, all of you, and let your King decide.'

'What do you mean, all of us?' Ektor asked.

'Any who wish to go are welcome. A representative of each of the interested parties may be more sensible. Father, it would be in part a journey through winter . . .'

'You think me too weak and frail?' Lamar snapped.

'No. These are Nathair's words. He suggested that Krelis or Ektor make the journey, as your representative. Or both, if you wish.' *One hot-headed, one cold as a dead fish.* 'Fidele, of course. Lykos, Peritus.'

'Me?' Lykos said, sitting up straight and his smile fading.

'Aye. Nathair wants you with him in Mikil.'

Lykos frowned at that.

'That does actually sound like wisdom,' Ektor said. 'Certainly a means of avoiding such terrible bloodshed. I hate to admit it, and I can't believe that I'm saying such a thing, but Veradis is making sense.'

Fidele glared at him.

'I cannot go,' Lykos said. 'I am regent here.'

'No longer,' Veradis said. 'At least until this predicament is resolved to everyone's satisfaction. And Nathair has asked for you, Lykos. You are leaving Tenebral.'

Lykos scowled at that but held his tongue.

'And what of Tenebral in the meantime?' Lamar asked, frowning. 'Who will govern here?'

'I will,' Marcellin said, attracting many shocked stares.

'Marcellin will remain in Tenebral,' Veradis said. 'He will act as steward of the realm until this situation is resolved. By our King. Not the needless slaughter of men of Tenebral.'

'It is not men of Tenebral that I would slaughter,' Lamar said. 'but Vin Thalun. They are vastly outnumbered.'

'I will not throw my men into needless battle,' Marcellin said.

'So it would be you that is outnumbered, Father,' Veradis pointed out.

Lamar's eyes narrowed, cold as flint.

He is more angry than I realized. But he is also a good commander, a man of strategy, knows when to fight and when to retreat. Now for the final role of the dice . . .

'If you choose to fight, then I will have no choice but to step in. I will fight beside the Vin Thalun.'

'Against your own people. Against your own kin?' Lamar said, bitterness dripping from his voice.

Veradis stared at his father. He'd known this point was coming, could not be avoided. *I will not falter now.*

'Yes. I follow the orders of my King. Your King. Lykos is ... was, his chosen regent.'

'Not any more,' Lykos muttered into his wine cup.

'If you raise a hand against Lykos,' Veradis continued, 'you are raising it against Nathair.'

'You would lose,' Lamar said, a muscle twitching in his cheek. Never a good sign.

'Who knows?' Veradis shrugged. 'All things are possible in battle. But you would be sorely outnumbered, and my eagle-guard are veterans, have been victorious many times.' He looked at Peritus, who had seen Veradis and his shield wall fight their way out of a river and win the day against overwhelming odds.

'I do not think we would lose.'

A silence settled over the tent.

'You have grown since last I saw you,' Fidele said, though to Veradis' ears it did not sound like a compliment.

'I agree,' Lamar said. It did not sound like an insult the way his father spoke it. There was even a tinge of respect in his eyes. *That is something I have never seen before – not directed at me, at least.* For a moment it broke Veradis' train of thought. Then he gathered himself.

'This meeting is at an end,' Veradis said. 'The choices are before you.'

'I for one have made my choice,' Marcellin said. 'It seems that I've walked a long way to sit with you all in this tent, but for better or worse I accept Nathair's proposal. I will not fight, and I will steward Tenebral until Nathair has sorted this mess out.' He scowled at them all with his bushy brows. 'As for you,' he said, pointing at Lykos. 'I hope Nathair exercises some sense and I never see your face in this realm again.' Then he stood and left the tent, his shield-man close behind him.

Fidele clapped her hands, slowly, looking at Veradis.

'You have manoeuvred us most skilfully,' she said. 'Divided

our ranks and left a route open for us to retreat without losing our honour.'

'It is not like that,' Veradis said. As much as he was battle-hardened, had been injured, stabbed, bruised, Fidele's comment hurt him more than any wound he remembered.

'No? I am well used to the world of politicking, and I recognize this for what it is.' She looked around at them all.

'Divide and conquer.' Her voice was steady, not quite calm, but Veradis saw the colour draining from her face, eyes drawn back to Lykos again. 'But some of us are not so easy to manipulate.'

'I am manipulating no one,' Veradis said, feeling his own temper stirring. He respected Fidele in many ways, but for her to sit there and accuse him, after all that she had done, and confessed to doing . . . 'The things I have heard said about you, my lady. I had dis-counted them as no more than gossip and rumour, but seeing you, listening to how you are twisting the truth, I am more inclined to believe the rumours.'

'Have a care,' Maquin said to him.

'I have few friends still breathing,' Veradis said slowly, turning his gaze upon Maquin. 'And I'd not lose you, Maquin. But you'll not threaten me again.'

Maquin shrugged. 'It wasn't a threat.'

Veradis stood. 'This meeting is over.'

His father rose, Ektor standing with him.

'Father, perhaps we could talk, soon?' Veradis asked him.

'Aye,' Lamar said. He passed a hand over his eyes. 'After we have reached our decision.'

Ektor nodded a farewell.

Lamar turned to leave, Ektor moving to hold the tent flap open for him. Fidele stood, face taut with anger, and turned to follow them.

'Fidele,' Lykos called after her. She paused and looked back.

'Soon,' he said and blew her a kiss.

Maquin's explosion into violence was so sudden that it took Veradis half a dozen heartbeats to realize it was happening.

Maquin leaped across the table, sent it flying as he pushed off from it, cups and jugs and chairs flying, smashing, wine spraying.

Lykos was still seated; he shoved himself backwards and disappeared as his chair rolled, Maquin a heartbeat behind him, somehow a knife in his fist.

He cannot do this – it is a rowan-meet, sacred.

Veradis drew his short sword, heard people shouting, willed his feet to move after Maquin, who slashed at the rolling Lykos, blood arcing. Then Lykos' shieldman Kolai was there, standing over Lykos, who was still tangled in his chair. Kolai and Maquin exchanged a flurry of blows, punches, chops, knife thrusts, too hard and fast for Veradis to follow. There was a wet punching sound, then, for a moment, everything was still, Maquin standing with his knife buried to the hilt up through Kolai's lower jaw.

The Vin Thalun collapsed, one leg juddering, and the chaos began again, more shouting, Veradis feeling as if he was moving through water, trying to reach Maquin. Voices were yelling outside the tent, muffled, eagle-guard piling in, weapons drawn, bodies everywhere. Veradis stumbled on something, slipped, then felt an impact on his shoulder, turned, yelling, and something slammed into him, staggering him back a pace. A man.

It was his father, Lamar, his arms around Veradis.

What?

Then Veradis felt something warm on his hand, looked down, saw blood slicking his fist. He jerked backwards, let go of his sword hilt, the blade buried in his father's belly. With a sigh Lamar collapsed.

CHAPTER FIFTY-NINE

LYKOS

Lykos scrambled on the ground, fists pulling up chunks of grass and dirt. Maquin's face loomed over him, standing over the corpse of Kolai.

He was scared, and angry with himself for being scared, but the fear was winning out over any thoughts of revenge, screaming at him to get *away*.

Maquin lost a few moments as he dragged his knife from Kolai's skull and shoved the collapsing body out of his way, moments that Lykos determined to use well. Finally he managed to roll out from the chair that he had become entangled in, rose to a crouch and leaped towards the canvas of the tent wall. Fumbling for his knife, he managed to draw it and slash at the fabric, tearing a rent large enough to fit his upper body through. He hurled himself through, crashing out into cold daylight to land on his head before a line of frowning eagle-guard, beyond whom his Vin Thalun were milling.

He clambered to his feet and ran, Maquin's snarling face appearing through the tear in the tent. Lykos lunged to the side and heard a knife whistle past his ear to thud into an eagle-guard shield.

'Stop him!' Lykos yelled at the top of his voice, the first ranks of Veradis' eagle-guard parting to let him through. 'Protect Veradis, defend your lord,' he bellowed, voice cracking.

The eagle-guard were moving, sweeping around the tent like a closing fist. Some of his Vin Thalun had seen him and were moving his way.

Faster. Move faster.

Lykos looked back to see that Maquin had cut his way out of the tent. He saw Lykos, seemed blind to the fact that Lykos was surrounded by eagle-guard, and a horde of Vin Thalun were growing closer with every heartbeat, because he just snarled and ran at Lykos.

Does the man not know when he is beaten?

Nevertheless that wave of fear that had only just calmed swept up again.

He killed Kolai in less than ten heartbeats.

Lykos looked about frantically, heard someone in the eagle-guard shout and saw shields thudding together.

Maquin threw himself against them, managed to pull one man out of position; Lykos saw the glint of iron as swords were drawn.

'Do not kill him,' Lykos yelled.

Someone clubbed Maquin with the hilt of a sword. Maquin staggered, grabbed a shield, was clubbed by more men.

Lykos sucked in a few breaths, felt relief, then anger sweep his fear away. Then a deep joy.

The Old Wolf is mine again. Then he smiled.

He heard a scream, looked to see Fidele half in and half out of the tear in the tent. She was looking at Maquin, trying to climb out, but hands were pulling her back.

Peritus?

Amazing the difference half a day can make. Life is looking far more promising than when I woke this morning. I will come and find you soon, he promised Fidele.

The first of his Vin Thalun were about him now, looking at him with confused, questioning glances. He strode towards Maquin, beckoning for his warriors to follow.

The Old Wolf was on his knees in the grass, a ring of eagle-guard about him.

'My thanks,' Lykos said to a serious-looking warrior who seemed to be in charge. 'I'll take him now.' The eagle-guard looked at him suspiciously.

'You'd best get inside that tent – your Lord Veradis has been attacked.'

The eagle-guard yelled some orders and they hurried away.

Lykos looked down at Maquin, Vin Thalun all around pointing iron at the pit-fighter.

'What a good day this is turning out to be,' said Lykos as he squatted down beside Maquin. Not too close – Maquin was bleeding from his scalp, but you could never be too careful with this man.

Maquin breathed deep through his nose, hawked and spat blood. 'I can smell your fear,' he said.

'No, you have that wrong,' Lykos said, leaning as close as he dared. 'You're mine now. And this time it will be forever.' He stood up. 'Oh, and you need to stop killing my shieldmen.' He spun and kicked Maquin in the head, stunning him.

'Take him to my quarters,' Lykos ordered. 'Twenty men on each shift.'

As his warriors bound Maquin and dragged him away, Lykos processed what had just happened, what he'd glimpsed inside the tent as he'd been rolling over in his chair.

Lamar with a sword in his belly. Marcellin the new steward of Tenebral. He snarled, glaring over at Marcellin and his warband, resenting Nathair and his decision to remove him from power.

I will get it back.

He looked at the rowan-meet tent, could hear the sound of grieving from within, people shouting. He called a dozen men to him and marched up to it, cautiously entering.

Eagle-guard were everywhere, hovering mostly, some attempting to clean up the mess Maquin had made. Kolai's corpse had been lifted to one side of the tent, where he lay staring at nothing, a red hole in his jaw, blood drying upon his chest.

An exceptional warrior. What a waste. Is there anyone that the Old Wolf cannot kill?

Veradis was kneeling in the centre, his sword discarded and red to the hilt, Lamar lying on the ground, head upon Veradis' lap. Veradis was stroking his father's head. Lamar was breathing, though he was as pale as the dead and it looked as if an ocean of blood had spilt into the grass about them.

How did that happen?

The silver-haired man who had been present in the rowan-meet was kneeling with them, hands stained red, bent over Lamar's wound.

Lykos only gave them a perfunctory glance.

There she is.

Fidele was standing beside a tent pole, Peritus with her, as well as Ektor, the sickly son of Lamar whom Lykos had never seen before. He had a stunned expression upon his face, like a man after a battle. It looked as if Fidele and Peritus were arguing. A trio of eagle-guard hovered close by.

'My lady,' Lykos said behind her.

She almost leaped away, fear washing her face. That made Lykos happy. Then she got angry and reached for a knife at her belt. Peritus gripped her wrist.

'Now, is that a way for a wife to greet her husband?'

She spat in his face. 'I'll put a knife through either yours or my own heart before I let you touch me again,' she hissed at him.

'You should be careful, the promises you make. You may have to fulfil that one.'

'I intend to. Where is Maquin?' she asked, something other than rage seeping into her voice.

'In my care,' Lykos smiled. 'He will be well looked after.'

'He is my shieldman, I demand that he be returned to me.'

'I don't think so. He is a slave. My slave, my escaped property.'

'You will give him back, unharmed, or I will have your head today, and no force in the world of flesh will stop me.'

She spoke with such utter conviction that for a moment he believed her.

'Don't worry, I have no desire to kill him, quickly.' He smiled. 'Living will be a greater punishment for him.'

'You will—'

'I will do as I *please*,' he hissed, feeling his anger begin to wax like the tide. 'And you will stop telling me what to do, unless you want Maquin's head as a gift.'

The three eagle-guards nearby stepped closer, watching him suspiciously.

I must tread carefully. They love her more than they do me, and I no longer have the effigy Calidus gave me, or the regency of Tenebral. Power is a fickle master.

He let his eyes wander her face and body. 'I had forgotten how beautiful you are,' he said. 'And look, you gave me this.' He lifted his shirt and twisted to show a scar low on his back. 'I treasure it,' he whispered. 'And when you are back in my bed, we shall discuss what would be a fitting punishment for betraying your husband so . . . thoroughly.'

Her fingers twitched for her knife again.

'As much as I would love to stay and chat, I have work to do. But we shall talk again.'

'There is nothing left to say until we are both standing before Nathair,' Fidele said. 'He shall decide the right and wrong of this.'

'This is a reprieve for you, nothing more,' Peritus said. 'Once we are before Nathair, you will know justice.'

'We shall see,' Lykos said.

'Return Maquin to me,' Fidele called after him.

Never, bitch.

Veradis' voice filled the room, shouting *No*, over and over. Alben was staring at him, shaking his head.

Lamar's chest had stopped rising and falling.

Krelis darkened the tent entrance, came staggering over, as if drunk.

Veradis looked up at him. 'He's gone,' he said, palms open and bloody.

Krelis snarled and punched down at Veradis, again and again, men rushing to pull Krelis off. He shrugged them away, carried on punching, blood spattering from Veradis' face. He made no effort to fight back, or even to pull away.

Then Alben clubbed Krelis across the back of the neck with the hilt of his sword, subduing him enough to enable warriors to pull him away.

Lykos left the tent, shaking his head.

Family.

The gates of Ripa's tower were open and Lykos strode through as if he owned them, a hundred Vin Thalun about him. *The Old Wolf is shackled, but he's not my only enemy.*

Veradis' eagle-guard had stepped in during the confusion of the rowan-meet's end, when rumour had spread and violence hung in the balance. The warband of Ripa had snapped and snarled like an angry dog, for the moment without clear leadership as Lamar was slain and Krelis was grief-stricken. Caesus, Veradis' captain, had brought up his warband and ordered the men of Ripa to stand down.

After a few tense moments they had, and now Lykos thought to take advantage of the confusion that had spread in the rowan-meet's wake.

That Caesus is one to watch – followed Veradis' orders without hesitation, and it was clear he'd have killed his own countrymen without any hesitation. Another fool too loyal to think for himself. He shook his head. *Where does Nathair find them?*

He strode through a timber feast-hall, through an arched doorway; the floor became stone as he entered the tower; a spiral staircase stood before him.

Up or down? Where are they? He sent half of his men up, took the rest with him and spiralled downwards, footsteps echoing as he wound his way deep into the rock of Ripa's cliffs. At every corridor he sent men to search, until he was left with only a dozen men about him. Soon he found what he was looking for. A bolted door, two guards outside – men of Ripa. They stood uncertainly before him. He snapped an order and quickly had them overwhelmed and disarmed, then unbolted the door and kicked it open.

'Ahh, here you are,' he said as he peered in.

The giantess Raina and her bairn Tain were standing against the far wall.

The first thing Lykos noticed was that their collars were gone from their necks.

He stepped into the chamber and Raina snarled at him like a cornered wolven. Tain appeared hostile, too, but in a more brittle way, the kind you'd see in a wild horse – fire that could turn to flight. He clutched a chair in one hand.

Lykos' men flowed into the room, Lykos pacing closer, drawing his sword.

'I have missed you,' he said, arms open in friendly greeting.

'Come no closer,' Raina growled. He saw a piece of chain in her hands.

'You do not tell me what to do,' Lykos snarled. 'I thought you learned that lesson long ago.' He stepped closer still, stopped a dozen paces away. 'I hope that you have enjoyed your respite, because it is over. You are mine again.' He looked at her hands. 'I see that you have kept your collar and chain. Very helpful of you.'

'To crush your skull with.'

Lykos sighed. 'Need we go through this? If you resist, I will kill your son. I don't need both of you – that is just a luxury, an extra surety. So.' He looked between them both, saw Raina's will wavering. He raised a hand and his men drew closer, spreading into a loose arc around the two giants.

'Well?'

Raina's eyes darted around the room, and she took a step closer to her son, part shielding him behind her. Lykos saw her eyes narrow and knew her answer. He drew his sword. She snarled and stepped forwards, hurling the collar at his face with startling power and speed, holding onto the chain, wielding it like a whip. He threw himself to the side, saw the collar crunch into a warrior's face behind him, the man crashing to the floor in a gurgle of blood and teeth.

A Vin Thalun grabbed the chain, which in hindsight was a mistake, as he was pulled hurtling forwards towards Raina, grabbed by Tain and pummelled with a chair.

Lykos and his men rushed in, some jabbing Raina with spears. They knew, whatever Lykos said to the giants, that he would personally flay anyone who caused either of the giants' deaths, so they were hesitant. While Raina was distracted with jabbing spear-points, Lykos sped in behind the furious Tain, who was still smashing what was left of a splintered chair-leg into the pulped head of his warrior. Lykos slashed Tain across the back of the leg and kicked him behind the knee for good measure, dropping the giantling to the ground. Lykos grabbed a handful of Tain's hair and yanked his head back, resting his sword against the throbbing vein in Tain's neck.

'Hold,' bellowed Lykos.

Raina froze instantly, then dropped her chain. Immediately the Vin Thalun were on them, tying their wrists with rope.

Footsteps echoed in the corridor and warriors walked in, a dozen, then a score, warriors of Tenebral in gleaming cuirasses with bright eagles on their chests. At their head strode the old man, Alben.

'Step away,' he said, eyes searching out Lykos. There was something about his stare that made Lykos wary.

'They are my prisoners,' Lykos said.

'They are prisoners of war, agreed,' Alben said. 'But not yours. Veradis ben Lamar holds the highest rank here, and these are his men. He has ordered these prisoners taken into his personal custody.'

'What? That is ridiculous,' Lykos said.

'Here are the orders, and his seal,' Alben said, waving a scroll at Lykos.

'Pfah,' Lykos grunted, waving an arm. 'Papers. We are all on the same side here. What does it matter whose custody they are under?'

'Exactly,' Alben said. 'So you will not mind if they are in Veradis' custody, rather than yours.' It was not framed as a question.

'They are *mine*,' Lykos snarled, feeling his temper fray. He was not used to dealing with so many disagreeable people all in the same day. He made to push past Alben, his Vin Thalun pulling the giants behind them. Alben stepped in his way.

Lykos put a hand to his sword hilt. Alben rested his hand gently on his. The hiss of swords being slowly pulled from sheaths sounded as the eagle-guard wrapped fingers around hilts.

Outnumbered. And I hate to say it, but those eagle-guard are Veradis' veterans. In close quarters like this . . .

With a twist of his lips he pulled his hand away from his sword and barked a command at his men. They dropped the ropes.

'And what does Veradis plan to do with them?'

'Take them to Mikil with him.'

Lykos raised an eyebrow at that. 'May I?' he asked, gesturing at the open door and Alben stepped out of his way.

Lykos marched away, a seed of worry taking root in his gut. *Mikil. Calidus will not look favourably upon that, and I will most likely get the blame. Ach, what a day. Still, it could have been worse. I need a good bottle of wine, and then I have an old friend to become reacquainted with . . .*

CHAPTER SIXTY

ULFILAS

Ulfilas walked with a limp through Mikil's keep, one arm bandaged and in a sling. He wasn't sure if he'd ever be able to use a sword with his old skill again. Yet he was thankful to be alive.

Though perhaps not for much longer.

He was about to see Jael, his first audience with the King since he'd been sent on his fateful mission in search of Haelan, the fugitive King of Isiltir.

A moon had passed since he'd led the attack on Gramm's hold, since he'd ridden out against a warband of warriors charging uphill with long, curved swords. If he'd known they were the most skilful warriors the Banished Lands had ever seen he'd have organized a retreat before they'd arrived and left Gramm's hold to them.

At least, the one that I fought was. And judging by the fact that I'm the only survivor of over three hundred men, I'm guessing that the others weren't half bad with a blade, either.

Dag the huntsman walked beside him, neither one saying a word to the other. Silently they climbed a staircase and entered a long corridor, at its end shieldmen in red cloaks and black breastplates standing guard before a door. Sounds of combat drifted out, grunts and thuds, the clack of practice blades.

Ulfilas and Dag were ushered in and stood before Jael, King of Isiltir.

He was not alone.

The room was large, before Jael's chair a space was cleared, in which two men fought. Ulfilas recognized one – the shieldman he'd seen win the bout in Dun Kellen, named Lafrid. The other he didn't know, but even at a glance Ulfilas could tell that he was good. Careful, never overextending, patient. As Ulfilas watched, his eyes drawn for a moment, he saw Lafrid make a feint, much like the one he'd used in Dun Kellen, but the other man just stepped back and smiled.

The bout went on.

Beside Jael, seated in high-backed chairs, were three other men, and standing behind them the bulk of a giant.

Not more giants.

This one was dark-haired, face impassive, a war-hammer slung across his back. Of the three men seated, Ulfilas recognized the first – King Nathair, though he had been a prince the last time Ulfilas saw him, at the council of Aquilus. The years had worn heavy on him, nothing of the enthusiastic boy left about him. Now he was lean, still handsome with unruly curly hair, but there was a gauntness to his features, a hollowness about the eyes that spoke of a deep weariness.

Being king will do that to a man.

Next to him sat an old man, silver hair and a neatly trimmed beard on a sharp-lined face, clusters of laughter lines at his eyes. Despite his years he looked full of life, with bright eyes and a certain tireless energy about him. And then Ulfilas saw the third man. He almost took a step back, his fingers twitching in the sling for his sword hilt – it was a warrior similar to the ones he'd just fought at Gramm's hold. Clad in black linen and dark mail, the hilt of a curved sword slung above his shoulder.

How can that be?

Perhaps the warrior felt Ulfilas' eyes upon him, for he looked away from the bout and stared full at Ulfilas. Again he felt the urge to step back, to recoil. The man's eyes were black, no pupil, no iris, just a black well. Ulfilas' fingers moved to form the ward against evil.

The man looked him up and down, slowly, then returned his attention to the duel before them.

It came to an end suddenly, the patient man enduring a blistering combination of blows from Lafrid, the last strike too powerful, unbalancing Lafrid for a moment. The other man's weapon darted out, struck Lafrid hard on the wrist, then it was at his throat.

'You're dead,' the patient man said.

Lafrid blinked, it had happened so fast, then nodded grudgingly and gripped an offered arm. 'Well done,' he muttered.

Jael clapped, Nathair and the old man following suit. The dark-clothed warrior didn't.

'Well, it seems I have found my first-sword. Unless you have come to test your blade,' Jael said, looking at Ulfilas.

'I am afraid not, my King,' Ulfilas said, looking down at his bandaged arm. The cut to his bicep had been the worst injury, slicing deeply through muscle.

'I see you have a tale to tell. Well, let's hear it.'

Ulfilas stepped forward, Dag following him.

'I attacked Gramm's hold, my lord, as planned. Ildaer and some of the Jotun joined us, and it was all going well, more than well: the gates were down and Gramm's warriors broken, fleeing. We were hunting for the child when two warbands were seen approaching – one on a small fleet of ships.'

Nathair and Calidus sat up straighter at that.

'The other a warband of riders, approaching from the south. I rode out to face the riders – we outnumbered them heavily.' He glanced at the black-clad warrior. 'They were like him. Clad in black war gear, no shields, curved swords worn upon their backs.'

'Tukul,' the black-clad warrior breathed, the word sounding like a curse.

'Tukul?' Jael said.

'My sword-brother. A betrayer.'

'We fought.' Ulfilas felt a flush of shame. 'They were better than us. The likes of which I've never seen before. I fell and later escaped when I saw the battle was lost.'

As he spoke of it Ulfilas remembered too vividly how he had been struck half a dozen times in as many heartbeats, somehow his reins slashed as well, and falling with a numbing crash to the ground. He'd lain on his back in the blood and dirt as the black clad warrior had loomed over him, thinking his death was moments away. Then he'd seen the warrior choose to fight a bear and giant instead. He hadn't stayed around to watch the outcome.

'Dag found me a few leagues south – he'd been tracking the men who took the children from Dun Kellen.' He dropped to one knee before Jael. 'I failed you, my King.'

'Yes, you did.' Jael sighed. 'But your honesty is refreshing, Ulfilas. Never any excuses from you. And did you make a mistake? I think not. Would anyone have had a different result in the same circumstances? Again, I think not. So I shall leave your head on your shoulders. This time.'

'I thank you for your mercy,' Ulfilas said, and he meant it.

'It seems our enemies have joined forces,' Nathair said. 'The Black Sun evaded me in Narvon, stole some of my ships, burned the rest. Now I know where he took them.'

The Black Sun?

'Well, we shall raise a warband and go pay them a visit,' Jael said. 'They will have Haelan with them now, no doubt.'

'They are not at Gramm's hold any longer,' Dag said. 'I found Ulfilas, but we didn't come straight back. Went and watched them for a while. They left later that day, near a thousand of them, by my reckoning, heading east. I put a few of my boys on their trail. We'll soon hear where they're going.'

'They're going to Drassil,' the old man said.

'What?' said Jael.

'You remember my father's council at Jerolin?' Nathair said to Jael. 'He spoke of the God-War, the polarization of sides between the Black Sun and the Bright Star. The prophecy that spoke of the Seven Treasures and Drassil.'

'I do,' Jael said.

'Well, that is what this is. It is happening now.' He looked hard at Ulfilas. 'Those who attacked you, one of them was the Black Sun, an upstart peasant named Corban, though he dares call himself the Bright Star.' His mouth twisted bitterly. 'The servants of Asroth are prone to lies and deception.' His eyes flickered to Calidus. 'This is why I am here, why a council of war must happen between our allies.' He pinched his nose, closed his eyes. 'Better to leave this conversation for the council. Are the others here?'

'Lothar arrived yesterday from Helveth, but there is no sign of Gundul yet.'

'Ach,' Nathair sighed. 'Well, we will wait, then. There is always the morrow. I need to sleep now. It has been a long road, but before I go and find my chambers, I have a gift for you.'

'That is most gracious of you,' Jael said.

'It is a little unusual, but I think that you will value it more highly than gold. Or even the head of this child pretender to your throne.'

'You have my interest piqued,' said Jael.

'Sumur. He is your gift. These are dark times and our enemies lurk in the shadows, waiting for any opportunity. A finer first-sword you shall never find.'

'These are dark times,' Jael agreed, 'and my enemies gather as we speak.' Though Jael was looking at Sumur with little joy. 'But, as you saw, my new first-sword is a very capable man. And the best in all of Isiltir.'

The old man spoke up now. 'No offence to your newly appointed first-sword, but Sumur is better.'

The newly appointed first-sword, Fram, snorted. He was looking at Sumur with interest, though, not anger, as some warriors would under the circumstances.

I like that about him. A calm head.

'Nathair fears for your safety,' the old man continued, 'and this seems to us to be the perfect solution.' He smiled genially, but there was more behind that smile. Daggers. An implied threat. *Do not refuse me*, it said.

Don't do it, thought Ulfilas. *Do not take him. How can you trust an outsider – not a man of Isiltir? No matter how good, how could you rely on his loyalty?* But Ulfilas remembered a conversation with Jael, how he seemed consumed with the fear of assassination. *He could be tempted, if this man is as good as they say, and if he is anything like the one I met, then he is.*

'Are you sure he is better than Fram?' Jael asked.

'Perhaps a demonstration?' Calidus said.

'Yes. I would like that.'

Sumur rose and stepped into the cleared space before them, shrugging off his scabbarded sword, laying it carefully on a table, then picking up the wooden practice sword that Lafrid had used.

Fram stepped into the makeshift ring.

'A friendly demonstration,' Calidus warned. 'No need for bloodshed or death. Or permanent injury.' As he said it he stared hard at Sumur, who returned the gaze with his flat, black eyes. He shrugged.

Fram and Sumur bowed to Jael, then turned to face each other.

Sumur just walked forwards, as if Fram were an open doorway that he intended to pass through. Fram shuffled his feet, sword raised, looked mildly confused.

He is a counter-striker, prefers to defend, and strike off of his opponent's blows.

Sumur's feet moved, a ripple through his body, starting at his ankles, and then he was striking two-handed at Fram, a blurred combination to head, throat, chest, groin and thigh. Ulfilas did not see which blow connected – perhaps one, perhaps all, but a few heartbeats later Fram was lying groaning on the floor.

The problem with being a counter-striker is that you first have to block the strikes made against you.

Sumur stood over Fram, looked as if he hoped the warrior would get back up, then dropped the practice sword and calmly retrieved his scabbarded blade and slung it across his back.

'Impressive,' said Jael.

'He is,' Nathair said. 'And he is yours. I will sleep better knowing you are watched over by one such as Sumur.'

'My thanks,' Jael murmured, 'but . . .'

'What? Ahh, I know. You doubt his loyalty. A shieldman must be prepared to give his life for you, and as he is not a man of Isiltir . . .'

'Exactly,' Jael said.

'Sumur is loyal, to the extreme,' Calidus said, leaning close in his chair. 'Tell him to put a knife through his hand.'

'That will not be necessary,' Jael said.

'I think it is. But the order must come from you, else you would still question.'

Jael frowned as Sumur padded closer.

Even walking he is graceful as a dancer.

'Tell him,' Calidus hissed.

'Sumur, put your knife through your hand,' Jael said, wincing as if the words tasted sour.

Sumur drew a knife from his belt, placed its tip against the palm of his left hand, and pushed. It was a slow, deliberate movement, the knife tip disappeared fraction by fraction into Sumur's hand. And all the while Sumur stared blankly at Jael.

Ulfilas felt himself wincing.

'Enough,' Jael said with a nervous laugh.

Sumur stopped.

'You are sure?' Calidus asked.

'Yes. Yes. Sumur, take the blade out.'

He did, one smooth pull, then cutting the edge of his linen shirt and tying a strip around his palm. Ulfilas saw one drop of dark blood hit the floor.

'Well?' Nathair said.

'He is loyal,' Jael said. 'Of that there is no dispute.'

'If you still have concerns then keep Fram as well. Who said we kings should only have one first-sword?'

Jael smiled at that, though Ulfilas could tell he was still not completely happy about this new arrangement.

'How can I take someone of such skill and devotion away from you, Nathair? If I am at risk from my enemies then surely you, our high king, are in greater danger, and so would need his skills more than I.'

Nathair smiled. 'That is not a problem – you must not concern yourself about that. And to prove it I'm going to leave you with another score of his sword-kin. Consider it an honour guard.'

'I must protest,' Jael said, almost squirming in his seat. 'You cannot set aside such fearsome warriors on my behalf.'

Nathair waved a hand in the air, a dismissal. 'I told you, that is not an issue. I have a thousand more making camp beyond your walls that are just like him.'

CHAPTER SIXTY-ONE

CORALEN

Coralen pushed a branch out of her way, stepped onto a rotted and fallen trunk and jumped down, avoiding a patch of dark-vine that would stick to her boots and burn her fingertips if she touched it, all the while moving through the forest as quietly as she could manage. She'd had years of practice during her years with Rath's crew.

But no amount of woodland hunting and living in forests could have prepared me for this.

Forn was like no other place she'd ever seen, dark, oppressive and enormous. The trees were on average as thick as a fortress tower, looming so high above that the forest canopy seemed like green-tinged clouds. Daylight was a nimbus glow high above, leaking down upon them like misted copper, most of the time the level of light hovering somewhere between twilight and full dark. The foliage upon the ground was sometimes just flat forest litter with clear spaces wide enough to pull two wains through, sometimes it was such a snarl of bush, thicket and thorn that Balur and his giants could not cut a way through it.

And they were not alone. The forest was alive with noise – during the day mostly birds and insects, though some of the insects were as big as her hand. Night was worse. There were the noises Coralen was familiar with: fox and owl and the occasional howl from a wolven – Storm always cocked her head at those. But also the sounds that she had never heard before. Strange clicking, scratching sounds and hissing, usually just out of the firelight's reach. Once there was a deep basal rumble that she felt reverberate into her feet through the ground. Balur told them all that it was a draig, and reassured them that it was leagues away. And of course there were the notorious Forn bats – a hiss above from wings almost as silent as breath, sometimes a distant screech. So far she had not seen any of the great bats, only the husk-like, dried-out remains of their victims. A deer, a boar, once an elk as big as a horse. After that she'd resolved not to wander in the forest alone, and to ensure her scouts travelled in pairs.

They'd left Gramm's hold almost two ten-nights ago, the first ten-night making good time, the second proving to be slower going. Even abandoning the wains had not proved the remedy that Coralen had hoped for.

'How can we travel any further through this?' Coralen muttered to Enkara, who was walking along quietly beside her.

'We are nearly there,' Enkara assured her, wiping sweat from her brow. By Coralen's reckoning they were well into autumn and approaching winter, but the weather within Forn was surprisingly mild, the thick lattice of branches high above keeping out all extremes of weather, apart from rain, which would still drip from leaves and find the back of her neck with annoying accuracy. They'd been walking since dawn, when the air was cold and they could see their breath misting, and it was not highsun yet, but it didn't take long to warm the blood when you were forging your way through a forest.

'Nearly there?' Coralen said, feeling a flare of excitement. 'Drassil is that close?'

'Not Drassil,' Enkara said, 'but something else . . .'

'Coralen,' a voice called from behind her.

They both stopped and turned, saw movement in the undergrowth and waited.

Dath appeared and Coralen frowned.

He is supposed to be on rearguard.

A figure appeared behind him, a dark blur in the foliage.

Kulla. Coralen rolled her eyes. She was like dark-vine where Dath was concerned.

Dath reached them, breathing hard and sweating heavily. He rested a hand upon his knee, opened his mouth to talk, realized he couldn't yet.

'Dath thinks we are followed,' Kulla said for him.

He nodded.

'You should be fitter,' Kulla said to Dath, poking him in the ribs.

'The Bright Star's closest friend, you shame him. How could you defend him if you'd had to run a little first?'

'I . . . am . . . fit,' Dath said, looking more hurt than angry.

'Followed?' Coralen said.

'Aye. I dropped back because I spied a doe pass us. Thought it would make a change from brot. I hunted it a while.'

'He is very good at that,' Kulla said.

'I thought I saw something,' Dath said.

'Saw what?'

'A glint of iron behind us.'

Coralen waited.

She had left Enkara to scout ahead and sped back past the long column of their warband, strung out over a league of forest, then carried on a little for good measure, gathering a few of her scouts along the way. Dath and Kulla were with her, along with Teca, the woman Coralen had saved from the Kadoshim in the woods of northern Narvon. She had the makings of a fine huntswoman. Yalric, one of Gramm's warriors who had survived the battle of the hold, was with them too. And Storm, of course.

The wolven was crouched beside her now, both of them sitting in thick foliage upon an embankment, the rest of Coralen's hunters spread loosely on the far side of the path. They'd been here maybe half a day, the glow of the sun above the trees steadily drifting westwards, waiting for whoever it was that Dath had spied. She rested her head against Storm's shoulder.

'I am glad you are healed,' she whispered, tweaking one of Storm's ears. The wolven had limped for a ten-night after her run-in with the bear at Gramm's hold, ribs bruised, maybe cracked. She was brave, though, tougher than any warrior Coralen had known, and had loped on day after day, league after league. Coralen had seen Corban's concerned looks, and had felt the same way, but one day Storm had uncurled from sleep, stretched and just seemed fine again. Coralen had felt a weight lift from her shoulders that she hadn't realized had been there.

Can't believe how soft I'm getting. Rath would be ashamed.

She felt a vibration and realized that Storm was growling quietly. She sat up, reaching slowly for her strung bow, half a dozen arrow shafts stuck into the earth before her. The odd ray of sunshine sloped into the forest from the west, motes of dust suspended in the amber glow.

'Easy,' she whispered to Storm, half-nocking an arrow, then concentrated on staying as still as possible. She focused on her breathing, as Rath had taught her, long, deep breaths, hold, slow release, over and over. Just when she thought Storm must have heard something else, there was a sound off to her left, a crackle of forest litter. Then, quiet but clear as the tree before her, a whispered conversation. Her skin prickled.

Dath was right.

Moments later a figure appeared in the gloom, pausing for a while on the path below her, then moving on, slow and steady, eyes sweeping ahead and the forest to either side. Then two more figures, further back, twenty paces apart, like an arrowhead. She waited longer.

No one else came.

A sound behind her, the scuff of bark, Storm's surprised snarl and she was throwing herself forwards, twisting as she fell, loosing the arrow half-blind into a shadow looming behind her. A scream, then Storm smashed into the figure, an explosion of blood.

Coralen lurched to her feet, trusting Storm with her back, reaching for another arrow. The men on the path were scrambling for cover, one down with an arrow through his throat that she knew instinctively was Dath's. Arrows whistled through the twilight, one skittered off a tree, another sank thrumming into a trunk.

Two men down there, at least two men.

Then she saw them – one flat against a tree, spear in hand, the other a dozen paces from him, crouched behind a fallen trunk. The one behind the tree peered around it, showing her his back and she put an arrow through it. He grunted and sank to the floor. The one behind the fallen trunk saw his comrade collapse, realized someone was behind them and leaped into motion. He was fast, running and leaping diagonally away from the others Coralen had placed on the opposite bank, but away from her as well. He weaved as he ran, Coralen releasing one arrow which missed him by a hair's breadth, then she was up and running. In a dozen paces she knew he was faster than her.

But not faster than Storm.

The wolven hurtled past her down the slope, bone-white fur blurring in the gloom as she raced after the huntsman. He heard the drum of her paws, turned panicked eyes towards her, fumbled with a knife at his belt and then she was on him, tearing at him as they rolled.

Coralen ran faster, saw them separate and Storm spring to her feet, twisting to get back at him. The huntsman struggled to rise, blood slicking his shoulder and back. Storm ran at him.

'Hold,' Coralen yelled at Storm, and the wolven skidded to a halt before the man, stood snarling and slavering over him. Coralen reached him, kicked his knife from his hand and then kicked him in the head. He dropped onto his back.

Dath emerged from the gloom, others close behind.

The huntsman on the ground groaned. 'Who do you serve?' Coralen said, drawing her sword and pointing its tip unwaveringly at his chest. He curled his lip and spat blood.

'That is rude,' Kulla observed. Her sword was in her hand, and although she made no move the man on the ground cringed a little.

'Look at me,' Coralen said to him. He did. 'I will have an answer to my question, one way or another.'

She held his gaze, preparing herself for what she might have to do. She'd seen Rath and Baird put men to the question, but never done it herself. Torturing defenceless men was not something she'd ever aspired to do.

But we need to know.

She remembered what Rath used to say in times like this, and sometimes it had worked.

'This is the end for you, one way or another. I'll not make you false promises, offer you your life. You'll not be seeing daylight again.'

She took a moment, let the words sink in.

'What I will offer you is a quick end, no pain. No flaying of your skin, or breaking of your bones. No putting your eyes out, or holding a flame to your stones. No giving you to her . . .' She looked pointedly at Storm, who was watching him with her fangs dripping red.

'So I'll ask you one last time. Who do you serve?'

He licked his lips, eyes moving around their group, from Coralen to Storm, Kulla, Dath, Teca and Yalric, all stern and silent. He must have seen no hope amongst them, and no mercy, for Coralen saw the decision in his eyes before he opened his mouth.

'Jael,' he said. 'I serve Jael, King of Isiltir.'

'He's no king of mine,' Yalric growled, hefting his axe.

Coralen tutted.

'How far behind us is Jael?'

'He's not following, yet. Far as I know, my master set us on your trail, went to report to Jael about the Hold, and you . . .'

'How many of you following us?'

'Four,' he said without any hesitation.

And four are here – three dead, you soon to follow. Coralen thought about breaking her word, putting him to the question. They weren't hard to follow, over a thousand of them and a few hundred horses tramping through the forest, it would be impossible to hide their tracks. But it was vital that there were no eyes on them – that's what Enkara had said. *No eyes watching us.*

But looking at him she believed him, and it made sense. It's what she would have done – put a few good men on the trail, told them to hang back and not lose them. Report back when there was something to report.

She shifted her weight and stabbed him through the heart.

'Get their bodies. Best we leave a message for those who come after,' she said.

'I like you,' Kulla said to her as they made their way back to the warband.

Coralen glanced at her and grunted. Kulla was short, slim, large dark eyes in an oval face. And a deadly killer. Coralen had seen her spar, seen her take lives at Gramm's hold with a deadly efficiency, as if she was harvesting crops.

'You are strong, here,' Kulla said, tapping her forehead. 'And here.' She pressed her palm to her heart. 'Back there, you did what you had to do, even though you did not like it.'

They had gathered the four dead huntsmen, wound rope around their feet and hung them from branches so that they dangled over the trampled path. Then Coralen had gutted them, slicing their bellies and spilling their intestines in tangled heaps below their hanging arms. She knew the warband that would eventually come this way would find them, half eaten probably and butchered like game after a hunt. It would sow seeds of fear.

She looked at her hands, still stained with blood.

'No, I didn't,' Coralen said.

'You will make a good match for our Bright Star.'

Coralen blinked at that, felt her neck flushing.

'Did Tukul talk to you?' she said, more abruptly than she intended.

'No,' Kulla said, wrinkling her brow. 'Why?'

'Never mind.'

She found that she missed Tukul, had enjoyed his company on the mad ride through Isiltir. All of the Jehar were stern and serious, but there had been another side to Tukul, a pragmatic humour that seeped into all he did or said. He had reminded her of Rath.

And now he is dead, too. Like Rath.

She felt grief clench in her chest, like a fist about her heart, slowly breathed it out, her thoughts turning to Gar. He had howled like an animal when Tukul had died, and his grief was still draped heavy upon him, his eyes hollow and angry.

I do not think there is one person in this entire warband that has not suffered the loss of loved ones because of this God-War. That made her angry.

We shall have our vengeance.

They were catching up with the warband now. Something drew her attention, from behind her. She slowed, turned, stared into the forest, head cocked to one side.

'What is it?' Kulla asked, staring with her.

'I don't know,' Coralen frowned. She could not have said what had made her pause – not a sound exactly, more a tingling upon her skin.

Like I'm being watched.

There was nothing, only the gentle rustle of a breeze through branches. She shrugged and carried on, leaving Kulla and the others as rearguard scouts, and sped up to try and get back to Enkara before it was full dark. Storm padded beside her, and when they reached Corban the wolven loped away to join him. Glancing down, Coralen noticed something red sprinkling the ground. She squatted to inspect it, saw it was paler than blood, almost pink. Then she heard Storm growl and looked up to see Buddai sniffing at the wolven. He frolicked closer to her, Storm gave him a swipe with a paw and he jumped away.

Hmm . . .

Corban reached down to run his fingers through Storm's fur, then smiled over at Coralen.

I'll have to report to him about what happened, but I need to find Enkara before it's dark.

She ignored him and jogged on. Soon she found Enkara, a darker shadow in the encroaching gloom.

'I've found it,' Enkara said, looking very pleased with herself.

'What?'

'Walk over here.'

Coralen did, past Enkara. For a moment she felt something, a kind of prickling against her skin, like the air before a storm breaks, but then something under her foot shifted and she looked down to pick her way. The ground was covered with deep forest litter, clusters of dark-vine here and there. She took some wide strides to avoid it. Then she stopped and looked back at Enkara, who was smiling at her.

'What?' Coralen asked.

'You can't see it?'

'See what?' She was getting annoyed now.

Corban was getting close now, Meical beside him, both of them leading their horses through thick undergrowth. Behind them the warband was a hulking shadow.

Enkara bent down and seemed to plunge her hands into the ground, then she saw the Jehar warrior lift up a thick knotted rope, leaning back and pulling on it. As she did, the ground shimmered and rippled, spreading out in circular waves from Enkara like a rock thrown into a pool. Coralen steadied herself, looked down to see that she was standing on some kind of wooden construct.

Enkara put her back into pulling. 'Some help,' she grunted, and Coralen hurried over. Together they tugged on the rope and with a creaking groan a wooden door rose up from the forest floor, a huge iron-banded and hinged semi-circle.

Coralen stood there with her mouth open, looking down at a wide stone slope that led down into darkness.

'A glamour,' Enkara said.

'What is this?' Corban asked.

'A tunnel that will take us to Drassil,' Meical said.

Balur smiled when he saw it.

'Good. You have found one, then,' the giant rumbled. 'When Drassil was abandoned they were hidden so well that those that came after could not find the way back.'

Ethlinn was beside him. She took a deep breath, closing her eyes. 'The glamour is strong upon these,' she said, her voice like the creaking branches.

'There's more than one?' Corban asked.

'Yes,' Enkara said. 'We found six of them, all beginning at Drassil. Tukul set us to clearing them – some were blocked, others crumbled and collapsed. Some had things living in them . . .' She shivered at a memory.

'But, how will we hide them from our enemy?' Corban said. 'We will lead them straight to Drassil.'

'No,' Balur said. 'The glamour is cunning. You cannot see them until they have been revealed by someone who has walked them. Once you have seen one, you can see them all.'

'I don't understand,' Corban said.

Neither do I, thought Coralen.

'When we are inside and the door is closed above us, the glamour will cover them again. No newcomer will see them, will notice anything other than the forest floor.'

'So how did Enkara see it?' Corban asked.

'Because she's seen it before. And now that you have, the glamour will no longer work upon you. You will be able to see all six of them, now.'

Corban thought about that for a moment, then looked up and smiled.

'Excellent,' he said.

The doors closed with a bang and darkness settled about them, broken by countless torches that burned a dotted line down the endless tunnel.

Ethlinn had remained behind with Enkara and Coralen, the rest of the warband marching on. Ethlinn lifted a huge wooden beam and slipped it through iron bars fixed to the enormous trapdoor.

'A precaution,' she said, 'though doubtless unnecessary.' She murmured a few words in giantish, Coralen feeling her skin prickle as it had earlier, when she'd stood upon the door and not seen it.

'There,' Ethlinn said, turning away.

'So Drassil is down there?' Coralen said.

'Aye,' said Enkara. 'It would take three or four moons of hard walking through Forn to reach Drassil from this point, and that is without the glamours and traps that surround the fortress. In this tunnel, mounted, we'll be there in a ten-night.'

'Onwards then,' Coralen said.

'Home,' whispered Ethlinn.

CHAPTER SIXTY-TWO

ULFILAS

Ulfilas stood with his back to the great doors of the feast-hall, checking all entrances and exits, making sure they were guarded by trusted men. Even though they were in the heart of Isiltir, in the fortress that had once been Romar's seat of power, Ulfilas had reached a point of permanent mistrust.

Perhaps Jael's paranoia is rubbing off on me.

He flexed his fingers and clenched a fist, felt muscle and tendon ripple and contract along his arm, the stitches in his bicep pulling. A ten-night had passed since he'd arrived in Mikil and met with Jael. His arm was out of its sling now, feeling weak, and aching as he'd never imagined, but slowly, oh so slowly, he was starting to feel a trickle of strength flow back into it.

The room had been converted into a council chamber, the fire-pit covered over with boards and a thick-legged carven table placed across it.

The fire-pit should be lit, if even just to lend some heat to this room. Summer had slipped into autumn and the winds blew cold across the rolling plains of Isiltir.

All the kings of the alliance were there: Jael at the table's head, with Fram close by and Sumur a black shadow at his back, then Nathair with his companions – silver-haired Calidus and the brooding giant, the outline of his war-hammer like a crow upon his back. Lothar, once battlechief to Helveth's ruler and now king of the realm. Ulfilas remembered him from the battle of Haldis, deep in Forn Forest. He had been clear-headed in council and fierce in battle. He sat now in silence and kingly splendour, the black hammer of his realm emblazoned on a white cuirass, a white cloak of wolven fur trimmed with gold around his shoulders. His face was predatory and hawk-like, his nose sharp and beaked. One warrior stood at his back.

And then there was Gundul, King of Carnutan, dark-haired and round-faced. He was the son of the traitor Mandros who had slain Aquilus, Nathair's father, and had his head taken from his shoulders in recompense by Nathair's first-sword, Veradis. Gundul had played a part in Mandros' downfall, and in return Nathair had supported him in his claim to the throne of Carnutan.

None of these men would be king now, if not for Nathair. It is no wonder Jael is indebted to him. But no man gives such favours for nothing. What will he ask for in return?

A man sat beside Gundul, with deep lines in a narrow face and an iron-grey beard, he sat straight-backed and alert, sharp eyes taking in every detail.

Belo, some relation of Gundul, and apparently more in control of Carnutan than Gundul is.

Gundul had only arrived yesterday, two hundred warriors riding with him as an honour guard. Jael had chafed at the delay, and so had Nathair, who had spent most of his days hidden away in his camp, which was built like a fortress around a huge wain, wheels as big as a horse. Nathair stood, and the murmur of conversation died out, a hush falling around the table.

'Well met,' he said, nodding to each king. 'It has been a long road since last we were all together – during my father's council at Jerolin. It was there that we made our pledge to one another, gave our oaths to this alliance; and now, look at us all. We are kings. Fortune has favoured us.' He raised a cup to them, his lips twisted in an almost-smile, as if at some unknown jest.

The kings raised their cups.

'I have helped you all, given aid when you asked. Lent my war-bands, their blood spilt in your causes. Now I ask that you remember the oaths that we pledged to one another, and the war that we committed to fight.'

'I remember it well,' Gundul said. His face was flushed, whether with wine or enthusiasm Ulfilas could not tell. 'And I for one remember with gratitude all that you have done on my behalf. Whatever must be done, if it is within my power to do so, then I am willing.'

Jael and Lothar raised their cups to that, though Belo's face did not look so pleased.

'The God-War has begun in earnest. The Black Sun is revealed as a warrior from Ardan in the west. He has gathered a warband about him of evil men and giants – Jael's battlechief has already crossed paths with him.' Nathair gestured towards Ulfilas, who stood blinking beneath the gazes of the kings of the Banished Lands. A silence grew.

'I fought them in the north,' Ulfilas said. 'It is true – giants and deadly warriors, the like of which I have never encountered before.' His gaze flickered to Nathair. 'I alone escaped with my life, my entire warband slaughtered.'

'In the north?' Lothar said. 'What were their numbers, and where are they now?'

'Over a thousand strong, and more joining them, so Jael's scouts tell us. They have travelled into Forn,' Nathair said, 'and seek to take refuge in Drassil.'

'Why in God's name would they do that?' Gundul asked. He dwelt furthest from the old forest.

All he knows of Forn is likely the faery tales and stories of its blood-thirsty inhabitants – draigs, wolven, bats and all manner of beasts that'll consider you a good meal.

Belo leaned forwards, resting his chin on steepled fingers.

'What do you propose is done about this Black Sun?' he asked.

'We go after him.'

'That would not be the easiest task,' Belo commented.

Nathair frowned, turning a brooding stare upon Belo. 'Did you ever think that a God-War would be easy?'

'I can't say that I've thought about it much at all,' Belo said. 'Gundul's and my time has been spent working hard in our own realm to heal the damage done during the succession.'

Nathair raised an eyebrow at that but made no comment.

'What would you have us do?' Lothar asked.

'Build roads into Forn, wide and straight like the giant roads of old. Each of you from a different location, set on a course to intersect at Forn's heart. From there, we build a fortress of our own. Drassil must be found, and the Black Sun dug out from the hole that he hides in.'

'Why not just leave him there?' Belo asked. 'If he is hiding, let him hide. Most that go into Forn are never heard of again.' He shrugged. 'Let the forest do our work for us.'

Nathair stared at him, took a deep breath, not quite a sigh. 'This is a council of kings,' Nathair said. 'Let your King speak for his realm.'

'I advise my King,' Belo said. 'And to do that, I like to understand the facts.'

Nathair pinched his nose.

'I have given you all the necessary facts. The Black Sun is in Forn. We must go after him. To bring the might of our warbands against him we have to build roads for them to march upon, to bring them supplies, to be able to fight without a tree branch getting lodged up your arse.'

I think he's getting angry.

'There may be other options.'

Nathair slammed a fist onto the table. 'I have not travelled a thousand leagues, fought myriad battles, dethroned kings and crowned new ones and stormed the gates of Murias to come here and haggle like a fishwife over *options*.' He was shouting by the end of the sentence.

Belo just stared at Nathair, fingers still steepled under his chin.

'This an alliance,' Belo said calmly, 'not a dictatorship. You do not rule here, or command the kings of the Banished Lands.'

Nathair went very still.

Calidus rose beside Nathair and touched his arm. The King of Tenebral had gone pale. He took a deep breath and sat.

Calidus faced Belo and spoke. 'There are weapons in Forn,' the old man said. 'Relics from the Giant Wars and the Sundering. We have to take them from the Black Sun. To leave him is to allow him to become stronger, and to consolidate his power.' Calidus' voice was deep and resonant, soothing in its pitch and cadence, and Ulfilas felt himself nodding in agreement with the old man's words. 'If left, one day he will emerge from Forn, stronger, too powerful by far, and prepared to annihilate us all.'

'That does not sound so good,' Gundul muttered.

'No. Best we strike now, before he grows stronger,' Jael said.

'That is our reasoning as well,' Calidus said good-naturedly.

Jael has a motive to fight this war, to chase this warband into Forn: Haelan. To catch one is to catch the other. But these other kings, why do they need to do this? To commit their warbands to such a mammoth task?

Ulfilas studied the faces around the table and could see that some at least were thinking along similar lines. Lothar was nodding thoughtfully. Gundul just looked scared. Belo, though, did not look impressed with the idea of carving a route through Forn.

'So you would have us build roads?' Belo asked.

'That is right. Summon your warbands and we shall begin our search for Drassil and the Black Sun.'

'Forn is a big place,' Belo said.

'Best then that we start sooner rather than later,' Nathair grated.

'There is someone missing from this table,' Belo said. 'Someone whom I have heard has joined your, our, alliance. Queen Rhin.'

'She will come,' Calidus said. 'She is securing her borders, but when we call for her, she will come, and bring a mighty warband with her.'

'Internal strife, then,' Belo said. He looked pointedly at Nathair. 'There are rumours of other realms that are struggling to maintain order within their borders. I have heard the word *rebellion* mentioned in connection with Tenebral. Is there any truth in this?'

'There has been—' Calidus began.

'It has been crushed,' Nathair interrupted. 'My first-sword has sent me word, Tenebral is at peace, and he brings the leaders of this so-called rebellion here, for my judgement.'

'Veradis, your *problem-solver*.'

It was Veradis who cut Mandros' head from his shoulders. Belo's cousin.

'Just so,' Nathair said, eyes fixed on Belo, who gave the first sign of any kind of emotion, a tightening in his jaw and narrowing of his eyes.

'I think it is time we retire,' Belo said. 'You have made your case clear, what you wish from us. Gundul and I shall discuss it at length.'

'That is not good enough,' Nathair said. Calidus put a hand upon his shoulder but he shook it off. 'Time cannot be wasted. I must have your answers now. This day.'

Belo shrugged and stood, his chair scraping. 'We don't always get what we want,' the ageing warrior said. 'And I for one am not sure I'll be advising my King to listen to a man who cannot even maintain order within his own realm. Come, Gundul,' he said, touching the young King's arm.

'Stop,' Nathair said quietly, venom in his voice.

Belo did stop, for a moment looking with angry eyes at Nathair.

'You do not give orders to us, King of Tenebral. This is a council of equals, and I take my orders from my King, not some upstart with a faded title, a realm in chaos and a reputation for murdering kings. Now, Gundul, let us—'

'Sumur, kill this thorn in my flesh,' Nathair said.

Sumur moved without a second's hesitation, walking calmly around the table, hand reaching over his shoulder for the hilt of his blade.

'This is not amusing,' Belo snapped. 'I will not be intimidated.' Ulfilas saw his eyes flickering between Nathair and Sumur.

'My patience is at an end. I will listen to your whining opposition no more,' Nathair said.

With a rasp, Sumur drew his blade.

'This is a council amongst allies,' Belo snapped, disbelief and fear mingling in his voice. He took a few steps back, hand reaching for his own sword.

'You are not my ally,' Nathair said. 'You did not take the oath, Gundul did.'

'This is outrageous,' Belo cried.

Sumur walked on, around the table.

'Alric,' Belo yelled, panic in his voice now, the shieldman behind Gundul shifting, looking between Gundul and Belo.

'Alric, now!' Belo shouted, and the shieldman moved, stepping in front of Sumur and drawing his sword.

Sumur curled a lip and rolled his shoulder, his sword snapping out, the shieldman moving too slowly, staggering into Gundul's chair, gurgling as blood spurted from his throat.

Sumur walked on.

Belo drew his own sword, backing into a column. Sumur reached him and struck an overhand blow, double-handed. Belo blocked it, but Ulfilas heard the unmistakable sound of bone cracking. Ulfilas, no stranger to battle, winced.

He's broken Belo's wrists.

Belo screamed, sword dropping from strengthless fingers.

No one is that strong.

Sumur raised his sword and struck again, Belo's scream cut short, then again, the sound of meat being cleaved, more bone breaking.

'Enough!' Calidus yelled and Sumur froze, looked back over his shoulder, blood splattering his face. He licked a drop from his top lip.

A silence had fallen upon the chamber, kings staring in horror, Gundul's eyes fixed on Belo's corpse. He whimpered.

'I was going to do this later,' Calidus said with a sigh, 'but perhaps it is appropriate now.' He gestured for the feast-hall gates to be opened. Ulfilas thought about questioning him, then looked at the pile of meat and bone that had been Belo and decided to move, nodding to his men to open the great doors. Daylight streamed in, along with a bitter wind. Footsteps thudded and warriors marched in, black-clad men and women like Sumur, a hundred, two hundred, more. They stood before the council table, eyes black and empty.

'They are a gift for my fellow kings,' Nathair said. 'One hundred warriors for each of you, a protection in these dark and dangerous times.'

A protection from whom? More your enforcers. Ulfilas did not like this, not one bit. He could see that the kings and their shieldmen felt the same way. The display of violence had been shocking, but the consequences of this were settling upon him now. Nathair was taking over this council of kings. If each of these warriors before him was half as capable as Sumur, then together they could carve up a warband.

This is Isiltir, not Tenebral. He looked to Jael, hoping that he would give Ulfilas the order to summon his warband and put an end to this. Jael just sat there, looking as shocked and scared as the rest of them.

'Now,' said Nathair, 'let us discuss our assault on Drassil.'

CHAPTER SIXTY-THREE

UTHAS

Uthas strode along beside Rhin, Dun Carreg towering above them upon its cliff like some predatory bird. Horns blowing, Rhin's honour guard rippled to a halt on the giantsway.

Honour guard! More like a warband – five hundred of Rhin's shield-men and fifty Benothi giants. Not a sight often seen in Ardan.

Uthas looked about him, drinking in the view like a half-parched man.

Ardan, they call it now, but it was only ever Benoth to me. There was a time when I thought I'd never see this land again.

Ahead of them Dun Carreg sat on its high cliff, at its foot the sprawl of a fisher-village, and all about them were rolling meadows, to the north the glitter of a pewter sea, and behind it all the cry of gulls. Uthas sucked in a deep breath, savouring the salt air and chill that filled his lungs.

'Was this your home, once?' Rhin asked him.

'Home, no,' Uthas said. 'I dwelt in Dun Taras, governed that part of Benoth for Nemain, but I came here often. I have . . . fond memories of this place.'

'The truth does not often live up to the memory,' Rhin said, looking up at Dun Carreg high above. 'Let us see what welcome Evnis has prepared for us.' She clicked her horse on and they headed through the fisher-village, the inhabitants hustling off the streets into houses as they saw Uthas and his kin approaching. They carried on up the winding road to the fortress, hooves clattering on the stone bridge as they crossed the chasm that separated the fortress from the mainland, the wind blowing up around them in great gusts.

Warriors lined the courtyard beyond Stonegate, turned out in their finery to greet their queen. With Rhin's warriors and fifty giants striding into the courtyard it soon became crowded.

'Where is Evnis?' Rhin said with a frown to the man who stepped forward to greet her, a captain named Andran.

'He rode south, my Queen,' Andran said. 'He received word of the rebels in Dun Crin.'

'How far is Dun Crin?' Rhin asked, looking annoyed.

'A ten-night down the giantsway,' Uthas answered. 'Through the Baglun and out the other side. Dun Crin is sunk in the marshes, though.'

Rhin nodded thoughtfully. 'Well, we do not need him for what we came for, I suppose. I just would have liked to see him.' She ordered her honour guard and mounts cared for, her warriors to be escorted to the feast-hall for a meal.

'Your giants should accompany them,' Rhin said.

'They may cause unrest,' Balur said.

Giants walking abroad in Dun Carreg – this has not happened for a thousand years. And the reaction they are likely to provoke is the reason Rhin came with us.

'They are my guests here. Any unrest will end with heads on spikes.' She said that loud enough for the whole courtyard to hear.

That should be enough. Rhin's presence in the fortress, combined with her commands, should be enough to keep my people safe.

'Eisa, you lead the kin,' Uthas said. 'Eat, drink, rest with our friends. And be courteous.' He held her gaze and raised an eyebrow. 'Salach, you will stay with me.'

'And now I will defer to you, Uthas,' said Rhin. 'Let us go in search of your Treasure.'

Uthas led Rhin and Salach through the streets of Dun Carreg, a sense of wonder filling him. He gazed about at the wide flagstoned roads, the stone buildings looming over them, and remembered when his kin had gazed back at him from shuttered windows and bairns ran laughing in the streets.

Soon they passed around the keep and into a wide courtyard, a pool with fountain and steps dominating the square. Then, further on, down the steps into the tunnel that led to the great well. It was all exactly as he remembered, even the damp smell, the drip of water, the echo as they entered the circular room with the wide hole that sank deep into the bowels of the cliff that Dun Carreg was built upon.

Uthas nodded to Salach, and he squatted beside the well-shaft, reaching down along the rough stone. He nodded as he found what he was looking for, then there was a click, a hiss and the outline of a door appeared on the wall to the left of them.

Rhin nodded approvingly and the three of them walked through.

'*Lasair*,' Uthas commanded, and the torch of rushes in his hand sparked into flame. He led them on into the tunnels beneath Dun Carreg, excitement coursing through his veins.

Nemain's necklace, one of the Seven Treasures.

Calidus had sent him to find them – necklace and cup, the Treasures he had promised to Asroth – and Rhin was to be his protector. Fifty Benothi giants wandering the west would not be much appreciated by the locals. Once he had them he was ordered to take them to Calidus, either at Mikil or somewhere closer to Forn and Drassil.

Drassil. This will bring me one large stride closer to claiming the fortress back for my kin. For all of the clans. The thought of it sent a thrill through him – sitting on Skald's throne, the chieftains of the five clans bending their necks before him. He realized he was grinning.

They spilt into a huge chamber, iron sconces holding unlit torches hammered into the damp walls. Uthas lit a few, sending shadow and light flickering about the room.

A shape was slumped in the middle of the room, crumpled and curled. The skeleton of a wyrm, not that large compared to the ones that had dwelt in Murias, but big enough, tattered scraps of skin hanging off strips of pale bone.

Its head was gone.

'This is a clean cut,' Salach said, kneeling beside the skeleton and examining the point on the spine where the head had been shorn. 'Not a bite wound, but a blade.'

So people had been down here, found a way in. And encountered a wyrm.

'This way,' Salach said, leading them to the left of the room, towards a mound of piled rubble, draped with thick web. Towards the tomb where Uthas had watched Nemain place the casket containing the necklace and book.

'This is where the casket was kept,' Uthas said as he held his torch higher.

Here and there the splintered frame of a doorway was visible, rock and boulder collapsed from the wall above to fill the entrance. Uthas exchanged a look with Salach, feeling a knot of worry growing in his belly.

How did this happen? A dead wyrm, the entrance to the tomb collapsed.

There was a gap in the rubble, high but too small for a giant to wriggle through, and Uthas could not imagine Rhin attempting to squeeze through, so he put his torch down and began to lift rocks. Salach soon joined him.

Uthas lost himself in the rhythm of lifting. He kept glancing at Rhin, the torchlight making her face shift, rippling between shadow and light.

She is changed since Uthandun. Humbled by Calidus. Shamed by him, in front of us all. That does not sit well upon a woman as proud as Rhin. During their journey south from Uthandun, through the Darkwood and into Ardan, Uthas had seen flashes of that change: not as calm, more prone to bursts of rage and melancholy.

She feels more dangerous now, not less so. What has Calidus done?

'That should do,' Rhin said, breaking into his thoughts. He looked and saw a hole amidst the rubble, large enough for him to stoop through. Salach lifted his torch, shrugged his axe from his back and passed through the doorway, Uthas and Rhin close behind.

They were standing in a circular chamber, smaller by far than the one they'd come from. At the far end of the chamber was a stone tomb, the lid lying cracked and broken upon the floor. Rows of giant axes and war-hammers edged the room, all thick with dust and web.

'These are still sharp,' Salach commented, running his thumb along the edge of one of the axe-blades.

They approached the tomb, treading over the flat stone lid, which was broken into slabs. Uthas held the torch higher and peered into the open tomb.

Inside was the skeleton of a giant, its hands clasped upon its chest, at its feet the broken shards of wyrm shells. Uthas glanced around the room, remembering the skeleton in the chamber without. Then he looked back into the tomb, eyes searching ever more frantically. Salach leaned in, ripped out the skeleton's chest cavity, ran his hand around the base of the tomb.

'It is not here,' Uthas growled, feeling his dreams of Drassil crumbing like sand within his cupped hands.

He stared at Rhin and she stared back at him, suspicion growing in her eyes.

'Evnis,' they both said together.

CHAPTER SIXTY-FOUR

CORBAN

Corban blinked as the trapdoor opened above him. Enkara went first, holding her hands up high, and iron glittered in the torchlight above her. He rode Shield up the slope, Storm loping beside him, and squinted as he entered a room that felt as bright as the sun after spending a ten-night in that huge, endless tunnel.

Blurred figures were standing in a semi-circle before him and he reined in. As his vision started to clear he saw they were Jehar. They drew their swords, dropped to one knee before him, bowing their heads and crying out, 'The Seren Disglair.'

'Please, rise,' Corban said as he slid from Shield's back.

There were ten of them, all older, between forty and fifty summers like Enkara.

I thought this kind of behaviour was all over. I've accepted who I am, but Seren Disglair or Bright Star or whatever they call me, it doesn't mean people need to get down on their knees in front of me.

'On your feet,' Corban said, more firmly, walking to the closest one and gently lifting him. They stood and sheathed their swords, looking at him with awe-struck eyes.

'Well met; I am honoured to meet you,' Corban said. 'I have been told much about you, and value your faithfulness in guarding Drassil for this day.' He had spoken a long time to Enkara about this, quizzing her during their journey through the tunnel of what to expect upon his arrival.

He greeted them all by name, again learned from Enkara; he thought it the least he could do, not able to imagine the dedication it had taken to spend sixteen years preparing Drassil for these times, then watch most of their comrades leave, knowing that they had to stay and guard an empty fortress.

'And you must be Hamil,' he said to the last one, a serious-looking man with iron grey at his temples and a hooked nose. The man dipped his head.

'Hamil, we have ridden far and there are many of us. Would you and your kin please help get them settled?'

'Of course, Bright Star,' Hamil said.

'Corban – please, my name is Corban.'

'Of course. One question.'

'Aye.'

'Where is Tukul?'

For a moment Corban did not know what to say. He missed Tukul, every day. For a man whom he had not known all that long, Tukul had had an immense impact upon him.

Then Hamil looked over Corban's shoulder and saw Gar. He stared a moment, then smiled, the expression transforming his face.

'Gar, is that you?' Hamil said.

Gar looked at him, blankly at first, then he smiled in return, though to Corban it looked wan. Nevertheless he slipped from his horse and embraced Hamil, who hugged him tightly and patted his back.

'Oh, how you have grown,' Hamil exclaimed.

'Aye. Seventeen years,' Gar shrugged.

'Where is your father?' Hamil asked him.

Gar's smile vanished, that stricken, hollow look returning to his eyes.

'He fell,' Gar said.

'What? No.' Hamil gasped. He took a long look at Gar and hugged him again. 'This world will not be the same without him.'

'No, it won't,' Gar whispered.

Meical was waiting patiently on the slope behind. 'There are many weary people down here,' he said.

'Of course, of course,' Hamil said, and then they were all moving, Hamil taking Shield's reins from him and allowing Corban to move deeper into the hall. People began to file out of the tunnel, an exodus squinting and blinking in the light. Buddai bounded over to Storm and they ran off together. Now that Corban's eyes had adjusted he took a moment to look around, and saw a huge chamber, bigger even than the hall in Murias where the cauldron had been kept.

It was roughly circular in design, the flagstoned floor that Corban was standing upon sunk deep into the ground, broad pillars of light slanting down into the chamber through vellum-covered windows. Wide stone steps led up to great doors of oak and iron. The steps would have stretched the length of the keep at Dun Carreg, so wide that they looked more like the tiered seats of a theatre or a gallery. But all of that was not what took Corban's breath away. High above, branches as thick as tree trunks in the Darkwood wound their way through the chamber, many of them breaking through the roof, or, as Corban looked closer, perhaps the roof was built around them, as there seemed to be some kind of design at work. A gentle breeze set branches and leaves rustling, as if a hidden host were whispering in the shadows up above them. He turned a half-circle, trying to take it all in, then froze, his jaw opening. At first Corban did not understand what he was seeing so he walked closer. Then he understood. At the centre of the chamber was a huge trunk, wider than Dun Kellen's keep, rising up and up, disappearing into the shadows of the high roof. The chamber he was standing in was built around the trunk, an outer ring of stone around one of timber, sap and bark.

Something was built into it, at its base, where the stone floor met the trunk.

Corban ran a hand along the bark. It was hard as iron, though not as cold. In fact, there was a sense of warmth, a tingle in Corban's fingertips. He walked slowly along the trunk, marvelling at it, then reached the construct he had seen.

It was a throne, partly wood, hewn into the trunk, and part stone, the arms carved in the shape of the great wyrms Corban had seen below Dun Carreg and in the cauldron's chamber in Murias. Sitting upon it, slumped within it, was the cadaver of a giant. Stretched grey skin, here and there patches of ashen bone, a tattered strip of leather or cloth. And in its chest, through its chest, piercing the chair behind it and on, deep into the trunk, was a spear. Sap had leaked and congealed about the wounded trunk. Corban ran a hand along the spear shaft, which was thick and smooth, darker veins twisting through it, a spike of black iron at its butt. When his fingers reached the metal he snatched them away as if burned. For a moment he'd thought he heard voices, a hissing chorus inside his head.

'It is Skald's spear,' a voice rumbled behind him.

Balur One-Eye.

'With this blow our high king was slain, the Giant Wars were begun, and the Sundering sealed.' Melancholy dripped from his voice.

'Who did it? Who killed Skald?'

'I did,' Balur said.

Corban looked up at him and saw tears running down Balur's craggy face.

A thousand questions rushed to the tip of his tongue but his voice faltered. The grief on Balur's face was too much to disturb.

The questions will wait.

They stood in silence a while, the warband emptying from the tunnel beneath Drassil like ants marching from a nest.

Ethlinn appeared at his other shoulder.

'Come, Bright Star, let Balur show us Drassil, first and greatest of the giant strongholds.'

'You have not seen it before, then?'

'No. I was born in Benoth, and like you I have only heard of it in tales.'

'Come then,' Balur grunted.

Corban walked the streets and courtyards of Drassil in a state of ever-growing wonder. The stronghold was built around a tree, although a tree the size of which Corban would have claimed was an impossibility. The main trunk was thicker and taller than any construct Corban had ever seen, more like a mountain rising into the sky than a thing of bark and timber. Its upper branches seemed so high that they touched the clouds. Branches sprouted from it, stone towers and walls spiralling and twisting about them as if set by some child-god's unbounded imagination. Here and there the ground was scarred and ruptured by roots rising out of the ground like the ancient knotted knuckles of some colossal sleeping giant.

Hamil appeared from a side street and hurried over to Corban.

'We have worked hard to prepare Drassil for your arrival,'

Hamil said. He wore the dark chainmail of the Jehar, and black linen beneath it, but he seemed less severe than most of the Jehar Corban had met.

'I am grateful for your commitment,' Corban said. That seemed to make Hamil incredibly happy and he gently took over as their guide, pointing out where vine had been sheared from walls, where stonework had been repaired, explained how they had made maps of the labyrinthine catacombs that burrowed for leagues beneath the stronghold and out beneath Forn. They passed a handful of cairns.

'Those are new,' Balur observed.

'Aye. They are raised over our Jehar kin who died here. Sixteen years we were here as the Hundred. Some died of sickness, others met Forn's predators. Daria is there, Gar's mother.'

Corban looked at the cairns, stone slabs dotted with moss and pale flowers. He had never thought of Gar having kin elsewhere; the man had been such an integral part of his life, it felt strange to think of him having a life elsewhere.

'Over there is the courtyard of forges,' Hamil said. 'You giants were very organized – nothing scattered, everything in its place.'

Balur just grunted.

'We have only used one forge while we have been here, but they are all prepared for use.'

'Thank you,' Corban said. 'We will need them all.'

'This way,' Balur said, changing their course.

'Ah.' Hamil smiled, but said no more.

Balur led them to a wide set of arched doors. He stood there a moment, hand on the iron handle, head bowed, and then tugged the door open. It was dusty inside, light streaming in on cobwebs thick as rope. Balur entered first, the others following.

It was a weapons chamber, as large as Dun Carreg's feast-hall, lined with racked weapons – axes, war-hammers, spears, longswords, daggers, along the back wall coats of chainmail and leather armour, shoulder plates, cuirasses, arm-bracers.

Balur smiled.

They tarried in there a while, Balur walking down each wall, trailing fingers against axe-hafts and hammer-heads as if he were greeting old friends. He stopped and pulled a spear from a rack and threw it to Ethlinn, who caught it with one hand and spun it, cobweb flying from its iron-spiked butt. Corban paused before a dagger, its blade wider and probably a little longer than his own sword. He ran his thumb across its edge and drew blood.

'May I have this?' Corban asked Balur.

'Of course,' Balur said.

Corban drew it from the iron rack, found a leather scabbard for it. *For Farrell, when he needs to chop heads from the Kadoshim.*

They left the chamber with some regret and entered a courtyard that was lined with stone buildings, hundreds of them, looking more like a row of stables than anything else, though taller and wider.

'The bear pens,' Balur said.

They were a hive of activity and appeared to be being put to good use. Corban saw some of the Jehar who had remained behind organizing the stabling of horses, removing tack, rubbing mounts down and providing water and food.

One line of the pens was built against a high wall, green with thick vines and hanging purple flowers. Hamil led them through the courtyard to a set of steps built into the wall and they climbed them. Meical came out of a stable, saw them and followed after.

The view at the top was not what Corban expected.

The branches of Drassil's great tree stretched out over the wall to cast dappled shadows over a deep meadow that ringed the fortress, a wide open space – *or killing ground.*

'That is not natural,' Corban observed, pointing to the open meadow.

'It is not,' Hamil said with pride. 'It was Tukul's undertaking, and took us many years to clear the trees and undergrowth so far back from the wall. On the south side of the fortress we have tilled fields of wheat, maize, rye. The harvest was good.'

'It is an amazing feat,' Meical said.

'So it is,' said Corban, 'and it will be most useful to us if Nathair and Calidus come against us here.'

'They will,' Meical said.

'You are sure?' Corban looked at the Ben-Elim.

'Yes.'

Corban took a deep breath. 'I have been so focused on just getting here that I have given little thought to what we will do now that we've arrived. We must talk of what comes next.'

'We should,' Meical and Balur said together, and Hamil nodded his agreement.

'But for now let us settle, find our places here, rest. Soon we will make our plans.'

Corban woke feeling unsettled, a pale grey light seeping into his chamber. It was the first night he'd spent in a bed since they'd left Dun Taras with the warband of Domhain, and yet he'd slept poorly.

A year ago. And my back aches more now, after one night upon a mattress stuffed with goose feather and horsehair than it did sleeping rough on the floor.

But his broken night's sleep was not just down to the mattress. He had dreamed again of the Otherworld. It had been similar to the last time, where he had been walking in a green valley, a lake in front of him, waters still and pure, and behind him tall cliffs that reared as high as the bloated, blood-red clouds.

That had struck him as odd. His memory of the Otherworld was of shades of grey, land, rivers and sky, but this place was lustrous in its colour. He'd wandered, the beauty of the place seeping into his very being, filling him with a sense of calm tranquillity. And then he had seen Meical, flying high above with great beats of his white wings. Somehow he had known it was Meical, although he was too high to distinguish any features, and he had remembered Meical's words to him, about Asroth hunting him, about the Kadoshim flying abroad in the Otherworld. *Promise me if you find yourself there again, that you will hide, do not move. Asroth's Kadoshim fly high, and they will see you before you see them.*

So he had found shelter beneath a red-leaved maple, sat and watched Meical as he had alighted on the cliff high above him. He thought he glimpsed other white-winged figures greeting him, but then they all disappeared into a dark hole in the cliff face. And then . . .

Then I woke up.

He dressed quickly, strapping on his sword-belt and pinning his wolven cloak about him. Something struck him as wrong. He looked about and realized that Storm was not with him, remembered now looking for her when he'd awoken during the night, missing her presence. Perhaps that had contributed to his restlessness.

Probably off exploring, sniffing every corner of this place. Still, it was unusual, and he'd rather have her at his side. He opened his door to find Gar standing there with a fist raised to knock.

'Sword dance,' Gar said by way of explanation, then turned and strode away. Corban followed him, the slap of his boots ringing in the empty corridor.

The weapons court of Drassil was enormous, like everything else in this fabled fortress, most of it hard-packed earth and worn grass, to one side an area flagstoned. Weapons bins stood full of practice blades, and even though the Jehar didn't use anything other than their curved swords, there were stacks of shields and spears, lined in racks, a row of straw targets at the far end of the field.

It is not so different from the Rowan Field at Dun Carreg.

Dawn mist clung to the ground, the air was chill and heavy with moisture, the sky above feeling as if it was pressing down upon them, clouds bloated and heavy with rain. As Corban hurried along behind Gar he saw Coralen, standing with Enkara and Kulla, Enkara showing them a combined rotation of shoulder and wrist. Corban recognized it as a technique that Gar had taught him a while ago, a way of getting a final snap into the strike of a two-handed blow.

The three women looked up as he approached them.

'Coralen, have you seen Storm?'

'Not since yesterday,' she said.

Corban frowned. 'Me neither. The last time I saw her was just after we came out of the tunnel. She ran off with Buddai.'

Coralen raised an eyebrow at that.

'I think I might know where they are, or at least what they're doing.'

'What do you mean?'

'I think Storm's in season.'

'What!'

Corban blinked, for a moment not understanding. Then Coralen's words sank in.

In season? Are Storm and Buddai making pups? In hindsight it was so obvious that he almost slapped his forehead. Her change in behaviour, her playfulness with Buddai. *Of course wolven have seasons, but I have noticed nothing. Too busy, too preoccupied to notice those around me. And she's run off with Buddai.* He thought about that a moment and then smiled. *They would make fine pups. Or cubs?*

'Corban,' Gar called to him and Corban hurried away, Gar throwing him a curved practice sword.

Corban loved the sword dance; it was like an old friend or a favourite place, such as the oathstone glade in the Baglun, somewhere that he would go where he felt safe and comfortable. Once he began, raising his sword high, two-handed into stooping falcon, everything else melted away. He did not even remember moving from one form to the next, flowing between them like liquid. The dance ended with a lunge and shout combined, a straight thrust that began in his ankles and ended with his blade through an imaginary opponent's heart.

With the shout still ringing in the air Corban blinked and looked around, sweat dripping from his nose. The weapons court was full with what must have been every single person that had travelled to Drassil with him. Corban saw Balur and the rest of the Benothi, villagers of Narvon, Wulf and the survivors of Gramm's hold, Javed and the oarsmen from the Vin Thalun ships, all mingled. Something white moved, and for a moment he thought it was Storm, but then he realized it was much smaller – the terrier, with Haelan standing beside it.

All of them were staring at him, and as he looked back he realized what a unique and varied warband they made, so many strengths and specialities amongst them.

We are a force to be reckoned with.

'This is the weapons court,' he heard himself cry out. 'Come, join us, for here we will forge the warband that will slay the Black Sun and his followers, and set the Banished Lands free.'

Where did that come from?

A silence settled about him, and then a huge roar, starting, Corban suspected, with Farrell and Dath, but growing into a bellow louder than a hundred draigs. As it died out and people began stepping into the court Corban marched over to Balur, Gar pacing behind him.

He won't let me get out of sparring, even if I am the Bright Star.

'Balur, I would ask something of you,' Corban said.

'Aye,' Balur said, eyebrows knitting together above the scarred socket of his missing eye. 'Ask then.'

'Would you spar with us? You and your kin?'

'Is that wise?' Gar said quietly.

'A good question,' Balur rumbled.

'At Gramm's hold we fought giants. At Murias I saw Benothi fighting alongside the Kadoshim. My guess is that we will be fighting giants again.'

If possible Balur's eyebrows knitted tighter and protruded further.

'So you want me to teach you how to kill giants?'

'Yes,' Corban shrugged. 'I wouldn't take it personally – we already practise how to kill each other, us men.' He glanced at the Jehar warriors about the field, many of them women, finally at Coralen, who was performing a particularly vicious move that ended up with Farrell on his back and Coralen's weapon thrust under his jaw. 'And women.'

Balur glowered down at him, then his brows unknitted.

'I was wondering if you would ask me. The answer is yes, it is wisdom. We will spar with you, though perhaps first some practice weapons should be fashioned for us – axes and war-hammers in the dimensions that we use.'

'Well, it's not like there's a shortage of wood,' Corban grinned.

Balur's face twisted and it took a moment for Corban to realize the giant was smiling at him.

Hamil approached Gar and whispered something in his ear. Gar frowned and Hamil pointed over at the Jehar, who were gathered together in a loose circle, seemingly every last one of them.

'What is it?' Corban asked.

'The Jehar are choosing a new leader,' Gar said, the frown still on his face.

'Tukul is gone.' Hamil shrugged. 'We follow you, Bright Star, but there should be a lord amongst us. That is the way it has always been.'

'Aye. So why are you frowning?' Corban asked Gar.

'Akar has put himself forward,' Hamil answered when Gar didn't.

Gar and Hamil walked away, towards the gathering of Jehar. After a moment's hesitation Corban followed.

The Jehar were standing in a ring, over three hundred and fifty of them, with Akar standing at their centre.

'How does this work?' Corban whispered to Hamil.

'A warrior is nominated, or nominates themself. If more than one is put forward, then the court of swords decides.'

Corban looked at Akar, standing stern and resolute in the circle's centre.

'I have waited the allotted time,' Akar called out, looking up at the sun. 'None have presented themselves, no one has nominated another.'

He is a great warrior; I've seen him fight, and he has proved himself many times over during our journey here. And he has led a company, proved he has the skills to lead. But he was fooled by Nathair, fought for him. Corban frowned, troubled at the thought of Akar taking up Tukul's mantle. *But who could take Tukul's place? No one.*

Except Gar.

Do I just think that because of how close I am to Gar? Instantly he knew the answer to that was *no*. He loved Gar like a father and brother combined, but above and beyond that he knew that Gar was a great man, deserving of leadership.

'Something troubles you?' Hamil asked him quietly.

'I think Gar should be your lord,' Corban said.

A smile twitched Hamil's mouth. 'I nominate Garisan ben Tukul,' he cried out in a loud voice.

Akar's head snapped around to him, as did the head of every other Jehar in the crowd. Except Gar. Corban saw his friend bow his head. He looked up at Hamil. 'I am not worthy,' he said.

'He is not worthy,' Akar said. 'I have spent my life in Telassar, I am already a named captain of the kin, have led warriors in battle. I am trained and proven.'

'Another has been nominated,' Hamil said. 'The time for words is passed, only the court of swords can decide this.'

'If he accepts the nomination,' Akar said, eyes falling upon Gar.

Gar looked at Hamil, about the crowd, then finally at Corban.

'You *are* worthy,' Corban said to him. 'No one more so.'

He sighed, then nodded. 'I accept,' he said, and strode into the ring to stand before Akar.

Hamil stepped out of the crowd.

'Akar ben Yeshua, would you stand against Garisan ben Tukul in the court of swords?'

'I would,' Akar said. 'He has been tainted by the world, softened and weakened. He is not fit to lead the Jehar.'

That made Corban angry. He fought to keep his mouth clamped shut.

'Garisan ben Tukul, would you stand against Akar ben Yeshua in the court of swords?'

Gar stood before Akar, head bowed, then raised his eyes and met Akar's gaze.

'I would,' Gar said. 'Because my father did not want Akar to lead the Jehar.'

Akar scowled at that. 'A dead man's words should stay with him, in the grave.'

Gar drew his sword.

What!

What are they doing?

'Why is Gar doing that?' Corban gasped, grabbing Hamil's arm.

'Because his father would have wished him to.'

Akar drew his blade, threw his scabbard to one side.

'No. Why are they using sharp iron?'

'This is to the death,' Hamil said.

Gar and Akar faced one another.

There was a pause, the calm in the storm before violence is unleashed, death's wings close.

Corban walked into the ring.

'No,' he said.

Everyone looked at him.

'You will *not* fight to the death,' he shouted. 'Asroth and his Black Sun outnumber us, threaten to overwhelm us. I need every warrior that can hold a blade – and two Jehar with a lifetime of skill and learning . . .' He shook his head. 'It is a waste. I will not lose either of you over this decision.'

Both men stared at him.

'What would you have us do, then?' Gar asked. 'This must be decided.'

'Let it be to first blood,' Corban said. 'If anything, that will reveal the greater skill.'

Both men stared at him, then nodded.

'Then begin,' Corban said and stepped back into the crowd.

The two men raised their swords and without any other sign attacked.

Their blades rang, a flurry of high blows from both men, neither giving ground. Then Gar stepped in close and kicked Akar in the knee. Akar staggered back, for a fleeting moment his cold face twisted with shock and anger. Gar followed him, striking in a long, relentless combination to head, neck, groin, gut, heart, head – Corban recognized each and every blow, one flowing into the next, fluid as a song.

Akar defended, something the Jehar did rarely, giving ground with a shuffling backstep, favouring, protecting his injured leg.

Corban felt a presence behind him, glanced back quickly to see crowds forming, seemingly every man woman and child in the weapons court. The sound of iron on iron had drawn them.

Gar did not let up, Akar's defence beginning to appear frayed, disjointed as he tried desperately to parry every blow.

Abruptly Gar stopped, took a step back and walked slowly around Akar.

'You are right to say that the world has touched me, moulded me,' Gar said, eyes never leaving Akar as he paced around the warrior, who was taking advantage of the respite, setting his feet, controlling his breathing.

'But you are wrong to say it has made me weaker.' Gar stepped forward, sword moving again, iron clashing, ringing loud. This time Akar did not give way and the two of them stood, chopping and lunging, blocking, stabbing, parrying, neither one able to break through the other's defence, each parry turned into a strike that was in turn blocked. Blow by blow they inched closer, until they were standing with swords locked above them, grating sparks, legs planted, leaning into their blades as if they were an extension of their bodies, both staring at each other, sweat dripping. Then Gar's head jerked forward, headbutting Akar on the nose. Blood spurted and Akar stumbled back a step, Gar's foot hooking behind Akar's ankle and then Akar was on his back, blood running down his chin, Gar's sword hovering over him.

Corban let out a breath he didn't realize he'd been holding.

Coralen's used that move on me a hundred times, and I eventually learned to do it back to her. Looks as if Gar's been watching us spar.

'You're bleeding,' Gar said. 'Do you yield?

It was an unorthodox move, something these Jehar would probably consider beneath them. But as Coralen always says – dead is dead.

Akar stared up at Gar, emotions warring across his face. Then something in him softened and he nodded.

'First blood is yours,' Akar said. 'I yield.'

'The world has touched me, but it has made me stronger, not weaker,' Gar breathed. 'Now, give me your hand, brother.'

Gar held his arm out.

A moment's hesitation and then Akar took it. A roar of approval rose up from about the ring, even the giants bellowing their approval, Corban's voice lost in the din of it. Then Akar dropped to one knee before Gar and kissed his hand. Other Jehar dropped to the ground, Gar looking about at them with a slightly embarrassed expression upon his face.

Now he knows how I feel.

Hamil stood and strode to Gar, gripped Gar's wrist and raised his arm in the air.

'Garisan ben Tukul,' Hamil cried in a great voice, 'Lord of the Jehar.'

CHAPTER SIXTY-FIVE

MAQUIN

Maquin swayed in his saddle, holding onto his mount with his knees as his hands were bound behind his back. Twenty paces to his right the dark waters of a wide river flowed, and to the north he glimpsed snow-capped peaks, a wind swirling down from them that set the long grass whispering and brought with it the faint chill of ice. He shivered. He was riding as part of a great column, close to six thousand warriors before and behind him, the combined warbands of Veradis' eagle-guard and Lykos' Vin Thalun. An honour guard of Ripa surrounded Krelis, Ektor, Fidele, Peritus and Alben. Ahead of him Maquin caught a glimpse of the two giants – prisoners again, like him – their long strides keeping pace with the mounted eagle-guard watching them.

More than a moon had passed since that day in the field beyond Ripa's walls, when the world had been turned on its end. Two warbands massed against Lykos, outnumbering him two to one – killing the Vin Thalun lord had felt inevitable.

And then Veradis had arrived.

As they'd stood in the rowan-meet, listened to Veradis' proposals on behalf of Nathair, any hopes he'd had of Lykos finding justice had been burned away. And then the final straw. After all that Lykos had done to Fidele, to see him in her presence, taunting her . . .

I thought my self-control was total. It seems that I was wrong.

Hooves sounded behind him and Lykos came into view on his left side. Maquin stared straight ahead, refusing to look at him.

'And how are you today?' Lykos said.

He kept his lips shut tight.

'Managing to sit straight?'

Maquin's back and ribs were bruised purple. Each breath brought with it an ebb and flow of pain.

One cracked rib, at least.

And when he had emptied his bladder that morning there had been streaks of blood in his urine. He gritted his teeth, buried the pain. He would not give Lykos the satisfaction of knowing how bad it was.

I've endured worse before, and I will no doubt endure worse if Lykos has anything to do with it.

'This is only a taste,' Lykos hissed, 'of what is to come. I am watched, you see. That bitch has told tales of me to Veradis, and even though he is not in his right mind at the moment, he watches me. So, no bruises that cannot be covered by your clothing, no broken bones, no pain that keeps you from your saddle . . . Yet.'

Lykos rode in silence beside him a while, almost as if they were old friends.

'What I am really looking forward to is when I can have both you and Fidele chained in the same room. I *will* have her back, you see, but before we can go back to how things were, she will have to be punished. Taught the consequences of her actions.'

Maquin's fists clenched, an involuntary ripple that bypassed his conscious mind – he tried to stop it when he realized his body was betraying him, willed his fingers to loosen, but it was too late – Lykos had seen. He laughed, low and intimate.

'You have a weakness now, Old Wolf. Fidele has charmed you, that is clear. After I have punished her and she has learned her lesson, when I have her in my bed again, perhaps I'll let you watch.'

I should have got her out of that tent, run with her, then and there, instead of chasing Lykos like some blood-crazed berserker.

They crested a ridge in the road and ahead of them, upon a hill beside a lake was Jcrolin, its black walls and tower gleaming in the weak sunlight.

'Ah, good,' Lykos said with a vicious grin. 'Tonight you will have a room rather than a tent. Thick stone walls to drown your screams.'

Not if I can help it.

Maquin had not screamed once during Lykos' visits. Grunted, winced, ground his teeth, bitten his tongue, but he had held his voice, regardless of Lykos' efforts. A voice in his head told him he was being stupid – *cry out and Lykos will stop, for fear of drawing attention.* But he had not, because he knew the Vin Thalun were listening, waiting to hear their lord break the Old Wolf. With each night's visit Lykos grew a little more desperate, a little more frantic, and Maquin knew what his warriors would be whispering around their campfires.

Lykos leaned close. 'Soon, I will break you,' he whispered.

Never.

Maquin stared at the fighting arena on the plains before Jerolin, remembering the last time he had been there. Facing Orgull in the circle, the rebellion, chaos, fighting Deinon and Lykos, fleeing with Fidele . . .

His horse was led to the stables, where hands dragged him from his saddle and led him unceremoniously into a cluster of buildings close to the keep. He was thrust into a stone room, the door clanging shut behind him.

The shaft of sunlight through a high window edged its way across the room as highsun came and went, sliding towards sunset. Maquin heard muted voices and the slap of booted feet beyond his door, saw the orange flicker of torchlight through the gaps as twilight seeped slowly into the world, then full dark.

No one came to his room.

He will come.

He felt a flutter of fear at the thought of what was to come, but immediately smothered it.

I may as well rest until it starts.

He lay down upon the bench and closed his eyes.

Keys rattling in the door woke him and Lykos walked in, silhouetted by torchlight that a warrior held behind the Vin Thalun lord.

'Good evening,' Lykos said amicably, two, three shieldmen entering the room before the door was shut.

He fears me still, even bound and beaten bloody. He felt a moment's pleasure at that thought.

Lykos drew a small knife from his belt, sharp and wicked looking.

'Help him stand,' Lykos said.

Two of his shieldmen grabbed Maquin, the third standing back, holding his torch high to illuminate the room.

Lykos cut away Maquin's cloak and woollen layers, exposing a web of bruising and lacerations. The Vin Thalun smiled.

'You *will* kneel to me. You *will* beg for my mercy. You *will* pledge yourself to me for all eternity,' Lykos said grimly. 'You remember Orgull, do you not? Your hulking friend. Do you remember seeing him broken, beaten, wishing only for death. *I* did that to him.'

You did not break his spirit.

'This night, you will beg; this night.' Then, slowly, carefully, Lykos stabbed Maquin with the knife – an incision about a thumb-nail deep, starting at his armpit, slowly working its way down to Maquin's hip.

Maquin grunted, ground his teeth, squeezed his fists together until it felt as if the bones in his hands would crack. He knew better than to writhe or try to pull away, that would only lead to greater injury, worse pain. Instead he endured, stared fiercely into Lykos' eyes – his look a promise of death should he get free.

Lykos stepped back, a slight scowl creasing his forehead.

'I will flay you if I have to,' he growled. 'Or perhaps an eye . . .' He raised the knife, rested it on Maquin's cheek a hair's breadth below his eyeball.

Maquin was staring at Lykos, but in his mind he was back on the bridge of swords, the Ben-Elim standing before him with his sword of flame.

You must make your choice, the Ben-Elim had said to him.

I did. I came back for three people: two to kill, one to love. If I'd known it would lead me here . . .

Fidele's face hovered in his mind. For a brief moment he felt her lips brush his, the tickle of her breath, the faint smell of roses.

I'd make the same choice. She is worth a lifetime of pain.

With a snarl Lykos pulled the knife away, left a thin cut in Maquin's cheek. Sweat stung it. Maquin blinked, saw Lykos turn away and snatch the torch from his shieldman.

'Perhaps a tickle of flame will coax something more from you,' Lykos hissed. He held the torch between them, inched it closer to Maquin's belly. He smelt the hairs on his body burning first, heat washing him in waves, felt the almost irresistible urge to move, to step away.

I cannot move, I am held fast. And to move, to scream, is to fail.

Sweat beaded his brow, dripped from his nose.

Lykos smiled and moved the flame nearer, just a fraction, but the pain surged and Maquin felt his skin start to blister. A groan escaped his mouth, a wave of pain behind it desperate to find release in screaming abandon.

He clamped his mouth shut.

'I should have tried this sooner,' Lykos said, leaning close to Maquin, studying him. Willing him to break.

'Scream, damn you,' Lykos snarled, the frustration growing in the Vin Thalun with every passing heartbeat. He twisted a fist into Maquin's matted hair.

Not in this lifetime you bastard.

A voice spoke behind Lykos. 'My lord, burns like that may kill him; at the very least he will not be able to ride on the morrow—'

'You'll be surprised what this man can do,' Lykos said. He took a step closer, the flame no longer a ripple of pain now, just a constant, searing agony. Maquin smelt his own flesh burning. He opened his eyes, saw Lykos' face hovering in front of him, that hateful face, smiling, eyes bitter and full of malice.

Maquin lunged forwards, for a moment taking his guards by surprise, too focused on holding him up to hold him back. His mouth opened, a huge roar escaping his throat, echoing around the room and then he snapped his mouth shut, teeth closing on Lykos' face – his nose, part of one cheek.

He bit down hard, ground his teeth into flesh, felt blood burst into his mouth, hot and salty. He shook his head like a wolven with a hare in its jaws.

Lykos screamed, high and piercing.

He was a lot quicker to scream than I.

Then Maquin felt a rush of heat sear his face, flame shooting up between him and Lykos. Maquin's lunge had squashed the torch to them both, ignited Lykos' linen shirt.

Good – let's see how you like it!

Lykos screamed again. He was sobbing and trying to pull away. Something crashed into the back of Maquin's skull and his legs turned to liquid. He sagged to his knees, blood slick upon his lips and chin, saw Lykos fall backwards, dropping the torch and slapping desperately at his burning shirt.

There was another blow across the back of Maquin's head that knocked him to the floor. He rolled over, watching Lykos screeching in pain, saw him ripping off his shirt, standing there, chest heaving, blood sluicing his face from where Maquin had bitten him.

Lykos was blinking and gasping heavily. He gingerly touched the blisters on his chest, felt his torn face and looked at Maquin with undisguised hatred. He drew his sword.

'You . . . are more trouble than you are . . . worth,' he breathed and raised his sword.

Footsteps suddenly echoed in the corridor, the sound of iron-shod sandals on stone.

Lykos paused, looked at the door, Maquin following his gaze to see figures there. Men with eagles on their chests.

'Put your weapons down,' a voice ordered, harsh and commanding, but vaguely familiar. Then: 'He is coming with me.'

'No. He is my prisoner – mine,' Lykos said, spitting a gob of blood on the floor.

'Not any more. He will stand before Nathair. After that, perhaps he will be yours again, but until then I am taking him into my custody.'

The voices started to blur in Maquin's mind, he was unable to make much sense of them.

'You keep taking prisoners from me; this is becoming a very bad habit,' Lykos growled. 'And I thought we were friends.'

There was no answer, only the pressure upon Maquin's back disappearing and firm hands gripping him. He groaned as he was hoisted from the ground, heard someone swear, then darkness closed in about him.

He woke to pain.

It was still dark, torchlight flickering somewhere. His torso was agony. He groaned.

Someone was bending over him, spreading something cool across his belly. He opened his eyes to see an old face staring back at him, framed with silver hair and beard.

'Alben,' he whispered.

'Hush,' Alben said, smiling, though it didn't clear the worry in his eyes. 'Drink this.' He lifted Maquin's head and gave him sips of something bitter from a cup.

'Will he live?' a voice said behind Alben.

Alben sighed. 'I don't know. He is strong, and the desire to live burns fiercely in him. But this is not a day's healing. A moon, maybe.'

'We must leave on the morrow. The mountain paths are closing.'

'He cannot ride.' There was no possibility of discussion in Alben's tone.

'A wain, then?'

'Perhaps,' Alben shrugged.

Maquin lifted his head. 'Veradis?' he whispered.

Veradis stepped into his vision, his strong face with short hair and close-cropped beard lined with cares, making him seem older than his age.

'I am sorry, for your father.'

Maquin had seen the cairn as they rode out from Ripa, seen Veradis, Krelis and Ektor standing before it with heads bowed.

Grief, raw and powerful swept Veradis' face.

'It was your fault,' Veradis said.

Maquin blinked at him, confused.

'You attacked Lykos in the rowan-meet; pandemonium broke out, shieldmen bursting in, shouting, shoving. My father was knocked, somehow. He fell upon my . . .'

'It was an accident,' Alben said. 'A tragic, terrible accident.'

'I didn't know,' Maquin said. *I am a fool. Should have kept my knife in its sheath.* 'I am sorry,' he mumbled. 'So sorry.'

Veradis ground a palm into his eyes. 'The past is done,' he said. 'I am sorry, too. I was not aware that Lykos was doing . . . this.' He gestured at Maquin's body.

'I am surprised at the friends you keep,' Maquin whispered. The pain was more bearable now, still there, a constant throbbing, but dulled.

'As am I,' Alben echoed.

'Lykos is not my friend,' Veradis snapped, then took a long, frayed breath. 'But he is my King's ally. I cannot understand the things that have happened here, what he is accused of doing.'

'These are not accusations – they are facts,' Maquin said, looking at the tapestry of scars and fresh wounds upon his body. 'He is evil, and must be stopped.'

'That is not for me to decide. Nathair will hear all – I promise you that. He will decide. Until then, I will keep him from you, and Alben is the best healer I know.' He shrugged. 'I would do more if I could.'

'It is enough,' Maquin said.

Veradis turned to go, but hovered by the door.

'Part of me hates you,' he said quietly. 'Because of my da. I cannot stop it.'

Maquin said nothing.

'And you should know, I cannot save you, even if I had a mind to. You broke our sacred law when you drew your blade. I should have executed you on the spot, and the only reason you are alive is because someone of influence has begged me to postpone your execution.'

Fidele.

'But you drew a blade in a rowan-meet; there will be no pardon, no way out from that. Once you stand before Nathair the inevitable will be decided. You will die.' He stayed a moment more, then shook his head and left. Maquin heard his voice in the corridor, and then another figure slipped in, a shadow wrapped in a cloak.

A muffled sob came, and then Fidele was kissing him, stroking his face, tears dropping onto him, mingling with his own tears.

'Elyon, but it is good to see you,' Maquin breathed.

'What has he done to you?' Fidele snarled, then swore in a very unqueenly way. He lifted a hand to her cheek.

'I tried to get you,' she whispered, 'I took Alben and a few score warriors to take you back from Lykos.'

'The eagle-guard stopped us, thought it would lead to war,' Alben said.

'They were probably right,' Maquin said. 'Veradis?'

'No, one of his captains. Veradis was in mourning, had passed over command for a time.'

The grey of dawn was creeping through windows now, and

Maquin heard the sound of iron-shod feet, guards changing shifts.

'You cannot linger, my lady,' Alben said. 'If anyone sees you . . .'

'I am a prisoner too,' Fidele said with a twist of her lips. 'To be judged by my son on the charge of adultery.'

'What!' Maquin tried to sit up but a fresh wave of pain convinced him to stop.

'Because of the farce with Lykos,' she said.

'So reports of you kissing an ex-pit-fighter will not help your cause,' Alben said.

'True enough,' Fidele said, a smile twisting her lips.

'Go,' Maquin said. 'This has been enough.'

She brushed her lips against his one more time, cupped his cheek with her hand, then she was slipping away.

'I will be back soon,' Alben said. 'Veradis has placed guards on your door. You are safe, from Lykos at least.' He frowned with worry.

'I will not die,' Maquin growled. *Three things to live for.*

Alben smiled, leaned down and whispered in Maquin's ear, then left too.

Maquin lay there, watching dawn claim the day, feeling his eyes grow heavy with sleep and the potion Alben had given him. As sleep took him he mused over the words that Alben had whispered in his ear.

Keep the faith.

CHAPTER SIXTY-SIX

CYWEN

Cywen sat at a long table in the great hall of Drassil. Corban had called a council of war, and many had come. Meical and Gar were sitting with Corban, and beside them Balur and Ethlinn, in chairs built for giants. There was Brina and Coralen, Hamil of the Jehar and Wulf from Gramm's hold, Teca the huntswoman to represent the people of Narvon, Javed and Atilius from the oarsmen, and also the child prince, Haelan, a shieldman standing behind him.

And there's me, Cywen the apprentice healer. Sister to, apparently, one of the most important people in the world. Madness.

And lurking off to one side, not at the table, but close, were Farrell, Dath and Kulla. Farrell had his new sword at his hip, a giant's dagger gifted to him by Corban.

Gar shifted beside Corban and whispered in his ear.

Gar has changed, since his duel with Akar. Six nights had passed since the duel, and Gar had lost the stoop to his shoulders, the bitter twist to his mouth. He was a fine leader and already the Jehar were saying how like his da he was. *How proud Tukul would have been.* While it was obvious that Gar still mourned the loss of his da, he seemed to have accepted it as well.

The first step on a long road. And I know what that feels like.

Corban stood up and the room fell into silence.

'We are finally here, in fabled Drassil,' Corban said. 'It feels as if we have completed a quest, just getting here. We've encountered our enemy, fought battles, lost friends and family.' He looked at Cywen and Gar as he said that. 'But now we stop running, and we make a stand. The God-War is happening, now,' Corban continued. 'We have been fighting it. But now that we are here we must decide not only how to fight this war, but how to win it.' He turned to Meical, who sat straight and tall, jet-black hair, silver scars down his face.

'Meical, you are the author behind all of this, the force that has bound us together and guided us here. Now, more than ever, your wisdom would be welcome. How do we win this war?'

Is this really my baby brother? The same brother I kicked Rafe in the stones for, because he'd bloodied Corban's lip? When did he get so eloquent?

'The answer is simple,' Meical said. 'From the outset Calidus' plan has been to use the cauldron to breach the wall between this world of flesh and the Otherworld, the world of spirit, where the Kadoshim and Ben-Elim dwell.'

'Hasn't he already done that?' Dath said. 'Those Kadoshim in Murias seemed pretty real to me.'

'No,' Meical shook his head. 'With the Seven Treasures a doorway can be opened that allows Asroth and the Kadoshim to cross over from the Otherworld in their own forms, and in doing so their forms would become flesh. What happened in Murias was akin to a possession, where some of the Kadoshim's spirits passed into host bodies. This was because there were only two of the Treasures present, and so only a crack in the doorway could be created. What happened in Murias, and those Kadoshim, is but a shadow of what Calidus hopes to achieve: Asroth and the host of the Kadoshim made flesh. And for Calidus to do that, he needs the Seven Treasures. He has the cauldron, and will be searching for the rest. But two of the Treasures are here.' He looked to Balur, who had the starstone axe slung across his back.

'The starstone axe and the spear of Skald are here.'

'What of the other Treasures?' Brina asked.

'Two more are in the west,' Meical said with a shrug. 'The cup and necklace.' He glanced at Balur and Ethlinn.

'That is true,' Ethlinn said. 'Uthas lost the cup during the retreat from Dun Taras, and the necklace was kept in one of the southern fortresses.' She looked at Balur. 'We do not know which one.'

'And the others?' Corban asked.

'The torc and the knife,' Balur rumbled. 'The torc was last recorded as being in the hands of the Jotun; the knife, with the

557

Kurgan. But that was over a thousand years ago – what has happened to them . . .' He shrugged.

'Whatever happened to them, Calidus will be bent on finding them. He will find them. And the knowledge that we are here will drive him. The thought of us in Drassil with two of the Treasures will consume him. He will think the longer we are here the stronger we will become – and he's right. Besides, there are other Treasures here apart from those forged out of the starstone. He will come as soon as he can,' Meical assured them.

'How do you know that?' Brina asked him.

'Because I know Calidus.' He sighed and shook his head. 'I have made mistakes, in the past been outwitted by him. That is because he knows me, too. He sought out the people I recruited for this war and has removed many of them from the board.'

They were people, not pieces in a game!

'We were one kin, once, before he fell,' Meical continued. 'I know him, and in this I am certain. He will come for us – and as quickly as he can mobilize his forces.'

Corban nodded thoughtfully, sharing a glance with Brina.

'And that leads us on to the next question,' Brina said. 'How will he come here? It is not exactly a pleasant stroll through sun-warmed glades.'

Meical frowned. 'We have all experienced the difficulties of marching through Forn, and we had the advantage of the tunnel. He will want to bring a lot of men – he will not want to risk defeat. How he will find Drassil, and then bring with him enough warriors to ensure a victory in his reckoning, I do not know.'

'Maybe we'll have longer than you suspect, then,' Atilius said.

'Maybe,' Meical replied. 'But one thing I have learned to my detriment; never underestimate him. He is cunning, and he is ruthless.'

'I have a question,' a small voice piped up – Haelan, the child-king of Isiltir. 'What of our allies? Do we have any?'

'Now that is a very good question,' Brina said. 'This warband is low in numbers, though made of exceptional warriors, granted. We total around eight hundred men and women who can wield a blade. Calidus and Nathair, I have no doubt, can rally many thousands more than that. If they do make it this far, we will be overwhelmed by sheer numbers.'

'There is Edana,' Corban said. 'Though we have no idea how she fares – alive, dead, a warband behind her?'

'Craf will know,' Brina said.

If we ever see the old crow again.

'Is there anyone else?' Haelan asked, looking to Meical.

'There are friends to our cause in various places, but none who could lead a warband, except, perhaps, the Sirak.'

'Who are they?' Cywen asked.

'The horse lords of Arcona,' Meical said.

'If we sent messengers, would they help us?' Brina asked.

Meical shrugged. 'Perhaps. Politics is an unstable affair. Those who are sympathetic to our cause would certainly try – but who is to say whether they are in power, or even still alive with Calidus' scheming?'

'And there is one other ally who has not been mentioned,' Corban said.

'Who is that?' Brina asked him.

'The Ben-Elim,' Corban said. 'Meical, you read from the prophecy, a line about them gathering beneath the great tree.' Corban gestured to the trunk that the chamber they were sitting in was built around. 'That is why you counselled me to come here, because of the prophecy.'

'Aye,' Meical said. 'Because of the prophecy.'

'So, where are they? When will they arrive?'

Meical gave Corban a sad look. 'I do not know, Corban. The prophecy is not clear.'

'But you are Ben-Elim, one of them. More than that – their captain. Surely you must know.'

'I do not. Neither do they. All that we know is that the prophecy says it will happen. So we must believe, we must trust. And remember, we accomplish much by our very presence here.' He glanced behind him at the spear embedded in the tree. 'With the spear and axe in our possession we know that Calidus cannot fulfil his aim, cannot breach the wall between this world and the Otherworld, cannot bring Asroth's destruction upon the Banished Lands.'

'That's all well and good,' Brina snapped, 'but what do we all do now?'

'We ready ourselves for the battle to come,' Meical said. 'A battle that will spill a river of blood, that will see us live or die, win or lose. And it is coming, of that there is no doubt.'

A silence fell upon them all.

'So we prepare,' Corban said. 'We train, we build, we organize, we use our surroundings. And we scout.' He looked at Coralen. 'We don't want to be surprised by a warband appearing at our walls.'

'We can use the tunnels,' Coralen said. 'There are six of them – Hamil has mapped them, and they run for leagues upon leagues, many with smaller exits along the way. If we man them, have fresh horses at each waypoint, I would be very surprised if any warband could come within fifty leagues of Drassil without us spotting them . . .'

'A fine idea.' Corban smiled at her. 'I would suggest that you and Dath take responsibility for that – recruit who you need for the task.'

'There is much to do,' Brina said, brusque and businesslike. 'We will need healers and a hospice ready for the wounded.' She looked at Cywen.

Ah, that is why I am here. Wonderful.

'We have a great store of supplies, linen for bandages, herbs and medicines; we cultivated a large garden for just such an end,' Hamil said.

Brina nodded grimly.

The meeting descended into a discussion of all that would be needed – the logistics of feeding near a thousand people day in, day out, of clothing, of firing forges, of making weapons, training, the maintenance and strengthening of Drassil's fortifications. Cywen found herself drifting in and out of various threads of conversation as the day wore on. She felt a weight on her foot and looked down to see Buddai had flopped upon her.

He had reappeared some days ago, following Storm. Corban had told Cywen of Coralen's suspicion, and to Cywen's eyes both Storm and Buddai had looked sheepishly guilty.

The chamber was darkening, someone was lighting torches, others quietly carried tables and benches into the chamber and lit fire-pits. Corban stood to signal the end of the meeting. Farrell and Dath accosted him before he could leave.

'Yes?' he said, raising an eyebrow.

'Everyone seems to have a job to do,' Dath said.

'Aye. Most have more than one job, including you two,' Corban said.

'True enough,' Dath said, 'but we'd like one more.' A grin slowly spread across his face.

Corban frowned. 'What are you two up to?'

'I'm not one for saying things, or making speeches,' Farrell said, shuffling his feet. 'But, you see, we want to be your shieldmen.'

'Corban blinked at that, looking from Farrell to Dath and back again.

'We *are* shield-brothers, sword-kin, all of us,' Corban said. 'And you two most of all, my oldest friends.' He paused a moment, swallowed. 'We've stood shoulder to shoulder, the three of us, saved each other's lives many times over. But there is no need for shield-men amongst us. I am no king. And besides, I have Storm . . .'

'Ah, that's where we disagree, you see,' Dath said. 'And we're not the only ones.'

The doors burst open and people poured in, a whole host filling the chamber, hundreds of them.

All of them, Cywen saw, *every last person that followed Corban to Drassil. What have Dath and Farrell been up to?*

It did not take long before they were all spread in a half-circle about Corban, tiered by standing on the wide steps about the chamber's edge.

Corban just stared at them all, looking completely bewildered. Brina stepped before Corban and ushered Laith forward. She walked slowly, solemnly, holding a pillow before her, something gleaming upon it.

'This is for you,' Brina said, 'made by your people for you, as a token of our esteem.'

It was a spiral of metal, dark like iron, but threaded with streaks of silver, two snarling wolven heads at each end.

'My people?' Corban whispered. He reached out and tentatively touched it.

'It is an arm-ring,' Laith said, voice like gravel. 'We thought to make you a king's torc, but Dath said you wear the torc your da made you, and that you would not change it. So, we made you a king's arm-ring instead . . .'

Brina plucked it from the pillow and slid it up over Corban's hand, until it rested about his bicep. Laith gripped it and gently squeezed, the metal moulding itself to the contours of Corban's arm.

'I don't know what to say,' Corban muttered, gazing down at the arm-ring, then out at the crowd about him. 'I have done nothing to deserve this.'

'You freed us,' Javed said, taking a step forward. 'We were slaves, we would have died with collars around our necks.'

'You came to our aid,' said Wulf, stepping beside Javed and Atilius. 'Our home was burning, our warriors broken; we'd have died without your help.'

'You saved us,' Balur rumbled. 'We would have perished in Murias without you.'

'And we'd have been slaughtered by the Kadoshim had you not intervened,' Teca from Narvon said.

Cywen stepped forward. 'You crossed realms and mountains to find me in Murias. In the middle of battle you came for me. I owe you my life.'

'You give me hope that all is not lost,' Brina said looking at him with a sharp smile.

Gar stepped close to Corban. 'You give me the strength to go on,' he said. 'You give my life meaning.'

'You will save all the Banished Lands,' Coralen said as she stepped forward. 'And I will follow you to the ends of the earth, or die trying.'

Corban was looking at all of them, tears streaming down his cheeks.

Meical stepped forward.

'Corban, give me your sword.'

Corban slid it from its sheath and shakily offered it to Meical hilt-first.

Cywen smiled through her tears.

My da made that sword. Fashioned the wolven head as pommel, worked the iron, bound the leather. He and Mam would be so proud of Corban.

Meical took it and held it high over his head.

'*Oscailte*,' he yelled and stabbed the sword down into the flag-stoned floor. There was a concussive crack and a flash of incandescent sparks, the sword sinking half its blade into the ground. Meical released it and stepped back, leaving the sword quivering, a fading hum emanating from it.

'Corban ben Thannon,' Meical cried out in a voice that swept the room like the north wind, 'our Bright Star, the Kin-Avenger, Giant-Friend, Lightbringer, Rock in the Swirling Sea, will you bind yourself to these people, be their sword and shield, the defender of their flesh, their blood, their honour, unto death?'

Cywen stared at Corban. Saw him look around the room and straighten with pride and resolve.

'I will,' Corban said. His voice trembled. He gripped the blade of his sword, his blood dripping down the cold iron, finding the fuller to flow into.

'People of the Bright Star,' Meical cried out, 'will you bind your-selves to Corban ben Thannon, become his sword and shield, the defender of his flesh, his blood, his honour, unto your dying breath?'

'We will,' they cried, Cywen raising her voice with the rest of them, the sound of their voices like a clap of thunder, making the flames in the fire-pits flicker.

Gar nodded to Dath and Farrell, and one by one they stepped forward and gripped Corban's blade, their blood mingling with his, then stood either side of him. Gar stepped forward and did the same, all the while his eyes locked to Corban's. He stood aside, let the next person step forward. Cywen followed, smiling at her brother as if it was Midsummer's Day, both joyful and solemn, then Coralen, Brina, all of Corban's captains. Then the crowd behind began to file forward, each and every one of them performing the same ritual, Corban sharing more than words with each one of them.

Eventually it was done and then food and drink was filling the tables, boar and deer turning on spits above fire-pits. Cywen finally fell into her bed exhausted, but also filled with a sense of something she'd almost forgotten.

Peace. I feel at peace, for the first time since . . . She did not know, giving the last shreds of her sleep-slipping attention to that thought.

Since Ronan was slain.
One last thought flitted through her mind before sleep took her.
We are going to win.

CHAPTER SIXTY-SEVEN

ULFILAS

Ulfilas wiped sweat from his brow. It was freezing cold, there was snow beneath his boots, and the ground was as hard as iron beneath that, and yet still he was sweating.

This road-making is hard work, there's no denying.

Behind him close to three thousand warriors laboured from sunrise to sunset, felling trees, levelling ground, laying a timber road wide enough for a dozen horsemen to ride abreast. At the rear of the column King Jael rode with his honour guard of twenty Jehar warriors, and Sumur. Ulfilas had ridden with them for the first moon, but he found those black, dead eyes of the Jehar harder to bear than the backbreaking life of a road-layer, so he chose to fill his days with hard work and his nights with exhausted, dreamless sleep.

Up ahead Ulfilas heard shouting, saw men stop what they were doing.

Better go and see what all the fuss is about.

Running feet caught him up as Dag joined him.

'What's that all about?' Ulfilas asked the huntsman.

'We'll find out soon enough.'

Ulfilas felt a flush of pride as he looked at the road they were building and thought of both the leagues behind them and the conditions under which they'd accomplished this mammoth task.

It was Tempest Moon, the heart of winter, and they had carved their way over sixty leagues into Forn forest, following the trail left by the warband that had abandoned Gramm's hold, following the markers left by Dag's scouts. Felling trees, stripping them of branches, cutting them down to manageable strips, clearing thorn and underbrush, and all while hungry predators watched, prowled and occasionally ate someone stupid or unwary enough to wander too far alone.

Then Ulfilas and Dag were at the head of the column, staring up at what had caused the commotion.

'Ah, well, at least we know what happened to your scouts, now,' Ulfilas said to Dag. Four corpses dangled upside down from branches directly in front of the route of the new road. Dag gave him a sidelong glance.

'They were good men,' Dag muttered. 'Huntsmen through and through; two of them I trained from before they were old enough to set foot in the Rowan Field.'

'Oh. My apologies,' Ulfilas said. He'd noticed himself making comments like that lately; insensitive, sometimes cruel. *That is not the man I used to be. What is happening to me?*

'Cut them down before word of this spreads,' he muttered to Dag. *Warriors won't like this. It's the kind of thing that festers into fear around a campfire at night.*

'Too late to stop that,' Dag said, looking back at a group of men supposedly working on tree-felling who were standing staring at the corpses.

Behind them Ulfilas saw a handful of riders approaching.

Jael.

'What is all this?' Jael called as he rode up. There were a dozen riders about him – Fram his first-sword and other warriors, the best in Isiltir. About them strode the black-clothed Jehar, Sumur close to Jael.

Jael has his own shieldmen, a bulwark between him and the Jehar. He remembered Sumur defeating Fram without breaking a sweat, and cutting down old Belo in Mikil's feast-hall. *I do not think they would protect him for long, though.*

The Jehar spread to either side of the new road's foundations, some looking up at the dangling bodies as men climbed trees to cut them down.

'What is all this?' Jael repeated, gesturing at the corpses.

'My scouts,' Dag said.

'Ah. Confirmation that we are on the right trail, at least.'

We've hardly needed that so far, the path left by the warband fleeing

Gramm's hold has been wide and deep. I could have tracked them, and I'm no woodsman.

Dag didn't answer.

'How long have they been up there?' Jael asked.

Now that is a sensible question. In other words, how far behind this Bright Star and his rabble are we?

Dag bent to look at the first corpse that was cut down, hitting the ground with a brittle crack.

'They are frozen,' Dag observed, 'and have been feasted upon by . . .' He waved at the forest, trees encroaching upon them. 'So it is hard to tell with any measure of certainty, but –' he poked and prodded strips of skin, sniffed – 'dead four moons, is my guess.'

Jael nodded. 'We are making good time,' he murmured, looking pleased.

We have a head start: a trail to follow.

After Belo had been cut down at Nathair's council they had spent the day discussing how exactly Drassil was to be discovered.

They had settled upon the plan put forward by Calidus, to build roads into Forn, each with a different starting point. Gundul's road would begin at Brikan, the old Hunen tower that the Gadrai had occupied as their foothold in Forn. Lothar's road would follow the course they had originally travelled to Haldis, the Hunen burial ground, and then work deeper into Forn from there. The theory Calidus had used to justify this course was that the giants had dwelt in Drassil before their Sundering into many clans, and so Haldis and Brikan most likely were linked to Drassil in some way, possibly even by giant-built roads.

Jael's road had been given a different starting point – the logical move to follow the trail of this Corban, 'the Black Sun', Nathair had called him, and his warband into Forn. Ulfilas suspected that they had the easiest course, and from Jael's expression so did he. It was not just personal satisfaction and pride in a job well done. Nathair had given an incentive that the leader of the first group that found Drassil would rule the three kingdoms of Isiltir, Carnutan and Helveth, the other two kings reduced to vassals. Looking at his Jehar warriors, no one had doubted that he could enforce the threat. *Or promise, to the winner.*

So the race is on.

'Onwards then,' Jael shouted, turning his mount to ride back down the road, the Jehar closing about him and his shieldmen like a black-gloved fist.

Ulfilas turned and stared ahead, into the gloom of the forest. A snowflake drifted down and landed on his nose, filtering through the leafless canopy high above. Trees filled his vision. *And out there somewhere is this Black Sun, with giants and the warriors that cut through my men like a scythe through wheat.*

And we are rushing to find them.

'What do you mean, their trail has disappeared?' Jael snapped.

'There are no more signs of their passage, my King,' Dag said. 'No boot prints, hoof prints, excrement, dung, scuffed rocks, trampled or broken foliage. Nothing. It is as if they disappeared.'

'Pfah,' Jael said, clearly unable to formulate anything more complex.

It would appear that our good run has come to an end.

'You must search harder,' Jael said, waving a hand vaguely at the forest.

'My King, I have over two hundred scouts scouring the surrounding area. If there is any sign to be found, they will find it.'

'Has there been any word from Ildaer and his ilk? The Jotun dwelt in this region once, they must surely know something.'

'No word from him, or any of the Jotun, my King,' Dag said.

We have heard nothing from them since Gramm's hold. What happened to Ildaer there? Does he even still live?

Jael threw a cup of wine at the fire; the flames flared.

'What use in dealing with giants if they prove to be useless,' he snarled.

They were sitting in Jael's tent, a huge, sumptuous reminder of Jael's new title, furs and tapestries draped extensively about, a richly decorated table and chairs in the centre laden with cups studded with jewels and gold platters heaped with untouched food. The pale dawn light leaked in through the entrance, the forest feeling dense and oppressive all about them.

'We'll keep moving forwards,' Jael said. 'Straight as an arrow from their last known position. And keep searching; take more men from the warband if you need them – just find that trail.'

And if it is not there to be found?

Yes, my King,' Dag said, bowed and left the tent. Ulfilas followed him, not wishing to endure the wrath of a petulant King. He knew Jael better than any man alive. There was a crash from inside as the tent flap swung shut behind him.

Ulfilas stood with one hand upon his sword hilt, looking down at the corpses strewn about the glade. Four men. They'd been part of a scouting team that had not returned to camp last night. Each man was lacerated with scars, two had had their throats ripped out, the flesh gaping in ragged strips. One of them lay amongst his own intestines.

'What did this?' Ulfilas asked, his eyes sweeping the trees about the glade, shadows moving with the creak of branches.

'Wolven pack?' Dag shrugged, though he was frowning. He crouched to examine one of the dead more closely.

'It happened early,' Dag muttered, prodding the pile of intestines that were frozen solid. 'Soon after dusk. And look.' He pulled the dead man's head back, the throat cut in three clear lines. Ulfilas frowned.

Those cuts look too neat for claws.

Dag looked up at him and raised an eyebrow. 'Looks iron-made, not animal,' he said.

'Whether iron, tooth or claw, Jael's not going to be too happy about this,' Ulfilas muttered.

'I know it,' Dag agreed.

It had been a ten-night since the trail of their enemy had disappeared, the road-building slowing to a snail's pace as more and more men were taken from work crews to scout the surrounding areas. Three nights ago men had started disappearing. These were the first that had been found. Yesterday, upon hearing of men going missing, Jael had half-throttled the messenger bringing him the tidings.

He doesn't seem best equipped for dealing with the pressures of ruling.

A sound in the undergrowth had Ulfilas and the six men with him drawing their blades, Dag reaching for his bow and quiver. Figures appeared from amongst the gloom between the trees, Dag's scouts.

'Something for you to see,' the first one said, breathing hard, then turned and disappeared.

'More dead men?' Ulfilas muttered.

They followed the man through thick undergrowth, finally climbing a slope and stopping beside the scout.

Dag looked around and then smiled.

'What?' Ulfilas asked.

'Look,' Dag said, pointing.

They were standing on a level area, an embankment either side. Dag nudged something with his toe, a rock. Ulfilas looked closer, saw that it had been shaped, an edge rounded.

'It is dressed stone,' Dag said.

Ulfilas looked further, saw more pieces of stone glinting with frost, sparkling a ragged line into the distance.

'A road,' he whispered.

CHAPTER SIXTY-EIGHT

CAMLIN

Camlin stood on the banks of the lake, watching Meg walk away from him. He'd just said goodbye to her. With a sigh he turned and stared out at the disjointed walls and towers of Dun Crin, islands of stone amidst the dark waters. Beyond them he could see the small fleet of boats that was carrying away so many of those who had started to make a new life for themselves around this lake.

Better to run and live than to stay and die. And better for the warriors that stay. They'll fight better knowing their bairns and kin are safe.

He heard footsteps and turned to see Edana walking towards him, Halion, Baird and Vonn around her.

Vonn. Edana's shieldman. Do I trust him so close to her?

'Walk with me,' she said to Camlin, and they strolled in silence away from the lakeshore, following a path that wound through tall grass and thick clumps of reeds, shadowing one of the many streams that fed into the lake.

'You are sure of this?' Edana said when the lake had passed from view.

'It is the only way. Even if I'm successful, it's still no guarantee, but it'll give us a chance. It'll slow them down, and bring them here from one direction. Much better knowing where they'll be arriving.'

Edana stopped and turned to face him, took hold of his hands and stared into his eyes.

'I will never forget this, or the countless other times you have risked your life for me. If there is ever a time when this is over, and I am Queen of Ardan . . .' She hesitated. 'I will not forget this.'

Camlin shrugged. 'I'm not doing it for a reward.'

'Why are you doing it, Camlin? A brigand from the Darkwood. You do not even come from Ardan, but from Narvon.'

He looked at Halion, Baird, then Vonn, finally back to her.

'Because,' he said with a shrug, 'you make me want to be a better man. Not just you, but all of you. Marrock, Dath, Corban. Never really had friends before, just fellow thieves. Doesn't make for a good night's sleep.'

Edana nodded to herself, as if hearing an answer to a long-asked question.

'Come back to us,' she said.

'I'll try my very hardest t'do that.' He grinned.

'And I want you to take someone with you. Halion, Baird or Vonn, my most trusted shieldmen.'

'No need,' Camlin said with a shake of his head.

'I think there is. And even if there isn't – it will help me sleep better at night. Please, do it for me.'

Camlin looked between them, at Baird's slightly wild grin – *a good man to have beside me in a fight, though I think he may pick a few that don't need fighting* – Vonn, as serious as a man standing at his mother's cairn, and Halion, calm, steadfast – *keeps his head in a scrap, a strategic man, better with a blade than most, maybe better'n Braith, even.*

'I'll take Vonn, then,' he said.

Don't like the thought of him left around Edana without me here to keep an eye on him.

Edana smiled and Vonn nodded, more to himself than Camlin.

'Right, I'd better be off, 'fore I lose any more light.'

Edana stretched onto her tiptoes and kissed him on the cheek. She turned to walk away and they heard footsteps rustling through the grass and reeds. Everybody's hand went to a sword hilt, including Edana's.

A shadow appeared amongst the reeds, a figure stepping out before them.

'Ah, I thought you were here somewhere,' Lorcan said. His eyes sought out Edana. 'I need to talk to you about something.'

Camlin lay on his belly upon a slight hillock, reeds a slatted screen before him, looking down upon a willow beside a twisting stream.

Three arrows were stuck into the soft earth before him, his bow lying beside him. A figure sat leaning against the willow tree, wrapped tight in a cloak, head drooped forward onto his chest, seemingly asleep. Yellow hair stuck out from a pulled-up hood. A spear leaned against the willow tree, just a handspan from the figure's fingers.

'How long do we have to lie here?' Vonn whispered. 'I can't feel my feet.'

Camlin ignored him.

He does have a point.

It was cold, the sky above was overcast with clouds heavy and silver sheened, threatening snow, the marshlands were a grey, damp, mist-filled world of mosquitoes and croaking frogs. They'd been lying on this hillock since sunrise, and the sun was now melting into the western horizon.

'Camlin, I—'

'Shut up,' Camlin breathed, pointing.

Something was moving, off to the left, a shiver amongst the long grass and reeds – a movement opposed to the wind. Steadily it kept creeping forwards, then stopped, within sight of the figure sitting against the tree. A hesitation, a hundred heartbeats, two hundred, then it was moving forwards again. Two men broke from cover, stooped low, moving swiftly and silently in a loop around the figure against the tree until they had the willow's trunk between them and the reclining warrior.

Stealthily they crept up, single file, the first drawing a knife from its sheath.

Camlin pushed himself onto his knees, tugged an arrow from the ground in front of him, slowly lifted his bow.

The first man was right behind the sleeping figure, by the spear. He raised his knife.

Camlin drew the arrow to his ear, held his breath, sighted, released. It struck the second man, piercing leather vest and linen shirt to sink deep into his back. At the same moment the first one buried his knife to the hilt in the sleeping man's chest.

There was an explosion of straw, the man with the knife tugging his blade free, looking at the shape against the tree, then at his collapsing companion, then straight up to the hillock where Camlin was drawing his second arrow.

It punched through the knife-wielding man's chest, hurling him onto his back. He thrashed in the grass a moment, movements weakening, then he was still.

Camlin and Vonn climbed to their feet, Camlin groaning from the stiffness in his limbs, and they hurried down the hillock.

'That's the third time this has worked,' Vonn said to him, shaking his head.

'Aye,' Camlin agreed. They'd been hunting these scouts for four nights now, each time using the straw man to lure their enemy in and then kill them. So far it had been remarkably successful. Six men dead in three nights.

Camlin checked the two dead but knew before he saw their faces that neither one was Braith.

Can live in hope, though.

He drew a knife, bent and cut his arrows free of the two dead men, checked them over for food and coin, then saw Vonn standing above him, frowning.

'Old habit,' he said with a shrug as he dragged and tipped one corpse into the stream. 'Check our friend, eh?'

'He's a straw man wrapped in a cloak,' Vonn said.

'Aye. Check the cloak's not ruined – can't have a pile of straw leaking out of his belly, can we?'

'He's fine,' Vonn said.

'Good. Give me a hand with this one, then.'

Together they lifted the second dead man and carried him to the stream, slipping the corpse into the slow-moving water as quietly as they could. Camlin grabbed the spear and with the butt-end pushed the body down into a snare of reed. Then they checked the area for any evidence of their having been there, Camlin emptying one of the dead men's water skins over a pool of blood, diluting and dispersing it. Vonn picked up the straw man and slung him over his shoulder, then they were moving off into the reeds, shadowing the stream.

Camlin froze suddenly, turned and looked back.

'What?' Vonn hissed, hand going to his sword hilt.

Camlin stood still as stone, head cocked to one side, eyes scanning the twilight and mist that curled languorously amongst the shadows. All he could hear was the gentle flow of the stream. Then a splash, almost nothing.

More long moments listening, then he shrugged and walked on.

'Wish you wouldn't do that,' Vonn muttered.

Camlin ignored him.

'So what now?' Vonn asked him.

'Do it again,' Camlin said. 'They'll be strung out in a loose line, but we'll move faster than them. We'll set up again in half a league or so, snare us some more scouts.' With each trap Camlin had edged his way back towards the lake and Dun Crin's ruins, imagining that Braith and his huntsmen would be inching their way ever so carefully inwards. So far he'd been right.

'How many of them are there?'

'Don't know,' Camlin shrugged. 'At least ten, probably closer to a score.'

'What if they come in bigger groups?'

'Doubt it. Braith always sent us out in twos – enough to watch each other's backs, not too many to make a racket or leave a trail.'

'How do you know where to put the straw man?'

'Don't know,' Camlin said. 'Just a feeling, mostly.'

'Most of this is guesswork, isn't it?' Vonn said.

'And a bit of luck.' Camlin grinned back at him.

Dawn came damp and grey. Camlin emptied his bladder, prodded Vonn awake and checked their straw man.

Just before full dark he'd found a spot that felt right. A cluster of alders beside a stream, a gentle rise in the land screened by a snarl of dogwood and briar.

'C'mon then,' Camlin grunted. He leaned the spear against an alder, adjusted the straw man so he appeared to be sleeping, then picked up his bow, slung his quiver over his shoulder and headed off towards the cover of the dogwood. He heard Vonn's footsteps padding behind him.

They settled behind the bushes, Camlin stabbing arrows into the spongy turf, and waited. Time was hard to measure, the clouds too thick and bloated for any sign of the sun. 'What do you think about that mad bird?' Vonn asked him as he strung his bow.

'Craf?'

It had been a shock to all of them when Craf had fluttered into their meeting. Camlin had felt a rush of excitement, thinking that the bird's arrival must precede that of its companions – Corban, Dath and the others – but the bird had quickly disabused him of that notion. It had been good to hear news of them, though. That they were still alive, most of them, at least.

The other things it had squawked at them all – Camlin still did not know what to make of all that.

Going to Drassil. A fortress of faery tales, and talking about prophecies and bright stars and the Seven Treasures. I remember Gar saying things like that about Corban, as we fled across Cambren. But now he's leading a warband several hundred strong, Benothi giants amongst them. Can that really be true?

'I don't know,' Camlin said to Vonn.

He lay flat in the grass, wriggling to find a gap in the bushes to peer through. Snow was falling now, soft and steady. It was getting darker, the snow adding a faint glow to everything.

Have to end this, soon. Too dark to hunt, and my bowstring's going t'get wet.

'It makes me think,' Vonn said quietly beside him. 'My da used to say strange things, about a God-War. Never came out and said it straight, of course, that's not his way. But he would allude to things, choices, sides, using your head, not your heart.' He tapped fingers to his temple and his chest as he did it.

He can see Evnis saying it to him now.

'It's like he knew it was coming . . .'

'Maybe he did,' Camlin muttered darkly. *Maybe he did. Maybe there's a reason we're on opposite sides.*

A movement drew his eye, down by the stream. He squinted, seeing movement through the falling snow.

'Best concentrating on staying alive through this,' Camlin whispered, pointing. 'Plenty of time later to think about God-Wars. The trick right now is to keep breathing.'

He pushed himself to one knee and reached for his bow.

Two men broke from a cluster of trees, moving stealthily, flitting from one clump of cover to the next. Sound was muted, the snow beginning to settle on anything that wasn't water.

Camlin frowned. *They're more cautious.*

He reached for an arrow, nocked and drew, deciding not to wait for these men to reach the diversion.

'Vonn, be ready to move quick,' he whispered, voice strained with the tension of holding his drawn bow. His arrow-tip tracked both men below him, only thirty or forty paces away now, settling upon the first, feeling his vision close in upon the man's chest.

'I'd lower that bow, right slow if you want to keep breathing,' a voice hissed behind him.

It can't be . . .

Camlin released his arrow, dimly registering a scream from down below as it found his target. Beside him Vonn spun around, scrambling to get his feet under him. Camlin heard a solid crunch, Vonn falling back, eyes rolling back into his head, blood matting his hair.

'You don't want to be killing him,' Camlin said. 'He's Evnis' boy.' Slowly he laid his bow down in the grass.

'I told you to lower your bow, not shoot one of my men,' the voice snarled.

'Didn't think cooperating would change your mind about killing me.'

'You're right there, Cam,' the voice behind him said. 'Now, turn around slow.'

Two men were standing looking at him. One with a spear levelled at Camlin's face, a young lad, fair-haired. Camlin recognized him, though he couldn't remember his name.

Beside him stood Braith, naked sword in one hand, a smile on his face.

'Thought you'd catch me with my own trick?' Braith said. 'I'm hurt.'

'Hello, Braith,' Camlin said.

CHAPTER SIXTY-NINE

CORALEN

Coralen bent low in the saddle, kicked her horse on and kept her eyes on her target, her spear held tightly and level with the ground. Frozen by winter's arrival it was as hard as rock, the horse's hooves pounding a staccato rhythm. At the last moment Coralen nudged a knee, twitched the rein, and her mount veered to the left, at the same time Coralen lunging with her spear, piercing the straw target approximately where a warrior's heart would be. She grinned fiercely as she reined in and cantered back to collect her spear. As her excitement faded she became aware of a pain in her shoulder and shrugged, trying to adjust the weight of her new chainmail shirt. It was rubbing on the bone between her shoulder and neck. She wasn't used to wearing one, but Gar had given it to her last night, told her that everyone was getting one.

We'll all be wearing them when we face Nathair and his warband. You'll be grateful when it turns a blade and saves your life. She'd frowned and he'd pointed a finger at her. *Wear it, practise in the weapons court in it, sleep in it. You'll need to be used to it when real battle arrives.*

She knew he was right, although right now it felt heavy, uncomfortable and restrictive.

And that's why we're supposed to train in them now.

She saw Dath hovering, looked at him enquiringly and he hurried over. He was wearing a new chainmail shirt, too.

'What is it?' she asked him.

'You know what I was talking to you about?'

'Aye.'

'Do you really think it'd be a good idea?'

'I do,' Coralen said, 'but it's not me you need to be talking to about it.'

'I know. I just wasn't sure, and you're, you know, pretty fierce. If you like the idea, then maybe . . .'

'Why don't you go and ask him?' Coralen said, spying Corban on the weapons court.

'Would you come with me?'

'Me? Why?'

'Because he takes your advice seriously. And you put him in a good mood.'

'Ach, you fool,' Coralen said, aiming a boot at Dath, feeling both angry and happy that he'd said that.

Do I?

'Please?'

Coralen sighed. 'Come on, then. Let's go and talk to him now.'

'Now?' Dath blinked.

'Aye. No time like the now if you want something done,' she said, and before Dath had a chance to object she was kicking her horse into a trot. She heard him running to keep up.

They passed rows of straw targets. Cywen and the giantling Laith were standing before some, Cywen throwing knife after knife from the belts strapped diagonally across her chest, each one hitting the target flawlessly. Laith had a similar belt of leather across her torso, knives as big as daggers sheathed in it. As Coralen watched, Laith threw one of them. It slammed into the straw target and hurled it to the ground.

I wouldn't want to be on the receiving end of one of those.

Further along, Wulf and a few score men hefting single-bladed axes were similarly practising.

His hands have healed well, Coralen noted as Wulf's axe *thunked* into the head of a straw man. She remembered Tukul and with a sigh determinedly banished those memories.

The future must fill my mind now, with what is to come.

There was a dense circle of people around the stone section of the weapons court, a fair number of giants dotted amongst them, all watching Balur and Corban. Coralen's eyes were drawn to Corban's arm-ring, the streaks of silver in it gleaming in the pale winter daylight.

A moon had passed since that night in Drassil's feast-hall when they had sworn their oaths to Corban, and he to them. Things had felt different since then, there was a unity amongst their disparate groups that had not been there before, and the moon had passed in a flurry of activity: forges fired, weapons and armour made, clearing more land beyond Drassil's walls, hunting, scouting, grinding of grain, shoring of walls, and then training and preparation for the battles to come. They were beginning to feel like a real warband, not just people hurled together by the whim of war.

'Never try and block a blow from a giant with strength alone,' Balur was saying in his rumbling deep bass of a voice. 'It will shatter your bones.'

I could've reasoned that out myself, Coralen snorted. *Any weapons-master worth his pay teaches that you guide a weapon away, not meet its momentum head on. Unless the only other option is death.*

To demonstrate the point, Balur hefted his freshly made wooden battle-axe. He swung it high and down at Corban's head in a whistling arc. Corban stepped to the right, swung his own practice blade and struck the axe haft a glancing blow, steering it to crunch into the frozen ground. As Balur was off-balance Corban slipped inside his guard and had his sword-tip at the giant's throat before Balur had managed to wrench his axe free of the ground.

Warriors around the court cheered and murmured.

'It would never be as simple as that,' Corban shouted. 'Balur held back – he could have hit harder and faster. But the key point is still the same; it's all about timing. Speed, balance, reactions. Whatever your choice of weapon, the same result can be achieved – sword, axe, spear, even a shield can be used to the same end.' He looked about the court and nodded. 'Come on, then,' he said, 'let's see you do it. And no broken bones, eh?'

Warriors paired up with giants and filled the courtyard.

Coralen took the opportunity and headed towards Corban. He heard the sound of hooves on stone and turned, smiling up at her as she slid from her saddle. Storm padded beside Corban and Coralen saw the swell of her belly. They'd guessed for a while now that she was in pup.

What are her cubs going to look like? Coralen couldn't help but feel excited about the prospect.

'Dath's got an idea he wanted to talk to you about,' Coralen said.

'What's that, then?' Corban asked.

'Something I've been thinking about for a while,' Dath said. 'It might sound mad to you, or wrong, or—'

'Just tell him,' Coralen said.

'It's about archers,' Dath said. 'About using them in battle.'

Corban frowned.

'See, I knew he wouldn't like it,' Dath said to Coralen.

'Just hear him out,' Coralen said to Corban, staring at him fiercely. She knew what it had cost Dath even to approach him about this.

Corban looked a little abashed and nodded.

Dath hurriedly continued, 'I know that the bow is not considered a weapon of war, that it is a huntsman's tool. And that the old way talks of honour in combat, of one warrior testing his skill against another.'

'Aye, that is how it has always been.'

'Well, I think times are changing,' Dath said.

Corban frowned again.

'Look at them,' Dath said hurriedly, before Corban had a chance to say anything. He pointed at Wulf and his men practising their axe-throwing. More than just the warriors of Gramm's hold were there Coralen saw Gar and a handful of other Jehar, as well as some of Javed's pit-fighters.

'Have you tried throwing an axe and making its blade hit the target first?' Corban asked.

'I have,' Dath said. 'It's not as easy as it looks.'

'No, it is not,' Corban smiled. 'There is great skill in throwing an axe.'

'Aye, there is,' Dath agreed. 'But tell me, is there more skill involved in a well-thrown axe or a well-cast spear than there is in a well-aimed arrow?'

'No, I suppose not,' Corban murmured.

'Wulf and his warriors – they use their axes in battle, sometimes a whole line of them, Wulf has told me. If there were enough of them it would be devastating against an enemy charge.'

'Aye, it would. Apparently a similar thing brought down a bear at Gramm's hold,' Corban said.

'Exactly!' Dath was becoming animated now. 'I often think of Camlin,' he continued. 'Remember how he organized our ambushes – always me and him shooting first, thinning the numbers, making our enemy scared, making them rush. Well, imagine ten archers doing the same, or a score, two score, three score. Chances are we're going to be heavily outnumbered in any battle we fight against this Black Sun – Brina said so herself – so why don't we do something to even the odds a little?'

A silence settled between them, Corban looking thoughtfully at Wulf and his axe-throwers, Dath shuffling his feet.

A sound drew all of their attention, a loud thud that Coralen felt through her boots.

Balur had buried his practice axe in the ground again, this time against Haelan's shieldman, Tahir. As Balur tugged on his axe Tahir spun around the giant, slashing his practice blade at the back of the giant's leg, sending him toppling to one knee. Another spin and the edge of Tahir's sword was rested against Balur's neck.

'Balur, I think you've just lost your head,' a giant shouted, laughing.

Balur stood and scowled at the young warrior.

'You've done that before,' Balur said.

'Aye, that I have,' Tahir said. 'I served with the Gadrai of Isiltir. Giantkillers, we were – no offence intended – fighting the Hunen out of Haldis.'

'None taken, little man,' Balur said. 'I *hate* the Hunen.'

There was more laughter at that, both men and giants.

'What do you think about Dath's idea then, Cora?' Corban asked.

'I think it makes a lot of sense,' Coralen said. 'And it could mean the difference between winning and losing.'

'All right then,' Corban said, turning back to Dath. 'See how many would like to join you – I'll not be telling anyone to do it, but if they're willing . . .'

'You won't regret it.' Dath grinned, clapping Corban on the arm.

Coralen rode out of the west gate with Enkara, Teca and Yalric of Gramm's hold. Gar was halfway up a ladder that leaned against the stone arch of the huge gates, Balur and a handful of giants with him.

They were setting the skulls of the Kadoshim they had slain into the stone of the archway. Gar had said it would send a fine message to the Kadoshim when they arrived here.

Coralen grinned at the thought of it.

The group headed north, skirting Drassil's outer wall. The area around Drassil was alive with activity, the hundred or so paces of land that had been already cleared doubled in a moon by close to a thousand willing hands. Trees were being cut down, branches lopped off and the timber dragged inside the walls of Drassil, the ground around the felled trees cleared of underbrush to create an open space around the entirety of the fortress. It was back-breaking work, as Coralen had learned first-hand.

I'd rather be out scouting than chopping up trees and doing battle with thorns as long as my fist.

They left the walls of the fortress behind them, following the broken remains of an ancient road, mostly reclaimed by the forest now, riding up a gentle incline that slowly steepened, trees felled as far as a high ridge. When they crested it, Coralen looked back.

The great tree of Drassil rose like an organic tower in the midst of the fortress, branches fanning out and framing everything. The sky was a pale glow far above, visible through leafless branches that scratched together in a strong wind. For a moment Coralen thought she saw a lone figure on the fortress walls staring back at her, then it was gone and she was kicking her mount over the crest, down the hill into a wall of trees, Enkara and Teca following.

They headed north the whole day, going slowly, stopping often to make notes on parchment. They were trying to map the outlying area of Drassil, concentrating on the swathes of land that spread between each of the six great tunnels. Coralen had put people in place in the tunnels, so that each had a small team manning the exit points along the way, horses changed every day so that if the approaching enemy was sighted word would reach Drassil on swift hooves. Their biggest threat came from the stretches of land between the tunnels, widening with every league that the tunnels bored beneath the forest. She only had so many scouts and couldn't watch everywhere.

It took them six days to travel twenty leagues, zigzagging through the forest whilst they filled reams of parchment, using the remnants of the old road as a marker, although that was faint enough, a raised embankment here, a crumbled flagstone there. Twice they found waypoints on the tunnels fanning out from Drassil and spent those nights in the tunnel with the teams posted there. It was dark, musty and dank, but far safer than sleeping above ground in Forn. One night the ground trembled above them as something huge passed through the forest.

On the nights where they had no choice but to sleep above ground they made no fire – it attracted moths the size of Yalric's shield, and a host of far more unpleasant creatures that watched them from the edge of the firelight's reach, their presence betrayed only by the reflection of eyes.

On the eighth day out they were riding through an area dominated by wide-spaced golden-wood; it was like an ocean of orange bark and red leaves. The trees were as straight as spears, with few low branches amongst them, and the ground was spongy with leaves, making the riding easier than it had been for days.

Coralen winced as a strange smell drifted through the forest, pungent and acidic. She looked at the others and they were all pulling similar faces.

'Do you recognize that?' Coralen asked Yalric – hailing from Gramm's hold he was the only one of them that had any experience of Forn.

'No,' he said, shaking his head. 'But I have never travelled deep into Forn. Strange things live beyond its fringes.'

As you've told me before. Yalric was deeply superstitious and always making the ward against evil, but Coralen had come to find him an intuitive tracker and as brave as Storm when he could see that he was fighting flesh and blood and not a demon from the Otherworld.

Wait until he meets the Kadoshim.

The smell became progressively worse. Coralen's horse started shying, the mare's ears flattening to her head.

'Perhaps we should stop, go back,' Yalric muttered, wrestling with his reins and snapping a command at his horse. 'Whatever is making that smell, it's nothing good.'

Coralen frowned at him. *We need to know what's causing them to behave like this.*

In the end Coralen slid from her saddle, the others doing the same. Teca stayed with the horses and Coralen led Enkara and Yalric on. The smell was so intense now that she was fighting the urge to gag.

About fifty paces ahead something appeared on the ground – a series of mounds, more of them coming into focus, Coralen counting thirty or forty as they drew closer. She paused before the first one, a mound about chest high. It was steaming – a few of them were, others were hard-crusted and frozen with the cold. The stench was overwhelming, crawling up her nostrils, coating the back of her throat. Coralen prodded the mound in front of her. Beetles seethed out from it, covered in viscous slime.

It's dung.

Something was poking out of it. Not seeming able to stop herself, Coralen grabbed it and pulled; a knobbly bone emerged from the pile of steaming dung.

This is not good.

Just beyond the dung piles there was a dip in the land, invisible until you were this close. Coralen crept to its edge and peered down a long, gentle slope. At its base there was a hillock, its peak not quite as high as the ground Coralen was standing upon, made of craggy black rock coated with thin soil and patches of grass. Caves dotted it, eight, ten, more than Coralen could see, dark openings that bored into the black rock.

Enkara touched her shoulder and indicated that they should leave.

Coralen nodded and started to inch backwards when in the darkness of one of the caves something moved. A hulking shadow emerged, lizard-like but huge, its squat body low to the ground, legs splayed and ending in clawed feet, a long thick-muscled neck with a broad, flat muzzled head and sharp fangs.

A draig.

The three of them stood frozen a moment, desperate to move, too scared to make a sound.

The draig raised its head, a long tongue flickering from its jaws, tasting the air. Abruptly it went still, completely motionless, then its head snapped up and it stared straight at them.

It roared.

Like a release from a spell the three of them were sprinting back towards the horses.

Coralen skirted a tree and saw Teca a hundred paces away.

She glanced over her shoulder, saw the draig explode over the slope, all fangs, muscle and jaws kicking up earth as its claws raked the ground.

Teca's eyes bulged and she leaped into her saddle, tried to lead the horses towards Coralen and the others but the horses were neighing wildly, rearing and kicking.

There was a huge crack behind Coralen, the draig ploughing into a tree in its haste to reach them. It roared, making the world shake. It sounded as if it was almost upon them.

Then Coralen was swinging into her saddle, her horse almost mad with fear. She saw Yalric yelling curses at his horse as it powered away past her, heard hooves pounding behind her, then a collision, a horse screaming, bones crunching.

Fear had her in a grip she'd never known before. She was too scared even to look back. *Ride, just ride, get away.*

Another scream from behind her, this time human.

Enkara.

She heaved at her reins, her mount slowing, skidding to a halt, and looked back.

The draig was crouched over a horse, one claw upon its neck, pinning it as it bucked and writhed, the draig's jaws slick with blood as it tore bloody holes in the animal's side. Enkara was squirming on the ground, one leg trapped under the fallen horse.

Before she could think Coralen was kicking her horse into movement, swearing and cursing at it when it resisted, eventually acquiescing to its rider and moving hesitantly back towards the draig. Teca appeared from the left, her bow nocked, Yalric riding back to them, an axe in his hand.

We can't fight it – look at the power of it. But maybe . . .

Coralen shouted to Teca and Yalric and then she was picking up speed, a trot to a canter, her mount back under her control now.

Enkara was still pinned, the weight of the draig upon the horse grinding her leg into the forest litter. Teca and Yalric rode at the draig, both of them sighting their weapons and loosing while their mounts were moving. Teca's arrow sank into the soft flesh between its foreleg and torso, Yalric's axe bouncing off of its head with a dull thud.

Thicker skull than a bear, then.

The draig swung its head about, confused for a moment, then bellowed, shifting its weight momentarily off of the horse. In an instant Enkara had pulled free and was on her feet, lurching into a hobbling run. Coralen guided her horse close and grabbed Enkara's forearm, swinging her into the saddle behind her and then she was off, kicking her horse hard, letting it do exactly what it wanted most in the world – gallop as fast as it possibly could away from the draig. A hasty glance over her shoulder and Coralen saw that Teca and Yalric were following behind, the draig obviously deciding that more chasing was not necessary when it had a tasty meal under one claw.

'Can we go back to Drassil, now?' Enkara shouted in Coralen's ear.

CHAPTER SEVENTY

CAMLIN

Camlin felt a sharp pain in his back, Braith's sword-tip prodding him, directing him to walk on. The snow had stopped falling now and was turning to slush under his boots. Vonn trudged before him, blood matting one side of his face, his hands bound behind his back, just as Camlin's were. Braith's companion, a lad holding a long spear, was leading the way, two grey hounds at his heels. They were tall and sleek, and they looked hungry, too.

Long as I'm not the meal. Wouldn't put it past Braith. He's probably been starving them and promising them me for dinner.

'You made it back home, then,' Vonn addressed the lad with the dogs. He turned and looked at Vonn.

'I did, no thanks to you.'

Camlin recognized him, then. The prisoner Coralen had caught in the hills of Domhain, the one who had told them about Cywen and Conall both being alive.

'Strange, Rafe, that we've ended up on different sides, when we were once such good friends.'

'Were we?' Rafe asked.

'I thought so.'

'Well, friends or no, I chose to stand by my oath – the one I swore to your da.'

'That's strange, too,' Vonn said, 'because I chose to stand by my oath – the one I swore to my King.'

Rafe looked back and scowled at Vonn then, one of the hounds doing the same and growling.

'Family should come before kings, or queens,' Rafe said.

Vonn frowned, staring at Rafe's back, and said no more.

They were walking down to the stream where two men waited for them, one of whom was sitting with his back to a tree, blood drenching his belly, soaking into his breeches, staining the white snow about him. He was screaming.

Might have something to do with my arrow in his gut.

Braith made an irritated sound behind him, though Camlin wasn't sure if it was aimed at him for shooting one of his men, or at the man on the ground for making so much noise.

'Sit,' Braith ordered Camlin and Vonn as he dumped both of their sword-belts and Camlin's bow and quiver against the tree, next to the straw man. When he was happy that Camlin and Vonn were both secure, Braith went and sat beside the wounded man. He unstoppered his water skin and gave the man some. He drank in short sips, panting in between with the pain.

'Madoc, this is going to taste sweet as heaven in your mouth,' Braith said to the warrior, 'but when it reaches your gut it's going to hurt like every demon in the Otherworld is trying to claw their way out of your belly.'

Madoc nodded, sweat slicking his face, his shirt sticking to his body.

'My boot,' Madoc breathed. 'Some coin for my Rhian.'

Braith nodded. 'I'll see it gets to her.' He lifted the water skin to Madoc's mouth and with his other hand drew a knife from his belt.

'You ready?'

Madoc nodded and Braith cut his throat.

'That's seven of my men, now, by my counting,' Braith said, wagging his knife at Camlin.

'Aye, that's what I make it,' Camlin agreed. He shrugged. 'It's war.'

'So it is,' Braith said, wiping his knife clean and sheathing it. He came and sat close to Camlin.

Not so close that I can reach him, though.

'But this is more personal than that, between you and me.'

'I was afraid you were going to say that.'

Braith barked a laugh.

'You see, Cam, despite everything, you can still make me laugh. You've poisoned me, cut me open with this blade on your belt.' He paused, pulled back his shirt at the neck and showed Camlin an ugly white ridge of scar tissue. 'Hurt, that,' Braith said.

'Aye, well, I've a scar of my own from you.' He pulled his shirt open. 'See. You shot me. The arrow had to be pushed through. That hurt a bit, too.'

Braith shrugged. 'Not that this is a contest, but you did dump me into the ocean for the fish to gnaw on.' He shook his head.

Camlin smiled grimly. 'If it helps, I did think you were dead at the time.'

Braith chuckled. 'But the thing that hurts most, Cam, is the *betrayal*. I thought we were friends.'

Camlin laughed at that. 'So did I,' he said, still chuckling. 'Perhaps we can be reconciled, eh?'

'I don't think so,' Braith said. The smile disappeared from his face. 'But I can even the score.'

He stood, looking about the marshes at the endless banks of reeds, willow and alder.

'Where is she, Cam? Your new Queen?'

'If you think I'm going t'be telling you that,' Camlin said, 'then you don't know me.'

'If you think you *won't* tell me,' Braith said, moving closer to Camlin, 'then it's you who doesn't know me.'

I've seen Braith put people to the question. He tries to be their friend first, gets what he can that way, then lights a fire under their feet, just to make sure.

'There'll be no torture here,' a voice said. Vonn, sounding just about as commanding as Camlin had ever heard him. 'You will take us to my father. We will not talk to men such as you.'

Braith smiled at Vonn, walked over to him.

'Get him up,' Braith said, the warrior behind Vonn yanking him to his feet.

'My father is the regent of Ardan, representative of Queen Rhin and—'

Braith punched Vonn in the gut, doubling him over. He grabbed a fistful of Vonn's hair and yanked him upright.

'Your father is not my king,' Braith snarled. 'I answer to Rhin, no one else, so your precious father can go kiss my arse. And you'll not be giving out your orders to me, or any of my crew. Is that clear?'

'All two of them,' Camlin murmured.

Vonn dribbled spittle.

'I said, is that clear?' Braith repeated, bunching his fist.

'Aye,' Vonn muttered.

'Good,' Braith said, letting go of Vonn's hair, the young warrior dropping to the ground.

You tried, lad, I'll give you that.

'Don't you worry, Vonn, I'll take you to your da soon enough. Not sure what kind of welcome you'll get, but at least you'll live to find out, which is more than I can say for my old friend Camlin.'

Braith spun around and kicked Camlin in the face. He fell back, pushed himself onto one elbow and spat blood, and a tooth.

'I'm going to leave you with that thought for the night. Come morning I want answers to my question. Where is the bitch, Edana? Answer true and I'll end it quick. No pain. If I don't believe you, well, I'll be taking this knife,' he drew it from his belt, the one he'd used to cut his man's throat. 'And I'm going t'start taking body parts off you. Think I'll start with the fingers on your bow hand.'

Camlin lay close to the stream, his arms stiff and the skin on his wrists rubbed raw. Beside him lay Vonn – sleeping, he thought, from the steady rhythm of his breathing.

Something had woken him.

Maybe the cold. He was shivering enough for his teeth to rattle. There were no clouds above now, the sky a panoply of stars, the thin crust of snow on the ground had frosted to ice and was glittering in the starlight. Trying not to make any noise, he rolled over, the snow crunching, sounding loud enough to wake the dead.

Braith was sitting against the tree, his head drooped to one side, his surviving warrior curled in a blanket while Rafe was standing on the stream's edge, spear in his hand, staring out into the darkness.

His watch, then.

One of the two hounds growled, its ears pricked. There was a rustle amongst the riverbank and they were both bounding forwards, snuffling amongst the reeds. Rafe followed them, spear levelled, then the hounds came out, tugging at something between them. Camlin heard the wet ripping sound of amphibian flesh.

Some poor frog's having a bad night. He thought of his fate approaching with the rising of the sun. *I sympathize.*

The hounds finished tearing apart whatever it was they'd found and settled to wolfing down their respective pieces. Rafe lowered his spear and went back to stamping his feet and blowing into his hands.

Camlin looked at Braith, felt a wash of hatred for the man, swiftly tempered by the knowledge that he was just a man, like him, who'd made his choices and was seeing them through.

Sometimes they lead to a pot of gold, other times they get you bitten on the arse, or see you watching your fingers go under the knife, one by one. What I'd give to take him with me, though . . .

He heard a *thunk*, behind him, between him and the stream. He looked about but no one else seemed to have heard it, Braith still with his chin on his chest, Rafe staring in the opposite direction. Even the two hounds now seemed to be sleeping deeply, chests rising and falling. He rolled over slowly, saw something sticking in the turf and snow. A glint of iron, a leather-wrapped hilt.

I love it when a plan comes together.

Slowly he rolled over again, his back and bound hands to the knife, shuffled backwards a handspan, stopped as Braith muttered in his sleep. Another wriggle backwards, then waiting, eyes checking Rafe, the hounds, Braith, the other warrior. Another wriggle, checking again. Eventually, as a grey pallor seeped across the sky, he felt leather brush his fingertips.

'Wake up,' Braith said and kicked Camlin's boots. With a groan Camlin squirmed onto his knees, holding the rope that had bound his hands tight behind his back.

'You're like a landed fish,' Braith said. 'Which is an appropriate analogy, because today I shall be gutting you, like a fish.' He smiled, no humour in it. 'But let it not be said that I am a cruel man. Dai, help him up.'

For all of his bluster Braith is a careful man. He will not step within arms' reach of me. I should be flattered that he thinks so highly of my prowess. He glanced at Vonn, who had clambered to his knees.

Rafe was calling the hounds but they lay still on the stream bank.

Camlin caught Vonn's eye, looked over his shoulder, wiggled the knife in his frozen hands. Vonn's eyes widened for a moment, then he looked away.

'No funny business,' Dai muttered, put a hand under Camlin's arm and hoisted him upright.

'Something's wrong with my dogs,' Rafe said, an edge of worry in his voice.

'What do you mean?' Braith asked, suspicious.

There's a reason he's lived this long.

'Look.' Rafe prodded one of the hounds with his spear-butt. 'Scratcher,' he called. It didn't move, though its chest still rose and fell, breath misting about its muzzle. Rafe fell to his knees, dropping the spear on the ground beside him and shook both of the hounds.

Braith's eyes snapped to Camlin.

'Hello,' a voice called behind them. Braith and Dai spun around; a figure stood on the snowy ground, surrounded by morning mist.

Meg. She looked more like a ghost than a person of flesh and blood. She stepped back into the mist, disappearing.

Braith reached for his sword and rushed after her. Dai let go of Camlin and took a step after Braith, then the knife in Camlin's fist was punching into Dai's back, through fur cloak, leather and wool into flesh, between ribs and into a lung. Camlin's other hand clamped around Dai's mouth, stifling the hiss of exhaled air. He pulled the knife free, stabbed again, and again. Dai slumped and Camlin let him go, grabbing his sword hilt as he dropped, the rasp of it sliding from its scabbard stopping Braith in his tracks.

'Almost had me,' Braith snarled as he stared at Camlin, hands free, a sword in one hand, bloodied knife in the other. It didn't seem to put Braith off as he charged at Camlin, shouting to Rafe, who was oblivious, still shaking the hounds, looking as if he was crying over them.

Camlin rushed to Vonn, slashed and sawed at the ropes binding his wrists, painfully aware of the crunch of boots on snow as Braith sped to skewer him with his sword.

With a gasp, Vonn's hands were free and then Camlin was turning, dropping the knife in the snow, for Vonn, Braith hacking at him, iron clanging as Camlin raised his blade in a hurried parry, staggering back, blocking a flurry of powerful blows.

He sidestepped, sweeping Braith's blade away, the rage in Braith's attack adding to his momentum, sending him stumbling off balance for a moment. Camlin hacked at him, chopped into Braith's hip, blood spraying.

There was shouting behind him, Camlin shuffling backwards to see what was happening while keeping Braith in his vision. Vonn and Rafe were circling one another warily.

Then Braith was coming at him again, blood sluicing from the wound in his hip. Another flurry of blows, high chops, swinging loops, all merging into a fluid assault, and a rushed retreat. Eventually they parted, a red line leaking blood across Camlin's shoulder.

'Last time you had to poison me to beat me,' Braith said, face pale from blood loss, but his eyes were sharp, voice steady and calm. 'What are you going to do this time, Cam? You're not my match with a blade, we both know that.'

'I'll just have to think of something,' Camlin muttered and darted in, his sword-point lunging straight at Braith's heart, dropping the blade as Braith sideswiped a block, carrying on his lunge to score a red line across Braith's ribs, cutting through leather and wool, blood seeping as he leaped back, away from Braith's backswing.

'Maybe I'll just bleed you to death,' Camlin said, circling Braith warily.

I've blooded him twice. Can't believe I've done that. If only the Dark-wood boys could've seen it. But luck doesn't last long against Braith, and he's right, he is better'n me. What I could do with is some help.

Camlin risked a quick glance at Vonn and Rafe, saw they were still circling one another. Camlin frowned. It sounded as if they were talking to each other.

'Vonn,' Camlin barked, 'less talking, more killing.' Then Braith was coming at him again. Camlin retreated before a withering combination of blows, his heart thudding in his ears, too fast to feel fear, just reacting, retreating, muscle and sinew straining as his whole body strived to avoid death. He held his blade two-handed, blocked another powerful blow that reverberated through his arms into shoulders and back, each blow weakening him a little more, his breath coming harder, his reactions a fraction slower. He saw a grim smile twitching Braith's lips, knew the end was coming.

Something moved in the corner of Camlin's eye, a stick spinning out of the mist and smacking into Braith's head, the wood shattering in an explosion of splinters.

Meg emerged from the mist, threw another piece of rotted wood at Braith, striking him on the shoulder. It didn't hurt Braith much, but it did give Camlin the opportunity he needed.

He turned and ran.

For a heartbeat, two, three, four, there was no sound of pursuit from Braith, then a snarl and heavy footsteps. Without looking, Camlin hurled his sword behind him, heard a clang as Braith struck it from the air, a curse as he stumbled, then Camlin was diving, rolling, one hand grabbing his bow, the other scrabbling for an arrow from his quiver. He came out of the roll on one knee, looking back, saw Braith bearing down upon him, sword raised high over his head, six paces away, four, Camlin's death in his eyes.

He nocked his arrow, drew, two paces, the sword swinging down in a glittering arc.

Release.

The arrow punched into Braith's gut, stopping him like a kick from a mule, sending him staggering back a handful of paces, sword swinging wild, hissing through the air before Camlin's eyes.

Another arrow from those scattered from his quiver. Braith snarling, cursing him, lurching unsteadily towards him.

Nock, draw, release. This one slammed into Braith's chest, sending him crashing onto his back, blood erupting.

Camlin stood, breathing hard, still wary.

Braith rose to one elbow, then to one knee.

Another arrow, nock, draw, release, throwing Braith flat on his back again.

'Stay down,' Camlin yelled, relief starting to seep through him. Another arrow.

'He's finished,' Vonn said, walking close. Camlin saw Rafe's back as the lad crashed through reeds and long grass, sighted his arrow, gazed along the feather and smooth shaft, iron tip to Rafe's back, raised it, adjusting for distance, to the left for the wind, all a process that was as natural as breathing, done in a handful of heartbeats.

'Let him go,' Vonn said in his ear. 'He's a misguided, scared boy, nothing more.'

'He's sat his Long Night, made his choices as a man,' Camlin growled, but he hesitated and then Rafe was gone, claimed by the mist and marshes.

Camlin lowered his bow and strode over to Braith, who was still trying to get up. Camlin made sure he stopped out of arm's reach of the woodsman.

Braith's woollen shirt was soaked with blood, leather vest stained dark with it, the snow around him churned pink.

'Looks like our score's settled,' Camlin said, looking down at his old chief.

'Not supposed to end like this.' Braith wheezed as he made a final effort to rise. Only his head moved. He coughed blood and lolled back into the snow.

'We don't always get what we want,' Camlin muttered and stood there, watching Braith's chest rise and fall, the gap between each breath growing longer. Blood bubbled from Braith's mouth and Camlin waited for another breath.

It never came.

Camlin looked about, saw his sword and picked it up.

'This time you're staying dead,' he said to Braith's corpse and he hacked down once, twice, the third time Braith's head rolling free from his body.

Meg emerged from the reeds and ran to him, throwing her arms about his waist, hugging him tight. He ruffled her hair.

'You did good, girlie, think I might just owe you my life, there.'

'There's no *think* about it,' she said, grinning up at him.

CHAPTER SEVENTY-ONE

HAELAN

Haelan searched the stables, Pots running at his heels, his tail wagging furiously. He looked inside every single stall – and there were literally hundreds of them, over half of them occupied with horses.

She won't be in one of those. He slammed another door shut, frowning. *An empty one.* By the time he reached the last stable he was sweating, despite the cold that seemed to seep through even walls of stone.

Winter is upon us. It was the Snow Moon and winter was holding Drassil in its tight and frozen grip.

Where is she?

He was looking for Storm, had overheard Corban talking of his wolven, how she was heavy with cubs, and if the birth cycle for a wolven was anything like a hound's then she should be whelping any day now. And then she'd disappeared.

She's in her den, ready to whelp, Coralen had said to Corban.

Haelan had been running chores in Cywen's hospice, a huge building situated to the west of the fortress, close to the herb gardens that grew within the walls. Coralen had been sitting beside one of the Jehar, a dark-haired woman lying in a cot with her leg in a splint and bandages. Slowly the conversation had drifted towards Storm, and the fact that she was missing.

That's what I thought, Corban had said. *I need to find her. I remember Da helping a bitch whelp; there can be all kinds of problems.*

Corban had sounded so worried that Haelan had decided on the spot that he would find Storm and her den, and had been searching ever since.

He left the stables disappointed; he'd been convinced they

would make the perfect hideaway for Storm, and began to wander the fortress aimlessly.

I'll never find her in this place. Someone could hide for a moon, every single person here searching for them.

Slowly he walked through ancient stone streets, past windows with the glow of warm fires filling them, then through courtyards and streets with empty buildings and dark windows. He pulled his cloak tighter about him, his breath misting, before eventually stopping in a courtyard.

He sat on a huge twisted root that broke through the stone of the courtyard like the spine of a great sea beast and fished around in his pockets for some food. He found half a biscuit, broke it, throwing half to Pots, then chewed on the rest.

He'd come to a strange conclusion. For most of the time that he had lived at Gramm's hold his thoughts had ever returned to his mam, to Jael, to the throne of Isiltir, and he remembered spending days plotting his vengeance upon Jael, or how things would be different when he was king, or how he would make someone else do his chores. He didn't think like that any more, couldn't remember the last time anything like that had crossed his mind. After much thought he'd decided that there was only one conclusion to be reached about that.

I'm happy. At first he'd felt guilty about that realization, his mam's face springing instantly to mind. *I shouldn't be happy. She gave her life for me, so that I could one day be king.* But he didn't want to be king any more, not really. He wanted Corban to be king instead. Never had he come upon a man whom he thought so highly of. From his first words Corban had made him feel himself, made him feel that he didn't have to pretend to be anything. And he liked that. And Corban was everything that he imagined a king should be. A skilled warrior, courageous – he'd heard the tales about him, fighting demons, wyrms and wolven, setting slaves free, and he'd saved Wulf and the others at Gramm's hold. Despite all this, and the demands on him, he made sure he had time for everyone who sought him out, always listening to their problems, big or small.

Pots whined behind him and he threw the dog some more biscuit.

And when Haelan spoke to Corban, he felt that he listened,

really listened to what he had to say. No one else had ever treated him like that, even Tahir, whom he loved like an older brother. He always looked at Haelan as if he was a duty he had to fulfil.

Which I suppose I am, to Tahir. To a shieldman.

His happiness had been tarnished with the recent news, though. A warband had been spotted, creeping in from the north-west, building a road. They were almost on a direct course for Drassil, though of course moons away as they had literally to cut their way through the forest.

It's Jael, I know it is. Am I never allowed to be happy while he draws breath?

Tahir had told him that Corban had led a few raids on the enemy camp, using the trapdoors situated along the tunnels – not large attacks, but hunting down their scouts and stragglers, and Tahir said that Corban and those with him had dressed in wolven furs, killed with their gauntleted claws.

Pots whined again behind him, scratched at something. Haelan rooted around for some more biscuit but couldn't find any.

'Sorry, boy,' he said as he turned around to stroke the dog, then saw what he was whining at.

Beneath the curve of the root was what looked like a pool of shadow, but as Haelan looked closer he saw that it was more than that. It was a hole.

Pots was digging in a mound of loose earth spread before it.

Haelan crawled up to the hole, saw that it was bigger than him, bigger than a full-grown man. He stuck his head inside, saw the root twisting and boring its way into the dark earth. Then the ground crumbled beneath him and he fell in, head first, sliding and rolling, soil getting in his face, his mouth. He came to a crunching halt, falling onto the root, the earth around it eroded away by rain and frost so that it made a kind of cavern, large enough for him to stand, if he stooped. Daylight seeped into the hole, enough for him to see that the root branched left and right. Pots was looking down at him, tail wagging.

'It's not a game,' he muttered, then, figuring he may as well explore while he was down here, he crawled to the left, following the root. Abruptly the root took a sudden twist, arcing down, almost vertically, and Haelan stopped. A strange smell leaked up from the hole here, strong and acidic, like rotting vegetables mixed with . . .

something else. Whatever it was, he wanted to get away from it, the smell feeling like fingers clawing their way into his mouth. He shuffled back along the root; the smell receded, and soon he was at the point where he'd fallen in. Pots started barking at him when he came into view. He decided to go the other way now, enjoying the thought that he'd found something new in this ancient fortress, something that only he knew about.

It could be my den, he thought, *my secret place.*

Den?

Then, from the darkness in front of him, he heard a low, terrifying growl. He froze. The growling rumbled on, then faded, and behind it he heard something else. A squeaking sound.

He shuffled back along the root as fast as he could, stood on tiptoes to climb out, jumped and caught hold of the edge, pulling and scrambling to get out. Leaping to his feet, he sprinted around a corner and saw Tahir marching purposefully towards him, pointing at him.

'I've been searching everywhere for you,' Tahir said as Haelan ran past him.

'Can't stop,' he blurted, not even slowing, heard the sound of slapping feet as Tahir ran after him.

He found Corban in the weapons court, holding sword and shield and sparring with Wulf. Gar stood watching them, his arms folded across his chest and a frown upon his face.

Haelan skidded to a halt, desperate to tell Corban his news, but saw he was in the middle of something with Gar.

'I'm not saying you should not train with a shield,' Gar said, 'only that I will not.'

'Why don't you like using a shield?' Wulf asked him.

Without saying anything Gar strode to Wulf, grabbed the shield rim wide with both hands and twisted. Wulf yelled in pain.

'If I twist this shield another handspan your arm will break,' Gar said matter-of-factly. 'For a weapon that is supposed to protect you, it can be easily used to defeat you.' He let go and Wulf stepped away, wincing. 'The best defence is a good offence.' Gar shrugged. 'I've seen a shield used well when it is strapped tight to your back.'

'Halion,' Corban said.

'Aye,' Gar nodded. 'It can be well used if you use a spin to manoeuvre around your foe, to protect your back and come out of the spin with some momentum for an attack.'

'Show us,' Wulf said.

Corban glanced away and saw Haelan, almost jumping up and down beside the weapons court in his excitement.

'What is it?' Corban asked him.

'Storm,' Haelan gasped. 'I've found her.'

Haelan stood in the courtyard with the tree root, a small crowd about him.

Corban slipped into the hole, his hand appearing and Gar passing him a torch, then Gar disappeared into the hole as well. Haelan heard a muffled protest from Corban followed by Gar's flat refusal, then silence. More silence, then a rumbling snarl that mutated into a snapping, slavering growl that made the ground vibrate and Pots whine and hide behind Haelan's legs.

A moment later Gar's head appeared out of the hole and he climbed out.

'Don't think she wants me down there,' Gar said with as much dignity as he could muster as he stood, dusting himself down.

'What about Ban?' Coralen asked.

'Oh, he's fine, Storm's licking him like she hasn't seen him for a moon.'

'And is Storm all right? Has she had cubs?'

'Oh aye,' Gar said. 'She's right as rain. And she's had six cubs. She's even letting Corban touch them. Me, on the other hand, she wanted to rip my head off just for looking at them.'

Tahir pulled Haelan away and looked at him sternly. 'What if you'd got stuck down there?' Tahir asked him.

Haelan knew the shieldman was angry with him, but proud of him too. He'd been brave, and he'd done something no one else had been able to do.

'I didn't, though,' Haelan said.

'What if you had?' Tahir frowned at him.

'Fools worry, the wise do, as your old mam used to say.'

Tahir blinked at him.

'You're getting too clever for your own good,' the shieldman muttered.

Haelan grinned.

CHAPTER SEVENTY-TWO

FIDELE

Fidele gazed in wonder at the trees shadowing both sides of the road she was riding on. They dwarfed anything she had ever seen before, thick as a house and high as a tower, their dense layers of branches reaching above and over the road, weaving and interlocking to form a latticed archway above them, weak sunlight occasionally breaking through to dapple the ground with pools of light.

So this is Forn.

It had been a long, hard journey, taking them almost three moons to reach Forn Forest. First they had crossed the Agullas Mountains into Carnutan, then ever northwards, across great plains, through rolling hills and snow-swept valleys until they crossed from Carnutan into Isiltir. A ten-night gone they had reached Mikil, only to find that Nathair had ridden east towards Forn a moon before them. So they followed him. All six thousand of them, give or take the few score that had died along the journey, succumbing to the bitter cold. She glanced over her shoulder, glimpsed Maquin riding amidst a circle of eagle-guard.

Not him, though. I knew he would not die.

At first Maquin had lain in a wain, semi-conscious and delirious from the pain of his wounds, Alben tending to him while they travelled, but he had been on the back of a horse for over a moon now. Their eyes would meet frequently, though always briefly, both of them mindful of Alben's advice and the charges that she was accused of. They were never allowed close enough to speak, Veradis' eagle-guard rigorous in their duties. Fidele did not mind so much, as she knew the same devotion to duty would keep Lykos and his Vin Thalun away from Maquin.

What they have done to him. She could still see the burns when she closed her eyes, could remember the smell of charred flesh as she'd entered Maquin's chamber back in Jerolin. Not for the first time a swell of rage filled her, coalescing about an image of Lykos in her mind. In it he was smiling at her.

I will see him dead. I will convince Nathair of the Vin Thalun's crimes.

Part of her was desperate for this journey to be over, so that the long-prolonged and avoided justice that Lykos deserved could finally be meted out, but part of her dreaded the journey's end, because then Maquin would stand judgement for his crime, and she could not see any other outcome than death for him, even with the mother of the high king pleading his cause. She felt a fist of worry clench in her belly just at the thought of it.

The road curved, and a building appeared ahead, framed by the arched branches. A grey-stone wall about a squat tower, thick with creeping vine, and beyond it the sound of running water.

We have reached Brikan and the River Rhenus, then. Am I about to see my son finally, after so long?

She was close to the head of the column, riding with the men of Ripa – Krelis and Ektor, Alben and Peritus and almost the full strength of their warband, more than eight hundred men. Veradis had suggested he only bring an honour guard, but Krelis had refused. Fidele knew it was because he trusted no one on this journey, not even Veradis.

Even with eight hundred, if the Vin Thalun turned on us we would be sorely outnumbered. And whose side would Veradis stand upon?

Ahead of them Fidele could see Veradis, sat upon a white horse, his young captain Caesus at his side, eagle-guard marching in disciplined ranks behind them.

He has changed, been changed by this war, but there is something I still trust about Veradis, something solid at his core. In truth it was Veradis who gave her a glimmer of hope about the outcome of all of this. He clearly tried his best to remain neutral whenever Fidele spoke to him of Lykos or Maquin, impartial and objective, but she knew, could sense, that deep down he agreed with her. And that he and Maquin shared an old friendship did not hurt.

There is hope. If Nathair will not listen to the counsel of his mother, surely he will listen to that of his oldest and closest friend.

The chamber was high in the tower, a fire and torches crackling both to warm the room and to brighten the constant twilight of the forest; they were only partly successful at both tasks. Fidele sat upon a long bench; an open space lay before it, then a raised dais, a tall, high-backed chair empty upon it. Beside Fidele sat Krelis, Ektor and Peritus. None of them was in chains or bound in any way, but Fidele felt as if they were captives on trial, with eagle-guard scattered around the room, along with the black-eyed Jehar watching them dispassionately. There had been hundreds of them in the courtyard of this old giant tower, gathered around a great wain that sat in the courtyard like some brooding beast. Once upon a time the Jehar had made her feel safe, the thought of them about her son comforting her through dark nights of worry for Nathair. Now, though, with their flat black eyes and dead stares, they scared her.

Veradis was also in the room, standing with his back to Fidele beyond the empty chair, staring out of a window at the forest and wide river beyond the tower, the noise of wains creaking, auroch bellowing, whips cracking, drovers yelling orders. Fidele had glimpsed a wide swathe cut into the far side of the forest, beyond a stone bridge. A road cut straight as an arrow through the trees, heading north-east, a steady flow of traffic travelling both ways.

A door creaked open, cold air washing into the room, and Nathair strode in.

My son.

Fidele felt her heart lurch at the sight of him. He had lost weight, making the bones of his face more apparent, and there were shadows under his eyes, though he still walked with purpose and confidence, more, if anything. And beneath it all, still her boy, the child she had held and comforted and laughed with. She took a step towards him and stopped herself.

This is a trial and I must be strong. Be seen to be strong. My son is two people: my son, and the high king of these Banished Lands, as I am two people, his mother, and the regent of Tenebral.

Calidus and the giant Alcyon walked at Nathair's heels, Jehar

behind them, moving with the grace and contained power of predators at the top of the food chain.

And behind them all, Lykos, walking with head down, eagle-
guard either side of him. He was led to the bench Fidele was sitting
on and ordered to sit. He did so without any complaint or hesitation. Fidele had never seen him so submissive.

'Mother,' Nathair said, and she looked up. Nathair had paused
on his way to the empty chair, was staring at her with a faint smile
upon his face. Then she was moving towards him, arms rising to
enfold him, but something in his look caused her to falter and she
stopped before him. He took her hand and kissed it.

'It is good to see you, Mother,' he said. He gazed into her eyes,
studied her face as if he had forgotten what she looked like. 'You
have changed.'

'As have you,' she replied. 'We have much to tell one another.'

'And to not tell,' he snorted with a twist of his mouth.

What does that mean?

'Nathair,' Calidus called, a tone in his voice that Fidele had
not heard before, and one that she did not like. Commanding.
Impatient. She thought of Ektor's chamber of scrolls deep beneath
Ripa's tower, of the hints she had read about Ben-Elim and
Kadoshim. As she returned to her seat her eyes met Ektor's.

Nathair strode towards the empty chair, saw Veradis and smiled,
something of the young man Fidele had bid farewell to returning to
his features. The two men embraced, and then Nathair was sitting
in the chair, Calidus and Alcyon standing either side, the Jehar
spreading behind them.

'We await two more,' Veradis said as Nathair opened his mouth
to speak.

'Who is that?' Calidus asked.

'Some strange prisoners I encountered in Tenebral,' Veradis said.

'What?' Lykos now, looking concerned, scared even, staring at
Calidus. 'I told you that Calidus must see them privately. They
cannot come h—'

The door opened once more, eagle-guard entering first, then
the giants Raina and Tain behind them. Iron collars were about their
necks, their hands bound.

'Stop!' Calidus shouted, the eagle-guard snapping to a halt, the giants stumbling behind them.

'There was a frozen moment, the whole room staring at Raina and Tain, the two giants looking around the room with disdain at those gathered there.

'Raina?' a voice grated. 'Tain?'

It was Alcyon. His face had drained of all colour, skin as pale as if he'd been dead a ten-night.

Then he smiled.

'Raina, Tain,' he repeated.

'Alcyon,' Raina whispered.

'Get them out of here,' Calidus hissed.

'No,' Alcyon said, taking a step, reaching a hand out.

'Now,' Calidus yelled.

The eagle-guard behind the giants must have tugged on their collars, for they were both jerked backwards.

'No,' Alcyon snarled, reaching for his hammer. Then the strangest thing happened.

He froze, his arm part-raised, then, slowly, tremblingly, he lowered his arm, his face smoothed of all emotion and he passively watched Raina and Tain as they were dragged shouting from the room.

The door slammed shut, the giants' cries fading down the corridor.

Calidus said something to Alcyon and the giant took a step back, resuming his position behind Nathair's chair.

Fidele frowned. She noticed that Veradis was looking concerned at the turn of events as well.

'So,' Nathair said, resting his elbows on the arms of his chair and steepling his fingers, appearing as if nothing unusual had just happened. 'Tenebral. Our home. There can be no conflict, no state of war within my own realm. Veradis has spoken to me briefly of the various grievances and accusations between you, but for the sake of clarity I will have him recount the disputes now, for all to hear. Then, if any disagree, they can speak up now. Once we have dealt with this I will not go back to it.' He looked at them all, then nodded to Veradis, who tore his frowning gaze away from the now-mute Alcyon and stepped forward.

Veradis stood between them and began to talk. He spoke of the rebellion within Tenebral, the factors that he thought had contributed – the insensitively handled influx of the Vin Thalun and their ways, including the legalizing of fighting-pits, the order of Peritus' execution, the wedding of Fidele to Lykos, clearly unpopular amongst the people of Tenebral, especially so when Fidele's first husband Aquilus had ruled the realm for so long and was a figure of such great popularity and respect. Veradis criticized Lykos' handling of the power given to him, his hasty resort to violence rather than negotiation, his inability to politick.

For a while Veradis' words filled the room, an ebb and flow to them as he recounted the facts as he understood them.

The reality was worse, far, far worse than you even begin to touch upon.

Fidele realized Veradis had stopped talking and was looking at her. He took a deep breath, as if steeling himself for battle.

'Lady Fidele has accused Lykos of terrible things,' Veradis said, 'misuse and abuse of power, manipulation, murder . . .' He paused again, took another deep breath. 'Sorcery.'

'Sorcery?' Calidus said. 'What exactly does that mean?' His mouth twitched as he spoke, a contained smile. 'Specifically?'

'The control of another's mind, and their body,' Veradis said.

He is trying to spare me.

All in the room looked at her now. She felt the desire to leave, to run from the room, to get away from their eyes. *I will not feel ashamed. I fought him with all that I am.* She raised her head and looked only at Nathair.

'Mother, that is a grave accusation.'

'Accusation? It is no accusation,' she said, feeling her anger stir. She wished she were back in the wild with Maquin, where you faced an enemy face to face with sharp iron, and where you trusted the man at your side. There was a simplicity to that, both appealing and utterly absent in this room. 'It is a statement of fact.'

'Fact?' Calidus said, frowning. 'It is a vague accusation which is open to a multitude of interpretations. Control of your mind? So Lykos somehow invaded your mind by his sorcerous powers.' There was a snigger to her left.

Lykos.

'And he forced you to do . . . what?'

Fidele just stared at Calidus, at that moment felt an overwhelming hatred for the man. She forced her gaze back upon Nathair.

'I would talk with you of this in *private*,' she said to her son.

'No, Mother. This must be open. I cannot, will not, be accused of nepotism.'

Fidele closed her eyes, bowed her head. 'Very well then. What I mean when I say that Lykos used sorcery to control me is that he *raped* me.' She looked away, swallowed, fought the tears. Saying it aloud seemed to give it a new power. She composed herself and looked back to Nathair.

Emotions swept across his face. Outrage. Anger escalating to fury. He glared at Lykos, then his head turned to stare at Calidus, who returned his gaze dispassionately. The old man said something, too low to hear, and slowly, incrementally, the emotion drained from Nathair's face. He cocked his head, as if listening to another voice, then screwed his eyes shut, some kind of internal debate consuming him.

When he opened them he regarded Fidele with a deep sadness, mingled with something else.

Pity?

'Oh, Mother,' Nathair said, and she felt a glimmer of hope that he would now set things right, that justice would be done.

'The loss of Father has hit you so much more than I ever conceived.'

'What?' *What does he mean, why . . . ?*

'Your grief has overwhelmed you, I fear. I should never have given you the responsibility of a realm, and so soon after Father's death.'

Fidele felt those strong walls that she had built within, layer upon layer of will and strength to protect her from the hurt Lykos had inflicted upon her beginning to crumble. She filled her lungs, slowly blew out. 'This has nothing to do with your father's death. Lykos—'

'Is a Vin Thalun sailor, a ship's captain, lord of his people. Not a sorcerer. Look at him.' Nathair waved his hand. 'He is a man of many talents, but a sorcerer?'

More sniggers, louder.

'His thirst for power drives him,' Fidele said, her voice sounding reed-thin in her ears. 'Whatever he has, he wants more.'

'Power?' Nathair said. 'I had already given it to him, appointed him regent of Tenebral, made him one of the most powerful men in the Banished Lands.'

'It was not enough for him,' she said, almost a whisper, feeling her strength and will fading away, draining from her.

'Mother, please,' Nathair said, still regarding her with that maddening pity in his eyes. 'It is clear to me that you are grief mad, and that in that madness, out of it, you have brought Tenebral to the brink of civil war. But I cannot punish you for it. You are not to blame. If anyone is, it is me, for placing too great a responsibility upon your shoulders. There will be no punishment for you, but you will retire, to somewhere safe and calm, away from all of the pressure and strain of these dark times.'

Am I really hearing this? Can my own son be saying this to me? It is some terrible nightmare. She wanted to say something, to convince him, but her mind was a blank.

'Now,' said Nathair, 'as for the rest of you, I can hardly believe what I have heard. Tenebral, my home, the realm of the high king of the Banished Lands, has collapsed upon itself like so many squabbling children.'

Krelis muttered at that, Peritus sitting straight and tense.

'The right of the situation clearly lies in Lykos' favour.'

Krelis made to stand, but Peritus and Ektor both held him.

'Ripa chose to defend a man sentenced to death – you, Peritus – and to take up arms against my appointed representative. I appointed Lykos – Mother, you saw my letter with my seal, and Veradis reported my sanctioning of him as regent of Tenebral. What you have all done is treason, and I could have you all executed.'

'This is outrageous,' Krelis exploded, lunging to his feet, Peritus following, trying to calm him.

Jehar were suddenly circling Krelis, swords half-drawn from scabbards. Krelis froze.

'Sit. Down,' Nathair commanded.

Krelis just stood, glaring rage at Nathair. 'My da was slain,' he growled.

'Please, Krelis,' a voice said – Veradis. 'Please, brother, take your seat.' And slowly, with a final glower, Krelis did.

'I could have you executed for treason,' Nathair repeated, holding Krelis' gaze, daring him to move. Krelis didn't.

'But I *won't*. I want peace in my realm, order, trust in those ruling so that I may focus on the real task at hand. The defeat of the Black Sun. What we are discussing is petty by comparison.'

Fidele's mind was swirling, a turmoil of shock and pain, that her own son would disregard her so utterly and completely . . .

I do not recognize the man he's become, do not know him. How could someone change so completely. Nathair was still speaking, though his words were a blur in her head now. Fragments began to coalesce, spinning together, like a broken window reforming, and slowly she began to see.

See Calidus meeting with Nathair, all those years ago, introducing him to Lykos, advising him to leave Tenebral, to chase after the cauldron, whispering in his ear, as he was even now. She glanced at Ektor, saw him frowning, gaze flitting between Calidus and Nathair, remembered his giant scrolls that spoke of the high king's counsellor being Kadoshim, a demon of Asroth. At that time they had been talking of Meical, who had been Aquilus' counsellor, but Nathair was high king now, and Calidus his counsellor . . .

'What have you done to my son?' Fidele heard herself say, loud and clear as she stood and pointed at Calidus.

For some reason she shocked everyone to silence.

'What do you mean?' Veradis said, looking between her and Calidus.

'I have done nothing but give good counsel, my lady,' Calidus said, his voice calm, reassuring. Suddenly she knew, beyond all doubt, every fibre of her being screaming the same thing.

'You are *Kadoshim*,' she said. Quietly, but seeming to impact everyone in the room.

Calidus pulled a face, part surprise, part sneer. 'You are mistaken, my lady,' he said.

'And if we needed any more evidence of her madness, there it is,' a voice shouted, Lykos, laughing.

'You are Kadoshim,' Fidele said, louder.

'What are you talking about, my lady?' Peritus called to her.

'Nathair, tell me it isn't so,' she pleaded with her son.

He stared at her, blinking, almost startled.

'Be silent, Mother,' he mumbled.

She looked around the room, Calidus regarding her as if she were an insect to be crushed, Veradis was confused, looking from her to Nathair, Alcyon the giant – hulking, solemn, sorrowful – the Jehar just staring with their dead eyes. A hand touched her wrist, Ektor.

'Not here, not now,' he hissed, shaking his head. She shook him off and looked back to Nathair, who was still staring at her.

'What have you *done*?' she whispered.

'Take her away,' Nathair said, looking away as if he'd been slapped. 'Her madness is deeper than I feared, she must be protected from herself.'

Eagle-guard moved forwards, Krelis and Peritus standing to protect Fidele. Swords were drawn.

'No,' Fidele said furiously to Peritus and Krelis. 'You will die here, for nothing.'

'You dare draw your blades, before *me*?' Nathair said, his voice rising from a shocked hiss to strangled yell.

'I have offered you all kindness and mercy, and you throw it back at my feet. Draw your swords in my presence. Well. I. Say. This.' Nathair was on his feet now, fists bunching. 'My word is law, and you will abide by it, whether you be my ancient friend or my closest kin, else you will lose your heads.' Spittle was flying now.

'Take them away,' Calidus said.

'Aye, that's right,' Nathair cried, voice still charged with emotion. 'Get them out of here, all of them, take them below. I want them under lock and key.'

Eagle-guard swept forwards now, firm hands steering Fidele towards the door; Krelis, Peritus and Ektor herded along with her.

As she reached the door she looked back and saw Calidus staring at her, eyes flat and dead, like one of the sharks in Ripa's bay.

CHAPTER SEVENTY-THREE

VERADIS

Veradis watched the door close behind Fidele, Peritus and his brothers.

What have I just witnessed?

A silence fell upon the room, Nathair slumped back into his chair, for some reason staring at the palm of his hand.

At the scar from our oaths to each other.

'Well, that could have gone better,' Lykos said.

'Shut up,' Calidus replied, almost absently, eyes still fixed upon the door.

'Your mother,' Calidus said to Nathair.

'Yes?'

'She is a remarkable woman.'

'She is,' Nathair agreed.

'What is going on here?' Veradis said.

No one answered him. Nathair was still staring at the palm of his hand.

'Nathair, Alcyon?'

The giant looked at him with sad eyes. 'I cannot say.'

'Nathair?' Veradis said, anger leaking into his voice.

Calidus' eyes rolled away from the door, fixed onto Veradis. 'A confusion,' he said to Veradis. 'Fidele is confused. Her grief—'

'She sounded lucid enough to me.'

'She—'

'Enough,' Nathair said. 'Calidus, Alcyon, all of you.' He finally looked up from his hand. 'Leave us.'

'Is that wise?' Calidus murmured.

'I say it is,' Nathair said. 'You have hidden things from me.

Lykos and my mother . . .' His face twisted as if with a surge of pain and he screwed his eyes shut.

'For the greater good,' Calidus said quietly.

Nathair's eyes snapped open. 'I will talk with Veradis now. It is time.' He locked gazes with Calidus. They stayed like that long moments. 'I must tell him,' Nathair said, almost pleadingly, a hand going to his temples, 'I need to tell him, else I go insane.' Still Calidus said nothing, then eventually nodded.

'As you wish,' he said and ushered everyone from the chamber, including the eagle-guard and Jehar, leaving Veradis alone with Nathair.

'What just happened?' Veradis asked.

Nathair stood and paced to the window, looked out of it.

'They look like ants from here,' he said tiredly. 'All those men working on the road to find Drassil, no bigger than ants. Do you remember, in the forest during my father's council?'

Veradis did. They had seen a host of ants on the march, millions of them, each as big as a thumb. Seeing them had been the seeds of Nathair's inspiration for the shield wall.

'I do,' Veradis said, joining Nathair at the window.

'Gods above and below, but it feels like a different lifetime.'

'It does,' Veradis agreed. He thought back. 'Nearly four years.'

Nathair fell silent, staring.

'Nathair, what your mother just said. About Calidus . . .'

'Aye.'

'Why did she say that?'

'Perhaps because she's grief mad.'

'I don't think so.'

Nathair sucked in a deep breath. 'History is a peculiar thing, is it not? Take the giants, for example. Our histories tell us that they are the enemy. That they were wicked – evil, even – and that our ancestors' war against them was righteous. That right was on our side. Is that not what our histories say?'

'Aye,' Veradis said, wondering where this was leading, 'that is what our histories tell us.'

'What if it was a lie?'

'It isn't,' Veradis said without thinking.

'How do you *know* that?' Nathair asked him. 'We were not

there. No one whose word we value was there. We only have the ancient record, and that was written by our ancestors, the victors. The people that fought the giant clans and took their land.'

'What of it?' Veradis asked. He had an unpleasant feeling in his gut, part sickness, part fear.

'I do not think that all giants are evil. Alcyon, for example. You would consider him a friend, even.'

'I do,' Veradis said.

'So, perhaps those that wrote our histories were biased. Twisted the truth to suit their perspective, even.'

I'm sure Ektor would have an opinion on this but Krelis and I were always more comfortable with a blade in our hands than a book.

'Why are we talking about this?' Veradis asked.

'What if those who wrote about the Scourging, about Elyon and Asroth, were equally as biased?' Nathair looked at Veradis now, eyes bright with fervour. 'What if the Ben-Elim were not the righteous ones, the Kadoshim not evil? What if they were just like the giants and us, two peoples fighting a war for their own ends, and the defeated were portrayed as the villains?'

'No,' Veradis said.

'What if Kadoshim and Ben-Elim are just names.'

Veradis' mind was reeling. He wanted Nathair to stop, the words feeling like a sudden flood in his mind, a river bursting its banks, changing the world as he knew it.

Or as I want to know it. What if Nathair's right, all that we know a mixture of truth and lies. He mind was swept on by the thought, more and more truths coming into question.

'Wait,' he said aloud, shaking his head to try and bring some focus back. 'What are you saying, Nathair? Are you telling me that Calidus *is* Kadoshim, not Ben Elim?'

Nathair turned from the window and looked at him, then nodded.

'I am.'

'Then all that we have done, believed, fought for . . .' He looked into Nathair's eyes. 'A lie?' He felt dizzy suddenly, his legs weak.

'No,' Nathair hissed. 'Think, man. Nothing has changed. Right and wrong, they are just ideas in our heads, meaning that we give to our actions. Our friendship is still the same, our oaths to one another still stand. That is what we must cling to. Our goals and our vision are still the same. Nothing of import has changed.'

'Nothing has changed,' Veradis echoed.

'Apart from the names,' Nathair shrugged. 'Ben-Elim, Kadoshim, Elyon, Asroth.'

'Bright Star and Black Sun,' Veradis said.

Nathair froze at that, his mouth a bitter twist. 'Aye, that too.' He shrugged. 'We must accept the hard truth, even if it hurts at first.'

'But what of Calidus? We *saw* him; he had wings. He is Ben-Elim.'

'Oh, he has wings, but they are not made of white feathers,' Nathair snorted. 'What we saw in Telassar was a glamour.'

Veradis ground his palm into his forehead. *This cannot be. Everything that we are has been devoted to this cause, and it is a lie.*

He looked at Nathair, saw his face was a kaleidoscope of battling emotions. Scorn, shame, hope.

'You are the Black Sun,' Veradis said.

'Whatever men call me, I shall rule, and rule well. You know that. I am still the same person, still your friend, and your king. Nothing but the titles we have imagined have changed.'

But that's not true, is it?

'Show me your hand,' Veradis asked.

'What?'

'Your *hand*.' Veradis held his own palm up, the scar of his oath to Nathair.

Slowly Nathair held his hand out, uncurled his fingers.

'You have two scars now,' Veradis observed. A seed of doubt and anger growing larger by the moment.

'Aye. A man can make more than one oath.'

'Who was it to?'

Nathair didn't answer, made to pull his arm away, but Veradis gripped his wrist, held the palm open.

'Who did you swear this oath to?'

'Asroth,' Nathair whispered.

Veradis threw Nathair's arm as if it were a viper.

Betrayal, it is all betrayal. And lies upon lies. How can he not see that? What else has he hidden from me?

'And you say nothing has changed,' Veradis snarled, pulling away from him. '*Everything* has changed.'

'Think on what I have said,' Nathair pleaded, 'on what is truth and lie. On our *friendship*.'

'I need to get out, some air,' Veradis mumbled. He was so furious he couldn't even look at Nathair as he made for the door, slammed it open to see Calidus striding towards him. Beside him walked a strange figure, a girl, tall, fair-haired and long-limbed. Something about her reminded Veradis of Tain, the giantling, though she appeared travel stained, half-dead, skeletally thin and shivering uncontrollably. They passed each other, Calidus' eyes fixing Veradis as he went by.

He is Kadoshim. His skin goose-fleshed.

Calidus steered the girl into Nathair's chamber.

A dozen paces along the corridor Veradis swayed, reached a hand out to the wall to steady himself. He heard Calidus' voice.

'You told him, then.'

'Aye. It was time.'

'He didn't look as if he took it too well.'

'What did you expect?'

'Perhaps I should bring him back,' Calidus said.

'No, leave him. Where can he go? We are in the middle of Forn Forest. All will be well, he just needs some time to think it through, to readjust. He will be back of his own accord.'

'We shall see.'

'He must come back to me, our friendship is too strong. And I need him . . .' That last was only a whisper.

'And who is this?' Nathair said, firmer again.

'Answer your high king, child,' Calidus said.

'My name is Trigg, my lord,' a frail voice replied.

'And tell your King what you told me, Trigg,' Calidus said. There was a new note in Calidus' voice that Veradis had not heard before. Excitement.

'I can take you to Drassil,' the girl said. 'I saw their secret way.'

'And why should I trust you?' Nathair asked her.

A silence settled, broken finally by the girl's voice. 'All my life I thought them my kin, my family,' she muttered. 'But they betrayed me, sent me away.'

'What are you talking about, be clear, girl,' Nathair snapped. 'Why should I trust you?'

'Because there are those in Drassil that I would see dead,' the girl snarled.

Veradis pushed himself from the wall and strode away.

Traitors. It seemed the world was full of them.

CHAPTER SEVENTY-FOUR

MAQUIN

Maquin sat in a cold cell with iron bars, off a corridor deep in the bowels of Brikan.

Life is strange, and cruel, he thought. *It was not so long ago that I sat in the halls above, and ate, laughed and sang with Kastell and my Gadrai brothers. Orgull, Tahir . . .*

The world has gone mad.

He was not alone in these cells. Earlier the giantess Raina and her bairn had been herded in and shut away at the very end. Maquin had heard them talking in giantish, like two landslides grating back and forth, and he had heard a sniffling sound which he had presumed was weeping. That had all ended some time ago, though, and since then the only sound had been the steady drip of water from walls.

A key rattled in a lock, the door at the end of the corridor swinging open and feet slapping on stone, splashing through puddles in the dank corridor, voices protesting. One of them making him stand and run to the bars.

Fidele.

She was being escorted into the corridor by eagle-guard, along with Krelis, Ektor and Peritus. At a glance it was clear that they were prisoners, their scabbards empty of swords.

The eagle-guard filed towards his cell, one of them muttering and rifling through a ring of keys. He stopped and opened the first cell, a few doors before Maquin's, thrust Ektor into it, the young man spluttering at the indignity, moved on to the next cell, where Peritus was thrown, then the cell the other side of Maquin, placed Fidele in there, and finally the last one for Krelis.

The eagle-guard filed out without a word, looking somewhat shame-faced and confused at having locked their own Queen away.

'Didn't think I'd be seeing you down here,' Maquin said, as close to Fidele's cell as he could get.

'As dark as things have become, my heart still skips to see you,' her voice came back to him.

He reached a hand out through the bars and felt her fingers lace with his.

'What happened?' he said.

'Nathair is a madman, that's what happened,' Krelis yelled, slamming his cell bars, sending a cloud of dust puffing into the corridor.

'Something terrible,' Fidele said, and proceeded to tell Maquin of the meeting with Nathair.

'More like a sentencing, not even a trial,' Krelis growled. 'We should have fought in Tenebral, killed Lykos when we had the chance.'

I remember advising that exact course of action.

You are blinded by your thirst for revenge, Ektor had said. *You're not seeing clearly,*

Not blinded. Driven.

Mind you, in light of the events in the tent, he does have a point.

'And we should never have walked into that tent, then father would still be alive . . .' Krelis was muttering.

'Ifs and buts will not help us now,' Ektor said from his cell. 'We must think of a way out of this, else we'll all end up in a group execution alongside Maquin.'

Comforting.

'And Fidele, perhaps you should not have accused Calidus of being Kadoshim,' Ektor said.

'It is the truth.'

'Like as not, you are right. I have suspected the same. But to stand and point a finger when you are surrounded by what, six, eight thousand men sworn to him and Nathair?'

'Aye,' Fidele muttered, 'the timing could have been better, I'll give you that.'

Kadoshim? The God-War that Orgull spoke of. Is there no escaping it? Will it suck us all into its jaws.

'So what do we do?' Krelis said. 'How do we get out of here?'

'We bide our time,' Peritus said. 'Hope for an opportunity, and if one presents itself, we seize it.'

If there is one.

The conversation went back and forth amongst them, daylight through a grate high in the wall slanting and fading to darkness. They spoke of Calidus, Ektor telling them of the giant scrolls and the hints they gave about the God-War, about Kadoshim and Ben-Elim, prophecies of fabled Drassil and the Seven Treasures.

'Drassil. That is why they are here,' Fidele said. 'That is why they are tearing down trees and building roads through this forest. They are searching for it.'

Maquin heard something, a grunt, maybe. Then the key in the corridor's door. It creaked open, footsteps, then Alben's face was looking into their cells. He held the ring of keys in one hand, an array of swords under his other arm.

'I found these in the guardroom,' he said with a nod of his head. 'Thought you might be needing them.'

He was greeted with a chorus of thanks.

'We must be quick,' Alben said, trying keys in Peritus' door, the first not fitting, nor the second. The third did, the door opening with a click. The ageing battlechief stepped out and slid his sword into his scabbard.

'Why are you doing this?' Ektor asked from his cell. 'With an apology we would most likely be forgiven in the morning. Now we will be fugitives.'

'If that is so then why are gallows being built in the courtyard?'

There was a stunned silence at that.

'That cannot be,' Ektor breathed.

'You're welcome to stay in here and see,' Alben said, 'but I'd advise you to come with us.' With another click Ektor's door swung open.

'I do not know what you did to fall so far from favour,' Alben continued as he moved to Maquin's cell, 'but something is happening here.' Alben tried keys in Maquin's lock. 'It is the middle of the night and warriors are mobilizing, thousands of them. Nathair's warband are already beginning to march across the river.'

'I named Calidus as being Kadoshim,' Fidele said.

Maquin expected a shocked response from Alben.

The silver-haired healer paused with the keys and looked at Fidele. 'Did you?'

'I did. Please, Alben, before you call me mad, listen to—'

'I believe you,' Alben said.

'What? How?' Fidele stuttered.

'I am a friend to Meical,' he said. 'I have been waiting for this day for many years. The sides have formed, the line is drawn. The time to act is here.'

There was a thud behind him – Peritus falling to the floor. Alben spun around, the sword aimed for his head stabbing him between the shoulder and chest, blood erupting. He slid to the ground, Ektor tugging the blade free, standing over Alben, blood-spattered and breathing heavily.

'What are you doing?' Fidele screamed. Maquin lunged a hand through the bars, his fingers snaring around Ektor's wrist, and heaving him into the cell bars. Ektor's face crunched against iron, blood spurting from his nose, the sword dropping with a clang from his fingers. Maquin slipped his other arm through the gap, trying to get a grip around Ektor's throat, but Ektor squirmed and lunged, panic fuelling him, and he tugged himself free of Maquin's grip, staggering back, choking.

Alben reached for the sword but Ektor kicked him and snatched it up again, pointing the tip at Alben's chest. Alben crawled backwards, away from him. He was bleeding heavily, looked to be on the verge of passing out.

'Don't worry, Alben, I'll not kill you now. Calidus will be very interested in having a conversation with you, I think.'

Ektor looked at them all now, each standing at the bars of their cells, a self-satisfied smile spreading over his face.

'I knew Meical had got to one of you,' he breathed, wiping blood from a cut above his eye. 'It has taken me years of patience to reach this moment. Calidus will reward me well for this.'

He stepped away from Alben and casually thrust his blade down into Peritus' body.

Krelis screamed, 'Ektor, you pale-faced little bastard . . .' and hurled himself at the bars, tears running down his cheeks. 'When I get out of here.' He grabbed a bar and heaved, twisted, veins popping in his neck. The bar creaked in its setting, started to bend.

Ektor chopped at Krelis' fingers, the big man throwing himself backwards just in time.

'Shut up, you oaf,' Ektor snarled.

'Ektor, what have you done?' Fidele said.

'Chosen wisely,' Ektor sniffed, curling a lip at her. 'You could have joined me. You still could.'

She spat at him through the bars.

'You have sold your soul to the devil,' Alben said from the floor.

'Perhaps,' Ektor shrugged. 'That I can live with, but I think I have chosen the winning side.'

'Why?' Krelis asked, calmer now, anguish leaking from his voice.

'You wouldn't understand,' Ektor said, 'you who have everything.'

'So did you,' Krelis growled. 'You want for nothing.'

Ektor shook his head. 'I. Had. *Nothing*,' he hissed bitterly. 'No respect, no loyalty, no future, outside of my scrolls. I was laughed at, mocked with whispers as I walked by. Father did not respect intellect, only brawn. Well, I showed him.'

'What?'

'How did you think he ended up on Veradis' sword, you idiot. *Someone* pushed him.' He smiled. 'It was not the only favour I have gifted to Calidus. How did you think the Vin Thalun scaled Ripa's cliffs?'

'I will *kill* you for this, I swear it,' Krelis said, a coldness in his voice more daunting than his rage.

'Unlikely,' Ektor shrugged, picking up the bunch of keys from the floor. 'Time to call some guards, I think.'

Footsteps sounded behind him, echoing down the corridor, the iron crack of eagle-guard boots on stone.

'Perhaps naming does call,' Ektor smiled.

Maquin peered down the corridor, saw a lone warrior in the black cuirass of an eagle-guard striding towards them. He passed under torchlight and Maquin saw who it was.

Veradis.

Nathair's first-sword, Maquin thought, bowing his head. All hope left him.

'Good timing, brother,' Ektor called out, 'though to be honest I could have done with your help a little earlier.'

Veradis paused when he saw Peritus' body, glanced between the fallen warrior and the sword in Ektor's hand, then stepped over Peritus and punched Ektor in the face.

Ektor staggered back, dropping sword and keys. Veradis followed and punched him again, flush on the chin. Ektor's eyes rolled up into his head and he collapsed, unconscious.

Veradis hurried to Peritus, crouched beside him, feeling for a pulse. He stood, shaking his head.

'What has happened here?' Veradis said. His voice was changed, the misery Maquin had heard in it the last time they spoke magnified a thousandfold.

What has happened to him?

'Ektor is an agent of Calidus, was thwarting Alben's attempt to rescue us,' Fidele said.

Veradis looked at them all. His eyes were red-rimmed, face pale as bone.

'Veradis, what has happened to you?' Maquin asked him.

'Fidele, you spoke the truth. Calidus is Kadoshim.' He hung his head, grief and shame dripping from his voice. 'And Nathair is . . .' He trailed off.

'The Black Sun,' Alben breathed from the ground.

Veradis sucked in a deep breath, looked down at Alben, at the keys on the ground. He bent and picked them up, put an arm under Alben and lifted him to his feet.

'I have been a fool, but no longer. You must leave here, now, under cover of dark,' Veradis said as he ripped a strip of material from Ektor's shirt, bound Alben's wound as well as he could and then set about unlocking their cells.

Maquin put his arms around Fidele and pulled her close, felt her sink into him and hug him fiercely.

Krelis pushed past him and retrieved his sword from where Alben had placed it. With no warning he swung it high and chopped down into Ektor, severing his head with one blow.

'No,' Veradis yelled. 'He was *still* our brother.'

'He killed our da,' Krelis said, nostrils flaring. 'He pushed him onto your sword. He confessed it.'

Veradis stared at Krelis, those words sinking in, then just nodded.

'Good, then,' he said.

'What do we do now?' Fidele asked.

'The warbands are making ready to leave,' Veradis said. 'Eagle-guard, Jehar, Vin Thalun. Many thousands of them. Dawn is still a long way off; it is chaos, your best chance is to escape in the confusion.'

'My men,' Krelis said. 'There are eight hundred men of Ripa up there. I would not abandon them.'

'They are ready and waiting for us,' Alben said. He was still pale, but Veradis' bandage had stemmed the flow of his blood and he seemed to have a little more strength about him.

'Can you ride?' Veradis asked him.

'I'll damn well ride away from here,' he said.

'But where?' Fidele asked.

'We must get to Drassil,' Alben said, as if it were a simple task. 'It is where Meical is, and the Bright Star.'

'You will have to race Nathair and Calidus,' Veradis said.

'Then that is what we will do,' Alben replied.

'It's a plan.' Maquin shrugged. 'But first we need to get away from this tower. I lived here, once. I know the pathways, I can lead us out. We should travel with those others leaving, at first, leave them once we're away from this tower.'

He looked about at them, their faces stern and solemn.

'Agreed?' he asked.

'Agreed,' they replied.

They made ready. Maquin took Peritus' sword, unstrapping the dead warrior's belt and scabbard.

'You have a good man's blade there,' Krelis said.

'I will kill many of his enemies with it.'

Krelis smiled, a grim and fierce thing. 'May that knowledge go with him across the bridge of swords.'

They were about to leave when Maquin stopped.

'There are more prisoners in here,' he said, looking to the end of the corridor.

'Who?' asked Veradis.

'The giantess and her bairn.'

Veradis frowned a moment.

'Calidus wanted them locked away, and that is a good enough

reason for me to set them free. Can you hide them, take them with you?'

'Hide them?' Krelis snorted. 'Not the easiest task.'

'We can try,' Alben smiled.

Veradis strode to the end of the corridor and unlocked their cell. Tentatively the two giants stepped out.

'Raina, Tain,' Fidele said, 'we are fugitives in this place, fleeing, in danger of losing our lives, but you are welcome to join us, if you wish.'

Raina looked from Fidele to the end of the corridor, the door open, torchlight inviting.

She is scared, thought Maquin. *Has been a captive so long, the alternative is a thing of fear.*

'It is a chance at freedom,' Alben said. 'You should seize it.'

'Better to die free than to live in chains,' Maquin said.

'Is it?' Raina asked, glancing between her son and Maquin.

'Aye, it is,' Maquin said with conviction. 'And no one knows the truth of that better than I do.' He felt Fidele's hand brush his back.

'We will taste freedom,' Raina said, 'even if it is only for a short while.'

They all strode down the corridor into a square room before a set of stairs. Two guards were sprawled on the floor. Alben shrugged. Krelis took their cloaks and gave them to the giants.

'Probably won't help much,' he muttered.

'I'll go up first, make a distraction for you,' Veradis said. 'When you hear it walk fast, turn right at the top of the stairs and—'

'I know the way,' Maquin said.

'Veradis,' Fidele said. 'You're not coming with us?'

'No,' Veradis said. His eyes flickered between them all.

'What?' blustered Krelis. 'But you must come with us.'

'No. I have something to do.'

Maquin recognized that look. Had seen it many times in his own reflection.

Honour. Or death. And sometimes one follows the other.

'Come with us, friend,' Maquin said, stepping close to Veradis.

Veradis just shook his head.

'We'll see you again, then,' Maquin said, squeezing Veradis' shoulder.

'Aye,' Veradis nodded grimly. 'This side or the other.'

'What are you staying here for?' Krelis called after him.

Veradis paused and looked back.

'Brother, please. Come with us,' Krelis pleaded.

Veradis shook his head. 'I cannot. But I will join you if I can.'

'Why? Why will you not come with us now?'

'Because I am going to kill Calidus.'

CHAPTER SEVENTY-FIVE

ULFILAS

Ulfilas reined his horse in, Dag beside him. He had ridden back from the front line to find Jael, passing over two thousand men filling the road they had carved through the heart of Forn Forest. He felt a thrill of pride at seeing the road receding as far as his eye could see, branches arching over it as if they bowed to some royal procession.

Quite a feat.

He felt another thrill of excitement at what he had just discovered, or more accurately been told by Dag. He wanted to give the news to King Jael himself.

We started out with closer to three thousand men, Ulfilas thought as he rode through the throng. Hundreds had been lost to the cold and the predators of Forn.

And some of them have walked away on their own two feet, I am sure.

Many of the losses Ulfilas and Dag had attributed to enemy raids. They had kept their thoughts to themselves, not wanting to fuel the rumours that the Black Sun and his demons were hunting them at night. Nevertheless the fear had spread. The only thing that had stopped men deserting in large numbers was the fact that those who did desert were usually found dead within a day of leaving, victims of Forn's denizens.

'There he is.' Dag pointed, and Ulfilas saw Jael standing before his tent, watching it being raised for another night in the forest. Winter was breaking now, the cold air fresh rather than bitter, the ground softer underfoot. All about them branches were flourishing with the green of new leaves. Days were lasting longer, allowing them to work later each day. Ulfilas jerked his reins and guided his horse down the embankment the road was being built upon, great lengths of timber laid over the crumbling stone of this ancient giants' road. Jael was surrounded by his usual guards, Fram and a dozen men, they in turn circled by a score of the Jehar warriors, Sumur close to Jael.

He is always close to Jael. A permanent reminder of Nathair and his threat, or promise, no doubt.

Jael looked up as Ulfilas and Dag approached.

'You have news?' he asked.

'We do, my King,' Ulfilas said.

'Come, then, tell me over a cup of wine,' Jael said and marched into his tent; servants inside were lighting torches, laying out furniture, food and drink.

Within short moments Ulfilas was handed a cup of wine that had been warmed over a fire. He drank, allowing Jael to settle himself into his fur-draped chair.

'Well?' Jael asked when he was comfortable, a jewelled cup in his hand.

'We've found Drassil,' Ulfilas said.

Jael blinked at that, the words seeping in.

'You're sure?' was the first thing he said.

'Aye,' Dag said. 'Seen it with my own eyes.'

'What's it like, man?' Jael asked, leaning forward. That had been the first question Ulfilas had asked of the huntsman.

'It's big,' Dag said. 'Like nothing you've ever seen.'

'How long?' asked Jael, looking both excited and scared.

'Half a day,' Dag replied. 'We can stop building the road now, make a base camp here, use the old road to get there on the morrow.'

'The old road? Is it fit for purpose?'

'Good enough. We'll have to walk, not ride. But clearing the way and laying the new road would cost another half a ten-night.' He shrugged. 'Depends how desperate you are to get there.'

'We are the first, then,' Jael said.

'Oh aye, there were no other warbands camped outside the walls.'

'So I shall be ruler of Carnutan and Helveth. Gundul and Lothar will be my vassals.' He smiled viciously.

'Do you think they'll just allow that to happen?' Ulfilas said, not able to keep the scepticism from his voice.

'Do you think Nathair lacks the ability to enforce it?' Jael replied.

Ulfilas remembered the display of Sumur against Fram, thought of a hundred like him. A thousand.

'No, I don't, now that you mention it.'

'Neither do I,' Jael said. 'So we shall march with dawn and attack on the morrow.'

'Would it not be wiser to wait?' Ulfilas said. 'Now that we have found Drassil. We could scout it out and wait for the others to arrive?'

'No,' a voice said behind them. Sumur, who had entered the tent silently. 'Meical is there. His puppet is there. I will taste their flesh before the sun sets on the morrow.'

They all looked at him in silence.

Taste their flesh!

'We have not carved our way through Forn to sit and wait,' Jael said, trying his best to ignore Sumur and avoid the flat stare of his eyes. 'Haelan is in there. I will not give him a chance to flee once again. And what of Gundul or Lothar? If we wait and they arrive from the south and west they will likely dispute my claim as first here! No. We shall be standing upon Drassil's walls by the time they arrive.' His grin widened. 'This is a good day. And the morrow will be better. Now, let's discuss how we are going to win the coming battle.'

CHAPTER SEVENTY-SIX

VERADIS

Veradis stood on the spiral of the tower steps and stared out of the window.

Below him was the courtyard of Brikan, where great iron pots blazed and crackled with fire, creating pools of light amidst the darkness. He watched as Fidele and the others, the giants stooping like ancients, ludicrous to any eyes that lingered upon them, made their way through the busy chaos. Horses were stamping and whinnying, men calling out, marching or mounting up. Making it worse, the cauldron's wain filled a large section of the courtyard, Jehar forming an unforgiving perimeter around it.

I have done all I can for them. My task here is too important to accompany them.

With relief he saw the escaping group pass through the arched gates that led to the encampment beyond, where – according to Alben – the men of Ripa were awaiting them.

Good.

He turned and strode up the stairs, grim-faced and determined.

Calidus' chamber was situated on the first floor of the tower, with two Jehar standing guard. Flies buzzed languidly around one of them. It didn't seem to bother him. They regarded Veradis with their black eyes as he knocked on the door and entered, not waiting for an invitation.

Calidus was bending over a small chest, silhouetted by a huge fireplace built into the wall. Unaware of Veradis' presence he was focused on placing something – a doll-like figure with crude arms and legs – into the chest.

Alcyon was standing to the left, before a huge unshuttered

window that looked out onto the river as it curled tight to the rear of the tower.

Focus on your task.

'Ah,' Calidus said. He closed the lid of the chest with a snap. 'I was starting to think you had abandoned us.'

'That is not who I am,' Veradis said. He glanced at Alcyon, saw the giant regarding him with sombre eyes.

'No, it is not,' Calidus said. 'But a man of your mind-set. I imagine it is hard to come to terms with such a shift in reality, almost like the ground changing beneath your feet.'

'I have had to think long and hard on it.'

'Indeed,' said Calidus, head cocked to one side, studying Veradis intensely, like one of the vultures that circled a battlefield. Veradis walked to a table and poured himself a cup of wine, unable to meet Calidus' gaze.

'Have you visited Nathair first?' Calidus asked him.

'No,' Veradis said, sipping dark red wine and taking a step towards Calidus.

'That is unexpected,' Calidus frowned.

'I had some questions,' Veradis said and took another step closer. 'For you.'

'I would be happy to answer them for you, Veradis. You are a valued part of our campaign. Deeply talented at what you do. There is much you can accomplish for us.'

What I do. Kill people. A blunt instrument of war. And, oh, how many I have killed for your cause already . . .

He felt shame and self-loathing rise up like a wave, threatening to engulf him. With an act of will he forced it back down.

But can I kill him, standing before me without a weapon in his hands? It may be murder . . . but in this case I'm willing to make an exception. Maybe then Nathair will see sense.

After leaving Nathair, Veradis had found an abandoned stairwell and sat in solitary silence, thinking over, reliving every moment since he'd met Nathair. Their first meeting with Calidus and Alcyon, when he'd leaped through a wall of fire to defend Nathair, the council of Aquilus, the ants, sailing to Tarbesh and fighting giants and draigs, Telassar and Calidus' unveiling . . .

And all of it is lies. I have been such a fool. And what more has been done without me by his side that I am unaware of?

And then the hunt for Mandros, Veradis leading a warband into Carnutan to hunt its King. He remembered Mandros' words in the glade, just before Veradis had slain him.

Nathair killed your King, not I.

'I understand that all is not black and white, that difficult choices must be made in war. I am no infant to expect anything other.' He drew in a deep breath. 'However, there is one thing I *must* know.' He looked up now and met Calidus' eyes. 'Truth now is all I ask. Did Nathair slay Aquilus?'

'Of course he did.' Calidus snorted. 'He had no choice. It was—'

'For the greater good,' Veradis finished for him, nodding. 'As is this.' He threw his cup of wine at Calidus' face, at the same time leaping forwards and drawing a knife from his belt. Calidus staggered back a step, right before the roaring fire, his arms raised, flailing. Veradis heard Alcyon moving, the table between them being overturned in Alcyon's rush, but he was too late. Veradis stepped in close to Calidus, ducked his flailing arms and buried his knife to the hilt in Calidus' belly, twisted and ripped, blood slicking his fist.

Then Alcyon's huge hand clamped upon his arm. Veradis kicked Calidus in the chest, sent the Kadoshim stumbling backwards, tripping over the chest and falling into the huge fireplace.

Calidus screamed as flames exploded in a roar about him, engulfing him. Alcyon hauled Veradis back a pace, twisting his arm, forcing him to his knees, pain screaming through his arm as tendons tore and sinew ripped, the shoulder close to dislocating.

'Do what you will to me,' Veradis snarled. 'Your master is dead.'

Alcyon just stared grimly at the fireplace and blazing flames.

A figure appeared amongst the roaring flames, man-like, for a moment the likeness of dark, shadowy wings unfurling about him. Then Calidus staggered out from the fire's embrace, stepped onto the cold stone of his chamber. His cloak was ablaze, his silver hair scorched black or burned away, and the flesh on his face was peeling and charred.

He undid the brooch of his cloak, let it slip to the ground, swatted at a flame on his sleeve. Annoyed and almost amused.

'As you can see, I am quite hard to kill,' Calidus said, voice deeper, harsher.

Veradis just stared at him in horror, his eyes drawn to his knife still buried deep in Calidus' belly. Calidus wrapped blistered fingers around the hilt and pulled it out, growling with pain like a wounded animal. He held the blade up between two fingers, grimaced and threw it over his shoulder.

'Well done,' Calidus said. 'It takes a rare man to get past my guard – and my guardian.' He shot a black look at Alcyon.

Veradis glowered at him, felt a surge of pure hatred for this man, this creature before him. The one who had corrupted everything, his friend, his whole world.

Calidus met his gaze and sighed.

'I can see we're not going to get anywhere with you,' he said. 'A shame.' He shrugged. 'Alcyon, kill him.'

Veradis stared into the giant's eyes, part of him wanting death, welcoming it.

I deserve it. The wise man lives a long life, the fool dies a thousand deaths.

'I am sorry, True-Heart,' Alcyon whispered and slowly raised his war-hammer.

'Who were those giants to you?' Veradis asked him.

Alcyon paused.

'Kill him,' Calidus hissed.

'What?' Alcyon rumbled.

'Those giants during the trial. Who were they to you?'

Alcyon's face twitched, muscles spasming. His lip trembled. A tear rolled from one dark eye.

'My wife. My son.'

'They are free,' Veradis whispered.

'You lie,' Calidus sneered, though an edge of doubt showed in his voice.

'I set them free,' Veradis said, fixing Alcyon with his gaze. 'Saw them walk out through Brikan's gates.'

'Alcyon, kill him.'

Alcyon's arm hovered over Veradis. It shook, as if caught by an invisible force.

'No,' the giant whispered.

'No?' Calidus frowned. He and Alcyon glared at one another, beads of sweat breaking out upon both of their brows. Time passed – a dozen heartbeats, a hundred, Veradis did not know. Eventually Calidus turned away, threw open the lid to the chest before the fire and reached inside. Veradis saw more of the clay figures contained within and suddenly remembered Fidele's explanation of Lykos' enchantment.

All I know is that he had a doll, a clay figure, a strand of my hair set within it, she had said. *When Maquin fought Lykos at the arena it was crushed underfoot, destroyed, and immediately the chains within my mind were broken.*

Veradis swept a leg out and kicked the chest into the fire. The flames flared about it, smoke billowing, the smell of burning hair wafting about them.

'You fool,' Calidus snarled, a feral rage twisting his face, and he drew his sword.

Alcyon swung his hammer into Calidus' chest, hurling him back against a wall. He slid to the ground, the wall cracked, fragments of stone falling about him. Slowly Calidus stood, shook his head.

'Legion,' he roared, his voice like a storm wind, and the door burst open, the two Jehar surging in. Veradis heard the buzzing of flies.

Veradis stood on shaky legs, the pain in his shoulder still screaming at him. He reached for his sword hilt.

Then a huge arm was wrapping about his waist, lifting him and carrying him across the room in great bounding strides. Towards the open window, Alcyon's foot on the sill, launching them out into open air and darkness. Then they were falling, tumbling, wind snatching his breath away, still held tight in Alcyon's iron grip, the black waters of the river below rushing up to meet him.

CHAPTER SEVENTY-SEVEN

EVNIS

Evnis sat in the tower on the northern border of the marshlands and brooded.

There had been no sign of Braith.

He left over a moon ago, and still no word. Yet Evnis trusted Braith – when it came to hunting, anyway. It was not the finding of Edana and her little band of rebels that concerned him, it was what he would do once he knew where they were. Once he had them.

Edana's easy, of course. She has to die. And apparently the bitch-wife of Eremon is with her, and her idiot son, who has a claim to the throne of Domhain. Rhin won't like the thought of him still breathing, so he'll have to die as well.

No, they were all simple.

All of it is simple, in fact. Kill everyone. Except . . .

Except his son.

What will I do with Vonn?

He loved his son, of that there was no doubt. And if there ever had been any doubt of that he had resolved the situation when against all judgement he'd stood up in a field full of enemies and called out his son's name.

But now men were talking about him. He knew by the looks as he passed, the whispers. *They are saying I am weak. That my love for my son is a vulnerability, that I am a risk, a danger. What if it happens again, they say, and our position is revealed?*

I must prove them wrong. Show them my strength. A ruler's power is his reputation. I cannot afford to be considered weak. Rhin hears all, and if she hears that . . .

He sipped from a small cup of usque, the liquor smooth and sweet, warming his belly, the glow spreading.

There was a knock at his door, it was Glyn his shieldman.

'Someone comes from the marsh, my lord.'

About bloody time. Braith at last.

It was Rafe.

Evnis stood on the wall above the gates, watching a boat slip through the marsh waters, a man inside leaping ashore and tying the boat off. A bag was slung across his back, which he set on the ground while he saw to the boat. Two hounds ran along the riverbank.

Why is he alone?

Evnis decided that he no longer liked waiting – *it feels as if I have been waiting my whole life.*

Evnis was almost at the riverbank when Rafe started walking towards him. The lad had been squatting beside his boat, patting his two hounds.

Sentimental boy. Not like his father.

Rafe's expression sent different signals to Evnis. He was feeling too impatient to work them out himself.

'Tell me,' he said simply.

'Braith's dead,' the young huntsman said, 'and all the others. We were hunted down by that Camlin.'

Evnis felt a muscle twitch in his cheek.

'So, a complete disaster, then.'

'Not exactly. I escaped, then followed them back to Dun Crin. I know where it is, can guide you there.'

Evnis grinned. 'That, my lad, is wonderful news. You said *them*. You followed *them*.'

'I did,' Rafe said. 'Camlin had help. Vonn.'

'Vonn helped hunt Braith down and kill him?'

'Aye. But he let me go. He could have killed me, always been better with a blade than me. He let me go.'

'Why?'

'He asked me to give you a message.' Rafe looked at Glyn.

'Go on, lad, Glyn's good at keeping secrets.'

'Said when you come for Dun Crin, and he knows you will, that he wants to talk to you.'

Evnis felt a rising hope.

'Did he now? Did he say what about?'

'He said he wants to talk to you about the God-War, the Seven Treasures, and the necklace of Nemain.'

Evnis was stunned to silence, almost took a step back at that.

'Someone is coming,' Glyn said into the silence, looking back up the hill. 'I think it's Morcant.'

It was, the young warrior striding with his usual grace and arrogance, a handful of warriors behind him.

More peacocks, like their master, though with lesser plumage.

'What news?' Morcant asked as he approached.

How is it that he even makes a question sound arrogant?

'Edana and her rabble have been found. We will set out on the morrow,' Evnis said, trying to sound as indifferent as possible.

'Good,' Morcant said, rubbing his hands together. 'I'm overdue a good fight.'

Evnis sat near the head of a long barge, thirty warriors about him. It was early, the sun not yet burning off morning's mist, wisps of it curling about the river, coiling up and over the side of the barge. Evnis shivered.

Morcant sat in the boat behind him, looking every bit the hero in his black and gold war-gear.

How I despise him.

And behind Morcant the boats of their small fleet were filling; fifty vessels, bought, stolen, built, not all of them as big as the one he was sitting in, but they carried over five hundred men between them.

More than enough to crush this rebellion.

The sensible voice in his head told him to wait for the extra men to arrive from Dun Carreg, a few hundred at least. Enough to make the outcome of this conflict a foregone conclusion. He knew that this was riskier, but had justified it, claiming that they must strike hard and fast now, before Edana's rabble grew, and that if they did not strike now there would be a high risk of Edana's rebels just moving base, and then they would never find them.

So it has to be now, Evnis had argued.

Good arguments, and true, to a point. But they are not the reason I am ordering an immediate strike.

I need to see my son, and resolve this once and for all.

CHAPTER SEVENTY-EIGHT

CORBAN

Corban woke to a knocking at his door. For a moment he did not know where he was. Then he remembered.

Drassil. And today we fight.

An enemy warband had been spied in the forest some moons ago, identified as Jael and the warriors of Isiltir. Kadoshim had also been seen amongst them. Since then Coralen and her scouts had kept track of it, and many night-time raids had issued from the tunnels in an attempt to whittle down the numbers and spread fear amongst the survivors. Yet still they had forged on, a few thousand swords, coming to Drassil to kill them.

And today they will be here. At the gates of Drassil.

The knocking sounded on the door again and he rose, shivered as his bare feet met the cold stone floor.

It was before dawn, grey light seeping through windows, the orange glow of embers in his fire seemingly the only colour in the room. He pulled his breeches on and padded to the door.

Brina was stood outside with a bowl in her hand, other faces behind her: Cywen, Dath, Farrell, Gar and Coralen. Buddai's tail thumped on the floor at the sight of him. Without waiting for Corban to say anything Brina pushed past him, the others following. They were all dressed in their war gear, gleaming with iron and leather and wood.

'Eat this,' Brina said, pushing him into a chair and passing him the bowl filled to the brim with steaming porridge.

'Has it got honey in it?' He frowned. 'I don't like porridge without honey.'

'Told you,' Cywen said as she picked up one of Corban's boots and began hunting for the other.

'Yes, it has,' said Brina, unusually patient.

He tasted some suspiciously, then smiled and ate.

'Almost as good as Mam's,' he said as he finished, scraping the bowl. 'Now, what's this all about?'

'We just wanted to see you, before . . .' Cywen said, who had collected a pile of clothes together and laid them upon his bed.

'Before people start stabbing each other,' Brina finished for her. They all came and sat around him.

'We've come a long way, eh?' he said.

'Aye, we have,' Gar nodded gravely.

He looked at all of their faces, so many memories rushing up with each of them, warming his heart. Too many memories to begin to mention. 'I don't know what to say,' he said.

'Neither do I,' said Brina, her eyes shining.

'That's a first,' Dath whispered, too loudly, as always.

Brina glared at him.

'Apart from one thing,' Corban said. 'And it is that I love you all. Would give my life gladly for any one of you.'

Gar stood and leaned forward, put his hands on Corban's cheeks and kissed his forehead. 'We love you too, Ban,' he said, the others murmuring agreement. 'And we are proud of you. And your mam and da would burst with that pride if they could see you now.'

'Well,' Corban said, sniffing, 'I did not think I would start the day with tears.' He smiled as he rubbed at his eyes.

'Me neither,' Brina said, wiping her own eyes. 'Now come on, best get you dressed; we haven't got all day.'

'Dressed?'

'Aye. Farrell's brought you a nice shiny new shirt, Coralen's sharpened and polished your wolven claws, I even got my stitching needle out.'

They helped him dress for war.

Farrell smiled when Corban put his arms and head into the shirt of mail.

'It's lighter than the one I've been training in,' Corban said as he rolled his shoulders, 'and it fits better. Much better.'

'Laith helped me,' Farrell confessed. 'She's an amazing smith.'

He patted Corban on the back, staggering him as Brina slipped his arm-ring over the shirt-sleeve, Farrell squeezing it tight around Corban's upper arm. A leather bracer was buckled around his right forearm, sewn with strips of iron, then Gar unfolded a black surcoat, an emblem upon its front. A white star with four points, like the north star.

'Brina made this for you,' Gar said.

'In case you forget you're the Bright Star, which I wouldn't put past you,' Brina muttered.

How can she manage to call me the Bright Star of prophecy and insult me with the same breath?

Corban just looked at them as Gar slipped it over his head and Cywen buckled his belt around it, adjusting his sheathed sword. 'I remember me and Mam making that scabbard, and we wound the leather on your sword hilt,' she said.

'Aye, you did.' Corban felt a lump in his throat stopping any more words coming out.

'Da made your sword,' Cywen continued, 'and your torc.' Brina slipped that around Corban's neck, the two wolven-head ends a comforting weight.

Coralen lifted his left hand, slipped the wolven-claw gauntlet on and buckled it tight. 'Don't try and scratch your chin with this hand,' she said as she adjusted the buckles over the mail shirt-sleeve, 'I've sharpened your claws. Think they'd cut iron right now.'

She slipped his wolven cloak about his shoulders, fastening the brooch and pausing to look in his eyes, smiling at him.

'We made you this, as well,' Dath said, slipping out of the door-way and grunting as he lifted something in the hall. He came back in carrying a shield, iron-rimmed, painted with black pitch, the same white star upon its centre as was upon his surcoat.

'I know you rarely use a shield,' Gar said, 'but you've trained hard with one in the weapons court, and it's better to have one and not need it, than to need one and not have it.'

'That sounds like something Brina would say,' Dath commented.

'And you can always use it like I showed you,' Gar said, strapping it onto Corban's back. 'So that your back is shielded in a melee. Which may happen today.' He shook it, made sure the strap was tight.

They all stepped back and looked at him.

'Thank you, all of you,' Corban said.

'You look almost like a hero, if I don't say so myself,' said Cywen.

Brina looked up at the window, sunlight streaming in now.

'Time to go,' she said.

They filed out of the room, Corban walking last, Buddai rising in the corridor to greet them. As he reached the doorway Coralen turned back to him, stopped him with a hand on his chest. She gripped a fistful of his surcoat and pulled him hard towards her and before he knew what was happening her lips were against his, warm and fierce. The world shrank to the two of them, for a few heart-beats all else fading as he kissed her back, then she was pushing away from him, turning her back, taking long strides to catch up with the others.

He stood there a moment, breathless, blinking, the faint taste of apples from her lips lingering, then he shook his head and followed after her.

Stairs wound about Drassil's trunk and they walked in silence down to the great chamber's stone floor, boots echoing. Gar and the rest of them paused, letting Corban walk ahead, and they followed close behind him.

Balur One-Eye was standing before the throne of Skald, the ancient King's skeleton transfixed by the spear a constant reminder of the centuries of war that had spiralled from that one moment. Balur's tattoo of thorns wound dark about both of his bare fore-arms, disappearing beneath the sleeves of a chainmail shirt; the starstone axe lay black and brooding upon his back. Ethlinn and the might of the Benothi stood behind him, grim and dour in leather, fur and iron. War-hammers and axes glinted. Even the giantlings were there, all ready for war. Corban saw Laith amongst them, her belts criss-crossing her torso, like Cywen, bristling with knives. Balur nodded to Corban and they followed silently behind him.

The great doors opened before Corban, light streaming in. A handful of the Jehar waited for him there, led by Hamil, dressed in black shirts of mail, swords strapped to their backs, each one wearing a black surcoat with a white star upon their chests. They parted for Corban and, as he strode through their midst, closed up behind him. He saw children standing in the shadows, running along with them. Haelan was one of them, his white ratter at his heels, and Corban beckoned him over, not breaking his stride.

'I have a task for you, if you would help me,' Corban said to the lad.

'Of course,' Haelan breathed, his face shining with pride, 'I'll do anything to help.'

'Good. Follow me, then.'

Corban led them through the streets of Drassil, not straight to the gates, but eastward, through a less-inhabited part of the fortress, finally stopping in a courtyard where the ground was ruptured by thick roots.

'Storm,' Corban called out as a silence fell in the square. His voice echoed back from the stone walls all about, and before it had faded Storm leaped out from the hole beneath the tree root and padded up to Corban, nuzzling his chest with her scarred muzzle. He buried his face in the fur of her neck.

More shapes emerged from the darkness of the hole: six cubs, running and bouncing to their mother's legs, standing in the shadow beneath her bulk. They were close to three moons old now, more balls of fur with teeth than anything else.

'Storm, I need you with me today. So I'll leave some friends to guard your cubs.' Corban looked at Haelan. 'Think you can do that for me?'

'Aye,' Haelan beamed, scooping one of the cubs up in his arms.

'I thought so, as I've seen you visiting these cubs every day and luring them out with scraps of food. Thought they might be happiest with you.'

Haelan's smile grew, if that was possible. 'Think I might need some help, though,' he added as he tried to scoop another cub up and missed.

'Wulf's bairns will help you,' Corban said, then turned to leave.

'Not you, Tahir,' Haelan said. 'I give you permission to go and fight today, not stand around in here watching me.'

Tahir smiled and ruffled Haelan's hair.

'Storm, with me,' Corban said and strode from the courtyard.

Storm hesitated a moment, looking between Corban and her cubs, then padded after Corban.

'And, Tahir,' Haelan called out after them, 'bring me Jael's head.'

'I'll do my best,' Tahir muttered behind Corban.

The rest of the warband were waiting for Corban before Drassil's great gates, the converted bear pens edging the courtyard. Although the plan was to remain inside the walls, horses were saddled and harnessed, prepared for any eventuality. Corban heard Shield whinny when he entered the courtyard, calling out to him.

A great host stood before the gates, every last man and woman who could wield a sword, and standing in front of them was Meical. Today he looked like one of the Ben-Elim from the tales of the Scourging, tall and commanding in a coat of gleaming mail, his dark hair tied back in a severe knot. He half-bowed to Corban as he led his followers to the gate.

'The Bright Star,' Meical called out, his voice ringing from the stone walls, drowned by a great roar from the warband.

Corban climbed a dozen steps on the wall, then stopped and looked about at them all, hundreds of faces staring back at him. A mixture of fear, of pride, of determination. Brave men and women, all touched, scarred in some way by Asroth and his servants.

I am dreaming. How has life come to this?

He took a deep breath.

'We have been hunted, hounded, our kin slain, our friends murdered. We have travelled hundreds of leagues, fled the dark tide that is sweeping this land. But no more. Today we stand. Today we fight. Now that's a tale our kin will be proud to tell.'

The courtyard rang with cheering. It slowly faded to an echo.

'Win or lose, live or die, I am proud to stand beside you.'

A great roar rose up from the courtyard then, feet stamping, spears banging on shields, swords on bucklers. As it died a new sound rang out. Horns blasted from the walls above.

They are here.

Corban felt a jolt of fear, his guts turning to water for a few heartbeats. He ground his jaw, refusing to let it rule him.

He drew his sword and held it high over his head. 'Truth and courage!' he yelled, punching the sky, then turned and strode up the steps to Drassil's wall. The courtyard rang with the echo of a thousand voices yelling the same battle-cry as they all went to find their places.

'That's a lot of men,' Dath commented in Corban's ear.

It is.

Thousands of warriors were pouring out of the trees to the north-west of the fortress, spilling into the open space like blood from a wound, gathering into a thick pool, edging forwards.

From this distance Corban could make out little detail, just a mass of iron and leather, red cloaks and fur. Most of the warband were on foot, and the disconcerting thing was that they just kept on appearing, more and more of them emerging from the shadows of Forn. Eventually riders appeared, a banner held aloft, a lightning bolt with a pale serpent wrapped around it.

I like my banner better, thought Corban, looking up to see the bright star on a black field snapping from the gate tower above him.

Slowly the warband moved southwards, skirting the edge of the land cleared over the last few moons, until they were massed about a thousand paces from Drassil's only gates. Then they began to edge closer, a semi-organized line stretching the width of the western wall, ten men deep at least. Corban began to make out details, the most troubling of which was the number of long timber ladders he spied being carried amongst their ranks.

'Two and a half thousand swords,' Gar whispered behind him.

Five hundred paces out and horn blasts rang from the cluster of riders, the warband rippling to a halt, a silence settling heavy upon them all.

'Is it just me, or is there a lot of waiting in war?' Dath muttered.

'Aye, you're right,' Farrell replied. 'Usually followed by a lot of dying.'

Dath took a deep breath.

'That's comforting.'

'Here to help,' Farrell muttered.

Hearing Dath and Farrell's bickering actually helped to calm Corban's nerves, something familiar in this most unfamiliar of circumstances.

The other battles seemed to just happen – Dun Carreg, Murias, Gramm's hold. This waiting and watching is worse.

Four riders separated from the others, riding at a steady pace towards the gates of Drassil, one clearly the leader, his horsehair plume tugged by the wind – *must be Jael, the self-appointed King of Isiltir* – another held Isiltir's banner, the third appearing to be a shieldman, obviously a warrior, sitting his saddle with an easy grace and clothed similarly to the other two, in red cloak, black cuirass and iron helm, sword at his hip, spear in one hand. The fourth appeared elderly, hunched over his saddle and wrapped in a voluminous cloak, the hood pulled up.

A loremaster, perhaps, come to tell me that I have no legal claim to be fighting against the King of Isiltir.

They rode steadily closer.

At least it looks as if the waiting's over.

CHAPTER SEVENTY-NINE

ULFILAS

Ulfilas rode one side of Jael, his first-sword Fram upon the other, their cloaked and hunched companion close behind them. As they drew nearer Ulfilas looked up at the walls of Drassil, the great tree towering behind them, its branches unfurling like some giant organic shield that touched the clouds.

The gates were huge, constructs of weathered oak and iron, as tall as a house from Mikil, and looked as thick as a wall. On the wall above, warriors stood in silent rows, peering down on them. Here and there Ulfilas saw the huge proportions of a giant.

Never thought I'd wish for the company of Ildaer and his Jotun. Where is he, the traitorous coward? Over a dozen messengers had been sent north into the Desolation in search of Ildaer and his giants. Not a sight or sound had been heard of them since the disaster at Gramm's hold, and eventually Jael had tired of sending messengers.

On one of the gate towers a banner rippled; as Ulfilas drew nearer he was able to make out a rayed white star upon a black field.

In the crook of his arm Ulfilas held the banner of Isiltir, the wind trying to rip it from his grip.

White star against the storm and serpent.

They were three or four hundred paces from the gates now, still closer to their warband than to the walls of Drassil, but nevertheless Ulfilas was starting to feel a little intimidated by the sheer scale of them.

Are our ladders even tall enough?

'Are you sure this is a good idea?' Ulfilas asked Jael, who sat straight and confident in his saddle.

Jael reined his horse in and cupped his hands about his mouth.

Too late.

'Who leads this rabble?' Jael called out, voice sounding small and insignificant as it battered against Drassil's walls. No answer came back to them.

'I've heard a name, and a title,' Jael called. 'Corban. Bright Star. Are you up there, Corban, but too scared to speak with me.'

He's always had a natural ability to get under the skin, has Jael.

'I'm here,' a voice came down to them.

'I've a proposition for you, Bright Star,' Jael shouted, managing to make the title sound like an insult. 'I've a lot of men under my care, and no doubt you've a fair few with you inside those walls. How about we decide this the old way, and spare the blood of thousands of men. Spare their lives.'

Silence.

'You against my champion. Winner takes the field.'

More silence.

'I'd wager that that has set the cat amongst the wood pigeons,' Jael whispered to Ulfilas.

'You lie,' another voice drifted down.

I recognize that voice.

A face peered over the wall. Wulf.

'Ahh, the son of Gramm,' Jael called out. 'How are your hands?'

I think he's genuinely enjoying this.

'You will die today, Jael. As will your lackey, Ulfilas.'

Well, I did spill his da's guts before his very eyes. I'd be surprised if he wasn't angry.

'Be quiet, you insignificant oaf,' Jael called back. 'I'm talking to your leader, not you.'

Curses drifted down and then Wulf's face disappeared.

'I do not lie,' Jael said. 'I swear an oath, before my people and any powers that deign to listen. If you defeat my champion I shall withdraw and leave you in peace.'

'I'll fight *you*,' the first voice came down to them.

'Ahh, tempting,' Jael said, 'but, no. I am a king. I have a champion, whereas you are no king, but profess to *be* a champion. The champion of Elyon, no less; or am I mistaken? That is what the prophecy says, does it not?'

More silence.

'So if you are the champion you claim to be, then come down here. Fight my champion, and spare the lives of your followers.'

Jael turned and grinned at Ulfilas. 'Either way, we win here. If he refuses, he loses the respect of his warband – they will not fight so fiercely for someone who had an opportunity to save them and chose not to. And if he comes down here, he dies. Their Bright Star. That will rip the heart out of this warband. They may even surrender after that.'

I'll give it to Jael, he is a canny one.

'But what if he comes down here and wins?' Ulfilas said.

Jael just pulled a face at him. 'Win? Please.' Then he frowned as he thought about it a few moments, finally shrugging. 'If he wins we'll just kill him, anyway. He won't get back to those gates before my mounted shieldmen could catch him.'

'That may inspire some anger amongst his warband, rather than dishearten them.'

'It may, you're right. But he'd still be dead, and that is the most important goal here, Ulfilas. To kill a snake you cut off the head.'

'I'm coming down,' the Bright Star's voice drifted down to them.

The gates opened with a grating of iron and oak and a lone figure stepped out. They closed behind him with a booming thud as he strode purposefully towards them.

'He looks quite confident,' Jael remarked.

'He does,' Ulfilas agreed.

The four of them waited in silence as the lone warrior approached them.

So this is the Bright Star that Nathair is so scared of. Corban. He is younger than I expected.

He was young, his face smooth-skinned apart from the short dark stubble of a beard. He walked with the easy gait of a warrior, of average height, broad at the shoulder, thick at the chest, slim at the waist, built more like a blacksmith, to Ulfilas' mind.

He's well dressed, though, Ulfilas thought, admiring his war gear. A well-fitting coat of mail, leather and iron on his wrists and feet, shield slung across his back and a large hand-and-a-half sword at his hip.

A big sword, too big to use single-handed. Strong but slow.

Ulfilas had seen this type many times before, strong but slow, their strength often their worst enemy, relying upon it to batter their opponents into defeat. He saw a strange weapon strapped to Corban's left hand, like a three-pronged knife bound into a leather gauntlet.

Like claws. Ulfilas remembered the wounds on many of those who had been slain in the night-time raids during the journey through Forn.

Something glinted on his arm, an arm-ring spiralling around his bicep, gleaming with silver.

Jael will want that once this man is dead.

He stopped about fifty paces from them, regarding them with dark, serious eyes.

'I am here, then.' Corban drew his sword almost without having seemed to move, his feet shifting, balance perfect. He rolled his shoulders.

Maybe not so slow, then.

'Brave of you,' Jael commented, 'and trusting.'

Not so trusting, that's why he stopped over fifty paces away from us.

Corban shrugged. 'Let's get on with this.'

'Not a conversationalist, then,' Jael said. 'As you wish.' He pulled on his reins and kicked his horse, turning to ride back to the warband. Ulfilas and Fram followed. Ulfilas looked back over his shoulder, saw the surprise on Corban's face as Fram rode away, then saw his expression change as the fourth member of their party slid from his horse and dropped his cloak.

This will most likely be over before we are back amongst our warband.

It was Sumur.

CHAPTER EIGHTY

CORBAN

For a heartbeat Corban froze, numb, shocked, then a jolt of fear hit him.

Sumur. Kadoshim.

I'm going to die.

I should have listened to Gar and Meical and not accepted Jael's challenge. Gar had insisted on accepting the duel, said that he was Corban's champion, that he had stood guard over him since birth, and it wasn't going to change now.

You can do much for me, Gar, but you cannot be me. Jael is right, I am Elyon's champion, no other. Gar had just stood there, looking into Corban's eyes, his face twitching with frustration.

Meical had grabbed Corban, ordered him not to go, and then when it became clear that wasn't going to work, almost begged. It was the most emotion Corban had ever seen from the Ben-Elim.

But I had no choice. How could I let so many die when I could have done something to stop it?

You tell me I am the Bright Star, Corban had said as Meical had gripped his arm. *I must do this.* Meical had regarded him with sad eyes, then nodded and let go.

As those behind him recognized who he faced they broke out with shouting and cursing. He recognized Gar's voice, Dath's swearing. Could imagine the look of fear on Cywen's face.

I have to put it out of my mind, he told himself. *If I want to last more than a few heartbeats I must put everything out of my mind except his sword.*

'Surprised?' Sumur said, having crossed over half the distance to Corban, only twenty or thirty paces separating them now.

'A little,' Corban muttered, taking a few steps backwards as Sumur strode towards him, inevitable as time.

It seems the Kadoshim have learned a little humour since they entered this world.

'I am going to carve out your heart and eat it,' Sumur said, the gap closing between them.

Now that's not so funny.

'Are you Sumur, or something else?'

'Sumur is still in here,' the Kadoshim said, walking closer, his black eyes boring into Corban. 'All of his knowledge, his skill, the instinctive responses of his body.' He rolled his wrist as he approached Corban, his blade twirling a slow circle. Corban recognized the movement, remembered seeing him do the same thing back in Dun Carreg, when Gar had faced Sumur, trying to purchase Corban time to escape.

Strange – the body and movement is Sumur's, but the voice is someone else's. Not someone, something. And if Gar couldn't beat him, how in the Otherworld can I?

'But Sumur does not rule in here, any more.' The Kadoshim put fingertips to heart and head. 'I am Belial, captain of Asroth.'

'I think I'll just stick with Sumur,' Corban said, shuffling back another few paces.

Sumur shrugged and continued striding forwards. 'Will you run from me?' he asked, his head cocked to one side. 'I can smell your fear.'

He is not trying to goad me, is just speaking the truth.

'All men feel fear,' Corban snarled and surged forwards.

Partly he was just sick of running and wanted to fight, but there was more to his attack than simply a knee-jerk anger. He had half-hoped to catch Sumur by surprise, maybe have half a heartbeat within which to find an opening.

That did not happen.

Corban's first strike was a two-handed chop at the head, using all his strength, from feet and ankles, through legs into his back, shoulders and arms.

Sumur met the blow easily, almost lazily shrugging it off. Corban's second, third and fourth blows – a combination that he was sure Gar would have stopped and applauded him for – all met with hard iron. He did manage to stop Sumur's advance, though, the Kadoshim planting his feet and gripping his blade two-handed. Corban swirled around him, one blow merging into the next, trying to move onto Sumur's left side.

Then, without any warning, no visible tell that Corban spotted, Sumur was pushing forwards, almost opening Corban's throat with his first blow, the blade-tip scraping off Corban's torc, the second strike glancing off his mail-covered shoulder, the third met with Corban's blade, the fourth deflected by the iron strips in Corban's bracer, the sixth avoided by a leap as Sumur tried to cut his feet from under him. Three more blows came at Corban's head in sharp succession, each one powerful enough to take his head off if not deflected. Corban rolled and rotated his wrists, elbows, shoulders, shifted his weight, sending the blows slipping a finger's width wide of his head each time.

It is like fighting a giant, his strength is incredible.

Sumur's blade came at him faster and faster, the strength building with each blow; the Kadoshim starting to move in circles about him, halting Corban's steady retreat back to the gates of Drassil.

Instinct overcame Corban's fear then, his mind shrinking to the man and blade before him, reading the shift of his feet, the contraction and extension of muscle, the tilt and bunching of balance. At first it was enough that he managed to block each blow, but slowly his body began working faster than thought, the constant drills of Gar and the sword dance flowing through his limbs without conscious direction, and he began to counter Sumur's blows. First one in three or four, then every other blow against him and he was striking back.

They exchanged another flurry of blows, Corban using every form within the sword dance, and while he managed to push Sumur back a dozen steps and defend against his attacks, he could not break through the Kadoshim's guard.

They parted, Corban breathing heavily, muscles and tendons strained and screaming for respite, bruises throbbing beneath his mail shirt where blows had sneaked through his guard, blood trickling down one leg from a shallow cut above his knee. Sumur was unmarked but looked . . . irritated.

I'm still alive, Corban thought. It came as quite a shock to him.

He knows the sword dance as if he were it, can strike with every conceivable combination, can counter the same. If that is all I can meet him with I am going to die – sooner or later I will tire, will slow down, and his strength and stamina are not changing. If anything his strength is growing with his anger. A memory flashed through his mind, of Gar standing over Akar in the weapons court.

'What's the matter?' Corban breathed with a forced grin. 'Can't you kill me?'

Sumur snarled at that, powered in at him, blows coming from every angle. Corban blocked them all, just, then forced his body to change course, stepped in instead of obeying instinct and swirling away. He headbutted Sumur full on the bridge of the nose, punched his sword hilt into Sumur's face as he staggered back a step, slammed his wolven-claws into the man's belly, punching through chainmail links deep into soft flesh, ripping the claws free as he swept away.

Thank you, Coralen.

Sumur paused, looked at him with his head cocked to one side, dark drops of blood smearing his lips, dripping from his mouth. He did not seem to notice the wound in his belly, even though blood was dripping, pooling about his feet.

I have to take his head. I can hardly touch him, and when I do, I deal a blow that would kill any other man and he does not even notice it.

The uselessness and frustration of it threatened to overwhelm him.

No. Gar's words from a million training sessions came back to him, ordering him on. *I endure. I try again.*

'Surprised?' Corban said. 'Perhaps I'll get to add your head to those of your kin that are decorating Drassil's gate.' He gestured behind him towards Drassil and then followed in before Sumur could respond. Their blades rang, a concussive, harsh rhythm, echoing off Drassil's walls.

Abruptly pain ignited along Corban's thigh, a line of burning fire, a downwards glimpse showing him a red line, bleeding heavily, soaking into his breeches. Sumur spun out of reach, Corban blocking a backswing with his wolven claws, taking too much of the power from Sumur's blow, a pain stabbing through his wrist.

This is how the end comes. The slow creep of a myriad small wounds, blood draining away, muscles bruised, worn, weary, tendons stretched too far, too many times, exhaustion squeezing in upon your mind and body, all combining to slow you by a heartbeat for that one fatal blow.

No, he screamed at himself.

Sumur smiled at him. 'Your heart, I can almost taste it.' He licked his lips.

If I'm going to die I'll make a song of it, at least. Don't want Tukul waiting for me on the bridge of swords without a smile on his face.

He hefted his sword, taking the weight in one hand, striking like a smith at the forge with both arms, blade and claw, on his fifth or sixth stroke he felt his blade slam into Sumur's chainmail, caught Sumur's sword between the blades of his claw, punched him in the mouth, pulled away, pivoted on a heel, taking two blows in quick succession upon the shield across his back, as he spun, catching fragmented glimpses of the world around him – men in red cloaks, silent and staring, a horse stamping a hoof – as he came out of the spin swinging his sword low at Sumur's calf, Sumur jumping over it, Corban using the brief moment Sumur was weightless to step in close, hook his foot behind Sumur's ankle as he landed and push with all his strength against the Kadoshim's chest, sending him crashing to the ground. Corban swept forwards, his sword rising and chopping down, into the churned dirt as Sumur rolled away, rising smoothly to his feet. Corban could hardly breathe, the exertion of that last attack draining him of all energy and will. He stood staring at Sumur, leaning on his sword, tip buried in the ground, heart thumping in his chest, mouth hanging open as he sucked in great lungfuls of air.

He is too good, too fast, too strong. They call me Elyon's champion? Where is he now?

Sumur walked towards him. His left arm and shoulder were hanging oddly, his clavicle was clearly broken, but it did not alter his movement, the pain not even registering upon the Kadoshim's face.

'You've done well,' Sumur said, his voice a demonic rasp, 'better than I'd ever have imagined, but the end is, has always been, inevitable.' Corban saw the coiling of muscle in his legs, the bunching of tendons in his wrist as Sumur prepared for the death lunge and knew exactly what the once-Jehar was going to do; he also understood that he could not stop him. At the same time he remembered another duel, one he'd watched so long ago, in a feast-hall on Mid-winter's Eve.

Tull.

As Sumur moved, so did he, flicking his wrist to spray dirt from his blade-tip into Sumur's face, blinding him for a moment. Sumur took a step back, raising his sword in front of him to defend against the blow that he presumed would come at his head, at the same time Corban spun in a circle to his right. He came out of his spin to Sumur's left, ending up almost behind the Kadoshim, Corban's sword chopping into the back of Sumur's neck, landing perfectly at the spot where the skull ends and the back and shoulders begin.

There was the wet sound of an axe splitting damp wood and Sumur's head flew through the air, a trail of dark blood arcing in its wake. The body collapsed, feet twitching, and a great black mist poured from the open wound, forming into a winged creature above the corpse.

Corban stood, feet planted wide, chest heaving, not quite believing what had just happened. What he had just done. Then he noticed the silence, heightened all the more by the thump and roll of Sumur's head as it hit the ground and came to a rolling stop.

The winged shadow above Sumur's corpse screeched in fury, its wings appearing to beat in a attempt to reach him, then the wind was tearing at it and in moments it became a tattered, shredded banner, and then, nothing – less than a sigh upon the air.

Corban looked up, saw Jael staring open-mouthed, behind him his warband, every last one of them silent in disbelief. Then he heard a roar from the walls of Drassil, rolling down to him like a great cascading wave, engulfing him, the sheer shock and joy of the moment making him grin. He punched his sword into the air and added his voice, exulting in his victory.

As the cheering died down Corban walked to Sumur's severed head, reached down and held it high by its hair.

'Keep your word, Jael,' Corban yelled. 'Your champion is defeated. Go back to Isiltir.'

Jael stared at him, something between awe, fear and rage flitting across his features, then he snapped a command to the mounted warriors around him. They looked at him, seeming to hesitate, but Corban guessed what was going to happen. Jael barked his command again and first one warrior kicked his horse and snapped his reins, then another and another, until a score of them were riding towards him.

Corban looked back at the gates of Drassil, knew he'd never make it in time, so he set his feet and held his sword high with two hands.

'Come on, then,' he said. And then, louder, he bellowed, 'TRUTH AND COURAGE,' more rage spilling from his voice than he knew he felt.

The enemy hooves pounded towards him, warriors bent low over their saddles, spears and swords pointing his way. The ground trembled. Dimly he recognized the sound of Drassil's gates opening, heard the enraged, frantic yells of warriors as they raced from the gates to his aid.

You will be too late, he thought calmly. *Go back.*

He concentrated on the closest rider, no more than two hundred paces away now, two score heartbeats, maybe less, focused on the rhythm of the hooves, the rise and dip of the spearhead in the warrior's fist. A part of his mind registered that it was one of the warriors who had ridden out with Jael, not the one with the banner, but the one he had thought was Jael's champion.

Strangely, out of nowhere, he remembered Coralen's kiss in the doorway to his chamber, could almost taste a hint of apple.

I wish I could see her one more time, if only to tell her . . .

A new sound had crept into his awareness, the rumble of hooves from behind him, closer than those in front, and mixed with it the thump of something else, something as familiar to him as his own heartbeat.

The sound of wolven paws.

As if to confirm it, he saw fear spread across the face of the closest rider bearing down upon him.

He looked back, saw Storm pounding towards him, her fangs bared, muscles rippling with each bound of her powerful legs, and beside her Shield, his mane whipped by the wind, hooves a hammer blow, the two of them matching pace. Behind them a swarm of warriors were pouring from the gates of Drassil, Balur and the Benothi forging ahead of them.

Before him the riders were closing, a score of warriors intent upon his death.

Then he knew what he had to do.

He sheathed his sword and turned his back on the enemy riders, took a deep breath, focused on Shield's hooves, the rhythm of his gallop, and he set his feet as the stallion approached. He bent his knees, went onto the balls of his feet, began to move, to run and then Storm and Shield were almost upon him, Shield a mountain of muscle and mane so close he could smell him, see the sweat streaks in his coat, and he broke from a run into a sprint, Storm pounding past him, both Corban and Storm's muscles bunching, leaping at the same time, Corban's heart thumping in time with the pounding of Shield's hooves. He reached out, grabbed a fistful of the stallion's mane, and used the horse's momentum to hurl himself into the air.

There was a heartbeat that felt like an eternity as he was weightless, flying, legs scissoring, then, with a solid *thump* he was in the saddle, hands reaching for the reins and Shield was angling away, pounding through a gap in the approaching riders and then he was free, galloping across open space along the front of Jael's warband, wind whipping his black hair out behind him like a banner.

Some of Jael's warband were actually cheering him.

Behind him the sound of screams rose up as Storm tore her target from his saddle and ripped him apart.

He guided Shield in a loop, slowing to a canter, glimpsed Storm leaping and snapping amidst the riders sent to kill him, saw spears rising and falling and felt a hot rage bubble up. From Drassil warriors were still pouring, Jehar on horseback amongst them, hundreds charging across the open space. Horns were blaring along the lines of Jael's warband and suddenly they were lurching into movement, stuttering forwards.

The plan was to stay atop the battlements, let their warband break upon the walls of Drassil. Guess we'll need a new plan.

He heard Storm growling and snapping, saw horses rearing and plunging around her.

With a snarl he drew his sword and urged Shield back to a gallop.

CHAPTER EIGHTY-ONE

ULFILAS

I have a bad feeling about this.

'Charge them, charge them, *kill them*!' Jael was screeching close to Ulfilas' ear.

The warband was moving, but sluggishly.

They are still reeling from what we have just witnessed. And in truth I do not blame them for being hesitant about joining battle with these people.

Ulfilas was still coming to terms with what he'd seen.

The greatest duel between two men that I have ever witnessed – maybe that has ever happened. I cannot believe that Sumur lost. It had been like witnessing two storms collide at sea, a maelstrom of furious, deadly movement, utterly beautiful to watch. At first it had seemed an inevitability that Corban would die – he was an exceptional warrior, clearly, but Sumur had seemed too perfect, too clinical, too fast and powerful, but then, slowly, almost by sheer, dogged will and determination, Corban had edged back into the fight, gone from just trying to stay alive for a few moments longer to having a slim chance, and finally, mostly by a combination of heart and wits and a general stubborn refusal to die, had taken Sumur's head.

And what the hell was that thing that came out of Sumur?

'What are you DOING?' Jael was screaming at him, almost apoplectic with rage. 'Lead the warband forward; you are my bannerman.'

Don't you think you should be leading them? You're our King.

Ulfilas ignored the sense of foreboding growing in his belly, grunted at Jael and kicked his horse forwards, warriors on foot behind him lurching after him. Horns were blaring. The score of riders that Jael had set upon Corban were dead or dying, that wolven the size of a horse ripping half of them to pieces and still running amok just a few hundred paces ahead.

And the first man that beast tore apart was Fram, Jael's first-sword; after Sumur, that is. So that's his two finest warriors down before the battle is even joined. Not the most inspirational of starts.

Ulfilas was rapidly losing heart for this conflict, but a voice in his head was shouting at him that to turn and run would be the end of him. *And that's true enough, I don't doubt. If we are broken here any that survive the battle will then have to survive the long march through Forn. Don't fancy that much, so we'd better get on and win this battle.*

The men of Isiltir were responding to the horn blasts and Jael's screams urging them on, sweeping forward and curling in upon the lesser numbers that had swarmed out from the open gates of Drassil.

That at least is a stroke of good fortune. At least they are coming out here to fight so we don't have to try and climb those walls. Our numbers may still win the day.

Ulfilas felt a warrior's respect for Corban, even if he was his enemy. That running mount had been a thing of beauty, undertaken with sharp iron bearing down upon him, mere heartbeats separating him between life and death. It was as if the running mount had been distilled into that one moment, learned and practised by every warrior in every realm throughout their youth for that exact purpose.

Warriors on foot swept past him, running into the battle, the score of Jehar the same as Sumur, which gave Ulfilas a flare of hope – *all of a sudden I'm wishing Nathair had forced a hundred of them upon us, like he did on Gundul and Lothar.*

He saw the Jehar slam into a knot of enemy warriors only fifty paces ahead of him, a mixture of giants and men who looked remarkably similar to the Jehar that were with him, except that they wore surcoats with the white star blazing upon their chests.

Ulfilas had a sudden memory of the warriors at Gramm's hold who had cut him and his riders down so easily. Instinctively he pulled on his reins, but the press of men behind him was too great and he was forced on.

I am no coward, but I am no fool either, and I have no death-wish upon me.

He saw that he was about to enter this battle whether he wanted to or not. He slipped Jael's banner into the leather cup on his saddle that usually held his spear, drew his sword and kicked his horse on, choosing a warrior who looked like one out of Gramm's hold.

Someone normal to fight.

His horse's shoulder ploughed into the man, sending him reeling, Ulfilas' sword rising and falling, crunching into the warrior's helm, dropping him instantly.

He kicked his horse on, swinging left and right with his blade, leaving a wake of bloody wounds and dying men. He started to think that they could still win this battle, though all was chaos and blood around him. It was almost impossible to tell how the battle was faring. He hacked at a spear jabbing at him, snapped the shaft, stabbed into the face of the warrior wielding it, heard a scream, saw the man go down, and dug his heels into his horse.

For a moment there was a lull around him. To his left he saw Corban, still upon his horse, hacking at men of Isiltir with maniacal energy; close to him there was a flash of white fur and fangs, and about the young warrior a knot of fighters gathered to protect him – a huge man with a war-hammer, a red-haired woman with wolven claws like Corban's, dripping with gore, and one of the Jehar mounted and trailing arcs of blood with his sword – he looked remarkably like the warrior who had unhorsed Ulfilas at Gramm's hold, only younger and more battle-frenzied.

Not going that way, then.

He yanked upon his reins and suddenly there was one of the Jehar in front of him – one of his Jehar – fighting a silver-haired giant with one eye and a black axe. The Jehar was fast, darting in and cutting at the giant's leg, eliciting a howl of pain or rage, but then a huge knife smashed into the Jehar's chest, hurling it from its feet. The injured giant lumbered forwards and swung his axe, taking the Jehar's head off as it tried to rise, and then there was a screeching shadow-demon materializing in the air right in front of Ulfilas, his horse screaming and rearing. He managed to control his mount, saw another giant striding forwards, smaller, slimmer – *female? It's so hard to tell the difference* – but still clearly a giant, two belts crisscrossing her chest with an abundance of those oversized knives sheathed in them. As Ulfilas watched, she bent down and recovered her knife from the chest of the decapitated Jehar and then looked about for a new target.

Her eyes settled upon him.

The bad feeling that Ulfilas had ignored reared up now, a flare of fear and foreboding, and he ducked low in his saddle as the air whistled over his head and something sharp missed him by a hand-span. He kicked his horse on. It was well trained and it stepped agilely to the left and leaped away, sending those about it reeling, friend and foe alike. For a handful of insane moments the horse rose and fell, forging its way through the battle like a leviathan through stormy seas, then it burst into clearer ground.

Battle still raged here, but it was islands of violence upon the plains surrounding Drassil, rather than a constant sea. Everywhere Ulfilas looked the red-cloaked men of Isiltir were falling to giants and to sword-wielding Jehar. He saw a tall dark-haired warrior in blood-spattered mail, at first thought him a giant, but then realized he was a little too short, and too slim and elegant, too graceful in his death dealing. Even as Ulfilas watched, this warrior cut down three men of Isiltir in as many breaths.

Further away he saw more of those shadow-demons appearing in the air, hovering like a dense mist as they screamed their rage and then drifting apart in the wind. He knew by now that their appearance marked the death of one of Nathair's Jehar.

Whatever they are – and I'm not sure I want to know – I do know that this battle is lost.

Always the pragmatic man, Ulfilas looked to the north, saw the remnants of the old road they had followed here. The prospect of fleeing through Forn was becoming more appealing with every red-cloaked death around him.

Run, live a little longer; stay and die very soon.

It wasn't much of a choice.

He lifted the banner of Isiltir from its harness on his saddle and dropped it to the ground, then spurred his horse to the north, moving at a trot, calling men to him as he went. Within a hundred paces he had close to two hundred men following him, then another hundred. He reined in as the land began to rise and looked back over the battlefield.

The warband of Isiltir was breaking apart, men beginning to

turn and run, heading towards the perceived safety of the trees of Forn. Soon it would become a rout. He glimpsed Jael on the far side of the conflict, still in his saddle, a knot of warriors about him as he moved steadily southwards towards the treeline.

Looks as if he has the same idea as me.

With a shake of his head Ulfilas spurred his mount up the slope, towards the trees.

Then the ground in front of him exploded.

Fifty paces or so up the slope turf and dirt erupted into the air, beneath it something dark and round emerging from the ground.

Ulfilas swayed in his saddle, jerked away, then realized what it was.

A huge trapdoor.

Men and women with long bows in their hands – ten, twenty, thirty, more – were surging out of the ground. Even as Ulfilas stared in frozen shock they formed a line, drew arrows from quivers, nocked, drew and released. Straight at him and the warriors about him.

He threw himself backwards, out of his saddle, heard the soft *thunk* of arrows sinking into flesh, his horse rearing and crashing to the ground, legs kicking, all about him men falling with feathered shafts buried in their flesh.

Ulfilas thrashed on the ground, one foot caught in a stirrup, flicked it free, rose to one knee in time to see the archers drawing and shooting again. He threw himself flat on his face, heard more screaming around him, dragged himself upright and stared frantically around.

The men who had followed him were wavering, though they still outnumbered the archers at least three or four to one.

Those archers stand between me and freedom. A good charge should see to them, Ulfilas thought, dragging his sword from his scabbard, waving it in the air, yelling to his warriors. He took a few steps forward, heard the boots of men following behind him, saw the archers in front snatching for arrows, saw panic stirring in some. He singled out one in the centre of the line, slim, small, resolutely drawing another arrow from his quiver, something about him saying that he was the leader of these archers.

I'm going to take your head, Ulfilas thought, the need to kill, to vent his frustration at this most disastrous of days rearing up within him. He started to run.

Then someone else climbed out of the hole, a lone Jehar warrior, small, a woman. She saw him charging at the archer and her eyes narrowed. She drew her sword. Behind her more men were appearing from the hole in the ground, men clothed in leather and fur holding single-bladed axes in their fists.

Gramm's men.

Twenty or thirty of them as well, forming a line and throwing their axes. Ulfilas threw himself to the ground again, a mouth full of dirt, a body crashing down beside him, face a bloody ruin with an axe-haft poking from it.

As Ulfilas looked up he saw the axe men start to run down the slope, pulling fresh axes from their backs, and behind them another wave of warriors pouring from the hole, these dressed strangely, scraps of leather armour wrapped around forearms and shoulders, most of them carrying bucklers and short swords or knives.

Bollocks to this.

Ever the pragmatist, Ulfilas scrambled to his feet and ran the other way.

Something thudded into his back, a hard punch that sent him sprawling and knocked the air from his lungs. He tried to push himself up but found his arms weren't working as well as they should, felt a dull ache in his back, a tingling numbness. He managed to get his right elbow under him, push up, but his left arm wasn't doing what it was told.

Must get up. To stay is to die.

He coughed, saw blood speckle the ground close to his face.

What?

Then there was a pressure upon his back – *someone's boot?* – an unpleasant tugging sensation, closely followed by a wet ripping sound. The pressure on his back disappeared, replaced by a tingling pain, a boot slipping under his chest and flipping him over.

He gasped, looked up into a bearded face.

'Well, well,' the face said, 'I was hoping I'd run into you.'

It was Wulf, and he was smiling.

He was holding an axe in his fist, blood dripping from its edge. He raised it high, above his head, and Ulfilas screamed.

CHAPTER EIGHTY-TWO

HAELAN

Haelan watched the battle from the walls of Drassil.

It had been Swain's idea, but Haelan had not been difficult to persuade. He felt proud that Corban had asked him to watch over Storm's cubs, but as the horns rang out from Drassil's walls, announcing the arrival of Jael's warband, he had felt a desperate need just to see. So when Swain suggested a way of him doing both of those tasks. Well . . .

So here they were, Haelan, Swain and Sif, standing upon a deserted patch of the western wall, each of them with a wolven cub under either arm, Pots was sitting at his feet, looking up at him like he felt a little left out. They'd put the cubs in a wide, deep basket of willow, the three of them carrying it all the way to the battlements. The cubs had become restless, though, so they'd decided to get them out for a while and let them watch the battle too.

They liked it, or at least seemed to, they were quiet enough.

Haelan was finding it hard to breathe, at various moments had felt that his heart was lurching out of his chest, that despair would overwhelm him, closely followed by sheer joy that he was sure would cause him to explode.

They'd reached the wall just as Corban had begun his duel with the black-clothed warrior, one of the Jehar obviously. Within moments Haelan was certain that Corban was going to die. Tears had blurred his eyes long before the end, and then he had cried fresh tears, these ones of joy when Corban had sent his enemy's head spinning through the air.

And then such treachery, Jael setting his shieldmen to ride Corban down, after what he had just survived, just achieved.

And then the running mount.

When he saw Shield and Storm pounding across the open space he had cheered, screamed, exhorted them to greater speed, the voices of Swain and Sif mingling with his own.

If there had been any doubt in Haelan's mind that Corban was the greatest hero the Banished Lands had ever known, that succession of events had confirmed it beyond all question. He'd fight anyone who dared to say differently.

And now the whole plain along the western wall boiled with battle.

'We're going to win,' Swain was yelling, putting his two cubs back in the basket and leaping up and down.

Of course we are.

After Corban's duel and escape from Jael's shieldman, it seemed that victory was inevitable. He was only worried now about who might fall along the way.

Tahir is down there, fighting for me.

His eyes scanned the field, but it was so hard to make out individuals amongst the press and heave of battle. Giants were easy enough to follow, Balur One-Eye particularly, with his silver hair and black axe, swathes of blood consistently bursting around him, from this distance looking like droplets of dew on morning grass. And Corban he could see, still mounted, with Storm always close to him, leaping and tearing.

The cubs under his arms began to squirm so he put them back in the basket, stroking his favourite, a brindle bitch with a face as black as night.

He saw Jael's banner flying in the centre of the battle, then it moved steadily northwards, a single rider breaking out from the heart of the battle, a steady motion towards the northern flank. Then the banner disappeared, the rider still visible, heading further and further out, men of Isiltir gathering in a great mass about him.

They are fleeing. Hope swelled in his chest, something telling him that the battle was coming to its last stages now.

Then he saw Jael, his white horsehair plume blowing in the wind, still upon his horse, a knot of warriors with him. They headed steadily towards the southern edge of the battlefield, reached the treeline, then stopped as a handful of giants stormed through them.

Haelan gripped the battlement walls, knuckles whitening, praying, begging for Jael to fall. All was confusion, flesh and iron and blood merging in a chaotic explosion for a dozen heartbeats. A giant fell, of that Haelan was sure, and then figures were disappearing into the trees. Jael was nowhere to be seen.

From Haelan's vantage-point it looked as if the whole battlefield paused for a moment, then rippled, like the death-spasm of a dying animal.

The trickle of those fleeing turned into a flood now, red-cloaks falling away from the mass of combat in tens and twenties, and then they were all fleeing, the warband of Drassil following, slaying with impunity.

Then a sudden thought struck Haelan.

Those men fleeing are men of Isiltir. My people.

'Watch the cubs,' he blurted to Swain and Sif, 'and don't let Pots follow me.' And he was running down the wall's stairwell, leaping steps two at a time.

In the courtyard before the main gates he climbed into the saddle of a fully tacked horse. It was a little big for him, the stirrups too long, but it was the most suitable of what was left and he was a good rider, had been sat in a saddle as far back as he could remember. Without any more thought he clicked his tongue and rode out through the gates.

It was a different world down here, the battle from above seeming to have something serene about it, playing out like the swirls of sea and sand as the tide comes in. Down here it was loud, filled with the screams of the dying and the yelling of the living, and it stank, of blood and metal and excrement. Everywhere was chaos. He scanned the field for Corban, could see men of Isiltir fleeing, giants striding amongst them wielding their axes and hammers, then he caught a flash of bone-white fur and headed for it.

Before he'd covered a hundred paces he heard running to one side, felt a flash of fear. *I am part of the reason Jael came here, led a warband of thousands through Forn Forest with the goal of seeing me dead.*

'What are you doing down here, laddie?' a voice called out, and relief swept him.

Tahir.

Relief at both Tahir being alive and the fact that it was not a warrior coming to separate his head from his shoulders.

'I've an idea,' Haelan said, 'and I need to find Corban.'

Tahir looked at him, was clearly wrestling with the idea of marching him straight back to the safety of Drassil.

'All right then. Shift along then, and I'll climb up there with you.'

They found Corban drinking from a water skin, drenched in blood, his hair plastered to his head. A handful of people were gathered around him, Gar and Meical, Coralen and Farrell and Laith, as well as Balur One-Eye and Ethlinn. And of course Storm.

The battle had moved away from them, or rather the chasing of the broken and fleeing warband, only here and there the sound of iron marking real combat, a few knots of men fighting rearguard actions and retreating in a more orderly fashion.

'Little one's got something to say to you,' Tahir said as they rode up.

Haelan looked at the fierce bloodstained faces around him and quailed a little. He swallowed his fears, knowing what needed to be said.

'These are my people,' Haelan told them. 'Jael is fled, I think, or maybe dead. I saw him from the battlements, over there.' He pointed south to the trees. 'The rest of them, they might stop if I ask them, if they are offered mercy.'

'Mercy?' growled Farrell.

'Yes, mercy,' Haelan said, holding his chin high. He looked at Corban. 'Some of them, many of them, were just following the orders of their King, yet still they cheered you . . .'

Corban looked back at him, dark eyes thoughtful, and behind that Haelan saw a well of exhaustion that Corban held in check.

'You're right,' he said. 'No need to go on killing. It's just how exactly we're going to do this.'

Haelan dangled in the air, Balur One-Eye holding him up high over his head, like a human banner. On one side of him rode Tahir, on the other Corban. Balur was calling out in a booming voice, proclaiming Haelan King of Isiltir and pronouncing mercy upon all those who would lay down their arms.

Over seven hundred men surrendered.

'Well,' Farrell said to Corban and Haelan when they were gathered before the gates of Drassil, 'I would imagine that it's rare to end a battle with more men than you started with.'

'Aye. I think it's safe to say we can call this a victory, then,' Corban said.

'That we can, Ban, that we can,' Gar said with a weary smile.

Just then a group of men and women approached from the northern end of the battlefield – Dath and his archers, as well as Wulf with his axe-throwers and Javed and his pit-fighters. Wulf held up a severed head as he drew near, and threw it at Corban's feet.

'Ulfilas,' he said. 'Jael's high captain, and the man that killed my da.'

'I am glad for you,' Corban said wearily. 'A day where much justice has been done, and injustices set right.'

'Aye,' murmured many voices around them.

Haelan noticed that Dath was looking up at Corban, the widest smile upon his face. One of the Jehar stood close to him, a small, pretty young woman, or so Haelan thought. She was smiling too.

'What are you smiling about?' Corban asked Dath.

'I'm getting married,' Dath said, his grin growing even wider.

CHAPTER EIGHTY-THREE

CAMLIN

Camlin sat and waited.

Feels as if I've spent half my life waiting for men to kill. Not sure which part is the worst. The waiting, or the killing.

Depends on who I'm waiting around to kill, I suppose.

He was sitting upon a raised knoll amidst a thick bank of reeds, a space flattened at its centre for him. From here he could peer out through the reeds and have a commanding view of the surrounding area, watching over a dozen streams and rivers that fed from the lake, flowing in the direction that he reckoned Evnis and his warband would come. Looking the other way he saw the lake, the village that had grown up along its banks deserted now, still and silent apart from the odd chicken. A moorhen pecked about in what had once been a fire-pit, claiming it for her own. At the heart of the lake Dun Crin reared from its still, black waters. If Camlin stared hard enough he could make out warriors along its ancient walls, standing in the shadows of its crumbling towers.

The sky above was a pale blue, a fresh wind welcome in this stagnant place, and bringing with it the scent of spring.

Least the bad weather's broken. Waiting's always better without the rain and snow.

He heard footsteps close by, peered through the reeds to see Edana's fair hair, Roisin, Lorcan and Pendathran with her, their shieldmen as well – Halion and Vonn, Cian and Brogan. He pushed through the reeds to join them.

'All's ready, then?'

'Ready as we'll ever be,' Pendathran said. 'You up to this?' the big general asked Camlin.

'Course,' Camlin grunted.

'Of course he is,' Edana snapped.

'Aye, you've proved yourself, that's for sure,' Pendathran growled. 'Don't mind me, I just get nervous before a fight, that's all.'

'Surely not you,' Roisin said, a purr in her voice that Camlin didn't like.

'So do I,' Edana said, eyes scanning the marshes with its countless streams and rivers and hidden approaches.

Don't we all? Camlin thought. *I've been in a hundred scrapes, more, probably, and my mouth still goes dry and my palms sweaty 'fore a fight.*

'It's the prospect of death,' he said matter-of-factly. 'No matter how many battles you live through, doesn't mean you'll see the end of the next one.'

They were all silent at that.

'Indeed, well, on that cheerful note,' Roisin said.

There was a flapping from above and a black speck dropped out of the sky.

'*Men, boats, spears,*' the crow squawked, alighting in the branches of a willow. They all stared at him.

I'm glad Edana talked him into sticking around, now.

'*CLOSE,*' Craf squawked, giving his wings an extra flap to emphasize his point, making them all jump, even Pendathran, who swore.

'This is it, then,' Edana said, looking at them all. 'You all know what to do.'

'Aye,' Pendathran said. He looked in their eyes, then grinned.

'For Ardan and Domhain, for kin and friends, for our Queens.'

They parted, Camlin walking back to his bank of reeds.

'Camlin,' a voice called after him, Halion striding after him. 'I'll see you again,' the warrior said. He held his arm out and Camlin took it in the warrior grip.

'Aye, brother,' Camlin said. 'This side or the other.'

Again, the waiting.

Camlin checked his bow, his string, lifted his blade in its scabbard to check it wasn't sticking, let it slide back with a *click*. Checked his arrows, the tips wrapped with foul-smelling linen. Flint and a pile of tinder and kindling set neatly to one side, not damp, not spoiled.

Good.

The reeds rustled and a head poked through them, scruffy red hair and a dirty face.

'Hello, Meg,' Camlin said. 'You shouldn't be wandering around at a time like this.' There was no force in his reprimand, though – he'd learned by now that the girl would damn well do as she pleased, no matter what he said about it.

'Don't need to worry about me,' she said.

He frowned. 'You happy with what you've got to do?'

Camlin had adopted a new strategy with Meg. He'd learned that if he kept her out of things in an effort to keep her safe she'd just follow him and get involved anyway. So now he was finding tasks for her to do, even in the most dangerous of situations. That was what he had done with the hunt for Braith.

And thank the stars it turned out about as well as it could.

Every night he put his head on his pillow he felt a sense of relief that Braith was no longer out there, hunting him.

'I am,' she said. 'I just came to see that you were all right.' She looked at him intently, then smiled. 'And you are.' With that she spun around and disappeared into the reeds.

Strange child. P'raps that's why she fits in so well around us. Around me.

Then he heard the creak of wooden boats, weight shifting within them, the sound of oars and paddles in water, quite but not silent.

Here we go, then.

CHAPTER EIGHTY-FOUR

EVNIS

Evnis sat at the head of his boat and blinked as the lake opened up before him. Beside him Glyn swore.

Whoever would have thought that such a place existed?

The lake was vast, its waters dark and still, and at its centre stone walls and towers reared, as if the lake were a black field about a broken fortress. Except that green algae and creeping vines grew upon this fortress, silent, sinuous things swirling in the waters about the walls. Birds clustered upon crumbling towers, taking flight and squawking their protests at the arrival of Evnis and his warband.

Rafe was in the first boat leading the way, his two grey hounds sitting in it as still as stone, like figureheads. Warriors behind Evnis rowed them deeper into the lake, more boats following, others filtering from a series of streams and rivers along the north-eastern bank of the lake. Before half of them had emerged from the marshland streams a boat appeared from between two towers that loomed out of the lake. It rowed towards them.

'Hold,' Evnis said, raising a hand, his men backing water, the motion continuing through the boats behind him.

The lone boat rowed closer, four or five figures within it, the first with long fair hair.

Surely not . . .

Oars backed water and the boat stopped, drifting for a moment until it was side-on to Evnis' boat, maybe fifty paces away. Half of Evnis' fleet were spread behind him, the other half still backed up in the streams and rivers.

Edana stood in her boat. Evnis smiled to see her. She was dressed plainly, looking more like a woodsman than a queen, in woollen breeches, a linen shirt and black leather vest, though she wore the grey cloak of Ardan around her shoulders, something that Evnis hadn't seen for a while. And she wore a sword at her hip.

He almost laughed at that.

'There does not need to be bloodshed here today,' she called out, her voice carrying across the still waters of the lake.

It's unlikely to be our blood, Evnis thought. *Perhaps you mean your own.*

Edana looked at the warriors in their boats, taking her time to meet their eyes. Men behind Evnis fidgeted.

'There are men of Ardan amongst you, true-born warriors of Ardan who fought for my father.'

Aye, there are, and now they fight for me. Most of them have always fought for me.

'Men of Narvon, maybe, Owain's men. And warriors from Domhain, perhaps, who once served Eremon.'

Two figures stood in Edana's boat, one dressed as a warrior, dark-haired, though Evnis could see he was little more than a lad, beside him a woman, tall and dark-haired, her chin lifted proudly.

A rare beauty, Evnis thought.

'This is Roisin of Domhain, wife of Eremon, and her son Lorcan, rightful King of Domhain.'

Excellent. This is most helpful of you, Edana, gathering all of the rats into one boat. You are making my life so much easier.

'You are fighting as pawns for a woman with a black heart, a manipulator, deceiver, a betrayer. Rhin is not a queen; she is a tyrant, a disease that must be cut out.'

Much to his surprise Evnis found himself *listening*, as if Edana actually had something to say. He pulled his eyes away from her, looked at the others in her boat, sitting at the oars. One of them was Halion, the warrior sitting calmly, his eyes scanning the boats behind Evnis. He looked to the other rower and started.

It was Vonn.

His son was staring straight at him.

A long silence passed between them, something unspoken communicated, and then, finally, Evnis nodded to Vonn, a small incline of the head, nothing more. Vonn saw and looked away.

Edana was still talking, something about peace and good men banding together.

'Can someone please kill her,' a voice shouted from behind Evnis.

Morcant, of course.

And I think I should oblige.

Evnis roared an order, oars and paddles splashing into water and they were moving again.

Edana, Roisin and Lorcan were all sitting down in their boat now, Halion and Vonn rowing hard, a sprint for the sunken fortress. From gaps in walls and towers other boats appeared, men in them, but for each boat with people in there was one that they towed by rope, empty. Evnis noticed it but did not have time to think too hard about it. He was closing on Edana.

Then he heard a huge tearing *whooosh* behind him, followed closely by screaming. He twisted around, rocking his boat, to see a wall of flames igniting along the lake shore, crackling through reed banks and somehow spreading across the streams and rivers that they had travelled upon.

How the hell have they done that? We're in a marsh, with more water than land.

Some of his boats were on fire, men jumping overboard, human torches, and separated behind them, on the far side of the flames were roughly half of his warband.

He cursed himself for a fool and set his mind on killing Edana.

CHAPTER EIGHTY-FIVE

CAMLIN

Camlin watched as Meg tugged on a long rope, dragging a rolled mat of dried rushes and reeds across a stream between two boat-loads of warriors.

Camlin touched his arrow-tip into the small fire he had crack-ling, the linen soaked in fish oil catching alight with a hiss. He raised his bow, drew and released, his arrow arcing and dropping into the mat of reeds. That, too, had been doused in fish oil and so the whole thing ignited in a heartbeat, flames roaring, men screaming, leaping from the boat, flames searing the flesh from warriors before and behind it.

Meg appeared at another spot on the bank, alongside the forms of other men hidden in the reeds. Clay pots filled with fish oil flew through the air to smash into boats. Camlin released another flaming arrow and a boat went up in flames. Along the bank other huntsmen fired flaming arrows and more fires were igniting, roaring into the air, more men screaming.

Camlin heard screaming all about him, the same happening on a dozen inlets.

He glanced out to the lake, saw Evnis leading over a score of boats towards Dun Crin, Edana a dot before them. Other boats were appearing from the walls, moving towards Evnis' splintered fleet.

Going to plan, then. That's a pleasant surprise.

Shouts and battle-cries drew his eyes back to the river before him. About a dozen of Edana's warriors were spread along this side of the bank with him, some doing the same as him. Others ran forward as Evnis' men began to reach the banks, some leaping, others swimming, not every boat on fire – some further back were not touched at all.

Damn, but there's a lot of them. Five hundred at least is my guess. Those weren't good odds, as Edana's warband numbered less than two hundred swords.

Mind you, we're evening the odds a little, now.

Spears began to fly, going both ways, and Camlin ducked as one hissed a handspan over his head.

He started aiming at men now, planting flaming arrows in chests, throats, backs, thighs, at least a dozen men falling to his aim before a handful of warriors reached the bank and charged at his clump of reeds.

Time to leave.

He grabbed his quiver of arrows, half-empty now, slung it over his back, waited a few moments as his enemy drew nearer, until he heard them crunching into the reeds, and then he grabbed a clay pot and threw it as he ran the other way, heard it smash down upon the small fire he had set, then the sucking in of air, like an indrawn breath before flames exploded, ripping through the reeds and scorching the onrushing warriors.

More screaming.

He flew out of the reeds, hearing flames rushing up behind him, and hurled himself out onto the lakeshore, rolling amongst abandoned huts. He came to his feet alone, the sounds of battle raging along the various streams and rivers behind him, and more dimly from the drowned fortress in the lake. He took a moment to stare, worry for Edana gnawing at him.

Fires dotted the lake, like bobbing candles on the water.

I bet it's not so pretty right close, though. As he watched, he saw one of the empty boats that they'd packed with jars of fish oil and dried rushes shoved with long poles into an enemy rowing boat, hulls crunching together, a torch thrown in after it. The vessel went up in flames, quickly setting the enemy boat on fire.

More screaming.

Think there's going to be a lot of that today.

Many of Evnis' boats were aflame, and Camlin could see shapes in the water – men swimming for land. Some of Evnis' vessels had made it to Dun Crin's walls and warriors were scrambling onto the cold stone. Camlin heard the clash of iron drifting across the lake.

There were only sixty warriors of Edana's warband on the sunken walls, the other hundred or so ranging the rivers and stream banks, where they'd hoped to contain the bulk of the enemy warband, and where they thought the fiercest fighting would be.

And talking of fighting . . .

Camlin looked between Dun Crin and the lakeshore, decided there was nothing he could do for Edana now except kill those enemies of hers that were closest to him.

He nocked an arrow and ran at a crouch towards the streams, veering around the wall of flames.

He burst into chaos, the world rapidly constricting to a score of paces at most in any direction. The blockade was still burning, but even if it hadn't been, no boats were getting into the lake now, as the first two this side of the firewall were roaring infernos, blocking the stream completely, dark shapes twisted within them. Further along the stream more fires raged. Some of the enemy were splashing in the stream, being skewered like fish with spears by Camlin's companions from solid ground. A few boats had managed to make it to the stream bank and their cargoes of flesh and iron and harmful intentions were unloading rapidly. Fifteen, twenty men, more on another boat behind them. Camlin recognized one dressed in black leather and wool, cloak of sable and a silver helm.

Morcant.

The old first-sword of Rhin led his men along the bank, cutting down two of Edana's warriors before they even realized the enemy were ashore.

Camlin ran to higher ground and started to loose arrows into them, knowing their strength of numbers could still sweep him and his dozen or so warriors from this side of the stream in short order.

Morcant was lost from view for a moment, so Camlin settled for winnowing their numbers.

One warrior spun and fell back into the stream with an arrow through his heart, another collapsing onto the ground, hands around the shaft through his throat. Then men spotted him and changed their direction to cut him off. He released another arrow, saw it punch into a thigh, then he was moving, pushing through a thick curtain of willow branches, circling right, into thicker reeds, pushing on to reappear on the stream bank, but behind the warriors who had been running at him. They were cautiously moving through the willow curtain. He put an arrow into a warrior's back, close enough for its iron head to punch through a leather cuirass and deep into flesh, nocked another, drew and released into a face as the enemy turned, teeth flying as the arrowhead tore through his mouth and into his brain. Then Camlin was running again, his fingertips brushing his quiver as he ran.

Three arrows left.

He weaved through long grass, jumped and squeezed through a coppice of alders, circled slowly around to his left, hoping to do the same thing to his pursuers.

He saw the willow tree he'd ran past earlier and headed for it, cautiously peered through the dangling branches, but could see no enemy warriors. The stream bank was hidden from view here, but the din of battle seemed less, now.

Is it nearly over?

Then something crashed into his back and he was falling, tumbling, his bow spinning from his grip. He rolled to a stop and saw Morcant emerging from the willow branches, grinning, sword in hand.

'I could have killed you then, but I didn't,' Morcant said, the smile still on his face. Other warriors appeared behind him, four, six, seven, more in the shadows.

'I remember you from the Darkwood,' Morcant said, still smiling, 'so thought it would be a shame to stab you in the back.'

'Very noble of you,' Camlin said as he climbed to one knee, his eyes flitting, looking for his bow. Morcant took a step and was beside it, kicked it away.

'Perhaps you should draw your sword,' he said as he advanced on Camlin.

Not that he thought it would do him much good, but Camlin did so, stood and set his feet.

'Excellent,' Morcant said.

His sword blurred, Camlin saw the tip lunge forward, spiralling somehow to curve around his attempted parry to scrape along his ribs. He grunted with pain, retreated, blocked an overhead chop and a slash at his belly, missed the thrust that pierced his thigh. Blood sluiced his leg and he stumbled back, realized that Morcant must have cut muscle as his leg gave way beneath him and he was crashing to the ground.

'Well, that was fun,' Morcant said as he stood over Camlin, sword rising.

Then an arrow punched into the meat of Morcant's arm, making him stagger back a step. He snarled, looked about.

'There,' a small, high-pitched voice cried, 'over there.'

Camlin rolled, concentrating on getting as far out of reach of Morcant's blade as he could, no matter how many arrows the man had poking out of him, caught a glimpse of Meg standing with the half-bow he'd made her, out of boredom more than anything else, certainly not expecting it to save his life one day. Meg was calling to someone behind her, hidden in trees and rushes, then Pendathran's bearded face appeared, blood-spattered and furious, a score of men at his back.

Morcant took one look at Pendathran and fled, his handful of warriors with him.

Boots thundered past Camlin's head as Pendathran charged past him, his men close behind, and then Meg was helping him to stand, tying a ripped piece of cloth around his leg.

'That's two you owe me,' she said with a smile.

'I'll not argue with that, lassie,' he said. 'How are things going out there?' he asked as he retrieved his bow.

'We are winning,' she said. 'In fact, I think we've won. They're mostly all running away, Pendathran, Drust and some of the others chasing them for the fun of it.'

'How about those on the lake?' He was thinking of Edana.

Meg shrugged.

They went to see.

Fires were still blazing out on the lake; along the shore a few of Evnis' men were staggering from the lake, those who had worn leather, not chainmail. Camlin listened and there was no sound of battle drifting over from the fortress. Then he saw two boats rowing for the shore, a little to the south, away from the battle. He and Meg stood in the shadows of an abandoned hut and watched.

The first boat crunched onto the sand, Edana getting out and stumbling off along the bank of a stream, quickly hidden by reed-beds.

The second boat was not far behind, beaching smoothly.

Two warriors climbed out, Cian and Brogan, Cian offering a hand to help Roisin ashore.

She glanced quickly about, then took long strides after Edana, Cian and Brogan following.

So. Camlin nodded to himself, looked at Meg and put a finger to his lips, then followed them.

He caught up with them soon enough, not making a sound even though his leg thumped as if a horse had kicked it and his ribs were on fire where Morcant had cut him. He and Meg stayed within the shadow of trees and watched.

Edana had stopped in a secluded grove by the stream, trees to one side, a thick bed of reeds blocking her way. She was resting a hand on her thigh, bent over the stream, looked as if she'd just vomited.

Roisin entered the glade, paused, then walked closer.

'Edana, are you well?' Roisin asked her.

'No,' Edana said. 'I've just killed a man.' She patted her sword hilt and Camlin saw the blood upon it.

'During difficult times, difficult things must be done,' Roisin said, walking steadily closer to Edana. Camlin noticed her hand rested upon a knife at her belt.

Edana stood straighter at that.

'Indeed,' she said. 'So. I take it you have come to kill me.' It was not a question.

'What?' Roisin spluttered, drawing to a halt. 'Don't be absurd.'

Camlin reached for one of his last arrows.

'Absurd? Maybe. All of this war and hunting and betraying and killing – it can take its toll on trust in the end, can't it?'

'Aye,' Roisin said, voice a whisper.

'I apologize if I have insulted you,' Edana continued. 'Put it down to battle-fatigue.'

'No insult,' Roisin said. 'Rather, a display of your intelligence. In another life we could have been friends, I think. We have much in common. But in this life you are just in my way – too popular, and that is growing daily. Even my only son adores you.'

She sighed.

'Cian, Brogan, please.'

Her shieldmen drew their swords and advanced on Edana.

'Roisin, you don't need to do this,' Edana said as she retreated before the two shieldmen.

'I'm afraid I do. Without you around Pendathran is my man. This warband will be mine, for my son, of course.'

'I think you are too used to killing anyone you consider a potential threat.'

Roisin nodded. 'You're probably right, but better a potential threat dead than a definite one still alive. That philosophy has worked well for me so far.'

Edana stumbled into the bank of reeds and stopped.

'This gives me no pleasure,' Cian said as he raised his sword above Edana's head. Then Brogan stabbed him through the back, his blade bursting out of Cian's chest, spattering Edana in a red mist.

Men stepped out from the reeds and trees. Halion, Vonn and Lorcan.

'You are my shieldman,' Roisin hissed at Brogan.

'Aye,' Brogan said sadly, pulling his blade free as Cian slipped to the ground. 'But only because of your son. I am his man, Domhain's man, not yours.'

Roisin screeched her rage, then looked to her son.

'It was for you,' she said pleadingly. 'I was doing it for you.'

Lorcan looked at her coldly. 'No, Mother, you were doing it because you are jealous. Because you love power. But you go too far.'

'So,' Roisin said, looking back to Edana, standing straight, regal again. 'What will you do with me? Trial? Prison? Exile?'

'Exile,' Edana said, her mouth a straight, hard line.

Roisin's face twitched, a bitter smile at first, then a tremble of the lips.

'Don't be ridiculous,' she said.

'Betrayal,' Edana said, her lips twisting as if the very word made her sick. 'I am so tired of people close to me seeking to betray me,' she continued. 'I have lost patience with it. Your days here are done.'

'This is absurd,' Roisin said, 'a misunderstanding.'

'All here heard you,' Edana said.

'Please,' Roisin whispered.

'Halion will take you from here, leave you where you will never find us again.'

Halion drew a cloth from his belt.

'You would blindfold me and abandon me?' Roisin said. Leave me all alone?'

'Better than you would have done for me,' Edana replied.

Roisin ran to her son, grabbed his hand. 'Please,' she said.

'I love you, Mam, but I could not let you murder Edana. I love her.'

'I'm your *mother*,' Roisin hissed.

'Aye, you are, but you should not have made me choose,' he said.

'Argh,' Roisin screamed, scratching at Lorcan's cheeks.

Lorcan turned his face away.

She staggered to Halion, grabbed his leather vest.

'Please, help me.'

'You murdered my mam. Gave her poison intended for me and Conall,' he said, face cold and hard.

'Mercy,' Roisin said. Her eyes swept the glade in desperation, fell upon Cian's body, his sword in the grass beside him. Before any could stop her she leaped into motion and swept it up. She held it two-handed, pointing the tip at Edana, her feet moving as if it wasn't the first time she'd held a blade.

Halion moved towards her.

'Hold,' Edana shouted and Halion froze.

'Fight me,' Roisin said. 'Exile in these marshes is a death sentence, you all know it.'

'Edana doesn't need to fight you,' Halion said. 'She is Queen. She commands.'

Fight me now in the court of swords,' Roisin snarled at Edana, 'show the backbone a queen needs; or are you a coward, happy to let others do your dirty work?'

Edana hesitated.

'I always knew that you were just talk, a spoilt, shallow child,' Roisin spat.

Edana drew the sword at her hip. Blood was still upon it.

'No,' Halion and Vonn called out, both of them moving in.

'Step back,' Edana snarled, eyes fixed upon Roisin. They paused, then reluctantly did so.

Roisin twirled the sword in her hand. 'Three older brothers who used to use me for practice,' she said, a thin smile twitching her lips. Then she rushed at Edana, who blocked, retreated, parried again, stepped to the side and punched Roisin in the mouth.

Roisin staggered back, spat blood. 'You'll regret that, you little bi—'

Edana lunged forwards, deflected Roisin's hurried block and chopped her sword into Roisin's wrist. Blood spurted and Roisin screamed, collapsed to her knees, staring at Edana in surprise.

Edana stood above her, blade raised high, tip pointed at Roisin's heart, quivering. A long silence stretched. 'You lose,' Edana said, lowering her sword. 'Halion, get her out of my sight.'

Looks like the princess has grown up.

As Halion moved forward Camlin lowered his bow and slid his arrow back into his quiver. Then he looked about the glade, realized one of their number was missing.

Where's Vonn?

CHAPTER EIGHTY-SIX

EVNIS

Evnis stumbled along the stream bank, pushing through tall reeds and hanging branches. The sun was sinking, a mist rising from the water, swirling lazily onto the bank. He was shivering, soaked to the skin, the clothes of his left side burned black, the skin on the back of his hand and the left side of his face prickling with pain.

But I still have my life. I will get out of this swamp, wait for the warband from Dun Carreg. He shook his head. *Outwitted by that little bitch Edana, the humiliation. It must have been someone else's plan – Pendathran, maybe. He was there, I saw him. And, let's look on the positive side, with any luck Morcant's dead.*

He saw a movement up ahead, a flash of grey fur, disappearing amongst a reedbed.

A hound? Rafe? He'll be able to get me out of this stinking dung hole.

He had lost everyone, his boat speeding after Edana so intent on catching her that he hadn't seen the empty boat being pushed with poles straight into his vessel – not until it was too late, anyway. And then the flames. Jumping overboard had seemed the only sensible thing to do, particularly in light of the fact that his whole left side had been on fire.

Oh, the pain . . .

Somehow he had made it to shore, though he'd lost his sword along the way – a knife still hung from his belt.

Not that it will do me any good.

He'd lain upon the lake shore for a while, covered in cold, sticking mud, which had eased the pain of his burns, somehow, and watched the chaos and carnage as his warband had been systematically set on fire and slaughtered.

Nothing like fire to cause a good panic. I must remember that.

Slowly a measure of strength had returned to him as he lay upon the lake shore, and the idea of running and living had grown in his mind. So that is what he had done. As the screams of his warband had rung out through the marshes, most of them already fleeing and the hunt beginning, he had dragged himself to his feet and run. The running hadn't lasted that long, exhaustion seeming to be never more than a few paces away, but he ran long enough to take him into cover.

And he was still trudging on. Occasionally he heard a scream ring out, usually it was cut short, he didn't know whether it had been the swamp or more human dangers that had finished it – neither thought was encouraging. He walked in the general direction that he thought he'd seen the hound, though he didn't see it again.

There was a fluttering above. He looked up and saw a black crow circling above him.

I'm not dead yet.

He walked on, slowly the sun sinking into the west until it was just a ball of bronze melting into the horizon. He heard the flap of wings again, closer this time, and looked up. The crow was now sitting on the branch of an alder a dozen paces ahead. It was the scruffiest crow he'd ever seen, feathers poking out at angles, a patch of skin visible here and there.

'*Wait here,*' the crow said to him.

He stopped and stared at it.

Did I just imagine that?

The bird flapped into the air, seeming to take a lot of effort.

'*Don't leave,*' it squawked down at him.

Usually this would have struck him as strange, but after the day he'd had, he just sat down.

He was starting to doze off when he heard footsteps and a man appeared – a warrior, tall, fair-haired, stern lines to his face and serious pale blue eyes.

Vonn.

'Father,' Vonn said.

Evnis stood, not easily, his body stiffening from his brief rest.

'There was a time when I thought I'd never see you again,' Evnis said.

'I have thought of little else but this meeting,' Vonn replied, a half-smile upon his lips. 'Though I did not imagine it here, under these circumstances.' He looked closer at Evnis. 'Father, you are shivering.'

'Yes, I am,' Evnis said, not knowing what else to say.

Vonn unclasped his cloak and wrapped it around Evnis' shoulders. It was Ardan's grey.

'I'd best not go back to Dun Carreg with this on,' Evnis said.

'You could,' Vonn answered, stepping back a pace.

'I don't think Rhin would approve,' Evnis snorted.

'You could ride back to Dun Carreg with Edana, her warband at your back.' He hesitated. 'Your son at your side.'

'And Rhin? The Queen of the west, conqueror of Ardan, Narvon and Domhain. What of her? What do you think she would think of that?'

'Rhin be damned,' Vonn snarled. 'She is overstretched, tried to conquer more than she can rule. Ardan is *ready* for Edana's return.'

'Don't be a fool,' Evnis said wearily. 'Rhin has powerful allies. To go against her is to die.'

'You're wrong.'

'I am not wrong.' Evnis felt his anger stirring, memories of his last argument with Vonn. He was convinced of his own opinion then, as well.

'I'd hoped you had changed, had grown up,' Evnis said. 'That life's hardships would have disabused you of your infantile notions of honour.' Even as he said the words he regretted the way he said them, angry, impatient, patronizing.

'I have grown up, learned many lessons,' Vonn said sadly. 'The main lesson I learned is that I think I have many more lessons yet to come.' He didn't meet venom with venom, which in itself was a change.

'Perhaps you have,' Evnis mused. 'But that doesn't change the facts. Rhin is on the winning side. That is partly why I have chosen her. She will not lose. Any resistance will only be fleeting. And why would I want to welcome Edana back? Daughter of the man who condemned your mother to death. Why would I want Edana to rule Ardan again, when it is mine already? I sit in Brenin's throne. I rule from Dun Carreg. Why would I give it up?'

'For me. Because it is the right thing to do. Rhin is evil. Father, what do you know of this God-War? Of the Seven Treasures?'

'Only a little,' Evnis lied, shrugging.

'I have heard things,' Vonn said. 'Of the cauldron, of a gathering in Drassil, within Forn Forest. Of a need to find the Seven Treasures.'

'I know a little about it,' Evnis said. 'But this is not really the time or place to discuss it.' Twilight was settling about them. A mosquito buzzed in Evnis' ear.

'There was a necklace in your secret room,' Vonn said.

'Aye. With my book, which you stole.'

'I did. I am sorry for that. I wanted to hurt you.'

Well, at least he's honest.

'You did hurt me. Can I have it back?'

'I don't have it any more.'

'That's not good. It's a powerful, dangerous book. Who does have it?'

'Brina.'

Oh, just wonderful.

'There was something else in there,' Vonn said. 'A necklace with a black stone.'

Evnis said nothing.

'Is it still there?' Vonn asked.

'Why?'

'I think it is one of the Seven Treasures. Nemain's necklace.'

'That's ridiculous,' Evnis said.

I had thought exactly the same thing.

'And if it were, what does that mean to you, anyway.'

'Corban needs it, in Drassil.'

'Corban – that arrogant fool.'

'Corban is the Bright Star.'

'What? Where have you heard such things? Who have you been talking to?'

For the first time Vonn looked a little unsure of himself. 'Craf,' he said quietly.

'Who's Craf?'

Vonn looked up, at the crow in the branches above him.

'A bird,' Evnis said.

'Craf's very intelligent,' Vonn said, a little defensively.

'*Craf clever*,' the bird muttered above them.

He actually is, Evnis thought, *for he seems to know more about this than I do, and I've been studying it all of my life.*

'Vonn, this is all very interesting – more than that, important. But this is not the place to discuss it. Please, come with me. Be my son again. I am sorry for the way things happened, the night Dun Carreg fell. I am sorry for the rift between us, for arguing, sorry that Bethan died . . .'

As he said the girl's name he saw pain flutter across Vonn's face.

'I ask your forgiveness for my part in it, and I hope that you can see I did not intend harm to come to her. I was acting out of what I saw to be our best interests. I betrayed our King, I know, but he betrayed me, betrayed us. Refused aid that would have saved my Fain, your mother . . .'

Words choked in his throat for a moment.

It never fails to surprise me how close the pain is.

'I want you to come back to me. Come back with me. Share my victory, help me rule Ardan, be my battlechief, my first-sword, my *son*.'

Please say yes, Vonn. Please, I beg you. If you do not . . .

Vonn was looking at Evnis with tears in his eyes.

'I cannot, Father. I would ask the same of you. Come with me, back to Dun Crin. I have hated you for that night in Dun Carreg, but I can understand the currents of your heart. Mother . . .' He paused, swallowed. 'I can forgive you for that night, but not for continuing on this path. Please, come back with me.'

Evnis felt such a wave of emotion, like a great hand tugging at strings attached to his heart, that he almost said yes, just to make Vonn happy. But then the feeling subsided, enough for him to see clearly.

I have come too far, done too much. He looked at his palm, traced the decades-old scar there. *I have made an oath, sworn my soul . . .*

'I cannot,' he said, grave and solemn.

Vonn's face fell.

'Then here we must say farewell,' Vonn said. 'And for my part, I hope that I do not meet you upon the field of battle.' He turned and walked away.

That is highly unlikely, Evnis thought, hardening his heart as he drew his knife from his belt, quickly following his son, a few paces behind, knife rising.

Please understand, I cannot allow my own son, my only son, to openly oppose me, to stand with Rhin's enemies. It will bring me shame and ruin in this new life I am carving.

Then something hit him in the chest, felt like a punch, and he staggered, stopped.

Vonn spun around, seeing Evnis' raised fist, the knife in it.

They both looked at Evnis' chest together.

A long-shafted arrow stuck from it, blood welling about the entry point, right above Evnis' heart. He opened his mouth to say something, but he couldn't get his lungs and vocal cords to work together. Breath hissed out of his mouth. His legs felt weak and he stumbled forwards, felt a numb jolt, realized he had dropped to his knees.

Is this dying?

He toppled onto his face, his son's boots filling his vision, darkness like a tunnel shrinking in upon him. He heard a voice, distant but terrifying, whispering, calling to him, remembered it from a night long ago when he had sworn an oath in a forest glade.

Asroth.

CHAPTER EIGHTY-SEVEN

CYWEN

'You're joking?' Cywen said to Farrell, almost feeling angry with him that he would make up such a stupid thing at such a serious time.

The hospice was full to overflowing with injured warriors. Cywen, Brina and the team they'd put together numbered nearly three score and they were still hard-pushed to treat everyone who staggered in or was carried through the wide doors.

Farrell was the first person to enter the hospice without an injury that needed treating, although that wasn't quite true. He had his fair share of cuts and scrapes and bruises, just nothing that would lead to imminent death or disablement if he wasn't treated immediately.

'I'm not, I swear it,' Farrell said. Cywen paused in the act of bandaging the leg of a Jehar warrior she was treating and looked up at Farrell.

'If this is a jest I will get my own back on you, Farrell. The chances are that someday I'll be wrapping a bandage around some part of you, remember. I know how to ease pain, and also how to increase it.' She raised an eyebrow at him.

'I would swear an oath if it helped you believe me,' he said, looking worried now, and also slightly hurt by the level of Cywen's mistrust.

'You really mean it, don't you?'

'Yes,' Farrell burst out, looking relieved. 'Dath and Kulla are to be wed. He's walking around with a grin on his face that the Kadoshim couldn't remove.'

'Well, I never,' Cywen murmured.

'Idiot boy,' Brina said from over by another cot.

Maybe it's not so stupid, Cywen thought. *This war has us all standing on death's doorstep. It reminds us how precious life is, and how much it should be lived.*

And of course the joy of victory had swept through Drassil like a summer wind, warm and pleasant, spreading relief and great joy. Cywen could already hear the celebrations beginning elsewhere. It took longer for that to seep into the hospice, where the harsh and stark reminders of the battle's cost were still all too plain to see.

'Good for them,' Cywen said.

'That's what I said,' said Farrell. 'After I stopped laughing, anyway.'

Brina shook her head, muttering.

'You haven't heard the best bit yet,' Farrell smiled.

'Oh, and what's that?' Cywen asked, going back to her bandaging.

'Dath wants Brina to perform the ceremony.'

'What?' screeched Brina.

Cywen stood with a smile on her face and a tear in her eye, soft spring sunshine breaking through branches above them to bathe the courtyard in sunset's amber glow.

The closing part of the handbinding ceremony of Dath and Kulla was taking place in a part of the fortress that was rarely used, chosen by Kulla because of the magnolia tree that grew within it. It had flowered early with the first flush of spring, huge pink petals hanging over the couple as they stood hand in hand before Brina.

Dath getting married. The boy who loved collecting gulls' eggs with my little brother. Seems like a lifetime ago. Guess we're all growing up.

The courtyard was full to overflowing, people crowding on the steps that climbed the walls, hanging out of windows, standing on flat roofs, every single person who now lived within Drassil come to the handbinding of the Bright Star's friend.

It had been a long and happy day, the first part of the handbinding ceremony beginning that morning with the first rays of dawn, Dath and Kulla's hands bound together for them to spend the day intertwined, a taster of the rest of their lives.

Not that it will be much different from a normal day for them; they are never far from each other.

It had been a beautiful ceremony, Brina managing to say words that made Cywen cry, even if the old healer had told Cywen a hundred times that she had no time for 'the nonsense of youth', but Cywen was convinced Brina was secretly as happy for Dath as the rest of them were. Cywen had smiled more than she remembered in recent memory, and so had Corban, she'd noticed. In fact all of them had, even Gar. And now they had gathered at sunset for the closing of the ceremony.

Brina raised her hand and the courtyard fell silent.

'Kulla ap Barin, Dath ben Mordwyr,' she cried in a loud voice. 'Your day is done. You have been bound, hand and heart, and lived the day as one. Now is your time of choosing. Will you bind yourselves forever, or shall the cord be cut?'

Dath and Kulla both grinned at one another, their joy infectious.

'We will be bound, one to the other, and live this life as one,' they said together.

Brina took their bound hands in hers.

'Make your covenant,' she said.

'Kulla ap Barin,' Dath began, 'I vow to you the first cut of my meat, the first sip of my mead . . .'

It had been a ten-night since the battle, the first five days spent tending to the wounded and building cairns over the dead. As heartbreaking as that was, the numbers of the fallen had bordered upon the miraculous. One hundred and fifty-seven dead from amongst the various peoples that populated Corban's warband and one thousand six hundred of Isiltir's warband dead, another seven hundred warriors from Isiltir surrendering and joining the people of Drassil, as they were starting to think of themselves.

And we have learned from the survivors of Isiltir's warband that two more warbands are building roads through Forn, trying to find us, as well as Nathair's own force of Kadoshim. The odds seem overwhelming, and yet I don't feel scared as I used to. I don't have that feeling in the pit of my belly that something bad is just around the corner.

It had been seeing Corban slay the Kadoshim, then escape in such dramatic fashion from twenty shieldmen bearing down upon him, and then watching him lead a warband against an enemy that dramatically outnumbered them and win, with minimal losses.

It was inspiring, and Cywen knew she was not the only one who felt that way. Everybody did. There was an atmosphere at Drassil now of quiet confidence. That Elyon was perhaps guiding her brother after all.

We are going to win.

She smiled to herself and focused back on Brina and the happy couple.

'Peace surround you both, and contentment latch your door,' Brina sang the closing words of the benediction. Then she held up a wide cup for Dath and Kulla to grip with their bound hands. They drank together, then Brina cast the cup to the ground and stamped on it.

'It is done,' she cried, and the crowd erupted into cheering, Kulla grabbing Dath and kissing him fiercely.

'Good, now let's eat,' Brina announced.

The great hall had been transformed, long rows of tables set with trenchers of steaming food, a score of spitted carcasses turning over fire-pits; barrels of mead found on the abandoned baggage wains of Jael's warband stood in a long line.

Cywen sat and watched it all go by, just enjoying being still and watching, when mostly life felt like one long rush of doing. As the evening wore into night and the fire-pits began to sink low she found herself feeling reflective, thinking over the last year as she sipped at a cup of mead.

It is almost a year ago to the day that I was in the great hall in Murias; when Corban and Mam came for me . . .

Surprising her, tears swelled in her eyes.

I miss you, Mam, and you, Da. You would be so amazed if you were here. So proud of Corban.

Someone sat next to her, the bench creaking with the strain.

Laith. She had a cup of her own and was smiling, her eyes shining.

'Tonight, life is good,' Laith proclaimed, raising her cup.

Cywen nodded and touched her cup to Laith's, wiping the tears from her eyes as she did so.

'Your arm,' Cywen said, pointing at the dark tattoo that now curled from Laith's wrist to elbow.

'It is my *sgeul*, my Telling,' Laith said sombrely. 'The record of the lives I have taken. The vine is my journey, my life, the thorns, each life I take.'

Cywen studied it, gently brushed it. The skin was ridged and peeling, hints of green and blue beneath the scabbed skin. She tried to count the thorns, reached fifteen and then lost count.

'It is a serious thing,' Laith said, 'taking a life. A sad thing, I think, though better to take another's than to lose your own. Many of my kin consider the thorns a badge of honour. I suppose it is that as well.'

'It is,' Cywen said. 'But something can be many things, or can mean many things, not just be confined to the one. Like us.'

Laith looked at her intently then. 'You are right. I used to think that you were just angry,' she said, 'but there is far more to you than just that. And you are wise as well.'

'Hah.' Cywen snorted and sipped from her cup. 'The wisdom of mead, maybe.'

Laith grinned. 'I'll drink to that,' she said, and did. 'Now,' she continued, smacking her lips. 'Where's that fine-looking Farrell gone?'

'Farrell?' Cywen spluttered into her cup.

'Aye, Farrell,' Laith said with a shy look. 'He's big and strong, got good bones, not like the rest of you. I've been thinking on him for a while now, and what with spring in the air . . .' She shrugged and smiled mischievously.

'You know he's sweet on Coralen,' Cywen said.

'Oh aye, everyone knows that. But everyone also knows that she's sweet on someone else.'

Yes, we do, Cywen thought. *Apart from the one she's sweet on!*

'So perhaps he just needs the way things are explained to him. I was talking to Balur about it—'

'Balur!' Cywen spluttered again. Try as she might, she just could not imagine the giant warrior dispensing advice about love.

'Aye – and can you stop doing that? Balur said to me that sometimes people can't see things as plain as the end of their nose, but once it's been pointed out to them they don't know why they went so long without seeing a thing.'

'That's very wise,' Cywen said. 'In fact, Laith, you're very wise. How old are you, exactly?'

'I've seen forty-two summers,' Laith said with a wave of her hand. 'But we mature slowly, us giants, or so I'm told. Like usque. Ah, there he is.' She pointed at Farrell and stood, swaying ever so slightly. 'Any advice?' she asked.

'Try arm-wrestling him,' Cywen said. 'I hear he likes that.'

Laith smiled. 'A man after my own heart. Will I have to let him win, though?'

Cywen was still laughing when Laith disappeared into the thinning crowd.

The bench creaked again.

This time it was Brina.

'I need to talk to you,' the healer said.

'Feel free,' Cywen said with a wave of her hand.

Brina frowned. 'Are you sober?' she asked, then her hand darted out and she pinched and twisted flesh on Cywen's arm.

'Ouch.'

'Well, you're still feeling pain, so that's good enough,' Brina said. She stood up and walked away, then paused and looked back. 'Well, come on then, what are you waiting for?'

Muttering, Cywen rose and followed.

Eventually they ended up in Brina's chamber, small and sparse, a bed and chair, a table with a half-melted candle upon it and a jug of water.

Only one cup, though.

'I don't get visitors,' Brina said with a shrug, seeing where Cywen was looking. She dug around in her cloak and pulled out the book.

'Isn't that heavy to carry around all the long day?' Cywen asked.

'Of course it is,' Brina snapped, 'but I'm hardly going to leave it lying around for someone to just come along and take, am I? A book hundreds of years old, containing wisdom both wonderful and terrifying?'

'I suppose not.'

'Sit down and pay attention,' Brina said. She sat on the bed, Cywen on the chair, and Brina opened the book at the back and started to read.

When she finished they both looked at each other. The worry and concern on Brina's face, she knew, was reflected in her own. 'We need to tell Corban,' Cywen said.

CHAPTER EIGHTY-EIGHT

CORBAN

Corban knew the place well now, this part of the Otherworld that seemed to call to him when he slept. The green valley, a lake such a deep blue that it was almost the purple of the sky as it darkens, just before full night. The red-leaved maple that he hid beneath, and of course the beat of Meical's wings, high above, like a heartbeat, sweeping him to the cliff face that he always landed upon, and the cave that he always entered.

And again as always, he remembered Meical's words to him, about Asroth hunting him, about the Kadoshim flying abroad in the Otherworld. *Promise me if you find yourself there again, that you will hide, do not move. Asroth's Kadoshim fly high and they will see you before you see them. And they are not the only dangers in the Otherworld. There are creatures, rogue spirits that would do you harm if they found you.*

Always he had obeyed. And yet, this time, he did not want to. Without knowing or even understanding why, just feeling that he must, he left the shade of the maple tree and began to climb the cliff. It was remarkably easy, the rocks not cutting into his palms, no sweating or straining of muscles, no dangerous up-draughts. Just a steady, constant motion, taking him up.

And then he was there, standing on a rock shelf, the entrance to a cave before him. It was a high, perfect arch, much higher and wider than it appeared from the ground, runes of the old tongue carved around it. Carven steps led into it, the flicker of torchlight within luring him on. He walked along a damp, curving corridor, down, curling in a deep looping spiral until the corridor opened into a great underground theatre, huge torches bathing the room in a flickering orange glow, a semi-circle of stone-tiered benches on the far wall full to overflowing with the white-winged Ben-Elim. And, standing before them, a small, fragile figure in the depths of the theatre; Meical.

'When?' a voice boomed from the massed Ben-Elim.

'I do not know,' Meical said. 'Soon.'

'It is always soon,' the voice replied.

Meical shrugged, a distinctly human gesture in this chamber, this world, so full of the other.

'We have waited aeons, brother, how much longer?' other voices called.

'How much longer?' a thousand voices reverberated around the chamber.

'We have waited aeons,' Meical echoed the speakers. 'A little longer will not hurt.'

'How much longer?' the voices demanded.

'Soon,' Meical repeated.

Corban woke with a start, looked about, a sharp pain in his neck and his hip. He was sitting in an alcove in the great hall, fires burning low. He shifted his weight, adjusting his sword hilt from where it was digging into him.

What am I doing here?

Then he remembered.

Dath has been handbound with Kulla. He smiled, a gentle joy seeping through him at the memory of his friend, at the depth of his utter, transparent joy. And then, as they seemed to do frequently and almost of their own accord, his thoughts drifted to Coralen. In truth he had thought of little else since the battle had ended. Or more specifically, of her kiss. He had wanted to talk to her, every day, had decided that he would, had steeled himself, practised the words, and then gone dry-mouthed and weak-kneed as soon as he'd seen her.

How is it that I can fight Kadoshim but I cannot talk to a woman?

Today. I will talk to her today. That gave him a pleasant feeling in his belly, part the flutter of fear, part something else.

The chamber was mostly empty now, the fire-pits a glow of embers. He stood, thinking of his bed in his chamber, then saw a figure standing before Drassil's tree, before the spear and skeleton of Skald.

Balur One-Eye.

Corban walked over to him, stretching his neck, blinking the sleep from his eyes, came to stand beside the giant, for a moment enjoying the silence.

Eventually the burning question had to be asked.

'Why did you kill Skald?'

Balur did not look at him, said nothing. Then he sighed, put his big slab of a hand over his face and rubbed his eyes.

'It was a terrible thing. I was his guard, his high captain. I seized his own spear from him and slew him upon his throne.' He said the words as if each one were a punishment.

Corban thought about that, nodded slowly. 'Aye, that is terrible. A great trust to betray. What I know of you, though . . .' He shook his head. 'I cannot conceive of you doing such a thing.'

Balur raised an eyebrow at that.

'He ordered Nemain killed. Ordered her strangled – here, before him, whilst he sat upon his throne.'

'But Nemain was his Queen,' Corban said.

'Aye, she was.'

'Then why would he do such a terrible thing?'

'Because she was with child. And it was not his.'

'Oh.'

Corban looked at Balur; deep grooves were etched in the folds of the giant's face. He was ancient.

'It was your child, wasn't it?'

'Aye.'

'Ethlinn?'

Another sigh. 'Aye.'

'So she is your Queen, then. Queen of the Benothi.'

'She is. Some would say she was Queen of all the Clans, even though she is bastard born.'

'And that is her spear, then.'

'Aye. By rights. But she will not take it. Will not claim it. One day, perhaps.' He looked down at Corban, his face full of melancholy.

The whisper of feet echoed down to him, and Corban turned to see two figures at the great doors. Brina and Cywen. Brina gestured to him impatiently. He reached out and squeezed Balur's hand and then he strode to Brina and Cywen.

'We've been looking for you everywhere,' Brina hissed, as if it were his fault that she couldn't find him.

'What time is it?' Corban asked.

'Late. Time to talk,' Brina said.

'It feels more like bedtime,' Corban muttered. 'Can't this wait until daylight?'

'No,' Brina said. 'We need somewhere private to talk.'

'My chamber, then,' Corban suggested. 'It's close, and I will not have to walk far to my bed afterwards.'

Brina tutted but did not argue so they made their way through Drassil's stairways and corridors to Corban's chamber. Storm was curled asleep at his door. She was starting to spend a little time away from her cubs now, and they were becoming braver and more adventurous, wandering from their den for short spells. Haelan, Swain and Sif never seemed to be too far from them.

Corban opened his chamber door, lit a candle, though a glance at the window showed the darkness turning to grey.

Dawn, then.

Brina pulled her book out and thumped it onto the table.

'A book?' Corban muttered.

'Ban, it's important,' Cywen said. The look on her face quelled the protest forming on his lips and he pulled up a chair.

'All right then,' he said. 'Let's hear it.'

Brina turned to a marked page, almost the last page, and pointed to a scrawl of old runes.

'Cywen, read this for me; my old eyes . . .'

Cywen bent over the book.

'*Is e an coire an ghlais,*' she read.

She was always good with her letters, but now she actually sounds like a giant – the tone, inflection. If I closed my eyes she could be Laith.

'The cauldron is the lock,' Brina translated.

'*Is iad na se seoda eile an,*' Cywen continued.

'The other six Treasures are the key.' Brina spoke in a flat voice, her eyes never leaving Corban's.

'*Na aris cheile is fiedir leo a bheith, go deo seachas nior clans aontu.*'

'Never again together can they be, forever apart did the clans agree.'

'*Uimh nios mo taobh le taobh faoi bhun an cran mor.*'

'No more side by side beneath the great tree.'

Corban sat back in his chair, a frown creasing his face, a sick feeling squirming in his belly.

'Forever apart,' he murmured.

Brina and Cywen stared at him, waiting.

'It doesn't make sense,' Corban said eventually. 'Why would Balur bring the axe here?'

'It has always niggled at me,' Brina said, 'but not as much as this. Why has Meical not ordered the starstone axe and spear taken to the far corners of the Banished Lands.'

Corban blinked, images filling his mind. Of a red-leafed maple, a high cliff, a dark tunnel . . .

Meical.

'It is as if he is using them,' Cywen said, 'but for what?'

'Bait,' Corban muttered. He stood and strode to the door, Storm following him.

'Where are you going?' they both called after him.

'To have a talk with Meical.'

Corban found Meical in the great hall, its sheer size making even the Ben-Elim appear small and insignificant. Apart from Meical and Corban the hall was empty, the silence in dawn's gentle glow almost a physical thing, a silent beauty. Skald's skeleton in its throne brooded close by, a malignant tumour spoiling the purity of the scene. Meical was standing beside one of the tunnel entrances, the one they had journeyed through, a smaller door within it open – all six of the tunnels were cleared now, a system of runners positioned in each one to relay news of any enemy sightings in Forn. Meical looked as if he was listening to, or for, something.

'There *were* no Kadoshim,' Corban said as he came to stand beside Meical. Storm peered into the small open door of the tunnel and cocked her head.

Meical blinked and looked at Corban, raising a questioning eyebrow.

'In my dream. In the Otherworld. I climbed the cliff. You told me not to, because of the Kadoshim in the sky. But they were not there.'

'Ah,' Meical said, for a brief moment his face shifting with emotions before he stamped his cold face upon them. He turned to face Corban. 'And what did you see?'

'An entrance carved with runes, a torchlit corridor. A stone theatre, filled with the Ben Elim. With you.'

Meical breathed in a long, deep breath, pursed his lips, his silver scars wrinkling.

'Soon, you said. What is it that you and your kin have waited aeons for?'

'This time. These days. Now,' Meical said with a dismissive wave of his hand.

'No. It is more than that, Meical. Brina has read to me from a book – a giant's book. About how the Treasures must be kept separate, never brought together again.' He glanced at the spear transfixing Skald's skeleton.

'What is going on?'

Meical sighed, a long, sad exhalation. Something flitted across his face.

He looks ashamed. Corban felt his doubt grow, become something firmer.

'You are hiding something from me,' he said.

Again the long, cold stare. Eventually Meical turned away.

'I cannot do this,' he muttered.

Corban grabbed his wrist and pulled him back.

'Cannot do what?'

'Ach, this task I have been given; its cost is greater than I ever imagined.'

'What do you mean?' Corban asked.

Meical stared at him long, silent moments. Emotions tore at his cold face like waves against a sea wall, until finally it began to crumble, revealing something else in Meical's eyes. A depth of sadness and regret that set a spark of fear in Corban's gut.

'Tell me,' Corban whispered and Meical took a deep breath, then began to talk.

'We are different from you, we Ben-Elim. We serve,' he said. 'We serve Elyon, that is our reason for existing. Duty. Honour. The joy of service to our Maker.' He looked at Corban, a wistful smile twitching his lips. 'He is beautiful to behold, is Elyon. To be in his presence would light a glow within your very being. Purity. Peace.

And then Asroth destroyed that, took him from us.' His face twisted in a snarl, hatred pulsing from it for a few powerful heartbeats, then the cold face was back. 'But we continue to serve. Hoping that he sees our efforts, our devotion to him, even in his absence.'

'It must have been very hard for you all, to be separated from him,' Corban said.

'Aye, it was. It still is. For a while we were lost, did not know what to do. But then we went back to what we did know, the only thing we had ever known. Serve him. So we looked to you, your race, this world. We never understood you. My kin still do not. But that did not matter, was not important. We knew that Elyon loved you, that he treasured you, valued you. Adored you. And that was enough for us. We did not need to understand you, only protect you for Elyon's return. A gift that would symbolize our devotion to him.' He looked at Corban and nodded hopefully, willing Corban to understand.

'And you have done that,' Corban said.

Meical's face shifted again, as if every emotion that he had ever felt was finally reaching the surface of his skin, eroding and breaking through the wall he had built.

'You understand, we did not comprehend you – mankind, I mean? My kin. Me. I am the only one of my kind to have lived amongst you. It has been . . . revealing. You are a race of great passions. So much of everything. A remarkable species. And you most of all, Corban.' He looked at Corban, something between admiration and affection flickering across his features. 'You have accomplished truly amazing things, and earned the love and devotion of so many.'

Corban shrugged at that, feeling uncomfortable, as he always did when he was the subject of discussion. 'Meical, you sound as if you are making some kind of apology.'

'I am,' Meical said. 'I am truly sorry.'

'I think I know and I understand,' Corban said. 'You've taken a risk, used the Treasures as bait to lure Asroth's Black Sun out. Rather than hiding the Treasures and taking the chance that they could be found in a moon or a year or a decade, you've risked all on a confrontation where you hope to defeat his champion decisively.'

Meical was staring at him now, his intensity almost unbearable.

'Yes, well done, Corban. You are right, or at least on the right path. But that is only part of it.'

'What do you mean?'

Meical put a hand to his face. 'I never knew how hard this task would be. To live amongst you, to form bonds of friendship, to see your sacrifices, your deeds of love and valour. I think, out of all of my kin, that I am the only one who understands Elyon's love for your race. And that is why I cannot deceive you any longer.'

He lowered his hand and faced Corban, his features racked with pain.

'Forgive me, Corban.' A single tear rolled from Meical's eye.

Corban was confused. Felt the seed of fear in his gut grow.

'Forgive you for what, exactly? Meical, you are scaring me now. You have set a trap, used us, which is a little underhand, I have to admit. But it does make sense . . .'

'No, Corban, you do not understand. It is *all* a trap,' Meical breathed. 'Us here, the Treasures, the prophecy . . .'

'The prophecy? How can that be a trap?'

'It is not true.'

Corban thought he'd misheard.

'What?' he said.

'The prophecy is not real. It is not of Elyon. *I* wrote it.'

Corban felt as if he'd been punched, the sick feeling he'd felt earlier spreading like an infection through his veins.

'But that's impossible.'

'No. I know. I wrote it. I made it up. Elyon did not choose you, Corban – I did.'

'No, it cannot be. There are things in it that you could not know . . .' Corban's mind was reeling; he felt dizzy, as if the ground were moving beneath his feet. He struggled to cling to something, to understand.

'Aye, that is true,' Meical said, his brow furrowing. 'Which gives me hope. Perhaps Elyon is stirring at last. Is noticing. Is becoming involved . . .' He shrugged. 'What I do know is that I wrote it with my own hand. But not all of it. The core of it came from me, whispered to Halvor, the giant, voice of Skald, as he dream-walked the Otherworld. But it has grown, become many times what I planted in his mind. But that is common, is it not? A tale is told, it will travel a hundred holds and villages, and when you hear it next the hero who slew the giant has now slain a giant clan, and draigs as well.' He shrugged. 'It did not matter, as long as the core remained the same.'

'But why? Why would you do this?'

'Because Asroth is predictable in his evil and his scheming. We knew he would strike at you, attempt to destroy Elyon's most beloved creation, an act of spite and malice against his Maker. But we did not know when; we did not know how. So we used the prophecy to lure him, but also to guide him. To control him. We gave him a path for his great malice to follow.'

'I do not understand,' Corban growled, rubbing his temples, anger beginning to boil within him. 'Speak plainly.'

Storm raised her head to look at Meical, her top lip curling back in a silent growl.

'Asroth hates Elyon, with a passion few could even imagine. But he also loves him, in a deep, hidden place. Despite everything, Elyon is still Asroth's Maker. We must never forget that. And Asroth trusts Elyon. Believes him. We knew that once he saw the prophecy, if he believed it was of Elyon's making, he would never doubt it. And he has not. He has followed it like a rule book – chosen his champion, sought out the Treasures. And now he will come here.'

Corban staggered, reached out to grip something, anything. He put his hand upon the shaft of Skald's spear and retched, bile splashing onto the stone floor.

'Truth and courage,' he whispered bitterly as he cuffed bile from his chin. He stood straighter, glared at Meical. 'What of that? How could you do this to us? Lie to us like this?'

'You have to understand, this was a strategic decision. We are unused to emotion. Remember, we are duty, we are honour. We viewed you as a race, a collective, not as individuals. As the stakes of an age-old conflict. What matter if a few of you were sacrificed along the way, as long as the majority were saved? It seemed logical, the obvious choice. For the greater good.'

'The greater good,' Corban whispered. 'My mam, da, Tukul – all died believing they were fighting for something more than this . . .'

Meical held up a hand. 'I do not say that I condone this now. I don't. I regret much.' He shook his head. 'I have never felt shame before, regret, but I do now. I have come to respect you, Corban, to feel genuine kinship for you, and your companions. Love, you would call it. That is why I am telling you now. I . . .' He paused, mouth twisting. 'I care for you, for your companions, feel something of Elyon's great love for you. I cannot bear to deceive you any longer. But the path is set, too late to change it now. We must see it through.'

'What path? There is yet more to this?'

Meical nodded, avoiding Corban's gaze.

'You just said you would deceive me no longer,' Corban snapped, 'or was that another lie?'

Meical flinched as if from a blow. 'You remember Coralen's straw men in Narvon? The distraction that allowed us to sink the fleet and steal the ships?'

'Aye.'

'This is the same.'

'How so? In what way? You are still speaking in riddles.'

'I cannot tell you any more. I have sworn to my kin.'

Corban turned away, took a dozen paces, wanting nothing more than to get away, to find somewhere alone where he could curl up and hold his head and wish it all away. He stopped, spun on his heel and strode to Meical.

'I am *not* the Bright Star?'

'There is no Bright Star. No Black Sun,' Meical whispered. 'Apart from the ones of our own making.'

'That is why you did not want me to accept Jael's challenge and fight the duel.' Corban shook his head, the myriad implications and consequences staggering him. 'What of truth and courage?' he hissed.

'I never said that to you,' Meical said, looking away. 'I could not say it to you. But in a way you are the Bright Star, as much as any man is anything. As real as any king. Because people have chosen to believe it.'

'That does not *make* it so,' Corban snarled.

'You think not?' Meical asked pleadingly. 'We are what we choose to be. What makes a king a king? Is there something different about him? Does special, sacred blood run in his veins? No. He is chosen; he believes it, and the people believe. He rises to the task, or he fails it.' He shrugged. 'It is no different with you. And you have risen to the task, of that there is no doubt, surpassed it in every way. You are a testament to the power of belief. To what can be achieved through combining belief with will.' He smiled, a faint, rueful thing. 'What you have done is truly staggering.'

Corban was shaking with fury. 'I have been lied to. Deceived. Danced to the tune of a prophecy that does not exist.' He felt his hand reaching for his sword hilt, a rage such as he had never known filling him, fuelled by a bottomless despair. 'And worse, you have made a liar out of me. I have *lied* to these people, fed them a deception hatched by power-mad immortal *bairns*.' He yelled those last words, spittle flying, Storm rising to her feet with a growl, her hackles bristling. His fist closed around his sword hilt as Meical stood and looked down upon him, a world of sorrow scribed across his face, leaking from his eyes.

'I am sorry,' Meical whispered.

'Sorry? We have armies coming to *slaughter* us. The only hope we had was based on a *lie*. My people will die – and you're *sorry?*'

Corban released his sword hilt as if it had bitten him.

'I cannot stand to look at you,' he said and strode away, heading for the nearest exit, which happened to be the small door in the tunnel. He walked through it into the flickering torchlight and dampness of the underground passage and marched furiously on, Storm padding behind him. He glanced back before he rounded a bend and saw Meical's blurred silhouette standing in the doorway. He turned his face from the Ben-Elim and, crying angry tears, he carried on into the darkness.

CHAPTER EIGHTY-NINE

RAFE

Rafe was exhausted. He had run, walked, staggered, crawled his way through the marshlands for over a ten-night. At one point he had collapsed, thought he was just going to lie there until he died, but Scratcher and Sniffer had licked, pawed, nibbled and dragged him back to consciousness. If spring had not arrived and brought with it milder weather he would have died. But instead he lived, and walked.

He was a good huntsman, and even in the horizon-spanning marshes he was able to find his way back, eventually one cool morning finding the river that flowed past Morcant's Tower, as he had come to think of it.

A pale mist lay over the land, rising up from the marshes to creep a little way up the hill that the tower was built upon. The sun was already burning it away, though.

The dogs ran ahead of him, seemingly as pleased as him to be out of the marshes, and they must have been sighted from the tower, for horns rang out, announcing his arrival.

Figures came out of the gates as he walked up the hill; all he could think about a warm meal and a soft bed. Then the dogs came running back to him, both of them with their ears flat and tails tucked.

He paused and looked at the figures coming out of the gate.

Something was very wrong there – one towered above the other, so either one was a dwarf and the other normal sized, or one was a giant . . .

Elyon's stones, it's Rhin. Not the person I most wanted to see. And she's got a giant with her!

Queen Rhin stood before him, a giant with grey hair and a spear the size of an oar stood beside her.

'I take it it's not good news,' Rhin said.

'News?' Rafe said.

'You're the only one back,' Rhin said impatiently, then looked at him quizzically. 'Has the marsh stolen your wits?'

'Hungry, thirsty,' Rafe mumbled.

'Yes, of course.' She clicked her fingers. 'Feed him, give him something to drink – not alcohol, he'll most likely sleep for a week – then bring him to me.'

Rafe was escorted to a huge tent on the meadow beside the tower and enclosure. Tents were everywhere, hundreds of them, warriors in Rhin's black and gold. Rafe also saw giants, at least a score of them together.

Strange days, strange days.

Scratcher and Sniffer walked with him, but they wouldn't enter Rhin's tent, just bounded off together as he walked in. That might have been because of the giant outside the tent entrance – not the one he'd seen earlier, but one that looked even more fierce if possible, a huge axe slung over his shoulder and a moustache that Rafe could have swung from.

It was cool inside the tent, not dark, but dim. Rhin sat at a table, behind her the grey-haired giant that had accompanied her earlier.

'Feel better?' Rhin asked him.

'Aye. Thank you,' he said, remembering his manners a little late. 'My Queen,' he added.

Rhin laughed and gestured for him to sit. He did, a cup of water already poured for him. He drank, savouring it. Most of the marsh water had been stagnant and rank, even the fresh water was questionable, and usually with something slimy in it. He looked up over the rim of his cup, realizing Rhin and the giant were both staring at him.

'So,' Rhin said. 'Where is Evnis?'

It was not the question he had expected, certainly not the first one, at least. He'd been expecting something more along the lines of *What happened?*

'I don't know,' he said.

Rhin sighed. 'Please, it is very important. Think. Hard.'

She looked scary sometimes, and Rafe suddenly remembered sitting with her in a dark room, watching a fire reveal pictures of Halion and Conall in a dungeon far below them. He shivered.

'He was in his boat, we were on the lake, all rowing at Dun Crin, chasing Edana—'

'Edana. Dun Crin. Chasing. Good,' Rhin murmured.

'Then there was fire – they set traps, started setting the boats on fire.'

'In a lake!' Rhin said, not sounding pleased again.

Rafe explained in more detail the battle of Dun Crin, the tactics used against them. He told her how his boat had capsized and how he had swum to the shore.

That wasn't exactly what happened. I don't like fire much. I paddled my arms off and got to the lake shore without even getting my feet wet. But then I tried paddling up a stream and men started throwing spears and pots of oil at me. I got wet then, capsized, swam a hundred paces underwater, scrambled out onto the opposite bank and ran like hell.

He told how the battle was lost by then, and he had escaped into the marshes.

'Hmm,' Rhin said when he finished, steepling her fingers. 'That's not very helpful.'

Rafe shrugged. 'Sorry.'

'Not very helpful at all,' the giant rumbled, which made him jump a little.

'I'm sorry. I was in front – I led the warband to Dun Crin – and Evnis was right behind me. But then it all went to hell – excuse me – fire and water and blood, and I didn't see any more of Evnis.'

'You were the master huntsman?' Rhin said.

'Aye.'

'What of Braith?'

'Braith's dead.'

Rhin sat back in her chair at that, looked genuinely dismayed, even as if she might shed a tear.

'By whose hand?' she asked, voice like sharp flint.

'Camlin. He was Braith's captain from the Darkwood. Gut-shot him, from as far apart as we are.'

'I've heard his name,' Rhin said with a hiss, 'and I won't forget it. And you escaped?'

'Aye.'

'You seem to be very good at that,' Rhin observed.

Can't blame a man for staying alive, he thought. *Can blame him for running, though, I suppose.*

He didn't know what to say, so he didn't say anything, just looked at the cup in his hands.

'I will want a detailed account of this place, the lake, Dun Crin, a map of the waterways in and out. Everything you remember. And numbers – people. Edana of course. Who else?'

'Roisin and Lorcan. They were in the boat with Edana.'

Rhin pulled a face at that.

'Halion.'

'He made it here, then.'

'Aye. Vonn.'

'Who's he?'

'Evnis' son.'

Rhin and the giant exchanged a glance. 'Go on,' Rhin said.

'Pendathran. Camlin, I guess, though I don't recall seeing him at the battle. But he's a sneaky bastard, probably hiding somewhere and shooting his arrows.'

Just then the sounds of a commotion drifted in through the tent entrance. It was pulled back, warriors entering, standing either side and another figure came in, another warrior, but this one battered and bloody, iron helm dented, a bloodstained bandage around one of his arms.

Morcant.

He saw Rhin and almost ran to her, dropped to one knee before her and kissed her hand. She seemed to like it, by the look on her face.

Should I have done that?

'My Queen,' Morcant breathed, 'I am overjoyed to see you.'

'Well, I'm quite pleased to see you,' Rhin said, the smile still flickering upon her lips. She wrinkled her nose. 'Though you could smell better.'

'The marsh,' he said, gesturing, looking offended.

'Of course. Your smell I can cope with, for the moment. We

were just talking to the first survivor of this disaster to return to us.'
Rhin waved at Rafe. 'You can go now, by the way,' she said to him.
'I would talk with Morcant a while. She stroked Morcant's cheek,
running a finger along one of the scars he'd earned in the court of
swords.

Rafe was more than happy to leave. He stood up and bowed
clumsily, then left the tent.

He collected a skin of watered wine from the kitchens, a shoulder
of cold lamb, and walked away from the crowds. Scratcher and
Sniffer soon found him and he wandered, somewhat aimlessly,
thinking back on Rhin's questioning and the battle. He reached the
river where all of the boats had been moored, where they had set off
nearly a moon ago, full of confidence, maybe arrogance. He walked
on, following the riverbank, knew where he was going now.

He turned away from the riverbank and walked a way into the
marshes, stopping eventually at the husk of a dead tree. He walked
round behind it to where its roots had cracked the ground, got down
on his hands and knees and reached into a dark hole beneath a root.
His hand scrambled around and then he felt it, pulled out his kit
bag.

He sat with his back to the dead tree, drank some of his wine, ate
some of the cold lamb, threw strips of fat to the two hounds and just
enjoyed the feeling of being relatively safe, for a few moments.

*What now, I wonder? Probably back into the marshes with this new
warband, have another crack at Edana, but maybe with giants on our side
this time.*

He opened his kit bag, pulled out his coat of chainmail. He'd
chosen not to wear it – stupid, maybe, as he'd been going into battle,
but the thought of wearing a mail shirt while in a boat, travelling
across rivers and lakes. No, the thought of drowning held a special
terror for him.

Then he took out the box, turning it in his hands. He tried the
lock again, but it would not shift. He shook it, something solid
rattling around inside, took out his knife and wiggled it in the lock.

It would not open. He pressed harder and harder, in the end his
knife slipping and cutting the palm of his hand. A flash of anger and
he threw the knife, then stood with the box in both hands.

Can't carry this stupid lump of wood around with me wherever I go.

He raised it over his head and smashed it down upon the tree root, as hard as old bones.

There was a loud crack and the lid flew open.

Pleased with himself, he sat back down again, the hounds coming over to be nosey, and he looked inside.

A cup sat in the box, not particularly fancy, dark. He lifted it up to the light and was surprised by how heavy it was.

It's made out of some kind of metal. He twirled it in his hand, saw it was mostly black and smooth, here and there a paler vein running through the metal. Around its rim old runes curled in a scrawling script.

Well, I've carried a cup five hundred leagues across the Banished Lands. He laughed to himself and hefted it to throw it in the river, then paused. Looking at it, he suddenly felt thirsty.

Might as well have a drink from it first, let it earn its keep.

He poured some of his wine into the cup, swirled it around a little, then drank it down. He'd intended to only take a sip, but then he was smacking his lips and the cup was empty.

Maybe it's a magic cup, he thought, *one that makes everything taste nicer. P'raps I won't throw it in the river.*

He could feel the wine in his belly, a warm glow. As he thought about it the sensation grew, felt as if it was spreading through his veins, warm and wonderful, like tendrils of gold.

He groaned in pleasure.

The sensation grew, spreading to the far corners of his body – toes, fingers, into his head, behind his eyes, swirling, intoxicating, better than the finest usque his da had ever let him sip. He heard laughing, realized it was him, and then he felt grass on his cheek. The cup rolled out of his fingers, into the grass.

Waves of pleasure pulsed through him, continued to grow, becoming uncomfortable in their intensity, too wonderful, an itch behind his eyeballs, feeling as if his heart was swelling in his chest. He groaned again, but not from pleasure this time. From fear, pleasure turning to pain. He curled his legs up to his chest, writhed and groaned and squirmed, the dogs sniffing and whining around him, ears back, licking his face.

Then he screamed, his whole body going rigid, sweating, every muscle in his body locked in an endless spasm. He tasted blood, realized he'd bitten his tongue. Darkness swooped down upon him, his vision blurring, the world around him fading, and then he knew no more.

CHAPTER NINETY

CORBAN

Corban marched along the dank tunnel, torches lodged high in sconces punctuating the darkness, the thud of his boots and whisper of Storm's footsteps echoing ahead of him.

He felt as if he was going insane.

The enormity of what Meical had just told him kept hitting him, rolling over him like endless waves upon a beach.

His first thoughts had been for his friends, of telling them. Of telling Gar.

He has lived his whole life devoted to the prophecy, and to me because of it. His father died because of it. It will destroy him.

How can I tell everyone else? So many who have lost so much for this strategy, *as Meical called it.*

What will they think?

What will they do?

Will they all leave Drassil? Go back to their homes? Give up?

And then, hitting him like a hammer.

What will I do?

The truth was that right now he did not know. All he knew was that he needed to be away from Meical. His rage had scared him in the great hall, knowing that he was only heartbeats away from drawing his blade on the Ben-Elim. And, despite everything, he did not want to see Meical dead. Or even try to kill him. There had been something raw and honest in Meical's confession, and as he'd listened to the Ben-Elim Corban had even felt an edge of sympathy for him – completely overwhelmed by all-out rage right now, but he knew it was there nevertheless.

He looked at Storm beside him, rested a hand upon her back and carried on walking.

Figures stood highlighted beneath the next pool of torchlight, two men, swords at their hips, one with a spear. Corban had lost track of how long he had been walking, just knew that his anger had started to recede – not fade or disappear, but at least to stop bubbling and spluttering in his mind like a thousand angry hornets kicked from their nest. And his stomach was growling, telling him to find some food.

The figures loomed closer – two guards set on the first trapdoor into Forn. He recognized them as he drew closer, the two oarsmen Atilius and his son Pax. Corban waved them a greeting as he drew near, and they both looked pleased when he addressed them by name.

Both of them bore marks from the battle before Drassil's walls: Pax had linen bandaged around his head and Atilius had a raw scar running down the length of his forearm, the stitch-holes still visible from where they had recently been cut and pulled.

They both were talkative, smiling and asking about Dath.

He was handbound yesterday! Was it only yesterday? A lot seemed to have happened since then. Corban found it hard talking to these two men. He'd grown accustomed to people wanting to talk to him and always tried to take a few moments to speak with anyone who wanted to, but that had been before.

Before I learned of the great lie. He felt ashamed before them, warriors who had risked their lives before Drassil's walls, all in the name of a prophecy and a Bright Star. They looked at him, thinking he was something that he knew he wasn't.

I need some air.

'Would you open the gate for me?' he said. 'I could do with some sunshine upon my face.'

'Aye, lord,' Pax said, running up the slope that led to the hidden door.

Lord! Corban thought as he and Atilius followed more slowly.

'Any news on the next warband?' Atilius asked him. He was an old soldier, a warrior of Tenebral, and clearly used to war.

'No,' Corban said.

'We'll show them, if they ever reach here,' Pax said as he threw the bolt, his da moving to help him lift the oak crossbar.

'I don't doubt it,' Corban said as the door was pushed open and broken sunlight streamed in. 'My thanks,' he said as he stepped out into the fresh air, Storm loping off to sniff at a patch of dogwood.

'My lord?' Pax said nervously.

Not that again. 'Aye,' Corban sighed.

'Where are your shieldmen?' Pax looked about the forest. 'Forn is not safe.'

'They're all sleeping off hangovers,' Corban said with a wan smile. 'But Storm is with me, and besides, I won't go far,' he said to the two men. 'I'll stamp on the door when I'm ready to come back down.'

'All right then,' Atilius said and they pulled the trapdoor closed. Pax stuck his head out just before it shut and threw something to Corban – a water skin and something rolled in linen. Corban smiled and then the door was closed, turf fixed to its top making it look like an ordinary patch of woodland.

He walked for a little while, drawn to the sound of running water, and soon he came upon a steep-sided river, fast flowing and narrow, its water foaming white and loud as it carved its way through a miniature ravine. Corban climbed a gentle rise that suddenly steepened until he emerged into a grassy glade on the brow of a hill, to the south the walls and towers of Drassil visible through the trees, behind and above the fortress the great tree spreading like a guardian of bark and branch. The sun was warm upon his face in this glade. He lay on his back and looked up, enjoying the sensation of not having a canopy of branches above him for a change. Cloud like faded gossamer veiled the sky, softening the sharp blue glare of spring.

From here the troubles of life seemed to fade, just a little, the storm of shock and despair that had been so overwhelming a short while ago receding to calmer waters. He propped himself up onto an elbow and unstoppered the skin Pax had thrown him. It was watered wine, not water, a little reminder of yesterday's celebration, and it tasted very good to his dry throat. Wrapped in linen was a chunk of cheese and a thick oat biscuit, which he shared with Storm. She sat and stared at him, perfectly still except for the drool dripping from one of her fangs. He threw her another bit of cheese and she leaped to catch it, jaws snapping, then padded over and bashed him with her head, knocking him onto his back again. She stood over him and licked his face.

He pushed her off and rolled over, felt a pinch in his arm and looked down to see his arm-ring, dark iron and silver thread curling around his upper arm, a thing of beauty. He remembered the night it had been given to him, Meical slamming his sword into the ground.

We are what we choose to be, Meical had said to him that morning. *The question is, what do I choose to be?*

He thought over Meical's words to him, every sentence, poring over them. He noticed the air starting to cool about him, a strong wind coming up from the south.

'Time to go back,' he said eventually to Storm. 'I can't sit here forever. And I have an announcement to make.'

Meical's confession still hurt, almost more than he could bear, like a wound that had pierced deep – unreachable, unhealable – but he knew that he could not just hide away in the woods, that he had to go back, if not for his sake then at least for those others who had believed the lie and followed him. And there was more to this God-War than titles and the strategies and games of immortals. There were people. Kin. Friends.

I may not be the great warrior prophesied to come and save the world that I once thought, but I am a man who has lost his mam and da to war. Lost my home, my King, my friends. I will not just walk away from that. Calidus and Nathair are still a great evil, and they still need to be stopped. I will not turn my back on that fight, avatar of a lost god or not.

As he stood, Storm looked northwards, down the incline and into the shade of the trees. She growled. At the same time a sound drifted up to him on the wind from the south. From Drassil. The wild blasts of horns. He strained to listen and thought he heard voices, screaming, the clash of iron.

Beside him Storm's growl deepened, turning into a snapping snarling, the ridge of her hackles standing. Corban spun around, felt the ground tremble, saw branches shaking as something huge approached through the forest.

He told his feet to move but for a moment remained transfixed to the ground. Then a mass of fur and jaws and teeth emerged from the gloom and the treeline: a great bear with a blond-haired, pale-skinned giant upon its back. He was wrapped in fur, a war-hammer slung across his back.

The giant from Gramm's hold that slew Tukul. Ildaer, warlord of the Jotun.

'I *know* you,' the giant grated at him.

Other bears emerged from the forest, two, four, five of them, each with a rider upon their backs.

Corban snapped a command at Storm as he turned and ran.

CHAPTER NINETY-ONE

CORALEN

Coralen kicked Akar's feet out from under him, saw him drop and attempt the roll that Sumur had executed so perfectly in front of them all during his duel with Corban, but Akar was a fraction slower and Coralen aimed a little higher, accounting for the attempted roll before it had fully begun.

The result was a dead Akar, or he would have been, if her sword had not been made of wood. He rose with a wince and a courteous nod, which she hardly even noticed. She was thinking about Corban.

I kissed him. Kissed him. And what does he do? Nothing. Even in her head the word was a snarl.

'Again,' she said to Akar. She didn't notice that he looked disappointed to be asked.

Their weapons clacked a staccato rhythm as they moved with the tempo of their contest. Akar was technical, fluid, perfect, like all of the Jehar; Coralen was movement and fury, but she was without her wolven claws, using just a practice sword. Akar broke through her guard with a feint and lunge and punched his blade against the flesh a fraction below her ribcage.

You just killed me.

That made her mad and she grabbed his blade, dragged herself up it and sawed her own weapon against Akar's throat.

'What was that?' he asked as he stepped away.

'You killed me, but not instantly. I was practising taking my enemy to the bridge of swords with me.'

He smiled at that and nodded his respect, then touched his hand to his throat, fingertips coming away bloody. Even though her blade was made of wood she'd managed to draw blood.

'I am not your enemy,' Akar said.

'What?'

'I am not your enemy,' he repeated, 'and I do not wish to die whilst training on the weapons court.'

'Sorry,' she muttered.

She'd been first on the weapons court this morning, expecting to see Corban, fully intending to give him as many bruises as was physically possible during a morning's training. When he had not turned up it made her angrier, her only option to take it as a personal insult.

He is avoiding me.

Akar had been the first unfortunate man who had asked her if she wished to spar with him.

This is not working. I need to see Corban and tell him what I think of him. What I think of a man who gets kissed by a woman and then avoids that woman for a ten-night. And especially when that woman is me. Me, who's punched and kicked and bitten a score of men that tried to kiss me, and now . . .

She screamed internally.

Coralen strode from the court, slamming her practice blade into a wicker barrel as she left. She strode through the wide streets of the fortress, heading for the great hall, her eyes scanning for Storm as she went. If Corban was not in there she would try his chamber.

She reached the great hall and walked through the open gates. This chamber still managed to fill her with a sense of awe. It was just so huge, the branches snaking across the roof high above. She stood on the steps that led down onto the main floor and took it all in. She thought of Dath and Kulla at last night's festivities and smiled, then remembered them kissing, which reminded her of something else, and she scowled.

She saw Meical sitting on a bench at one of the tables, alone and with his head bowed.

It's the first time I've seen him still. He is usually doing something every moment of the waking day. Maybe he's seen Corban.

A horn blast echoed through the chamber, off from the right. She looked about, not seeing anyone, frowning, then realized what it was.

One of the tunnel alerts.

'To arms!' she bellowed. 'Foe in the tunnels. To arms, to arms.' She was running, a sword in her fist without realizing how it got there, searching for the tunnel with the horn-blower. The blasts kept coming, people taking up her cry, Coralen hearing it spread through the chamber and out of the gates into the courtyard beyond.

Must close the tunnel, seal the doors.

Glancing left and right, she saw Meical running, speeding after her, others heading for the gates. Then she saw the tunnel. A warrior was standing at its rim blowing on his horn, others heaving on the huge trapdoor. A giant joined them to help, but then the horn-blower was shouting at them, gesturing for them to stop.

Then Coralen was there. Strange sounds echoed out of the tunnel, hooves and feet and what sounded like a great wind.

'Close it,' she yelled at the men and giant standing with ropes on the huge trapdoor, holding it hovering.

'No,' the horn-blower shouted at her, a huntsman from Narvon who had joined her team. 'We have scouts in there – my brother is down there.'

Coralen paused a moment, looking into the tunnel. It sloped down gently, a hundred paces in two pools of torchlight revealing only emptiness. In theory any enemy in the tunnel should be at least half a day away, the scouts inside equipped with horns and fast mounts to spread the alert as quickly as possible. But she didn't like the sounds coming out of that tunnel.

They could be a long way back – sound travels far in those tunnels, especially if it's made by those in a hurry.

Then the clatter of hooves separated from the others, growing louder with every moment, and suddenly a rider was visible in the tunnel, galloping through the torchlight, hurtling up the slope towards them. His mouth was moving, shouting, but nothing could be heard over the crashing of his mount's hooves and the strange sound rushing up behind it, a scraping, grinding sound, like a thousand knives scratching at stone.

'Close the gates,' the rider screamed as he exploded from the tunnel, Coralen rushing to take his reins, his horse sweat-streaked and foaming at the mouth. The rider's eyes were wide with panic.

Coralen was planning on asking a few questions but instead she turned to the men holding the huge trapdoor and yelled and screamed at them to close it. Its hinges creaked as it began to come down.

A huge roar boomed through the tunnel, bursting up into the chamber like a blast of wind in the worst of storms, a physical thing that rattled chests and burst eardrums. In the tunnel something appeared, something huge, a flat muzzled head with small eyes, long fangs, thick powerful legs with razored claws.

No.

'DRAIG!' screamed Coralen and the door came crashing down, all efforts at lowering it with control gone. Coralen had one last glimpse inside the tunnel, the draig looming close, someone upon its back, and behind it warriors, some mounted, others running, iron glinting, then the door was down, a cloud of dust billowing up.

Men were at the bolts, trying to throw them across, the giant and others reaching for the great oak beam that slotted through iron collars across the door.

Someone grabbed her arm and spun her. Meical.

'What did you see?' he asked, voice calm, controlled.

'A draig, a rider upon its back.'

'Nathair rides a draig,' Meical said.

'Aye, it was him,' Coralen breathed. She would never forget the sight from Murias. 'And the Kadoshim are with him, hundreds of them.' She looked up at the scout rider. He was wild-eyed, in the grip of panic. Gripping his wrist, she shook him.

'How are they so close?' Coralen asked him. 'Where are the other scouts?'

'They move faster than the wind,' the scout said, 'that draig . . .' His face spasmed, remembering something terrible. 'They caught up with the other scouts, ran them down.'

The giant slid the oak beam through the first iron collar. Warriors were everywhere now, a few hundred at least, iron in their fists but most not in their war gear. More were pouring into the chamber as the horn blasts spread warning through the fortress.

'Where's Ban?' Coralen asked Meical, grabbing his arm as he turned away.

'He . . .' Meical paused, a mixture of grief and guilt crossing his face. 'He took Storm down one of the tunnels—'

'What!'

'Not this one – this one goes south, yes?'

'Aye.'

'No, the one by Skald's chair. He is safe.'

'Why did he do that?'

There was a huge, concussive boom on the trapdoor, shaking it, dust boiling from its edges, locks rattling, some of the bolts flying loose.

It's not going to hold. Coralen knew beyond any doubt.

'Make ready,' Meical yelled at the top of his voice.

Gar swept through the doors, a few score Jehar at his back, other people appearing from all directions – Wulf and a handful of axe-throwers, Javed with his pit-fighters, Coralen saw Brina and Cywen standing upon the stairwell that led to Corban's chamber, Dath and Kulla bleary-eyed and tousle-haired behind them.

At least he has his bow.

'Where is Ban?' Gar yelled as he drew near.

'In the north tunnel; Meical says he's safe,' she said, nodded a greeting to Enkara, who was along with him, her leg not fully re-covered from when her horse had fallen upon it.

Another impact upon the trapdoor, the oak beam the giant had slid across splintering with a piercing crack, another dust cloud rippling outwards.

'Back, get back,' Coralen cried, trying to herd them all away from the trapdoor. *They are too close: if the doors break, a hundred men will be slain in the explosion.*

Meical and Gar added their voices, then others, and slowly the milling, confused mess edged backwards, forming a ring about the trapdoor, leaving a space of ten or twenty paces.

And that will be our killing ground, Coralen snarled to herself, bouncing on the balls of her feet, eager now. *Wish I had my wolven claws. Have to do it the old-fashioned way.* With her left hand she drew a knife from her belt.

There were a few moments of silence, dust settling, armour creaking as everyone waited.

Then the trapdoor exploded in a deafening burst of wood and iron, a dust cloud billowing out to envelop them. The draig within the tunnel roared its fury and crashed into the chamber, shadowy figures swarming behind it.

Then all became chaos.

The draig ploughed a way through the ring, eviscerating a dozen men too foolish or too brave to leap out of its way, Nathair hacking from side to side with a longsword. A horde of enemy surged after the draig, breaking through the immediate ring and hurling themselves into the warriors who were gathering deeper into the chamber. Meical did not wait for the enemy but strode into the dust cloud behind the draig, one man sealing the gap against so many, his sword a dull gleam as he was obscured; moments later a shadow-demon screeching into existence in the air, and Coralen knew Meical had his first kill.

Gar ran in after him, bellowing, 'TRUTH AND COURAGE!' and Coralen followed, screaming at the top of her lungs, all those in the circle adding their voices and surging forwards.

Kadoshim were everywhere, but among and behind them emerged other warriors – ones clothed like the pirates they had stolen the ships from in Narvon, in kilts and vests of leather with short swords and bucklers. Coralen liked them; they were much easier to kill than the Kadoshim. In what felt like no time at all her sword and knife were slick with blood and half a dozen men were dead or dying in her wake.

The Kadoshim were shrieking like the demons they were, frenzied in their killing, and wherever they went the people of Drassil fell. A handful of paces ahead of Coralen Gar and Meical stood like an island against them; almost every other heartbeat a shadow-demon formed like a black marker above them.

A face surged out of the press at her, iron rings in an oily beard, an iron-bossed buckler punching at her face. She swayed to one side, slashed the arm behind the buckler with her sword, stepped in close and punched her knife into a belly, ripped sideways as she stepped away, giving the warrior a shove in the chest to send him stumbling backwards, leaving a trail of his intestines on the floor. Another warrior stabbed at her, blinked when she was no longer where he expected her to be, then choked on his own blood as she raked his throat with her knife.

Then a Kadoshim was coming at her and she was retreating, slashing with sword and knife, opening a wound across its thigh, a wrist, along the ribs, but it did not seem even to feel the injuries, let alone be slowed down. Blood seeped from the wounds, but slow and thick, not sheeting like she expected. Step by step she retreated, forced steadily out of the ring, towards Skald's throne and away from the warriors who fought desperately to contain the warband that was forcing its way up and out of the tunnel. A sliver of fear worked its way into her belly as her defences became frantic and ragged. She felt her body weakening, her lungs burning as the Kadoshim pressed on, unrelenting, blow after blow merging into one seamless, constant attack. She blinked what she thought was sweat out of her eyes, but it was blood, a cut over her eye appearing that she hadn't even felt and the blood wouldn't stop flowing. The sliver of fear grew.

I may die here. How did Corban make fighting these things look so easy?

Then a warrior swept around her, black-clothed, wielding a curved sword, Akar. He spun around the Kadoshim, coming to a standstill with his back to them both, sword held out to his side in a two-handed grip, dripping black globs of blood. The Kadoshim staggered on a few steps and its head rolled to the side, then toppled to the ground with a thud, its body following a few moments later, mist like black ichor forming in the air, hissing its rage at the world and then evaporating.

Coralen nodded her thanks to Akar and then he was gone, a dozen Jehar moving with him, chopping into the tide of Kadoshim and Vin Thalun that were flowing from the tunnel.

She ripped a strip of cloth from her shirt and tied it around the cut on her forehead, took a moment to look about the room.

More warriors were still entering the chamber. She glimpsed the child-king's shieldman, Tahir, leading scores of Isiltir's red-cloaks in a charge down the steps at Nathair upon his draig.

The ring that had formed around the trapdoor was getting steadily pushed back, thinning and starting to fray as more enemy kept emerging from the tunnel, though the numbers of the fallen enemy seemed uncountable, piles of them stacked in an ever-widening circle.

We cannot hold them much longer.

Even as she watched, a break came in their circle and Kadoshim and Vin Thalun poured through it like a flood, spreading into the chamber, turning back to attack the defenders from behind.

Coralen looked about wildly, trying to find her friends in the chaos, having a mind to fight beside them if this was going to end the way she thought.

I wish I'd spoken to Ban. Please, Elyon, let him be safe. Let him live.

A great roar echoed through the chamber, for a moment drowning out the din of battle, and Coralen looked to see Balur One-Eye standing upon the steps before the gate, black axe in his hands, Ethlinn and the might of the Benothi behind him. With another roar he strode down the stairs, began to run towards them, the Benothi following like an avalanche, the ground trembling. They hit the Kadoshim and Vin Thalun that had broken through the circle, scattering them like straw dolls, axes taking Kadoshim heads, warhammers crushing Vin Thalun to pulp, and behind them the defenders started to rally. Coralen saw Dath had gathered a dozen archers to him and they were lined along the staircase that led to a higher floor, raking the enemy with flights of arrows. To the other side Wulf had rallied his axe-men to him and they were hurling blades at Nathair's draig and the enemy that thronged around him. Elsewhere she glimpsed Javed, soaked in blood, a knife in each hand, Vin Thalun dead or dying all about him. He was smiling viciously, his pit-fighters about him carving a bloody swathe through a knot of Vin Thalun warriors. Coralen felt a new surge of hope and with it energy, and she leaped back into the battle, wanting to find Gar and stand beside him.

He was still standing close to Meical, the two of them blood drenched and ringed by a tideline of corpses. Coralen joined them, protecting one and then the other as Vin Thalun and Kadoshim hurled themselves at the two warriors. She stabbed and hacked and chopped until her arms grew heavy and her hands slippery with blood.

Others joined her, spreading in a half-circle to guard the flanks of Gar and Meical – Enkara and Hamil, Akar and a dozen other Jehar.

The flow of enemy from the tunnel started to slow, one last wave surging towards them. Coralen turned a blow with her knife and buried her sword in a Vin Thalun chest, blade sticking between ribs as she tried to tug it free. Another Vin Thalun saw and lunged at her, sword plunging towards her unprotected side.

Something smashed into his chest, hurling him away from Coralen in an explosion of blood. He hit the floor and rolled, Coralen seeing one of Laith's throwing knives sticking from his chest. Laith bounded up, a fresh knife in each hand, covered in cuts and other people's blood. Farrell was with her, his war-hammer slung across his back, the giant dagger in his hands slick with blood.

'Better for Kadoshim,' he growled. 'Where's Ban?'

Before she could answer a new sound rose from the tunnel. Battle lulled around them and many paused to look. A rhythmic *thump* rumbled out of the tunnel, reverberating in pulsing waves. A line of new Kadoshim emerged, flies buzzing about them, a warrior at their head, tall, lithe, gripping a longsword and clothed in mail, but Coralen's eyes were drawn to his face, parts of it burned charcoal black and peeling, silver hair growing in tufts on his head, elsewhere singed to stubble or burned clear.

'Calidus,' Meical snarled.

Behind him and the new Kadoshim marched more warriors, these in disciplined rows with long shields and short swords in their hands, iron caps on their heads. Coralen remembered them from Domhain, when she had been part of a night raid against Rhin's invading force. They had been the only force that hadn't panicked, and days later she had been told that their wall of shields had broken Domhain's warband.

Hundreds of them were marching from the tunnel, an endless column of men twenty shields wide. Coralen felt her heart sink.

Calidus saw Meical, sneered and strode straight at him. Meical stepped to meet him, their blades clashing with blinding speed; the sheer sense of power rolling off their blows was staggering. Then one of the Kadoshim was lunging in, something different about him from the rest, flies swarming around him. He lashed out at Meical, caught him a glancing blow and sent him crashing to the floor, rolling backwards. Calidus followed and Enkara stepped between them, sword raised high, turned Calidus' blow as it swept towards Meical, a backswing from Enkara slashing across Calidus' eyes and sending him reeling. Behind her Meical pushed himself to his knees, then the other Kadoshim was lunging at Enkara. He had no blade in his hands, just grabbed her, somehow swaying past her curved sword and gripping her wrist. He gave a savage yank and her sword was spinning away, Enkara pulled close to him. With one hand he gripped her face and twisted.

Coralen heard Enkara's neck snapping from twenty paces away, the Kadoshim discarding her lifeless body to the ground.

Coralen screamed and ran at him.

CHAPTER NINETY-TWO

CYWEN

Cywen burst into the hospice, chest heaving, lungs burning. People were sitting up in their cots, some shuffling about on crutches, others trying to pull boots on and find weapons. They all froze and stared at Cywen.

'Out of here,' she gasped, then louder, 'the enemy are in the great hall. If you can wield a blade, go do it, if not, you need to get somewhere safer.'

The room burst into motion. Brina stumbled in behind Cywen.

'Thanks for helping . . . an old . . . lady,' Brina said.

'Sorry,' Cywen said.

They'd both stood in the great hall, staring dumbstruck as the draig had smashed its way through the trapdoor and the warband of Kadoshim and Vin Thalun had come boiling out of the ground. It had not taken long to realize that the warriors of Drassil were hugely outnumbered and in fighting the Kadoshim, unlike the battle beyond the walls, were battling against a foe that was at least their equal. Added to that, the Kadoshim seemed to be limitless in their numbers and supported by a screaming horde of Vin Thalun pirates. As the circle of defenders trying to contain them had broken down Brina and Cywen both looked at one another and realized the same thing – *the hospice.*

If the Kadoshim reached here it would be a bloodbath.

So they had run through the streets of Drassil, chaos everywhere, Cywen pulling ahead of Brina.

Still breathing hard she started to help people from cots, tugging on clothes, dishing out seed of the poppy. Brina was stuffing herbs and vials into a bag. Once the hall was close to empty Cywen saw the other thing that she'd come here for – her two belts of throwing-knives.

She slipped them over her head and ran her fingers along a row of leather-wrapped hilts, their comfortable weight reassuring.

'Ready?' Brina asked her, a slim spear in one hand, bag slung across her shoulder. Cywen raised an eyebrow at the spear.

'As much to help me walk and keep up with you as anything else,' Brina snapped.

And then they were heading back to the great hall, slower this time, the din of battle growing louder with each step. Men and women were running in all directions, panic thick in the air. Battle had spilt into the courtyard before the great hall, knots of combat here and there, Kadoshim and Vin Thalun a constant trickle through the half-open doors. Cywen saw a Kadoshim leap through the air, covering at least twenty paces to crash into a handful of Wulf's men, scattering them. As Cywen ran past she saw the Kadoshim squatting upon a body, jaws slick and dripping with blood, the throat of the warrior beneath it torn and ragged.

As they approached the hall's half-open doors, running up the few steps that led from the courtyard, there was a deafening roar and something slammed into them from the other side, one door crashing from its hinges, falling with a resounding *boom* upon friend and foe alike. The draig surged out from the wreckage, Nathair upon its back, the beast powering into the courtyard, its head swinging from side to side, jaws lunging, snapping. It veered away from them, chasing a mass of fleeing warriors, leaving the gates momentarily empty.

'Now,' Brina said, running towards the entrance.

A Vin Thalun ran at them as they reached the open gateway. Cywen put a knife through his eye, dropping him in a twitching pile. She paused to retrieve her knife, then ran through the entrance, colliding with Brina's back.

Then she saw why the healer had stopped at the top of the stairs that led down into Drassil's great hall, staring down into the enormous chamber, the sight almost breaking her heart.

The hall stank like a slaughterhouse, the dead and dying everywhere, all manner of noise filling the air, battle-cries, death cries, men and women screaming, mewling or weeping with pain, the clash and grate of iron on iron, giants bellowing defiance, the Kadoshim's ululating screeches.

The trapdoor that the enemy had emerged from was abandoned, the ring of Drassil's warriors broken, reduced to knotted islands in a sea of the enemy. And marching through the middle was the shield wall of Tenebral's eagle-guard, thousands strong, pushing through the surge and press of battle with irresistible force.

Veradis. Is he down there?

Even as Cywen stood and stared, horns rang out from the shield wall, and before her eyes it split, not in panic, but in organized motion, parting to form new, smaller squares that branched off into a sweeping arc, systematically clearing the battle before them.

'This is over,' Brina said beside her.

The words still in the air Cywen heard a great roar from the far side of the chamber, saw the Benothi giants, felt a flare of hope, but that was instantly dashed as she saw a handful of them retreating, carrying a slumped form between them, silver hair hanging and matted with blood.

Balur One-Eye is fallen.

'Aye,' Cywen grunted.

Elsewhere she saw warriors of Drassil starting to break and run, here and there a more organized retreat – Wulf and his axe-men had joined with Javed's pit-fighters and were disappearing around the curve of the great tree's trunk; closer to her a hundred or so red-cloaked warriors were retreating slowly, a forest of long spears holding back the press of the enemy.

'We need to find Ban and get out of here.'

'Where do we go?' Cywen mumbled, the shock of defeat washing through her like a poison, murdering her will, draining her spirit.

It cannot be.

'There,' Brina said, pointing with her spear.

The trapdoor before Skald's throne was a surging sea of battle, bodies rising and falling like storm-racked waves. At the centre of it Cywen saw her friends. Gar and Meical were standing together, dealing death. Even as she watched screaming shadow-demons burst into momentary existence and then faded about them. Cywen caught a flash of red hair, saw Coralen fighting like a lunatic banshee of legend, close to her Farrell and Laith, Dath and Kulla, a few score others, mostly Jehar. She realized that their numbers were dwindling – not because they were falling to enemy blades, but because they were disappearing one by one into the smaller door of the tunnel's trapdoor.

They are escaping.

'We need to get to them, now,' Brina hissed, grabbing Cywen and pulling her down the stairs.

They were moving against the tide, most now trying to reach the gates. Cywen pushed, shoved and slipped between people, one hand in Brina's. They reached the bottom of the stairs and broke into a run. Cywen used two of her knives on Vin Thalun who fixed their eyes upon her or Brina, leaving her blades in their corpses, and then they were at the mass that was pressing against Meical and the rest.

Brina skirted it, running around to the flanks of the half-circle that was closing like a fist upon their friends. Brina buried her spear in the back of a Vin Thalun; another turning, seeing her, raising his sword, fell gurgling with one of Cywen's knives in his throat. They moved into the press, Cywen catching a glimpse of Laith ahead of her, and Farrell.

Then a Kadoshim was before them, its mouth open in a feral snarl, black eyes fixed on them, curved sword rising. Brina buried her spear in soft flesh, just above the rim of its chainmail shirt, below its throat. The blade sank deep – dark, almost black blood welling around the wound like cold porridge. The Kadoshim slashed at the spear, snapping the shaft, leaving the blade in its flesh. It seemed unconcerned about that, advancing on Brina as she stumbled back.

Cywen threw knives, one, two, three in quick succession, the first crunching into its skull, second bouncing off of the mail shirt, and third piercing its links to sink into the Kadoshim's belly. It took no notice.

I can't take its head with a knife. She drew the sword at her belt and hacked two-handed into the creature as it sliced at and just missed Brina's face.

Cywen's sword sliced into its neck, flesh parting, blade grinding against bone.

That got its attention.

It turned its black eyes upon her and lunged, wrenching her sword from her fingertips, leaving it embedded in the Kadoshim's neck. It ignored that as well, seemingly intent upon Cywen's death. A hand snaked out and grabbed one of her knife-belts, dragging her closer to the Kadoshim's sword-tip. Then Brina was there, in the corner of Cywen's eye, arm raised, and she was shouting something in giantish. Amongst the garbled words from Brina's lips Cywen heard the word *lasair*, for fire, then Brina threw something – a vial that exploded in the Kadoshim's face – and it erupted into fire, spreading in heartbeats down the Kadoshim's neck and consuming its torso, flames hungry and devouring, the instant smell of charring flesh and burning hair billowing out with waves of heat and smoke.

Cywen threw herself backwards as flames snaked along the Kadoshim's arm. She slammed onto the ground, saw the Kadoshim stagger away, reeling like a drunkard to crash into a Vin Thalun, the flames leaping onto him and in moments he was a human torch. Both Vin Thalun and Kadoshim collapsed to their knees, screaming, toppled to the ground, limbs thrashing, the Kadoshim stiffening and then going still, the now too-familiar sight of a shadow-demon appearing in the air above it.

So, the Kadoshim are not fans of fire, either, although it's not the instant victory the taking of a head gives.

Cywen staggered to her feet, Brina nodding with a satisfied expression upon her face.

A slavering, screeching howl drew their attention and they both spun to see a handful of Kadoshim running at them. Brina's hand frantically scrabbled inside her bag and pulled out another vial.

I thought they were medicines – what has she been up to?

More giantish words issued from Brina's mouth and she hurled the vial at the first Kadoshim, just a few paces from Cywen now. There was a blinding flash, a concussive explosion and then Cywen was flying through the air; the last thing she saw before darkness closed in upon her was Brina's face, an expression of profound surprise upon it.

'Well, what a pleasant surprise,' she heard a voice say, somewhere above her. She opened her eyes, decided that was a mistake, pain thumping in her skull, and closed them again.

A boot kicked her in the ribs, more pain in different places now, all clamouring for attention.

She opened her eyes again, looked up into a burned face, but still familiar.

Calidus,' she said, voice hoarse. As she said his name he reached up and tugged at a blackened strip of flesh on his lip, it came away with a soft tearing sound. He grimaced and flicked it away.

'Indeed,' he said. 'And what a pleasure it is to see you again. A feeling that I'd imagine is not mutual.' He smiled, a ghastly expression with half a lip missing.

She didn't bother replying, just pushed herself to her knees, realized her hands were bound in front of her.

She was still in the great hall, sitting on the wooden trapdoor she'd been so desperately trying to reach, though now it was mostly populated by the dead. Further away she saw Meical, pressed and held to his knees by three Kadoshim. He was covered in blood, no way of knowing if it was his own or his enemies'. Cywen suspected mostly the latter.

Calidus walked away from Cywen, towards Meical.

'Hasn't turned out quite as you'd hoped, has it?' Calidus said cheerfully.

Meical just looked at him, stare flat, emotionless.

'So. Let's get to the heart of this. Where is your puppet? Your champion? Your Bright Star?'

Just more silence from Meical.

A group of Kadoshim strode up, one stepping forward, flies buzzing about him in a cloud. He held something out in his hands. A black axe. Cywen had to stop herself from grinding her teeth when she saw it.

The starstone axe, taken from Balur.

'Excellent,' Calidus grinned. 'Most satisfying. That makes two Treasures in one day.' He glanced at Skald's spear, still sunk into the great tree, the giant's skeleton draped about it. 'Now, all I need to make my day perfect is your Bright Star's head on a spike. So . . .'

There was a crashing, pounding rumble from behind Cywen, the now-familiar scrape of a draig's claws on stone.

'Where is he?' Nathair cried from the draig's back as he drew near, glaring down at Meical. 'Where is your Bright Star?'

'I was just asking the same question,' Calidus said. 'And now it's about time for an answer.'

'Safe,' Meical said. 'He will come for you – he is a force of nature, Elyon's own wrath. You'd both best be looking over your shoulders from now on.'

'Oh, please.' Calidus laughed.

'This is far from over,' Meical growled.

'Ah, now that's where you're wrong.' Calidus sighed. 'At least for you. I must admit that I'd hoped for more, Meical, and I'm sad to say it, but you're boring me. Legion, take his head.'

Meical struggled in his captors' grip, but the three Kadoshim held him fast, two dragging his arms wide, the other pushing on his back with a booted foot until Meical's cheek ground into the stone floor.

The Kadoshim holding the axe raised it high and swung it down. There was a crunch and a resounding crack as the axe cut through Meical's neck and buried itself in the stone floor beneath him. His severed head rolled in a half-circle, eyes bulging. A mist formed in the air above his twitching torso, a stern-faced warrior, great white wings spread about him.

'See how it feels,' Calidus said.

The wraith-like Ben-Elim glared at Calidus, then let out a bellowing, mournful roar – rage, frustration, defeat mixed together. The great white wings beat once, the air momentarily a gale, and then it was gone, evaporating.

Calidus turned to face Cywen, a triumphant smile fading from his scorched features.

'Now tell me, you little bitch,' he snarled. 'Where is your brother?'

CHAPTER NINETY-THREE

CORBAN

Corban ran, the blood pounding in his skull, branches whipping his face. Storm was a blur through the trees just ahead of him.

He'd run down the hill and headed deep into thick underbrush, hoping it would halt the passage of the giant bears. By the sounds of crashing and snapping behind him his plan hadn't worked. He ploughed on, vine, root and thorn snaring and snatching at him. He stumbled, rebounded from a tree, carried on, the crashing behind him louder, closer.

I need to try something different.

He veered right, burst out of the undergrowth into a patch of soft forest litter and wide-spaced trees, put his head down and sprinted.

The sounds of bears and giant cries faded behind him, each stride opening the gap between them. He tried to work out his position, the direction he should be running in, heard the sound of running water to his left – *the river* – and headed towards where he thought the trapdoor lay.

Sounds faded behind him.

I'm going to do it.

Then there was a ground-trembling explosion of undergrowth, sounding like whole trees were torn and uprooted, the pounding of huge paws and then a roaring that staggered him, sent him stumbling, then falling from his feet.

He rolled on the ground, glimpsed claws and fangs and fur bearing down upon him, the pale skin of a giant somewhere high above, heard more bears bellowing, further away, to left and right. Then he came to a halt, litter and leaves in his hair, up his nose, in his mouth. He reached for his sword.

Ahead of him he saw Storm skid to a halt, turn and look back for him.

'On,' he commanded.

She did not move.

'ON,' he shouted.

Still she stood and stared at him.

Run on. Please. Go, he willed her.

A bear and giant crashed out of the forest behind him.

Storm snarled, legs bunching, and ran back towards him, her head low, a vein bulging in her chest as muscles pumped in contraction and extension.

He rolled to one knee, drew his sword, then Storm was bounding past him, legs coiling to leap at the bear converging upon them, her jaws gaping.

They slammed together, bear and wolven, a collision of flesh, bone, fur, tearing teeth and ripping claw. Storm sank her fangs deep into the bear's shoulder, her claws scrabbling for purchase, the momentum pulling her loose, tearing her free, leaving a great fold of flesh torn and flapping on the bear's flank. It bellowed in pain as Storm fell to the ground, the giant's war-hammer swooping through air, missing her head by a handspan. She rolled on the ground, gathered herself for another leap.

Then Corban was up and running, the bear's charging momentum carrying it on, leaving Storm behind, surging straight at him. Corban swerved to the side, swayed out away from a slashing paw and talons and hacked two-handed with his sword, all his strength smashing it into the fur and flesh of the bear's side, blood spraying, ribs crunching and cracking. There was a stirring of air above him and he swayed backwards, dropped to a crouch and a war-hammer hissed over him, the giant wielding it snarling in frustration.

If the wound Storm inflicted had caused the bear pain, this one gave it agony. It screamed its torment and halted its charge, sliding, tearing up the ground, crashing into a tree, the timber splintering and spraying, then the bear was rolling and its rider was sent flying through the air, hurled into the gloom and undergrowth. Storm bounded forward, leaping onto the bear as it lay on its side, trying to rise, blood frothing from its nose and mouth. She sank her teeth into its throat, the bear thrashing, trying to rise, but its lungs weren't working properly, its legs scrambling for purchase. Then Storm shook her head, a violent twist and there was a wet tearing sound and a gouting fountain of blood and the bear was sinking into death.

Corban ran to Storm, put a hand on her shoulder.

'Good girl,' he murmured. 'Now let's get out of here.'

'That's the second bear of mine that you and your kind have slain,' a voice said from the shadows.

Ildaer, warlord of the Jotun, emerged from the gloom, his war-hammer held loosely in one hand, his huge frame wrapped in leather and fur. At the same time two more bears and their riders crashed into view, lumbering towards them.

'I remember you,' Ildaer said, moving closer. 'You stood over your friend at Gramm's hold.'

'Why are you here?' Corban asked, eyes scanning the forest for routes of escape.

'To give Jael my aid,' Ildaer said. He paused and cocked his head, listening to the faint sounds of battle that drifted up from Drassil.

'Jael is defeated, his warband broken,' Corban said.

'Then who is it that attacks you now?' Ildaer asked.

Corban looked nervously towards Drassil.

'I don't know.'

I must get back there.

Ildaer's eyes looked Corban up and down. 'You have a new arm-ring since Gramm's hold, I think.' He cocked his head to one side, frowned. 'Are you their lord?'

'Come any closer and I'll be your death-giver,' Corban said.

'Ah, I like that.' Ildaer nodded, looking at his warriors about him. 'Good spirit.'

There was a hissing sound and a spear punched into Ildaer's shoulder. He cried out and staggered back, fell against a tree, slid down it.

Two men burst out of the trees behind Corban: Atilius and Pax.

'Corban,' Atilius yelled, and Corban didn't need calling twice, he turned and scrambled over the dead bear, slid down the other side and set off running, Storm bounding beside him, red tongue lolling.

They caught up with Atilius and Pax in a dozen strides and then they were all sprinting through the trees.

There was some shouting and snarling behind them, then more crashing as bears lurched into motion.

'This way,' Atilius said and veered left, taking them into thicker cover, squirming beneath and around a clump of huge trees that had fallen in some great storm, roots exposed like the husks of great wyrms.

'Bears can't follow us here,' Atilius said. Beyond the fallen trees lay a thicket of long-thorn, Corban discovering how aptly it was named as he tried to navigate his way through, following a narrow fox trail that Atilius seemed to know well, the sound of water growing louder all the time. It was a long time later when they spilt into an open glade that edged a sharp drop to the river. They all paused to fill their lungs, Atilius passing Corban his water skin. Storm stood staring into the undergrowth.

'My . . . thanks,' Corban breathed.

'We heard the bears,' Pax said. 'Didn't know what they were when we heard them, mind, but we knew it wasn't good, and that you were out here somewhere.'

'We need to get back to Drassil,' Corban said, suddenly remembering the horns he'd heard from the hill, the sounds of battle.

'Aye. We'll follow the river, takes us close to the trapdoor,' Atilius said.

Storm growled.

There was a whistling, sound, a *whump, whump, whump*, as of something huge spinning through the air. They all had a moment to look up, then Atilius was hurtling backwards, blood and bone spraying in his wake, crunching into a tree, where he remained, pinned by the giant axe that had carved him near in two.

Pax screamed and a giant thundered out of the undergrowth.

Corban grabbed Pax, shook him, the lad's eyes fixed on his da's body.

'Drassil. Pax, you have to get back to Drassil. Get help if you can.'

Pax looked at him, crying, then nodded and ran.

Corban drew his sword and turned to face the giant.

It came howling into the glade, pulling a dagger as long as his sword from its belt, eyes flitting to its axe in the tree. Corban did not wait for it, moved forwards, Balur and Tahir's voices sharp in his mind – *deflect the blow, nudge it, guide it, use your speed, your size as an advantage.*

Then Storm leaped, jaws clamping around the giant's wrist, blood spurting, the dagger falling. Corban lunged in as the giant raised a fist and punched Storm in the head. She didn't let go and then, before the giant even saw him, Corban was burying his blade in its belly, angling his blade high, under the ribs, slicing through a lung. Blood sluiced and it was sinking to its knees. Corban ripped his blade free, cut its throat and kicked it backwards.

He turned to follow Pax and something crunched into his knee, pain exploding, stealing his breath away. He dropped like a felled tree, saw a giant towering over him, war-hammer in its hand, another behind it holding a thick spear.

He rolled away, used his sword to lever himself onto the knee of his good leg, raised his sword.

The giant with the war-hammer laughed and kicked him in the chest. Corban heard ribs snapping, a thunder-clap in his head and he was rolling over and over.

The giant advanced. Corban's hand searched for his sword hilt, couldn't find it, pain pulsing from his chest and leg.

Then Storm was standing over Corban, crouched low, snarling. The giant hesitated, the one behind with the spear moving into view. Before either could move, Storm was leaping, slamming into the first giant before he could swing his hammer. Her jaws snapped for his throat, teeth ripping, both of them crashing to the ground, rolling.

Corban got to his feet, couldn't put any weight on his damaged leg, found his sword and used it as a crutch to hobble after them.

The giant was punching Storm as they rolled, repeatedly, heavy fists crunching into her ribs. Corban heard a crackling sound, then snapping. Storm whined, then her jaws were finally clamping around the giant's throat. She gave a savage wrench of her neck and head and blood jetted, the giant slumping, then lying still, Storm sinking across him. She whined as she tried to stand, then the other giant was standing over her, spear rising, Corban a dozen paces away. The spear came down, punching into Storm above the shoulder, angling down into her chest, at the same time Corban hurling himself at the back of the giant's knees, toppling him to the ground, leaving his spear in Storm.

Corban howled with rage and fell onto the giant, his pain threatening to overwhelm him. He dragged his blade up as the giant tried to rise, stabbed it into the giant's groin, severing the artery high in the inner thigh. He collapsed upon the dying giant, struggling to breathe. He'd never felt pain like it, pulsing through him, a sharp spike in his chest every time he took a breath, but only one thought filled his mind.

Storm.

He left his sword buried in the giant, did not have the strength to tug it free, rolled onto his front and saw Storm lying flat and still, the spear protruding from her chest. He dug his hands into the ground, pulled, dragged himself towards her. He was sobbing, his vision blurred by the hot tears streaming down his cheeks. He must have been saying her name as well, for she raised her head and looked at him, whining pitifully. Her tail thumped weakly on the ground, blood foaming from her mouth. Her front legs shifted, paws scratching in the dirt, and she moved, just a fraction. Then she did it again, and again, dragging herself towards him.

That was how they met, both battered, bloody, bones broken, upon a grassy ridge above a white-flowing river. Corban gripped the spear buried in her chest and pulled it free, Storm yelping. He threw it away, tried to stem the flow of blood that pulsed from the wound with his hands. Storm licked his face and then laid her head upon his shoulder. He buried his face in the fur of her neck and held her close to him.

There was crashing in the undergrowth, giant voices.

How long have I slept?

Corban groaned, lifted himself from Storm's side. She was still breathing, though in short, sharp breaths, not the long, deep movement of her chest that he had slept against so many times. She lifted her head to look at him with glazed, pain-filled eyes.

Hold on, girl. After everything I've lost I'll not lose you as well.

The voices again, closer.

Got to move.

He tried to stand, pain exploding in his chest and leg, collapsed, almost fainted with the effort.

Right. Walking's out of the question, then.

He listened to the sound of the river.

The thud of feet in the undergrowth, so close.

If they find us, they will kill us.

He gritted his teeth and pushed against Storm. Pain was pulsing in huge, rolling waves from his leg and chest. He ignored it, pushed again, strained harder. Storm whined, high-pitched, almost snapped at him. Then they were both slipping over the cliff edge, sliding down slick, sharp rocks, falling, then splashing into ice-cold water. The current took them, Corban clinging to Storm, desperately trying to hold her head above the water, spluttering and choking himself. He bounced off a rock, spun, his head ducking under the water, for a moment not knowing which way was up, then he was clear, gasping air.

The water calmed a little, carried them on until the current spat them out onto a rocky shelf, the steep sides rising over them, not much higher than one of the bears they'd been running from. Corban checked Storm, saw she was still breathing, then collapsed against her, utterly exhausted.

He woke with dawn, wet and shivering. Storm's breath came in a wet rattle. She opened her eyes when he moved, just lay with her head on the rock, too weak to move, looking at him.

He stroked the fur of her cheeks, above her amber eyes, remembered that first day when he'd saved her as a cub, Evnis looming over him, demanding her death. How he'd refused. And since that day she'd been his constant companion, his guardian, protector, friend.

He put a hand on her chest, felt her heart fluttering.

I have to get help for her. She needs a healer. She needs Brina.

His leg felt numb so he risked moving it. Pain erupted and he rolled over and vomited in the river.

Then he was lurching upwards, being dragged, hanging suspended over Storm, her head rising a fraction, eyes tracking him. He lurched up again, dangling in the air, something hooked under his belt.

Another lurch and he was looking at two giants, one with a rope in its hand, attached to an iron hook that it removed from Corban's belt.

'You were right to follow the river,' one said to the other.

'Let me go,' Corban coughed.

'Ha, I think not,' the giant said in common tongue. 'You have led us a merry chase. The others are searching for you all over Forn.'

'We should put a spear through his heart,' the other one growled.

'Ildaer wants him,' the first giant said.

'What about that?' The other giant jutted its chin at Storm.

'I'll not be going down there,' the first giant said with a shake of its broad head. 'Besides, there's no need. She is finished.'

As the two giants dragged Corban up the slope and through a glade, pain lancing through his leg and chest with every movement, every breath, he heard Storm howl behind him. It was a rattle, weak and fluid, yet long and mournful, and Corban felt his heart was being ripped apart.

They took him deeper into the forest, and soon Corban discovered the one thing that broke his heart more than listening to Storm's weak and fading howls.

The moment when she stopped howling.